To Bob Crane
One of the best.
A Marine
with appreciation!

P9-EEB-027

CV

TERMINAL POLICY

Liam McCurry

WITHDRAWN

MONTEREY COUNTY FREE
MARINA
CALIFORNIA
LIBRARIES

Ashleigh
Publishing Group

ROSSVILLE, KANSAS

Ashleigh
Publishing Group

PO Box 93
St. Marys, Kansas 66536
www.ashleighpublishing.org

Author: Liam McCurry
Terminal Policy ©2009 Liam McCurry

10 9 8 7 6 5 4 3 2 1

All rights reserved. Except as permitted under the U.S. Copyright Act of 1976, no part of this publication may be reproduced, distributed or transmitted in any form or by any means, or stored in a database or retrieval system, without prior written permission from Ashleigh Publishing Group.

Library of Congress Control Number: 2009910452

ISBN-13   978-0-9825513-0-1
ISBN-10   0-9825513-0-4

First Printing November 2009

Printed in the United States of America

For information regarding special discounts for bulk purchases, please contact Ashleigh Publishing Group Sales at www.ashleighpublishing.org

Cover Design: Paul Hotvedt, Blue Heron Typesetters

This book is a work of fiction. Names, characters, places, and incidents either are the product of the author's imagination or are used fictitiously. Any resemblance to actual events, locales, organizations, or persons, living or dead, is purely coincidental and not intended by the author.

ACKNOWLEDGEMENTS

To voice thoughts inspired by the writings of Robert Emmet and William Butler Yeats, let it be said "No man writes alone" — for it requires the writer AND a reader. My truly great fortune is that, because I have such friends, "alone" is an unnecessary word. Accepting that such is the case, I gratefully dedicate this "entertainment" to those friends who have contributed so much in so many ways:

To "Foghorn" (USMC) who suggested the game; Maria Dennison (USMC), President of Ashleigh Publishing Group, who put the ball into play; Cindy B, dispenser of encouragement; Big Brad "The Enforcer" (USMC); "Suspected Spook" Rick P; "Master Guns" Bob W. (USMC); "China John" B. (USMC); Stan R. (USMC); Rolf S. (USMC); Howard T. (USMC); Ray A. (USMC-Hon. & "Wing Nut"); "Frogman" Russ H. (USN); Robert (The Wiz) W. (USN); "Tattoo" Jeff (USMC); Dave the Knife (USMC); "big Don" H. (USMC); Bob H. (Marine medic/USN); Glen G. (USMC); Marjorie T. (NIH); "Killer" Bryan K. (USMC); "Buffalo Head" Frank B.; "Hoser" G. (VA-rep) and my own "#1"- Bill (That's William, Sir) L. (USMC). Also Chelsea and Debbie along with Erin, Marie and Beth. To anyone feeling "left out," please know that only the limits of space, time, and my own fallibility are the culprit.

Most of all, my limitless gratitude to my wife Marguerite (that's "Margie," says she) without whose tolerance, assistance, understanding, support, encouragement and PERSISTENCE this "entertainment" would never have been completed.

Thanks, Gang.
Dia Dhuit. — in Gaelic, God Bless

PROLOGUE

The events related in this book occurred mostly in the time period between 1983 when the Islamic Jihad claimed responsibility for the bombing of the U. S. Marine Barracks in Beirut, Lebanon that killed 242 Americans, and the 2009 release of Abdelbeset Ali Mohmed al Megrahi.

The Libyan was convicted of murdering 270 people four days before Christmas, 1988, by blowing up Pan Am flight 103 over Lockerbie, Scotland. Serving a life term, al Megrahi was freed from prison by a Scottish Justice who cited "compassionate" grounds. He received a boisterous welcome when his plane landed in his native Libya. A large crowd, waving flags and honking horns greeted al Megrahi at the military airport in Tripoli.

The above facts are real, and terrorism is always with us. Might there be terminal policies?

The reader can decide.

CHAPTER 1

New Mexico Desert

The van lurched heavily around the corner, tires squealing against hot asphalt. The man in its enclosed back strained his eyes to follow the luminous sweep of the second-hand on the expensive watch strapped to his wrist. His sweat beaded face would have been recognized by only a few among the millions who lived in the western world. His decisions affected the lives of most of them.

At the predetermined speed of 35 miles an hour, it would take only a half-minute to reach the airfield where his heavily guarded private jet waited. A mocking smile, nearly a sneer, lifted one corner of his mouth.

He'd beaten the bastards!

· · ·

The shock of the explosion came milliseconds after its booming blast. The concussion flung his body from its seat and the van disappeared behind a swelling ball of pulsing red, with darting streaks of yellow.

The thundering roar was still echoing from nearby hills when a voice sounded. "That's it! You're dead!" The words were metallic and amplified. "Climb on out; let's take a look why." The man speaking held a bullhorn. He drew close enough to the scene to make its use unnecessary.

The rear doors of the still intact van opened slowly. A second man climbed out, carefully avoiding the dripping residue of the explosion. As he paused to examine his clothing for smears of the bright crimson paint, he was joined by two men who had exited after him. He massaged a bruised shoulder and glared at the man holding the bullhorn.

"You misrepresented," he snarled. "You implied it would be a kidnap attempt." His security men, now standing at his side, exchanged glances and relaxed. It seemed they were not to be blamed.

"Misrepresented?" The bullhorn man grinned. "Not damned likely," he remarked softly.

"But you said a kidnapping. Nothing about a bomb."

"Rocket. Low velocity, paint-filled. The van's armored to take it. The real thing would have exploded inside."

"Goddamn it, Raker, you said . . . ."

"Hold it!" The man lifted the bullhorn to his mouth. "Okay, Brick," he said, his voice crisp. "Get the crew out to clean up for the next batch of *ass*-umers." He grinned, turning his head to face his quarry. "That's the story; you assumed."

The cleanup crew approached and was joined by the driver and another guard who'd been in the separated cab of the van. They shuffled nervously to a location which they hoped was out of sight of the man for whose safety they were responsible.

The man addressed as Raker eyed each of the apprehensive security men in turn. "Relax," he said softly, "you only share the blame." He flicked flinty eyes toward their employer. "Most of the fault lies with the wheel here."

He handed the bullhorn to one of his cleanup crew and started to walk toward the airfield. "Let's go, children. It's back to kindergarten." There was no amusement in his voice.

He led the way toward structures standing near the intersection of two graded airstrips: one was a metal aircraft hangar, the other a windowless concrete building which looked to be thick and sturdy. It was. A single door appeared to be its only entrance. It wasn't.

The building was the nerve center of Prevent Incorporated, a private enterprise dedicated to the training of clients in anti-terrorist countermeasures. Founded at a later date than many of its contemporaries, the company was rapidly achieving a position of prominence. Many businesses and individuals who had cause to feel vulnerable were switching from the older firms and aligning themselves with Prevent, as its successful operations became known.

With the men from the van now seated in front of him, Beverly Martin Raker stood with his arms folded across his chest, smiling sardonically at his client. No one had called him Beverly, more than once, since he was a child.

"Questions later," he said. "For now, you're still dead." He turned to the large drawn-to-scale chart which portrayed the square mile-plus of his training site in an isolated and starkly rugged area of southwestern New Mexico. He picked up a swagger stick from the table near him and placed its tip against a small diagram of the false-fronted building from which the van had begun its journey.

"All you had to do was get from here," he slid the pointer up, "to here." He paused to set the stick down. His eyes impaled his client. "You say I told you it would be a kidnap attempt." He walked behind the table, sat down and leaned forward.

"Bullshit! You said it. You decided they would be trying an abduction." He shook his head pityingly. "I just didn't bother to tell you any different. My computer says they would just as soon have you dead." He paused to let his words make their impression.

"That's the weak spot with so damned many of us, isn't it? The old ego." He looked pointedly at his client. "Remember," he said gently, "we are rarely as important as we think."

There were nods of reluctant agreement.

"Very well." He stood erect and reached a hand inside his jacket. It emerged with fingers wrapped around the butt of a long, thick-barreled, .357 Magnum, Colt Python Hunter revolver. He aimed the weapon directly at his client's head. To the man looking down the muzzle, the black hole in the dark metal seemed gigantic.

"Never-trust-anyone-completely," he growled. His voice inserted hyphens between the words.

"Even me," he finished softly. And pulled the trigger.

NEW YORK CITY

The letter arrived at the Manhattan executive offices of PanGlobal Assurance with the Monday morning mail. It bore a New York City postmark and was addressed to Mallory Fleming Mitchell, president and chairman of the board. Below and to the left of the address, in hand-printed block letters, heavily underlined, was the legend PERSONAL AND CONFIDENTIAL.

Victoria Genn, Mitchell's executive secretary, slit open the envelope with practiced skill, eased out the contents, and unfolded the single sheet of paper. She read the lines, typewritten in capital letters:

> THIS IS FORMAL NOTIFICATION THAT WE ARE TERMINATING THE POLICIES OF CERTAIN SELECTED CLIENTS OF YOUR ORGANIZATION. YOU WILL BE NOTIFIED IN THE NEAR FUTURE REGARDING DETAILS AND CONSIDERATIONS INVOLVED WHICH MAY ALLOW YOU TO MINIMIZE YOUR LOSSES.
>
> $

There was no signature. Beneath and to the right of the last word, hand-drawn in red ink, was a large dollar sign.

• • •

Lifted eyebrows arched semicircles across Victoria Genn's elegant forehead. She replaced the sheet of paper in its envelope, marked it for her employer's attention, and turned to her other Monday morning chores.

After a moment or two, her eyes flicked toward the envelope. It might be better to deliver it immediately. She put down the letter opener, picked up the envelope, and reached for the intercom to Mitchell's office. The discreetly small and unobtrusive clock on her desk indicated it was 9:23 a.m., New York time.

NEW MEXICO

In New Mexico it was 6:23. The morning sun had just begun to show over the low mountains southwest of Las Cruces and north of El Paso, Texas. Its light silhouetted the outlines and cast long shadows of the bunched structures which, viewed from certain angles, could well be those of a small village. Closer observation showed them to be more closely related to the false-front buildings found on motion picture sets. Areas of pavement and curb wandered and angled in a mixture of geometric and random array. Stretches of railroad track came from and went nowhere. Well away from the buildings stood a large, domed, metal structure. High above its curved top, a bright, orange windsock fluttered weakly in the prevailing northwest breeze.

Some few hundred yards in front of the hangar could be seen the "X" formed where airstrips crossed. Except for artificial light visible through the doors of the domed building, most observers would see no indication of activity anywhere on the 640 acres of land. In the growing light, a network of sinuously twisting, narrow and randomly spaced roads was becoming visible; some were gravel surfaced, others merely scraped earth.

Inside the low building flanking the hangar, Beverly Martin Raker sat at a heavy walnut desk placed in a corner well away from the structure's single outside door. That is, its single public outside door. Without taking his eyes from the papers spread before him, he picked up one of the two telephones on the desk and started to dial. He glanced at the open door leading from his office to the reception area and replaced the instrument.

"Theresa," he called.

"Yes?" The melodious voice was bright and alert. The hour made no difference to Theresa Maria Chavez. She gladly worked any hours asked by Raker. Often far more.

"Get Colt, will you? New York City. At his office." He returned his attention to the papers in front of him. It seemed only moments before Theresa's voice called out.

"It's Mr. Colt, Rake. On one."

Raker punched a button and picked up the phone. "Jimmy boy," he greeted. "How's the claims avoidance expert?" Colt was vice-president for claims investigation for PanGlobal Assurance— and of far more importance to the iron-fisted man who ran that company than his title alone would indicate.

"My God, it's Attila the Hun, himself." Colt's pleasure was evident in his voice. "And the answer is no! There's not an insurance company in this mortar-forking world that'll approve you for a policy. How in the hell are you and what do you want?"

"A bit of info, James. Any rush of casualty claims overnight? Big ones?"

Colt was silent for a moment, then spoke. "No . . . nothing noted yet." His tone brightened. "How about out there in mañana land? Any excitement going on?"

Raker gave a short, one-note laugh. "Satisfying session with a pompous tycoon type." A three-note laugh. "Bruised ego, wet pants and probably dyspepsia."

"What in the hell is dyspep-whatever?" asked Colt.

"What in the hell do you know about UTRACO?" Raker countered.

"Universal Trade Company," mused Colt, dividing it into syllables. "Acronym for Universal Trade Company. One of the larger holding companies around. They talk billions up to trillions. Are you dealing with them?"

"I'm looking into it. Preliminary. They've been having some trouble with the 'baddies.' Seems they've had an exec or two nabbed. I'm to meet with them tomorrow to see if we like each other. Thought as long as I'd be out your way we could get together and rehash old times over a jar or two."

James Travis Colt mentally eyed Raker, feigning suspicion.

"No doubt it'll destroy my saintly reputation to be seen with you," he said. "When you coming out?"

"This evening. Theresa is booking me through now."

"Want I should meet you?"

"Too inconvenient. Don't have my precise schedule. Anyway, I don't want to endanger my life with your driving. Why don't you check with my hotel, say eightish, and leave word if I'm not in yet. The Sheraton up by the park."

"Why there? Would think all your vast riches would have you staying at one of our super plush jobs."

Raker grunted. "I like the anonymity that goes with indifferent service." He looked down, thought, and paused a moment. "I hear Himmler junior is working there with you. Is that right?"

There was a long moment's hesitation before Colt answered. "It's not right, but uh-huh, Webb is here." His voice was flat. "Want me to give him your regards?"

"Not in this lifetime," said Raker.

The two men exchanged a few more pleasant insults, reaffirmed their meeting, and ended their call.

In New Mexico it was 6:37 a.m., MST.

New York City

"Colt," he said, picking up his PanGlobal office phone.

"Mr. Colt," came Victoria Genn's calm, smoothly professional voice. "Mr. Mitchell has called a special meeting and all are expected in the boardroom immediately. Is that convenient?" It was not really a question.

"On my way, Victoria," he answered. He was one of three people Victoria Genn enjoyed letting use her first name. The fact that she had addressed him as Mr. in private conversation informed Colt that the meeting was to be of the sort that she liked to call "heavy duty."

· · ·

Access to the boardroom of PanGlobal was close to running a gauntlet. As he left the elevator, Colt's smooth, athletic stride carried him through the outer reception office where two secretarial aides greeted him politely, and on through the doors of Victoria Genn's office. "Go right through, Mr. Colt. He's in the boardroom with Mr. Webb."

"Anyone else?"

"It's to be only the three of you."

Colt nodded and went into the boardroom. Unlike Mitchell's bright and airy room, the boardroom had no windows. The walls were solidly paneled with dark wood that matched the massive table and chairs which nearly filled the room. Fluorescent lighting illuminated the scene evenly but starkly. The only other furnishings were a pair of huge file cabinets. The floor was deeply carpeted, but there were no decorations of any sort on the walls. There were to be no distractions when Mallory Fleming Mitchell held court. As Colt entered he lifted his head and spoke. "Come in, James. Come in. I want you to look this over." His fingers flicked toward the paper in front of him.

As he approached the table, James Colt nodded toward the man standing near Mitchell. He was Harlan Webb, director of security for the company—looking, Colt noted, his usual erect, starched-and-creased self. Webb returned the nod crisply. Well-dressed and immaculately groomed in civilian attire, Webb was able to convey the impression that he was wearing a uniform.

"Sit down, Webb, sit down," growled Mitchell as he pushed the letter toward Colt. "Tell me, James, what you think of this."

Colt read the short, capitalized note. "Extortion attempt, obviously."

"Obviously," repeated Mitchell dryly. "Webb, here, suggests that we turn it over to the . . . authorities." He lifted heavy, rumpled eyebrows to look at Colt expectantly.

Colt snorted. "We can't advertise that we are being black-mailed!"

"Exactly!" thundered Mitchell, slapping the table with the flat of his hand. "And I'm not about to let some goddamn kook force me into any precipitate action. Webb?"

Webb shrugged without disturbing his parade-rest posture. "You're the boss," he said.

"Damn right I am," replied Mitchell. "Any suggestions?"

"We wait, I think," mused Colt, "until we hear something else about this. In the meantime I'll have our lab check for fingerprints and anything else we can learn from this . . . communication."

"From paper?" asked Mitchell.

"There's the old iodine process, some new laser procedures . . ." A pause. "Many more." He knew the man knew.

Mitchell swiveled in his chair.

"I want as few people in on this as possible," he said. "Can you handle it?"

Colt studied the letter and envelope he now held. "Common dime-store material," he said. "Written on a typewriter with changeable type. Little likelihood of tracking that down, I'll venture." He sighed. "For prints, I'll guess nada except for mail handlers and our own people. Anyway, I'll process them, of course." His expression hardened.

"We can hold any results in private until we decide to turn it all over to . . ." he paused to glance at Harlan Webb, ". . . the authorities," he finished.

Mitchell's head bobbed as he gave a small snort. "James doesn't seem to share your enthusiasm for our protectors of law and order, Webb."

"That is his history," agreed Webb.

"Yes, well, do not forget, Mr. Webb, that when one attains the stature that this company has achieved, you . . . I . . . become the authorities. I know your damn authorities, and their security leaks like a punctured tire!"

As he stared pointedly at Webb, the chime on the intercom sounded. Mitchell allowed no telephones in the boardroom. The only communications permitted from outside while the board was in session came solely through Victoria Genn directly to Mitchell.

"Yes, Victoria."

"I believe I'd better come in for a moment." Her voice came quietly, but with a trace of tension. "There is something you should see."

• • •

"Come, do," said Mitchell. He turned to Colt and Webb. His fingers drummed on the table top in short, staccato bursts until the door opened.

"A young woman is in the outer office," said Victoria Genn. "She had a sealed envelope, addressed to me personally. I opened it and immediately contacted you." She extended her hand. "This is it."

Mitchell extracted the paper from its envelope, muttering ". . . to you, huh?" As he unfolded it, the others could see —below several typewritten lines — a bright, bold dollar sign drawn in red. Mitchell placed the sheet of paper on the table where it could be read by all, and smoothed it flat with his hand. They read:

MS. GENN:

THE BEARER OF THIS COMMUNICATION HAS MATERIAL FOR PRESENTATION DIRECTLY TO MALLORY FLEMING MITCHELL. IT IS IN THE BEST INTERESTS OF ALL THAT YOU FACILITATE IMMEDIATE DELIVERY.

NOW, ASSUMING THAT YOU, MR. MITCHELL, ARE READING THIS, BE ADVISED THAT THE TOTAL KNOWLEDGE OF THE BEARER

REGARDING THE PROJECT AT HAND IS RESTRICTED ONLY TO WHAT
SHE HAS BEEN TOLD, ALONG WITH SUCH DATA AS SHE HAS BEEN
AUTHORIZED TO WILLINGLY OFFER REGARDING THIS DIRECTORATE.
SHE HAS BEEN EMPLOYED SOLELY AS A MESSENGER AND KNOWS
NOTHING MORE THAN WHAT SHE WILL VOLUNTEER.

WHILE YOU WILL IMMEDIATELY RECOGNIZE THE IMPLICATIONS
IN THE MATERIAL SHE BEARS, SHE WILL NOT. IT IS, THEREFORE,
TO YOUR ADVANTAGE TO OFFER HER NO INFORMATION SHE DOES
NOT ALREADY POSSESS. SHE IS, IN ANY AND ALL EVENTS, TO BE
CONSIDERED IMMUNE FROM ANY INTERFERENCE OR INQUISITION.

ANY ACTIONS TAKEN AGAINST HER, PAST THOSE PERMITTED BY THIS
DIRECTIVE, WILL BE MET WITH IRREVERSIBLE AND DEVASTATING
RETALIATION.

$

"It would seem," said Mitchell, "that the plot is about to do
the proverbial thickening." He turned to Victoria Genn. "By all
means, show the lady into my office."

Unfolding his lank frame from the chair in which he was sitting,
Mitchell faced the other two men already on their feet. "Come,
gentlemen, let's see just what illumination is to be cast on this little
drama." He began to pick up the letters from the table.

"May I suggest," said Colt, "that we leave this material in here?
The timing of the letter and the visit sort of defy coincidence, but
the fact that she may actually be only a relatively innocent go-
between would seem to make that the wisest choice."

Mitchell looked from the papers to Colt's face and back again.
"You're quite right, James, quite right." He dropped the letters on
the table and motioned toward the door. "Shall we?"

• • •

Mitchell's office was as open as the boardroom was closed. Glass
walls, attractive furnishings, fine paintings, and an array of live
greenery gave the large room an inviting air of tasteful opulence.
The massive, ornately carved desk and matching high-back chair

lent the room Mitchell's authoritarian stamp of proprietorship. The desk also served as an effective barrier between the man sitting behind it and those on the outside. All other seating in the room was, though comfortably upholstered, low and deep. Sitters were forced to slouch back and look up at the great man, or perch uncomfortably on the front edge of their seat.

Mallory Fleming Mitchell could, however, still be the gracious salesman when so inclined. As Victoria Genn ushered the caller into the room, he rose quickly to his feet and moved from behind the desk to approach the visitor, a broad smile brightening his craggy face.

"Come in, come in, please," he said, arms extended in welcome. "Have a seat anywhere, Miz . . . "

"Miss," said the young woman, looking around at the available seating. "Maguire. Pagan Maguire." She selected a chair close to where Colt and Webb were already seated.

"I have small use for general terms." She sat forward on her chair, briefcase-like handbag on her lap, knees together, legs comfortably slanted to the side, ankles quite properly crossed.

"Now," she said, "would you mind sitting somewhere that I don't have to crane my neck to look up at you?"

A slight flutter of surprise crossed Mitchell's face but did not affect his salesman's smile. "But of course, my dear." He chose a chair across from the others, leaving the low table between them. Habit is hard to break.

"Now," he said, "these gentlemen are confidants I've asked to meet with us. I'm sure you won't mind if I get right to the point. Just what is this business all about?"

"It's that I've been employed to deliver this communication to you. And then I'm to try and answer any questions you have." She removed a sealed envelope from her bag and handed it to Mitchell.

"Thank you, my dear, thank you," said Mitchell, taking the proffered material. "While I'm reading this, could I have some refreshments brought in to you?"

Pagan smiled brightly. "Don't be after bothering with the blarney, Mr. Mitchell. I'm only here to perform the job I was hired to do."

Mitchell rose from his chair and stood to survey the girl levelly for a moment before speaking.

"Right," he said. "Of course. Excuse me." As he moved to his huge desk the girl turned her head and smiled tentatively at Colt and Webb.

"You're staring," she observed.

Webb remained seated at attention, arms folded across his chest to dispel any familiarity. "Did I understand you to say that your name is Pagan? Does that signify a predisposition?"

The girl turned intelligent and remarkably lovely eyes toward Webb, studying him for a moment before replying.

"To disbelief, you mean?" she shook her head. "Perhaps that I'm hard to convince. Actually, it only signifies a father with a sense of humor. He was a delightfully irreverent man who liked the play upon the Irish small-name, Pegeen. Mr. . . . ?"

"Webb." Her smile showed she had already remembered. "Does that indicate a tendency toward entrapment, Mr. Webb?"

James Colt stifled a laugh. "Well done, Miss Maguire," he said. "But I'm afraid you'll also have fun with my name. It's Colt. Hopefully it signifies ordinary horse sense." His grin was infectious.

"For a fact," Pagan said, "in Irish or American, the word signifies friskiness."

Colt's grin spread. "Touche,:" he said.

"Are you of Irish ancestry?" Pagan inquired.

"I'm American hash, Miss Maguire. And you? You're Irish?"

"I was born in America," she said. "Virginia, it was. But my parents were Irish."

Colt was interested. "Then you have dual citizenship?"

"I travel on a United States passport."

"But you qualify for an Irish passport," insisted Colt.

"Do I now?"

Colt dropped the topic. "Would it be proper for me to ask just what, or at least how, you came to be involved in this . . . assignment?"

"It would," answered Pagan, glancing toward the desk where Mitchell was poring over the contents of the envelope he had been given. "But I think I should wait until Mr. Mitchell has finished with the communication there."

Colt nodded reflectively. He thought to himself: Pretty girl. No! More than just pretty. Striking! And bright. And those enormous, luminous eyes! Emerald green, and sheltered by long, sweeping, dark lashes. At the last thought, Colt almost laughed at himself. Christ, he thought, here I am, involved in the opening moves of an extortion attempt, and I'm waxing poetic over some twenty-what? Twenty-three or twenty-four-year-old girl who might well be more than the simple courier she seems. There was no doubt that she was intelligent and capable. No doubt at all.

Pagan Maguire kept her eyes on Mitchell as she reflected on the two men seated near her. Colt, she thought, she understood. Mid-thirties or just possibly a bit more; quite attractive in a lean, strong-featured way; and charmingly polite and attentive. But for all of his charm there was a certain something about him—not appearance, not in the way he walked. More like something from inside, something she had sensed in a few of her brother's friends. It was just that it was there—a sense of threat, a sort of harnessed and controlled violence.

The other man she understood better. Webb, it was. She knew well his kind. They commanded brigades on both sides of the "troubles." She had seen the type with both the Irish Republican Army's Provisionals, and with that scurvy lot who did the filthy work advocated by that black-hearted Paisley. Webb would be tough and hard as blackthorn, and disciplined as only the fanatical can be. In his favor, one would always know where one stood with Webb. Her brother had been like that, she thought reluctantly. Her dear, sweet brother! And they wanted to know why she was here? Well, they would have answers, but they'd not learn of her brother. And she thought of how she herself had learned, less than six months ago.

CHAPTER 2

The telephone system hadn't worked well anywhere in the Republic of Ireland for years—especially in Dublin. It required three tries to complete the "urgent" call to the number she had received in a brief, unsigned note pinned to the door of her residence. These attempts included one call to Directory Inquiry which yielded the information: "That number has been changed. Please deposit the correct monies and dial again." All without divulging the secret of the new number. But persistence prevailed.

"Yes?"

"I was told to call this number."

"Miss Maguire?" It was a male voice.

"Herself."

"Miss Maguire, you do not know me, but I have news of your brother, Colin."

Pagan's heart soared. Colin! Dear Colin. So many years, so many long years unheard from. "Oh, sweet Mary, Joseph and Patrick! Where . . . what . . . where has he—"

"Please! Wait. I can't speak on the phone. I must meet with you."

Oh, no, she thought. No! They're still after him. He's still running. Damn the Brits! Damn the government! Damn the IRA! "Anywhere, anywhere," she pleaded, "just tell me when."

"Do you know the Davy Byrnes?"

"Of course!" Many of the young, theatrical crowd made it their local.

"How long will it take you to come here?"

"I'm not far, and transportation runs nearby. Perhaps twenty minutes?"

"Can you call a taxi?"

She hesitated. "That will probably take longer."

"Twenty minutes, then. What are you wearing?"

A pause. "A gray, tweed skirt, an off-white jumper. Black pumps."

Jumper? Of course, a sweater. "It's misting a bit," he said. "Will you wear a coat?"

"I will. Light tan, beige."

"Wear it over your shoulders without your arms through the sleeves, and carry a book. Hold it in your right hand, hugged to your chest."

"I will that."

"Twenty minutes, then. I'll be waiting." The line went dead.

• • •

In less than the time estimated, Pagan Maguire stepped from the bus to the pavement at the stop nearest Duke Street, deep auburn hair bouncing, book clutched close to her breast. Before she could take four steps toward her destination, a voice called her name.

"Miss Maguire."

She looked up quickly as a man detached himself smoothly from the building he had been leaning against and approached her. He appeared broad and sturdy in a belted trench coat. He was hatless. His head was completely hairless, either shaved or naturally bald. He wore a heavy, drooping, dark mustache which matched thick eyebrows over dark eyes.

She looked at him inquiringly.

"I'd prefer to change our meeting place," he said, taking her arm. "Phones are too easily listened in on."

Pagan grasped the front of his coat with her free hand and pleaded, "Colin? What of Colin?"

The man gently urged her to his side. "Not here. In a moment."

As they walked north through the misting rain, Pagan, head down against the wet, asked, "You're American?"

"Canadian," he said. It was the end of conversation as they headed up the street. Occasionally the man would pause before a shop window and study their fellow pedestrians and the automobiles on the street. Just short of O'Connell Street Bridge, he guided her around a corner, down the narrow road, and through old weather-beaten doors, into a dimly lighted pub. Leaving her seated on the upholstered bench against the wall, he went to the bar where he ordered a hot punch for her and a pint of Guinness for himself. Pagan sipped from her glass, wanting to speak, but feeling a sense of apprehension.

"I wanted you sitting down," said the man, eyes avoiding hers.

"Oh, no! Please God, no."

"Yes." It was that simple. Not easy. Just simple. "You must have known."

Pagan leaned her head back and closed her eyes. "I feared it," she said limply. "I think we all feared it." Her hand clenched the stem of her glass. "How? Where? When?"

"It's who, you should ask. Where and when don't matter that much."

"Who? Why who?"

"He was murdered, Miss Maguire. A calculated assassination, that's how." The man removed a hand from his pocket and placed a photograph in front of her. "And this is who."

Pagan looked with horror at the photograph which was a portrait detailing the faces of a man and a woman. There was a marked resemblance between the two. They were extremely attractive, the man almost effeminately so. Their expressions were of self-satisfied aloofness.

"I've . . . seen . . . " started Pagan, slowly.

"Yes. You've seen their picture before. That's most likely. At least his. Their name is Gordon. Elizabeth and Alec Gordon. They are twins. And violent supporters of the northern separatists. They are well known to . . ." he hesitated, ". . . well known to friends and associates of your brother," he finished.

Pagan nodded slowly, staring intently at the photograph, etching the faces into her memory. "Yes," she said, "I've seen their pictures before. And heard of them. They're evil. But how . . . ?"

"How did it happen? Your brother didn't know about him, or them, when it happened. It was only after . . . after your brother was murdered that we found out about the Gordons. Here," he took another photograph from his pocket, "this was taken just days before . . ." and he left the sentence dangling as he handed her the photograph.

Unwanted tears filled Pagan's eyes as she looked at Colin's face smiling broadly from the snapshot, bearded as last she had seen him, and with his mop of curly hair tumbled low on his forehead. He was posed with one knee on the ground, holding some sort of weapon across his other leg. Next to him, holding a rifle, was Alec Gordon. Pagan breathed deeply, and used a finger to brush the wetness from her lashes. "I see," she said. Her voice was deathly cold. "And how do you know it was Gordon?"

"I found Colin, shot in the back, where he'd fallen. He'd been on guard with Gordon. I never saw Gordon again until I learned he was back in England."

"England? Aren't they Northern?"

"English. They were told that Colin had been responsible for the death of their older brother who was an officer with the Brits up north."

Pagan was jarred. "And was he?"

"Come, Miss Maguire. Your brother was active with the Provos for years. You knew that, even at your tender age. He may well have been responsible for the deed." He leaned toward the girl and tapped a finger against the back of her hand in emphasis. "But that was war, Miss Maguire. Not trusted companion shooting friend in the back."

"The Provos aren't always that careful," she replied quietly.

"No, they are not," agreed the man, "but the Gordon brother was a soldier." He touched her face with a finger to turn her eyes up to his. "Does it matter? Is it all right if it simply evened the score?"

"It is not!" Her eyes flashed. "It certainly is not. That man must be brought to justice."

"Not just the man. He was the instrument. The sister was the power."

"Then they must both pay."

"Pay who, Miss Maguire? No jurisdiction wants them. Colin

was buried, with words said over him, in a country far from here. No one cared about a missing guard hired to protect a rich man's home in a backward country. Pay who, Miss Maguire?"

"There are friends who care. There are certainly friends, and family." She studied the man intently for a moment. "Is that what he . . . you . . . were doing? Guarding a rich man's land, Mr. . . . ?"

"Coleman," supplied the man. "Owen Coleman. Yes. That's what we were doing."

"And where abouts, Mr. Coleman?"

"Where doesn't matter," he replied, "but I think these do." He reached into a side pocket of his raincoat and brought out a loosely wrapped package. He handed it to Pagan.

She silently unwrapped it. It contained only a weathered passport, a small clasp knife, a religious medal strung on a chain, and the engraved identification bracelet she had given her brother on his 21st birthday. As she fingered the bracelet, reading the short inscription which said simply, "With love to my biggest brother— Peg," her eyes started to mist. She tossed her head, shaking off the emotion and clasped the bracelet tightly in her hand.

"I'm sorry," said Coleman.

"So am I," answered the young woman. She composed herself. "Now! From all this, I assume you can help in . . . in . . . delivering up these . . ." She hunted for words. ". . . these rotten bastards?" The words sounded uncommonly evil coming from her mouth.

The man who called himself Coleman waited a moment before answering. "I can," he said, "and more. I can deliver them, and be of great assistance in helping to put a stop to others like them. But I'll need help and cooperation from you. And others."

She met the man's gaze and slowly nodded her head. And as he talked, Pagan Maguire continued to nod her head in agreement with his proposal.

After a time, Coleman took a small notebook from an inside pocket. Removing the top from a soft, felt-tipped pen, he started to write.

"When you have made the necessary arrangements," he said, "you may notify this number that 'all is ready.' I will understand

and communicate with you. That will prevent unnecessary contact between us."

She took the small sheet of paper. Her fingers, damp from the glass she had been holding, smeared the ink.

"I smudged it," she said apologetically. "Those soft tipped pens do that so easily." She examined the written numbers.

"On the other hand," said Coleman, with a knowing smile, "they don't leave impressions on the surface below, now do they? Can you read it?"

"No," said the girl. "I fear I've ruined it. Have you a regular pen?"

Coleman shook his head. "Never use them." He took the slip of paper back and placed it carefully in his pocket. "I'll write it again."

"It would be safer if we do not leave together," he said, handing her the second slip of paper. "I'll wait until you are well on your way before I leave."

She nodded.

"I'll be expecting to hear from you," he said.

"And that you will, Mr. Coleman." She stood, clutching her handbag and the book. "That you will."

CHAPTER 3

NEW YORK CITY

"Well, now." Mitchell's voice broke the silence in the room high above the New York City streets. He cleared his throat with a cough. "Most interesting. Most interesting, this."

He held up the papers he had been reading and waved them. Folding them, he moved from behind his desk to rejoin the others. He faced Pagan. "Are you familiar with the contents herein, Miss Maguire?"

"I am not, sir." She answered coolly and truthfully. "I was instructed to only read material addressed specifically to me."

"Yes, yes, of course," harrumphed Mitchell, struggling to regain his salesman's smile. "You realize that you have brought us some rather disturbing information, don't you?"

"That is apparent, sir. I was told that what I was bringing would not be to your liking, and . . ." she paused momentarily, "that I might be subjected to some rather intensive questioning. I've been instructed to answer what I can, but I must say I know little more than I've just told you."

"Quite. Yes, quite. So I've been given to understand." He removed the half-glasses with which he had been reading, polished them with a handkerchief and returned both the glasses and the handkerchief to his pocket. It was an obvious delay to allow him time to think. "I see. Is there any way we can contact you, Miss Maguire?"

"I have been told that such would not be prudent, Mr. Mitchell," replied the girl. "But I have also been instructed to call your office each day in the morning and again in the afternoon to make myself available to anything you may want to tell me, or ask me."

"Excellent! Excellent, fine." Mitchell placed his hands on the arms of his chair and hoisted himself to his feet. It was a gesture of dismissal.

"I think that will do for now, Miss Maguire." He took her by the elbow and walked her toward the door. "Mrs. Genn will show you out. We will be anticipating your telephone call. May we assume tomorrow morning?"

"Or this afternoon, if you like."

"No," said Mitchell, opening the door, "tomorrow will be quite fine."

As the girl exited, he closed the door and whirled.

"God damn!" he exploded. "God damn it!"

He strode back to sit in the chair he had recently vacated. "Some clever and rotten son of a bitch has got a hand on our nuts and he's ready to squeeze."

The tough old man seemed to sag in his chair. He took the envelope from his pocket and threw it on the table between him and the other men.

"Read the thing, gentlemen." He jerked his hand viciously toward the envelope.

"Read the motherfucking thing and weep!"

YOUR COMPUTERS HAVE BEEN ACCESSED AND YOUR CLIENT FILES COMPROMISED. ENCLOSED YOU WILL FIND NEWSPAPER CLIPPINGS DETAILING TRAGIC EVENTS. EACH EVENT REPRESENTS A FINANCIAL LOSS TO YOUR COMPANY.. NONE OF THE EVENTS WAS AN ACCIDENT. EACH WAS PLANNED AND EXECUTED BY ME.

DISCOUNTING POLICY VALUES PLACED BY YOU WITH RE-INSURERS, THESE LOSSES TO YOUR COMPANY TOTAL NINETY MILLION, SEVEN HUNDRED THOUSAND DOLLARS AS ROUNDED TO THE NEAREST THOUSAND.

YOU MAY VERIFY. ADDITIONAL "STRIKES" ARE BEING EXECUTED TO INSURE YOUR FUTURE COOPERATION. TO PRECLUDE DOUBT REGARDING THESE FUTURE POLICY TERMINATIONS, IDENTIFYING MATERIAL WILL BE PRESENTED QUITE SOON, WHICH WILL SERVE TO PREVENT MISUNDERSTANDING BEFORE THE FACT.

TERMS TO BE MET BY YOU WILL BE DELIVERED ONLY AFTER THE
POLICY TERMINATIONS. THESE TERMINATIONS SHOULD INSURE
YOUR UNDERSTANDING OF MY SERIOUSNESS OF INTENT.

$

The letter closed with the red dollar sign.

•••

James Colt stood at the east wall of plate glass and looked down
on Manhattan from forty floors above the street. Mitchell had
moved to the huge chair behind his desk. Webb was still seated,
military posture temporarily forgotten, as he continued to pore
over the paper Pagan Maguire had delivered.

"Well," started Mitchell. "What about it, James? Is it as bad as
I feel?"

Colt turned from the window and started to walk slowly back
and forth across the thick carpet. "Yes, I think it's that bad. And
too damn clever by far. They want us to sweat. And the timing is
too perfect. First the letter; then immediate contact by the girl—
and now we know it's too late to even try to stop them before
damage is done. He glanced toward Webb and the paper he held.
"You'll check those out?"

Webb nodded. "Immediately." The newspaper stories concerned several hotel fires, transportation accidents and a vanished
oil tanker.

"And there'll be more to come, if we're to believe it."
Webb dropped the papers he'd been studying. "Believe it," he said.
"There's no bluff here. I think that now even you will agree that we
must call in the . . ." he hesitated, reluctant to use the word. Ego
won out. ". . . the authorities. There has to be an inside contact,
and it'll take more time than we can muster to combat something
as organized as this appears to be. He stood and clasped his hands
militarily behind his back. "And the girl . . ." his voice trailed off.

"What about the girl?" asked Colt.

"Right now," Webb replied, " she's the only hope we have of
breaking this thing. We've got to go after her with everything we've
got." He looked up at Mitchell. "I don't know why you didn't give
me the opportunity to at least have her followed."

"Don't be precipitous, Webb," lectured Mitchell. "You read the first communication. Any interference might well be too costly."

"I didn't build the largest company of its kind in the world just to see some demented sick, lazy, shit-head threaten me out of it." He stood as his anger grew. "I'm a business man, and a goddamn tough gutter-fighter." His thick eyebrows slanted into a V over eyes that gleamed defiance.

"No, by God! I'll not see my empire—that's right, empire!—destroyed by fear. We'll fight them!" His fist thundered against the top of his desk. "Fight them!" He glared at Webb. "Maybe we'll come to your way, Webb. But what we need right now is a smarter way." He turned eyes to Colt.

"James? We've got the best investigation department in the business, maybe in the whole world—and information on damn near everyone in it—all filed away in our computers. Isn't there some way we can run the show ourselves?"

Colt had moved back to the window. He turned slowly. "Yes," he said. "I have an idea there is." He moved to the edge of the desk as Mitchell reseated himself. "Do you need to let the board in on this?"

Mitchell scoffed. "That gaggle of ninnies do what I say. I'll let them know what I decide when the time is right." The ninnies of whom Mitchell spoke represented some of the wealthiest names on both sides of the Atlantic Ocean.

"Why?"

"We need professional help," said Colt. "Not Webb's 'authorities'," he injected hurriedly, "but a professional. I'm not certain we can get him, but I know one. I also know he'll be damned expensive."

"Expensive!" exploded Mitchell. "Fuck expensive. What I'm facing could ruin my company, *all* my companies. Piss on expensive. Tell me about him."

"Have you heard of an outfit called Prevent Incorporated?" asked Colt.

Mitchell reflected momentarily. "Vaguely," he said. "Something about a subscription newsletter on terrorism or such?" He showed interest. "You're not serious?"

"Dead serious," said Colt.

"Are you familiar with the organization, Mr. Webb?" inquired Mitchell.

"More than familiar. It's run by one of the most dubious individuals you or anyone else is likely to meet. A man—well, there is a tony British word that fits the bastard: Blackguard! The sonofabitch is a genuine blackguard."

Mitchell looked at Colt. "James?"

"His services are used by some of the most reputable companies in the world. He not only compiles data concerning terrorism, but has an operation headquartered in New Mexico where he trains personnel in terrorism countermeasures—measures he calls avoidance, detection and disassembly." Colt looked over his shoulder at Webb.

"Harlan there and Raker had a run-in some years back when Raker's operations conflicted with Harlan's criminal investigations for the Army."

"The bastard was stealing arms," objected Webb.

Colt shrugged. "It was never proven," he said.

"Hell no, it wasn't," fumed Webb. "He was protected by you . . . " Even in his anger he reconsidered what he had been about to say. "By your damned CIA," he finished. He jammed his hands into his pockets and thrust his jaw forward aggressively. "Your crew supplied him for years."

Mitchell followed the interchange with interest. "That, also, has never been proven," said Colt. He sounded amused.

"Webb," said Mitchell, turning to face the man directly. "Through the years has there been a case of Raker being accused of violating a trust?"

Webb shouted, "No!"

Colt turned back to Mitchell. "Sure, there have been charges and investigations about illegal activities." He shrugged. "Again, nothing proven. It always turned out that he was hired, apparently legitimately, as a consultant to certain governments."

"Certain governments!" snorted Webb. "He was a full-blown mercenary commanding one of the hottest commando battalions around, and you damn well know it. Didn't your own CIA supply him? And weren't you his liaison a good part of the time?"

Colt smiled. "Some have claimed that," he said gently. "Again, never proven."

"Cool it, you two," interrupted Mitchell. "Let me sum it up. Webb, is this . . . what was it? Raker? Is this Raker effective?"

Webb once again folded his arms across his chest and stood erect. He took a deep breath and nodded his head sharply one time. "Yes. He's effective."

"Is he dependable?"

Webb shifted uncomfortably from foot to foot. "Yes. He is reputed to be dependable by his employers."

"James, you seem to know Raker rather well. Is he trustworthy? Tight-lipped?"

Colt considered the question for a moment before answering. "There are times, when it is to his advantage, that Raker will talk for hours, but without reporting a thing. And you can stake your life on his trust-worthiness. Many have. He is also the last man in the world I would cross."

"And you, Mr. Webb. How would you feel about crossing this man?"

Webb showed his discomfort. He chose his words carefully. "There are few things I fear," he said. It did not sound like a boast. "I *do* fear Raker. It will only aid my point when I say that he is undoubtedly one of the most dangerous men in the world."

Mitchell was impressed. "And just how old a man is this Raker?"

Webb and Colt exchanged puzzled glances. The question had never occurred to them.

Mitchell read their expressions. "Never mind. I'm sure he's in the computer." He came to a decision. "Then I see no need to quibble. He appears to be capable and qualified, and I'd trust damned near anyone to keep their mouths shut rather than those 'authorities' Mr. Webb seems to regard with such reverence." He thought a moment. "One more thing, James. Does he have the resources we might need?"

Again, Colt took time to study his reply. "Without a doubt. He certainly has the trained personnel, and he has evolved certain methods in protection and prediction that none of the other companies such as his seem to understand. He's also evolved a program for running computerized psychograms that have proven to be surprisingly accurate in predicting and identifying both targets and terrorists. Coupled with our own resources," he shrugged, "he just might be able to make government agencies look foolish."

"Weaknesses? Failings? Anything like that?"

Again, Colt took time to consider his answer. "He is one of the most disciplined, emotionally uninvolved persons I've ever known. If it's a weakness, he has always been unfailingly loyal to his associates. I think the only thing in the world Raker gives a damn about is his daughter. Weaknesses?" Colt grinned. "He does have a few. Raker insists on running things."

Mitchell gave a short laugh. "That may be tough for an old war-horse like me to take," he said, "but I'll work on it. Can we get him?"

"I'll have to see," answered Colt. "I thought of him immediately because he called me quite early this morning. He will be in the city sometime this evening. He has a meeting with Universal Trade Company."

"Universal Trade Company," echoed Mitchell. He grinned. He—well, he and the others—owned Universal Trade Company.

"If they want him, we want him more. Hell, the bastards may be killing clients right now. Get him, James. Get him. And I hope . . ." he hesitated.

"Hope?" encouraged Webb from across the room.

"Just thinking about profits," said Mitchell. "Just hoping that whoever those poor bastards are that they're going to kill, that they all have small policies. Or that we've farmed them out."

• • •

Returning to his office three floors beneath Mitchell's throne room, Colt's face bore an expression of grimness which caused his secretary to cock her head to one side and ask, "Bad?"

"Bad," said Colt. He paused at her desk to smile wryly. "Get 'Prevent Inc'. on the phone, will you? Raker probably will be gone. Make sure you're talking to Theresa Chavez. Find out when Raker will arrive, airline, time, you know," he waved a hand. "I'll be back in my office."

"Will do."

• • •

Janet Fremont had been Colt's secretary ever since he had been persuaded to join PanGlobal. He had known her long before that while they were both employed with the Central Intelligence Agency; Janet at a desk with the Directorate of Management and Services, James Colt in the field with the Special Operations Division.

When Colt left the agency in protest during the period which saw certain politicians—some now voted out, too many still in office—deliberately attempt to castrate the CIA and destroy the intelligence capabilities of the government, Janet had joined him for an extended vacation. They had traveled and lived together comfortably and happily for months, enjoying and respecting each other, neither demanding more than the other willingly offered.

When Janet found another man who kindled her interest, their affair ended in friendship and without rancor or resentment. Their present association was one of business, closeness, friendship and continuing respect.

Colt sat idly at his desk, repeatedly and unconsciously flipping a pencil and catching it, and contemplating the developments of the morning, when the intercom signal sounded. Voices or ringing bells never blared at PanGlobal. It was always a soft chime.

"Yes?"

"He's off," said Janet Fremont, "and flying. He left from El Paso a short time ago. He'll be in early this evening." She went on to give Colt the particulars.

"Thank you, Janet."

"What I'm here for," she replied. "Just a moment, James. There's a call . . . ."

He waited until her voice came back. "It's Daskalos," she said, "on hold."

Colt punched the flickering button and picked up the phone. "Colt."

"It's done."

"Yes?"

"Junior had his bird dogs out."

Webb had the girl followed. "Yes."

"To the nest. Want the site?"

"Not on the phone. Spotted?" Colt knew Daskalos loved the "code talk" game.

The man's voice sneered. "Not mine. Used trips."

"Good. Send up a memo. Hand carry it."

"Gotcha. Stake out?"

"If it can be invisible."

"I'll check. Report on its way."

Colt glanced at his watch. It was not yet noon! How, he thought, can so much have happened so early? From the code-like conversation, Colt knew Pagan Maguire had been followed by Webb's men. They, in turn, had been followed by Colt's crew.

Daskalos's men had used a decoy system with three followers. One to serve as an obvious tail if the girl was suspicious, another to lie farther back, and yet another to actually stay in front, dropping back when necessary. The system worked unusually well with all but the most professional evaders. Colt hoped the girl was not one of those. From his experiences of the past, Daskalos's men were so far superior to Webb's recruits that chances were slim they had been spotted.

When Daskalos delivered his written report to Colt's office, his judgment was verified. Daskalos reported that they had not been noticed by either the woman or Webb's trailers, and that she had been followed to a single family dwelling in the village not far from Washington Square. Colt instructed Daskalos to check the ownership of the residence; get any information regarding its present occupancy, but do it delicately.

At least they had a start, and he knew where Maguire was if he needed her. But then so did Webb! At the thought, he told Daskalos to, at all costs, keep Webb's men away from her—just in case. Daskalos left.

C'mon, Raker, thought James Colt. Get your butt into town.

CHAPTER 4

Colt stood at the bar in the mostly stand-up, pseudo-Victorian pub near the escalator leading from a concourse at Laguardia Airport. Colt had situated himself so that he could watch out the open doors near the moving stairs. He had elected not to meet Raker in any more public area than the bar for he knew Raker's inherent suspicion: all departing and deplaning passengers at the world's major and/or port-of-entry airports were photographed.

As he waited amid the noise and tumult created by the rapid turnover in clientele, he studied those coming and going as well as the stayers. He thought idly of how Raker would be, even weeks from now, able to recognize the faces and even the various walks and mannerisms of those he studied. It was but one of the many unusual talents that had kept Raker alive for so long.

Colt recognized Martin Raker as he stepped off the escalator at the bar's level. "Rake!" he called.

Raker's head swiveled toward the sound of Colt's voice. He lifted his free hand in greeting, and carried his bag and an attaché case toward Colt.

"Well, now," he said, "for once you finally picked a civilized place to meet."

The men shook hands briefly.

Raker dropped the folded travel bag to the floor and shoved it forward to the base of the bar where he could stand guard over it. He placed the case on the bar top.

"Almost missed you," said Colt. "What's this? A new image?" He looked Raker up and down. He was used to much closer cropped hair and casual clothing. "That beautifully barbered head of hair, was it that gray before? And that fancy banker's suit! My, my! Aren't we the corporate one?" He was grinning broadly.

"The new Raker. A true gentleman."

"That's good. Never cared for the old one much." Colt nodded his head sagely, and looked at the hand he had just shaken.

"One thing's certainly not changed," he said. "That hand. Feels like an elephant's tusk. Evidently you've stayed with the old Japanese martial arts."

"On and off," agreed Raker, "along with the Korean and Chinese. Keeps one occupied."

"Yeah, occupied," scoffed Colt. "You're black belt, as I remember. What dan?" He was asking what level, or degree, Raker had reached. "Still seventh?"

"A little above that," said Raker, not as a boast. "And you? As I recall you were approaching black. Did you go on with it?"

"Yes," admitted Colt, somewhat reluctantly.

"And . . . ?" asked Raker.

"Third dan."

Raker eyed him with interest. "We'll have to arrange a little get-together one of these days."

Colt laughed loudly. "Not on your life. Not while you're still breathing."

Raker didn't pursue it. "Now tell me," he continued, "to just what masochistic flair of altruism do I owe this untypical courtesy of being met by you?" He caught the harried bartender's eye and pointed down at Colt's glass.

"It's scotch," said Colt.

"Who cares?" asked Raker. "Back to my question." He wouldn't finish the drink anyway.

"I'm a-coming beggin', massah," said Colt.

Raker tossed money on the bar as his drink was delivered, took a sip, gave an exaggerated "ahhh!" and made the pretense of wiping his mouth. "Don't you always?" he grinned. When Colt didn't smile back, Raker sobered his mood. "You're serious."

"Deadly," said Colt. "And I've put your name in as our savior. We've got a problem."

"We, meaning PanGlobal?"

Colt nodded. "How tied up with UTRACO are you?"

Raker hesitated. He knew that the controllers of PanGlobal were the controllers of Universal Trade Company. Should he let Colt know he knew? Not for now. "I can handle more than one thing at a time. What do you have in mind?"

"Probably a full-time thing for your personal attention. Can you handle that? Now? Immediately?"

"Whoa, boy. I've got to know something about it. Did you drive out?"

Colt nodded.

"And probably parked a long cab ride away. All right, let's get me into town. You can fill me in on the way." He took a small sip and pushed his glass away. "Or can you talk and drive in this city's suicidal traffic?"

"Shouldn't be too bad at this time of evening."

"It's always bad," observed Raker. "All right. Let me leave first. I'll see you out where people wait for those little busses to Grand Central."

"Right," said Colt. He watched Raker's broad back as the man moved out through the entrance toward taxis.. He remembered Mitchell's asking about Raker's age. It hadn't seemed to matter. Middle-aged or something like that? Whatever, thought Colt, for his years and size, he moved more like a shadow than bone and muscle. Colt was waiting when Raker returned.

On the drive to the city, Colt outlined the day's developments.

Traffic had slowly thinned as they left the airport and passed older homes, trees, and jutting gray rock outcroppings. Now, as they approached the tunnel, the traffic increased.

"Not heavy traffic?" inquired Raker.

"This is light," said Colt.

"Sure. Light. In New Mexico I can drive for an hour without meeting ten cars," observed Raker.

"Yeah? Well here in Manhattan we have cars that run. You can actually start them without jumper cables."

"Un-huh, and bigger and better siphon hoses. Nope. Scratch that. I understand that here they take the whole damn car."

Colt was silent for a moment. "You amaze me, Rake. Here I

am telling you about death and destruction and all that good stuff, and you, you're making with the jokes."

"Sure. I save the heavy stuff for business."

"This is business."

"I'm not in it yet. Not until I meet your Mr. Big."

"How about the UTRACO deal?"

"That's in the morning. Set up a session with Mitchell at, say, 1:00 p.m.?"

Colt nodded. "Can do."

As they neared Raker's hotel, Colt asked, "Do you have a little time for some more . . . what do you call it out there in the desert? Palaver?"

"We call it bullshit," grinned Raker. "Sure. I'd like that. But just where in this concrete beehive can you park this heap of yours?"

"You forget, my plebeian comrade, my new-found eminence— or at least that of my employer. We possess our own subterranean parking facility. It's one of the perks to which I have prostituted my undying loyalty."

"I'm duly impressed. And where is this automobile Valhalla?"

Colt told him. It was within walking distance of Raker's hotel.

"Good," he said. "What would you say . . . " he paused to check the time on his watch. It was probably early enough. "What would you say to joining me for a few at Rick's Place, and perhaps one of those corned beef or pastrami sandwiches?"

"Rick's Place? My God, I'd forgotten that. Sure. I'd like it. Hell, no wonder you stayed at the Sheraton." He had forgotten the nearness of the neighborhood tavern.

"Haven't been there in over a year," said Raker. "Would like to see if John and Joe from the auld sod are still about."

With Colt's car safely ensconced, the two men walked to the corner of 55th and 7th where, after a brief friendly reunion with the bartenders, who were indeed still there, Colt and Raker settled at a table away from the juke box at Raker's recommendation. They carried with them schooners of beer along with sandwiches.

"It's good to see you again, Rake," said James Colt around a mouthful of corned beef on rye. "And not just for business."

"It is," agreed Raker. "We've been through a lot together, Jimmy boy."

"Have you . . . ?"

"Go on," urged Raker.

"Have you seen . . . heard from . . . you know, your daughter?"

Raker chewed for a moment, then took a swallow of beer. "No, I haven't."

Colt felt discomfort. He shouldn't have brought it up. He watched in silence as Raker smiled wistfully. "Should never have let you know about her," he said. "No. That's not quite right. I simply would prefer that things hadn't . . . that is, things weren't . . . like they are," he finished lamely.

"I don't know the whole story, Rake. Don't want to know. But she's your only child; she needs you."

Raker's expression had grown hard. "Drop it, James. Drop it."

Colt shrugged. He looked around the nearly empty bar, then back at Raker. "Tell me something, Rake. Why is it that so many times we meet, it seems to be in places like this? Or that place down around the Statler. You know, that little ten-foot-wide joint."

"The Treaty Stone," supplied Raker.

"Yeah. The Treaty Stone. How come?"

"Realler people, James. Their food and booze are a lot more important to them than to the Fancy Dans who are out to see, be seen, and impress."

"But it seems that—what would you call us? Outsiders? Newcomers?—that we seem to attract attention in these places."

"Only briefly. Unless we ask for it. Passing curiosity, then disinterest. They've got their own problems, James. They're not interferers unless we do something to disrupt their routine."

Colt nodded. "I suppose that's true. I guess I just envy the fact that you seem as much at home in a truck stop as you do at old George Sank in Paris, or London's Savoy."

Raker grinned. "Or Harry's in Venice?" He shook his head. "You and those goddamn little bells!"

Colt donned an air of injured innocence. "Simply collecting a souvenir," he said with dignity.

"Yeah," said Raker dryly, "and expediting an unplanned trip to the Tyrol to avoid the police." Raker smiled in fond memory.

"Sure. And a damned good thing, otherwise you'd never have found the village of Matrai am Brenner."

Raker's memory surged pleasantly. Matrai. Especially Alt Matrai—the tiny town down below the road, and on the edge of the tumbling river, high in the Tyrolean Alps. A setting seemingly designed by Walt Disney, music by Wagner. He chuckled. Real people, but of another world and time.

"Touché, Jimmy boy. That was special, wasn't it? Anyway, regarding your original question: I save a hell of a lot of money by visiting places like this."

"Just a peasant at heart, Raker old man. You're just a peon. You probably even like *pulque*."

Raker grinned. "As a matter of fact," he agreed. "After you get past that first slippery mouthful. I recall a little *pulqueria* . . . "

Colt groaned loudly. "Oh, no. Spare me. I'm not about to sit around while you wax nostalgic. You can stay here and reminisce, <u>cuate</u>, since your bed awaits just down the street, but I've got miles to go, so I'm going to drag my high class butt out of here."

Raker grinned. Colt's apartment was in the east 60s, a luxury address allowed through the money accumulated by a family who, for five generations, had almost always shipped the most profitable products, whether imported or exported, legal or not. His place was only blocks away.

"Well, far be it from me to deprive you of your badly needed beauty sleep."

Colt paused. "You're certain UTRACO won't interfere?"

Raker waved off the suggestion. "It's not a selling job. They want us. I'll pay them the courtesy of an in-person visit then turn it over to the crew. Hell, they do the work anyway."

Colt knew that wasn't the case, but said nothing about it. "Then I'll see you at 1:00?"

Raker nodded. "Your office? 1300?"

"Screw you," grinned Colt.

They parted.

BALTIMORE-FELLS POINT

Alec Gordon stood just outside the Wolf's Eye Pub, across from the decrepit remains of, in Bawl-morese, the old "peckin' house" complex. No longer active with the "laborin' class," but underway as classy millionaires' penthouses, across the dark, quiet waters of the Inner Harbor. Behind and over the outline of dimly-lit buildings, brilliant stars glittered invitingly in the pleasantly smog-free sky.

Gordon moved up the three steps leading over the ubiquitous Baltimore bar dog, his eyes searching the large, loud, almost riotous crowd of drinkers, laughers, and appreciators of Irish music. He slipped to a spot barely available against the bar. It was a little crowded, but he moved in. The busy bartender lifted his head and his voice.

"Yeah? What ya goin' ta hav'?" It was more Bronx than Baltimore.

Gordon hesitated a moment before replying. "Whiskey, with water."

The barman frowned. "C'mon, buddy. We've gotta lotta whiskey. Rye. Bourbon. Vodka. Rum. Malts galore. What'll it be, fella?"

"Scotch," said Gordon. He was as annoyed as the tavern owner, who sighed.

"Name one. Malt blend, Highland, Lowlands, Island . . . " he stopped, a slight mocking expression on his rugged face. Gordon realized he was being twitted. He forced his frown away.

"A nice single malt would be fine." He hoped his voice was friendly. It wasn't. Almost nothing about Alec Gordon, or his fraternal twin sister Elizabeth, was friendly. Gordon clenched his jaw and turned his head.

The *doin'* underway in the pub was in honor of Dairmud Sullivan, a large, friendly, billionaire who enjoyed the finer but commoner rewards of a hard working life, devoted to structure removal and demolition, construction components, forceful labor organizations and other generally violent business and social activities—some legal—who was the object of Alec Gordon's quest.

As he studied the layout of the room and Sullivan's location, Gordon's drink came. He sipped at it, and as Sullivan's eyes swung toward him he averted his gaze to study the walls. Mirrored signs advertised different brands of Irish whiskey. The man's eyes narrowed as he saw other signs. They annoyed him. Anything Irish annoyed him.

"Let's be havin' some music there, lads," roared Sullivan. "And none of that 'don't offend the pommies' garbage. How about *Four Green Fields*, or the like?"

One of the musicians grinned back. "How about *Off to Dublin*?"

"Grand!" Sullivan clapped his hands.

The assassin gritted his teeth. As the music started, he tried not to hear the words of the rebellion song. He studied the back bar, and felt his fury rise until it was a tangible thing, burning in his throat. The signs! The goddamn signs. FREE IRELAND NOW! Oh, those pig-faced mother-sodders. On the mirror behind the bar was plastered what appeared to be a bumper sticker, depicting an arm and sleeve marked with a Union Jack and a hand grasping the northeastern part of a map of Ireland. Another hand gripped the wrist of the Union Jack clad arm. The sleeve from which it extended bore the tricolored flag of Ireland. On the sign in bold letters was the legend, "Put It Back, Thief, Now!" The fair-haired man gripped his glass with both hands and pressed them against the bar top to stop their shaking. He closed his eyes to shut out the sights. A roar in his ears drowned out the words and music in the room.

I'll kill the pig now! The man's mind screamed silently. His hand moved toward his pocket, then stopped. It was no good. He couldn't crowd close enough through the throng around the man. Stiffly, he lifted his glass and drank. Placing the empty glass down on the bar with careful, controlled gentleness, he turned and, almost numbly, pushed his way through the people between him and the door.

Once outside, he stopped to stand erect, face lifted, and take several deep breaths. The tenseness began to abate. He turned to study the buildings on either side. There was a dark area to his left, only a few feet from the open door. It was a wide opening, deep enough to shield a man from the light.

Moving swiftly, the man crossed the street to his car. He took out the package which concealed an automatic weapon. No larger than a box which might contain a woman's dress or sweater, the package contained one of the world's most compact, rapid-fire, silenced weapons. The covering on the side decorated by a bow was only tissue paper. A second to tear through the thin covering, another second to pull the weapon free, and he would be ready to kill. He crossed back, and settled into the dark doorway.

"Hey buddy," whined a cracked voice. "Got a buck so I can eat?"

The killer jerked his elbow free from the touch he felt as he heard the voice. "Get the hell out of here," he spat, voice venomous.

The dimly lit figure's rumpled clothing reflected light as it recoiled from the voice. "Jeez, sorry buddy. Didn't mean to . . ."

"Get away!" Damn, he thought. Too intent, too damn intent. Should have been aware. He watched the retreating figure. At worst I should have given him something to get rid of him. He watched as the man turned into the pub. No way to do it now. The bastard may mention "the man outside." Can't be sure of getting an accurate burst off into that crowd. Experience took over. The man, making a quick decision, moved silently across to his car, placed the package carefully on the seat, sat down, slouching low in the seat, and closed the door. He watched the opening into the Wolf's Eye.

• • •

A moment or two passed, then two figures, neither of them Sullivan, came outside, looked up and down the street, then went back inside. He had made the right decision. He slid down even further in the seat to lessen his visibility. I can wait, he thought, and he smiled. Before it had been general duty. Now it was personal! As he thought of killing Sullivan, muscles relaxed and tension eased from his body to be replaced with a warm, satisfying glow deep in his groin. The wait was short.

Sullivan's voice carried across the wide road and through the car's open window as he boomed his "good nights" to his fellow drinkers. As Sullivan backed out and pulled his car into sparse traffic, the man followed him at a safe distance, only close enough to be certain that Sullivan was returning to his 40-foot sport-fisherman berthed at the inner harbor.

...

As they arrived at the waterfront parking areas, the lights of Baltimore's Harbor Place had dimmed, though some of the businesses appeared to be open. As Sullivan parked his car and started his walk, the follower gave fleeting thought to taking him in the open, but quickly rejected the idea. He'd wait until the man was aboard. Then he too would saunter down to the south end of the dock area, quietly board Sullivan's boat. He paused and gave a quick, soft laugh. Yacht, not boat. Yes, that was better. He had much rather kill someone aboard a yacht than on a mere boat.

The thought pleased him, and his walk was casual and jaunty as he started the trip leading to his kill. He nodded pleasantly at two uniformed police officers walking toward him, a nod they acknowledged. The encounter pleased him even more. Right under their noses, he thought. He turned his head to spit softly at their retreating backs. After all, most American police were Irish, weren't they?

There were no lights on any of the boats tied near Sullivan's but there were lights aboard her. Moving silently, he stepped aboard and moved to the hatch of the main cabin. He rapped softly. "Sully," he called. "Hey, Sully."

There was a pause long enough that he was set to call again when the answer came. "Yeah? Who is it?"

"Murphy!" That was a filthy Irish name, wasn't it? Certainly Sullivan knew a Murphy.

"Whaddya want, Murphy, at this hour?"

"A present. From the Wolf's Eye bunch."

"Ah, now." The voice was closer. "You lads didn't have to go and do that. Just a minute."

The killer waited. He heard noises from the door latch, and then it swung open. Sullivan was outlined against the light from inside the cabin.

"Come in," started Sullivan, backing a step, then, "You're not
. . . . What the hell?"

A woman's sleepy voice interrupted. "What is it, Sully. Who's
there?"

The intruder's right hand tore through the flimsy tissue paper
wrapped around the lethal package and jerked the weapon free,
quickly switching the firearm to rapid fire. The silenced noise
seemed louder in the close quarters than it was, but the burst was
short. Sullivan had actually managed to take a step forward against
the hail of bullets which slammed him backwards before he fell.
The woman who had just appeared lay in a crumpled heap.

The man moved to Sullivan and poked at him to make sure he
was dead. One look was sufficient. He turned to the woman. She
too was dead, and next to her was the body of a child, motionless. The man frowned. He hadn't seen the child. He shrugged. It
didn't matter. The job was done. Fourteen rounds. Less than two
seconds. If the woman hadn't appeared, it would have taken only
one or two rounds. Now, there were three lifeless bodies.

He hunted the light switch, found it, and turned off the lights
before leaving the cabin. He shut the hatch behind him and stood
silently, listening. He heard only the water lapping against the
boats and seawall, along with a few distant city sounds. He jumped
from the gunwale to the jetty, holding the weapon at his side after
changing magazines. He wanted firepower—just in case. But he
met no one. He would dispose of the Ingram after cleaning it of
any possible finger prints, from the clip and cartridges as well as
the weapon itself. He stepped off the boat and checked around. A
couple of uniformed policemen were over near the Crab House. He
headed for them, giving a wave as he jogged past, joining the other
early-morning health trotters.

What a nice day, he mused. Not only had he killed that Irish
pig, but—a shadow passed over him at the thought—The Man will
be pissed off at the wife and kid business. Screw him. It was a good
hit.

Inside the boat, the sound had been loud. Outside the boat, no
one probably heard more than the busy wharf noises of an early
morning weekend.

He didn't know or care that Sullivan's life was insured by Pan-Global. Nearly five million euros.

NEW MEXICO DESERT

Somewhat more than half a continent away, a massively impressive truck, what its driver called his "many-wheeler," sped over the narrowing two lane highway reaching toward its "four corners" destination. That's reaching *toward*—not reaching.

In the driver's seat sat Clay Sizemore, a lean, hard-faced man whose sun-and-wind textured skin had some of the appearance of well-tended and carefully-used saddle leather. A best guess would have put his age at somewhere around forty. He'd probably looked that age since he was twenty and would until he was eighty. Seated next to him, lounging comfortably with his big body taking up most of the room on the passenger's side, was Victorio Largo. His age defied guessing, his copper-hued face smooth and unlined beneath straight, obsidian-black hair worn long and banded with a red, folded kerchief.

"You sure them turkeys'll be making a stop up at Cuba?" he asked.

"Yup," allowed Sizemore. "No doubt." He played Cowboy to Largo's Geronimo.

"Damn well better be," said the Indian. "Sure as shootin', The Man ain't gonna abide us not comin' through with our contract."

"Ain't never missed yet, have we?" He glanced toward Largo. "And when the hell you start talking like that? Sound like some damn cowboy-hippie from over'n Madrid." Sizemore put the accent on the first syllable, thereby distinguishing the tiny New Mexico town from the Spanish city. Its mining-days-of-glory a thing of the past, the village had become a mecca for the mostly unwashed and long-haired commune migrants of the early seventies.

"Learned from you, white-eyes."

"Shit," drawled Sizemore, "you redskins never learned nothing from the white man since we brought civilization to your savage ancestors . . . 'cept maybe scalping."

Largo grinned. "How about oral sex?"

Sizemore considered the question. "Well, now, you just might have something there. If you count ass-kissin'. I reckon those early U.S. Indian Agents were purty expert at brown-nosin' them politicians." He glanced over at his companion. "Course, some of y'all got pretty good at that, too."

"Navajos, maybe, white brother, but not the Apache. I've never took kindly to that sort of shit."

It was Sizemore's turn to grin. "There you go again. Hippie-cowboy talk." He shook his head, scraping his wide brimmed, deeply curved dogger's hat against the rifles on the rack across the truck's rear window.

"Anyway," he continued, "all you Amerindian types got one thing in common."

"And that is . . . ?"

"You all got fucked."

"That we did, cowboy. That we did." He was silent a moment. "And here you are, getting set to do it again."

"How's that?"

"Why I always got to be the heavy? How come you never start the fight and get all whupped up on?"

"Intelligence, redman, intelligence."

"I know the joke," said Largo. Sizemore smiled.

"Fact is, Victorio, that my enlightened paleskin friends just naturally think all you folks are born trouble makers. Now me, if I tried to start something, they'd just smile and make room or apologize. They'd recognize me for the sweet, loveable type I am."

The quip wasn't worth Largo's reply.

"How long they stay at the café?"

Sizemore glanced at the clock in the dash. "Another hour, at least. They pulled in around fifteen-twenty minutes ago. They'll want to nap, then be in Farmington about time to start making deliveries."

"Routine never varies?"

Sizemore shook his head. "Nope. Damn near set a clock by them."

"And we nail only the load?"

"Yup. And the truck."

"Not the men?"

"You know The Man. It'd be our butts if we wasted anyone unnecessary-like."

"Yeah. Funny about that. No compunction about destroying anything if it's a barrier, but he'll walk around lots of things if they're just an inconvenience. A most peculiar man." Largo shook his massive head.

Sizemore glanced at him. "You seem to've lost that funny accent somewhere, *cunado*. Better be careful. Your education's showing."

Largo shrugged. "That's the hazard in leading all those hunting expeditions into the hills. Only ones who can afford me seem to be educated folks." He thought a moment. "Odd thing is, Clay, most of them are pretty damn decent people."

"Yeah," drawled Sizemore. "Just having money don't make an asshole out of a person. Matter of fact, I know more poor-garbage than rich-pricks. Trouble is, rich-pricks can afford to be really *big* pricks."

"Well I'll be damned," said Largo, affecting a tone of awe. "I'm traveling with a damn philosopher. Texas's answer to Will Rogers."

"Don't I wish," grinned Sizemore. "Hell, I'm just a poor country boy who happens to be the best damned oil-rig diver in the whole fornicating world and, according to testimonials, the best lay on the whole Gulf Coast."

"And so modest," agreed Largo. "Speaking of that side of your many-faceted talents, how did the Irishers take to the skin-diving clinic?"

"Hell, you saw them," growled Sizemore. "Took to it like crabs to ripe chicken necks." He glanced across at the Indian. "Ever been to Ireland?"

"No. Well, yes. But only at the airports. Shannon, Dublin."

"Haven't spent much time there myself, but what I saw, it's so damn wet that I get the feeling all those folks are born with fins or webbed feet anyway."

"Well," mused Largo, "they've sure as hell learned to keep their powder dry."

"Yeah," Sizemore nodded. "Sure took to your explosives training, didn't they?"

"More'n that. I learned a few tricks. Not that they were used to really sophisticated equipment." He lifted a big hand and waved it. "But they sure as shootin' have learned to make do with basic materials."

"Un-huh," agreed Sizemore. "They'd a been a pretty decent bunch if we could have just got them to like to drink."

Both men laughed long and loud. On more than one occasion during the time they had worked with the six Irish recruits, teaching them free diving and the use of explosives underwater, they had found themselves with massive morning hangovers while their charges appeared bright and fresh.

"Jeezus, yes," said Largo. "Never saw the like of it. God, couldn't they put it away."

"My old grand-daddy used to say it was a good thing the Irish drank so much, otherwise they'd probably rule the whole damn world."

"Your dear old grand-daddy must have been an Irish hater," offered Largo.

"Nope," said Sizemore, "just jealous."

"There it is," interrupted Largo. "The great city of Cuba, New Mexico."

As they topped a small rise, a dome of light glowed faintly from over the next hill.

"How's our time?"

"Fine," said Sizemore. "One thing: just remember not to drink any more coffee than you have to. Gawd, but their water is awful."

"Not as bad as in Santa Rosa," objected Largo.

"No. There you're right. Gyp water! Rotten."

Sizemore slowed as they neared the all-night café on the south side of the highway, and pulled off the road a block away. The streets were empty except for a few parked cars. Three huge trucks were parked next to the café, as well as one car and two pickup trucks.

"Looks good. Shouldn't be too much activity, but enough," said Largo.

"Right. I'll let you off here. Give me a few minutes to get things all taken care of and get settled down and unnoticed before you make your entrance. Sure you'll know the driver and his gopher?"

"Good God, yes," groaned Largo. "I've looked at those photos until I can't stand the sight of them."

"Great," said Sizemore. "Then you shouldn't mind starting the to-do."

Largo eyed Sizemore. "No one, white man, likes to be beat upon."

"Get out, Geronimo, and mop on the war paint."

• • •

After parking the pickup where it was not visible through the windows of the café, and taking care of the preliminaries, careful not to be seen, Sizemore entered and selected a stool at the counter. His entrance created little interest, and by the time his coffee and pie had been served, his presence had been dismissed by the other men seated around the long room. Those of interest to Sizemore and Largo were seated at a table against the wall away from the door. The restrooms were past them. Sizemore relaxed and waited.

The wait was short. The front door opened noisily and a different man from the Victorio Largo that Sizemore had recently left, entered. The big body lurched into the room, eyes fuzzy, face slack, and as he slammed the door with too much force, the eyes of the diners and the lone waitress all looked toward the source of the noise.

Largo reeled heavily toward the counter, slammed his hands down on it and flopped onto a stool. He muttered something loud and unintelligible. The waitress looked at him with unfriendly eyes.

"Coffee." The word was slurred but understandable. "Where's the crapper?" The words were clearer.

The waitress looked at him with distaste and pointed toward the back of the restaurant. Largo mumbled and struggled to his feet. He stumbled past Sizemore and as he neared the table where their subjects were seated he seemed to trip and fall forward. He banged heavily into one of the men, knocking dishes to the floor.

"You goddamn stupid Indian," said the man. He stood angrily. He was big and square. He glared at Largo, fists clenched. "I
oughta whip your butt."

The man with him was also on his feet. He was as large as the
first man.

"Do it, Henry. Bust the bastard up."

All eyes were now on the source of the commotion. Largo, leaning on the table with both hands, slowly lifted his face. The eyes
weren't as fogged as they had seemed, but the men, in their anger,
didn't notice. Nor did they notice the tiny smile that played at the
corners of Largo's mouth.

Sizemore, unnoticed, slipped off his stool and moved to the
exit. "Yeah," said the first man. "I'm gonna do just that. Stand
up, you scummy bastard. Get your hands off that table. I'm gonna
haul you outside and kick the Indian shit right outta your sleazy
hide."

Largo straightened.

Sizemore slipped out the door.

Largo's eyes were bright and clear as he stood to his full height,
some two or three inches taller than the man who had addressed
him. The twitch on his lips turned into a full smile. And as he
looked at the man, his hand shot out and pistoned into the chest of
the other man. The force slammed him backwards over his chair,
and as he fell, Largo's other hand slashed out and the back of it
caught his tormentor full against the side of his head. The man
stumbled to the side, dazed, but not knocked down. Largo had
not meant to; he wanted the fight to continue for the time being. It
did, and as it did, the roar of the diesel powering the huge sixteen
wheeler sounded loudly in the café.

"Hey, Henry!" hollered one of the men watching the fray. "Your
rig! Your truck's pulling out."

Confusion reigned, and as the others rushed toward the windows to watch the truck's lights recede into the darkness, Largo
quietly moved away from them, and away from the door.

"God damn it!" shouted the man called Henry. "Who'll drive
me? Who'll help me catch the bastard?"

"Who was it?"

"Who the hell knows?"

"Who gives a shit? Wally! Drive me!" The restaurant emptied as the crowd spilled out onto the graveled lot and moved toward the two remaining trucks and three other vehicles nearby.

Largo eased out behind them and walked silently the short distance to where he knew Sizemore had parked their pickup. It was the only vehicle near the café which would be moving. At least it was the only vehicle near the café which would be moving until extensive repairs had been made to their ignition systems. They would soon find that their CBs were also out of order, as was the café's telephone. It would take only minutes before they managed to find other CBs or a landline, and cell phones were out of range in that open country—but those minutes would be enough.

Largo drove south before turning back to bypass the café and drive the four miles to the La Jara turnoff. When he arrived at the designated point he stopped the pickup and turned the lights on and off in a pattern.

"Any scars?" Sizemore asked as he opened the passenger side door.

"Naw," smiled Largo. "Even enjoyed it." The pickup pulled out and headed up the road near Regina and safe storage only minutes away. "Did it go well?"

Sizemore grunted. He swept locked hands up together and released them to show an explosion. "Ka-whoom!" he said. "It was beautiful."

"Heard it. Would have liked to seen it," said Largo, somewhat wistfully. He sighed. "Well, scratch one magnificent truck for Superior Imports Ink."

"Yeah," said Sizemore. It was his turn for sorrow. "And just imagine, all that magnificent, beautiful, expensive hootch. Yep, it was their once-a-month, high-priced run." He shook his head sadly. "Shame to waste it." He was silent a moment, as a smile started and spread. "But it sure was one hell of a ka-whoom," he said.

"Next time, dammit," said Largo, "I get to do the ka-whoom, all right?"

Sizemore studied the question before replying. "Next time, old buddy, it'll be both of us." He looked across at the Indian.

"And those," he added, "will truly be some kind of ka-whooms indeed."

• • •

The truck and liquor shipment belonged to Superior Imports Incorporated and was insured by PanGlobal Assurance for around $1,500,000. The driver and his helper, while bruised and bowed, were both still alive.

New Mexico time was 1:46 a.m.

WASHINGTON, D.C

In Washington, D.C., Robert Emmet Kavanaugh's grand experience had started earlier in the evening. It would have happened even if he were not a notorious womanizer. That fact only simplified the procedure.

It had been said of Kavanaugh that he was "over-sexed, over-moneyed, and over-Irish." The phrase was, of course, a play on the British comment during World War II concerning the trouble with the American military personnel in Great Britain; they were "over-sexed, overpaid, and over here." It was a fact that Kavanaugh worked to develop the reputation of having great sexual appetites, and he was, indeed, wealthy—a result of the fortune amassed by his family in their ventures as demolition contractors.

He was also one of America's heaviest contributors to the offshoots of the IRA Provisionals. Unsubstantiated rumors had it that he had helped finance the purchase and shipment of the most sophisticated arms available, from Russia to a militant group outside the IRA, a Marxist group who called themselves the Irish Freedom Force.

Whether these rumors were true or not was unimportant. They had been submitted as fact to the attractive young lady who had been flirting with Kavanaugh for the past four days. Kavanaugh had noticed the striking woman on more than one occasion, but each time he had tried to approach her it seemed that she would simply disappear, or at least manage to place distance or obstacles between them. On this night it was different.

Robert Emmet Kavanaugh operated on the principal that the only true aphrodisiac was variety. As a result, he seldom courted the same young lady twice. On this night, as was his custom, he was dining early in preparation for his nightly quest, prowling the city's most lively singles spots.

As he sat at a choice table against one of the glass walls of the Gang Plank restaurant, he admired the view of the Tidal Basin with its yachts and small craft, most moored, some in motion. As his eyes roved, examining the talent in the restaurant on the off-chance that there would be something to be found worth pursuing, the woman walked into his view, standing serenely next to the maitre d', her lovely, cat-like eyes surveying the room as though hunting someone. As he watched, the woman said a few words to the host, smiled politely, and moved into the restaurant in Kavanaugh's direction.

She's walking over to me, thought Kavanaugh. No! Not walking—gliding. But, good God, what a glide! And what an incredible body, at least from what he could see of it. Long legs, fine, nice turn to the hips, a slim, firm waist. And what knockers! High and sweetly curved, and just enough flesh bulging delicately over the dress top; almost but not quite veiled by her light evening wrap. Marvelous eyes, and while her makeup might be just a touch too much, it went well with the short, beautifully styled hair which seemed to be a black halo around her fine aristocratic features. A winner, he thought. This time, by Holy Patrick, he would damn well get to know her!

She sat at his table.

Kavanaugh blinked in surprise as she flashed him a remarkable smile, placed her elbows on the table, and rested her chin on locked hands.

"You really shouldn't be surprised, Mr. Kavanaugh," she said, throatily. "I've been noticing you, too." Her eyes seemed to glow with warmth.

"Yes," said Robert Emmet Kavanaugh, for lack of something better.

"I've seen your eyes following me," she continued, "and I must admit that I've watched you keenly too. I even asked your name."

What a wonderfully sexy voice, he thought. It fits her.

"But," she continued, "the time just wasn't right." Her eyes held him. "Tonight," she continued, "it is."

It was that simple, but that hadn't really mattered. Whatever the circumstances, the outcome would have been the same.

• • •

It was early in the morning, before dawn, when Robert Emmet Kavanaugh sighed deeply, with pleasure, in spite of the wet grass beneath him and his drizzle-soaked clothing.

"You," he said, "are fantastic." It didn't matter that the woman had insisted she wanted to make love in the outdoors, had wanted to feel the earth beneath her, and the soft rain bathing them. It didn't matter that there was the chance that they might be found, their clothes open and disheveled, on the grassy, shielded slope of the bank alongside the Potomac.

If he had looked, he could have seen the dots of red light atop the Washington Monument and the white colonnades of the Lincoln Memorial. But his eyes were closed.

"NOW," breathed the woman. "NOW, get on me. Get in me." She pulled at the man as she spread her legs.

"Yes," he said. "God, yes." He fumbled with a hand, trying to guide himself.

"I want to feel you in me. I want to feel the heat, the throb." Her hands finished what he had started. "Easy. Let me feel . . . oh, yes. There!"

Their bodies rocked, moving together in gentle rhythm, and as the man started to quicken his movement the woman's hands moved from his body to his head, fingers playing about his ears.

"Tell me," she breathed, almost moaning, "tell me when you're ready. Oh, God. That's wonderful. Tell me . . ."

Their movement quickened.

"Now," he rasped, "oh, my God, *now* . . ."

And Elizabeth Gordon drove her icepick-thin stiletto into his ear.

• • •

Kavanaugh was insured by PanGlobal for fifty million dollars.

CHAPTER 5

It was 8:15 a.m. when the phone call came from Pagan Maguire. James Colt had been at his desk since 7:30., as had most of the upper echelon of PanGlobal. He was carefully preparing the material he would present to Raker in the afternoon, and rehearsing questions he anticipated both from Mitchell and his friend.

"Yes, Miss Maguire?" he said into the mouthpiece.

"I preferred to call you, Mr. Colt, rather than Mr. Mitchell's office or that Webb. I hope that is quite all right?"

"Certainly. What can I do for you?"

"It really is what I'm supposed to do, I believe," said the girl. "I've received another communication I'm to deliver to you. I wanted to be certain that I could do so promptly."

"We will be here, Miss Maguire." He hesitated. He mustn't let her know that he was aware of where she was staying in the city. Even now checks were being made to determine who owned, and who had leased or rented the house. "Are you very far away?"

The girl's laugh was pleasant. "I'm not ringing you from where I stay," she said. "I'm quite near your office building right now. When will you have time to see me?"

"Miss Maguire," said Colt solemnly, "I can assure you that the most pressing business we have at the present-time is our business with you. When can you be here?"

"I should think easily by half eight," came the reply. "Will that be acceptable?"

She must mean within fifteen minutes, thought Colt. "That will be quite acceptable," he said. "And Miss Maguire?"

"Yes?"

"Please come directly to Mr. Mitchell's office. We'll be there waiting." He depressed the button, then dialed Webb's office.

"Colt," he told the secretary.

"Webb speaking," came the crisp voice.

"The girl is coming in again," said Colt. "Fifteen minutes. We'll meet upstairs."

There was a pause before Webb replied. "Bad timing. I'm up to it in a matter of fraud. Internal."

"Can't it wait?"

"Not if I'm to nail it down." Colt was silent.

"Mitchell knows all about it," said Webb.

"All right," said Colt. "He'll tape it, of course. You can check it later."

"Right, James. Later." The line went dead.

Just as well, thought Colt. Better, from a point of preference. The girl felt animosity toward Webb, it had been obvious from her words and tone. She might be easier to elicit information from without Webb there. Colt smiled. She was a very bright young lady, he thought. He doubted if she really knew much more than she was telling, but even if that was not the case, it would be difficult to find out anything she wanted to hide, at least without careful preparation. The thing he would like to know, mused Colt, was how she came to be involved in the affair, even if innocently. There must be some Irish connection. But the amount of business done by PanGlobal in Ireland was not great. Still, there was some. Colt shrugged. That would be for Raker to consider. That fox has connections everywhere, thought Colt. Hell, the CIA should work through him. He dialed Mitchell's office to notify him of her impending visit.

• • •

As Pagan Maguire was shown into the inner office by Victoria Genn, Mitchell's inherent salesmanship allowed him to be as cordial as on their previous meeting.

"Come in, my dear young lady, please come in. Have a seat." He was smiling broadly over concerned eyes.

Pagan perched comfortably on the front edge of the chair she had previously occupied. Mitchell, obviously remembering her comment of the previous day, sat across from her. "A good day to you," she smiled. She nodded brightly toward Colt.

"And to what eventuality do we owe the pleasure of this visit?" inquired Mitchell. His tone was edgy.

"During the evening I received another sealed communication," said Pagan, "along with instructions to deliver it to you at the earliest possible time. I am doing so now." She stood, and taking an envelope from her handbag, walked across to hand it to Mitchell.

"Yes," said Mitchell. "Yes, indeed." He looked apprehensively at the envelope, then back up at the girl. "Please excuse me a moment." He walked to his desk.

He's afraid, thought Pagan. She felt a twinge of sorrow. Whatever the messages she carried, they were of frightening impact on the old man. As she resumed her seat, she studied Colt covertly. The tension was also apparent on his strong, good-looking face. Her brow furrowed as she looked down at her hands. Her role was to be that of messenger, helping force this great insurance company to settle a claim they were reluctant to honor. What was so terrible about that? She took a deep breath and looked up to watch Mitchell as he slit open the envelope she had handed him.

All she knew was that by performing her duties as agreed, she would see the killers of her brother brought to justice. And for that, she didn't just have Coleman's word. She had the assurance of others, friends of her brother, that Coleman was to be trusted. Her lovely, young face settled into an expression of grim determination.

Mitchell seemed to age before the watching eyes of Pagan and James Colt. He spoke without looking up as he extended a hand holding the communication.

"It's all here, James. This is it. There's no doubt now, not that we had any before." He stood, with an effort, and moved from behind the desk to stand before the glass wall looking down on the city.

"No," he said softly, as though talking to himself. "No doubt at all."

Colt unfolded the sheet of paper he had been handed and read:

COMMENCING AFTER MIDNIGHT LAST NIGHT, TERMINATIONS
BEGAN OF CERTAIN PANGLOBAL ASSURANCE POLICIES. THEY
WILL CONTINUE THROUGHOUT THIS DAY. FOR PURPOSES OF

VERIFICATION, THE FOLLOWING INITIALS MAY BE COMPARED WITH
LOSSES SOON TO BE REPORTED TO YOU:

spi/cn}!; ds/bm; aqj/le; at/pph; rek/wdc.

CASUALTIES WILL DEMONSTRATE AUTHENTICITY AND INDICATE
FUTURE ABILITIES. SCOPE, TIME AND DISTANCE ELEMENT
WILL DEMONSTRATE MY REACH. TIME WILL BE ALLOWED FOR
VERIFICATION OF YOUR LOSSES PRIOR TO PRESENTATION OF
MY PROPOSAL. I AM CERTAIN THAT YOUR EFFICIENT STAFF HAS
VERIFIED PREVIOUS INFORMATION TENDERED.

AGAIN, EMPHASIS IS PLACED ON THE FACT THAT THE BEARER OF
THIS COMMUNICATION IS TOTALLY UNAWARE OF ITS CONTENTS,
AND KNOWS ONLY THAT SHE IS ENGAGED IN HELPING NEGOTIATE
A POLICY SETTLEMENT. ANY INTERFERENCE WILL BE SUMMARILY
DEALT WITH THROUGH INCONCEIVABLY EXPENSIVE COSTS TO YOU
OVER AND ABOVE THOSE SCHEDULED.

$

At the bottom of the text was the, by now familiar, red dollar sign.

• • •

"Well, James?" Mitchell's voice had regained some strength.

Colt cleared his throat. To Pagan he seemed visibly shaken. What was in that letter?

"It appears . . . thorough," said Colt before Pagan could speak, "quite thorough."

"Yes. It does, indeed." Mitchell walked toward the others. He stopped to look down at the girl. "Is that everything, Miss Maguire? Is that all you have for us today?"

Pagan stood. Her eyes nearly on a level with those of Mitchell. It seemed to her that yesterday he had been taller. "Yes," she said softly, "that is the entire material delivered to me."

"I see," said Mitchell. "It was really quite enough. Quite enough."

"Could I ask just how this was delivered to you, Miss Maguire?" asked Colt.

The girl turned to him. "By messenger. Last night. They are all delivered by messenger." At least that was true. She had not seen Coleman since their first meeting. All other communication had been by prearranged telephone, and by written instructions.

"I see," Colt said, nodding. He would be able to check on that. Daskalos's men would have had the place under surveillance.

"And could I be asking something?" inquired Pagan.

"Why, certainly," said Mitchell. "Ask away."

"It is obvious to me, gentlemen, that these communications I bring are most unsettling. Far more than I would expect an effort to settle an unhonored claim to be. Is there more to it than that? For that's what I've been told." She waited.

Mitchell looked at Colt. "James?"

Colt studied her for a moment, face expressionless. "It is certainly that, Miss Maguire," he said finally. "It is certainly an attempt to settle a claim against this firm." He paused. "It is perhaps," he continued, "a much larger, and to us a somewhat more controversial claim than we feel can be settled without considerable . . . consultation."

The girl nodded slowly. "I think I understand. You're telling me, then, that you're contesting the claim." It was not a question.

"Not exactly," said Colt. "It is simply that it requires . . . study, and . . ."

"Yes?"

"And it appears that it will represent a quite considerable sum of money, even for a company as large as mine . . . ours." Mitchell waved away his reluctant correction. Pagan smiled tentatively as she dipped gracefully to pick up her handbag from the low table at her side.

"That would explain it, then," she said. "I can understand the case being one to cause upset." She looked at the men gently, her huge, emerald eyes soft behind thick lashes.

"I'm truly sorry I have to be involved in creating unpleasantness. But . . ." she paused, "if the claim isn't settled, there will probably be great unhappiness on the other side." She considered her statement, then nodded in agreement with it. "And I suppose the hurt to be greater the other way. Don't you think that possible?" Again the two men looked at each other.

"Miss Maguire," said Colt, choosing his words. "I think I can certainly agree that if the claim is not settled, and rather soon, then others will surely suffer great hurt." He turned toward Mallory Fleming Mitchell. "Would you agree with that?"

The older man's resilience had flexed and Mitchell had visibly regained confidence. "I think that is a very fair summation, James. Very fair." He stepped forward and placed one of his big, hard-used hands on Pagan's shoulder. "Young lady, I feel you are quite honest. I hope so. I want to think you know no more about this affair than you've told us." There was a hint of question in his tone.

"Of that I can assure you," she said. But what was it that she shouldn't know? No matter! It was no concern of hers. She was only to deliver the messages. She looked at Mitchell with candid eyes. He seemed to have grown taller and she was pleased.

He patted her shoulder. "Good!" He walked her toward the door.

"Very good. And you will, of course, contact us immediately with any new information you receive?"

"Most certainly, sir," she replied. I like the man, she thought. And the other one. But then, she'd liked Coleman, too. "I shall call at once, have I something to bring." She looked at Colt. "And a good day to you, Mr. Colt." She flashed the men her bright smile and was quickly gone as Mitchell held the door for her.

Colt reached for the phone on Mitchell's desk and dialed rapidly. Mitchell watched with interest. "Daskalos?" Colt nodded.

"Colt. She's on her way out." He was silent for a moment, listening.

"All right. Did you have someone there last night?" Silence. "Was there a delivery?" Quiet. "Good. That checks. Any other visitors? Okay. Stay low. Let me know." He hung up and turned to Mitchell.

"Is that wise, James? You know what the letter said."

"We're not interfering. But if we can trace just where that messenger came from, we may find a lead. Doubtful. Daskalos was already on it. Looks like the message was taken to the delivery service by one of the street people. If so, it'll probably be a blind end. And Daskalos won't push too hard."

Mitchell settled comfortably into one of the low upholstered chairs. "How much does Daskalos know?"

Colt shrugged. "Nothing. Only that we're interested. You know Gus, no questions past need-to-know."

"Yeah, you have a good man there." Mitchell stretched hands up to smooth back his rumpled hair. "Now, James, let's get ready for that visit from your miracle-worker friend. What was his name?"

"Don't kid me, boss man," grinned Colt. "You probably sat up all night reading a computer printout on the dude. Raker. Martin Raker. As you damn well know."

"Yes. Raker," said Mitchell. "Beverly Martin Raker, I believe?"

"Yes, but don't ever use that first name," said Colt. His tone was serious.

"I know," said Mitchell. "That I know, but not a hell of a lot more. The man seems to have been a genius at covering his tracks. And our information is as good as any there is."

The phone on Mitchell's desk chimed.

"What the hell now?" muttered Mitchell. "Want to get that, James?" Colt lifted the phone before the second series of tones sounded.

"Yes, Mrs. Genn?" He waited. "Put him through, please." He turned to Mitchell.

"It's Daskalos. Yes, Gus? Not yet?" Colt glanced at his watch and looked toward Mitchell. "She left the office more than ten minutes ago. Nearer fifteen." His brow furrowed. "Stay there. She may have taken a break on the way. Check the other floors and elevators. I'll work from this end." He replaced the phone tentatively and turned to Mitchell.

"The girl. She hasn't reached downstairs yet." He gnawed at his lip.

"Women, James. You know . . . probably stopped to freshen up." Mitchell looked at the younger man. "Is that what they still say? Freshen up?"

Colt didn't bother to answer. His eyes were pensive. Suddenly a mental alarm sounded. "Son of a bitch!" he exploded. "That ignorant bastard!" He snatched up the telephone and dialed.

• • •

"What is it, James?" asked Mitchell.

"Webb knew the girl was coming. I'll stake a pile that overanxious, eager-fucking-beaver put the arm on her."

Mitchell waited, eyes watching Colt's face.

"Give me Webb," snarled Colt into the telephone. A pause. Colt slammed the phone into its cradle without comment and started rapidly for the door.

"The son of a bitch is 'temporarily in conference'," he called over his shoulder and was out of the room in quick, long strides. As decreed by Mitchell early in his career, there was always an elevator waiting on the floor which housed his executive offices. If his private elevator was in use, automation brought one of the other elevators to his floor and kept it there until the private car had returned. As a result, Colt was at Webb's office several floors below within just over a minute from the time he had placed his call.

Webb's secretary looked up quickly at Colt's sudden noisy entrance.

Her hand started to move.

Colt's voice grated as a file on metal. "Touch that button and I'll break every finger on your dainty little paw."

The secretary looked at him in fear; hand suspended and motionless. "Is the door locked?" he asked.

"I . . . I don't know."

"Never mind," he snarled. "Call him. Tell him you have a note from Mitchell."

"I . . . I can't do . . ."

Colt was at her side in one long step. He poised a finger which pointed directly between her eyes. "Do it. Now!"

Unable to take her eyes from the threatening finger, Webb's secretary fumbled at the intercom. His voice sounded annoyed. "Yes?"

"It's a note, Harlan," she said, voice shaky, "from Mr. Mitchell." Her eyes were still on Colt. "Shall I bring it in?"

There was a pause. "No. I'll come and get it." The annoyance had grown.

Colt patted the secretary gently on the shoulder, pushed her away from the desk, and held a finger to his lips. She thought his smile looked like that of a shark.

He waited by the side of the door to Webb's inner office. He heard noise from the lock mechanism, then saw the knob start to turn. As the door moved, he slammed into it with the full force of his 190 pounds.

Webb caught the blow as the door blasted open, was knocked backward into the room, lost his balance and tumbled to the carpet. Colt was inside and towering over Webb's prone body before he could rise. The force of the blow had dazed the man momentarily, and as he shook his head, focusing his eyes, Colt glanced at the chair near where Webb had fallen. Sitting in it was Pagan Maguire, face flushed, hair in disarray. She appeared to be struggling to rise, and Colt saw that her arms had been secured behind the back of the chair.

He looked down at Webb who was starting to rise from the floor. "You rotten, goddamn son of a bitch!" He spat out each word. "You ignorant bastard. If you twitch a single muscle I swear I'll kick your balls into your throat, you simple minded pile of shit."

Webb looked up at him. "You never saw the day you could take me, Colt."

"Just move! Just twitch," Colt pleaded.

"I'm down," objected Webb. "Let me get up and I'll show you."

"Shut your stupid mouth, you bastard, or you'll become a cripple right where you lay." He jerked his head toward the girl. "How's she tied?"

Webb glared up at Colt, fear fighting fury. "Handcuffs," he said.

"The key," said Colt. His weight was on one foot, the other poised in threat. "On your face before you move a hand," he warned.

Webb rolled slowly onto his face and then reached a hand into a trouser pocket.

"Toss it," said Colt. "Gently."

Webb did as told.

"Put your hands in your pockets," ordered Colt.

"Colt," started Webb. "Colt, I'll get you for this."

"Shut your mouth." Colt's voice was deadly in its softness. As Webb silently stuck his hands into his trouser pockets, Colt pulled the man's jacket down over his arms. "If you move before she's out of here you'll either have trouble walking or eating for the rest of your life," he told the prone man. He turned to the girl. "Did he hurt you?" He removed her bonds.

She shook her head. "No. Just roughed me up a bit. But I do think it's a very good thing you came in when you did." She rubbed her wrists.

Colt looked at her. "Are you all right?"

She took a deep breath and tried to straighten her hair. "Yes," she said, "I'm fine, now." She experimented with a smile.

Colt returned it. "Yes, I think you are. Go on now. I'll finish up here."

Pagan Maguire looked at him apprehensively. "Is it . . . all right?"

"You'll be fine now."

"And you?"

Colt grinned. "Don't worry about that."

The girl looked at him carefully. "No," she said, slowly, "I don't think I'll have to worry about that." She started toward the door, then stopped. She turned. "Will you . . . ." She hesitated.

He couldn't call her. She mustn't let him know her number or where to find her. She smiled. "I'll call *you*, if you don't mind," she said.

What a lovely smile, thought Colt. Beautiful girl. "No," he said gently, "I won't mind that at all. Now go, before our . . . chum here decides to take a chance on my not being attentive."

The girl hesitated. "All right. . . .James?"

"Yes?"

"Thank you."

Colt smiled. "No charge," he said. "Now, on your way."

Pagan left.

• • •

"All right, you stupid bastard," he said, turning to Webb. "You can get up now."

Webb disengaged his hands, shrugged his coat up off his arms, and scrambled to his feet. He took time to straighten his clothing. Wrinkles seemed to disappear as if by magic. "I suppose you'll make a real case out of this," he said. He'd had sufficient time to realize that his job could be in jeopardy.

"Don't be more of a damn fool, Webb. No. I'll not make a case out of it. Not for now. You're in this thing with us—at the moment. But damn it, man, do you realize what might have happened if you'd harmed the girl?"

"She knows more than she's telling, Colt. I could have gotten it out of her."

Colt sat on the edge of Webb's desk and looked at him with scorn.

"I doubt that. I don't think she knows more than she's telling us. At least not anything that would help. But if these bastards are serious—and we have every reason to believe they are—then your stupidity could have made it unbelievably complicated." He stood and walked to the door where he stopped. He turned toward Webb.

"And another thing, Harlan. In this echelon, I'm your boss. It may reach a point where what little you know won't justify keeping you around. Do you have that loud and clear, Mr. Webb?"

Webb glared at Colt before answering. He shrugged.

"As you say, you're higher up the echelon."

"Then stay out of it. Check everything with me or the boss-man. Got that?" Webb hesitated angrily before answering.

"Got it." He bit off the words.

"Good. Don't forget it." He turned to leave.

"Colt," called Webb.

"Yes?"

"I can still take you."

Colt paused a moment before turning. He surveyed Webb coolly. "I suppose you really believe that," he said. "And I suppose that before long we just may have to find out." His grin, as he left, infuriated Webb.

His anger now under control, Colt returned to his employer's office and explained the circumstances of the apprehension of the girl to Mitchell. He offered the opinion that less harm would be done by keeping Webb on a tight rein rather than by dismissing him. His knowledge of the threat to the company could create the very complications they were trying to avoid. Mitchell agreed, and said he would confirm to Webb that Colt was, indeed, running the show, and that Webb's future with PanGlobal depended on him "toeing the line," as Mitchell phrased it.

By the time procedures were running smoothly again, Colt noted that it was four minutes until 10:00 a.m. It didn't seem possible that so much could have happened in so short a time.

LONDON

In London, England, it was past afternoon closing time at the Spaniard's Inn, a pleasant, thoroughly English pub on the edge of Hampstead Heath. The attractive, suntanned, well-dressed young-looking man sitting at a table alone next to an old, paned window lifted a wrist to check the time, raised his half-pint, thumb-print mug to drain the last swallow of Danish lager, folded his newspaper carefully, and rose from his chair. Quietly, with practiced grace, he strolled past the bar, nodding pleasantly at the barmen, and exited into the small parking area at the opposite end of the building.

Outside, he paused, raising his face toward the clear sky, breathing deeply in appreciation of the fine day, moving aside as other patrons came out. Then he walked to his indeterminately ordinary black car and slid inside with supple ease. He appeared to be in no hurry. He methodically stored his newspaper in the door panel pocket, took time to adjust the rear view mirror, then took a pair of sunglasses from over the visor. Holding them to the light, he inspected the lenses for smudges and cleaned them with his breath and a soft tissue. Finally, apparently satisfied, he started the car and pulled out to follow the beautifully maintained vintage Bentley sedan in front of him.

As the cars merged smoothly into light traffic and swept past the curve and up over the rise bordering the edge of the tree-covered woodlands to the left, the man down-shifted and accelerated past the Bentley. He waited until he estimated there was perhaps fifty yards distance between the two automobiles, placed a hand into the left side pocket of his jacket and removed a relatively small, rectangular metal box. He opened the lid which gave a slight click, pushed one of the two red buttons, then—waiting a moment for passing traffic to clear some distance from the Bentley—pressed the second red button. The Bentley, now some 70 yards behind him, disintegrated into flaming shards.

The occupant of the Bentley was—or more correctly, had been—newspaper publisher Anthony Quiller-Jones. His life had been insured for two million English pounds by PanGlobal Assurance. He had been represented in the list of initials as AQJ/LE. The code, of course, represented the name of the victim, Anthony Quiller-Jones, and the location of the termination, London, England.

HAITI

It was midmorning in Port-au-Prince, Haiti, when Toussaint Salanet stopped his 1968 Dodge sedan outside the relatively new Holiday Inn near the downtown section, remodeled from the old Hotel Le Plaza, not far from the previously Grand Palace of former President for Life, Jean Claude Duvalier, otherwise known as Baby Doc.

He stepped from his automobile—or more properly, taxi—shining black face glistening above his gleaming white, well-starched and ironed Haitian version of what is commonly called a Mexican Wedding Shirt. He moved toward the hotel doorway with an athletic lightness which belied his corpulent body. After exchanging a few words with a similarly attired taxi driver, he leaned easily against the side of the entrance and waited.

Within but a few minutes a colorfully bedecked, middle-sized and middle-aged couple came through the door. Looking about with an air of "they all look alike to me," the man saw Toussaint strolling toward them, smiling; he nudged his slightly taller wife. "That's him," he said. "Hi there, fella."

"A most good morning to Madame and Monsieur," replied Toussaint, white teeth matching his shirt. "I am desolate." The smile was replaced with a sorrowful frown. "It is that I had forgotten when we arrange me to drive you that I had made a previous engagement." The smile returned quickly. "But that is of no consequence. I have here the nearly-equal substitute for Toussaint, with the excellent English almost so perfect." He motioned to the man with whom he had spoken earlier. "This is," he said, "my finest friend, Willamette. He will guide for less because of my subsidy to him for the compensation of my dreadful memory."

The visitors couldn't care less, except that they did like the idea of paying less for the inferior service offered by natives such as these. As they walked away, hooded eyes in Toussaint Salanet's now expressionless face followed them with contempt. When they had driven out of sight, he entered his car, and pulled out into streets swarming with pedestrians, decrepit automobiles, busses, and the garishly painted "tap-taps." These unique vehicles were little more than old pickup trucks with high sideboards and a top of sorts which careened the streets, coming only to rolling stops to pick up and discharge passengers.

Toussaint drove at an incredibly rapid pace through the packed machinery and throngs of humanity clotting the streets. He was followed only by an occasional obscenity from a pedestrian forced to leap from his path. His driving seemed an indication of the value placed on life in Haiti by those on an economic level which allowed them to own motorized vehicles.

Toussaint followed the road through thinning traffic, past the omnipresent roadside peddlers hawking their wares, on through the market town of Petionville, continuing up the steep mountainside, finally stopping near the village of Furcey. Women with baskets on their heads stood patiently at the edge of the pavement, stoically waiting for some tourist to make a purchase. Artists with their vibrantly colored paintings shared space with vendors displaying clothing, carved wooden figures and other art objects. They and the other merchandisers looked through, around, over and past Toussaint as he walked up the roadside and turned in to a rock-and-concrete building conspicuously obvious among the frame and rusted-tin buildings adjacent to it. Black paint on a white board proclaimed it an art and souvenir shop owned by one Aristide Tissot.

In the democratic republic of Haiti, it is advertised that the dreaded "Tonton Macoutes" of Papa Doc Duvalier no longer exists, even though some of its former members still are seen on the streets. But memories are long, and there are those who whisper that maybe, just maybe . . . but then, one doesn't talk of such things. And it had never been confirmed that Toussaint Salanet was even a member. In any event, no one chose to see Toussaint as he pushed through the strands of hanging cord which fly-guarded the entrance to A. Tissot, Objects d'Art.

The only person in the room was a slender man, neatly dressed in dark, pressed slacks, pale blue shirt, and a maroon and gray rep stripe necktie. "Good day," he said, "May I—oh," he switched quickly from English to the local patois which the Haitians call creole. "It's you. Welcome, my friend, welcome. You have made sales for me?"

Toussaint smiled broadly. "Of the largest, my friend. I have of the authorization to make selections myself." He spread his hands and raised his head proudly. "I will need to see the many beautiful paintings you so carefully store in the back," he said, throwing a friendly arm around the other's slim shoulders.

"Only the paintings? I have so many of the other . . . "

"I fear it is only paintings this time," said Toussaint, urging the man toward the door at the rear of the room. "Next time I will do my utmost to pursue the sales of your beautiful rock and wooden articles."

"I would show great appreciation," said Tissot approvingly. "Here they are," he said, as they stepped into the back room. He motioned at stacks and rows of paintings covering tables, walls, and the floor of the room.

"Yes," said Toussaint Salanet quietly, sliding his arm up from Tissot's shoulder. "It is true." He braced his hand against the side of the man's head and at the same time wrapped his arm around Tissot's neck, and with a powerful, skillful motion, he snapped it.

Artistide Tissot had been insured by PanGlobal Assurance for fifty thousand American dollars. It was not very much money, but then Haiti is not a very rich country.

The man worked his small farm with other Haitians—whom he kept drugged and captive and barely fed. Such victims had given credence to the myth of there actually being zombies.

CHAPTER 6

Beverly Martin Raker stepped from the elevator into the hallway outside Mitchell's outer office with two minutes remaining before his 1:00 o'clock appointment. He appreciated the efficiency with which his progress, since entering the building, had been reported before he arrived at each station.

Victoria Genn greeted him with a warm smile, the one reserved for persons she was told would be of use to her employer, announced him to those waiting inside the inner office, and ushered him through the doors.

"Thank you, Mrs. Genn," said Mitchell. He walked briskly from behind his desk to greet Raker near the door, extending a hand in welcome.

"Thank you for coming on such short notice, Mr. Raker. Most gracious of you. Most gracious. Would you please be seated?"

Raker studied the arrangement briefly and smiled. "No, thank you. I'd prefer to stand."

Mitchell's smile matched Raker's. He understood. "And I shall not try to intimidate you by keeping my rather ostentatious desk between us. Would you sit if I'd join you out here?"

"I'd really rather stand."

"As you wish, of course. As you wish." Mitchell hesitated, then elected to sit. "I must say that you come highly recommended, Mr. Raker. Quite highly."

Raker's eyes swept past Colt to Webb. "Not completely, I'll wager," he said.

Mitchell permitted himself another smile. "No. You're quite right. Not completely. There seem to be some reservations in certain quarters." He watched as Raker walked to the wide, glass wall to look down upon the city as Mitchell himself had done earlier. "Quite a view, isn't it?"

"Quite," said Raker. He turned. "Mr. Mitchell, I did not come here to exchange pleasantries or engage in small talk. I understand that you have what you consider a serious problem on your hands. I'm told that I may be able to help. Do you want to discuss that?"

Mitchell was taken aback. He was not accustomed to being cut short in such a manner. Slowly, he smiled. "Very good, Mr. Raker. Very good, indeed. Take them off balance, eh? The unexpected?"

Raker simply looked at him. "I didn't apply for a job. A friend asked me to come."

Mitchell stood. He wasn't tall enough to look down on Raker. He walked to his desk and sat. "Mr. Raker, do you realize the size of this company? Do you realize the power that I can bring to bear?" He waved a hand to ward off any comments. "PanGlobal has been the mother. I'm the sire. And between us we've birthed some of the biggest God-damned companies around. We own 'em, and property you wouldn't believe."

"Then you don't need me, do you?" asked Raker, voice deceptively mild.

"Don't be cavalier, Mr. Raker. Of course I need you. *We* need you. I'm not telling you this to impress you with how powerful we are. I want you to understand what we have to protect."

Raker nodded. "I'm impressed. But I know all this, you see." As Mitchell's eyebrows climbed, Raker continued. "It's my business to know who owns what, and who's interested in doing something about it."

"I see. Very good." Mitchell flashed a look at Colt, his expression one of approval.

"Please forgive me, Mr. Raker, for asking what you may feel is an unjustified question. But although you appear to be most competent, I took the opportunity to look over these anti-terrorism businesses since the . . . events of yesterday, and I understand that there are a good many well-accepted companies who are engaged in the business." Mitchell leaned forward to concentrate his gaze directly into Raker's eyes. His expression assumed the stony, eagle-like stoicism which caused so many of his peers to squirm uneasily.

"Why you?"

Raker's eyes locked on Mitchell's. With no change of expression nor flicker of emotion, his voice came from behind lips which didn't appear to move. "Your question is justified. You're speaking, of course, of a couple of organizations who use the word 'risk' in their names, and probably another two or three who refer to themselves as 'international' something or other. I don't like either word. My object is to minimize risk on the one hand—and if an organization has to assure you that they are, indeed, international, then they may protest too much. There are well over sixty counter-terrorist firms of one sort or another if you'd like to interview them all."

As Raker spoke, Mitchell had looked down at papers on the desk in front of him.

"I'm sure that the material you have there tells you that one of the larger and older organizations you are referring to was, as a matter of fact, actually organized by an insurance group in England some years ago."

Mitchell nodded.

"Then you also know we operate differently. My aim is negation, not negotiation. We are Prevent, Mitchell. We don't want to simply lessen risk or losses. We want to prevent them."

Mitchell leaned back in his chair. "What you are intimating then, Mr. Raker, is that you undertake actions which are usually considered to be in the province of . . ." he paused to glance briefly at Webb, ". . . the authorities. It is my understanding from Webb here that your experience includes mercenary activities in certain troubled areas of the world."

Raker affected an expression of wounded innocence. "That would be a criminal offense in this country," he said. "In the U.S. Criminal Code, Title 18 specifically bans the participation by a U.S. citizen—barring conditions of legal war—in any armed action against the property or persons of any foreign country, whether here or overseas, and expressly prohibits the aiding or abetting of, and I quote, 'foreign expeditionaries.' The experience you probably have reference to is that I have certainly aided in the formation and training of counter-terrorist, and counter-insurgency groups, but only within the proscriptions of the law."

Mitchell waved a huge, gnarled hand as though shooing flies. "I'm not at all interested in your methods, Mr. Raker. Only results." Once again he started to pin Raker with his piercing stare, but remembering the outcome of the first clash of eyes, looked down at his desk. Then, face composed, he said, "You certainly seem to know the law regarding the subject."

Raker remained silent.

"Can you stop this attack upon my company?" asked Mitchell.

"If anyone can, I can."

"You're not modest."

"No," agreed Raker.

"Then perhaps you can tell me what the success of this . . ." he looked down at the papers on the desk once again, ". . . this 'risk' outfit as you call it, the one organized by that English insurance group, has been?"

"I can," said Raker quickly, without reflection. "They are negotiators. They are at their best in dealing with hostage situations where they can reduce losses. It is my understanding that they have acquired the release of a good many hostages, and have saved their clients some fair amount of money . . ." His voice trailed off, leaving words unspoken.

"And you don't approve of that?" asked Mitchell.

Raker shrugged. "I always approve of saving money and lives. It's just that I don't think that's the option here."

"Oh?"

"From the material you've received to date I don't think you face negotiation."

For the first time, Webb spoke. "And just what does your expertise tell you we *do* face?"

"Action. Demand after the fact. No hostages."

Mitchell, Colt and Webb looked at each other.

"You seem to be remarkably astute, Mr. Raker. Today's communications would seem to indicate that you are quite a seer."

"You've had further communications?"

"Yes," said Colt. He looked at Mitchell who nodded. "Here." He went to Raker and handed him the letters received to the present time.

Raker scanned them quickly, then re-read them as the men waited.

"Well?" asked Colt.

"Brilliant," said Raker. "Ingenious. You're vulnerable as a mullet at a porpoise picnic."

"Any recommendations?" It was Mitchell.

Raker was silent a moment before speaking. "Let me outline the situation as I see it. A lot of this will be conjecture and surmise."

Without moving, without raising the tone of his voice, his presence now overwhelmed the room. "But," he continued, "it is the result of experience and familiarity. So listen, and realize the problems that PanGlobal faces, for all its size and power."

As they listened, Raker explained that when hostages are held by terrorists, whether persons or property, there is a locus of possible counter-action and, if the threatened group is willing to sacrifice the persons or property held hostage, the possibility exists of capturing or destroying the terrorists. In many cases such threat-removal can be accomplished with a minimum of loss. In other cases, sufficient protection can be offered—when the threatened persons or property is known or predictable—to make the possible losses to the terrorist threateners not worth their possible gains.

"In short," said Raker, "when the targets are known, and the location is known, a decision can be made to (1) pay up, (2) counter-attack and hope for the best, or (3) simply ignore the threat. In the last two cases, the victims may be sacrificed, but the nation, government, business, or whatever the threatened entity . . . it will continue to exist." He watched their faces as he spoke.

"However, in the projected actions against PanGlobal, none of this holds true. There are no hostages being held; there is no locus, no site for counter-attack; and with the millions of possible targets, there is no way to know or predict them, thus making protection sufficient to discourage attack impossible. And even that is not the worst. The threat is not simply to specified individuals or property—call them fingers and toes—but it is to the company, the entity. And that is the heart and the brain. This threat is to the very existence of your company.

"It isn't just a matter of sacrificing certain policy-holders or

insured property and the money that would cost; that would probably amount to only an insignificant percentage of PanGlobal's
profit. A few pennies a share. But what if the news media becomes
aware of the situation? What if policy holders are made to feel that
their property and their lives are in jeopardy by being on a terrorist
hit-list as long as they are insured by PanGlobal? How long will it
take the vast majority of them to switch to the seeming safety of
another company?"

As Raker had been talking, the listening Mitchell, Colt and
Webb had become more and more discomfited. Even the perpetual
military bearing of Harlan Webb had shown signs of wilting. Colt
stared at Raker as though in a trance. The jaw-muscles of Mitchell's face were knotted with tension.

"But they couldn't . . . wouldn't . . ." Mitchell's voice came in
a raspy, near whisper. "They would defeat their own purpose."
Color began to return to his face, which had become ashen during
Raker's discourse. "Such an operation would cost them money—a
great deal of money—and they would have no profit to show."

"There are other companies, Mr. Mitchell," said Raker, quietly.

"But how . . ."

"They infiltrated your security," interrupted Raker. "They have
obviously, if you will allow me to verbalize a noun, accessed your
computers, as stated in their communication. There is little chance
they haven't done the same with at least one other major company.
In this day of space-craft and shuttles, nearly everyone has learned
the imperative of having a backup system." Silence emphasized his
dramatic pause before he added, "And you can bet the existence of
PanGlobal on that."

A gray pallor had again washed Mitchell's craggy features.
"Then it's refuse the bastards," he observed, eyes watching his
knotty hands twist at each other, "and lose everything, all I've
spent my life building, or . . ." his voice trailed off. He swallowed,
lifted his huge head to look directly at Raker, " . . . or meet their
damn blackmail demands. Is that it, Mr. Raker? Is that the choice
I have to make? Is that what you're telling me?"

All eyes followed Raker as he moved across the room to stand
with his back to them, looking out over New York City from the
40th floor of the PanGlobal building. He turned to face them, legs

spread, hands clasped behind his back. The pose seemed somehow aggressive.

"No," he said softly. "There's another option."

Mitchell's shrewd eyes studied Raker carefully. "And just what might that be, Mr. Raker?" It was not a challenge.

"Destroy them. Totally." As the others started to speak, Raker silenced them with an upraised hand. "Wait! First, I'd need the total cooperation of your organization, if I decide to take on the job. All the facts regarding everyone concerned with PanGlobal—clients, investments, personnel, information on all stock holders. I'd work up psychological profiles and sociograms on them all." At Mitchell's look of surprise, Raker added, "Prevent has that capability. Especially in conjunction with your system; it has served us to good purpose."

"But the board—investors—why would anyone who benefits from our success want to damage the company?" asked Mitchell.

"Profit. Greed. Anger. Power. Insanity. Any number of motives," answered Raker. "There is no doubt that someone inside is helping the scam. But the greatest danger is in the structure of the attacking force. We can't just cut off a part. It's like a Medusa—or a cancer, if you prefer. It's obviously too wide spread, too organized to contain. It will have to be destroyed down to the last spore."

The calm intensity with which Raker spoke cast a physical chill upon his listeners. Mitchell, Colt and Webb exchanged looks of consternation.

"But you think, you feel, that maybe there's a way?" Mitchell asked.

"We could start by stalling. They would expect that. It would probably cost a few lives, some losses. But it would give me time to play ferret with what information we have." He picked up the clipped-together sheets which comprised the communications received up to now.

"They won't mind hitting you with a few extra losses if it will help insure their success. Just don't do anything to annoy them, past a little stalling."

Webb looked uncomfortable. Colt told Raker of the man's earlier actions against Pagan Maguire. Raker said nothing, simply stared at Webb coldly. He focused attention on Mitchell.

"Get ready to pocket some losses. No doubt they'll carry out their threats. But if I knew what targets had been hit, and how, I'd have some indication of their procedures. There might be some sort of pattern. More importantly, it would probably disclose their technique, and, quite probably, their first strikes will indicate the limit or extent of their reach."

No one spoke.

"And that would give me something to work with. Once I had something concrete, something to examine, there is a chance that I could put a name to the group involved. It has to be a group. No individual could hope to operate on this scale . The strikes occurring during a brief time period shows that."

Mitchell cleared his throat roughly before speaking. "And you think there is a chance you actually might be able to identify their MO? Is that the phrase?"

Raker smiled slightly. "It'll do. Yes, it may indicate a modus operandi which my computers could recognize. If so, there would be little problem after that."

The three men listening to Raker brightened visibly.

"I would also be very surprised if that occurs," added Raker.

"But you said . . ." began Mitchell.

"I said it would give me something to work on." Consternation! He glanced at his wrist watch. "You can be certain that within the next twenty-four hours you will know just who, or what, those initials represent. Right now it is a matter of wait and see." He paused in concentration. "How about those newspaper clippings the girl brought? Were they actually clients of PanGlobal?"

Mitchell's face showed surprise. In his distress he had forgotten them.

"Webb?"

"I'll check." He hurried to the phone.

• • •

Raker addressed Mitchell. "How do you like being a terrorist?" Mitchell looked quizzical.

"Come on, now," said Raker, his tone chiding. "Isn't that what it is? The insurance business? You deal in fear, Mitchell. You, of all people, should understand this terrorism business."

"You sound inimical," said Mitchell.

"No," replied Raker. "Perhaps envious. No one in your business wants to talk about motives past that bullshit concerning how one must fear for their survivors; how they must protect their investments from God-knows-what terrible consequences. You scare the shit out of people, Mitchell. You deal in terror as a matter of course. Without fear of the future, fear of loss, fear of the unknown, the insurance game couldn't exist. You deal in people's misery. It's possibly the oldest, nastiest 'terror' business around, yet you people have made it admired and appreciated through a propaganda campaign second, perhaps, only to Joseph Goebbels, and the big lie technique."

He grinned as Mitchell's face showed signs of approaching apoplexy.

"I'm not talking about you, personally, Mallory Fleming Mitchell. Compared to some of the ones I'm thinking of, you're a moderate. But the idea of an insurance company being in business to 'help others' is a bale of camel dung. Insurance companies deal in people's fears and best of all, insurance is indispensable. There can be no commerce without it." He smiled. "You have a ball-lock on them."

Mitchell, recognizing that he was being baited, had relaxed. "You, Mr. Raker, have the unhappy facility of calling a spade a fucking shovel, it would seem." He surveyed Raker through narrowed eyes, then nodded his head. "Yes, I suppose you might be entitled to think all that, although no one has said so to me before. But it's the money business, sir, and until the machinations of our own beloved countrymen helped foreign oil producers understand the temporary power they could wield, I've been told... insurance was the largest money business in the world. And of that group, I am the largest."

"As a successful bettor, then, sir," Raker threw the title back at Mitchell, "I'll wager that each of those newspaper stories concerning recently-past disasters will involve one of your clients."

Mitchell had no chance to reply, as Webb's voice filled the room.

"Then get it down here, damn it. Now!" Webb's voice was thunderous as he spoke into the telephone. He slammed it down.

"They've completed the report," he said, voice tight and hollow.

"And?"

Webb looked away. "To quote our records department, there seems to be a positive relationship."

Mitchell pursed his lips and blew out his breath as though exhausting steam. "It would seem, Mr. Raker, that you are a knowledgeable gambler."

Raker shrugged. "No gamble. A sure thing. The material wouldn't have been sent if the subjects weren't clients of PanGlobal."

"Then it appears that they have made previous strikes?"

Raker shook his head from side to side. "Not necessarily. All they would have needed is access to your client list, and they obviously have that. They could have picked the stories ex post facto. I would have to run the data through my computers before I could make a decision on whether they really were responsible."

Mitchell squirmed slightly and cleared his throat once again. "This computer of yours," he started, "you've mentioned it several times. Just what does it do?"

"What we order. It is programmed with information that allows it to be the brains of Prevent," replied Raker. "It contains all the information our organization has been able to compile regarding any and all actions which seem to have any connection with possible terrorist activities."

"And the terrorists?"

"Especially the terrorists. And those with the slightest connection."

Mitchell eyed Raker levelly for a moment. "You are most informed, Mr. Raker, most informed. Therefore it will come as no surprise to you to know that we consider PanGlobal to have the most extensive information system in the world stored in our own, and I'm sure more technologically advanced, computer system."

Raker only nodded.

"The vast majority of the population of this country" continued Mitchell, "and an appreciable part of the rest of the civilized world, have been carefully categorized and filed away for easy access. People who've never dream that we have any record of them are there, as you know. Anyone who has ever applied for a driver's license, bought anything on credit, opened a bank account, paid a utility bill, been to a doctor, ordered anything by mail," he waved a hand in circles, "and on and on and on."

He stood, stepped down from his elevated position behind his desk, and joined the others. "All these fine people, and many others, have quite complete and highly private information about them stored away in our system. People who have had no dealings with us. Your system can't begin to approach ours." Mitchell shook his head in denial.

"Then you'll not be needing my help," said Raker. "Just punch a button saying 'terrorists' and pick out the bunch threatening you."

"Not meant that way, Mr. Raker, not meant that way at all. I only submit the information, and offer it to you as an adjunct to your own specialized system."

"And a helpful adjunct it would be," agreed Raker. "It would certainly be of assistance in determining who potential victims might be." He paused to tap a large finger against the side of his nose. "And if my system were to deliver up a profile of who or what we are looking for, then maybe, just maybe, your system could spit out the names for us."

He lifted his head briskly, musing ended. "That would be the first order of business," he said. "I could work out the input material and query my system tonight. I'd need the information on the newspaper stories, and copies of all communications."

Mitchell looked toward Colt and Webb.

"Here are copies," said Colt. He handed an envelope to Raker and glanced toward Mitchell. "I anticipated him," he explained. "But we still need the records report."

"Where the hell is . . ." started Mitchell. He was interrupted by the chime of the intercom.

"Yes, Mrs. Genn?"

"An envelope from records."

"Check and see if there is a duplicate copy, Mrs. Genn. If not, please have one made immediately."

"Certainly, sir." The soft buzz of the intercom went silent.

"Is there anything else we can do for you, Mr. Raker. Anything else you'll need?" Mitchell's mobile eyebrows arched high. "But of course. I thought . . ."

"You assumed?" Raker's tone bordered on sarcasm.

Mitchell composed himself. "I did, indeed, assume, Mr. Raker. I certainly did assume. Would it be proper if I were to ask if you were willing to represent PanGlobal in this affair?"

Raker smiled, guilelessly. "Quite proper. I will be happy to accept. It is only that I do not like to be taken for granted. I hadn't said I'd take the job; I simply said what I could, and would, do, *if* I were handling it."

"I shall remember that, remember it indeed." Mitchell tried on a smile. "And your fee?" he asked.

Raker thought only briefly. "Expenses, one hundred thousand dollars a week, fifty million dollars upon the successful completion of the job."

Mitchell achieved a real smile. "Like that? No hesitation, eh?" He chuckled. "I like that. It is obvious that you did not answer that quickly just off the top of your head. You had decided prior to my inquiry?"

"Of course."

"And that is your standard fee?"

"I have no 'standard' fee."

"You are not inexpensive, Mr. Raker."

"I am not ordinary, Mr. Mitchell."

Mitchell laughed aloud. "No, by God! I don't think you are." He extended a hand. Raker took it and they shook. "I'll put it in writing, of course, but it will have to be covered under some heading other than . . . terrorism."

"Don't bother," said Raker, holding Mitchell's hand firmly. "The handshake is good enough for me. After all, we have to trust each other."

• • •

Victoria Genn entered the office quietly and handed papers to Mitchell. He studied them briefly, then offered a set to Raker.

"The newspaper correlations. It's all there."

Raker placed the papers with the others already in his pocket. Pulling a felt-tipped pen from his shirt pocket, he jotted a number on a corner of one of the pages and tore it off.

"I'll start processing them immediately." He moved to the door where he paused and turned to face the three men.

"I will be in continual contact," he said. Not continuous, continual. "Webb. Fix me up with identification that will allow me complete access to the entire complex. Everything. Call me an efficiency expert, or whatever. First, I'll start looking for the inside man—or woman. James, you know my hotel. Here's the phone number and room. Don't hesitate to inform me of any developments."

He turned and placed a hand on the door knob. Without facing them he said, "And leave Pagan Maguire alone. That can only lead to severe complications. Leave her completely alone. I'm sure that you had her followed. Call them off. For now I don't even want to know where she is. If we're watching, so are they." He turned the knob, stepped out, and closed the door behind him.

The three men looked toward the door for a moment then turned to face each other.

"Well, gentlemen?" asked Mitchell.

Colt answered first. "Raker is always Raker," he said. "Webb?"

"He's thorough. I'll get his identification papers processed today. He's efficient, I never said otherwise. That doesn't mean I have to like him."

"No," agreed Mitchell. "I don't think that's important, least of all to Raker. He's intuitive, and the computer says he's as tough as you two indicated, and competent." He chuckled. "And damned secretive, too. The data only goes back to his military service record . . . and that's pretty far. But there isn't enough personal information available, except for those records, to satisfy even nosy neighbors. Only business and credit information, and great gaps of time while he was, ostensibly, traveling."

"I could have told you that," Webb muttered.

"You didn't." Mitchell walked to the window where both he and Raker had stood earlier, and looked at the city.

"I think he is the right man. He's tough, he seems competent, he's intuitive, and, by God, he certainly isn't impressed with us 'big shots,' is he?" He chuckled. "I think you picked a winner, James." He turned toward the other men. "If anyone can be our salvation, by thunder, I think it must—*may*—be Raker." Hope lit Mitchell's countenance. "Interesting man. I wish I knew more about him."

CHAPTER 7

RAKER

Beverly Martin Raker was born in a small mining town in southern Colorado sometime after the stock market crash. He had never known his natural father, who had died in a mining accident only weeks before Raker's birth.

The boy's mother named him Beverly after her own mother, and—perhaps as a comment on her attitude toward her late husband—Martin, after her own father. Only two weeks after being delivered of the only child she would ever bear, she went to work as live-in cook at a boarding house whose residents were, for the most part, miners.

Any memories the boy might retain of his first years were pleasant. The male residents of the boarding house, sympathetic to the circumstances surrounding the boy and his young mother, treated the child as their special mascot and his mother with great respect. Their attention and their rough-housing ways during his early years delighted the youngster and developed him into what everyone agreed "had the makings of a real man's man."

When Raker was still a child, his mother, after careful consideration of the prospects, remarried. Her choice, which was made from a not inconsiderable list of swains, was a huge, gentle-seeming, quiet man who operated a grocery and meat market, and trapped and traded with the Jicarilla Apaches in northern New Mexico. It was an area where few men were willing to do business.

There was no doubting that the man's energy and astuteness, his obviously growing wealth and property holdings proved that. His name was Emil Raker, but it was said by some that it had been changed from some unpronounceable Polish or Bohemian name. Others said it had been German, and was changed by the man's father during the Great War. Still others—the older ones—whispered that Raker was not the name at all, but the name taken in remorse of another man killed by him. Whatever the truth, most people liked and respected the man.

Oh, it was true that there were some who looked upon the large man with disfavor. These, however, were the few village toughs who had been given reason. Emil Raker had never been known to start a fight. He did, however, specialize in ending them—quickly, quietly, and efficiently.

There were others, of course, as there would be in any town or village, who found fault with the match. They would have found fault with any match. To these few it seemed peculiar that a young, attractive, church-going woman could accept a seemingly uncultured man who spent so much time away from home. It somehow just didn't seem consistent for a man in such a safe, solid business as that of grocer and butcher to waste so much time wandering the mountains.

They would watch and wonder, when Raker would saddle one of the two huge mules he maintained, outfit the other as a pack animal and—allowing his single employee to run his store—be gone for weeks at a time in the mountains. Oh, certainly he brought back animal pelts, and Lord knows what other goods from those near-savages to the south, and there was probably good profit in it, but it just didn't seem proper. It just wasn't what one would expect of . . . well, it just wasn't the way a grocer should behave. And when Emil started taking his young step-son on his shorter trips, these same people were scandalized. One simply did not expose a mere baby to such things. Why, the boy couldn't be more than five or six! How terrible! But they should have consulted the boy.

He learned to track game, to follow spoor, read sign, and blaze trail. He learned to live off the land, and he discovered the secret of following water downhill to where you would always find people. By the time he was seven, he could tell who, or what, had passed a certain spot, in what number, and how long before. He could spot a wild turkey resting on a limb against the trunk of a tree, and could close, without being seen or heard, to within an arrow-shot of a watchful mule deer, though it would be a year or two before he could bend such a bow. Before he could read well in his own language, he could converse—with a basic vocabulary—in at least two Indian dialects.

These early experiences were idyllic for the boy, and for his mother and step-father as well. There was much affection and tolerance, and everyone seemed to have time for each other. Emil Raker, especially, was never too busy to pay attention to the youngster. Not once did a question go unanswered, even though perhaps not fully explained. It was during this year that Emil formally adopted the boy, becoming a father in fact as well as love. It wasn't until the fall after the boy's sixth birthday that any trouble began.

Young Raker had developed the usual number of neighborhood friends, if not more. This circumstance was partly a result of the fact that the family never lacked for material goods, even during the difficult times of the depression years, and they were always willing to share them. Raker's young friends were always made welcome with better food and treats than most of them received at home. Mothers liked the family because Emil seldom refused credit to those who asked; fathers also liked the family, or at least seemed to, if their attendance at the room reserved for them at the rear of Emil's grocery was any indication.

Prohibition notwithstanding, many of the men were seen to leave the room in a better mood than when they entered. And to Emil's credit, it was known that he never permitted a customer to leave his grocery store annex in a mean mood or in an obviously drunken condition. A few—not many—had discovered that Emil was extremely effective in convincing them to sleep it off in an area he had carefully prepared for just such contingencies. If the men had families, they were notified of the circumstances and condition of the men. Such consideration was appreciated, and times were good for Raker's family—until it came time for school.

Young Raker was enrolled in the first grade by his proud mother; enrolled by his full name, not simply the Martin which his father had insisted upon using. So, on his first day, there it was for all to see, carefully spelled out: Beverly Martin Raker.

It took two days for the trouble to start.

• • •

The taunting questions at first.

"How come you got a girl's name?"

"What kind of name is that for a boy?"

And then the insults: "Hey, Bev-er-lee, do you do like the girls, and squat to pee?"

Raker fought. He was strong, quick, capable and willing; and he inflicted damage. His rough-housing with the young Apache boys he had met on his trips with his father paid off well. But he was badly outnumbered, and after the first brawl he turned up at home with damage to his fists, clothing and face, in that order. His mother worried over him and reassured him as mothers often do, and told him to ignore the teasing. Emil, after first assessing the damage, told him that if he stood his ground firmly enough the boys would soon leave him alone. The pleasure would not be worth the pain.

Emil was right.

After only one major, and two minor, frays, his classmates concluded that the damage they were suffering as a result of the boy's tenacity and aggressive, practiced violence was more than the price they were willing to pay. At first, in a face-saving gesture, they simply ignored him, but the ridicule stopped. Soon Beverly was forgotten. He was Martin once again, and slowly, oh, ever-so-slowly, friendships were renewed.

Beverly Martin Raker had learned that he could win.

• • •

In the tiny mining communities of Raker's youth, there were no organized sports in the lower grades. Such luxuries were simply too expensive, and furthermore, there were far too many chores to be done for the children to waste their time in such unproductive ways. The situation suited Martin perfectly.

He delighted in helping his father in the store, becoming of real value as a surprisingly good meat cutter, stocker and delivery boy. He was bright, alert, strong beyond his years, and took great satisfaction in pleasing Emil—in just being around the big man. And when the grocery closed in the evening, Emil, for an hour before he would open his grocery "annex" to the thirsty townsmen, would show the boy tricks with hatchets and knives. He taught him respect for and the use of the cutlery designed for butchering, but the boy's greatest delight came from the impressive collection of hunting and sporting knives and tomahawks as he learned their use.

Emil had built a thick wooden target against the back wall of his storage area, and there had taught the boy to throw knives with eyebrow-raising accuracy. And while he could not yet duplicate his father's feat of throwing a knife to pierce a silver dollar pinned against the wood, the knives and hatchets he threw were difficult to pull from the target.

As the years passed and the boy grew tall and strong, prohibition ended, and the entrance to the grocery store annex was walled up, its front glassed in and decorated with lights, and a huge sign spelling out TAVERN spanned the front.

The village had grown—so slowly at first that only those associated with the one bank and two real estate firms had paid much attention to its expansion. They and Emil Raker. As his fortunes improved, Emil added carefully selected employees to his two businesses, and began to spend more time away from work, and more with his son. While he had quietly been purchasing undeveloped land around the village, as well as houses and more distant properties, he had acknowledged his wife's gift with figures, and turned over to her the responsibility for handling their accounts.

She felt important and needed—more than just a wife and mother—and it showed as she blossomed with assurance and vitality. She didn't even mind too much when Emil, during the summer months while school was out, extended his sojourns with his son to a month or more. The man and boy were delighted with the freedom to roam and wander the mountains and high desert, and as the man enjoyed teaching, the boy delighted in learning that men could live well without the protection and comforts afforded by towns and cities.

As these months together wore on, young Raker's proficiency in the outdoors began to approach that of Emil's. He had always marveled at how the older man could pass through brush leaving signs that could be discerned only after the most painstaking search. And how he could suddenly seem to appear out of nowhere without a sound. And now, occasionally in their games, the boy would succeed in eluding his father, once even came from behind to touch him, completely undetected. In the summer of his thirteenth year, young Raker was a masterful hunter and stalker, and as a result of his natural physical strength and the skills he had learned from his Apache friends developed with additional coaching from Emil, became more than a match for many grown men.

The boy had always been fascinated by Emil's knowledge of Indian culture, the mountains, and the outdoor life, but whenever he had attempted to question the man about how he had learned so much, Emil would only say, "Someday, Martin, someday I'll tell you all about it." That day never had a chance to come.

• • •

As the family's economics flourished, the boy's mother had been spending more and more of her time tending to the business of rental property and leases. At times it seemed to young Martin that his family must own most of the buildings and much of the land around their small town; he could still recall the discussions about mineral rights, and how his mother wanted to allow their holdings to be developed, and how Emil would say he didn't want the land scarred. And during the year past, it seemed that whenever Emil and the boy would return from one of their expeditions, there would always be some man from some company or other at the house. His mother would explain that they were asking her to convince his father to sign papers that could make the family a lot of money. He could remember his mother pleading with Emil, but the man stood firm in his decision.

The boy remembered one particular conversation in which his mother said, "If you wouldn't be so stubborn, we could make enough to get away from this awful hole, and move to a city where I could live a decent life." The thought of living in a city horrified Martin, and he was delighted when Emil said that he would never consider such a thing, and he would talk about it no more.

There was one of the men that young Raker especially disliked. He was the one around the most often. He smiled too much, was too well dressed, and called Martin "my little man." His name was Forbes, and he had something to do with real estate. He annoyed the boy sufficiently so that he took much pleasure on the evening Emil ordered the man from the house, telling him that he never wanted to see him there again.

Angry words followed the incident as his mother berated his father for his action. The boy took little notice, for such clashes were becoming more and more common. When they occurred, the boy simply went for a walk in the hills, and upon returning, the house was usually quiet.

On the morning following the most recent incident, Emil awakened the boy early, and they set out on an unexpected trip. But this trip was not like the others. Emil was quieter than usual, and the boy's questions, for the first time he could remember, went mostly unanswered. Perhaps even unheard.

When they loaded the pickup truck, the boy expected they would head out to their small farm where Emil stabled the animals. Instead, Emil drove past the turnoff and continued on the narrow strip of paved road which would lead, eventually, to Durango. The boy's father said simply that he had some business to conduct in the larger town, and once there, Martin was exiled to the darkness of a motion picture theater for the afternoon movie. To most of his youthful contemporaries, such an event would have been a treat. For young Raker it was not. He wasn't familiar with the characters in the weekly serials, and the movie version of cowboys and Indians held nothing of the reality he knew. It was with relief that he left the theater when the necessary hours had passed and met Emil back at their parked truck.

The man was silent on the way home, as he had been on their trip over. His breath smelled, uncharacteristically, of whiskey. He said only that they must get back so that he could "take care of some business." They would set off for the mountains on the morrow.

By the time they reached their destination it had grown quite dark, and Emil stopped some distance from their home.

"Wait here for me, Martin. I have to see about something."

The boy watched his father start down the street, and as soon as the man turned the corner, he slipped from the truck to follow him. He knew something was wrong. He could still feel the almost physical aura of tension which had surrounded them on the trip home.

The boy followed carefully, with the skill he had learned in the mountains. He knew it would not be enough if Emil had been his normal, alert self, but it was obvious to the boy that the man's attention was focused elsewhere.

Keeping at a distance, and in the shadows, the boy quickly surmised that Emil was headed toward their house, and with youthful agility and the knowledge gained from boyhood excursions through the neighborhood, he slipped between houses and over fences and was already hidden by the huge lilac bush near the front of their home when Emil turned the corner. As had the boy earlier, Emil recognized the car parked in the shadows of the trees across the street. It belonged to Forbes, the man Emil had ordered from the house the previous evening.

Martin watched as his father paused momentarily near the front steps, then moved silently up them to open the door slowly and softly. Alarm prickled the neck hairs of the boy, and after only a brief hesitation he hurried from behind the bush and started toward the house. The inner door was still open; only the screen door impeded his progress. He eased it open, and had started into the room when the silence was shattered into a nightmare of noise.

He would ever after remember the sound of his mother's voice, shrill and piercing, half-scream, half-plea; his father's great bull-like roars of anger, and the clatter and crash of upset furniture. In the half-light from the upstairs hallway, young Raker saw struggling figures, then suddenly a body came thudding down the stairs, and almost before it landed, his father got to the bottom of the steps in two great bounds. His huge hands reached down and grasped for a hold on the figure at his feet. The man wore no clothes, so Emil's powerful fingers fastened onto flesh and hair and lifted the struggling body from the floor. He surged toward the front of the room, and with a mighty heave threw the man through the screen door, tearing it from its hinges.

Eyes huge with fear, Martin watched his father stand at the open door, legs spraddled, hands clenching and unclenching at his sides, chest heaving, head lowered as he glared fiercely through the doorway, ignoring the presence of the boy.

Raker went to the front window and looked through it at the form of the man struggling to his feet. The naked body was stained and marked, but in dim light Raker could not tell if from dirt or blood. In spite of the fear he felt, Raker was struck by the fact that without his fancy clothes, the man looked bony and almost funny as he managed to stagger to his feet.

Gasping, the man lifted his face toward Emil. "Raker . . ." he started.

"Get out," said Emil.

"I . . . I need my . . . my keys . . . I need my . . ."

"Your clothes," said Emil flatly. "Do you want to try to come and get them?"

The man hesitated only briefly, then turned and started toward the street, seeming to gain strength as he walked.

As he reached the darkness near the lilac bush where the boy had hidden, his voice came to them in a hissing whisper. "You're dead, Raker. Dead!"

"Go, you son of a bitch," snarled Emil, not moving. "Go before I come out and kill you." And he stood silently looking out into the night.

Remembering his mother's cries, the boy raced up the stairs toward his parents' bedroom. As he looked through the open door, his mother, long hair streaming loosely, quickly gathered the bedclothes around her. But not before the boy had seen that she was nude. He stood in shock. So much had happened so fast, that only now was he fully aware of what had happened. As he looked at his mother, disgust filled him and glared from his eyes.

His mother held a hand up toward the boy. "Martin," she said, "Martin, please!" She reached hands forward as though begging.

The boy wheeled and sprinted down the stairs, out past his father still standing in the doorway, and he ran. He ran to the stream near the house, then turned to run along its rocky banks and up into the hills. When he finally stopped, it was from exhaustion. He sank to his knees, miles from the scene he had witnessed. He lay back against the grass, not minding, not feeling, the rocks digging into his lean body. He studied the sky and listened to the sound of the water and the night noises.

He would not think of what he had just witnessed! He remembered how Emil had taught him to force unwanted thoughts from his mind. Choose the most absurd word you can think of, then tell yourself that you must not think of that word. He thought of rhinoceros. That was not just an absurd word, it was an absurd animal. He would not think of the word.

He fell asleep thinking, "Rhinoceros."

• • •

When he awoke, the sun was a bright, gleaming halo behind thin clouds. As the boy blinked away the last vestiges of sleep, the horror of the night returned. He washed in the cold, flowing water and slowly grew aware that through the years he had stopped knowing his mother. So much of his time had been spent with his father that there had been no time for her, except when the three of them were together. And those times had been less and less. He realized that he didn't really know if he liked her or not. She had simply been there; convenient; handy; taking care of things like clothes and meals. But that was all there had been. And now, even that was over. He wouldn't go home, not with her there, not after what she had done to his father.

His father! It was Sunday. He would be down at the store, reviewing happenings of the past week and getting things ready for the next. He would see what his father was going to do! No! What *they*, the two of them, were going to do. Maybe go to the mountains for good. He started for town at a rapid pace, comfortable and quick, not like the exhausting run of the night before.

He turned onto the main street near his father's business. The only sound to be heard was the light flutter of the awning stretching in front of the town's jewelry store, left rolled down in the Saturday night hurry to close. The green and yellow striped canvas rippled gently in the early morning breeze. The street was small-town Sunday morning, barren of pedestrians, and with Emil Raker's pickup the only vehicle in evidence for two blocks.

The boy hurried past the squares of yellow tile and opaque glass blocks which surrounded the adjacent cocktail lounge's window. The thin neon ropes which, at night, combined to spell Cocktails & Beer in glowing red, were glassily dull.

The knot of distress and anxiety which had been suppressed into a sluggishly twisting mass in his stomach tried to force its way to his throat. Without conscious thought, he forced it back and let his mind dwell on what wonderful things he and his father could do together.

The door of the grocery was closed, an unusual occasion on warm summer mornings when Emil did his bookwork. The out-doors was Emil's life, and doors were only closed to keep out bad weather and pests. The boy tried the latch and found the door unlocked. He stepped inside. The lights were off. He listened, no sounds. "Dad," he called. No answer. He walked farther into the store, down a narrow merchandise-walled aisle.

"Dad? Where are you?" He walked on toward the desk where Emil worked at his Sunday morning chores.

He heard something. Not quite a voice, but wet, raspy breath-ing.

"Dad?"

The sound grew louder. It was a voice, but thin and broken, like the whine of a wounded animal.

"Dad!" cried the boy, and raced toward the back of the store. He stopped suddenly as he almost stumbled over the sprawled body of his father.

In the sparse light from the single, goose-necked lamp on the nearby desk, Martin could see the blood. It covered almost every-thing. It splattered unopened cartons, the side of the desk; lay in pools on the wooden floor, and covered the man lying on the floor. The face was an unrecognizable, red mask. The only movement was the faint stirring of a hand, fingers moving slowly in a feeble, beckoning motion.

The boy dropped to his knees. "My God, oh my God! What . . . ? Oh, Jesus!"

"Hush!" The word bubbled and fresh foaming blood appeared on the lips of Emil Raker. "They . . . shot me." More foam, and now bubbles on the front of the blood-soaked shirt. "Shotgun.

Three . . . men. Forbes . . . one . . . Forbes." The bloody chest heaved with the effort of speaking. The bloody hand which had moved, now slid forward and gripped the boy's wrist with some force. "Get . . . him. Them. Mustn't do . . . this . . . anyone else."

"Yes, Papa, yes," cried the boy. He hadn't called the man Papa in years.

"Must take care . . . your mother. Not . . . her fault."

The boy tried to hold his father's head. He would not answer.

"Must," insisted Emil. "Must take care . . . her. Promise . . . me."

Tears welled in the boy's eyes and he choked back the bile rising in his throat. "I promise," he said.

"Get . . . him . . ." The voice stopped, and the open eyes, white-rimmed in the bloody face, went opaque. The bubbling ceased. Emil Raker was dead.

The boy lifted his face toward the ceiling. He opened his mouth and uttered a shrieking squall which seemed torn from his throat. It was more war cry than wail.

The boy rose from his knees and stood staring down at the lifeless form of his father, the anesthesia of rage numbing his grief. He would kill them! Each of them. He knew the one. He would find the others.

The police! If they knew of the trouble between his father and Forbes, they might connect him with the killing. Mustn't let them do that. He, himself, had to kill the man. He remembered his father's dying words, "Get him . . ."—and he had promised. And to take care of his mother. At the thought of his mother the boy clamped his eyes shut and put his hands against his head, trying to squeeze out the memory of the previous night. She had been the cause of this! All right. He had promised to take care of her. He would. But he would never forgive her.

What to do first? He looked around the room, saw the telephone hanging from the wall. Call the police? No! Not yet. A robbery! Must make it look like a robbery. His father had attempted to stop them and they had killed him. If the police believed that, then they would have no reason to think that Forbes had been involved.

The boy moved around the body and walked behind the desk.

The drawers from the cash registers of both the grocery store and the cocktail lounge were sitting on the scratched and worn wooden surface. They were empty of all but a few coins. The bills were stacked neatly alongside the drawers.

Raker put the money into his pockets along with the coins, then walked around the long, center aisle island of stacked merchandise, and behind the meat display case. He found the wooden orange crate where his father and the butcher disposed of clean up rags and dirty aprons. From under the pile of blood-stained cloth he pulled the canvas bag which his father left for whoever was to open the store each Monday morning. He eyed the bag thoughtfully. Better leave it! Only employees and his mother—his thoughts paused as he swallowed to clear his mouth of the sour taste even the thought of the word brought. That woman. Only employees and "that woman" knew about the bag, so better leave it rather than have the police suspect that the killers—and robbers—had been someone who knew Raker's habits. He put the bag back and covered it with the cloths. How could he reconstruct it? They might have jimmied the door, relocked it, and surprised Emil. Not really, thought the boy, he would have been too wary. They must have tricked him. The boy made an unconscious vow never to trust anyone, without reservation. But the police might believe it.

The boy hurried quietly up the aisle and looked cautiously out the paned windows. There was still no evidence of any activity on the street. The only movement was that of a rumpled scrap of paper as it slid and quivered down the empty street, impelled by the capricious breeze.

He opened the door just enough to examine the area around the lock. It was unmarred. He hurried to the back and returned with a hammer. Carefully, staying inside the store, he used the peen end to scar the wood and the metal around the lock on both the door and the jamb. It looked all right. He started to replace the hammer, then hesitated. Could they tell that it had been used on the door? Better to take no chances. He stuck the wooden handle into his belt: He would dispose of it in a few minutes. Safely. Just as soon as he had decided what he would tell the police.

His deception was successful. The police found evidence that the door had been forced. And they accepted without question the boy's account of how he had come down to help his father with the Sunday routine, and had arrived just as a car with out-of-state plates was pulling away from the store. It had been too far to read the numbers, but the color of the plate was the same as those of New Mexico, the state to the south. The description of the car that he had given them fitted many of the cars on the road. There had been two men in the car. It had driven away in the direction of Pagosa Springs. The car and men, which did not exist of course, were never found.

Martin managed to be civil to his mother in public through the time of the funeral, although when alone he refused to talk to her. She didn't press the issue, but withdrew into her own silence, a fact which made confrontation unnecessary. It was two days after the burial of his father when the thirteen-year-old boy took action.

• • •

It was shortly before midnight on the fourth day following Emil Raker's murder when Jackson Forbes parked his car in the driveway alongside his home. He walked, somewhat unsteadily, toward the steps leading up to his front porch, fumbling clumsily at a ring of keys. He heard no sound, but sensed a blur of motion from above his head just before a searing shock of pain sent streaks of brilliant light flashing outward from the blinding ball of fire in his head. There was a brief moment of stomach-wrenching sickness before he dropped unconscious. Raker had dived headlong from the porch roof, slamming the flat of one of his father's collection of tomahawks accurately against the temple of the man below him.

Forbes groaned and stirred. He felt sick to his stomach and his head seemed to be splitting with pain. He tried to put his hands against his temples to ease the agony, but he couldn't move them. They were tied tightly behind him.

He opened his eyes, the effort causing him to wince. The room was quite dark, illuminated only by a flickering candle. Forbes rolled over on his side and attempted to sit up. The effort was too great. He toppled back and groaned.

"Just lay there, Mr. Forbes," came a voice.

"Who . . . what . . .?" Forbes's eyes searched for the source of the sounds. "Don't you know me, Mr. Forbes?" The boy leaned forward until the light from the candle was on his face. "Don't you recognize me?"

"You're Ra . . ." Forbes averted his eyes as he swallowed the last word.

"Can't you say it, Mr. Forbes?" The boy's voice was mocking. "Yes. I'm Emil Raker's son." The boy moved his face to where Forbes could feel his warm breath. "I'm the son of the man you killed."

Forbes looked at him, fear growing into panic. "Killed? Me? I didn't. I don't know what you mean. I don't have any idea . . ."

"Don't lie!" Martin's voice came hard and edged. "He told me, Mr. Forbes." The boy fastened a hand in the hair of the prone man and pulled his head from the carpet. "He lived that long, Mr. Forbes. He lived long enough to tell me." He dropped the head abruptly. As it struck the floor, a blaze of fresh pain washed across Forbes, causing his body to shudder. He moaned. "No! No! I had nothing to do with it. It was a robbery. A robbery."

"I made it a robbery, Mr. Forbes. You killed him." The voice was flat. He was not arguing, only stating a fact. "And I want to know who the other two men were. That information just may save your life."

Forbes's eyes were those of a trapped animal. No thirteen-year-old had the right to seem so deadly. "I . . ." he swallowed, then started again. "I didn't . . . that is, I don't know anything. Don't you understand? I didn't kill him." His voice was pleading.

"You're a liar, Mr. Forbes, and I'm losing patience." Raker placed the sharp tip of a broad-bladed Bowie knife against Forbes's forehead at a point directly equidistant between, and just above, the eyes. "I will not ask again. Who were the other two men?"

Forbes moaned. "I don't know. I didn't . . ." His words were interrupted by a yelp of fright mixed with pain as the boy's wrist flicked the knife up his scalp. Warm blood flooded his eyes and flowed saltily into his open mouth.

"Scalp cuts bleed like hell, Mr. Forbes." The knife tip moved to a new location. "And just maybe I'll decide to take the whole damn thing." A hand tugged at the hair on the top of Forbes's head. "Now, once more. Who were the other two men?"

Forbes, eyes squeezed tightly shut, turned his head and tried to spit blood from his mouth. "I . . ." He paused. Fear of the knife was now the only reality.

"Stash," he said. "Big Vince and Stash."

"I want more name than that, Mr. Forbes."

Forbes's voice came as almost a wail. "That's all I know them by. Stash and Big Vince."

"How did you recruit them, Mr. Forbes?"

Forbes hesitated and the knife tip moved against his skin. "Laughlin," he stammered. "They work for Laughlin Mining. My God, take that knife away."

The knife stayed against his forehead. "I need to know more, Mr. Forbes."

"I knew they did rough work for the mining company." Forbes moaned loudly. "Goddammit! I hired them. I hired them to kill the man that made a fool of me." Forbes's body was rigid, bouncing stiffly on the carpeted floor. "Kill me, God damn you! Go on and kill me if you have the nerve." He was shouting.

"Yes, Mr. Forbes," said the boy. "Yes. I think that's a good idea." He lifted the knife from the man's forehead and snapped the long, wide blade in an arc which reflected the flickering candle's soft flame. The honed edge sliced smoothly through Forbes's throat, severing both arteries and biting deeply enough to grate across the vertebra at the back of the neck.

The boy stood, quickly and smoothly, avoiding the sudden spurt of blood, and stood staring down unemotionally at Forbes's dying body.

It would take some time to clean up the floor, he thought. By then it still would be early enough to load the body on the extra horse he had brought to town and haul it to the deserted mine shaft where it would be found, if ever, only as bones. He considered taking the man's scalp, but rejected the idea. As he worked, he thought how fortunate it was, considering how many horses were spooked by the smell of blood, that his father had trained his ponies for hunting and carcass hauling. After tonight, he would have to let them rest before he sought out the other two men.

•••

On the second day following the disappearance of Jackson Forbes, Martin Raker paid a visit to the offices of Laughlin Mining Company. The fact that Forbes had not told anyone of any plans to be absent from his real estate and insurance office was the cause of some conversation. But it was widely known that "good old Jackson" was something of a philanderer, and his absence was met mainly with suspicious speculation and not a few knowing leers and winks.

Raker read the sign outside the offices of Laughlin Mining and found that the company not only had an office in this town, but also in Denver. It appeared that the owner, or at least the president of the company, was one T.J. Laughlin, so it seemed to Raker that he was the man to ask for.

The office held a large desk, two large tables, some chairs, and several filing cabinets. A trim, attractive young woman sat behind the desk. A large man, roughly dressed in plaid shirt, corduroy trousers, and heavy boots was seated near a window, thumbing through a newspaper. The young woman behind the desk smiled at Raker. "May I help you?"

"Yes. I hope so. Does Mr. T.J. Laughlin run this business himself? Or is he in Denver? I want to see him."

The young woman—more a girl, thought Raker—assured him that Mr. Laughlin did, indeed, run this business himself, and that he happened to be spending most of his time here, and not in Denver, at the present time, for here was where most of the mining activity was taking place.

"May I ask about what?" inquired the girl, politely.

"It's business, ma'am," said Raker solemnly. The girl was very pretty, he thought. "I think he will want to see me."

"I see," she said, smiling nicely. "Very well. Just a moment. And who shall I tell him is calling?"

"Raker, ma'am. Martin Raker." He paused only a moment.

"Beverly Martin Raker." He leveled his eyes directly at those of the girl.

"Yes," she said, not changing expression. "Just a moment, Mr. Raker, I'll see if he has time right now."

As she moved gracefully through the door into the inner office the boy watched her, thinking that he had never seen as attractive a girl before. The man reading by the window appeared to have no interest in either the boy or the conversation.

Raker waited only a moment for the girl's return.

"Mr. Laughlin will see you," she said. "In here, please." She held the door open, smiling, and Raker entered.

The room was much larger than the outer office. The windows were heavily and, even to Raker's inexperienced eyes, expensively draped; the furnishings were like those seen in the town's bank. The man behind the desk looked like a banker. At least at first. As Raker examined him, he saw that he was harder and tougher than any banker he had ever encountered in his limited experience. Except for the clothes, the man looked like he belonged to the outdoors.

"Good day, Mr. Raker," said the man. "My receptionist says that you have some business to discuss with me." His tone was neither patronizing or smug.

"Yes," said Raker, "I do. Do you know my name?"

Laughlin surveyed the boy quietly. He nodded. "Yes. The girl told me your name."

"I mean, do you recognize the name Raker?"

"Yes. I know the name. Was he your father?" The boy nodded silently.

"I'm sorry. He was a good man."

"Yes, he was. Did you have anything to do with his death?"

Surprise, then anger: "Just what in the hell do you mean by that?"

"Did you have anything to do with getting him killed?" The boy's tone was matter-of-fact.

The man started to rise to his feet, but stopped short. Face flushed, he placed his hands on the desk and seemed to shove himself back from it.

"Why you little . . ." He swallowed the rest of the sentence and composed himself. He looked with interest at the youth across from him. There was, at the same time, something old, tough and wise about the boy, yet young and vulnerable. He felt, in spite of the boy's youth, an intense threat of violence emanating from him.

"And if I did?" Laughlin asked softly. A veteran rough-and-tumble fighter, survivor of the brawling mining-camps of Colorado's earlier days, he waited warily, ready for any reaction.

In what seemed an uninterrupted move, the boy's hand swept behind his head, then forward. Light glinted on shiny metal as it flashed toward the man behind the desk. Later, Laughlin would seem to remember that he had known what the boy was going to do. As the knife made its single turn, streaking toward him, he lifted the heavy ledger from the desk and held it in front of his body. The force of the thrown knife speared the heavy blade through the ledger's thick covers, and Laughlin felt the shock as the hilt thudded against the book, stopping the weapon's flight.

The boy stood impassively in front of the desk, a near-smile lifting one corner of his mouth.

Laughlin turned the ledger over to look at the blade impaling it. He looked from the location where he held it, to his own body, then shook his head. "It would have missed," he said.

"I meant for it to," said the boy.

Laughlin laid the book down gently. Supported by the knife's blade, it tilted on its edge. He nodded slowly. "Yes. I think you did." He leaned forward and rested his chin on locked hands. "It was a hell of a throw."

The boy shrugged lightly.

"I see," said Laughlin, "not unusual, eh? All right, then. Why did you miss?

"I don't think you had anything to do with it."

"Your father? I didn't. I liked him. Why did you think I might have had something to do with his death?"

"Jackson Forbes was screwing my mother. My father caught them. Forbes killed him. Helped by two of the men who work for you."

Laughlin's eyebrows lifted high. "Two of my men? Who says?"

"Forbes. He said they're named Stash and Big Vince." Laughlin's face flushed again. "By God, I'll see about that." He raised his voice. "Murdock!" He called loudly.

The door opened immediately. The roughly dressed man who had been reading in the outer office when Raker arrived quickly entered the room. His eyes surveyed the scene and he relaxed visibly. "Yes?" he said.

"Get Jackson Forbes over here. Now!" he said.

"He's dead," said Raker quietly.

Both men looked at him with surprise. "Dead?" asked Laughlin.

"I killed him," explained the boy.

The two men exchanged glances. The man called Murdock looked at Raker with interest.

"This," said Laughlin, nodding his head toward the other man, "is Timothy Murdock. The best trouble-stopper, mine-boss, and friend a man can have. Tim, this is Emil Raker's son. He says his father was murdered by Forbes and two of our men."

Murdock lounged against the wall, arms folded. He nodded, saying nothing.

"You don't seem surprised."

"Forbes was a slimy bastard."

Laughlin turned to Raker. "All right, son. Tell us the whole thing. I'll guarantee you that none of my men will get away with working for anyone but me."

The boy told them everything from the night he had followed his father to their home up until the moment he had cut Forbes's throat.

"And what did you do with the body?" asked Laughlin.

The boy smiled slightly as he slowly shook his head from side to side.

"Is it . . . out of the way?"

"It won't be found."

Laughlin studied the boy's face. "I'm sure it won't," he said. He turned to Murdock. "Where are Stakowlski and Musso now?" He glanced at Raker. "That's Stash and Big Vince," he explained.

Murdock grinned. "Supposed to be waiting for Forbes. Supposed to protect him on his trip to bid on that high plateau property. Suppose they're still waiting. They're the ones?"

"Yeah," growled Laughlin, nodding grimly. "Get them over here. No, wait!" He turned to the boy. "If it turns out you've told me the truth, I'll—hold it!" he said hurriedly as the boy started to his feet. "I'm not saying you're lying. I'm just going to check for myself. Settle down."

Martin sat back.

"As I was saying, if it turns out they've sold out to Forbes, then we, Murdock and I, will do anything you want done with them. Do you want them killed?"

"No," said the boy.

Laughlin was surprised. "You don't?"

"I want to kill them."

"I see. Very well." He nodded at Murdock. "Get them, Tim."

• • •

Both the men were big and hard looking. Musso, or Big Vince, was slightly shorter than the towering Stakowlski, but broad and thick, with beetle brows shadowing deep-set eyes. His arms hung near his knees. Stash was simply big all over. He looked at Laughlin from out of pale blue, bulging eyes in a face that seemed rounded and doughy, without planes. Both men stood in front of Laughlin's desk. Murdock remained in back of them. Raker sat quietly in a far corner.

The two men stood casually at first, but as Laughlin fixed them, unsmiling and unspeaking, with a steady gaze, they began to shift uncomfortably. Seconds dragged into minutes during which time the men exchanged furtive glances.

When Laughlin finally began to speak, Murdock moved silently to the wall beside the door and took down a belt, holster, and revolver from where they had been hanging on one of a row of pegs. Without a sound he strapped them on. To young Raker he looked much the image of a gunfighter on a movie theater poster.

"So," said Laughlin, addressing the two men standing in front of him, "you did do it." He spoke softly.

The men looked at each other. "Did what?" asked the one called Stash.

"Yeah, what?" echoed Big Vince Musso.

"Forbes tells me that he hired you two to help him kill Emil Raker." The men were flustered. Apprehension showed.

"Aw shit, that ain't true," said Stash. "We just work for you, T.J."

"Yeah, like he says," growled Musso.

"There were witnesses," barked Laughlin. "You were stupid."

"Witnesses? That's a crock of shit," said Stakowlski, "there couldn't a been no . . ."

"Stupid turd, shut up," snapped Musso. He glared at Stakowlski. Both men knew it was too late.

Stakowlski swallowed with difficulty. "What I mean is . . . there ain't never anybody up that early in this burg."

"How early, Stash?" purred Laughlin. "Just how early was it?" The fingers of Musso touched the lapel of his coat.

"You'll never make it," came Murdock's voice softly. In the quiet following the words, the unmistakable click of the hammer of a revolver being cocked came jarringly loud. The boy hadn't even seen Murdock's hand move, though he had been watching. Now it held the long-barreled .44 Colt. The hands of the two men stayed at their sides.

Laughlin kept his eyes on the two of them, his expression showing distaste, as he addressed the boy. "I apologize, son, for any doubts," he said. "What do you want to do with them?"

"Look, now," protested Musso. "There ain't no proof."

"Shut up!" snapped Laughlin, his voice as grating as cinders scraped under a shovel. "We've got all the proof we're interested in."

"Do you know Bridger's Canyon?" asked Raker, voice quiet and unemotional.

Laughlin looked at him with interest. "Certainly." It was a narrow, blind canyon, half-a-mile deep, some ten miles north of town. High sandstone walls on both sides and at the east end made it accessible only from its mouth at the west. A spring at its upper end fed a small creek which encouraged the growth of trees and shrubs along its floor. In the past it had been used to round up cattle and horses. Miners had explored without reward. It now stood mostly unused except for occasional Sunday picnickers.

"Can you take them up near the spring, then turn them loose?" Laughlin exchanged quick glances with Murdock. Murdock nodded. "We can," Laughlin said.

"Now?"

"Yes." He paused.

"Without their pistols, of course."

"No!" objected Raker. "With their pistols."

"That's damn foolishness, son," started Laughlin, in protest.

"Let him, T.J.," said Murdock. "I have a feeling he knows just what he's doing."

As the two men in front of him turned their heads to smirk at each other, Murdock shook his head in sympathy. "Enjoy it, cocksuckers. This here little boy is the son of the man you killed. And I think you've bit off a hunk that's going to choke you to death." He turned his head slightly toward the boy, keeping his eyes on the two men. "Would you like a couple of hours to get ready?"

Raker thought a moment. "That will do fine."

"I'll get someone to drive you," said Laughlin.

"No need. I have a horse."

Laughlin was not surprised at the boy's independence. "Weapons?"

"I have what I need."

Laughlin laughed aloud as Murdock smiled. "I'll just bet you do," he said. "Yessir, I'll just bet you do."

As the boy left, nodding politely to the young lady in the outer office, he said, "Thank you, ma'am." He received a flashing smile in return.

• • •

The afternoon sun glared brightly up the box canyon as Laughlin and Murdock brought their car to a stop as near to its end as they dared drive on the soft sand. The back wall of the canyon, where the pool of the spring lay, was some forty or fifty yards to the east.

"Out," said Laughlin to the two men.

They climbed from the car under the watchful eye of Murdock whose arms now cradled a rifle instead of the revolver which had held them motionless in the back seat during the drive.

"How about the rods?" asked Musso. "The punk said we could have them."

"Yes, the boy said you could have them," agreed Laughlin. "Foot it on up the way. We'll throw them after you when you're well away."

"Throw them? Jeezus. Don't do that. The sand and all. It'll foul them up."

"Then you'll just have to clean them, won't you?" drawled Laughlin.

"Damned fool weapons for this country, automatics, anyway," said Murdock.

• • •

As the killers of Martin Raker's father moved away from the car and up toward the end of the canyon, glancing nervously over their shoulders, they saw Murdock take each automatic weapon and work the mechanism, unloading the magazines of both. The cartridges ejected into the sand. They would take some finding, he thought. He removed the magazines and tossed them away, then threw the handguns after them. From a distance, Musso and Stakowlski watched, faces ablaze with helplessness and hatred.

"I'd just leave them there till we're way out of sight," drawled Murdock. He waved his rifle at them. "This has a considerably longer reach than your fire power." He looked down into the sand. "That is, if you have any."

As the car pulled away, Murdock continued to watch the two men standing together, not moving.

"Damn shame," said Laughlin. "They were mighty handy for convincing folks. Going to have trouble replacing them."

Murdock only grunted.

"But, God damn it, people work for me, work *only* for me."

"You writing them off already, T.J.?" asked Murdock. Laughlin looked at him. "Of course. Aren't you?"

"Well, now, just let me say that I don't much imagine that

anybody'll be seeing much of them anymore. But that young 'un, now, I 'spect we'll be seeing him around."

"Funny," mused Laughlin, "we don't know much of anything about him, and he's just a boy, so why are we so damn sure he can handle a couple like Stash and Musso? Hell, Forbes presented no problem. Those two do."

"It's the insides, T.J." said Murdock. "There's a feeling that kid causes. Outside he's around thirteen-fourteen, and maybe 134 pounds. Inside he's all flint and steel, a full growed man, and I suspect he's got a fighting weight somewhere around half-a-ton."

"Shall we wait here and back him up?" asked Laughlin.

"He wouldn't like that."

He paused. "No. I expect you're right," he mused softly.

The two men drove back into town, in silence, not looking behind them, to wait.

• • •

Stakowlski reached the weapons first. He picked them up, face twisted in fury. "Goddamn sumbitch," he snarled. "Tried to ruin 'em. Come on, let's find the shells and clips. Watch your damned fat feet. Don't step on nothing. Gonna be hard enough cleaning all this fuckin' sand off anyhow." They finally located the magazines and all the shells except one which eluded them. They cleaned the weapons as best they could, glancing around the canyon. They were tough, brutal and capable, but the outdoors wasn't their normal hunting ground. The stillness was disconcerting.

"Think that little shit's gonna really try to take us?" asked Musso.

"Who knows?" shrugged Stakowlski. "If so, prob'ly with a rifle from up there." He pointed vaguely toward the top of the canyon walls.

"Yeah," agreed Musso. "Let's get outta here. Keep your eyes peeled."

They started down the slight slope toward the canyon mouth, eyes surveying the rims above them. The bright afternoon sun shown directly into their faces, making it difficult to see straight ahead.

"Wait a minute, Vince," said Stakowlski. "I don't like the

fuckin' sun in our eyes like this. Suppose the punk is up ahead drawing a bead?"

Musso considered the question. "Could be. Let's split up. Take that side of the stream, I'll take this. You check over my head and I'll cover yours." He looked around them. "There's enough brush and trees here. Let's try and keep it between us and the sun. Ready?"

"Yeah," growled Stakowlski. He grinned wolfishly. "Now that kid's gonna become the hunted!"

The two men separated and, keeping as close to the walls of the narrow canyon as they could, worked their way slowly toward its mouth. Branches slapped and tore at their loose clothing and sand filled their low-cut shoes.

Suddenly the voice of Musso rang out. "Get low! I seen something up over your head!"

Stakowlski dropped quickly to the ground and edged close to a thicket of scrub oak. He listened. There was only the sound of water trickling softly, the sibilant breath of air through foliage, and insect noises.

"You sure?" he called.

A pause. "Not exactly. Coulda just been a shadow or something. Goddamn sun in my eyes blinds me."

"Yeah," agreed Musso. "Well, let's head on down." He rose from the ground, slapping at the sand on his clothing. "Wait up," he called, "I gotta dump some of this stinking sand outta my shoes."

"Me too," came the answer from across the canyon.

Musso leaned against the nearby rock wall and pulled a shoe off. He dumped it upside down, shook it, then tugged to undo the knotted lace prior to putting it back on. He felt rather than saw a shadow suddenly appear at his feet. He looked up into the sun just in time to see the dark silhouette flow swiftly upon him. All at once, he dropped the shoe, reached for his holstered pistol, and opened his mouth to cry a warning. He was too late. The razor edge of the Bowie knife sliced through his throat, nearly decapitating him. He dropped without a sound except for what small noise is made by flowing blood. The shadow moved silently down the canyon and disappeared into the mottled light and dark of the scattered trees and shrubs.

"Y'got it, Vince?" called Stakowlski. Silence.

"Hey, Vince!" Stakowlski waited. "Come on now, don't be funny. Answer me . . ."

The trickle of the water seemed to grow in the silence.

"That's not funny. God damm it, Vince, answer me now or I'm gettin' out of here." He waited. This wasn't like Vince—he didn't play damn fool games. Maybe the punk kid had . . . naw! No way. The hair on the nape of his neck prickled. But still, Vince didn't kid around.

"Okay, Vince. I'm hauling my ass outta here. It's your fault, so don't blame me." Stakowlski moved away from the small clump of trees he'd been standing near, and after looking carefully around him, started toward the canyon's mouth at as rapid a pace as he could maintain through the brush, leaving behind him a string of muted curses. The sun was getting lower and shining more directly into his eyes. Shit! I can barely see enough to keep from running into things, he thought. A pine tree, larger than most of the other mixed variety of growth, loomed in front of him, leaning out toward the small rivulet of water.

Stakowlski veered to his right in order to pass between the tree and a clump of brush growing from near the base of the canyon wall, and as he did, he felt his legs tripped from under him. He spilled heavily forward to the earth, momentarily stunned. He tried to scramble quickly to his feet, but it was too late. He felt the weight hit squarely on his back, felt something grasp the hair on his head and pull it up strongly, exposing his throat. The stroke was so swift, the edge so keen, that Stakowlski never felt the blade of the knife that killed him.

Raker untied the trip rope from around the tree, shook it free of the sand with which it had been covered, and coiled it carefully. Once again he cleaned the blade of the knife, then sheathed it. Only the removal of traces and the short trip for the horses remained. Then he could dispose of the bodies—in a different mine shaft from the one holding Forbes—and he would go back to town to thank Mr. Laughlin and Mr. Murdock for their help. The air smelled clean, and the sun was warm on his face as he walked.

• • •

Laughlin looked at the face of the pocket watch he held in his hand and chewed on the unlit cigar in his mouth. Watching him from across the desk, Murdock reflected that Laughlin was the only man he knew who consumed cigars only from the wet end. He had never known the man to light one.

"Three hours," said Laughlin. His fingers thumped the desk top. "It should be over by now."

"I reckon," observed Murdock. "It'll take time for . . . clean up and disposal. The boy is thorough."

"You're still certain about his ability." It was a statement.

"Uh-huh, I am." Murdock leaned his chair back against the wall and locked his hands behind his neck. "You're experienced in judging men, T.J.," he said. "Matter of fact, there was a time no one was better. Don't tell me you didn't notice certain things about the boy."

Laughlin stood and then came out from behind his desk to pace the floor.

"Yeah," he said. "He is different, isn't he? Doesn't move like any awkward adolescent. Like most kids flop when they sit, thump when they walk, and can make crunching noises eating whipped cream. But not this Raker." He stopped pacing and looked down at Murdock. "Did you notice? He moves like oil and doesn't make a sound." He shook his head. "Damn spooky when you think about it." He resumed pacing.

"Learned it from his old man, I suspect." He paused again. "You knew about Emil Raker's past?"

"Heard stories. Apache raised. Now there was one, for all his size, could move like a shadow. Stronger'n a grizzly and deadlier'n a rock rattler." Murdock smiled in remembered admiration. "Looks like he did a good job of passing the old ways on to the boy."

Laughlin nodded. "A good man," he observed, smiling wryly. "Tried to talk him out of his mineral rights, but he couldn't stand the thought of seeing his land torn into." He stood silent a moment. "Damn it, Tim, if those bastards got that kid I swear to God I'll track them down and tear them apart myself."

"You'll have my help," said Murdock.

The sound of the knock was loud in the room.

Laughlin, closer to the thick door, snatched it open. Martin Raker stood before him, smiling faintly.

"Just wanted to thank you and Mr. Murdock," said the boy. "The front door was open."

Laughlin looked at Raker a moment, then placed his hands on the boy's shoulders, hands squeezing, feeling the hard muscle and thick bone structure.

"Glad you're here," he said.

"Welcome, boy," said Murdock, not rising. "Get it done?"

"Yes, sir. And the traces removed."

Murdock lowered his face, hiding a smile, and began to clean his fingernails, using the nail of a little finger.

"Sit down . . ." Laughlin hesitated. "I can't remember what it is you're called," he apologized.

"Martin," said the boy. He sat near Murdock, facing Laughlin. "It is Beverly Martin Raker, but I don't like to be called Beverly. My . . . father called me Martin."

"Martin, it is," agreed Laughlin. "All right. Martin. Are you satisfied now, Martin? Is it over?"

The boy considered the question. "Nearly. There is still my mother. I don't want to be around her, but I promised my father I'd see that she's taken care of."

The men exchanged glances.

"Yes. Well." started Laughlin. He cleared his throat. "Perhaps we can do something about that." He studied the boy carefully. "How old are you, Martin?"

"Thirteen. Nearly fourteen."

"You seem older."

"My father taught me much."

"Maybe we can find a place for you with the company," mused Laughlin. "Something that'll keep you interested and let you finish school. Tim?"

Murdock ceased his nail cleaning and looked up. "Yes, I think we can really use Martin," he said. "And it won't be just making a place for him. It will be a position that probably only he can fill."

Laughlin's expression showed puzzled interest.

"I'm thinking of Kingsford and Leacock." Murdock's voice

was bland. Laughlin's face was blank, then came enlightenment.

"You don't mean . . . ?"

"I do," said Murdock. "Think about it, T.J., think about it. None of us can get near them. The boy probably can."

Laughlin chewed on his unlit cigar. "But hell, we can't ask a boy to take on something like that. It wouldn't be . . ." He searched for a word. ". . . right," he finally finished.

"Martin isn't just any boy, T.J., is he? And it certainly isn't like he'll be losing his cherry or whatever."

"That's damned true," agreed Laughlin. He considered the unstated proposal, and then came to a decision. "All right. The bastards must be dealt with, and this just might be the way. But only if the boy is completely willing once he's filled in." He turned to Raker.

"Son," he started, "Tim has just suggested that we employ you to kill two men for us." He watched for Raker's reaction.

The boy's face was stoic. "Is there a good reason for it?" he asked. The two men once again exchanged looks.

"There is. A damned good one," said Laughlin.

"Eighteen good ones," added Murdock.

Over the next minutes the men explained to Raker how in the battle for mining claims and mineral rights, lawlessness pervaded. The large mining conglomerate operated by two men named Kingsford and Leacock was the most notorious. Losing the battle for a large, productive mine to Laughlin, the company had, in an act of vengeance and in an effort to prevent any future competition, resorted to tactics designed to create fear and terror among employees of Laughlin's company. They had been responsible for the dynamiting of the mine they'd lost. Eighteen of Laughlin's men had been killed in the explosion.

And the insurance policy Laughlin had paid for had, apparently, never been consummated.

"Can't you prove they did it?" inquired Raker.

The two men smiled grimly. "They covered themselves all too well," said Laughlin. "And they pack a lot of power, to boot."

"But they're guiltier'n sin," interjected Murdock. "Look, boy, T.J. and me, we aren't no angels. We've done our share of rough playing. But we never done nothing like that. We don't start things. And we don't hit at innocent people." He rubbed a finger under his nose. "Course, we sometimes do a little tough-guy bluffing. But this here's different. These damned treacherous sidewinders, pretending to be real gentlemen, are nothing but slaughterers."

"They know we're after them," said Laughlin. "They know we can play rough too. That's why we kept thugs like Stakowlski and Musso around. They'd like to take us out. And as for us, Kingsford and Leacock are hiding out behind an army of bodyguards, have been ever since it happened. We can't get close enough to them to do anything without recruiting an army and declaring all-out war."

The steady eyes of the boy looked out from his tanned, old-young face and fastened on Laughlin's own eyes. "I think it is right for you to want to get even for them killing your men," he said. "If you and Mr. Murdock think I can help, then I will be more than willing to do it."

There was awkwardness in the ensuing conversation as both Laughlin and Murdock fought to repress any feelings of guilt in using the boy to complete their plans to avenge the death of the miners of Laughlin Mining. Finally, but not without difficulty, they were able to integrate their actions and emotions with their genuine concern for Raker. It would work! It would be good for everyone—Kingsford and Leacock excepted.

"I think this calls for a drink," offered Murdock.

"Most certainly," agreed Laughlin, and he pulled a bottle of whiskey and glasses from the bottom drawer of his desk. "Martin? Would you like to join us?"

Raker grinned, shyly. "I tried it once. Didn't like it."

"Would you like something else?"

The boy looked down for a moment, then back up. "Yes. I would. If you don't mind, I'd like a glass of milk . . . and a hamburger or something." He paused. "I haven't eaten for some time," he said, apologetically.

Laughlin replaced the bottle, the men locked the office behind them, and led Raker past the town's small diner to its one complete bar and grill.

While the men enjoyed their drinks, Raker demolished the huge meal Laughlin and Murdock had insisted on ordering for him.

"Did you ever see anything like it?" asked Murdock as they watched the boy top off a huge meal with a whole pecan pie and a quart of milk.

"It's a genuine miracle," said Laughlin with mock awe.

Raker grinned around his mouthful of food. He enjoyed the bantering. There was nothing patronizing or condescending about the men. They obviously accepted him for himself, and recognized him for what he was: not quite a man, but almost.

As Raker now sat sipping a cup of black coffee as he and his father used to do at the end of one of their meals in the mountains, the flush of alcohol was on the men.

"You mentioned virginity earlier," said Laughlin to Murdock.

"I did?" asked Murdock, surprised.

"Well, didn't you?"

Murdock thought. "Well, sorta. You mean about the boy not losing his cherry, don't you?"

Laughlin nodded. That was it. He looked at Raker. "Son," he said, "are you a virgin?"

"I think of that being for girls," said the boy. The men exchanged smiles.

"Well, it sorta goes for men, too," said Laughlin. "Have you ever laid . . . have you ever been with a woman . . . girl?" Childless himself, Laughlin had often laughed at the problem others expressed about talking with their children concerning the birds and bees, or whatever they wanted to call it. But damn it, it was difficult! "You know what I mean," he finished.

Raker studied his empty plate. "No," he said softly. He looked up at the men. "No, I haven't done that."

Laughlin slapped the table with the flat of his hand, spilling liquid onto the red and white of the checkered tablecloth. "Then, by God, it's time. High time." He looked at Raker with fondness and placed an arm around the boy's shoulders. He grinned at Murdock's smiling face.

"Today, Martin, you become a man." His expression grew serious. "But who?" He looked toward Murdock whose eyes were busy following the back of the retreating waitress.

"Aw, hell no," he groaned. "Gotta be something fancier than that," he mused. "How about the House?"

Murdock considered the suggestion. "Naw. Not a good crop right now. Let's us think." He was silent a moment before addressing Raker. "Boy, do you have your sights set on anything . . . anyone, that is?"

The boy looked at him blankly.

"You know. Have you seen anyone you would like to . . ." he swallowed. He had discovered the difficulty as had Laughlin earlier. He started over. "Have you met any young ladies you would like to . . . spend some . . ." He stopped and leaned forward. "Do you know any girls you'd like to fuck?"

Laughlin roared.

Raker blushed behind his deep tan, then grinned sheepishly.

"Well?" insisted Murdock.

"I don't know many girls," started the boy, "but . . ." he hesitated.

"Go on," said Laughlin.

"Well, there was that real pretty girl in your front office." Laughlin blinked.

Murdock's eyebrows lifted and he laughed loudly. He slapped Laughlin on the back. "Janelle," he said. "Janelle, for God's sake. Sure!"

"I don't know," said Laughlin, reluctantly.

"C'mon, T.J.," urged Murdock. "You can't keep that private stuff to yourself all your life. What's more, you're too damn old for the girl. Hell, it ain't as if she was something sacred or like that."

"No," said Laughlin, "but she is a damn fine lady."

"Sure," agreed Murdock. "Don't you see? That's why she's the perfect one. A lady, a mighty fine person, and a real looker, to boot."

"B'God, Timmy, you're dead right." Whiskey was starting to slur the men's words. "Dead right," repeated Laughlin. "But she'll have to agree, of course. Not going to order her or something."

"Never fear, T.J., once we explain the facts to the lady she'll most likely snatch the lad right away from us."

Laughlin looked at Murdock suspiciously, not sure exactly what he'd heard. He looked then toward Raker. "Martin, lad. I want you to know that I wouldn't do this unless you were like a son to me."

The boy smiled his shy smile. It was hard to imagine the events he had performed during the past few days, thought Laughlin.

Raker knew he should feel some embarrassment, or thought he should, but all he was aware of was the warmth and the tingle he could feel spreading from his groin.

Laughlin rose from the table. "Waitress!" he called loudly. "The check, please. We must be off on an errand of mercy."

• • •

The trip was a short one, and as the car pulled up to the front of the house, a light could be seen through the tall, wide, curtained windows.

"She's awake," offered Laughlin. Something close to disappointment tinged his voice.

"It's only 9:30," observed Murdock.

"True," sighed Laughlin, "but somehow it's like giving up one's most prized possession."

"C'mon now, T.J., you don't own the girl."

"All too true, Timmy. All too true," said Laughlin, sadly filled with Celtic sorrow. "Well now. You'll have to do it, Tim. Make the arrangements. I just can't bring myself to it."

Murdock laughed with delight. It wasn't his girl. "And that I will," he said, "with pleasure."

Murdock and young Raker left the car and walked toward the front steps of the neat, white, two-story house. Laughlin seated himself on the curb, legs stretched before him, hands clasped between them, head down, his back to the house. He wouldn't look. It might be easier that way.

"Wait here," said Murdock as they reached the bottom of the porch steps. He moved up them, and tapped on the door. It opened.

The attractive face of the young woman from Laughlin's office appeared in the opening.

"Why, Tim," she said.

"Hello, Janelle," he murmured. "I . . . that is, we . . . have something to talk to you about." She waited. Murdock hesitated.

"Yes?" she encouraged.

"It's the boy," he said. He pointed toward Raker standing at the foot of the steps. "The boy from the office today."

"Yes?" Expectantly.

Murdock cleared his throat. "Well, Janelle . . ." he swallowed. "Well, it seems as if he's quite taken with you."

"Yes?"

"And it seems as if you're the only girl . . . woman he knows—or at least wants to know."

"I see."

Murdock shuffled nervously. "No. I'm not sure you do. That's 'know' in the biblical sense."

"Oh, really!" Not shocked, rather interested.

"Y'see, Janelle," stammered Murdock, "the lad's . . . pure. Y'know . . . hasn't ever been . . ." He turned his hands palm up and shrugged. "You know," he finished lamely.

"And T.J.? What does he say?"

"He drove us here." Murdock couldn't meet the girl's eyes.

"Send the boy up here, Timothy," said Janelle. Gratefully, Murdock turned away. "And Tim . . ."

"Yes?"

"It's a nice thing to do," came the girl's voice, softly. "Really. Tell T.J. that. I mean it." She stood in the soft light at the door, looking prettier than Murdock ever remembered her. Not pretty, he thought. Delicate. Feminine and beautiful. Lucky kid, he thought, as she raised a hand and beckoned toward Raker.

The boy moved slowly, tentatively, up the steps. Murdock turned away toward Laughlin's seated figure, but not before he saw the girl hold up her hands and place them lightly against the sides of the boy's face, drawing him inside. The door closed softly.

Murdock seated himself beside Laughlin. "It's done," he said.

"Yes," said Laughlin.

"Want a drink?" inquired Murdock.

"Not a drink, Timmy my boy. A whole goddamn barrel!" He looked over at his companion. "Have one?"

"Not a barrel. But a bottle." Murdock rose, went to the car, and returned with the bottle. "Make it last; we may be here for a while."

Laughlin groaned. And drank.

• • •

The cold of the late night drove the men from the chill of the concrete curb into the softer seating in the car. The first silvery light of dawn was starting its daily battle with the morning mist when the boy returned.

"Mr. Laughlin! Mr. Murdock!" came the voice, softly.

"Don't shout," growled Laughlin. "We're not deaf." Laughlin elbowed Murdock, and at the same time swished his tongue about in an effort to lubricate his mouth. He stared through fogged eyes at the smiling, glowing face of the boy. He was surprised at the warmth he felt upon seeing the youth. "All . . . rested?" he asked.

Raker's smile grew. "Not exactly," the boy said. He seemed to have grown. Gone was the shyness, replaced by certain self-assurance.

The realization made Laughlin somehow sad. He studied the boy's face as Murdock stirred and awakened. It was a one-time-only thing, he thought, never to be recaptured. He smiled gently, shaking his head. A foolish, sentimental thought, he reflected, not to be dwelt upon.

"Get in, Martin," he said softly. "Come alive, Timmy," he barked. "Time to be moving along. Our colt's been bred, and damn well from the looks of him." He started the motor as Murdock reached out a hand to clap Raker on the shoulder. "Us men have a lot of ore to dig."

"Or traps to set," observed Murdock, grimly.

Laughlin nodded. "True. Let's get about it." And they did.

• • •

It was just thirty days later when Walter Kingsford, co-owner of Kingsford & Leacock Mining Properties, was found dead in the public men's room of the Brown Palace Hotel in Denver, Colorado. His body was found crumpled at the foot of a urinal, a knife wound from the back having pierced his heart. No one remembered the young newsboy who had walked unnoticed around and through Kingsford's small army of armed men.

Less than two weeks following Kingsford's death, and in spite of increased security, Jervis Leacock was killed as he stepped from the door of his car to the driveway just feet from his front door. A three-foot wooden shaft, steel tipped and feather tufted, had severed his spinal cord. It had been launched with only the soft twang of a bow string, unheard from thirty yards away.

Leacock's bodyguards instantly swept across the grounds of his large estate, but they found no one. Raker was already twenty feet above the ground, silently finding hand holds for his strong, young fingers in the joints of the brick-sided house, even before the search reached the spot from where he'd launched the arrow. He quickly reached the top of the three-story mansion, lay quietly in the darkness until early in the morning, then easily descended the same way he'd gone up. The dead miners of Laughlin Mining's Pandora #3 were avenged.

CHAPTER 8

NEW MEXICO

In the days that followed, T.J. Laughlin had little trouble convincing Martin's mother that it was in the interest of both her and her son that he, Laughlin, should look out for the boy's welfare and education. It was even less trouble to convince her that she should sell the property Laughlin had tried to buy from her husband. She had always wanted to be rid of it. To Laughlin's credit, he had consulted with young Raker about the purchase before he approached the woman. With his father dead, Martin had no objections to the sale of the property and mining rights, and it would assure that his mother would be, as he had promised his father, taken care of.

It was Murdock who, indirectly and unknowingly, caused the death of Raker's mother.

In an effort to heal the breech between mother and son, Murdock had paid a visit to the woman and told her that the affair with Forbes, and the resultant death of her husband, was only the product of human frailty. Believing only half of what he said, Murdock assured her that both Forbes and Raker had been fine men, and she was not to be blamed for their deaths.

The woman asked how he knew that Forbes was dead. Murdock was flustered. He thought he covered it well by telling her that he really didn't know that, but in as much as Forbes hadn't been seen for so long, he must be, to have left a beautiful woman like her alone.

But the woman knew her son. And while she would not allow her mind to dwell on it, she realized the awful truth. On the seventh day after Murdock's visit, the widow Raker drove the family car—not the pickup, but the new Plymouth sedan—far from town, up to the top of the pass on the route to Durango, and drove it over the sheer cliff bordering the road. She was killed instantly.

"A tragedy!" the townspeople said. But if young Raker thought so, he didn't show it. It was as though he had been told of the death of a total stranger. And when Laughlin, who represented the boy in the probate of the estate, told him that he was now a modestly rich young man, Raker only shrugged. Money meant little to him. What did matter was that with Laughlin and Murdock, the boy had recovered part of the association he had enjoyed so dearly with his father. He didn't want that jeopardized, although he knew that as a minor his fate rested with the court. Laughlin handled the situation well, and using his influence and perhaps the knowledge of a closet skeleton or two, was appointed Martin Raker's guardian.

He was enrolled at New Mexico Military Institute at Roswell, New Mexico, and while missing his friends Laughlin and Murdock, found the school's curriculum and competitiveness to his liking. He quickly became a leader among his classmates, was discovered to be adept at the sports he had been denied in his early school years, and proved to have an insatiable thirst for knowledge. His proficiency in languages, history, literature and war delighted his instructors, both academic and military, and it was predicted that they might well have the makings of a future General on their hands. But as much as Raker enjoyed the school, it was the summers he liked most.

• • •

During the next three years, Murdock and Laughlin filled in the blank spots in Raker's education. From Murdock the boy became proficient in the use of firearms, especially handguns. He learned brawling and rough-and-tumble fighting from both men, an art which coupled nicely with the craftier skills he had learned from his childhood Indian friends.

From Laughlin, Raker became an expert in the use of and respect for explosives, and was an exceptional "powder monkey" before his sixteenth birthday. When World War II involved the United States, he was well on his way to becoming a complete warrior.

Eager to enter the conflict, Raker joined the Marine Corps, and established an enviable record during the war. He remained in the service through the Korean campaign, where he commanded a company which saw men competing fiercely to serve with him. After two wars, Raker had reached near perfection as a fighter, confidence inspirer, and leader of men.

DENVER, COLORADO

On his return to Colorado following separation from the Marine Corps, Raker flew directly to Denver to surprise his friends. Never good at letter writing, Raker had not written or heard from either Laughlin or Murdock for over two years.

The thought didn't bother him. It had been a busy two years, and the old men were indestructible. Of that he had no doubt, and now, as the taxi dropped him off at the address of Laughlin's office, his heart was light with anticipation. He took the elevator to the top floor, and as the car stopped, then moved jerkily to align itself properly, could hardly wait for the doors to open. They were still in sliding motion when he slipped through them. Glancing at the wall where arrows directed one toward the desired office number, Raker strode briskly to the door he sought. The letters on the frosted glass seemed somehow faded, and as Raker turned the knob and pushed, the door resisted. It was locked. He glanced at his watch—3:30 p.m. They couldn't be closed, could they? Not at this hour?

Raker looked around for a telephone; and not finding one in the corridor, punched the elevator button.

In the lobby he located a pay phone and quickly flipped through the phone book, looking for the office number. He found it and dialed. There was no answer. He hung up and turned to survey the lobby. There was an attendant at a small desk near the front doorway.

"Excuse me," he said.

The elderly man turned. "Yes?"

"I just called on Laughlin Mining. They seem to be closed. Do you happen to know why?"

"Laughlin Mining, you say? Just a moment." The man thumbed through a clipboard of sheets in front of him. "Yes, here we are. Laughlin Mining. Yes, they're closed, all right." He looked up at Raker. "Rent's paid for another six months, though." He reflected a moment. "Seem's as how I recollect something about a government lawsuit. Like that. Not sure, but it seems like."

"Government lawsuit? That can't be. T.J. devoted the last ten years to helping his government. It can't be."

The old man shrugged. "Possible. Don't know. But it seems like I recomember something about it. Anyhow, ain't nobody up there. Damn government, anyway—no appreciation for nothing. Damn politicians only take care of themselves anyhow."

"Yes. Of course," said Raker. "Thank you." He turned to walk back to the telephone. He looked up the number listed for T.J. Laughlin and dialed it.

"Yes?" It didn't sound like T.J. or Murdock.

"Is this the Laughlin residence?"

"It is."

"Is T.J. Laughlin in?"

"This is T.J. Laughlin." The voice had wrinkles.

"Well, T.J., you old pirate, this is your former ward, Captain Beverly Martin Raker. Why in the hell aren't you down at your office taking care of business?"

"Martin? Martin! Damn, boy, where in the hell are you? Get your no good, half-Apache ass over here right now. Hear me? I mean right now."

The voice had recovered its former life.

"You bet your sweet ass I will," said Raker, grinning into the phone. "Can we get old Tim over there too?"

Silence. When the voice spoke it was old again. "Can't do that, Martin." Sadness filled the pause. "He's gone, boy. Dead more than a year." The line hummed. "Sure do miss the old buzzard. Bet you will too. Now get on over here. We got lots to talk about." The voice was brighter.

"On my way, T.J." Raker replaced the ear piece and checked the phone book to be certain of Laughlin's address. Tears were foreign to Raker, but he already felt the empty space created by the loss of Murdock.

"Damn it," he muttered aloud, "should have written." He shrugged. The world was overflowing with should-haves.

Raker pulled open the door of the taxi he had quickly found and gave the driver the address.

"That's pretty far out, buddy." The driver remarked hoarsely as he turned a fleshy, pockmarked face to peer at Raker from over his shoulder.

"And that will make you more money, won't it?" inquired Raker mildly.

"Ain't the problem. All you damn doggies come scuffing back, running off without paying, stiffing us cabbies. I gotta see your cash up front."

Raker's teeth showed in a smile as he leaned forward. His right hand snaked out quickly and grasped the taxi driver's throat in a paralyzing grip.

"Sir," he said, his voice hissing softly, "I am a Captain in the United States Marine Corps. You may call me a gyrene, a sea-going bellhop, a jar head, a snuffy, a grunt, buddy, or even Mr." The driver's face flushed deeply, white showing around his bulging eyes, veins standing out prominently at his temples. "But you may not call me a 'doggie.' Is that understood?" His hand forced the driver's head back against the seat.

The driver made gagging sounds as he tried to nod his head.

"That's fine," said Raker, releasing his grip and leaning back. "I'm glad we understand each other." He unbuttoned a breast pocket of his tunic and extracted some folded bills as the driver gasped for air, hands at his throat.

"As for the money, what do you estimate the fare will be?"

The driver's face had lost most of the redness, and he eyed the money in Raker's hand hungrily, tinged with fear. "Probably around fi . . . say ten bucks," he said.

Raker smiled. "Five, you say?"

The driver's eyes shifted uneasily. This wasn't no average doggie he had picked up. Something about him scary. And jeezus, that hand could bend steel, he thought. His eyes avoided Raker's smile. He shrugged. "If that's what you heard."

"What I want to hear," said Raker, "is a lot of silence." He shoved a bill toward the driver. "Here's twenty. Will that buy it?"

"Mr.," said the driver reverently, "that will buy you damn near anything." He stuffed the bill in his shirt pocket, animosity forgotten. Hell! The guy was okay after all.

• • •

The trip took just over thirty minutes. Raker, remembering Laughlin's fondness for Irish *uisce beathadh*, the "water of life," as the old man called it, had the driver seek out liquor stores which might stock what, in those years, was a somewhat uncommon product. With luck, he found a supply of Jameson's at the second stop. As a precaution, the driver had been urged to accompany Raker into each store.

After an abortive attempt or two to start a conversation, the driver had lapsed into silence, but as he delivered Raker to his destination he spoke. "Mr.," he said. "I like your money, but do me a favor? Next time you need a hack, call someone else, will you?"

Raker laughed. "Fair enough," he said. "We got off to a bad start, but it turned out good. Here," and he held out his hand, proffering another twenty dollar bill.

The driver took it and looked up through the cab window at Raker. "I've changed my mind, Mr. Next time you need a cab, call for Augie at Yellow Cab." He touched his forehead in salute. "I mean it. S'long."

Raker looked after the departing cab, shaking his head. The guy was okay. He shouldn't have been so touchy. Poor bastard had probably lost plenty of money being stiffed by doggies. He turned up the walk leading to the big brownstone house surrounded by towering evergreens.

• • •

He had taken only a few steps when one of the wide, double doors was thrown open.

"Took your damn, sweet time, didn't you?" It was Laughlin's voice, but thin and flat, the power gone out of it, Raker thought.

"You cantankerous old coot," said Raker, hurrying forward. "I broke every speed limit in the city." Holding his package in one hand, he threw an arm around the old man. Sadness filled him. The body felt fragile and hollow-boned, not at all like that of Laughlin of the past with his heavy muscles and ruddy vitality.

"Aged, haven't I?" asked Laughlin, leading Raker through the open door.

"Not much," lied Raker. "Just a few more miles showing than before."

"Horse apples. Now what we got here?" asked Laughlin, taking the package from Raker and peering inside. "Whiskey! Hell, boy, I've got more whiskey in this camp than old Scarface ever peddled. What are you, some God damned Greek bearing coals to Newcastle, or something?"

"Just a miner bearing gifts," replied Raker soberly. It was good to hear Laughlin still pretending to be half-educated as he perverted adages and quotations.

"Not bad," laughed Laughlin. "Not good, but fast." He stood silent for a moment, studying Raker from head to foot. "You look good, boy. Damn good." He lifted the bottles. "C'mon. Let's get down to business."

Raker followed him down the hall, admiring the marble and dark wood of the house's interior and its immaculately maintained Victorian furnishings. The old man had aged terribly, but he hadn't let go.

As he followed Laughlin into what was obviously his library, Raker considered the old man's age. He had absolutely no idea how old he was. It had never seemed important. He thought back to when he'd first met him. What had he been then? Fifty? Sixty? Could have been more or less. Both Laughlin and Murdock had seemed so . . . permanent. Sort of ageless and indestructible. Raker shook his head. Object lesson in the mortality of us all, he thought. The old man must be in his seventies at least. It didn't seem possible.

Across the room, Laughlin took the bottles from the brown bag and held them up. "Well, you certainly do have acceptable taste, son. Must say that." He looked over at Raker. "Wish old Tim could be here with us." He cleared his throat roughly. "But then, he sorta is, isn't he?" He laughed. "Should have been here for the wake, boy. It was a beaut. Eight cases or more we drank. It was a genuine ten-roller."

Raker looked puzzled. "Ten roller?"

"Toilet paper, boy. Toilet paper. Ten rolls of toilet paper. That's how you judge a party. By the number of rolls of toilet paper used up."

Raker assumed an expression of seriousness. "Never considered that," he mused thoughtfully. "Makes perfect sense."

Laughlin looked up from the bottle he was opening. "It does? Then by God I'll just have to ignore it from now on."

Both men laughed as Laughlin finished opening both bottles. He walked across to hand one to Raker.

"No glasses needed, Marty boy. We're going to hold our own wake for Timmy." With effort he lowered himself to the carpeted floor and leaned back against the front of a heavy chair. "Join me, boy. No sense taking a detour when we can go direct. Hell, it's where we're going to end up anyhow."

Raker removed his jacket, placed it across the back of a chair, and seated himself on the floor, facing Laughlin. He watched as the old man lifted the bottle and took a long drink.

"What happened, T.J.?"

"Timmy? Old age, I guess. The old body just plain wore out."

"You, T.J. Yourself."

Laughlin looked down at the floor. "Dragon got me, bucko. An old fire-breathing dragon's chewing me up." He patted his stomach. "This here stuff is the only thing that seems to keep his fire doused."

Cancer, thought Raker. And far gone. "And the business?"

Laughlin lifted the bottle once again before answering. "That? Well, we just got too small for our britches."

"Too small?"

"No joke, Martin. We spread out too thin during the war. Wars," he corrected. "Tried to do too much. Diversify and all that."

"So?"

"We didn't have enough eggs in any one basket. The big boys ate us up."

"But how, for God's sake?"

Laughlin drank again. "Drink up, boy. Damned if I'm going to get roaring drunk alone. Haven't had much chance to compete since Timmy deserted. Drink!" He lifted his bottle.

Raker drank deeply enough to please Laughlin although he didn't care for alcohol that much. The size of his draught brought a smile to Laughlin's wizened features.

"How, you ask? Government, Martin. The big boys let the government do their dirty work for them. Held the hoop and government jumped. There must be some philosopher's law around that covers it, cause it's sure as hell a fact. When you got enough power, even governments squat to shit on command and ask "what color," for a fact." He lifted the bottle to his lips again before continuing.

"It was first one thing then another. Accusations of us being practically claim jumpers. Then investigations about price fixing. Claims of unfair labor practices and disregard of safety precautions. Hell," the old man spat, "we took better care of our men than any other company ever dreamed of doing." He drank and wiped his lips with the back of his hand.

"But again, we found out the damn insurance policies we had paid for didn't cover squat when it came right down to it."

Raker noted that the old man's color was improved and that juices seemed to be flowing in him once again. Juices! He smiled inside. Sure is that. Whiskey juices. But if it works, what the hell. He saw vestiges of the Laughlin he had known in the early years.

"We never let our men down," continued Laughlin. "Never. But you can't fight them, Marty boy. Can't fight power at all. Not unless you got the biggest cannon." He shook his head. "And we'd let ours be spiked, Timmy and I. Had let our contacts slip. Just didn't have the old fighting spirit any more." He looked down sadly at the bottle of whiskey in his hand. "Just didn't have it." He looked up at Raker. "Guess when we spent time coming up with that special alloy during the fracas with the Nips and Krauts, we figured we'd done our part." The old man shrugged and wiped the neck of the bottle with a finger. "What the hell, we'd had our fun."

"Then they broke you?"

The old man looked up slyly. "Shit no, they didn't break us. It just got to where it wasn't worth fightin' with our ammunition running out. But Timmy and I sure didn't let the money run out." Laughlin grinned broadly. "Wasn't a whole hell of a lot of it, but enough to hold us in style for some while. We had it stashed, Marty. lad. Stashed away carefully and safely."

He winked at Raker. "And now it's all yours."

"Mine? Hell, T.J., I don't need . . ."

"The hell you don't need money," roared the old man. "Every goddam body needs money. That's a farting stupid thing to even think. It's always been a weak spot with you—throwing your loot around like it was confetti at New Years." He snorted. "The shit you don't need it. You think that piddlin' little dab you got from your father and mother will last? Won't even buy a decent yacht nowadays."

"Who the hell wants a yacht?"

"Figure of speech." Laughlin waved it away with his hand. "Just don't knock money. It's second only to power in getting what you want."

The young man studied the old man's face before he spoke. "I don't know, T.J. I'm not sure those are the most important things."

"Bullshit, boy. Bullshit! What else is? Respect? Money and power buy it. Admiration? You can sure as cows-got-gas be admired a whole lot easier with money and power than without it. Love? I never heard of a romance breaking up because of having money. And health?" The old man leaned forward. "Well, maybe you can't buy it, but you can sure as hell get well quicker, or die more comfortably with it than without it."

The long speech had dried his mouth, and Laughlin lifted his bottle to drink. He grimaced. "Foul stuff. Worth it. No matter. What I'm getting at, Martin, is that just like old Machiavelli preached way back before you was born, it's a hell of a lot better to rule than serve, even if you rule in Hell, and the most effective way to rule is through fear rather than love. And money and power can create a whole lot of fear."

Raker grinned broadly. Laughlin was at it again. "I think it was Milton who preached about it being better to rule in Hell than serve in Heaven."

"No matter. All the same, those wops. But bright, mighty bright." The men drank. Raker was well aware that Laughlin knew the words he had paraphrased were Milton's, and that the man had been English.

"One exception to that," said Laughlin.

"Wops being bright?"

"Naw. Fear and love."

"And that is?"

"Love your own. And take care of them. Hard to do sometimes."

Raker nodded slowly. "It is that," he said. Had he ever told his father he loved him? Or Laughlin? Or Murdock? Probably not.

"Now old Timothy and me, we never had any children of our own. Too busy out skinning our knuckles against the rocks and then playing too hard when we played." He looked across at Raker with damp eyes. "But we had you, Marty boy. And you were . . . are . . . like our own. We tried to take care of you."

"You did, T.J., you did that."

"Maybe not like we should have. Anyway, everything we had is yours now. And that, along with what you have from your folks, will give you a good start. No—!" Laughlin held up a hand to stop Raker before he could speak. "Hear me out. We've invested your money pretty good. It's grown. And where we put our money, well, it's all right here, everything you need to know."

Laughlin reached into his inside coat pocket and pulled out a thick, brown envelope and tossed it to Raker. "It's all easy to get to, and all you'll need to take possession is what's in that envelope." He raised the bottle yet again. "And it explains other stuff as well."

"But you? What about you? You'll need . . ."

"Shit, boy, you'll take care of what I need." He paused thoughtfully. "Always do that, Martin. Always take care of your own. Take a look, boy; you'll understand a little about it."

Raker opened the thick envelope and read. After a time he looked up at Laughlin who had continued to sip from his bottle.

"So that was it, T.J.? That's how they got to you?" he shook his head.

"Yeah," drawled the old man, "that was sure enough it. Hell, boy, never before did it take more'n a handshake to seal a deal." It was Laughlin's turn to shake his head. "Never before," he repeated. "Just took me'n old Timmy too damn long to learn that there's times even those you help will betray your trust." He straightened his shoulders and lifted his head.

"But enough of this maudlin horse crap. Let's be getting on with our personal wake for The Murdock. In the cabinet over there," he motioned toward the far wall. "Fetch us two more bottles. Save a trip later. Don't think I have this brand, but you'll find something that'll do. And bring us that old green bowler you'll find settin' inside."

Raker did as instructed. He looked at the worn, bedraggled green derby he had found. "Been through the wars," he offered, "and this looks like a bite taken out of the brim."

Laughlin laughed, bringing on a short spasm of coughing. "That it is, bucko, that it is. One St. Patrick's Day I won "the game" and Murdock, in a fit of pique . . . that's a good word, isn't it? In a fit of pique, he took a bite out of the damn thing."

Raker grinned broadly as he remembered. Though he had never taken part, he knew the game. Each St. Patrick's Day, when both the men had been together, Laughlin and Murdock had armed themselves with a plenteous supply of whiskey, found a quiet room in which they could remain undisturbed, placed the green derby on some tall piece of furniture, and drank, drink for drink, until only one of them could rise to claim their prize. If one man rose to grab the hat, as long as the other could manage to place a hand on the derby as well, they would reseat themselves and continue to drink until only one could rise. On more than one occasion the hat had remained unclaimed as the men peacefully slept away the rest of the night in alcoholic bliss.

"You don't mean I'm finally to join in on this?"

"You are that, Martin. Have you a place to set it?"

Raker looked around and finally selected the top of a floor lamp near him. He balanced the hat precariously on the wires across the top of the shade.

"Whoa, boy. Isn't that a little far from me and close to you?"

"I'm not totally stupid, T.J.—with all your experience I figure it is the least handicap you should allow."

Laughlin chuckled delightedly. "Sit down, son. Less talk and more drinking." He lifted a bottle toward the ceiling. "Here's to you, Timmy boy. And many more to come."

Raker lifted his own bottle in salute and the men drank.

"Just one thing, Martin, before I drink you into oblivion . . ."

"Yes?" asked Raker, already feeling the effects of the whiskey.

The old man's eyes moved about as he searched for words. "I'd like to ask you to do something for us. All of us. Me and Timmie and you."

"Sure, T.J., anything I can."

Laughlin peered intently at the younger man. "Fight the bastards, Martin!" He formed a fist and shook it. "Don't let the bastards get to you like they got to us. Build a power base. Fight 'em! Pick the biggest motherfucker of the bunch and knock him down. The others will jump into line." He licked dry lips. "You've got all the equipment, son. Nobody's better equipped physically, and you're downright bright with your book-learning and all. But you're not suspicious enough. Change that, boy. Don't trust anyone that hasn't proven trustworthy . . . and then only trust them as much as you have to. And fight! But if you're out for revenge, don't hurry it. Wait till the bastard's got something worth having before you take it away from him. Or him away from it." He paused to drink, and as he pulled the bottle away from his lips he laughed.

"Listen to me," he said. "I sound like Conor talking."

"Conor?"

"Conor, or maybe it was Cormac. Anyway, a famous old Irish king. Gave grand advice. Mighty fine literature. Read it sometime." It was Cormac MacArt.

"I will, T.J.—you can count on it."

"I'm counting on you all the way, boy." His face grew serious. "You can be something pretty spectacular, Martin. You can, you know. Hell, you might even end up running this damned country one of these days. Now! Let's get on with this here now contest." Laughlin drained his bottle, and with a wink, reached for the other which was sitting on the floor near him.

• • •

Morning came.

Raker forced his way to consciousness, and disregarding the dehydration, the squirming mass in the pit of his stomach and a pounding headache, he crawled across to where Laughlin sprawled near the chair against which he had been leaning. One hand held the green derby.

Raker touched him. From his past experience he knew at once that the old man was dead. It couldn't have been for long, he thought, for the body was still warm and limp. It came as no surprise. It seemed as though Laughlin had only been waiting for him, and had been bidding him goodbye ever since he'd arrived.

Raker forced himself erect and found a bathroom where he doused himself with cold water. In the medicine cabinet he found a bottle of aspirin and spilled two tablets out into his hand. He eyed them for a moment before deciding that he would rather have the headache than anything in his stomach. He dumped them into the lavatory.

He returned to the library where he gently lifted Laughlin's body from the floor and carried him up the stairs. The body seemed weightless. He quickly located the old man's bedroom where he placed him on the bed and removed the urine stained clothing. It was the only sign of body excretion; the old man obviously hadn't eaten for some time. Using a soaked towel he cleaned Laughlin, dressed him in pajamas he found in a chest, placed him in the bed under the sheet, then carefully brushed his hair. Finished, he stood, smiling down with affection at the body of his friend.

"Go with dignity, old man," he said. His smile twisted into a grin. "Hell, by tonight you and Murdock will be throwing a drunken reunion in some corner of somewhere, if there's any such place."

As he reached for the telephone, he thought of what Laughlin had expected of him. Okay, T.J., he thought, I got it, and I'll sure as hell give it a go.

Beverly Martin Raker was grown.

NEW YORK CITY

Now, these many years later, Raker stepped through the doors of the PanGlobal building, turned onto the avenue of its east front, turned again down the cross street, and walked west. It was 3:12 p.m. His phone call would have to be placed in only 18 minutes.

Quickly calculating the time and distance, Raker slowed his stride and strolled into the lobby of the Sheraton at 3:23. He wanted to allow at least five minutes in the event all the public phones were in use. They weren't. He lifted a receiver to his ear while keeping its cradle depressed as he seemed to fumble for change. At precisely 3:29:30, he dialed. The phone at the other end was lifted almost before the first buzz came—the noise which is fed back to the caller to make one think it is the sound of a ring.

"Hello?"

"How did the morning go?" asked Raker.

"Somewhat awkward. Nearly most unpleasant."

"How so?"

The girl told him of her encounter with Webb, and of Colt's rescue. "Are you all right?"

"Yes. I'm all right now. Will I have to return?"

"Not likely at all," answered Raker. "You have the schedule for my future calls?"

"Of course."

"And the emergency—the 'in person' schedule?"

"Yes."

"And the key to the safe room?"

"I have."

"Then that's all you'll need. Just be certain you follow the schedule. If there's any future threat of harassment, go to the safe room, following the security precautions I detailed. Understood?"

"Certainly," came the reply, archly. "It's all committed to memory."

"Fine," Raker's voice had softened. "You've done a remarkable job. Get to your home now, and be cautious. If you need me, you know how to reach me. Just be sure it's necessary."

"I will do that. Is that all?" The question went unanswered as the line remained silent.

Raker smiled as he replaced the phone. Pagan was sincere and devoted, and had performed exactly as she had been coached. Raker was not surprised. He had felt that she was dependable ever since the first day, in Ireland, when in the role of Owen Coleman, he had recruited her as an uninformed pawn in his scheme against PanGlobal Assurance.

CHAPTER 9

La Amenaza
Mexico

It had taken years for Beverly Martin Raker to select his target and refine his plan of attack. It had taken yet more time, as well as unwavering determination and brilliant manipulation, before he had access to the barest information required to start his actions. The sacrificial victims of his attack would all have at least one thing in common. They would all be insured by PanGlobal Assurance.

The formation of his termination force had been accomplished quite easily and in a remarkably short time, especially considering the widespread field of action. It was not luck that his lifestyle had given him the associates he needed. Its accomplishment did, however, require money and time. Raker had both.

Following the successful completion of arrangements with his chosen personnel in the United States, Raker had begun his foreign recruiting. It suited him well that his first stop would be in Mexico.

It was a simple matter for him to arrange to be driven across the Rio Grande from El Paso to Juarez, Mexico. Clay Sizemore had been quite ready and not at all curious about the trip. Border formalities consisted of a uniformed man wearing a macho frown, stooping to peer at them, then give them an arrogant and disdainful wave of his hand to indicate they could proceed. Raker would return to the country by the same route. Photographs, surreptitiously taken at all such border points and transmitted to a central computer, presented no problem for Raker. His appearance offered him that security, and the car had no connection with him. There would be no record of him having left or entered the United States.

Once across the border, his telephone call to an old acquaintance, stating that he was on his way for a visit, required only a little less time than the trip, via AeroMexico airlines, to the Distrito Federal, and Mexico City.

The trip was uneventful and the required tourist card had been filled out in route. As the bus-like mobile lounge deposited Raker and his fellow passengers for a check by aduana inspectors, Raker did not have the bother of waiting to claim his luggage. Even for extended trips Raker had learned to travel light, and carried only a bag and a carefully designed dispatch case.

He extended his tourist card and passport—which authentic in themselves, did not bear his name—made the necessary declarations to the immigration official who met him with near-tolerable haughtiness, then waved him through into the jumble of taxi drivers who were poised for combat in their battle for fares.

Although he did not see the party who was to meet him, Raker felt the presence. The sense went far beyond intuition, it was a part of Raker's almost telepathic ability which had helped to keep him alive for so long.

Suddenly he smiled. There she was!

As the woman swept through the crowd toward him, heads did not simply turn, they snapped. She was, if nothing else, spectacularly magnificent. Not only in appearance, but in intellectual and physical abilities.

She stood in front of him, her eyes on a level with his, legs spread in an aggressive stance, hands on hips, and a welcoming smile on marvelously curving lips. Obsidian black hair, luxuriously thick and gleaming, was parted in the center and swept back on either side of her face where it seemed to flow like falling water, reaching nearly to her waist. It framed her face dramatically, as though designed for that specific purpose, and its sheen gave the impression that if you looked closely enough, you could see your reflection in it.

Her Aztec heritage was obvious in the superb bone structure and sculptured features of her face. Her skin tone was a rich, bronzed copper, made more striking by huge, exotically shaped eyes which were a nearly golden topaz in color, yet with the ever-changing, iridescent overtones found in fire opals. They were the only indication of the Spanish conquistador who was one of her ancestors.

Any makeup the woman might wear could only diminish her perfection. Her looks went much farther than mere beauty.

She wore a peasant-like dress, deceiving in its simplicity, tailored of rich, bright, turquoise velvet. It was long sleeved, its neckline cut to a length and width which tantalized without flaunting, and was gathered at the waist by a wide, exquisitely engraved and hammered silver concho belt.

Beneath the low hemline of her dress could be seen the handtooled leather of boots, their toes capped with silver to match her belt. In spite of her great height, the boots were high heeled. Angela Esperanza Castillo Diaz was totally confident and self-assured.

To the women who viewed her, on any occasion, her appearance and bearing seemed totally unfair.

"*Bueno acogida, mi Colonel*," she said. Her voice was like the woman herself—for all its power and distinction, hearing it was a pleasant experience. Raker set his luggage down and held his arms out from his sides. It was not quite an invitation for the woman to come to him for a hug; it was the prelude to one of their games.

She smiled and stepped forward. Her hands went under Raker's arms, she bent her knees slightly, then lifted. Her strength was considerable, but Raker's body did not move. The woman dropped her arms and her smile grew even larger.

"More training is necessary," she said simply. "I can press more than eighty kilos, it is true, but you, mi Colonel, are still the hulking, muscular beast as always. I thought the years would have diminished you." She moved into his embrace and held him tightly.

"You are more magnificent than ever, *querida*," said Raker, his mouth barely above her ear. Her natural scent was of sunshine, fresh breezes, and the sea.

The woman moved back and bent to pick up the larger of Raker's bags.

"Let us be away from this *bola*," she said, locking her arm through Raker's. "My car is not far." She gave a throaty chuckle. "It is illegally parked, with nearly an army of *policia* guarding it."

Raker made no effort to stop her from carrying his bag. "And with drawn weapons, I should imagine," he said. It would not, in reality, have surprised him. Whole armies had done far more for this magnificent female.

• • •

Beverly Martin Raker had first encountered the woman—girl then—not too many years before when he had been consulting with the leaders of a small country well beyond Mexico's southern border. The government in power at the time was aware that insurrection was in the offing—a fact which, in that area of the world, was not at all unusual.

Once upon a time, or so it is reported, a visitor was attending a bullfight for the first time, and made the observation that the country's most popular sport most definitely was revolting. The host admitted that the observation was quite accurate—but that bullfighting was certainly the second most popular sport.

At the meeting, Raker had found himself competing for employment with another mercenary. He knew the man and intensely disliked him. If it had not been for that fact, as well as the considerable sum being offered for Raker and his crew to train the country's own personnel, Raker would have withdrawn at once.

With the decision made that Raker—though certainly not known by that name—was to be their "advisor," the meeting adjourned. The rejected competitor, angrily ignoring the waiting limousine, stormed away through the gates outside the ornate Capitol building, and walked into the squalor and hunger beyond the heavily guarded wall which enclosed the luxurious grounds.

As he emerged, there was a sudden flurry as a figure dashed forward from the scattering of people on the street and flew at the man. He was dead before the automobile bearing Raker and the country's leader arrived at the scene. The man had been ripped open from his abdomen to his solar plexus.

The knife had been wielded, powerfully and expertly, by Angela Esperanza Castillo Diaz. She was sixteen years old at the time.

Guards had immediately pounced on the girl, roughing her up in the process. Raker had been able to minimize the mauling by sudden and violent action. The men he so capably handled would have liked nothing better than to have dismembered the *violente forastero*, but they knew of his importance to their leaders.

It required time, negotiation, and a readjustment in Raker's recompense for him and his mercenaries—as "advisors"—before the girl was released into his custody. Raker did not, however, reduce the figure more than a token amount. He knew that the dead man would have been just as dead if he had driven away in the waiting limousine with its driver and "bodyguard." It would not have been *discreto* to let the man depart with the knowledge he had gained during the negotiations.

Later, Raker learned that the girl had trailed, for nearly a year, the man she had killed. While visiting a tiny southern village on the Pacific side of Mexico, he had encountered the girl who was swimming in a quiet *charca* formed by the bend of an isolated stream. The date was June 24th. It was the Day of St. John the Baptist, a day when it is customary in Mexico for believers to go swimming or bathe at dawn. On that day the girl ceased to be a believer.

The man's companions, minor officials, for whom he had performed certain services which had included murder and other odd jobs, left. It gave him their tacit approval.

He raped the girl.

In the process he had been forced to injure her. The injuries, as it turned out, had not been severe enough. The man was found dead—and emasculated.

Following her release into Raker's custody, the girl had joined his command. There had been little hesitancy in Raker allowing her to do so. He remembered his own age and actions when he had joined Laughlin and Murdock.

Angela proved to be an apt pupil, and developed into an incredibly effective *guerrillera*. She was completely fearless, and her size, strength, and stealth had made her the equal of most men, even at her young age. Perhaps not as professional as Raker's carefully selected men, but of most.

She was soon accepted as a peer. That came after it was discovered—and in a few cases with long remembered pain and scars—that she was not to be approached with careless hands or proposals of lustful activities.

The men soon named the girl *La Amenaza*: The Menace. The

name stayed with her even after Raker's command disbanded. She became a young legend to many of her people—the poor of Mexico. They were the vast majority. She had championed their cause, and her popularity made it nearly impossible for public action to be taken against her. Her precautions, learned from Raker, had prevented the success of attempted covert actions aimed toward the disposal of her annoying existence.

Beverly Martin Raker, a man of limited compassion, had at least one good thing to say about the first man *La Amenaza* had killed. Without him, Raker would never have met the woman.

• • •

"No," said Angela Esperanza Castillo Diaz from behind the wheel of her car as she guided it expertly through the suicidal traffic of the city. "You will most certainly not be staying at the Fiesta Palace, nor even the Presidente. They may be excellent choices for touring groups, even the Japanese." The Fiesta was one of those travelers' favorite stops. "But the air, *Madre de Dios!* It is not breathable for more than a few hours at a time. Not anywhere within the city."

It was true. While the *Paseo de la Reforma* is surely one of the world's more attractive main thoroughfares, it becomes increasingly difficult, day by day, to see anything—even the hood of one's own car—as the ugly, sulphurous smog grows thicker.

"No," she continued. "You will come to my hacienda for your visit. It is north, past the cordillera, and beyond this *jofaina de suciedad.*"

Raker agreed readily.

"I have moved my studio," said the woman, "and consolidated it with my home."

"Gymnasium and all?"

"But of course. It is more convenient for teaching." The woman was a sought-after coach for aspiring gymnasts. She instructed when not busy championing the cause of people she felt were improperly used.

Raker smiled. "For the teaching of what?" he inquired. "Insurrection or athletics?"

It was the woman's turn to smile. "I would be foolish to admit to the one. I do have one most promising student in the other."

It seemed to Raker that she meant a gymnast.

"Also," continued the woman, "I have branched into the production of motion pictures. I find it challenging and profitable."

"There is," said Raker solemnly, "absolutely nothing wrong with either."

"*Como se llama ahora?*" he asked suddenly. How are you called—now? The woman's proper name was Angela Esperanza Castillo Diaz. It was not what he was asking.

Her eyes flicked across toward Raker with amusement. Her head nodded up and down, slowly. "Yes. You would ask that, wouldn't you." She was silent for a moment. "The same."

"Ah, yes," he said. "As I recall, you are the ABCs of discomfort to the ruling classes." He smiled. The woman had been named, by others, Amenaza Bellaqueria Cuartelada. To some, she was indeed a menace. She was also cunning, and was most certainly an advocate of revolution. Her *nombre de guerra* most certainly fit.

"Well," he commented, "with your country's financial problems, you do have yet another cause to support now," said Raker. "Have you taken to robbing the nationalized banks?"

"Why? The money is worth nothing. No, I fight for the land for the *campesinos*. The land, and the people, are all that are worth anything."

"And your motion picture making? That tells your story to the people?"

"Hardly. They make money to finance other ventures," said the woman. "*Pero basta' de ese pal ya.*" It was enough of such talk. "Let me instead ask what you are called, *mi Colonel?*"

"You can try Coleman," said Raker. "Owen Coleman."

The woman shook her head. "No, I think not . . . I prefer *El Hombre.*"

The car was approaching the tall pedestal atop which stood the statue of the Golden Angel. Its gleaming finish was haloed by smog. "Just where is it we are going?" inquired Raker. "I thought you spoke of your *hacienda.*"

"I seldom come to the city," smiled the woman. "I desire to

feast on a portion of that fine cheese and onion pie served here in the Zona Rosa. And to wash it down with great swallows of Bass ale."

That the woman would think of food came as no surprise to Raker. Her appetites, in all things, were great, and the food of Mexico City was as varied and wonderful as that of any city of the world. He knew the place she meant. It was named the Piccadilly Pub, and was situated in the cosmopolitan area of Mexico City where the streets bore the names of foreign countries.

The woman swung around the traffic circle and doubled back to drive only a short distance before turning on the narrow, attractive street named Copenhague. The pub with its handsome interior and outside sidewalk tables was at No. 23.

"You'll find no parking here," said Raker. The beautifully maintained lane was solid with shops and dining establishments.

"I will," she said, swinging her car quickly, narrowly missing a man serenading listeners at a nearby sidewalk café. His music was made by an old fashioned organ-grinder's instrument. Raker had not seen one since his last visit to the city. "A friend has a parking area under his apartment. I can always use it."

"And if he's there?"

Angela Esperanza Castillo Diaz shrugged. "He will have to move it," she said.

He did.

Raker and the woman snacked deliciously. The food was quite authentic. One of the husband and wife team of owners was English. Raker had never felt it important to find out which one.

Following their light repast, they reclaimed the woman's car and swung back into the crush of Mexico City traffic. On the small lane it had been easy to forget that the metropolis is one of the world's largest cities.

"Now home," said Raker's companion. "But first, a small stop."

"Another surprise?"

"Perhaps. Have you ever tried the *pulque*?"

"No. It may be one of the only potables I have not tried," he said. He looked at the woman. "It is potable, I presume?"

"Deliciously so. And a small *pulqueria* is quite near. The drink is far better than the after-dinner drinks of your *ricachon*. And it has *cojones*. Women are not permitted," she said. "However, I am."

"Lead on then, my man. Lead on." It would have surprised Raker if the woman had been unwelcome anywhere.

$$\cdots$$

The *pulqueria* was only a few blocks away, near the Reforma. The street was lined with shops but there were amazingly few pedestrians, only moderate traffic, and they were able to park quite nearby, choosing one of several available parking places. It was a different world from the Reforma, and the Zona Rosa. The woman moved in front of Raker and pushed open a plain, paint-flaking door which did not have a latch. The interior of the tiny room was dimly lighted and smoke filled.

"*La Amenaza!*" cried a voice. Other voices immediately echoed the words. Bedlam reigned as a bustle of white-clad figures stirred, the commotion not unlike the wild jumble of a disturbed colony of ants.

The woman, nearly as tall as Raker, towered over the men who crowded around her, each reaching out in an effort to simply touch her . . . arms, hands or shoulders. The words *La Amenaza* continued to be heard over the other welcoming shouts.

La Amenaza—the menace. The woman seemed a conquering hero to the clientele of the *pulqueria*. Her menace was to the users of such people. It took several minutes for some order to be restored and for The Menace to introduce Raker to her near-worshipers. The *senor* was most welcome. The tiny unpainted tables in the half-a-box-car sized room were surrounded by plain, nearly unfinished wooden chairs, all resting on a rough-surfaced concrete floor. The only light came from a bare bulb hanging toward the side of the room where the bar stood—or leaned. It more resembled a packing crate for a piano. Atop the bar sat two dairy cans.

"*Ordinaria*," said Raker's companion, her voice loud without effort, in response to the smiling, unvoiced question of the gap-toothed, robust man behind the tall cans. "The other kind is flavored," she told Raker.

The serving man's smile grew as he sat two large glasses on

the counter top, then dipped a dented tin cup into one of the open cans and poured thickish, milky-looking liquid into the foaming containers.

Raker offered money. It was refused with a look of accusation.

Angela Esperanza Castillo Diaz lifted one of the glasses and turned to face Raker, saluting the rest of the room with her raised hand. Raker picked up his own drink.

"*Salud*," said The Menace.

The room echoed the word.

"*Arriba!*" said the woman, holding her glass high. The men did the same, again echoing her words. As she continued the ritual, the men followed her lead.

"*Abajo!*" The glass was held low. "*Izquierda!*" The glass moved to her left. "*Derecha!*" It went to the right. "*Al Centro!*" The glass was held to her stomach. "*A dentro!*" She lifted the glass and drained its contents in one draught.

Raker lifted his glass and drank. His mouth and throat rebelled. He hesitated. His resolve stiffened and he drained the contents, forcing the last swallow down.

The room exploded with applause. The Menace smiled broadly.

"Damn near got you, didn't it?" Her expression was one of delight. Raker made no pretense.

"That first slippery mouthful is unbelievable. The texture is like overcooked okra, mashed oysters and not-quite-shredded pineapple."

"And the taste?"

"Better than many things I've encountered," Raker smiled. "Would it be an obnoxious *yanqui* showing off if I offered to show approval by setting up the house?"

"It only would be appreciated," said La Amenaza. It was how Raker had, at the first swallow of the drink, begun to think of her. Truly, The Menace.

"But only," she continued, "if you drink with us."

"I would have it no other way," said Raker. He meant it. *Pulque*, he had decided, was a quite worthwhile drink.

The cost of the round was as close to nothing as can be imagined. When La Amenaza thought it was necessary to leave, it required more touching and many protestations. While the ritual ensued, Raker quietly left enough money with the manager to set up many more rounds. For some reason, he knew the man would do so. The same could not be said at many of the far fancier places in which Raker had imbibed.

• • •

"You are a wonderful companion," said the woman. They were on the road north which led toward Teotihuacan. She laughed lightly. "I think you truly liked the *pulque*."

"And the company," said Raker. He meant it. The men of the *pulqueria* had been as gracious, polite, and as good company as he could ever ask. Quality, he thought, does not come with education, indoctrination, or one's manner of dress.

"Nice to say." The woman was silent as the car hummed quietly. "You did not come just for the visit," she said, finally. "With *El Hombre*, it is always a proposal of excitement." Her eyes left the road for a quick glance. "Just what is it this time, *mi Colonel*?"

"Someone I would like you to kill," said Raker. "Someone I think you will agree needs it."

The woman showed no surprise. "Who?"

"Zangano. Xavier Ybarra Zangano."

The woman spat. "That one! He should have been killed many years ago."

"You know of his latest business?"

"Which one? He has many. All harmful to others."

"The leading of immigrants into the United States."

"There can be no profit there now," said the woman. "The *tortilla* curtain is full of holes for my people."

"Not just your own," said Raker. "He recruits also from farther south. Ybarra took several refugees, at high price, across the border into Arizona and when it seemed that he might be discovered, he left them. They died in the sun. Dehydrated. Dead from thirst. Can you imagine such a death?"

The woman remained quiet for a time. "No. I did not know of that. I will not ask what was to be my next question: Why? I now know."

"It will be worth much profit to you," said Raker. He knew the woman was un-buyable except when she was willing to sell. "You can do much for your people with the money I speak of."

"I listen," said La Amenaza.

Raker detailed the dollar figures and the processes needed for complete payment. The sum was great.

She nodded.

"As a beginning," he said, "there is already half a million dollars on deposit in the United States. The necessary credentials to allow you to claim it will be yours when you agree. It will cover expenses."

•••

Angela Castillo had already decided. There was, however, still the game, another of the ones she enjoyed competing in against Raker. He was the only man she knew who represented a challenge she had not been able to meet. This would be the time. When he called, she had immediately put her mind to work. She had also called upon the *Bellaqueria* part of her *nombre de guerra:* The Cunning. Preparations had been made.

"Well?" asked Raker.

"I think on it." They were nearing the turnoff to her country home.

It was still light enough for Raker to see the broad fields of young century plants. Angela turned off the main road onto the graveled road that stretched in a straight line toward the sprawling fortress-like mansion she owned. Each corner of the taller central structure was bartizaned with balistraria tops on each, the openings through which weapons could be fired with some safety. The tops of the other walls were similarly crenellated. The structure was as ancient as it appeared, but fully restored; its additions had adhered faithfully to its architecture. It sat stark and nearly treeless near the center of the broad fields of cactus plants.

"Maguey?" asked Raker, looking at the plantings.

"Blue agave," said the woman. "For prime tequila . . . the quality plant. The other kind goes mostly for inferior products. But also for the *pulque*." She glanced at Raker to see if he shuddered. He didn't.

"Inside is much like the outside now," said the woman. "Once there we will talk more of your proposal." Her voice was bright with the pleasure of his company.

• • •

La Amenaza, thought Raker. He combined it with her birth name, Angela. He laughed. It fit her.

"You laugh," observed the woman, "but with wicked over-tones."

"Not really. Just thinking. I have composed a new name for you. I shall call you by it. Some of the time. Angela del Amenaza."

The woman joined in his laughter. Quite good. She not only enjoyed his company, she felt great affection for him. It would be a wonderful night for both *El Colonel* and *Angela del Amenaza*: The Colonel and The Menacing Angel.

• • •

The sound of Angela Castillo's car must have been heard as it approached the castle-like building, for they were greeted at the open door. "Hello, you two." The voice was full of life and welcome. "I'm glad you're here. With everyone gone, this is a spooky old place." The girl speaking was as lively and bouncy-seeming as her voice. The contrasts between her and Raker's hostess were remarkable. The girl came only to Angela's shoulder, and her coloring was the distinct opposite.

Silvery, almost platinum, hair flowed as gossamer threads of silky, molten metal from her head, falling straight down in the back and cascading forward to the front, where it reached her shoulders. Her eyes were a deep, mid-Pacific blue, and her complexion was cream and roses.

Her neatly arched eyebrows were a dark shade of rich, golden brown. The only similarity in the two females was their figures. In spite of the great difference in size, both of their bodies were lithe and athletically slim while still being curved and feminine. To Raker, most women were lovely, no matter what the exact configuration of their features. These two were superb.

"Colonel," said Angela Castillo, "permit me to present my

friend, Gisella. Gisel, this brutal looking beast is *El Hombre*." She indulged herself with a laugh. "Otherwise known as The Colonel. His proper name is absurd, and of no consequence."

The girl extended a hand. Raker took it. Her grip was firm and warm.

"I have much pleasure in making your acquaintance," said Gisella. "It is a pleasing event to see our Angel so happy." The girl was clad in a stylish and obviously expensive warm-up suit of the sort worn by top athletes. Her feet were bare.

Raker acknowledged the welcome with appropriate words and leaned forward to kiss the back of the girl's hand. It was an "event"—one he reserved for rare occasions, and then for only the quite young or the very old.

"Watch him, Gisel—when the old lecher does that trick he's up to no good." The woman's obvious pleasure belied the words. "Her Spanish is quite good," said Angela. "But she's of your country."

As the threesome walked from the entryway into the great receiving hall, Angela Castillo was aware that Raker, without making it obvious, was studying the furnishings of the house. They were barely adequate and quite spartan.

"I see you notice," she said. "None of my old paintings or other expensive decorations." A foot tapped the floor. "And now native rugs cover the floor in place of the Persians."

"Of no importance," said Raker. "Luxury can be enjoyed only by those who have the stomach and the time for it."

"The luxuries went to buy necessities," said Angela.

"But not for you," added Raker.

She shrugged, and smiled. "I have need for little. I do not deprive myself—but enough of this. I am for the game. Are you?"

It was Raker's turn to smile. "Do you really think you're up to it?"

The comment was expected. "More than ready, *hombre*. On this day you meet more than your match. That is, if you will abide by the rules."

"New ones?" inquired Raker.

"I'll show them to you. They are written. But there is yet another thing at stake, I now realize."

"And that is?"

"Your request." The woman was now the cunning one again. "You seek my cooperation. You may have it if you abide by the rules, and if you defeat me."

"And if I don't?" That event had never occurred in all the previous games. It was not that Angela was not good—she was; Raker had trained her. It was only that Raker was better.

Angela considered his question. Her smile grew more wicked. "If you do not prevail, if I win, then I will still perform the task you ask, but only if you agree to be my obedient servant for a period of 24 hours."

Raker's eyebrows went up in surprise. He did not like serving anyone. His eyes narrowed.

"You do not like the idea. Very well, I will change it. You need not become my servant. You must become my slave."

Raker stared at her.

"And if you hesitate longer, the terms will become even stricter." She smiled pleasantly. "Well?"

Raker considered. There was little if any chance that the woman could win in any game she named. Still . . .

"Two qualifications," he said. "First, I must see the rules you have written. Then, if I am agreeable, I will make it for 12, not 24 hours. That is only because my schedule requires I stay here no longer than that."

The woman's expression said that she was once again only Angela. "That is reasonable, *mi Colonel.*" She turned toward the girl who had been listening to the exchange with interest and a knowing smile. She already knew of the rules.

"Gisel," said Angela Castillo, "please give *El Hombre* a copy of the rules we so carefully worked out after he called." She turned back to Raker. "Immediately that you called I set to work, Colonel. I have devised what I think is a game that will allow me a small chance to beat you for once."

The girl handed Raker a sheet of paper. It was written in English. "So there will be no misunderstanding, Colonel, no matter how good your Spanish is. If you agree, I want your word that you will adhere to all that is written."

"You'll have it," said Raker. He was reading. The rules were simple. He and La Amenaza were to engage in person-to-person combat with the single objective being to break a tiny ampoule which was to be worn tied to the neck. It would be fastened so that it hung just at the hollow of the throat. Their hands were to be thickly encased in the softest foam rubber—for safety's sake—with only the very tips of the fingers uncovered. Striking any portion of the opponent's body with hand or foot would result in the immediate loss of the game. Only the fingertips could be used to strike. The exposed portions of the fingers would be painted with colored grease paint which would show where any unfair strike was made.

That, thought Raker, would require great skill. He had it; Angela must have increased her ability or she would not have included the article in the rules.

Clothes were not to be worn. The abilities and great strength of Raker would allow him to grasp loose clothing with teeth or even toes, or between foam rubber-covered hands. It would give him too great an advantage over the woman.

The Colonel must compete with one hand only. The other was to be secured behind his back.

Gisella was to serve as referee. Her only duty would be to see if marks of the grease paint were left by either competitor, and to check that the combatants did not manage to rub the paint off on the floor or on their own anatomy.

Raker considered the rules. They were acceptable.

Did he really need the woman's help? It would certainly facilitate his schedule. She was effective and totally dependable.

"Very well, my large and menacing angel. You have yourself a deal."

The woman smiled broadly, and Gisella clapped her hands in glee. It would be such fun to watch. Angela had told her of El Hombre's prowess.

"Very well, my old friend," said the woman. "We prepare. After, we shall bathe and dine, and make great happiness. Are you prepared?"

"At your service," said Raker. "Are there to be any other witnesses?"

"Certainly not. Everyone—that is, the few employees I've managed to retain—they have been given a holiday." It was *Cinco de Mayo*.

"And your trainees?"

"I have only the one at the present," said Angela. She nodded at the girl. "It will be only the three of us. We can use the training gym. Come!"

• • •

It seemed time-consuming to Raker that he and his opponent should be given separate dressing rooms. In only minutes they would be facing each other without clothing anyway. Oh, well; perhaps it was the feminine mystique. He finished hanging his clothes on the convenient hangers nearby and started to leave. As he moved, his mind flashed suddenly.

No way! He stopped where he stood, a smile of awareness curving his mouth. No way indeed. They would *not* face each other, both naked. Absolutely not! It seemed that his body would offer a far too convenient "holding" element. No clothing, indeed! The possibility he had just become aware of would be far more convenient to grasp than clothing—and incomparably more painful. His smile grew. That was probably the edge—or was it handle?—of advantage the truly cunning woman had counted on. He opened the door of the dressing room and raised his voice.

"A protest, my lovely angel!" His voice was loud. "There is no way I'm going to give you such an unfair advantage."

The adjacent door opened just a bit. Angela Castillo's voice came to him, riding on laughter. "So, my large one, you have considered the possibilities!" He could hear the laughter of both the females.

"It is all right, my friend. I will not insist on the advantage. You will find a suitable elastic guardian for your manhood inside the first locker." Laughter was still in her voice. "Though I wish you had not become aware until it was too late."

Raker was smiling. The woman invariably brought him pleasure. "Two minutes, mi Colonel. We begin."

It took less for Raker to don what he considered to be absolutely necessary protection, and the waist belt which would secure his right wrist to his side.

"Choose your target," said Angela Castillo. She pointed to the two red-filled ampoules attached to black ribbons which Gisella held out between the two contestants. "They are thin plastic."

"That," grinned Raker, "is obvious. Just let the girl tie them in place." His eyes admired, not lusted after, the beautiful form of his opponent. Perhaps in deference to Raker's athletic supporter, she had donned a tiny bikini bottom. Her figure was magnificent and purely feminine, yet the smooth highlighted gleam of well-conditioned muscles could be seen just under the satin surface of her skin. Gisella still wore her warm-up suit.

"Go on, Gisella," said La Amenaza, and both she and Raker waited as the girl, in turn, tied the ribbons around their necks. The ampoules were positioned directly at the hollow of each of their throats. It was the place where a terribly damaging blow could be struck. To break the ampoule without such damage would require great skill. It also required great confidence in one's opponent.

The man and the woman bowed, ritually, and the contest began.

• • •

Angela suddenly looked to be quite truly The Menace. She slid, quicksilver fast, toward the right side of Raker on which his hand had been secured to the belt, her own left hand streaking forward, then sweeping back toward his throat with cobra-like speed.

If she was the snake, Raker was the mongoose. His body turned slightly to follow her movement and his left arm lashed across his body, countering her thrust much like sword meeting sword. The woman's motion pulled her back from the rapier-like thrust of his fingers which came at the end of his parry.

They smiled at each other.

"Very good," he said. "You've improved." His hand dropped to his side. The words were to throw her off. His hand flashed forward and up, fingers lightly extended. The speed was more than the eye could follow. He felt the tips touch. The contest was over.

The woman danced back. The ampoule was unbroken.

Raker frowned. He felt he couldn't have mistaken the contact, yet there was not even the mark of red greasepaint on Angela's throat.

Her body leaned quickly forward, her left arm crossed in front of her. She levered it down, crowding forward, letting the arm block Raker's which he had withdrawn to look at his fingertips. Her right arm lanced forward and Raker barely escaped the thrusting fingers.

It was no time to be concerned with misses. He raised his arm quickly, up even with his throat, to guard the ampoule. He spun backwards, away from the woman and to her left, and his arm swept forward, fingers flicking. Angela drew back, swinging an arm upward to defend against the blow.

Once again Raker thought he felt the tip of his finger touch the thin plastic ampoule. It was still unbroken. He stopped, looking in amazement at the woman's throat and at his fingertips. In the split second, her hand flashed forward and he was suddenly aware of the flow of red which spilled to cover his neck and chest. Her blow had broken the ampoule around his neck.

Raker stared in disbelief as the liquid flowed down his chest.

It simply couldn't be. Had he become so old? So out of training? He shook his head. It was not possible—and yet his ampoule was broken. That of the one tied about the lovely throat of Angela Ezparanza Castillo Diaz was not.

"Touché," smiled the woman. She looked at Raker, seeing the worry etched on his features.

Gisella, standing aside, smiled but gave no other indication of favoritism.

"I saw you look at your fingers," Angela Castillo said. "You assumed. I think you thought you had made contact. It threw you off."

"Of course," agreed Raker. It was the terrible flaw of which he warned others. Assuming. He would not allow himself to be a bad loser. Later he would reconstruct the contest. He would be able to replay every move. There simply must be a reason! For now he must be gracious.

"I congratulate you," he said, "*La Amenaza,* you were superb." He looked up from the red staining his flesh. "Now where can I wash this red badge of loss from my body?"

"In the dressing room," said Angela. She felt the doubt Raker was suffering. "Don't worry too heavily, *mi Colonel.* I upset you with all my planning and you were limited to but one hand, re-member?"

"Yes. Of course." It should have made no difference. Raker turned to head for the locker room and a shower. He felt like a pitcher pulled from a world series game with the bases loaded.

"Gisella and I will shower and meet you in the dining room, off the reception hall." She smiled again, this time looking like the evil one. "And I'm afraid that you'll have to serve it. Remember? After all, for the next 12 hours, you are my slave."

Raker stared at her. He had forgotten.

"Or are you going to renege?" asked Angela.

"In no way, madame," said Raker, dropping into the role. "In no way. I shall honor my commitment."

"Fine. You may not find it as trying as one might think. Hurry now."

• • •

Serving the dinner consisted of carrying platters from the refrig-erator to the already set table. While the food was not hot, it was superb and wondrously abundant. Guacamole salad, marvelous gazpacho soup, shrimp, crab, and roast meats of every description including chicken, pheasant, beef, *cabrito* and ham. The vegeta-bles were white asparagus and pickled corn, carrots, onions and chiles. There were freshly baked breads, and a huge selection of exotic fruits as well as delicious *empanaditas* for dessert, served with a honey and cream sauce. The beers and wines, all Mexican, were extensive in selection and superb in taste. The meal ended with coffee and native Mexican brandy.

"Shall I clear the table, madame?" asked Raker after the three of them had finished the lusty dinner.

Angela Castillo smiled graciously. "No, *mi esclavo*. We shall only store the food and then we may leave the room. The food will go to feed others. The dishes will be taken care of tomorrow. I have different need of you."

"And that is?"

"Your company. We have much to discuss, you and I."

"And I," submitted Gisella. The girl had enjoyed everything since the interesting man had come to the house.

Angela smiled at the girl. "Of course. And you. If you won't find it boring."

"Oh, never," exclaimed the girl. "Not with you two." Her smile brightened the room.

"Perhaps you can have your prodigy perform for us," suggested Raker.

"Gisel?" The woman looked at Raker.

"You said you had one pupil only, who was a truly promising gymnast."

"So I did," said Angela. "Yes, I did, didn't I." She looked toward the girl. "Yes. Maybe that's a good idea. Maybe we should do that."

"Would you like that?" she asked the girl. "Would you like to perform?"

The girl looked slightly embarrassed. She hesitated. "Well, of course, if you really want me to."

"But we do, my dear," said Raker. "I'd really like that."

"Very well, then. I will be most happy. Angela says that I have much talent. That I show great promise for a successful career."

Angela Castillo nodded. "I did, indeed. And so you have, Gisel', my little one. All right then, you go and get ready. The Colonel and I will be along shortly." The girl bounced from the room.

"One last brandy?" asked the woman.

Raker was relaxed, already having discounted the defeat at the hands of this woman.

"Why not?" His remarkable extrasensory perception detected no danger at all. It should be a pleasant visit. He was truly looking forward to the evening with Angela, and watching her lovely athletic prodigy perform. "I," he said, "will pour. It is only my duty."

Both of them smiled.

Angela led Raker from the dining room, down the wide hall, and up a short stairway whose landing faced a heavy door.

• • •

"In here," said the woman.

"My, how fancy." Raker grinned. "A special viewing area, is it? Do you maintain it for judging students?" He turned the knob and opened the door.

"In a way, Colonel, in a way. Certainly for viewing." There was the threat of a sardonic smile in her voice.

They stepped inside and she switched on lights. The room was larger than Raker had anticipated, and comfortably furnished with upholstered chairs, a chaise lounge, and bed. He turned to look at Angela with surprise.

"This is not exactly what I had in mind," he said. "Not that there is anything wrong with it."

Angela smiled. "Oh, no, Colonel. There is most certainly not anything wrong with it. And it's perfect for our little performer." Her smile had grown much wider.

A trace of understanding began to light Raker's features. "Then Gisel isn't . . .?"

Angela shook her head. "No. She isn't. Not my promising gymnast. A prodigy, yes. She's my budding little star for motion picture ventures. And most lovely, don't you think?"

Raker nodded. "At the least." He studied the woman's face. "And your movies are—?"

It was Angela's turn to nod. "Quite right, *mi Colonel*. They are slightly pornographic. I would say more heavy "R" than "X." And very profitable. I think that whatever wrong there may be in such an endeavor—if there is any—is more than made up for by the good the profits do."

Raker was interested. "And just how does our little lady perform for us? Audience participation?"

"No. Certainly not with me in it," said the woman. "But you'll see. You will, indeed, see." Her hand motioned toward the far wall which was flanked by mirrored walls.

"In the meantime," she said, "please remember that for the next . . ." she paused to glance at her watch, "for the next 10 hours you are still my slave. I must ask you to divest yourself of your clothing. I look forward to watching your reaction."

Raker sighed. What the hell! He had agreed to the terms. And the thought of performing with the young and lovely girl did not exactly turn him off. He began to undress.

"We," continued Angela, her voice coming from behind him, "can watch from back here." Raker turned. The woman was lounging comfortably on a deep-cushioned chair at the back of the room. He was, then, not to be a performer? Once again nude, he carried his clothing back to where the woman sat.

"You'll find space to hang them in that closet," she said. "It won't be more than a few moments. Little Gisel likes to look her best, so she's been prettying up."

Raker found the closet and hung up his clothes.

"As for me," said Angela, although Raker was once again thinking of her as The Menace, but not without affection, "I think I just might join you. You look most comfortable." She lifted a hand as though in warming and shook a hand at Raker. "But you are not to touch. Is that understood?"

Raker shook his head, not as a negative, but in quiet despair. "You ask an incredible thing," he complained.

"But you are my slave," said the woman, "and you must do as I say." The smile was again wicked. Raker gave another sigh. It was better than weeping.

As Angela started to remove her clothing—slowly, ever so slowly—the door opened and the lovely Gisella entered. She was clad in a nearly transparent and obviously expensive negligee which covered an equally transparent and expensive but quite abbreviated night gown. One could almost, but not quite, see all of her body through the flimsy material. She smiled at both members of her audience and moved toward the bed.

She stopped. "Would you mind?" Her words were addressed to Angela. "I forgot the lights. I'd like the nice soft ones, I think."

"Surely, my dear. No spotlights. We'll just pretend this is a rehearsal."

"It is," said Gisella, "it is, and one I shall enjoy." Her eyes lingered on Raker.

Angela, now as naked as Raker, sat on the chair next to him. Raker, in spite of his eyes being fastened upon the lovely young girl, was acutely aware of his friend's presence. There was that wonderful scent of the woman again. Sunshine and fresh air. And warmth. Oh, yes—warmth. The two of them settled back to watch.

• • •

Gisella, standing near the bed, bent her head, eyes closed, then slowly looked up. She looked somehow different. She lifted her arms and slid them up the sides of her neck and back behind her head to lift her shining hair, drawing fingers through it.

The show had begun.

Her role was, apparently, that of a girl at home, bored, alone and feeling lonely. As Raker and Angela watched, they saw her become aware of herself. Her hands began to move across her own body as if she was discovering it for the first time. Her negligee went. She stood before one of the mirrors, admiring, then touching, testing the feel of herself. Her hands became bolder.

The tiny nightgown lifted and moved as hands slipped inside and under it, giving only glimpses of what it covered. Then the hands became more insistent as the girl's eyes seemed to glaze. Almost in a trance she slipped smoothly to the bed and sat, head lifted, hands undoing the tied front, then letting the gown slip from her shoulders. The hands slid up from her waist, cupping her delicately curved breasts. Fingertips began to gently pluck and explore. Slowly, the girl stretched flat, legs coming up sensuously to spread wide on the bed.

If her platinum-colored hair was bleached, thought Raker, she bathed in the stuff. Up to this moment, the show had been at least attention-getting to the watchers. But that had been nothing compared to how the beautiful creature began truly to caress herself, slowly, tantalizingly, and lovingly.

And, thought Raker, amazed at his reaction, with magnificent skill. It seemed a certainty she was no longer aware that there was anyone watching, and even if there was, it didn't matter. It was self-adoration and the search for perfect satisfaction that the girl practiced, and she knew every move, every nuance of the techniques her body craved. When it seemed that she had reached an end, time after time, it was only to see her body quiver and jerk with deeper and fuller convulsions, as her face proclaimed her ecstasy.

Raker was entranced. He would not have believed that voyeurism could have such a tremendous impact on his libido. Beside him, he could hear the shallow breathing of his partner, competitor and friend, Angela.

"Are you sure about the no touching?" he whispered.

"Quite sure," she whispered back. Raker sensed, more than saw, her body rising. It didn't matter, for his eyes were fastened on the girl's writhing body, and talented hands and fingers. He realized that he, even he, Raker, was learning things.

"Colonel?" The voice was Angela's. It was soft, throaty, breathy.

"Yes?" Maybe she had changed her mind. God, how he hoped so.

"Up, *amigo*. Onto your knees. Lean on that love seat."

Raker was startled. He looked around.

Angela stood behind him, hands on hips, tall, with shoulders back, her magnificent breasts pointed at him. Strapped to her hips was an aggressively threatening dildo.

Raker's eyes widened and his jaw dropped. No way, by God! No way in the world! He shook his head.

Angela leaned forward. "Your word, remember?"

Raker groaned. He felt himself responding. La Amenaza could undoubtedly, he thought, harden whipped cream. He started to roll his body over, lifting himself. Her arm slid across his chest to hold him fast, back against the bed. One of her strong legs swung across him and she rose to straddle the man.

"My turn," she said.

• • •

The woman—now simply Angela—lay with her head on Raker's broad shoulder, his arm around her.

"*Mi Colonel?*" Her voice was soft.

"Yes?"

"It is not yet twelve hours. Still, you are released. You are no longer my slave."

Raker smiled to himself. Except for one incident, it had been a great adventure. "Thank you, my large angel." Yes, he was most certainly "released."

"And Colonel?"

"Yes?"

"The contest. You did not lose."

"No?"

"No. It was a cheat. Gisella was instructed which ampoule to tie to my throat. It was unbreakable."

"I know," said Raker.

He had known it within a moment following their contest. It had not mattered.

"And Colonel?"

"Yes?" he said.

"I will delight in performing your task for you! The money will go to my people."

"Will the killing give you trouble?"

The woman laughed. "Not at all. The man is at my beck and call, though I never call. I shall, though, on the date you set. We will journey to the Pyramid of the Sun."

It was the towering structure at Teotihuacan.

"There? It's close to your *hacienda*—but why there?"

Her laugh was from pleasure within herself. "It would be a nice place to make love. High up on a monument of my Aztec ancestors. That is what I will say. It is not what I will do."

Raker was silent.

"The sun, do you not see? The beast let the sun and thirst kill his victims. The Pyramid of the Sun will be the death of him. I will throw him down from the top." She chuckled. "After all, did not my ancestors call the grand avenue below 'The Way of the Dead'?"

Angela Esperanza Castillo Diaz drove Raker to the airport. Neither of them believed in farewells. The parting was swift.

Raker was headed for Ireland, with only a preliminary stop at one island in the Caribbean. He would speak briefly with one Toussaint Salanet.

CHAPTER 10

CONNEMARA, IRELAND

His first meeting with Pagan Maguire, the sister of one of his former mercenaries—now deceased—had been accomplished with only a minimum of difficulty. Primarily, a difficulty with the telephone system in Dublin.

Now, as he and Pagan drove northwest from that city, his meeting was scheduled with the man who represented the only reason he had made contact with the young woman at all. Although the meeting place was completely across the waist of the Republic of Ireland, the distance was not great. As Raker—Coleman to Pagan—steered the rented Ford Escort with precision and care across the gently rolling countryside of the Irish midlands, she spoke.

"You must drive a good bit in Ireland, or at least England," offered Pagan Maguire, the car's only other occupant.

"Knowing the left, you mean?"

"Yes."

"I enjoy driving in Ireland," said Raker. It was true. He thoroughly enjoyed the country. Ireland had a particular beauty for him which he had found in no other place. Certainly it lacked the grandeur of the soaring Alps, or the magnificent starkness of the desert; its few decent beaches were easily excelled by most any other oceanside country, and while reforestation was underway, its woodlands had been nearly eradicated centuries ago by their British overlords.

Still, the charm of Ireland was undeniable. Stark but green, rough and wild yet gently shaggy. One could drive for miles, never knowing what lay behind the tall stone walls or hedgerows bordering so many of the smaller roads. Like the Irish themselves, thought Raker . . . enigmatic and unpredictable. For those not knowing of the troubled history of Ireland, it would be difficult to conceive of the intensity of the people if one looked no deeper than the surface helpfulness and charm so often encountered.

It took little work, however, to uncover the facts behind the facade. G.K. Chesterton had recognized them when he wrote some lines about the Irish. With what Raker considered pretty good insight, Chesterton poeticized something about how 'heavenly folk' had gifted Irish *Gaels* with the great fun of battle and the great tears of songs. Something like that. Anyway, other writers have opined that most Irishers are born laughing, but they then write and play some pretty sad music . . . and that the world was probably wacky!

Perhaps, reflected Raker, it wasn't any God that had made the Irish mad. Perhaps it was the 800-plus-year occupation of their island by the British. But that was of little more than passing interest to Raker. What did concern him was the willingness of Chesterton's great Gaels to fight for whatever cause they adopted. Manipulated correctly, it could be used with deadly effectiveness.

Raker remembered the observation of an instructor in military history, a man he had greatly admired. While giving a short course on guerilla warfare, the instructor had covered the tactics used by the Irish in combating the overwhelming military might of English forces who had conducted their ferocious campaign of slaughter with devastating consequences. Said the instructor: it was no wonder Ireland was so green; blood makes a wonderful fertilizer.

Raker, with Pagan Maguire, had left Dublin early in the morning, taking the road northwest to Mullingar where they turned southwest to cross the Shannon at Athlone. From there he had chosen a route that followed the maze of small country roads which continued to lead them west. The lanes, almost empty of traffic, made it nearly impossible for them to be followed by car without Raker's knowledge. Occasionally, he would stop the car and turn off the motor to listen while he scanned the skies for signs of an airplane or helicopter. Bypassing Galway, they reached Kinvarra, and Raker was reasonably certain that they had not been followed. He drove slowly through the magnificently desolate Burren area, down to Lisdoonvarna, and then chose a narrow road to the coast.

The lane was the only road to a tiny village which Irish maps and the postal service insist doesn't exist.

Several whitewashed cottages lined the right side of the road, each connected to its neighbor. On the front of the first home could be seen the painting of an Irish harp. It was the hamlet's only decoration. The houses, except for one which boasted a gray slate roof, were topped with thatch from which sprouted green tufts. In the distance could be seen the mist-shrouded, mauve outlines of the Atlantic-pounded Aran Islands. From the small hamlet the islands were nearly in line with each other and appeared as one mass of land in the blue-gray water between North and South Sounds.

"At the pub," directed Pagan Maguire, indicating the location with her hand. "There is a certain amount of trust here, Mr. Coleman." Her eyebrows knitted into a slight frown. "Not that it will do you any good to know of this site. The people here know nothing of illegal activities. But they do know who are strangers. And the word of such strangers' arrival does spread rapidly in all such villages."

"Of course," agreed Raker. "Ireland is a nation of watchers." And like hell they don't know what's going on, he thought. "Do they know you?"

Pagan paused with her hand on the door latch of the car. "I've been here before," she replied.

Inside the pub, Raker found it to be much like many of the other small, Irish country places he had visited. The part of the bar nearest the door served more as a counter for the sale of merchandise than a drinking area. As Raker and the girl entered, a woman behind the counter was busy selling one egg—"new laid," she assured her customer—and a quarter of an oversized loaf of bread.

Toward the rear, the counter turned an L to the right, and around the turn sat three men with a stone fireplace at their back and pint glasses of stout before them on the bar top. One wore knee-high rubber boots and a rain slicker. His head was bare. The two other men were dressed in worn dark suits; shirts open at the throat. Irish tweed caps slanted across their heads. The man in the middle glanced up at the newcomers, nodded his head to the side toward a separate room whose entryway was barely visible to their view, and turned his attention to the glass in front of him. Nearly everything in the bar looked comfortably worn and used. Even the anachronistic vinyl and chrome of the barstools and the Formica bar top.

Raker followed Pagan to the back and turned into the side room. A man sat alone at one of three tables. He had chosen the location furtherest from the door.

"*Dia dhuit, a Phadraid,*" said Pagan.

"*Dia a's Muire dhaoibh,*" replied the man, his words including Raker in the greeting. "*Tar isteach. Cad e mar ta tu?*"

"*Ta me go maith, buiochas do Dhia.*" She moved a hand toward Raker.

"This is the man."

"Is it now? I thought you'd brought someone else."

"Kevin's a comic," apologized Pagan, "or so he thinks." She turned to the man. "You're rude."

The man stood. "So I am. Please," he motioned to the chairs at the table, "have a seat, Pagan, Mr. . . . Coleman?" The girl's name had come out as Pegeen.

"Coleman," reaffirmed Raker, seating himself.

"And a famous name it is, being one of our great saints. I welcome you." He extended his hand. Raker took it.

"The girl here tells me you have an interesting scheme to propose."

"I have."

• • •

The man studied Raker at length. "I'm Kevin Brennan. I can say yes or no to your proposal."

"I thought she greeted you as Patrick?"

The man showed surprise. "You have the Irish?"

"Only a few words. Your accent is Ulster."

"Donegal." He looked at Raker with interest. "The name is Patrick Kevin Brennan. For true, I use the Kevin to honor another martyred Irishman." He turned to Pagan. "Would you be bringing us a couple of jars, darlin'?"

As Pagan left the room he addressed Raker again. "We have no fear of interruption here, Mr. Coleman? I regret having to take all these precautions."

"I approve of precautions."

"Would you be Catholic now, Coleman?"

"Does it matter?"

"In some cases." A wry grin twisted Brennan's square-jawed, old-young features. "But many times, no."

He waited as Pagan returned with three foaming glasses. He drank, then continued. "Many are the names familiar as martyrs for Ireland who were Protestant. And while there is convenience of identification in labels, the British press, along with religious fanatics, has made more of it than it should be. The only true religious freedom on this entire island is that here in the south.

"They try to say they fear unification because of religious persecution. But they really don't want to pursue the subject. I suspect it was an embarrassment when their own Prince Charlie got married and had it bandied about that it was forbidden for him, and by English law, mind you, to marry a Roman Catholic. Not just out of his own religion, now. He could have married a Moslem, a Jew, a Hindu . . . whatever. Anything but a Catholic. And don't be forgetting that there's no separation of church and state in Britain. It is, by God, The Church of England, and its head is the monarch.

"Yes, Coleman, if there's a religious war, then it was started by the Brits themselves. The Republic here has no state religion." He flipped a hand as though waving off a small annoyance. "Oh, sure now, there was at one time a constitutional provision which gave, as the old ones liked to call it, 'special position' to the Catholic church, but that was most wisely repealed in 1972. And repealed, Coleman, by a majority of the 90% Catholic population of the Republic. That, while the invader is trying to paint us as bigots, and accuse us of waging a religious war. I haven't noticed them doing anything to mend their misguided ways.

"But then they've not been known for their charity, now have they? As a matter of fact, I believe it was their own Queen who, publicly, and to an American mayor of Irish extraction I think it was, referred to the Irish people as pigs."

He smiled contemptuously. "Yes, Mr. Coleman. You'd be wise to know how religion is being used in an effort to avoid the more accurate terms."

"And those are?" asked Raker.

"Nationalist and Invader," said Brennan. He lifted his glass to take a long drink. Wiping the foam from his clean-shaved chin, he grinned. "And that's from a position of bias and resentment, it is. The terms are Nationalist and Unionist. It's those who want Ireland whole again, and those who want the thieves to keep their stolen part."

"I didn't come here for a lecture on Ireland," said Raker.

"But you've had one now, haven't you? No worries, you'll not be getting many. But before you present any proposition to himself," he jabbed a thumb against his own chest, "you'd best be knowing what the circumstances are."

Raker nodded. "All right."

Brennan leaned forward, elbows on the table, and stared fixedly at Raker.

"There was a time, Mr. Coleman, when these precautions we've taken today weren't necessary down here in the Republic. Now they are. Every stranger, even some who aren't strangers, could well be the enemy. Deadly ears are everywhere. Our own Republic's jails are full of patriots who only want to see a whole, unamputated Ireland once again." He leaned back slightly in his chair. "We're being sold out by some of our own. We need all the help we can muster, and we'll take it from whoever can give it to us."

Raker nodded his understanding.

"Pick up a paper, Mr. Coleman, anywhere out of Ireland. How often do you read of the atrocities of the other side? How many even know of all the groups—have even heard the initials? The UDR? Possibly, for it's supposed to be a legal group. The UDL? The UDA? The UVF? Too few people know of those, Mr. Coleman, and their dirty work. And any comment I make would be from a highly biased point of view, you might be saying. But all those usurpers who adopt Ulster into their name are as sure terrorists as any other of the ones you read about across the world.

"Ulster indeed! They take the name of their stolen province and try to make it their own. They're made quasi-legal like that black-hearted Ulster Defense Regiment, armed with the approval of the invaders, and allowed to wreak their havoc as they see fit and with only token wrist slapping. Dark of night shootings and bombs in pubs, is it? Sure, now, and it is. But it's both sides, Mr. Coleman, both sides. And it should be neither, it shouldn't." Brennan's voice was not loud. His anger was cold and controlled. "It's the enemy we're after. The British. The terrorists who hide behind a hedge of innocence. But as long as the British press controls the media, we'll never be recognized as soldiers fighting the invader."

Raker seemed about to speak and Brennan raised a hand.

"That's the recognition we want. That's not how it is, of course, but we'll keep trying to make it that way." He raised eyes to meet Raker's. "Did you know that there is not a single, major news service or television network from America that permanently stations a newsman over here? Those who cover the troubles are sent from England, at English expense, with English guides, to cover those occasions. Did you know that, Mr. Coleman? Now just how much 'truth' do you think such so-called journalists learn?"

"I can't do anything about that," said Raker mildly.

Brennan stared at Raker for a moment before replying. "No," he said, "of course you can't." He straightened his chair. "And that's not why you're here, is it now?" He inclined his head toward Pagan. "The girl tells me you can offer us the bodies of a pair of assassins, and worse. Do you mean alive or dead?"

It was Raker's turn to lean back in his chair. He spoke from over arms folded across his chest. "Either way you want them."

"You interest me, Mr. Coleman, you do that. You interest me greatly. We don't know that your story of the killing of the Maguire lad is true nor untrue. We have no reason to disbelieve it. The Gordon twins have done in others, and in disgusting ways. We would have had them by now, but they seem to hide rather well."

"Not from me."

"We want them."

"Alive or dead?"

Brennan paused to glance at Pagan. "I don't want the girl in on this."

"And I'm not wanting in on it," she said. "I'll be in the other room." She rose gracefully, paused to acknowledge the men with her eyes, and left the room.

"You please me, Brennan. I want the girl totally innocent in this affair. She'll be only a messenger. No more."

"And quite right, too," agreed Brennan. "You asked 'dead or alive.' Either way, Mr. Coleman, as you said. But you could save us trouble and, if I might be saying it, show your good faith by doing the job. We would, of course, want to be assured that you had . . . delivered the goods, as it were." His lips smiled but his eyes did not.

"You'll have someone around who can . . . reassure you? Even if the event occurs in say, Canada or America?"

The smile reached Brennan's eyes. "Just let us know. We'll be having someone around."

Raker nodded. "All right, you've got it. Now, Brennan, let's knock off this sparring shit. I have things you want, need. And I can deliver. You have services that I want. Let's work on it."

"To the point, and rightly so," said Brennan, all business now. "What is it you'll be wanting of us?"

"Possibly the killing of a couple of your enemies, and definitely destruction of a little of their property." The words came calmly, with no emotion.

"The thought is not disturbing," said Brennan. "And what do we get in return, in addition to relief from those demon Gordon twins?"

"Money. Immediately."

Brennan nodded.

"Also arms and ammunition, delivered to wherever you say."

Surprise showed. "You can do that?"

"I can do that," said Raker simply. "The money in your hands or any bank you specify. The delivery of an assortment of LAWS and TOW rocket launchers, with rockets; grenade launchers with grenades; and an assortment of automatic weapons including the highly concealable Ingram MAC 11. Are you familiar with it?"

"By hearsay only. I know the MAC 10."

"Improved model, larger caliber," said Raker. "Rapid fire, silenced, and extremely effective for close range hit and run."

Brennan's eyes looked greedy. "And you can deliver to the north?" There was disbelief in his tone. "The border is becoming more near impossible, day by day."

"That depends on how, and to whom you ship."

Brennan was composed. His eyes shown with anticipation. "Upon receipt, then, we'll agree to perform your requests. Within reason. You did say, didn't you, that our actions would be against our enemies and their property?"

"I did."

"Then it will be done. And afterwards? You can supply more of our needs?"

"Can and will. Can I be certain you will deliver?"

"Have you ever known an Irishman to lie?"

"Often."

Brennan grinned broadly. "That's true, isn't it, now? Among the world's greatest, I'll be admitting. But you can take my hand on it as the absolute truth."

Raker surveyed the man and his extended hand. He took it. They shook.

"Yes," said Raker, "I'm certain of that." He returned Brennan's smile. "Now, another pint of stout and let's get down to the details."

Brennan hesitated. "Would you object if, instead, we had a little stroll?"

"Is the outside secure?" Raker matched question with question. Brennan's slight smile hid secret knowledge.

"It is that, Mr. Coleman, it is that. We can even leave through the front, right enough."

A strange place, thought Raker as they walked, to be plotting death and destruction. The men had emerged into the soft, silvery light and were strolling along the narrow road which bordered a small creek. To their left cattle grazed lazily on the slopes of shaggy grass. As they approached the ocean on their right, Brennan spoke.

"It's Europe's window ledge, Mr. Coleman." He motioned past the rolling hills to the south. "Down below, only a few miles away from here tower the Cliffs of Mohr, 700 feet high, rising sheer from the lovely waters, and with nothing between them and America but the ocean."

"I know," said Raker. "And it's lovely they are, the cliffs."

Brennan eyed him suspiciously. "Is it making fun of the brogue you are?" he asked softly.

Raker grinned. "Hardly." He was remembering the phrasing of his last sentence. "It's just that the lovely, lilting way you Irish speakers sing the English language. It's infectious. It's downright catching."

Brennan nodded as he took a pipe from his pocket and began to fill it with dark tobacco. "You have the blarney, Coleman, but it's right you are. It's one of the few things the invaders left us that we've improved upon." He stoked the pipe into flame. "But enough. I'd like to know more about the weapons you mentioned."

"Top grade," said Raker, "as I told you."

"Is there a chance that you'd be having access to some specialty equipment I'm having in mind?"

"And what would that be?"

"Sniper rifles. With light amplification telescopes. Or infrared devices."

Raker considered the question. Such equipment would be frighteningly effective in the towns of Northern Ireland. Patrols would be terrorized to find that they could be effectively attacked in the dark.

"Well?"

Raker hesitated.

"Is it a promise you're wanting that they'll not be used against anyone but the Brit patrols? No war on innocent civilians and all that blather?"

Raker stopped walking. "Brennan," he said, "I don't give a rat's ass what you do with your weapons. As long as you don't interfere in my plans, and as long as you deliver what you agree to." He resumed walking. "I was considering if I'll be able to obtain what you want."

"And?"

"I can. You'll want the equipment for use in the cities?"

"Primarily," Brennan answered.

"Then I think it's the starlight scope you'll get the most value from. At least in the cities where there is more available light."

Brennan nodded agreement.

"All right," said Raker, coming to a decision. "Twenty sniper rifles, complete with starlight scopes. But there's a price."

"And there always is."

"Do you have any men who are experienced scuba divers?"

"Underwater breathers," mused Brennan. "Some. Not grand at it, but some experience."

"That'll do. I'll supply the training to make them expert. I'll want your best men."

"That's all I'd offer."

"And they should have knowledge of explosives."

Brennan's expression became incredulous. "Mr. Coleman, sir. All my men are knowledgeable with explosives. Why, haven't you heard? We're simply grand at blowing up infants in their baby carriages and all that sort of misinformation disseminated by the Brits." He snorted. "We war on the enemy, Coleman: The British—who have no legitimate business on my island—and their transplanted lackeys who bear arms against us."

"Spare me the lectures, Brennan. I just want to borrow six brave men who know something about free diving and explosives."

"All my men know explosives. You'll have the best combination. But I must be knowing for what purpose."

"First, so they can recover the weapons I'll have dumped into over 100 feet of water. I'll get them that far." He could get them closer, and on land, but why tell? "You'll have to get them from there."

Brennan glanced skeptically at Raker. "And how in the devil's name will we ever find them?"

"Underwater signals. I'll supply the equipment and specified coordinates." And it would be good training for their real mission.

"All right. But there's more, now, isn't there?"

"There is. They'll need the experience so they can effectively destroy a good portion of the British oil terminal in the Shetlands."

Brennan stopped as if suddenly frozen. Slowly, a smile spread across his hard face. "Well, now, Mr. Coleman. We seem to have found a happy, mutual interest. The oil terminal, you say. What a lovely thought! What a grand, lovely thought. It won't do their economy a bit of good, now will it? Losing all that valuable oil and all?" The grin grew as wide as his face would allow.

"No," agreed Raker. "It certainly won't help their gross national product."

As they strolled near the water, Brennan's mood darkened, reflected by his expression. "Six men, you say. Not enough. That terminal is heavily guarded."

"And I know just how it's guarded," said Raker. He looked knowingly at Brennan. "And then, there are over 800 Irish working in the area, aren't there? Don't tell me that some of them aren't yours."

A slight smile brushed Brennan's lips. "Perhaps one or two, now that you mention it. Perhaps one or two."

"We'll supply the demolition devices, the necessary equipment, and teach the skills required."

Brennan nodded.

"We'll supply the schedule and detailed plan. You decide who'll handle it."

Brennan considered Raker's words. "It'll work," he said. "By the Holy Family, it'll work." He stopped to relight his pipe. Raker waited. "And how long will it take to prepare?"

"Soon enough," said Raker. He looked at Brennan's pipe. "You don't seem like a pipe smoker to me, Brennan. I think of pipe smokers as being slow minded. Not unintelligent, mind you. Just slow and overly thorough."

Brennan's expression mirrored a child with his hand caught in a forbidden jellybean jar. "Noticed that, did you?" He stuffed the pipe into his pocket. It had already gone out. "I'm a cigarette smoker. And many of them."

"I know," said Raker. At Brennan's quizzical expression, Raker pointed a finger at the man's hand. The thumb and first two fingers were stained a deep, yellow-brown.

"Yes," said Brennan, "I see. But the pipe does allow time to think things over without seeming to stall."

"Perhaps over here," suggested Raker.

"And just what does that mean?"

"Among American politicians and so-called scholars, it has been overused to the point where only the truly dim-witted and the immature think it fools anyone. Not," he added, "that there aren't those who truly enjoy smoking a pipe. But they keep them lit."

"I see," laughed Brennan. "But then, we're not over there, now, are we?"

"No," agreed Raker, "truly we're not."

Brennan pulled a box of Sweet Afton cigarettes from his shirt pocket and lit one. The two men continued their walk near the water. Raker was aware that they were under constant surveillance. From time to time a motionless watcher could be seen in the distance.

"You're quite right, Mr. Coleman," said Brennan, seeming to read Raker's mind. "They're all about us. They are ours." He drew deeply on his cigarette. The smoke seemed never to come back from his lungs. "Tell me more about those sniper rifles you mentioned. And that—starlight scope?"

Raker considered the question carefully. "All right. I'll give you what I know as if you are not familiar with the weapon or the scope."

"That'll do just fine." Brennan paused near a large, flat, striated rock embedded in the earth near the ocean's edge. "Let's rest a bit while I listen."

"The rifle will be a specially altered one used by the United States Marine Corps," started Raker. "It is a Remington, actually a quite modified M-14 converted to bolt action. Uses .308 caliber ammunition which compares to the NATO 7.62mm. It has a milled bolt and a changed barrel. One with tightened rifling which spins the round faster. The conversion from automatic allows far less of the charge to escape, thus giving a higher muzzle velocity to the rounds fired. The weapon, in normal daylight use, has an effective sniper range of as much as 1,000 yards or more in the hands of an expert shot. Even a moderately good shot can achieve excellent results at lesser distances. At night, with the starlight scope, the range is drastically reduced. The limitation of the scope, of course. It depends on available light. But given a bit of moonlight, say 50 yards in open country, up to 100 yards in the city."

Brennan nodded in pleasure. "More light in the city, certainly."

"The starlight scope itself is a unit capable of great light-intensification. It utilizes phosphorescent rare earth, electrically charged, which enables the sniper to see the target as a ghostly green, but identifiable, figure. The more light, the better the image. The major disadvantage of the unit is that it requires special battery packs for its operation. It is not suitable for prolonged use." He glanced across at Brennan. "But then I should imagine you'll want it for only brief periods at any one time."

"Indeed. Our boyos do have to keep on the move."

"I should imagine," said Raker dryly. "And that's it. For your purposes it should be nearly perfect. And probably more suitable than the infrared system."

"I'll trust your judgment," said Brennan. "And when can we have these . . . miracle weapons?"

Raker thought. "The first ones I mentioned, those will be delivered immediately. I'll tell you where, how, and when. The night systems, well, they'll be delivered in the water, in watertight containers, the same as the others, and just as soon as the placement of my devices is completed at the oil terminal in the Shetlands."

Brennan nodded. "I think you said something about 20 of those starlight systems?"

"I did."

Brennan showed pleasure. "With those, we'll be able to introduce an entirely new dance step to the Ulster *ceili*."

"No doubt about it," agreed Raker. It was none of his concern. Only the oil terminal, insured in appreciable part by PanGlobal, was of interest to him.

"Tell me . . . Coleman?"

"Close enough," said Raker to the knowing Brennan.

"Tell me, what is it you'll be wanting out of this? I see more to our advantage than yours."

Raker surveyed the nearly silent ocean as Brennan smoked, waiting patiently for an answer. One hell of a question, he thought. Too complicated to answer, even if he was so inclined. How to explain the promise he'd made to old Laughlin? How to explain that the only person he loved, his daughter, he had deserted in a nightmare of violence, and that as long as violence was still his business he could never face her? How to explain that he would use violence to enable him to get out of the business of violence? It couldn't be explained, he thought. But when he had succeeded! Then, he would at least have kept his promise to old T.J. Laughlin—fighting the insurance bastards.

He looked across at Brennan whose eyes were focused on the sea. I could tell him, he thought. He might even understand.

Raker shook off the thought. No! There was no way to explain the obsession that had kept him searching, while developing the methods and the plan that would let him achieve his goal. By the time he returned home he would have completed the creation of his strike force. All that would remain would be to set it in motion.

Raker picked up a small stone and tossed it in a high arc out into the ocean. He watched the splash-rings spread in a wide circle across the gently surging water. A feeling of self-satisfaction settled upon him. Not just anyone could pull off his plan. But he could. He, Martin Raker. No! Beverly Martin Raker. *The* Beverly Martin Raker. He gave a short laugh.

"Funny, is it now?" inquired Brennan.

"No," said Raker. "Not funny at all. It's just that I can't answer that last question. Not at all."

"Can't or won't?"

"Can't. Oh, part of it is simple. I'm in it for personal gain, of course. It's the *why* that I find troublesome."

Brennan grunted. "Don't feel bad, me boyo. Don't feel bad at that."

He was years younger than Raker. "At times I can't tell you the why me own self," he finished sadly.

Raker looked at the man with understanding. Perhaps they were alike, this Irish terrorist and himself. Maybe he isn't a terrorist at all. Perhaps just a patriot lost in time. Maybe history would judge the Brennans of present day Ireland as it had done the rebellious Minutemen of New England in their battle against the same enemy—the British. It was not for him to decide.

Brennan cleared his throat and spat toward the sea. "You said something about wanting us to . . ." he paused as if trying to remember. "It was about us killing a couple of our enemies." He looked at Raker with narrowed eyes. "Did you mean your enemies or my enemies?"

Raker answered without hesitation. "Your enemies, my targets; though some of your enemies may well be mine."

"You know we make no moves against targets over in your land, don't you?"

"So I've been told." Raker's tone was doubtful.

"It's so, it is."

"Without exception?"

Brennan hesitated. "Almost without exception, not counting informers. Would have to be a most unusual case."

"No matter," said Raker. "The targets will not be on the North American continent. Furthermore, it quite probably won't even be required." To Raker's mind, the lie was forgivable.

Brennan showed approval. "Speaking of that, you told the girl you are Canadian. You're not."

"I'm not?" Raker feigned surprise.

"Not a bit of it," said Brennan. "American."

"What makes you think so?" It didn't matter. He hadn't tried to fool Brennan.

"I know so, never mind how," smiled Brennan.

"Does it matter?"

"Does not. As long as we'll not be asked by you to act over there."

"And that, I'll not be doing," said Raker, a lilt to his words.

"And there you go, mocking me brogue again," said Brennan.

"Sure, and not a bit of it, now," answered Raker. Both men grinned. "You're all right, Coleman. All right." Brennan rose from their rocky bench and brushed at his damp seat. "I'll swear the eternal water seeps up through the very stone," he said. "Let's be heading back to the pub for a last jar. The little cailin will be wondering where in the world we got off to."

As the men approached the pub they could see Pagan waiting outside the door. As they neared, she ducked inside the building, reappearing just as they reached the doorway. She was smiling. In her hands were two glasses nearly full of clear liquid.

"*Tar isteach*," she said, pretending severity, "*agus suigh sios ag an tine agus dean do seith. Ta se iontach fuar inniu.*" The Gaelic was too much for Raker to follow, but Brennan grinned broadly.

"*Go raibh maith agat*," he said. "*Leoga, nil se te inniu ceart go leor, ach nil se fliuch ach oiread.*"

The girl extended the glasses. "*Seo braon beag uisce beathadh. 01 siar e.*" She lifted a hand, indicating the men were to drink. They did.

"The real thing, Coleman. Good poteen. Illegal, it tastes better."

"And has authority," replied Raker.

"Did you get all that now?" asked Brennan, grinning.

"Not a word except about the whiskey." He wiped his mouth. "That is an impossible language—to read or understand."

"Not at all. She simply invited us in to sit at the fire. Says 'tis cold today. I allow as it may not be warm, but 'tis not wet. The girl says to drink the drop of whiskey. Simple."

Raker shook his head glumly. "Easy for you, difficult for me."

Pagan laughed, delightedly. "I know that. Señor Wences," she said.

"You're too young to remember television that far back," said Raker.

"I grew up some in the States. Reruns," she said, "I remember well." Her father had been assigned to an embassy.

"Amazing girl," said Raker, addressing Brennan who seemed relaxed.

"She's all of that, indeed," agreed Brennan. He walked toward the bar.

"Two more, Joseph, me boyo," he said to the man behind the counter.

"Are you gentlemen through with your planning and all?" asked Pagan.

"Not quite. Almost. Only a few details to iron out."

Pagan smiled brightly. "Then while you move back to your dark, secret room, I'll just stay up here and listen to Micho play the whistle." She nodded toward the back, beside the fireplace, where a large man was seated on a small stool.

Sweater-clad, face ruddy beneath a cap cocked sideways on his head, the simple tin whistle he played seemed to be a concert instrument in his huge hands. Raker listened as he watched one of the man's feet tap perfect time with the brisk tempo of the music.

The Irish, he thought. The damned, unfathomable Irish. On the surface, good humor—at times rowdy—and occasional quick anger. Inside, bottomless depth.

CHAPTER 11

The Aer Lingus 727C completed its turn over the green checker-board of eastern Ireland and crossed the muddy tidelands of the coastline on the Irish Sea. Raker smiled to himself as the thought struck him that the airplane had departed on time. It was the first thing that had happened on time since he had been in Ireland. After a while, one learned to roll with the punches, and even enjoy the idea that perhaps perfect punctuality was not always an imperative in the ordinary course of events. The important thing was that, when it mattered, you could count on the Irish being at hand.

Still, it would seem that they could give better directions than "down the road a piece, and over the brow of the hill." Raker grinned. A sure way to enjoy a show was to ask a group, of even two or three, how to get somewhere. You could sneak off quietly, and be long gone while the conversation and controversy continued to rage.

Raker was satisfied with his Irish connection. Brennan would deliver, of that he had no doubt. With Raker's help he could do more to harass the invaders, as he had called them, far more effectively than in the past—even with the disliked-but-accepted Libyan arms they had been forced to take. And the Maguire girl would make a perfect go-between. He frowned. He liked the girl, and hoped it would not be necessary to sacrifice her. He shrugged away the thought. Tough! If it happened, it happened. Still, the possibility was troublesome enough for Raker to try to refocus his thoughts. He stared down at the tops of clouds and cleared his mind of the present.

The passenger next to him tried to start a conversation. Raker silenced him quickly with a fierce scowl. It was an expression Raker had developed for just such occasions.

Now, he thought, eyes closed in concentration: Where do I stand?

Angela—La Amenaza—of course. Toussaint Salanet, the imperturbable Haitian, had been eager. He, as the others, had all proven themselves. Largo and Sizemore were set and waiting. They were as dependable as he could ask and, like the others, disassociated from his present life.

LeBlanc, the impossible cajun. Shrimp boat operator, expert seaman and aviator, and pathologically brave. He, too, was only waiting. DelSarto, the Italian, he would soon be seeing. And Grunewald, the good, Teutonic Don Quixote. Wolfgang would take on anything if a cause could be made of it. Fragonard? The fearless old man would be more than willing, thought Raker. But a shadow of a doubt crossed his mind as he considered the Frenchman. It would be up to him to take out a female. That would run against the grain of the old man's chivalry. Still, he and Raker had been through more together than most of the others. No—Fragonard could be counted on. Raker brushed the doubt aside. And then there was Cheney.

Raker smiled, eyes still closed. The damned, treacherous, volatile, conniving, and ever dangerous Cheney. What a role player! The most nefarious, insincere scoundrel he had ever met, but as dependable as a Swiss railroad schedule where Raker was concerned. Raker knew the man had been born within the sound of Bow bells, the criterion upon which the East End natives of London base their claim of being true cockneys. Somehow, however, Raker could not conceive of Phillip Cheney, or whatever his true name, ever speaking like a cockney. No more than he could imagine LeBlanc speaking without his cajun accent.

Phillip Cheney, the man Raker trusted nearly as much as Fragonard. A man who had proven that his loyalties lay only with Raker. It would be Cheney, and Cheney alone, who would know most—oh, not all, not by a long shot—but most of Raker's plan. Cheney would join in with great delight. And Cheney could put him in touch with the Gordon twins. Then Raker could deliver them dead, as agreed, to Brennan or his men. But only after they had served their bloody purpose.

Raker tensed as he thought of the pair. His grin tightened evilly.

Someone should have done something about them before. He did not mind the thought at all. But only after they had been recruited, and had played their double-duty role in his drama. In the meantime, he'd make the most of them.

The other girl, the wife of his long-dead-enemy's son? That, unfortunately, had to be. One had to avenge! Maybe that wasn't exactly what old T.J. had said, but it was what he meant. It had to be done, and it would be done.

Raker remembered the day he found the name in the limited and synoptic list of widely scattered PanGlobal clients he had first received, after researching Laughlin's policies. He had demanded from his inside contact that he have names from England, France, Italy, Germany, Mexico, the Caribbean and the United States. They would be necessary in order to show the distance his threat could reach; it would become wider.

And there he had found the hated name: *Bequerel!*

Mr. and Mrs. Henri Etienne. The target would be the wife of Henri Etienne Bequerel! The memories flooded back bringing the sour bite of acid to his mouth. Henri Etienne Bequerel! The son of Edmond Bequerel. The man . . . Raker closed his mind. He thought of a word, then tried to push it from his mind for thirty seconds. He was, of course, still thinking of the word when the flight attendant asked softly, "Would you care for something to drink, sir?"

Raker opened his eyes. He smiled. "You caught me napping. Yes, I would. Do you have Irish?"

"For certain we have, sir," said the woman, smiling her approval through copper hair framing her freckle-sprinkled face. "Be right back."

Rhinoceros, thought Raker. Ridiculous! Now why in the world should I think *rhinoceros?*

Rome

Rome is an ugly city. Congested, stained, and aging, it is littered, illogical, and dirty. Raker had never been certain of any particular moment, or of any period of time when he had become inured to its flaws and came to think of it as beautiful. But he did. He had always appreciated its long and magnificent history, had walked its ancient ways and felt the ghost of its once awesome power, but he didn't know when he came to love the city for what it was today.

Raker stood at the sound-proof double window of his immaculate and very expensive room in the Excelsior, The Hotel of the Via Veneto, considering that—for all its magnificence—he *had* selected it because of the single circumstance that kept it from being perfect: that was the increasing number of loudly obnoxious, brassy, and ugly-tourist types who sought out the quite superior hostelry because of its location and reputation. Because of the negative attention such residents drew, Raker, despite of his air of immense presence, was paid only respectful notice. It was what he desired.

Raker left the hotel, silently respecting the extreme tolerance of its staff as they coped with the trashy but affluent loud-mouths they were attending. He suspected that many of the tongues of the service personnel must bear self-inflicted teeth marks.

On the Via Veneto he turned up the slope and walked toward its far end. On the corner was an elderly man, stooped over as he worked at achieving a diamond gloss on the leather-clad feet of the man sitting in his one-client shoeshine stand. The one client was reading a newspaper. Raker paused at the corner for only a moment, crossed the street, and proceeded at a casual pace. He descended into a long, store-fronted tunnel, and then surfaced into the park bordered by the Viale del Galoppatoia.

He walked slowly, aware that he was being followed, and made a slight detour to stroll toward a small yellow building with a tile roof, nestled among trees and other foliage. The narrow path led him to a row of very public outside urinals which were set against a weathered wall. Their only covering was a rain shield above them. Raker stopped, not out of necessity, but rather amusement, and faced one of the utilitarian porcelain basins. The path just at his back led to the yellow building which was the ladies room. Raker had often wondered if one should tip his hat to those females passing by.

The man who had been following him took his place at one of

the receptacles nearby. It was the man who had been having his shoes shined. Both he and Raker were satisfied that there had been no particular interest in their progress.

"I would have wagered where you would lead me," said Niccolo DelSarto. "Have you decided?"

"To tip or not?" asked Raker.

"But of course." It was a long standing joke between the men.

"Certainly," said Raker. "For myself the decision is easy. I never wear a hat."

DelSarto laughed. "Then perhaps you should salute," he said. DelSarto had needed the stop.

The men turned and retraced their steps. They were in excellent physical condition, and while the distance their walk took them would have taxed the stamina of much younger persons, the subject of their discussion caused them to be unaware of the distance or time involved.

Their travels had taken them up past the Piazza del Popolo, down past the Tomb of Augustus, through the lovely Piazza Navova where DelSarto suggested they stop for food and people-watching. The automobiles were barred, said DelSarto, and the female legs, along with that which they supported, were magnificent!

Raker said he had other plans.

They proceeded past the Pantheon, up to the Piazza Collona, then onto the comparatively broad Via del Corvo. At the corner of Via Della Croce, Raker turned to the right and led DelSarto to where they would eat. Their business had been mostly completed. Successfully.

"I do not believe you, Colonel," said DelSarto. His eyes studied the esoteric decorations of their surroundings. "Do you not realize we are in Rome? In delicious Italia? Why in the world are we to eat here?"

"We are here, my old friend, so that you may awaken that jaded palate of yours and partake of great delicacies. I recommend the Kaiserfleisch." The restaurant was the Wiener Bierhaus.

DelSarto rolled his eyes. "In the land of frascati and saltimbocca, I am at the mercy of a Goth-loving barbarian." He smiled. His friend and former mercenary commander knew him well. He was offering him an excuse to deviate from his strict, self-inflicted, health food diet. DelSarto was a physical fitness addict who loved rich food, never smoked, and supplied smuggled cigarettes to distributors.

This would be a rare treat! He would have not only the Kaiserfleish, but a bratwurst and possibly a wiener schnitzel. All to be accompanied by liters of fine cool, foaming German beer.

Yes, he told Raker, between mouthfuls, he would be most delighted to eliminate the man Ugo Pascoli. Was not he, Niccolo DelSarto, a moralist? And Pascoli an abomination?

Within a certain time period? A specified 24 hours? But certainly! It presented no problem to Niccolo DelSarto. It would only require him to draw more heavily upon some of his many and varied skills.

Raker left Rome, pleased but not surprised. He also considered that he should find some place to take his next guest so they could enjoy Italian food. They would be in Germany.

MUNICH

Munich was as scrubbed and debris-free as Rome was littered. As he walked down the traffic-free streets to Marienplatz, admiring the blaze of spring flowers growing from every available empty area where soil or a container could be placed, Raker refused to compare his feelings about the two cities. Weisswurst and proscuitto, he thought. How do you decide which is better? Just enjoy, and let it go.

He strolled casually down the immaculate mall, past the clock tower of the Nieu Rathaus, turned left, and wandered his way to the Hofbrauhaus.

It was early in the evening, the lower floor was already crowded, and the small band was busily oompah-ing from their slightly-elevated bandstand. Americans are certainly here, somewhere, thought Raker. The band was playing *Yellow Rose of Texas*, with a distinct tuba sounding the beat.

A diminutive, pigeon-bosomed waitress took his order for a liter of *helles*, and when she returned he marveled at how such a small woman could carry so many of the huge steins without a tray. As she approached him, she paused, seemed to take a hitch in her grip, then wove her way through the crowd to serve him and others at the long, heavy table. His stein was still nearly full when Wolfgang Grunewald sat next to him.

"*Guten abend*," said the deeply tanned, youthful appearing man, nodding politely.

Raker returned the nod. "I'm sorry," he said, "I do not speak German. I'm Canadian." In fact, his German was nearly as perfect as Grunewald's.

A smile lighted the square-jawed face of the blond man. "I am so happy, then, that I have the English. Welcome to my tavern."

Raker feigned surprise. "You own this?"

Grunewald laughed. "Of course not. It is just that my family have been drinking here for many years."

Raker frowned. "They must have quite a capacity."

A smile flirted with Wolfgang's mouth. "You misunderstand. I, perhaps, did not phrase it correctly. For some generations, my family has been coming into this beer hall to drink." He thought about his words. "Upon certain occasions, from time to time," he added.

• • •

As the youngest of Raker's mercenaries, with the single exception of Angela Castillo, Grunewald had become used to the jokes about the German lack of a sense of humor. He found it funny.

Born too late to have had any part in the Hitler Youth groups, but from a family who had been involved, Wolfgang Grunewald had developed a deep sense of guilt about his inescapable heritage. Consequently, he had become a self-appointed defender of the oppressed, quickly taking up any cause for a seeming underdog. His devotion and respect toward things Jewish had created distrust in many who did not know him well. Raker knew his feelings were honest.

Accepting his "new" acquaintance's offer to show him part of the city, Raker joined Grunewald to stroll the streets. Grunewald listened while Raker talked. When they parted, Raker had another commitment for the demise of a PanGlobal policy holder. This one, even Raker—who normally kept emotionally removed from his analytical determinations—would be happy to see terminated. His name was Heinz Keppler. He was a successful manufacturer of plastic and paper containers. He had been a guard at one of the Third Reich's death camps, and had been acquitted of any wrong-doing when the only available witnesses who could have definitely identified him, either disappeared under mysterious circumstances, or died in what could have been—*could* have been, mind you—accidents.

It was Keppler's habit to attend the playing of the *glockenspiel* and to watch the figures in the tower of the new city hall each morning near 11:00. Wolfgang Grunewald considered that he would like to kill the man while he was watching the mechanical knights in the tower joust, if that was all right with Raker? It fitted well into Wolfgang's *Weltanshaung*.

It was.

Raker did not, after all, take Grunewald to dine on Italian food. Instead they enjoyed a magnificent meal at the Kafer Schanke.

Paris

Paris never failed to please Raker. He found beauty in all its seasons, even August, when the tradition—if not the actuality—of terrible heat drove multitudes of its inhabitants to the seashore, and many of Paris's best restaurants closed. If he had a favorite time, it was now, in midspring, with the flowers in bloom, trees fresh and green, the streets full of people, but tourists not yet arrived in insufferable numbers. And the threat of rain producing the Miracle of the Umbrellas.

Through the years, even before the advent of collapsible, telescoping, miniaturized umbrellas, those of Paris had seemed to appear from nowhere at the first drop of moisture. And the miracle was no less now, even with the compact style, for if one were to watch carefully enough a Parisian lady carrying only a tiny handbag and with no place to hide anything larger than a credit card, the umbrella would appear—no, materialize!—with the first raindrop. That they were somehow concealed on the person or in a handbag, there could be no doubt. It was simply that he preferred to overlook the logic and think of it as the Miracle of the Umbrellas.

This was one of those days, and as the umbrellas came and went, Raker, equipped with his carnet of Metro tickets, left his hotel not far from the corner of Rue McMahon and Rue des Ternes, and walked up the gentle slope of Rue Wagram to the Arc de Triomphe. He paused to watch the huge French tricolor suspended at the arch flap majestically in the breeze. *Formidable*, he thought with a French inflection.

He sauntered down the Champs Elysee toward the Place de la Concorde, pausing en route to stop briefly at the Renault showroom and restaurant where one could eat and drink from, on, in and over Renault automobiles of various vintages. Following this, and other stops along the way, he felt reasonably satisfied—though one can never be sure in France—that his presence had drawn no unwanted attention. For insurance he switched his routine, alternating walking with riding the Metro.

Reaching the Odeon stop, he lingered in the area of the Boulevard San Michel and St. Germaine to wander the side streets, savoring the special aromas floating from the many small restaurants and cafés which lined the narrow streets, pausing to eat a slice of watermelon from a street vendor.

Finally, he made his pilgrimage to the Closerie de Lilas, although it now resembled the old haunt of Hemingway and other literary immortals less than the McDonald's which dispenses its wares from alongside a Place Pigalle establishment proclaiming "topless" on a huge banner stretched above photographs of totally nude human forms.

As the appointed time neared, Raker descended to the Metro. After the filth and vandalism of New York and Boston, and the screaming brakes of the Washington, D. C. systems, the French subway seemed nearly silent and hospital-clean. Only Munich's U-bahn could be compared with it, and it was but a single line.

He surfaced at Invalides and walked the short distance to stand before the impressive structure which stretched wide and solid behind its rampart of cannons.

Into the courtyard, past the display of ancient, giant weapons, and under the statue of the Emperor, he continued through, obtaining his ticket, and walked into the Church of the Dome to stand silently before the massive, stone sarcophagus which was Napoleon's Tomb. As with no other monument at which he paid homage, Raker again felt the overwhelming aura of power seeming to emanate from the giant coffin. It was as if the life force of the man was still hovering in the air.

"Imposing, is it not true?" The voice came from just to his left. Raker glanced casually at the speaker, his expression not revealing the pleasure he felt at seeing the familiar face with its broad, jutting chin and monumental nose.

"The power marches." Raker spoke in French as had the man he now answered.

"The bench by the fountain of pigeons?" The man's eyes remained focused on the granite tomb below.

"The place of the old ones," answered Raker. "At nine." He nodded politely, and turned to walk slowly, almost reverently, from the domed chamber, into soft, filtered sunlight.

Raker was pleased. Yves Fragonard, for all his years, seemed much the same. He had no doubt that Fragonard understood the message, knew where the meeting was to be, and would remember to divide by two the number given at the time to meet, subtract one, and thus know the actual time for their rendezvous. It would be at 3:30 p.m.

Algerian-born French, Fragonard had always been a survivor. As a youth he had distinguished himself with the French underground in their harassment of the German occupation forces, and had been commissioned an officer in the Free French Forces. No mean feat for a man of his middle-class social and economic background. He had served as an officer with the French Foreign Legion in Vietnam, and in a remarkable demonstration of ingenuity, bravery and ruthlessness, had escaped from the debacle at Dien Bien Phu. He had led five men, only one of whom had survived with him, on a route to safety in Thailand. He had left in his trail a residue of death and destruction which had caused his pursuers, in the last days of his trek, to remain at a distance which would allow them to live to boast of their chase.

A temporary hero upon his return to France, Fragonard had sided with the *Colonels* in their rebellion against the DeGaulle policy to provide separation for Algeria. Captured by DeGaullists as a result of betrayal by an informer, his prison term had been shorter than his acts might have warranted, because of his past honors. Following his release he had joined the mercenary corps in the Belgian Congo where he distinguished himself by his ferocity against any enemy, and with his unauthorized one-man forays. The informer met death, shortly afterwards.

Unable to adjust to the discipline required by his leaders, Fragonard had gravitated to a special group who seemed to operate on the same principals Fragonard approved; those based upon the use of devastating terror-tactics.

The commander of this unique mercenary commando was known only as Colonel, to his face, and as "The Man" at other times. Of the members of the group who survived service with The Man through assignments in Africa, South America, the Near East, Central America, and the Caribbean, only a very few men knew who their commander really was.

Of these, Fragonard was one. It mattered little to the others. Their pay was always on time. Insurance coverage in case of casualty was generous and free—by virtue of the fact that their true occupation was hidden. And, as most of them used fictitious names, the ability of The Man to have them supplied with adequately authentic passports and travel documents was looked upon as ample reason to stay with him. And it was The Colonel who had made the team's earlier disbandment happen. And now some of their allegiances still could exist.

Unlike most other mercenary groups who were broken up through some catastrophe or misadventure, their disbandment had been quite nearly ceremonial. The group had met, traveling separately, tickets prepaid, to Quebec, Canada. They had entered the country at separate points, meeting under the guise of an international group of hot air balloon enthusiasts. In the banquet room of the hotel, The Man made a formal announcement of the disbandment, and while the men understood the words he spoke, outside listeners would have found nothing in them to rouse their suspicions.

"Men," he had said, though there was one woman present. She didn't mind. "We've been together through many events that will forever change our lives. The time has now come for us to each go his own way, each spreading his expertise in the way best suited to him. I am proud to have been associated with you. Among those of you here, none has ever let the other down. I dislike farewells, so let's just forego that. And before the party really gets going, let me add that all your loyalty in the past has paid off for all of us." He held up a small notebook.

"I'll be moving around, seeing each of you one at a time." He paused. "We are all aware that it takes money to be . . . balloonists." He smiled. "And no matter how you've been conducting your own affairs in the past, I want you to know that our mutual affairs have shown profitable growth." He lifted a glass from the table. "Now, enough of the hot air. Let's get to the partying."

The message was clear to each of the men in the room. It was over.

It took some seconds for the murmurs to grow into talk, and some minutes for the room to grow noisy, but that it did. And as the men talked, joked, drank and reminisced, Raker went to each in turn, giving him the number of a secret bank account, and in lieu of a signature, the answers to questions which would serve as proper identification at the diverse banks where funds had been deposited. In the years The Man had led his group, the profits had been good, and the investments better. The least amount, paid to the sole female, amounted to just under $200,000. The largest amount went to Yves Fragonard and Phillip Cheney who would find something over one million dollars in their accounts. It was not a case of Raker trying to buy gratitude; it was simply a case of reward following loyalty, as surely as death would follow betrayal.

• • •

Raker thought of the clothes worn by Fragonard when he had just seen him at the tomb. Dark suit, white shirt, black shoes. All of the best quality, but all, while not threadbare or seedy, certainly on the downhill side of used.

Raker grinned to himself. The old crocodile! There was little doubt that with his shrewdness, Fragonard had made the most of his money, and was in no great financial bind. On the other hand, the man's love of life and his free-handed way of entertaining strangers would require constant replenishment of his funds. Fragonard needed company, and it changed often. It was simply that he was uncomfortable when he allowed people to become too close to him, so he preferred the company of strangers. While his favorite haunts were far removed from the level of Maxim's and the Tour d'Argent, it still required money to entertain.

Raker shrugged off his thoughts. It didn't matter! Whatever Fragonard's economic status, he could count on him.

From Invalides, Raker rode the Metro to the Louvre, changing lines, and with time to spare before his 3:30 p.m. meeting with Fragonard, paid his way into the grand museum. It was another of his small joys—the quick visit to view the magnificent products of human minds and hands.

To Raker, the Louvre was like the Smithsonian in Washington—one could never really see it all. It was an inevitable delight whenever he could take the time to pay even a short visit. Time now allowed him to stand at the bottom of the staircase and gaze up at the magnificent statue of Nike, The Winged Victory. He enjoyed climbing the stairs slowly, allowing the marble creation to loom to its true, immense proportions of beauty and power as he ascended. Time would not allow him other sights, but that would only make the visit better the next time.

Leaving the museum, he wandered a seemingly random route which took him along the slow-moving Seine, past the soaring spires of Notre Dame, down side streets, and around the corner of a large, open-front market where Parisiennes searched for something of special value.

Pushing his way gently through the crowd, he strolled aimlessly for several yards, then turned into a small passageway. He waited a moment, then quickly emerged and turned back up the street. No one paid him the slightest attention. Muscles relaxed. The precautions he had taken on his trip since meeting Fragonard had reassured him he was not being followed, but one could never be too careful. Especially now, in France. He turned once again and walked the few steps to enter the doors of the small café named the Tartine.

It looked the same as the first time he had stepped inside. High, tin-squared ceiling, wall-seats behind square, bare, wooden tables. The stand-up bar to the right ran two-thirds the length of the front section of the café; tables and chairs filled the back. The black and white tiled floor was modestly clean—or slightly littered, depending on one's viewpoint.

The large blackboard was still there, above and in back of the cash register, with its chalk-written names and prices of wine, along with a limited selection of food. Fragonard sat with his back against the wall, a half-filled wine glass and plate of bread before him. He raised a hand in greeting as Raker approached.

"The Rhone," he said, nodding at his glass. "Superb."

"Like you, old friend. Rough and raw." Raker surveyed the blackboard.

"I think I'll try the Mouton Cadet."

"To the weak, the weak," shrugged Fragonard. He tore a piece of crust from the bread in front of him and dipped it in his wine. "Tell me, great rogue, of your troubles."

"First, how does one obtain service?" inquired Raker.

"One waits," replied Fragonard stuffing the wine-soaked bread into his mouth. "However," and he raised a hand and snapped his fingers with a reverberating click, "this one does not."

He smiled as a black-clad, white-aproned waitress sped the short distance from the bar where she had been engrossed in conversation with the woman behind the counter.

"What now, old one?"

"Service, my little cabbage, if you can remember what that is. For my valued friend here."

She looked at Raker, a hint of a smile on her wizened visage. "The Rhone," said Raker.

As she left, Fragonard lifted one of his heavy, arched eyebrows while the other didn't show a twitch. It was a feat in which he took pride.

"You learn. There remains hope," he said.

"Tell me, vintage lecher, do you believe this is actually the café where Marx and Lenin drank during their respective times in Paris?"

"But of course," answered Fragonard. "Of a certainty. I have it on the most *peachable* authority." The adjective was said in English.

"You mean *im*-peachable."

"I mean peachable. I wouldn't believe any bastard historian if he told me there were sewers in Paris."

He sighed. "But if Marx and Lenin did come here, then you may be certain that these very same ladies served them their wine. Or whatever the cretins drank." Fragonard disliked communists, capitalists, socialists, fascists, organized religion and atheists with the same jovial zeal. "Now. What is it you would have from me?"

"I want you to kill for me." The tone was the same as their banter had been.

"This is true?"

"This is true."

"There is, of course, a reason."

Raker nodded. "Reasons. Business and personal." He frowned slightly. "But a cautionary: you probably will not appreciate the nominee."

Fragonard put one of his solid hands over Raker's even larger one. "I have no choice, my friend." He gave a Gallic shrug. "I owe you my life." It would be, obviously, insane to argue the point.

"And I, to you, mine."

"There are debts that one does not equalize—the name?"

"First, you must know that it will have to occur on a schedule."

"You have your reasons. I have my duty. The name?"

Raker kept his eyes turned to Fragonard's face. "Bequerel," he said softly.

Surprise swept Fragonard's features. Both eyebrows went up. "But, he is dead these many years."

"He had a son."

"That is true."

Raker paused grimly and clasped his hands together in front

of him. Fragonard waited. "And the son has a wife." Raker said, looking into his wine glass.

Enlightenment showed, as Fragonard raised a hand, palm up. "It marches. The so-long memory. And—how did you used to tell me one of your American generals phrased it? Strike them where they exist not?"

"Hit 'em where they ain't," said Raker. "But no, this is more a case of hit them where it hurts."

"I do not like to . . . harm the women."

"I have this one coming."

It was Fragonard's turn to study his glass. After a long pause he spoke. "Perhaps." He looked up at Raker with used eyes. "You can be a man of the hard heart, old friend."

"We can both be men of hard heart, old friend." Raker waited.

Fragonard spoke first. "I will do it, of course."

"I did not want to mention it before, huge camel, but there is much money in the operation," said Raker quietly.

"It does not require the payment."

"Hear me, old one. There is more to be done, and better to your liking. I wanted to speak of the worst part first." He clasped Fragonard's wrist. "The game is on again. Only the rules have changed."

Fragonard lifted his head, interest showing in his expression.

"When we leave here, we will walk, and I will tell you all," said Raker.

The grizzled head of his companion nodded slowly. "One can, of a certainty, use money." He tore a piece of bread and looked at it. "Allow me, however, a moment to assimilate the idea of becoming a slayer of women." There was bitterness in his voice. He dunked the bread in his wine and put it in his mouth. The two men sat silent, each with his own thoughts.

• • •

It was—what? Fourteen? Fifteen years ago? Raker toyed with dates. Somewhere around that. After Tshombe at Stanleyville? It was named Kisangani now, he thought. After Oman? No! Before. Was it during the time break in between Kenya while helping Kenyatta set up forces to stop the incursions by Somalian herdsmen, and his commando's move to Nigeria during the Biafran campaign? Anyway, the date didn't matter, did it? Summer? No, spring. Early spring. April? Perhaps May.

It was not that he had forgotten. It was that he did not want to remember.

He had paid the men off handsomely, banking for them, without their knowledge as was his custom, a good part of their money. They could rendezvous in 60 days back at Mombasa where they had earned the gratitude of Kenyatta, not to mention special rewards made possible by Kenya's ousting of business-owning Asians. His mind carried him back to those long ago, sadly recalled days.

FRANCE

Home! The thought had made Raker glow with pleasure. Home, which at that time was lovely Geneva. Home, to his beautiful wife and beautiful daughter. Home, in time for the girl's birthday. Her seventh? Eighth? No matter. He had managed to obtain remarkably swift transportation considering the number of borders he had to avoid. The closest airport to which safe transport could be arranged was the one at Nice. It had been close enough.

The temptation to telephone ahead, once he had landed and checked into a hotel on Rue Victor Hugo, was overwhelming, but the thought of the pleasure of surprise he could give by actually being home on his daughter's birthday gave him the strength of will to replace the phone firmly in its cradle.

He walked the tree-lined streets and the sea-walk, strolled the twisting, cramped streets of the old town, and visited the bars. Real, or so labeled, American bourbon eased his tension and he had partied. But not with the girls. He didn't need that, not now. He would be home tomorrow.

Unable to obtain flight reservations easily, and not willing to risk calling attention to his presence in France, Raker had settled for renting a Citroen with which he could easily reach Geneva on the following day. He had planned to leave early, but the extent of his evening of pleasure, coupled with the emotional and physical relaxation which accompanied his return to civilization, had allowed him to sleep late for the first time in years. It was of no importance. He still had plenty of time.

Avoiding Cannes, he turned north to drive to Digne and continued on, following for a great part of the way the route of Napoleon during his final "Hundred Days." That worthy could have felt no better than I, thought Raker, as he hurried happily toward his home.

He was well into the city when the thought struck him: Presents! He hadn't bought any presents for his daughter. He laughed aloud, alone in the car. That would be part of the pleasure. The hunting, the mind searching, the finding of just the right thing. He had already neared the train station and the road toward Lausanne where his home was. His home!

Remembrances in Rome

Following the death of Laughlin, Raker had been willing to accompany other friends who had found employment in the service of a group who were helping to finance the training of military personnel for the Israeli republic.

With his value as a military expert, particularly in guerilla tactics, established, Raker had found ready employment, without regard to politics or religion. During these years he had developed skills in the events which make up the Olympic pentathlon, and though he had passed what he considered the suitable age to compete himself, he had sought and found two young men he thought, with his coaching and training, had the potential to become champions. He had the time and the money, and it was with high expectations that he had taken his two charges to Switzerland for intensive training. It was there in Geneva that he met the beautiful, charming and socially prominent Simone Dumoriez.

She had been captivated by the rugged charm and dynamic personality of the man; he discovered in her an air of culture and breeding which made her an object to be, if not loved, at least possessed and fiercely protected.

When the couple wed they purchased a pleasant and respectably expensive home overlooking Lac Leman, and Raker was over-joyed with his good fortune and his newly acquired showpieces. It was the first home, real home, he had known since the death of his father.

There had been no lack of money. The inheritance from his parents and the money left by Murdock and Laughlin had been wisely invested, and his expertise in the training of guerilla forces for certain middle eastern powers had paid him well. And Raker—but mostly his beautiful wife, Simone—had spent it.

Oh, not all of it; not even most of it; but enough to awaken Raker's concern. A year after the birth of his first, and only, child, he knew it was time to put his talents to work. He had hugged and kissed a reluctant farewell to Simone and his infant daughter—named Jennie, after his mother, not in forgiveness, but from guilt—and departed to his private and profitable wars. He had not been back until now. Oh, there had been telephone calls; and letters and photographs. But the business of war and money had taken priority in Raker's mind, and the remembrance of the glow of happiness his family and home had brought him had been diminished in the excitement and the sense of power.

Damn! thought Raker. If I had only been one of those bankers, or brokers! Something like that. A magnate. That was the word, magnate—a big business magnate. That would have done it. I could have stayed with my family like they do.

He laughed at the absurdity of the word and the thought. He knew that with his heritage and experience, he could only be what he was: a doubter and a man of action. The word killer never entered his mind. Moreover, there was still his vow to Laughlin.

• • •

While the streets of Geneva were familiar to Raker, he could not remember any particular area which might offer him the opportunity to find gifts suitable for his young daughter. Following the practice of experienced travelers throughout continental Europe, he headed to the central railroad station where he knew he could obtain the services and information he needed.

After changing money, at a rate somewhat less than he could

have obtained at other banks, he took a taxi and asked to be delivered to the area with the highest concentration of quality shops where he might find a selection of gifts to please a young girl.

As the taxi sped him over the river flowing from the west end of the lake, the lowering sun bathed the tall flume of water of the *Jet d'Eau*, or "*Jeddoe*," which spewed high in the air. As sunlight reflected on the upward sprays and the falling droplets, it gave the illusion of fireworks hovering over the fleet of small craft riding easily on the waters east of the bridge. The beauty, coupled with Raker's adrenaline-fed high of anticipation, had erased any lingering memories of the suffering and despair of the areas of Africa he had so recently left. He was at peace, enjoying the swirling glow of happiness which seemed to spread from his stomach and physically fill his chest to overflowing.

The deposit of 200 Swiss francs, with the promise of more to come, put the cab driver at ease as he waited the hour and slightly more that it took Raker to return with his purchases. The size of the tip he received when he dropped the man off back at the railroad station left the driver nearly as happy as Raker.

The sun had disappeared below the mountains by the time Raker had transferred his parcels to his rented car, but with the discipline practiced in nearly all things, he forced himself to drive toward the reunion with his family at a moderate speed.

Nearly halfway to Lausanne, he turned toward the sloping hills to follow the road to his home. Old and solid, the house loomed above him darkly, except for the lighted windows on the ground floor. From the steep driveway, the wide balcony porch shielded the windows of the upper floor, but Raker thought he could see reflected light glowing on the underside of its slanted roof.

A twinge of doubt nagged at him as he pulled his car to the front of the garage that he'd had built attached to the house. There should have been activity. It was his daughter's birthday. There should be people, and noise, and laughter. But all was silent. Only one sleek, dark automobile was in evidence. It was parked at the front of the house in the circular drive that continued down the other side of the hill he had just driven up.

The glow that had filled him only moments ago faded, and was replaced in Raker's gut by a heavy, leaden knot. He sat quietly for a moment, hands tightly gripping the steering wheel. Then, leaving the gift-wrapped packages in the car, he got out, opening and closing the door softly, and stalked silently up the steps to the front door. He listened. He heard nothing.

Raker tried the door latch gently. It was locked. From his pocket he carefully removed a key ring. From the few keys it held, Raker easily selected the one for the door. It had been with him throughout all the years, in every situation. It was his constant touch with home. He hesitated, a chill of apprehension prickling his scalp. Something was wrong. Would the key even fit? Had the lock been changed? Was he on the outside once again?

Slowly, ever so slowly, he slid the key into the lock. The lock moved. He turned it gently and slipped inside. He felt as though he were an intruder, a burglar. He pushed the door open quietly.

He stopped to listen.

Not a sound to be heard. The light inside the entryway glowed softly. Another light illuminated the room to the right of the entry. Then he heard the first sounds since approaching the house. Soft, quiet, almost indiscernible. It was music flowing gently down the stairs in front of him. And other sounds. Human. Too human.

In future years, Raker would not be able to remember exactly what went through his mind at that moment. A flashback to the past, perhaps? The memory of other stairs, and other sounds, and another man charging up those stairs? And the terrible, crashing noises? But those events he had only watched. This moment was his. And the one thing he knew he wouldn't do was charge up the stairs. He walked up, softly, quietly, and as the sounds became so terribly identifiable, he shut off his mind from hearing. The door to the bedroom, their bedroom, was ajar, and as he pushed it open, he couldn't shut off his sight.

His wife, his lovely, beautiful wife, knelt in ivory-skinned splendor on the floor at the side of the bed. Their bed. Her glorious mane of golden hair swirled down her nude back and across the thighs of the man lying across the bed. The fingers of his hands could be seen holding her golden head tightly to him as he moaned in pleasure. Raker roared!

Before the two people could move, Raker was across the room. A hand grasped the golden hair and lifted the woman, his wife, his beautiful Simone, high off the floor, and with his already considerable strength amplified by his fury, Raker hurled her across the room. His face contorted into a maniacal mask as he turned to the man who had raised his upper body from the bed onto his elbows.

Bequerel! His friend, Bequerel! His banker, Edmond Bequerel! Edmond Bequerel who was trusted to look after his family. With a feral snarl, Raker lunged forward, hands grasping. Bequerel, face contorted in terror, tried desperately to move back on the rumpled bed but failed. Raker's right hand clamped fiercely at Bequerel's groin and encircled the man's scrotum and now flaccid penis. He tore the screaming man loose from the mattress at which he clawed in agonized desperation.

"God, oh my God," wailed Raker's wife from across the room where she curled in fear. "My God, don't kill us! Oh, God, oh, my God!" She folded her arms across her bare breasts and doubled over, head against her knees.

Raker held Bequerel's legs and lower body off the floor, the man's head bouncing against the carpet, arms thrashing futilely about as he moaned and whimpered in paralyzing pain that spread sickeningly throughout his body.

Raker looked at his wife with loathing as he continued to hold the churning body of Bequerel in his savage grip. The hot fury of moments ago had been replaced with a terrible, chilling hatred, so intense it filled the room.

"Where is my daughter?" His voice was almost a whisper.

"She's at a party. My God, she's at a party." Simone lifted her streaked face. "It's her birthday. She's at a birthday party." She spread her hands. It was really so simple. Couldn't Raker see that?

"Without her mother. While her mother is fucking, sucking, her father's best friend?" Raker lifted and shook the dangling Bequerel whose body flopped on the floor in pain.

"Cover your body, slut!"

Raker, still maintaining his grip on Bequerel, dragging the man, moved across the room to shut off the soft music coming from the phonograph. He looked at the bedside table where a silver bucket held a bottle of champagne.

"How romantic! Music. Champagne. One hell of a way to celebrate your daughter's birthday, isn't it, whore? With your lover boy here."

He lifted his arm and shook Bequerel's genitals at his wife who had by now donned a robe. As she faced him, Raker could see a sudden look of horror fill her face. She wasn't looking at him. She was looking past him.

Raker turned. Standing in the open door was a young girl, face white with shock, eyes wide in disbelief. It had been years and the girl had been only an infant, but there was no doubt in Raker's mind.

It was Jennie. He looked down at the fist holding the now unconscious Bequerel's lower body off the floor. He opened his hand to let the body fall limply, and took a step toward the girl. "Jennie," he called.

The girl whirled and raced from the opening. "No, oh no, no, no!" Raker could hear her voice fade, and then the slamming of a door. He turned to his wife whose hands now clasped her robe closely around her.

"She was . . . she was to spend the night." Her voice was pained. "She wasn't . . . to come home until . . ."

"It doesn't matter now," said Raker.

He looked at the limp form of Bequerel, then back at his wife. "It doesn't matter at all, now." His voice was void of emotion. The change in him caused his wife to cringe away toward the wall at her back.

Raker laughed. A rough, harsh snort. "You're safe, slut. You and . . ." He kicked at the limp form of Bequerel, not hard, just a nudge of contempt, ". . . this slime."

He turned and walked slowly to the door and paused with his back to the room. Without turning around he said, "You're both safe now. I think I was going to kill you. Now I won't. Can't." He turned slowly to fix his wife with cold, hard eyes. "And I can't face my daughter now. But let me tell you this, and you hear me ever so perfectly. If I ever see him again, I *will* kill him." He paused. "Tell him. And if you are with him, I'll certainly kill you."

He placed a hand on each side of the doorway, waiting for an answer. Simone kept her eyes averted.

"Do you understand me?" She nodded, eyes squeezed shut. "I will make arrangements for her. For Jennie's security. And you may be sure that there will be watchers to make certain she is well cared for by you. Do you understand that?" Again the nod.

"If I were you," said Raker to the woman, "I would try to take every precaution against ever letting me see you again."

He left as he had come, quietly and softly, without another word.

CHAPTER 12

BEQUEREL'S REVENGE

In the days that followed, Raker drove back down to France where he traveled the coast from Marseilles to the Italian border, staying minutes ahead of the law. He left behind broken furniture, broken bottles, and broken bones, and by the time his fury had abated enough for him to turn to plans for the future, compensatory terms had been made to re-establish his right to return—if not his welcome—to the towns and cities he had vexed. In the meantime, Bequerel had healed.

It was days before Raker's former friend was able to leave his bed, and many more days before he could walk normally. But once the pain and fresh memory of terror had passed, the humiliation remained, and Bequerel set about avenging his treatment at Raker's hands. He had the money and the resources, and within three weeks had located Raker in Nice and, with the help of certain unsavory contacts all bankers would deny they have, he'd recruited two men he was assured would do anything if the price was right.

The plan was simple: They would abduct Raker, and while the two hired hoods held him, or made him helpless, he, Bequerel himself, would castrate him. He would spend his life remembering that one does not embarrass Edmond Bequerel.

The abduction was almost too easy, considering Raker's experience in guerilla warfare, and his native cunning and survival consciousness. As he walked beside the iron-railed edge of the promenade atop the seawall along the stony beach as was his custom each evening, Raker was approached from the front by a tall, large-framed man who stopped him to ask for a light for his cigarette.

As Raker supplied the flame, a car drew quickly alongside, the door opened, a large caliber revolver was produced, and Raker obediently slid into the back seat. As the car sped away, Raker asked, "Would you care to tell me just what this is all about?"

"You will learn, too soon," sneered the driver.

The man with the revolver, sitting alongside Raker, said nothing. The car followed the road west toward Cannes, then took the turnoff which would lead to Digne. Raker, mind alert, remained quiet and relaxed. It was by far the best thing to do. The car sped up the hills toward the north.

It was somewhat over thirty minutes when the driver turned off the pavement and up a narrow dirt road, through a heavily wooded area. As the car drew to a stop, and before the headlights were turned off, Raker could see the shape of an old wooden structure which appeared to be the remains of a deserted farmhouse.

"We are here," said the driver, unnecessarily. "Out!"

With the revolver still pointed at him from a safe distance, Raker followed the driver into the structure. As the door closed a match flared and a lantern was lit. The flame was adjusted, and Raker saw the face of Edmond Bequerel grinning above the pulsing light.

"You did not truly imagine that I was through with you, did you?" Bequerel's voice came from behind the flame, bitterly, smoothly, hissing.

Raker sighed. "You are beneath contempt, slime," he said. "You were told never to let me see you again."

Bequerel's teeth gleamed through a sneer. "I received your threat from your wife . . ." he paused in preparation for the enjoyment of his next words, ". . . your wife, my lover. Yes, I received the empty threat you made to my lover. And this is what it has earned you."

Bequerel held up his hand so the lantern's flame could reflect off the surface of the wicked-looking skinning knife he held. He turned the blade slightly back and forth to better catch the light.

"I am going to let you live, animal, but as for breeding purposes, you will serve only in an advisory capacity." He chuckled obscenely at his own humor.

"Then you set the penalty," observed Raker mildly.

Bequerel looked momentarily puzzled. He paused. "Yes, I set the penalty. Take him!"

At the last words, the tall man holding the pistol on Raker switched his aim ever so slightly and fired. The sound was not as loud as a clap of hands. The man who had driven the car to the meeting collapsed backward. The hole in the middle of his forehead was not large. There was almost no back of the head.

Even as the man was falling, Raker struck forward with snake-like speed to close his powerful hand around the wrist of Bequerel, whose hand held the skinning knife.

The swiftness of the move found Bequerel looking at an empty hand almost before his sense of touch told him the knife was gone.

"No!" cried Bequerel. He tried to draw away from Raker and seemed to shrink inside his clothing. "No! It can't be. No!" He held his free hand in front of him, palm facing Raker. "No. It can't happen like this!" His eyes darted from side to side, looking for escape.

Raker's smile was wolfish. "Oh, but it *is* like this." He fastened a hand onto the front of Bequerel's coat and pulled him forward to place the sharpened side of the knife lightly against the man's throat. "And you set the penalty, remember?"

His eyes turned to the tall man. "What in the hell was that you fired? For so large a weapon it spoke rather softly."

The man smiled wickedly. "Single shot. Of my own design. The amount of powder, I have reduced. And its voice I have subdued."

"You've been spending your time in better ways than I have, obviously."

Raker turned eyes to the trembling Bequerel. "Allow me to introduce you to my second in command of my—overseas activities." He studied Bequerel's frozen features. "You really should investigate your assassins more thoroughly," he advised. He turned to Yves Fragonard. "How did you get in on this?"

Fragonard gave his eloquent shrug. "Through the pipelines of Marseilles, *mon ami*.. I heard your name mentioned as a neck to be put on the block for the axe man. Naturally I thought it would be productive if I were to make a little extra profit. It proceeds well, does it not?"

"It most certainly proceeds well," agreed Raker. He turned his eyes back to Bequerel but continued to speak to Fragonard. "See if you can find me a huge nail, or perhaps some lengths of good, sturdy wire?

"But certainly," replied Fragonard. He moved about amid the litter of the room.

Bequerel's fear had grown to abject terror. He was as some small animal irretrievably caught in a trap, not yet resigned to its fate. By the time Fragonard returned with a jumble of rusted wire, Bequerel had lapsed into an almost trance-like state.

Raker cuffed him lightly on the side of his face with an open hand.

The eyes twitched, and then looked into Raker's face.

"You set the rules," said Raker, voice graveside quiet. "Remember that. But I'll let you make a final decision." His hand holding the knife slashed down at Bequerel's middle with practiced skill, severing the man's belt, then the sharp edge shredded his outer and under clothing, exposing his genitals.

"This is the last way I saw you," said Raker. "It will be up to you to determine how anyone else ever sees you. Or if at all."

"I will be outside," murmured Fragonard, and moved from the room. Even the strength of terror could not help Bequerel as Raker completed his preparations for the man's incision. He twisted the wire in several tight loops around Bequerel's scrotum and penis, then twisted the two ends into a spiral securing the loops. He hauled the terrified man to one of the thick posts holding up sagging ceiling beams. There was sufficient wire to wind several times around the post, and still twist the ends together with many tight turns. Bequerel was securely bound by his genitals to the post, unable to turn, and without sufficient movement to have any hope of untwisting the wire holding him.

Raker stepped back and looked at the pathetic figure. His face showed no emotion. "You were warned," he said, "and you made the decision." He moved forward, and with a quick thrust, stabbed the knife into the post some several inches above Bequerel's head.

"Now you have a last decision."

The bound man's eyes followed him as he moved away.

Raker surveyed his handiwork. "Given time, you just might be able to untwist those wires, or at least hack through them with the knife. It might be worth a try." He grinned evilly. "That is, if you can pull the blade from the post in time."

He moved about the room, gathering scattered papers and other flammable debris, piling them only a few feet from Bequerel. "But I don't think this old building will last long." He picked up the lantern from the worn table and lifted it toward Bequerel as though in salute.

"Do what you think is right," Raker said, and threw the burning lantern sharply against the floor amid the pile of tinder he had built. The lantern smashed, oil splattered, and the flames quickly blazed high and hot as Raker moved out the open door to join Fragonard at their vehicle.

The two men were well down the dirt road, nearing the paved highway, when the flames had grown bright enough to be seen over the surrounding trees.

"You left him but little choice," said Fragonard. "Of which option do you think he will avail?"

"Who?" asked Raker, slumping casually into his seat and closing his eyes.

• • •

Raker was torn from his reverie by the touch of Fragonard's hand on his shoulder.

"You have been remembering, is it not?"

Raker slowly nodded his head. "I have been remembering."

Fragonard's mobile eyebrows drooped dolefully. "Is that not enough? Must you, we, carry it . . . to this? If you must, then why not the son?"

Raker met Fragonard's gaze. "As you said, my old one, some debts are never equalized." He leaned forward, expression intense. "If it were the son, then there would be no Bequerel to agonize over the loss."

"As you have agonized over yours?"

"He took my life from me," said Raker.

"Your life!" scoffed Fragonard. "You life has been the war, the conflict, always the battle."

Raker waved away the comment with a sharp flick of his hand. "It might not have been."

"As the shark might not smell the blood?"

Raker was not listening. "He pursued her, even from the grave." His voice was flat. "The car wreck was no accident. You know that."

Fragonard nodded in reluctant agreement. Only three months after the aborted attempt to kidnap and castrate Raker, his former wife had driven, at high speed, into the low, stone wall alongside the narrow road of the Moyene Corniche near Eze. The high-powered sports car had flipped from the force, catapulting it and its driver to their destruction. The first car wreck of many years ago hadn't mattered. The second had.

"It left a daughter alone, with a father whose shame would not allow him to see her." Raker's voice was barely audible.

CHAPTER 13

LONDON

Raker had a reluctance concerning airports. It had nothing to do with flying. It was simply that in his experience, surveillance at airports was far heavier than at many other entry points. Given time, he would have preferred to have driven to his appointments in Rome, Munich, and Paris. Under the right circumstances, and avoiding troubled times, really thorough luggage checks were almost a thing of the past at borders between common market countries. Searches were for weapons and identity, and Raker always made certain that he carried nothing which could cause him concern. Weapons could always be obtained, along with all other necessary items. Except his passports.

These were carefully fitted into specially constructed pockets in his compact leather case, so skillfully designed that they defied discovery short of its actually being torn apart. Even the most esoteric product for smuggling could not be carried in such a small space with any hope of worthwhile profit. It was just that Raker always preferred to be noticed only when he desired. At airports, one could only take limited precautions. In view of this, as he prepared to depart Paris, he gave consideration to taking the train from Gare Nord to Calais, the hovercraft to Dover, and the train to Charing Cross station.

The time, however, was not worth the lessened visibility. He would fly, and to Heathrow, although he had for the last few years preferred Gatwick. It was less cluttered, less noisy, and farther from decay. But it was also much farther from where he needed to be.

· · ·

Since his last visit to Heathrow Airport, the "tube" had been extended and now the underground connected the airport with the city. He felt momentary surprise that it had been so long since he had been here.

Clearing customs quickly, as Owen Coleman, Raker resisted the temptation to experience the ride in on the subway and instead obtained a taxi. The fewer people he saw in his Coleman mode, the better. He would keep the name for now, but minor modifications in his appearance would make it less likely that some chance encounter would identify the man who entered the country as the man who was to be seen later on the streets of London.

Disguise, reflected Raker, wasn't difficult—if it was kept simple.

He felt that the photographs, which he was certain had been taken of all incoming passengers, would eventually be studied and compared with uncommon activities. He could take care of that. If I could just figure some way to disguise earlobes, thought Raker, quite irrelevantly. He had no intention of pursuing the idea.

"Know a good public house out from downtown?" asked Raker of the taxi driver he found.

"I do that, guv'ner. I most certainly do. Do you know the city?"

"Some."

"Uxbridge?" It came out Oxbridge.

I didn't quite have that far out in mind, thought Raker. It didn't really matter. "I think so," he said. "That's the end of the tube, isn't it?"

"There's some who think it's even farther, your honor. Yes, indeed. Certainly some who think so."

"There's a decent place there?"

"There be," said the driver. "Crown and Scepter, it's called. Animal heads all over the place. Nice pub."

"And you think I could secure a room there?"

"Don't know as how secure it'll be, but I'll wager a quid or two that you'll find lodging there."

Raker laughed. "I'll just take that, wager, old horse. If I find lodging there then I'll pay five quid extra. Deal?"

"A deal, guv'ner—a boney fidey deal."

Raker had always admired the skill with which London taxi and bus drivers navigated the maze of twisted streets in and around the city. This one was as adept as any. At their destination, he invited the man in to help ascertain that he could, indeed, obtain lodging.

He could. He did.

"You've been a great help," said Raker. "Here's the fiver." He placed it in the driver's ready hand. "Here's the fare, and," he hesitated, "here's another five for service above and beyond the call of duty."

"You are a true gent, guv'ner. A true gent." He touched a finger to his forehead. "Could I be treating you to a pint?"

Raker smiled. "I'll be delighted to join you," he said. "But if you buy, then I'll have to stand my turn, and then we may be joined by others, and they'd buy, and then it would be your stand again. Then mine. We could still be here at closing."

The driver considered Raker's logic. "Don't have no closing for guests, guv. Could be here longer'n that."

Raker spread his hands. "See?"

The driver scratched his head. "Somehow, I've seemed to've lost me way," he smiled. "I think you're saying you should do the buyin'?"

Raker snapped his fingers. "Got it!" He draped an arm around the shoulders of his newfound friend. "Shall we?"

They did.

● ● ●

In the morning it was raining. It helped Raker's plans although it would have presented little problem if the weather had been clear. He left, paying his bill and exchanging pleasantries with the publican, at 10:00 a.m., after passing up the invitation to an "eye-opener."

A hooded, plastic poncho covered his head which had miraculously sprouted a thatch of well barbered, dark hair. It was out of view of the pub keeper, therefore excited no interest. If the man noticed that the heavy, drooping mustache was now much trimmer and straighter across the lip than it had been the night before, he said nothing. And the change in the color of his customer's eyes was not mentioned. In fact, the public house's proprietor would not have noticed anything, including the most excellent toupee, even if he were looking at it. This morning he was quite sober. He even waved at the pleasant Canadian as the man left with the driver of a taxi he had called for him.

"Where to, guv?" asked the driver.

Do they all talk like that? wondered Raker, knowing they didn't. Maybe these last two were of a family. "The London Hilton, please. And there's no hurry. As a matter of fact, I'd appreciate a leisurely drive around some of your more worthy sights. Is that amenable to your schedule?"

"Guv," volunteered the driver, dropping the car into gear, "I'm totally yours to command as long as you can afford the pelf."

The trip allowed Raker the opportunity to be reasonably certain that he was not under observation, as well as time to place a telephone call.

· · ·

The man answering recognized his voice. "Yes?"

"Would it interest you to inspect the perching habits of the gargantuan, toping, multihued, flying sloth?" asked Raker.

There was a hesitation while the words were sorted out. "Sounds frightfully exciting, old top," came the reply. "Could I inquire as to when the performance is to be?"

"Better to get there as soon as the box office reopens," said Raker.

"I'll try and do that. Is that it?"

"Quite." He replaced the phone, smiling.

· · ·

By late afternoon, the rain had stopped, and the skies were nearly clear as Raker left the British Museum through the front entrance, turned right, then walked several yards to cross Great Russell Street and stroll down the intersecting road.

He appeared to saunter casually, pausing briefly at times to examine shop windows. He stopped in front of a small antique shop to study an ancient, three-wheeled pram, the body of which was fashioned of woven straw, then, spinning rapidly on his heel, he returned at a more rapid pace to the building he had just passed. He stood at the open doors of the Bloomsbury Carriage Company, admiring a vintage Jaguar roadster whose long, leather-strapped bonnet and squarish grill dated it no newer than the late '30s. The attendant, busily occupied dusting the automobile's gleaming finish, glanced up at him.

Raker nodded at the machine with a wry smile and winked as he gave a palms-up, "too bad I can't afford something like that" shrug, and continued his walk back toward the museum corner. He was satisfied he had not been followed.

At the corner he turned to his right and walked up the road to the Museum Tavern. The pub had just opened after the required closing period, and some of its clients were still waiting for a first drink with which to break their tradition-created drought.

Raker looked about the well-appointed room which was softly lighted by the lowering sun shining through the etched and frosted windows.

Behind the bar a flamboyantly dressed man in a tan plaid suit, bright red shirt, and violently contrasting green paisley necktie rambled back and forth greeting customers while two barmen moved efficiently around him and each other, busily filling orders which seemed to consist mostly of mugs foaming with brews of various hue.

From the familiarity of the greetings by the colorful "guv'ner" and the number of clients already comfortably settled and studying newspapers as they lounged on the cushioned seats against the wall, it seemed apparent that the pub had its share of regulars as well as the tourists and other museum-goers one might expect from its location.

Raker moved to a chair across the table from one of the customers already sipping a frothing half-pint of brew.

"Do you mind?" he asked politely.

"Not at all. Please," said the man, motioning toward the chair. "But I'm afraid you'll have to fetch your own. No table service available after lunch."

Raker thanked him and, after obtaining a pint of ale, returned and seated himself.

"Pleasant place," said Raker. He sipped, then nodded toward the bar. "Nice touch that."

Behind the counter, the flamboyant proprietor was engaged in playing with a large, caged South American macaw that would, on cue, flop upside down on his perch as though drunk. The bird's plumage was as vivid as his owner's clothing.

"Quite," said the man opposite Raker. "Makes a nice diversion for the unoccupied mind."

"Is this your local?" inquired Raker.

"Oh, no, just get by once in a while." The man paused to take a sip of his ale. "Afraid most of my favorite places are down in the heart of things."

"I don't really know many places," said Raker. "Be nice if you could recommend a few interesting spots for me."

"Be more than happy to," said the man, showing teeth gleaming white against his sun-lamp tan.

"Here," he said, taking out a notebook and pen. "Let me write out the names and addresses of a few of my favorite spots."

"Really appreciate that," said Raker, returning the smile. He sat silently, sipping at his glass, as the other man wrote.

In a few moments he spoke. "I'm sure that's quite enough. I won't be staying in London for too long a time."

The man's smile became a grin as he looked up from the notebook he was busily writing in. "Perfectly all right," he said. "I'm adding a few sundry notes to the addresses."

"I thought perhaps you were."

The man completed his writing, tore the page from the notebook, and extended it to Raker. "Here you are."

Raker accepted the folded paper and put it in his shirt pocket without looking at it. "Very good of you. Thanks."

"Quite all right. You're not English. American?"

"Canadian."

"I see. Would I be out of line in asking what sort of business you're in?" asked the man. He swallowed the last of his drink.

"Profit," said Raker solemnly.

The man eyed him evenly for a moment. "I see. Yes. Good business, that," he said. He stood and extended his hand. "Well, I fear I must be moving off. Pleasant chatting with you, old boy. Perhaps we'll be meeting at one of those places before you have to be leaving our fair city." He motioned a finger at Raker's pocket which held the written information.

"Yes," said Raker. "I would like that."

"Until another time, then," said the man.

Raker watched the tall, lean figure as it moved lithely toward the door, then he rose from his chair and slid smoothly into the still-warm seat against the wall.

Lifting his glass with one hand, he used his other to remove the folded page from his pocket. Printed neatly on the sheet was a name, address, and room number. The hotel was close to Green Park on Half Moon Street. Following that, information was written:

LIFT WILL TAKE YOU ALMOST TO THE TOP, THEN YOU'LL HAVE TO CLIMB THE STAIRS. TWO LIFTS. TAKE THE BLUE. GIVE ME AN HOUR OR MORE TO CLEAR MY TRAIL. DON'T YOU TRUST TELEPHONES FOR THIS SORT OF THING? AND HOW DID YOU REMEMBER WE COMPARED THAT DRUNKEN PAROT TO A SLOTH?

Raker pushed his glass aside, idly watching the antics of the caged macaw. He not only didn't trust telephones, the truth was that he trusted completely only one thing in the world: Raker trusted Raker.

He had decided, in the beginning, that Cheney would be his Number One. It was now truly imperative that he not be followed. Cheney would manage his end.

Raker had his taxi follow a circuitous route which eventually deposited him near the Nelson Monument at Trafalgar Square. He strolled a little distance, turned down a short, narrow street which led toward the Thames, and stood momentarily outside the door of a small corner pub whose sign proclaimed it to be The Two Chairmen. Raker had planned the stop carefully. As best his practiced eye could tell he had not been followed. No other taxi or automobile paused to disembark passengers in the direction from which he had come. No pedestrians approached the pub or lingered at the entrance to the street.

Standing at the bar of the pub which was still crowded with office workers and junior-executive types avoiding the incredible post-work transportation crush of downtown London, Raker ordered a half-pint of lager from one of the two surly barmen.

The notion idly crossed his mind that perhaps he should return at closing time and teach them some manners. It was not a serious thought. Wiping the bottom of the dripping mug on a small, gaudy rectangle of toweling which took the place of a cocktail napkin or coaster, Raker sipped at his beer, casually surveying his surroundings as he memorized the faces around him.

He allowed twenty minutes in the pub, leaving his beer unfinished, then walked the short distance to Charing Cross station where he once again obtained a taxi. Following his habit of seldom going directly to his destination, he had the taxi drop him off at a small restaurant some hundred yards past the hotel selected by Cheney for their meeting.

Confident that Cheney had taken similar precautions against being followed, he returned down Half Moon Street, noting carefully for future reference the cars and people he passed.

Cheney opened the door immediately at Raker's knock. He held a small transistor radio in his hand. It was playing loudly. "Insurance," he said, holding up the noise maker. "I did a quick run-through and it seems clean," he continued, eyes indicating the room, "but if I'm wrong, let someone try to untangle our words from this."

A double bed and large wardrobe nearly filled the room. Under the single window stood a wooden cupboard-like structure housing an apparatus for heating morning rolls and coffee or tea. The hotel apparently, and wrongly, considered itself out of the bed-and-breakfast category and had, sadly, moved itself to the continental breakfast mode. In the cramped space between the bed and the window was a small, low table, flanked by two chairs. Upon the table rested two glasses and a bottle of Haig and Haig whiskey.

The bottle was the one Americans call "pinch" and is referred to as "dimple" by the English.

"Welcome, Colonel," said Cheney, "or whatever you're calling yourself these days." He placed the blaring radio on the table between them as they sat.

"I damn near didn't recognize you in that get up."

"Good," observed Raker.

"You look terribly fit, old boy. Still doing those punishing press-ups and your marathon runs?" He made a circular motion with his hand. "And whatever other body-stressing exertions you persist in?"

"As often as I can," said Raker. He eyed Cheney. "You don't seem to have let that lean physique of yours get too far out of hand."

The other man eyed Raker accusingly. "The result of habits roughly instilled by a demanding Colonel—Colonel. You have that knack, y'know. Now what," he asked, changing the subject, "is the occasion for all this hush-hush?" He poured glasses two-thirds full of whiskey. "What's it been? Three years? The Moroccan affair, wasn't it?"

Raker nodded. "Something over three years."

"Righto." Cheney nodded. "And obviously you've got a fiddle of some sort going again."

"You could call it that."

"Surprising. Thought you were retired from the game, and on your way to becoming the Buffett or Getty of the anti-terrorist business, what?"

Raker held up his glass and twirled it, eyeing the liquid. He sat it down, untouched.

"It's made me moderately comfortable, Phillip lad. Moderately comfortable. But after all the chestnuts we've saved from scorching for some of the real nabobs, I think it's high time I joined their exclusive ranks."

"And you have a plan?" It wasn't really a question.

"I have a plan," said Raker evenly.

"And my role?"

"It will be a death strike, or strikes, that will happen through your machinations—and the pay will be considerable. Bother you?"

"Not if my funds are in some other currency." Cheney was pragmatic.

"That'll be up to you," said Raker.

Cheney nodded. "You've still not said who."

"Maybe more than one. But first, Anthony Quiller-Jones."

"That filthy sod? Be a bleeding pleasure. With that daily rag of his he's stirred up more hate and violence than most other newspapers put together. Except, of course, for your *Washington Post* or the *New York Times*."

"I'd like him taken out with a blaze and a pop."

"Like it was the IRA, eh?"

"Yes. And it must be on a certain day."

"No problem there. The vulture's habits are disgustingly regular."

"Good. All strikes must be according to schedule for maximum effect."

"I see. And how many—strikes—are scheduled?"

"Irrelevant at the moment. Several, however."

"And the—I think you said probable—decrease in the value of the pound?"

"I'm hitting hard at your natural resources."

Cheney considered the statement. Understanding lit his face.

"Oil! You're going after our rigs, or the terminal. Good God, man, those places are protected like . . . well, like your Fort Knox."

"I have ways," said Raker mildly.

Cheney sipped his whiskey. "Yes," he said, nodding. "I'm sure you do. Am I to be in on that?"

"No. Does that relieve you?"

Cheney thought. "Not exactly," he said finally. "Might be a real banger of an experience. Big thrill, and all that. Somewhat daring."

He looked at Raker expectantly.

Raker grinned broadly. "Your talents will be needed elsewhere, Phillip."

"You seem to have recruited plenty of help." It was a question.

"It's building," said Raker.

"It's obvious you're putting the bite on someone," said Cheney. "Am I to know who the victim is to be?"

"The victim, Phillip boy, can damn well be almost anyone among a goodly percentage of the population of the western world. And on any social or economic level."

Cheney looked puzzled.

"An insurance company, lad. THE insurance company. Any of their clients, or any insured property, can be the target."

Cheney digested the information. "If the company is of that size, then the potential targets are practically limitless," he said, realizing the implications.

"And in the most part, unprotectable." Raker studied Cheney's face. "Are you in?"

"I'm in. It's brilliant. That is, I'm in if I can afford it. It's obvious that the money can't be paid until the—until after you come to terms with your pigeon."

"You can afford it. You'll receive $250,000 up front. Now that will cover expenses with some to spare, won't it?"

"It *will* do that."

"And you can handle the Quiller-Jones affair without difficulty?"

"A piece of cake."

"There may be another, you know."

Cheney shrugged. "In for a penny, in for a pound." He smiled. "That's two clichés in a row, isn't it?"

"All right then. Let me run through the details for you. Here is the way it's set to operate, with precautions built in."

In the following minutes Raker outlined, succinctly but thoroughly, all the information Cheney would need to know: All strikes would be scheduled, with the target known in advance to the individual responsible for making the strike. These strikes were to be canceled only if an advertisement in the personal column of a designated newspaper ran within the three days preceding the scheduled date. In the unlikely event that the two strikes did not produce the compliance of the insurance company, a third strike would be made. This strike would include the at least partial demolition of the Shetland Island oil terminal.

The individual targets would be identified by additional advertisements containing information giving the title of the book that would enable Raker's associates to decipher the number code left in their possession. These numbers would determine the page, line, and letter to be used in spelling out the name and location of the target. This precaution was deemed necessary to insure that none of the participants would decide to take matters into their own hands.

Following the time set for each strike, an answering service in New York City was to be called. Prearranged, innocent-seeming messages left would identify the caller and indicate the success or failure of the mission.

Any required actions past those planned would be announced in the same manner in the advertisements in the same paper. It would be checked on a regular basis until terms were reached with the insurance company.

In the unlikely event that Raker should be "taken out," then sealed and coded instructions had been left with two separate law firms which would, upon not hearing from Raker according to a prearranged schedule, forward the sealed envelopes to Cheney. The use of two addresses would help preclude Cheney not receiving at least one. Uncoded, they would detail the remainder of the plan, and allow Cheney to follow it to a successful conclusion.

Cheney interrupted. "And what if I were to decide to have you taken out myself?"

Raker looked at him with grim humor. "First," he said, "if I thought that was a remote possibility, I would not have chosen you for my Number One. Second, I will not be available. Third, you know better than to even think of it."

Cheney was not offended. He nodded in agreement. "I have full appreciation of that."

Raker continued to outline the time and place for delivery of the necessary information, along with the promised front money.

"I'll need time to get all arrangements in place," Cheney said. "When do you need to know?"

"Tonight, early tomorrow. Soon," Raker replied.

Cheney nodded. "I'll have it for you. Phone all right?"

"There are always listeners," said Raker. He knew there weren't. At least, not always. But better to think so. "Still . . ." he thought a moment before continuing. "If you come up with a telephone number, reverse it and add one to each digit. If it's an address, do the same with the numbers, and give me the name of the next closest street starting with the same letter and paralleling the real street. In the unlikely event there are such streets equidistant on either side, use the north or east street name depending on which direction the street runs."

Cheney was refilling their glasses. "You're on. One for the road?" he asked. "Or should we make it one for the money?"

Raker lifted his nearly full glass. "I still have some."

"Yes," said Cheney. "So you do." He smiled knowingly. "But then you always do." He looked amused. "Tell me, Raker old man, as often as you hold glasses, but as little as you drink, why is it that you always seem to arrange meetings where liquor is served?"

"Because those are the places where total strangers have a right to be. And they are where one can sit quietly, observing, but being unobserved except by those who have either an insatiable curiosity or a more threatening interest. And you can do something about either." He grinned and mollified Cheney with a small sip from his glass. "You can't really tell when you're being watched in a museum, a church, or walking the streets. Pubs are nearly always available, and there's anonymity in crowds. But not so much that I can't tell who's showing up too often in the small crowds of the places I choose." He raised his eyebrows quizzically. "Or do you have some other suggestions?"

"Great heavens to the Venerable Bede, no, my dear mentor," said Cheney in exaggerated protest, holding up his hands. "It was only that you've mastered the art of appearing to drink when you're not." He took a packet of Rothman cigarettes from his pocket and started to light one with an expensive looking lighter.

Raker reached out a hand and grasped Cheney's wrist. "Sorry to see you've fallen by the wayside, laddy boy."

"Off the wagon, you mean?" said Cheney, looking sheepish. "I know, I know! Slave to a fermented weed and all that. Still, we're not in the bush any longer, are we?"

Raker released his wrist. "Really?" he scoffed. "We're always in the bush, Phillip. Us, and the others like us." He sipped at his drink. "Ever consider how many are still out there who'd like nothing better than to split you from crotch to cranium?"

"One tends to want to forget," observed Cheney.

"Well, bucko, they's just as dangerous in these here now civilized places as they were out yonder." He was silent a moment. "Remember us finding the Basque's head with a cigarette still stuck to the lips? The smell gave his position away."

Cheney stabbed the unlit cigarette into the ash tray. "You really do have a facility for breaking a habit, haven't you?" As Raker watched, Cheney took the pack from his pocket and tossed it into the nearby waste basket. Raker estimated that he would have it replaced within the hour.

"You look in top condition," said Cheney, changing the subject. "Hard as diamonds, like always. It's that damned discipline, I suppose?"

"Have to, at my age," said Raker.

"Shit, Rake, you're ageless. Never saw the day that any of us even dreamed we could take you. Never entered our minds." A new thought entered his mind. "And how are our old companions doing these days?"

Raker eyed him obliquely without answering.

Cheney laughed openly. "I see. So I'm not to know just who's in this with us. Fair enough. Then how's that lovely child of yours? If that's not classified info, also."

"No, it's not classified. She's fine. Fine. Real well." Damn. Why had he ever let anyone know he had a daughter?

"That's good. Glad to hear it. She still in Geneva?"

"Yes. School." Hell, she was almost too old for school. "Upper school, college. You know."

"I see. Yes." Raker's discomfort was apparent to Cheney.

Shouldn't have brought it up, he thought. He was vaguely surprised to see Raker show so much concern about anyone, then he remembered that the daughter was the only thing the man had ever displayed real emotion about. Dismiss it, he told himself.

"Then when will I see you again?" he asked.

Raker was relieved at the change of topic. "Don't know that we should, until after this affair is over. You have all the information, or soon will have, that you'll need to contact me in an emergency. Let's leave it there. For safety."

"Good," agreed Cheney. "Then we can get together and celebrate another successful foray." He lifted his glass in toast.

Raker touched his glass to Cheney's. "Then," he corrected, "we can get together and celebrate you becoming filthy rich." One of those like his well remembered friend, The Menace, thought Raker.

They drank.

• • •

The hallway outside the room was empty, and Raker left the hotel feeling that his meeting had gone unobserved. Now, he thought, a relaxing evening, and a good meal in an entertaining establishment. It would be at Vecchia Riccio on upper St. Martins Lane. It was a delightfully uproarious ristorante, and the food was superb. Raker would finally have his grand Italian dinner. Later, he would retire to his hotel for a review of his plans as he awaited Cheney's call. Tomorrow?

Tomorrow, Elizabeth Gordon.

• • •

It had taken Phillip Cheney more than five hours on the preceding evening to track down Elizabeth Gordon's phone number and address. Few others would have been able to do it at all. The address had not been in Kensington, but rather Knightsbridge.

A female voice answered Raker's call.

"Do I have the honor of addressing Elizabeth Gordon?" he asked.

"This is Elizabeth Gordon," came the reply.

"You do not know me, I'm afraid, not directly, but I am a former associate of your brother, Alexander."

"Alec? You're a friend of Alec?"

"We have spent time together, yes. Perhaps you have heard him refer to me?" Raker left the question hanging.

"And just how would he have referred to you, Mr.—?"

"Perhaps he might have mentioned "The Man?" or "The Colonel," quite possibly?"

The phone was silent for some seconds before Elizabeth Gordon replied.

"Yes, he has mentioned you, quite more than casually, Colonel." Some stiffness had crept into her voice. "My brother is not here in London at this time, however."

"I did not call to talk to your brother, Miss Gordon. It is *Miss* Gordon?"

"Unless you're American. You sound that. There, I think your mindless educators, spineless journalists, and overpaid robotized government employees prefer the asinine Miz designation."

"And you obviously don't."

"The *Times* certainly doesn't, and we must heed the *Times*, mustn't we?" A slight note of humor had crept into her voice.

"Most certainly, Miss Gordon. And in any event, I am Canadian. And I did not call to speak to Alec, but to you."

"To me? Whatever for?" Demure. Overdone.

"I find that my interests coincide closely with those of yourself and Alec." And I know who runs the show, thought Raker. "I felt it would be of more than passing interest for us to spend an agreeable luncheon while discussing them."

"I am not in the habit of dining with those to whom I have not been formally introduced, Colonel." The words did not match the warmth of the voice.

"I can appreciate your caution, Miss Gordon, however I don't feel that such is the case in hand. After all, your brother and I were quite close, so that does present a different aspect, does it not?"

Slight hesitation. "Perhaps." Tentative and non-committal.

Raker affected a light laugh. "Come, now, Miss Gordon. I would expect any meeting to be most circumspect. Let us say that

we shall meet for lunch in the bright of day at say, the Mirabelle?
12:30?"

"You are most persuasive, Colonel. Allow me to check my
calendar." Raker could discern no sound of the telephone being
set down, or any other noise to indicate movement. After a short
pause the throaty voice came back to him.

"That appears to be quite suitable, Colonel. How will I know
you?" The words that followed, quickly, were amused. "Now isn't
that like a line from some melodrama? In fact, how *will* I know
you?"

"Not necessary, Miss Gordon. I most certainly will know you,
and will be able, perhaps, to inveigle the maitre d' to perform that
formal introduction."

Her laugh seemed real. "That will be quite unnecessary, Colonel.
I shall look forward to our luncheon with pleasure."

The voice, thought Raker, didn't go with what he knew of
Elizabeth Gordon. But then, he was all-too-aware that things are
almost never what they seem. It was nearly 11:00 in the morning.
He just had time to prepare for the luncheon. It would not take
place at the Mirabelle.

• • •

At five minutes past noon, the taxi pulled to the front of the large
gray stone home and came to a stop. Raker walked the several steps
from where he had been standing against the adjacent building.

"Plans have changed," he said to the driver, extending his
hand.

In it was a ten pound note. "Will this cover your inconvenience?"

The driver took the note with alacrity. "Right enough, it will.
Not to worry." He touched fingers to his cap and drove away.
Raker watched, his back to the Gordon residence, until the taxi
was out of sight. He turned and mounted the steps to the front
door and rang the bell.

"Right there," came the voice he recognized.

In a moment the door was drawn open. Elizabeth Gordon's
mouth opened, then closed quickly. Eyes widened in surprise.
"But . . . I . . . you . . . I was expecting . . ."

"You were expecting your taxi," finished Raker. "I sent him on his way."

Elizabeth Gordon started to speak.

Raker lifted a hand. "Wait! I have reason, certainly. Please hear."

The woman looked up at the man standing in front of her, carefully evaluating what her eyes saw. Well and expensively dressed. Taller than she, but not quite towering. Modishly styled and expertly groomed dark hair was cut short over a tanned, rugged and interesting face. Neat, precisely trimmed mustache and keen, dark, penetrating eyes. She felt a sense of authority about the man. And competency. Certainly that. Her pale, tiger's eyes narrowed slightly. A challenge, by God! She kept silent.

"It was important that I see you, Miss Gordon. And the foolish preliminaries were necessary to help insure that I meet you without the company of others who may be interested in my, or your, activities."

Clever sod! Intrigue the girl, she thought. He had succeeded. "And just why might others be interested in your—our—activities?"

"I hope they will be just that, soon. *Our* activities. And, Miss Gordon, if so, I'm certain you wouldn't like any outside interest either."

The woman cocked her head to one side and studied the man in front of her. Yes, she was definitely intrigued. Just what did he know about her? And her brother? Yes. It was certainly worth finding that out.

"Just what is it that you are suggesting, Colonel?"

"Please call me Ian. Ian Campbell. The Ian will do." A possibility existed that the Gordons would hear of a man named Coleman working with the Irish.

She continued to study him, head aslant. "All right, Mr. Ian Campbell, just what is it you propose to do to insure that there is no 'outside' interest? Take the trusting girl into her own parlor—or yours?"

Raker was up to the game. "Perish the thought, ma'am," he said, holding a hand across his heart. "Heaven forbid! I simply thought it would be more proper for us to share victuals at another location than mentioned. I don't trust the privacy of telephones. And I thought it far wiser for me to drive us there, to make certain that we are not followed by any of those intriguing outside parties."

The bastard! He knew she was intrigued. He was indeed a challenge!

"Well, as you can see, I am prepared to travel. And ready for lunch. What do you suggest?"

Raker reached for her hand and gently removed the keys she held ready to lock the door. He pulled the door shut, turned the lock, and tested to see that it was firmly secured.

"We stroll casually to yon carriage, and seek out some interesting and diverting location in which to converse and eat." He eyed the woman's svelte figure. "Modestly. By all means, we must eat modestly. I would never be a party to changing by one centimeter that loveliest of forms."

"Isn't that a little forward?" asked Elizabeth Gordon. Her voice held no rancor.

"It is. But it is most certainly an honest and accurate evaluation."

Elizabeth Gordon slipped her arm through Raker's as they descended the steps. "I have the distinct feeling," she said, "that you are a charming and unmitigated bastard. And I will most probably like you very much."

They laughed together as Raker walked her the few yards to the hired Jaguar sedan.

• • •

Raker had been able to find parking not far from their destination. It was nowhere near Curzon Street and the Mirabelle.

"Have you been here?" inquired Raker.

"No," said Elizabeth Gordon. "I've heard of it, of course. Is there some reason you have avoided Mirabelle?"

Raker nodded. "Several. In addition to hired help who have become terribly impressed with themselves, and service which now borders on dis-service, I seldom go where I've said I'm going."

Elizabeth Gordon smiled in understanding. "The ever-cautious Colonel. Alec has told me of the trait."

The two were seated at and in Eleven Park Walk. The name and the address were the same. Raker did not tell the woman of the other reasons he had chosen the restaurant. Where the Mirabelle was one of London's most sophisticated haunts, its clientele was far too international, and there was too great a chance that—in spite of his changed appearance—he and his companion would be recognized. It was an event to be avoided. Mirabelle is a place for those who want to be seen and recognized; Eleven Park Walk is a place for those who want to be adored, if only by themselves.

The restaurant swarmed with sweet young things bedecked in the latest, high-fashion apparel. The two mirrored walls of the main floor offered patrons the chance to admire themselves from many angles. A lacily-banistered, curving staircase offered a display case for shapely legs beneath the swirling skirts of distaff patrons. Its steps were kept very busy. Probably, thought Raker, so were the legs. In the brightly lighted surroundings one might expect to see the faces of not-quite-top models, and new, hopefully rising stars of cinema and stage. One would be right. Moderately loud "in" music infused the air which made conversation require close attention, and eavesdropping quite impossible. It was the main reason Raker had selected the place.

The food and service had been adequate if not outstanding, and Elizabeth Gordon was pleased with the beauty around them. She held her glass of champagne in front of her and lifted it to peer across its top with narrowed eyes.

"Quite a lovely place, Colonel." She extended her hand toward Raker. He took it. "Are you ready to explain your rather intriguing remark about having interests which coincide closely with those of my brother and me?"

"Yes," said Raker. "There is that, isn't there?" During their meal the woman had changed moods sporadically, switching from haughty lady to little girl. Now it was the business woman.

"I suppose I just became distracted with more interesting things." He let his eyes sweep across the woman's face and upper body.

"Good. I like that. But I would also like to know what you meant." She looked around, pointing with her eyes. "There is certainly no one who can hear."

"True. Yes." Raker pretended reluctance. It was easier without her brother here, for Alec knew that "The Colonel"—though he did not know Raker's true identity—was never reluctant. Moreover, the woman was the leader.

"All right," he said. He paused and cleared his throat. "We have similar interests in seeing that the IRA doesn't force the union of Ulster and the Republic of Ireland." He made it sound a distinct possibility.

Shock showed on Elizabeth Gordon's face. And anger. That such an event could actually happen had never been given serious consideration by her.

"My God, no! Is that your interest?" She grasped his hand, hard, not flirting this time.

Raker nodded solemnly. "That's my interest, yes. And don't think for a moment that it isn't an imminent possibility."

Slowly, she shook her head from side to side. "No," she said, hesitantly. "No! That will never happen. Just never happen."

Raker waved off the approaching waiter.

"No," she reaffirmed. She shook her head more vigorously. Her deep hatred of all things Irish was dramatically obvious. "It isn't possible. Even with our government's token negotiations with those filthy Irish pigs, it will come to nothing. You don't appreciate the ability of the British to sidestep agreements of convenience."

"I'm quite up on the English facility for betrayal, Miss Gordon," said Raker dryly. "If you'll pardon the commonness of the adage, practice makes perfect."

The woman eyed him suspiciously. "That sounds terribly anti-British."

"Not at all. Just a statement of fact. You British have become expert at wearing black hats and making the world think they are white."

"Is that some Americanism?"

"Of no consequence, lady. I'm just agreeing with you. But you're dead wrong about it not happening." He emphasized the word dead. He leaned forward, holding her quiet with his eyes.

"Without the full support of the British people, you Northern Ireland separatists won't have a chance."

"I'm not any kind of Irish, Campbell." Indignation bristled.

"No. Certainly not. But you and your brother are so damned committed to maintaining the Empire's hold on Ulster that it's an obsession." He leaned back and made his expression less intense.

"You forget that I've worked closely with Alec. I know how your older brother met his end."

He waved toward the hovering waiter and ordered Cognac and coffee. The woman asked for B&B. During the short wait, he remained quiet, allowing Elizabeth Gordon to digest the implications of his words.

"All right, Mr. Ian Campbell," she said, finally, after the waiter had come and gone. "Now that you've stopped your foolish game of "charm the lady," just what is it that you are trying to tell me?"

"I'm notifying you that union is on the way. I'm informing you that without the full support of England, all the Ian Paisleys of Ulster and their shadowy Ulster Defense, or whatever groups, will have their dicks knocked in the dirt."

Her expression showed she didn't grasp the full meaning.

"Castrated," he said. "Emasculated. De-balled, your Grace."

"Crude," she replied, but the hint of a smile pulled at the corner of her finely curved lips.

"It's a matter of money, lady. Pure and simple." He reached out to tap the back of her hand with a finger. "Look! While those damn fools were busy starving themselves to death out at Long Kesh, Irish-Americans increased the rate at which they were contributing money to a degree you people can't even begin to imagine. Believe that—it's a fact. And they are still giving. That money can be used to arm and equip forces that your Unionist para-military groups can't begin to match—not without the cooperation of the British government such as they've had in the past."

"And still have," objected the woman.

Raker looked at her sympathetically. "Be realistic, Duchess. Public opinion is fickle. For all the hysterical jingoism generated by such acts of terror, the masses do tire of the fear and long to see it ended. Whenever you or your newspapers or your leaders start spouting about how the Provos, or any other Irish group, are on their last legs, just remember the PLD as only one example. There was a time when their particularly vicious brand of terrorism kept them hiding out in dark places, shunned by all decent governments. Look at them now! Look at the reception given the late Arafat, by countries such as Austria and Greece. By religious leaders, for God's sake! Good Lord, woman, they even have a seat at the United Nations! And the Irish nationalists' actions, while not acceptable, are damned near benevolent compared to those other bastards' actions."

"You are defending them."

"I am stating facts, lady. You'd better realize it. Unless something is done to stop the money coming in, home rule is coming to Northern Ireland, and you can put that in a collection plate."

Elizabeth Gordon looked skeptical. "I can't believe that."

"Are you willing to take a chance on it?"

She poured her B&B into the coffee and stirred it as she thought. "I'm practical, Campbell. Of course I'd rather not take a chance on it. Do you have any suggestions?"

The nibble! He nodded his head slowly. "I have," he said simply.

"And . . . ?"

"Cut off the funds at their source." Now, thought Raker, will come the part she'll like.

"And just how do you manage that?"

"I don't. You do. You and your brother." The baited hook bobbed delicately upon his words.

"Oh? And just what are we to do?"

Raker delivered his wolfish grin. "Easy—you eliminate the major donors," he said quietly.

The woman didn't change expression although her eyes windowed interest. It seemed that murder was a quite suitable discussion to be held over a luncheon table.

"You see," continued Raker, "I know just who those major contributors are, and I have the means to put you within striking distance."

"That's really a very foolish thought, Mr. Campbell. Whatever in the world makes you think my brother and I would have any part in such a hideous enterprise?" Her obvious interest belied her words.

"Come now, Miss Gordon. I told you that word spreads." The bait had been taken. Time to set the hook. But not too swiftly. He lifted his brandy and downed it. He raised a hand to catch the waiter's eye.

"Best be toddling along," he said. Let her stew over his words.

• • •

Elizabeth Gordon's agitation was obvious as they walked to the car.

Raker remained silent as he politely opened the door for her. She remained quiet as he pulled onto the street and into traffic. He waited for her to break the silence.

"Really, Mr. Campbell," said the woman finally, "whatever gives you the idea that we would be remotely interested in, or even dare think of such a thing as murder?"

Raker glanced at her, quickly. By God, he thought, she sounds like she's drooling.

"I know . . . things," he said, drawing out the last word. "And more than you dream." He sensed the line was drawing taut. The woman squirmed in the seat, twisting sideways to look at him.

• • •

"Suppose," she started, "just suppose that I—we—might be interested in such an adventure.

What would be in it for us?"

"Fewer Irish," said Raker simply. Now! Time to play her toward the net.

Elizabeth Gordon nodded without realizing it. "I see, and you think that is sufficient enticement?"

"I do," replied Raker. "But in addition, you'll receive a lovely, all-expenses-paid holiday, and quite liberal payment to boot."

"You intrigue me, Mr. Campbell. Most definitely; though I would never never be a party to such activities."

Raker kept his voice light. "I think the proper reply to that is 'Bullshit!' my dear. You've done it before."

There was no surprise forthcoming. "Have I, really?" She was more amused than concerned.

"You have. Would you like me to list names, dates, places?"

She regarded the question. "No," she said following a short silence. "No, I don't think I would like you to do that." Damn the bastard! He *does* know. "Not admitting for a moment that your insinuations are remotely true, fact and conjecture are poles apart," she said.

Raker simply looked at her knowingly.

"Furthermore, you're a fine one to be judging others. Alec tells me that you are one of the most bloodthirsty savages he's ever known."

"Who's judging, lady? You're wading in unnecessarily deep water. I'm on your side. Remember?"

Elizabeth Gordon settled back into her seat, somewhat mollified. "Yes," she said, a bit reluctantly. "I suppose you are." She looked at him. "You weren't exactly accusing, were you? Mind, I'm admitting nothing." Kill Irish sympathizers? Actually be able to kill those stinking papist pigs? How lovely! She felt a sexual tingle start to spread from deep within her body.

"What you're hinting at would be terribly dangerous." Oh, how delicious! To be paid, actually paid, for doing what she and Alec had rather do most. Well . . . nearly most. The tingle intensified.

Raker laughed. "Hinted? Somehow you've missed my words, lovely lady. I've hinted nothing. I'm offering you the opportunity to kill your enemies, and at my expense."

The woman was silent for several seconds. Not quite ready for the net just yet, thought Raker.

Finally she spoke. "A small concern," she said. "Just how do I know that you are who you say you are, Colonel whatever-your-name-is Campbell? I've only your say-so for that."

"Fair enough," admitted Raker. "I appreciate your caution. Do you know much of your brother's activities during his time with me? With 'The Man'?"

"We are very close, Alec and I. Yes, I do know."

And I know just how close, thought Raker. However-loving close. "Good," he said, "then you can ask anything you please. You should be able to come up with queries that only I can answer." He waited.

Elizabeth Gordon thought for several moments, as Raker drove smoothly with the flow of traffic. Finally, she began to ask questions. He was impressed with her knowledge of her twin brother's activities while he had served with Raker's commando. Especially the more gory details. An excellent memory, thought Raker. It was now filed in his mental dossier about the woman.

Finally, Elizabeth Gordon seemed satisfied.

"It would seem, at least on the surface, that you are truly, The Man, or The Colonel, as you prefer. Is Campbell the name?"

"Certainly not."

"No. It wouldn't be. Very well. I'll consider your proposal. But I will make no decision until Alec has had a chance to identify you in person, and until he approves of any arrangements."

"When did that start?" inquired Raker. "When did you give up command and allow Alec to make any decisions?" His tone took the sting out of his words.

She smiled. "I see. You do know the program, don't you?" She would have spelled it programme. She paused to light a cigarette. Raker did not object.

Brow furrowed in thought, she tapped a pink-pearl enameled fingernail against her front teeth. "All right, Ian Campbell," she said, coming to a decision. "I'll consider your game. But with a condition."

Into the net, little fish, thought Raker. Flop right in.

"And just what might that be?"

"I want to find out what you're made of," she said, smiling seductively. "Just how—basic you are. I've heard all these stories of how cold-blooded and hard you are, but I want proof."

"Proof?" Good God, did she want him to kill someone in particular? Well, that would depend on just who it was. *He* wanted the Gordons.

"I have a favorite little pastime of my own, and if you're what you make out to be, you'll not mind joining me in it." She put a hand on his thigh and slid it suggestively up and down.

"You should even enjoy it." Her fingers curled and she raked her nails, not gently, up his leg.

"Oh?" he asked. He knew of the games she and her brother

liked. A nice afternoon of friendly torture? Is that what she had in mind? Not on this old carcass, he thought.

"Over there," she said. "Ahead. The hotel on our left. Stop there."

He lifted his eyebrows. "An afternooner? How lovely." He made his mood light.

Her smile was faint. "Hardly yet." She said. "It requires more than merely an attractive man's proximity to prime me. No, foolish man. I've a call I want to make to check on something." She looked at him from under lowered lashes. "Not," she added, "that the other possibility doesn't bear some later consideration."

"Have you money?" she asked as the car pulled into the parking area.

"Telephone? Certainly." He reached into his pocket.

"No, silly. Well, I'll take that too. I mean real money. A goodly sum, I suppose you could say. What I'm planning may be quite expensive."

"I can manage," drawled Raker, making it sound as if his funds were unlimited. "Are you curious to see if I can really make good on my offer?"

She shook her head. "No. I will not even discuss that until later. I'm thinking of the payment for our . . . entertainment. Now. Today. If it happens to be on."

"No problem, Duchess, no problem. Make your call."

As Elizabeth Gordon walked to the small hotel, Raker considered what it was that she might be planning. He shrugged. No matter. He couldn't let it faze him, whatever the case, as long as it did not endanger him. He needed the Gordons to complete his preparations. He would have to go along with anything within reason, and there was little doubt her idea of entertainment would be esoteric. It might be a most interesting day.

When the woman returned she was obviously elated. Her eyes sparkled with an unnatural brilliance. She slid into the seat past the door which Raker held open for her.

"Must have been a successful call," he offered.

"Successful?" she leaned across and kissed him on the cheek.

"Oh, yes." She leaned back in the seat, eyes closed. "Ever so much so. Our timing is perfect. Tonight's a big, special event." She seemed to shiver delightedly.

"And just what big event, Duchess?"

She looked up at him slyly. "Never you mind . . . but it couldn't be better. Tonight's is a once-a-month affair."

Raker considered the information. It could be possible to recruit the Gordons without playing the woman's game, but he would prefer the twin's willing cooperation if he could get it. Coupled with the fear he would instill later, it would deepen their commitment. However, he would in no way endanger his personal safety. At the moment, his highly developed sense of self-survival was not alarmed by the woman's actions or her obvious excitement; it seemed caused by past experiences with whatever entertainment she was anticipating.

"Am I permitted to ask just what it is that I'm to join you in enjoying?"

Elizabeth Gordon affected a pout. "That would spoil it. I want it to be a surprise." She was now the little girl.

"And if I'm not willing?"

"That, my dear fellow, is what I want to find out. And if you can't accept that, then I will be forced to bid you a quick farewell."

Best to call, and see if it's a bluff, thought Raker. "In that event," he said, "I'd blow you a kiss as you departed."

"I see," she said. Fingers drummed against her leg. "And just what do you wish to know about the entertainment?"

"That it isn't harmful to one's—well being."

She laughed. "Oh, my goodness, no. Not to us. Quite the opposite. It's . . . it's exhilarating! It's a club, a social club that meets regularly in a large old mansion well out past Hempstead." She turned to him, eyes glowing. "Have you ever heard of the old Hell Fire Club?"

Raker nodded. "I have. Some of your royalty and even old Ben Franklin himself were reputed to be involved in it. Is that the one?"

"That's it. Well, this club is built somewhat along those lines.

It's for those who like, who enjoy, rather esoteric forms of pleasure."

"I see," said Raker.

She stroked his leg. "If you're what I've heard, you'll enjoy it quite as much as I."

• • •

So be it, thought Raker. I will at least let you think I enjoy it as much as you. And, he added, I just might. After all, there was very little that Raker hadn't experienced, or at least seen.

"Is there a name for this club?"

"Initials. Only initials. M-D-S, it's called. The M-D-S Society."

He considered the letters, then smiled faintly. Should have known, he thought. MDS. Not subtle. Not subtle at all. Marquis De Sade. The Marquis De Sade Society. Okay, thought Raker, that'll be fine. As long as I'm not on the receiving end.

"All right," he said. "But we mustn't overdo. We'll have to practice a little healthy discipline." He had paused to emphasize the last word. "I'll be happy to make that painfully clear."

She smiled. "Awful man," she said. "I guess you're . . . bound . . . to do it?"

She giggled and slapped the back of her hand against his arm. She felt the hard, resilient muscle under the fabric. She looked up at him.

"Not this sweet, young girl." She regarded him with sensuous eyes. "But oh, how much I'd like to have you . . . bound to please."

Raker laughed. "Not hardly, m'dear. Not hardly. Not my game, either—though I certainly won't mind trying to please."

"I'll count on that." She squeezed his arm. "Then let's you and I not get all—tied up in it." She was proud of her comment.

Raker acted his approval, with a smile. "And just how much time do we have?"

"Oh, oodles. We won't be admitted for a few hours yet. That gives us plenty of time."

"Good. I have a call of my own to make. After I take care of that, I'll escort you on a tour of the local dungeons and chambers of horror."

"I've seen them," she said.

• • •

Raker found a telephone within the next few blocks and made his call. It was to Phillip Cheney at the office he maintained in his role as a freelance journalist. On occasion, he had even written stories that had been published.

"Cheney here."

"Mr. Cheney, I'm calling to research an article I'm considering."

"I'll try to help." No name was to be used.

"I've heard of a group that calls themselves the MDS Society. I know little about them. Do you?"

"MDS, you say? Let me think. MDS . . . Yes. As I recall, a rather quaint little club. Into bondage and discipline . . . that sort of thing. Is that the one?"

"That would sound like the group. Are they . . . dangerous?"

Cheney's voice came back amused. "Not to their members, I understand. Supposedly many rather respectable types are reported to belong. Quite hush-hush. Very circumspect. If something of that sort can be. Quite discreet. Willing victims and all that. In the most part."

"Willing? Most part?"

"Yes, some for pleasure. Some for high pay. A few of the weird ones for their own perverse pleasures."

"And the others?"

"It's rumored that a few subjects are not exactly willing. Some members are very influential folks."

"I see. Then if one were invited, you think it might be safe to attend a meeting? Is there much chance of it being a trap?"

"Oh, I should think it safe. Quite highbrow, too. And ultra-expensive. Are you thinking of joining?" Cheney had his needle out.

"Oh, no. Just that a lady acquaintance of mine was telling me what little she knew about the group."

"Well, with luck, perhaps you'll be invited to attend a session. Understand they can be—how shall I say it? Arousing?"

"Yes, so I've been given to understand. Thank you very much, Mr. Cheney. I'll continue to search for articles by you."

"Good of you. By the way, I didn't get your name."

"No," said Raker, "you didn't, did you?"

He hung up, smiling. It appeared that it would be safe to accompany Elizabeth Gordon, and find out just what kind of evening she had planned. One thing, it was most certain to be different.

CHAPTER 14

INDOOR SPORTS

With some hours to spend before the appointed time, Elizabeth Gordon had teasingly asked Raker if, seeing as how he knew her town so well, he wouldn't give her a guided tour. In the following few hours she was slightly startled and moderately impressed to discover just how much she did not know about the city and its surroundings.

"You truly are an intriguing bastard," she said, finally, as Raker swung the car around Regent Park and onto Wellington Road which would lead them toward their destination. "I've thought that since we first met." She considered her words. "But you knew that. Planned it, did you not?"

Raker managed to look enigmatic. If she liked intrigue, so be it.

He had discovered facets of Elizabeth Gordon's personality that had not been included in his computer file on her. The basics had been there, but now he could add, if it mattered, emotional instability and mercurial mood changes.

He was not surprised. Only interested. It fitted with what he knew of her and her twin brother. He had tended to credit her with more solidity and less capriciousness. And, perhaps because of the cold violence of some of her past activities, he had not been quite ready for the extreme attractiveness and inescapable sensuality.

Why, he thought, do individuals so often equate brutal actions with ugly people? Perhaps because brutality is, in itself, ugly?

"There!" cried Elizabeth Gordon. "Just ahead. The big pillars and iron gate." He could hear the excitement in her voice.

It was still quite light, and as Raker turned the Jaguar into the driveway, he could see, through the heavy ironwork of the gates, the immense spread of the estate behind high stone walls. A broad tree-lined road swung in a wide curve past the gates and disappeared behind what appeared to be a garage.

"And what are you thinking?" she purred.

"Nothing unusual," he said. "Just thinking that it is quite orderly and well organized."

"Yes," agreed Elizabeth Gordon, "it is." She turned to face him, hand on the door handle of the car. She narrowed her cat-like eyes and affected a tantalizing smile as she cooed seductively: "Now, please step into my parlor, Colonel."

Her expression, thought Raker, would have suited a leopard as it contemplated a grazing fawn. He smiled. Or was it simply the woman eyeing a faun? Unworthy, thought Raker. He came much closer to a satyr than a faun.

Never mind, he thought. When you can't whip them, join them. He leaned across and slipped a hand behind the head of Elizabeth Gordon, fastening his fingers in her hair. He lowered his face, and holding her firmly but gently, nibbled at her lips. Her mouth parted in response and her arms came up toward his neck. He grasped her wrists in his free hand and held them securely, without effort.

"No." He said it softly and gently, smiling. "Not yet, Your Grace." She was startled at how easily he held her immobile. Try as she might, she could not budge her head or arms, yet he did not seem to be using any force.

"Damn you, Campbell," she said softly. There was no anger in her voice.

"Shall we?" he asked. For the moment, it had become his game, not hers. It was his invitation. She had to be made to believe that anything she could do, he could do better.

She stared at him, realizing that something had changed, not quite sure what or how. "Yes," she said, "let's. This, my good man, is going to be an experience you will long remember, if you can long endure."

She took his arm, and led him to the rear of the garage where she pushed a button next to a door. The panel slid open to reveal a small vestibule. As they stepped inside, the door slid quietly shut.

"And what now?" inquired Raker.

"You'll now appreciate the care and planning with which my club allows complete privacy to those so desiring."

"Those so desiring?"

She nodded. "Some do, others don't. If one wants to mingle and mix, one can."

"Otherwise?"

"Otherwise, one can have all the seclusion one wants."

"And if one wants to participate?"

She smiled. "One certainly may."

"And you prefer . . . ?" He let the question dangle.

She smiled enigmatically. "It depends."

"I see. And just how do we get out of here?" He looked around the small, wood-paneled room.

"We tell them what we want," she replied. "Here." Her hand indicated an array of buttons at the back of the tiny antechamber. "When one's wishes are known, the door will be opened from the outside, at a time that will allow us to continue unobserved except by those whose presence is necessary to attend our wants."

Raker's appreciation of skilled organization surfaced. "Admirable," he observed. "And just what have we decided?"

She wanted the upper hand again. For now, that was all right with Raker.

The woman crossed her arms over her breasts and leaned back against the wall to look him up and down. "It has been a long and busy day," she mused. "I think that perhaps a bath is in order."

"Friendly thought."

"And then, to the merchandise."

"Merchandise?"

She smiled. "Or menu, if you prefer. Tonight is auction night."

It was Raker's turn to be intrigued. Skillfully done, he thought. "And that means?"

"Never mind—you'll see." Her fingers became busy at the array of buttons. "There." She smiled up at Raker. "All done. I've told them just what we want."

Raker's curiosity was aroused. Stay alert, he warned himself, and learn. "And now?"

"Now, we wait."

The words were hardly out of the woman's mouth when the rear door slid open to reveal a large, ornately decorated chamber of red fabric, red carpet, white marble, polished wood, and gleaming, crystal lighting fixtures.

"Impressive," allowed Raker. "Lead on, Madame."

"We'll be led," she smiled, and as if on cue, a tall, suave, sleek man appeared, accompanied by a young woman. The man was dressed in the manner of an Edwardian-era retainer. The girl wore an abbreviated, coquettish costume meant to represent that of a French maid.

Raker smiled inwardly. She appears to have just stepped out from some porno-parlor peep show, he thought. But undeniably attractive.

"Sir. Madame." The man bowed his head the barest fraction of an inch. "Welcome. Your baths are being drawn."

Baths? Not bath? Cute, thought Raker. Tease and tantalize. Or was it a slip? He glanced at Elizabeth Gordon. She was smiling slyly. It was, indeed, to be the plural. Baths.

They followed the maid through another door, and were ushered to separate chambers on opposite sides of the corridor. As Elizabeth Gordon started to move through the door of her room, she turned to smile at Raker and lift her shoulders, hands out from her body, palms up, as though saying, "What can I do?"

Clever bitch, thought Raker, almost with admiration. Her quick changes of mood, her emotional instability and his knowledge of her psychopathic tendencies had made him forget that. She was deliberately trying to keep him guessing as to her game. Offer, suggest, then pull back. Strategies that used to earn a woman the title of prick teaser. And probably still does, he thought.

"When M'sieu completes his toilet," said the maid, cutely and with a theatrical French accent, "M'sieu should put on the robe to be found on the clothing rack, and slippers."

M'sieu would also find his clothes rejuvenated when the evening was over, he was informed, and M'sieu should also take his personal property from his clothing. He would find the pockets of the robe of sufficient size to permit such a course of action. M'sieu should, of course, ring when he was through, or if he happened to need something else. Raker wondered idly just what needs might be serviced by the "serving maid."

The water felt good to Raker. Its temperature was hot enough to prevent the lassitude which so often follows a simply warm bath. Emerging from the water, Raker rubbed himself dry with the large, thick, velvety towels provided, used the razor present on the wash basin to scrape the stubble from his face, and checked to make certain that the claims for the adhesive used to hold his "undetectable" toupee in place were true. They were.

He transferred his bulky wallet, handkerchief, pocket knife, comb, and key chain to the pockets of the sleek, silky robe, thrust his feet into the accompanying slippers, and pulled the tasseled cord hanging near the door. As he waited, he casually studied the room for indications of a concealed camera. If there was one, it was skillfully hidden. There were no mirrors flush-against the wall behind which viewers could lurk, and no vents or other grillwork to hide prying eyes or lenses. Perhaps they weren't used. It was possible that Phillip Cheney was right, and this was, as he had indicated, a discreet club.

He closed his eyes and concentrated. No, there was no sense of impending danger.

He opened the door to see Elizabeth Gordon standing in the hallway, smiling tentatively. She looked soft and feminine in a robe similar to his. Her tawny, shining hair framed her face in loose, feathery curls. Raker saw none of the hardness he knew was part of the woman. Well, now, he thought. Here we have the lovely, defenseless maiden, bravely ready to face what unknown perils the evening holds. How long, now, until I see another facet of the Gordon character?

"You look marvelous," she said, slipping her hand through the crook of his nearest arm. "So virile." It was almost a purr.

Careful, thought Raker. Your innocence is slipping. "And you, Duchess, are ravishing."

She looked at him from cruelly teasing eyes. "Isn't that for you to do?"

Again, the purr.

The innocence, thought Raker, has most certainly slipped. With this one, it could not last long. He tried a roguish grin. *"En garde,"* he said.

The "butler" was once again at hand, and as he bowed, more with his head than his body, he said, "Madame. Sir. Are you ready for me to conduct you to the viewing room?"

"But of course, Jellico," said Elizabeth, grandly.

The tall man hesitated, eyes on the woman.

"Yes?" she quesioned.

"It is only, Madame, that I have been asked to caution . . ." he stopped abruptly in midsentence, deliberately, thought Raker. "That is far too harsh a word," he apologized in a perfunctory manner, ". . . it is just that I have been requested to advise Madame that she must exercise more restraint on this occasion than when she was last here." Short pause. "Accompanied by her brother." The pause followed by the breech of secrecy was an obvious warning.

Elizabeth Gordon's eyes flashed in quick anger. She maintained her poise only with difficulty. "Very good, Jellico." The pleasures she derived from the club were far too exquisite to endanger.

The haughty man smiled icily. "Very well, then. Please follow me."

The man called Jellico led Raker and Elizabeth Gordon up a wide, curving staircase and to a door opening from one side of a hallway which curved out and away from the stairs in horseshoe fashion.

Lighting in the room they entered was soft and warm. Raker could see what appeared to be a broad, deeply cushioned chaise lounge at the elevated rear of the room, while in front of them were two heavy, comfortable looking chairs, facing a large glass window. Against a wall was a small sideboard which supported bottles, glasses, and an ice bucket.

"Drink?" inquired Elizabeth Gordon. Her anger still showed.

"I'll mix," said Raker. "What was that all about?"

"What was what all about?"

"The warning. About you and your brother. Exercise restraint?"

"Oh, that. Nothing at all."

From their afternoon together, Raker was aware of the woman's taste in liquor. He mixed their drinks and as he handed one to her he said, "No. I don't accept that. I think I'll just have to make very sure that I restrain you." He said it with emphasized insinuation. She played the cat's-eye game again over the rim of her glass.

"That just might be a lot more difficult than you think, Colonel Ian Campbell." The words were drawn out, soft and slow.

"Un-huh, sure," said Raker, then for effect: "What do we do now, screw?"

Her eyes widened with amusement. She set her glass down and placed her hands on his chest, pushing the robe slightly apart to slide fingertips across his chest.

"Not-fucking-likely, Colonel Campbell. Not just yet." She turned away abruptly and picked up her glass. She moved down to sit in one of the chairs before the dark and opaque window.

"There'll not be a long wait. Never is. Things run well here."

"And just what is to happen?" inquired Raker, seating himself beside her. "The merchandise, did you call it?"

"The merchandise." She nodded her head. The pink tip of her tongue slid forward and played across her lips. "The menu, I prefer."

A tiny frown creased her smooth brow. "I've been slightly remiss, I fear. I said it might be expensive. Would you consider it crass of me to inquire, just what kinds of funds you have?"

Jesus Christ! thought Raker. In the middle of this blatant introduction to what every indication says will be an evening of highly esoteric, erotic, and most likely perverted pleasure, the bitch wonders if it's crass to ask about money! At least, he thought, she is consistently inconsistent.

"I would hazard a guess that it is quite sufficient, Duchess. What's the normal fee?"

She accepted the question lightly. "More tonight than usual. As I said, it's auction night. Cover charge this evening will be at least five hundred pounds each, I think. Payable when we leave. But I shall most certainly want to buy some merchandise. That can be quite expensive."

To hell with the cost, lady, thought Raker. It will just come out of what would be your share. "And just what does expensive mean?"

Elizabeth Gordon's eyes gleamed brightly. "That depends on what I see on the menu." She considered the question. "I've seen bidding go as high as, oh, 3,000 pounds."

Be reluctant, thought Raker. But not too reluctant. He frowned. "That's a lot of money for a little entertainment."

"It's a lot of excitement for a little money," said Elizabeth. Raker would swear he could hear her pant. "Do you have it?" she asked.

"I have it," he said, "and more."

She leaned toward him, placing a hand on his knee. Her eyes caught and tried to hold his. "I'm going to challenge you, Colonel. I'm damn well going to see if all I've heard about you is true." She slid her hand up and down his thigh.

"And just what does that infer?" Her eyes had dared him.

"That you're up to anything. Those are Alec's words: The Man is up to anything." She patted him. "We'll see."

A voice broke the momentary silence, softly yet distinctly.

"Ladies and Gentlemen," it said from a speaker overhead, "the bidding will be underway shortly. If I can have your attention please?"

There was a thin whir and the opaque, tinted panel slid up past the wall of glass in front of them. A figure clad in a toga-like garment stood in a spotlight focused on a platform in the center of an arena slightly below them. There was now one-way viewing from their chamber.

The voice continued. "Tonight's merchandise will be displayed in order of the draw, except for the final presentation which will be a triple offering. Opening bids will commence at 500 pounds, and will proceed in 100 pound increments. The first offering is blue starred."

"It's starting," whispered Elizabeth Gordon, unnecessarily. Her eyes gleamed.

"What's the star biz?" Raker asked.

"Shh! Later!"

To Raker it was reminiscent of what motion pictures depicted as ancient slave markets. In turn, victims—for that is the way he thought of them—were led forward into the bright lights and presented for viewing through binoculars furnished with the bidding chamber. The presentation was, he acknowledged, carefully staged.

The first item of what Elizabeth Gordon had called the "menu" was a strikingly beautiful girl with dark, sleek hair which hung low about her bare shoulders. She was shoved roughly to the center of the platform by two burly men clad in the manner of Roman soldiers according to Cecil B. DeMille. Across her shoulders lay a stout pole along which her arms had been stretched and securely tied. She was clad, as was all the female "merchandise," in a sheer, chemise-like garment without shoulder straps. It opened down one side, that side being secured with two knots, one just under the arm which seemed to hold the thin slip up; another was near the waist. The garment hung to just below the top of the girls' thighs, and the nearly-open side allowed enticing glimpses of flesh. The simple and cleverly designed covering was far more tantalizing than a naked body.

No doubt, thought Raker, watching, that there is something arousing about seeing a beautiful object appear helpless and defenseless. He felt his interest quicken as he watched.

Bidding was conducted silently as buttons inside each cubicle were pushed which caused bidding light to glow outside the glass where the "slave-master" could see it. The girl, it was announced, had been claimed by Box Eight. The sum was 2,500 pounds. Elizabeth Gordon had watched carefully but did not press her bidding button.

The second presentation was a handsome, golden haired young giant of a man who was wrestled to the platform with difficulty. His body, clad only in an abbreviated loin cloth, gleamed with perspiration or oil. He was announced as another blue star.

"He's fighting," observed Raker. "Part of the show?"

"Most times. Not always." She watched the young man through her binoculars. "Sometimes the subjects are not all that willing."

Raker looked at her with interest.

"A small service of the club to offer disciplinary measures for members who have been affronted by certain individuals." She smiled.

"And?"

"I like those," she said. "They're the gold star offerings . . . often aren't as protected. Shhh! There's more coming."

The young man had sold for 2,400 pounds, and Raker and his companion watched as the next three presentations were sold; two girls and one man. It soon became apparent to Raker that bidding prices fell into a rather predictable range. The high had been 3,700 pounds, and the low, 2,500. Until now, all had been red or blue star.

"How many more?" asked Raker. He was enjoying watching. All the merchandise had been either handsome or beautiful, with the labels not to be applied, necessarily, as one might expect, to male and female respectively.

Elizabeth reflected momentarily. "It depends on how many boxes are full. They always make certain that there will be competition for the final bid. It will be, by far, the highest." Her eyes glowed in the dim light. "And the best." She licked her lips.

"And that's what you're waiting for?"

She had not yet made a bid. "That is exactly what I'm waiting for."

"And what if the last presentation is not to your liking? What if it's female?"

She looked at him from predatory eyes. "It doesn't matter. It doesn't matter at all."

CHAPTER 15

Marquis De Sade Society

Her wait was short. After only one other girl and a young man became the evening property of unknown club members, the original master of ceremonies came to the center of the platform.

"They know their people," said Elizabeth Gordon. "So far, four females, three males. And all sold well. Now, let's see just what the *piece d'resistance* is to be."

"Ladies and Gentlemen," said the chief auctioneer, "this evening's final presentation will include use of the Caligula Suite." He paused.

It meant little to Raker although he understood its implications. "A real chamber of pleasure," said Elizabeth Gordon. Her hands slid up and down her thighs in anticipation. "All kinds of . . . goodies up there."

"The bidding will commence at 4,000 pounds, and will continue at 500 pound increments." The toga-clad speaker paused once again. "This is a gold star offering. Bring them forward."

Raker expected the toll of a gong. One did not sound.

From the dark surrounding the platform emerged what seemed to be a struggling crowd. As the group came into the light, viewers could identify six of the armor-clad attendants hauling three struggling victims to the center of the lighted area. Raker caught his breath. The girls were astonishingly beautiful. He picked up the binoculars for the first time.

Slim, curving bodies swelled under the sheer and skimpy costumes the females wore. Their arms were tied tightly behind them, forcing their breasts out against their garments. The outline of hardened nipples could be seen jutting into the thin material.

One of the girls gleamed gold and ivory, with a cascade of glistening hair tumbling about her head. The other girl's long, chest-nut-brown hair reflected highlights of bronze and copper as she twisted and tugged against the hands restraining her. The young man was as striking as the females.

He stood slim and tall, beautifully proportioned and muscular, but with the trimness of a gymnast rather than the bulk of a weight lifter. His finely chiseled features were topped by locks of dark, unruly hair, and large, dark eyes glared at his captors. As he struggled, muscles played across his chest, stomach, and bare upper abdomen above the abbreviated loin cloth.

"My God," ached Elizabeth Gordon. "They're beautiful. All of them." She looked at Raker. "I want them, Colonel. I want them." She said it fiercely.

"Then get them. Bid until you have them." Hell, he thought, I'll find use for those ladies myself.

• • •

Evidently other bidders felt the same attraction, for it cost Raker over 20,000 pounds. That, thought Raker, will be relatively cheap recruiting, for it would come out of the Gordons' fee.

"Where do I pay?" he asked.

"There," said his companion, pointing. "There's a pneumatic tube. If you were a member they would take a check. Do you have the cash?" She eyed Raker's hand holding the fat wallet.

Raker handed her the money. "Tell them to keep the change," he said.

"Oh, no," she replied. "That will be returned when we leave." She placed the bank notes in the cylinder and sent it on its way, then picked up the telephone from the sideboard. "Now, Colonel," she said, voice filled with anticipation, "now we'll find out what you're made of."

Following Elizabeth Gordon's call, they were escorted to a lift that carried them up to what Raker estimated must be the top floor of the mansion. They were then shown into a room not at all like what Raker had expected.

The large chamber was lushly furnished, with a high ceiling and broad French windows opening onto a wide balcony which looked down upon a spacious courtyard. As he surveyed their surroundings he mused that he had, probably because of Elizabeth Gordon's intensity and all the showy preliminaries, been prepared for a dark and somber dungeon with stone walls and floor, racks, chains, wheels and bare tables for furniture, and with whips, tongs, pincers, and glowing braziers of hot coals as its decoration. Nothing of the sort was in evidence.

"Surprised?" inquired Elizabeth Gordon, as though reading his mind. She stood, hands on hips, eyeing him with amusement. "We're really quite sophisticated, you know. But all is not really what it seems." She reached out a hand to stroke his cheek. "Just you watch, love." She turned to their escort.

"Our property is gold star?" she asked.

The man cleared his throat gently. "Yes. They are not, er . . . ." he broke off as a slight smile twitched at his lips, ". . . not as protected as others might be," he finished.

"They are not volunteers?" persisted the woman. "They have been, let me say, somewhat uncooperative in their dealings with certain influential parties." The tiny smile was still there.

"You are quite right, Madame, in assuming that normal restrictions are not in effect on this particular lot." He held up a hand and waved a finger at the woman. "But, I must say, that the ultimate restrictions are still binding, with no recourse."

She had expected it. She smiled. "Not to worry, Jellico. I would never think of marring such lovely merchandise. Only permissible attentions."

"Quite. Very good." The dignified man turned his eyes toward Raker.

"Would you and the gentleman consult as to the placement? Or perhaps," he said, eyeing Raker's size and physical appearance, "he would like to do that?"

"Oh, not for now, I think. We may rearrange later. But for now, I think that terribly handsome young man should go over the horse, there. It should offer the finest view of his magnificent little bum." She looked around the room. It was obvious to Raker that she knew its potential.

"The lovely blonde girl—spread there, I think," she pointed toward the huge, upholstered, bed-like platform in the center of the room. "And our gorgeous, chestnut-haired beauty? On the little bench there, so we can allow those fine, long tresses to cascade freely." Her eyes sparkled with anticipation. Leather and metal straps gleamed from the four corners of the bed, the bench, and the bottom of the four legs of the sawhorse.

"As you wish, Madame," said Jellico, bowing once again. He clapped his hands loudly, and the entourage of guards entered, dragging with them their victims.

"Come, Colonel," said Elizabeth Gordon, taking Raker by the arm.

"Let's mix a refreshing drink as our entertainment is made ready." She tugged him toward a bar against the far wall.

• • •

As Raker poured, feeling somewhat awkward, but nonetheless aroused, he asked, "What normal restrictions, and what permissible games? Are those things I should be aware of?"

"Oh, that." She sipped at her glass. "We've been quite lucky, you see." She motioned at the room, vaguely. "These lovely little playmates of ours are not the normal . . . merchandise. They haven't sold themselves for money, or thrills, or anything like that. These are being punished for some offense or other they committed against the wrong party, or parties. In their case, nearly any game I can think of is permissible." She watched one of the girls being tied as she had requested.

Raker grinned at her. "And perhaps some I know that even you haven't heard of."

She looked at him with interest. "I hope so. I dearly hope so. As for the restrictions, those always apply. No blood, no scars, nothing broken. No permanent damage." She brushed the subject away as unimportant.

"Restrictions which you, and Alec, evidently went past on at least one occasion?"

She shrugged. "We were a tiny bit overzealous with a young couple. Nothing important." Her eyes were looking over Raker's shoulder.

He turned to watch with her. Not exactly my bag, he thought, though he was acutely aware of his growing sense of anticipation. Hell, it was something different. A little of the sadist in all of us, he thought. Try it, make it look good. Convince her you are as wanton as she. As he looked at the lush bodies of the young females he realized that it would not be difficult.

The handsome young man had been bent over a narrow, waist high, padded bar which was supported by sturdy A-frame legs, securely fastened to the floor of the room. The young man had his legs forced wide apart and strapped to the bottom of the structure's base. His arms had been pulled down over the rail and each wrist had been strapped opposite an ankle.

Raker viewed the youth's plight with interest. A most helpless and exposing position, he thought. He realized the potential for a variety of attentions Elizabeth Gordon might be planning to pay the youth. As they watched, together, the lovely blonde girl was spread-eagled on the low, bed-like platform and each wrist and ankle was tied firmly in place by the straps attached to each corner.

The girl with the beautiful chestnut hair, tresses reaching almost to her hips, was placed upon a low, narrow bench which was perhaps no more than a foot wide. Her legs were spread and her ankles tied to rings fixed to each side of the bottom of one end of the bench. Her wrists were tied together, her arms stretched up and back of her head, then pulled down and held taut by a rope run through a ring on the floor at the other end of the bench. It looked to be most uncomfortable, thought Raker. It was. But again, the position offered a great many possibilities for Elizabeth Gordon's kind of games. Raker's co-purchaser of tonight's merchandise had been right about the girl's hair. It tumbled in soft swirls about the stretched body, reaching the floor.

"Thank you, Jellico," said Elizabeth Gordon. "Very nice."

"Good evening, Madame. Sir." The man dipped his head. "Have a most enjoyable evening. I think everything you'll need will be found in the cabinet." He paused. "But then," and he looked at the woman, "you know that, don't you?"

It was his parting reminder to Elizabeth Gordon in regard to some past misjudgment.

"Well now," said Raker as they stood alone with the exception of their trussed and helpless property, "and just what is first on your agenda?" He was aware that excitement was building, and he could feel the throb growing in his groin.

"Don't hurry, dear man," smiled the woman. "We have oodles of time." She stalked slowly around the bound threesome. Finishing her examination she moved back to stand alongside Raker.

"I must say, they are truly a nice prize," she said, slipping an arm through Raker's. She turned toward him and pressed her body close against his. "My, we are getting a rise from the events, aren't we?"

She squirmed against him. As his arms started to draw her even closer the woman pulled away. "Wait, Colonel old boy. I have a little questioning to do first."

She pulled completely free and moved among the young, bound threesome. As she swayed her way around their tied forms, her hands fondled them as she talked.

"I know," she said, her voice soft and sweetly evil, "that I have the dear Colonel here who will be more than willing . . ." She paused as she reached the bent body of the young man, "and I'm certain that this nice young lad would not mind joining in, but what I'm interested in finding out is just which one of you young ladies I might persuade to take part in making love to me. I do love the men, but the attentions of beautiful girls do so add to the festivities."

She moved away from the male and circled around to the girl tied to the bed. "You?" she asked. "Wouldn't you like to join in with the men and see how much fun that might be?" She fastened a hand in the blonde hair and pulled the girl's head up. "Wouldn't you? Wouldn't you like to have a go at making love to me?"

The girl squinted her eyes against the pull of the hand in her hair but said nothing.

"Well?" insisted Elizabeth Gordon.

"N-no," said the girl. It was almost a whisper.

Elizabeth Gordon only smiled. She loosened her grip on the girl's hair and moved away to kneel next to the girl tied to the bench.

"And you?" she asked softly. "You heard the question. Wouldn't you like to do it?" She raised her hand and squeezed the girl's cheeks fiercely. "Wouldn't you?" Her voice was sharp.

"No!" said the girl. "Never." Her voice was defiant. Elizabeth Gordon sighed and rose to her feet.

"That is really too bad," she said, mildly. "Too, too bad." She moved back toward Raker. "Before this night is over, both of you will be begging for the privilege." She smiled up at Raker. "Stubborn little things, aren't they? But they will come around. They always do."

The woman leaned against Raker and her hand slid down his chest, parting his robe and fluttered lightly across the pulsing, hardened flesh at his groin. She spun away quickly with a laugh.

"Patience, my dear Colonel. Patience. The waiting only makes it better."

It was her game, Raker knew, and there was no doubting the woman's love for others' discomfort. All right, he could stand it, although it was getting harder. At the thought, Raker burst into laughter.

Elizabeth Gordon arched an eyebrow at him. "Something funny?" she inquired.
"Only anticipations of pleasure, Duchess. Now be getting on about your business before you end up the victim of sudden rape."

It was Elizabeth Gordon's turn to laugh. "You'll hardly find that necessary. You'll find me only too willing. When the time is right," she said. "And then there are our lovely guests for you to service. Again, when the time is right. We'll have to make them sing a bit first." She had walked to the cabinet indicated by Jellico earlier.

She opened its doors and took out a flat broad paddle which appeared to be made of soft leather. She slapped it against the palm of a hand. It made a resounding crack. She nodded in appreciation.

"Quite satisfactory, I think." She slapped the leather down once again. "Oh yes, quite suitable."

She walked slowly over to the youth strapped across the sawhorse-like bench. "I must say, this is certainly a nice prize." She turned her head to look at Raker over her shoulder. "Modest young chap, isn't he? Must do something about that." Her fingers busied themselves at the boy's hips, and then she pulled his loincloth free.

"Magnificent!" she exclaimed. Her voice was breathy. "Absolutely smashing little bum, what?" Her hand slid over the exposed bottom, testing and teasing. She slid her hand between the boy's legs, massaging and squeezing his vulnerable and swelling flesh.

"Now, isn't that better?" she cooed, leaning over the boy, addressing her remarks toward his head which was bent low across the frame. "We don't have to worry about all those cumbersome old clothes, do we?" Her hand kept up its movements. When the boy didn't comment, she tightened her grip, squeezing hard. "Isn't that nice, I asked?" She tugged. The young man moaned.

"Yes. Yes, it's nice," he groaned. "Please. It's nice." Elizabeth Gordon released her grip and patted him gently.

"That's better. That's a good boy. You'll just have to learn not to make mum angry, won't you?" Her hand slid backwards, and up. A finger with its sharp nail picked and probed, not deeply.

She looked toward Raker. "Isn't that a lovely little posterior, I ask you?" Her hands massaged the muscular bottom. "Truly lovely." She sighed.

She straightened and stood erect to undo the sash holding her robe closed. She shrugged it off and tossed it away. She knelt on the carpet behind the tied youth, hands at the clasp of the string of pearls around her throat.

"While you play, my dear Duchess," said Raker, "I think I'll take the opportunity to do a little exploring of my own."

"No, please," said the woman, quickly. "Wait. I want you to watch this. Then I'll join you."

Raker watched as she gently spread the boy's nether cheeks then, carefully and slowly as his hips twitched against the padded bar, she pushed the pearls, slowly, one by one, inside the boy. Very good, thought Raker. But with pearls? He knew the sensation of the game. A most novel and expensive innovation, he thought.

Finished, with only an inch or so of the strand now visible at the boy's rear, Elizabeth Gordon leaned forward, lifting her head to trail kisses across his firm flesh.

She stood, retrieving the paddle from the floor where she had placed it. With carefully measured strikes she began to spank the boy's elevated rear, alternating sides. First slowly, then faster, each stroke came slightly harder than the one before. The crack of the paddle had grown loud by the time a sudden, sharp cry was torn from the boy's throat. At the sound, Elizabeth Gordon halted the punishment she was delivering.

"That's a good boy," she said. She stretched out her hand to gently touch the angry, red welts the paddle had raised. "Those little decorations are most becoming," she said, "and I'm sure they'll keep you warm for awhile." She patted the boy. "I'll be back, little love. Yes, indeed. I will be back. But right now the big man and I must not deprive your lovely companions of our attention." She patted one final, firm goodbye which was accentuated by a gentle tug at the visible end of the string of pearls. "Be a good boy while mother's gone."

She turned to Raker. "How about our little blonde lovely, my dear partner?" she asked lightly, moving to sit alongside the spread-eagled girl. "Shouldn't we be taking a closer look to see if we received good value?" She raised innocent eyes to Raker. "Come here."

Raker did.

Slowly, deliberately, Elizabeth Gordon reached over the tied girl and loosened the two knots holding her scanty clothing about her. She pulled away the sheer cloth as though unveiling a new work of art. It was that, indeed, thought Raker. The girl's supple body, spread open and defenseless, seemed flawless. Pink tipped nipples topped firm, young breasts which managed to hold their arched curve though she was stretched on her back. Elizabeth Gordon's hand slid over the satiny flesh to nestle in the triangle of soft curls between the girl's wide-spread legs.

"Beautiful," she breathed. "Absolutely beautiful. See for yourself, Colonel," she said, moving away.

Raker needed no urging. He slid his hands over the smooth skin, finding and lingering in the areas where he felt the girl's body quiver in response. The soft tangle of curling hair was damp in spite of the girl's situation.

"And you, you gorgeous creature," said Elizabeth Gordon, kneeling beside the girl bent and stretched along the low bench.

"We mustn't ignore you. That wouldn't be fair, now would it?" She untied the knots holding the girl's only covering and pulled it away. "Oh, my," she breathed. "Please look at this, Colonel. Perfection!" Her hands caressed the taut body.

Raker took time from his work to look their way.

"Oh how thankful I am that we wouldn't be called on to judge a beauty contest between these two." Her hands captured the girl's coral-tipped breasts and she lowered her face, parted her lips, and nibbled gently at the nipples, sliding one hand down to let her fingers explore in the warm, soft darkness between the girl's legs.

The sight heightened Raker's arousal. There had been no intimation that Elizabeth Gordon was a lesbian, or even bisexual. From her actions until now it appeared certain she was most definitely the latter. That, or more likely, her sexuality allowed passion for any object upon which she could practice her beloved techniques of pain. He would think about that later. Not now.

Elizabeth Gordon placed a gentle kiss on the girl's cheek and raised herself from where she knelt. "First my dear Colonel, let's do a little decorating on this lovely lass with the long, long hair." She walked back to the cabinet from which she had taken the paddle used on the boy. Raker noted it was the second time she had spoken of decorations.

"These," she said, collecting items from inside the open doors, "have proven most effective on past occasions." She turned and held up her hands. They were filled with small metal clips, not unlike ordinary clothes pins. "When placed on certain sensitive areas of a body, they not only look quite nice, but they do bring forth the most extraordinary reactions and sounds." Her smile, thought Raker, was what the word wicked was all about.

"At first," continued Elizabeth, walking back toward the girl bound to the bench, "the sensation is quite uncomfortable but nearly tolerable." Her eyes flashed with anticipation. "But after a time the pain continues to grow and grow until it truly becomes unbearable. You'll see. Come, help me."

Raker, filled with the need for sexual release, hated the woman. He had never enjoyed or approved of causing others to suffer. Rather the opposite. Nonetheless, he was aware of the connection between pain and sex, and realized that his reasons for joining

Elizabeth Gordon in her torments were not only because he was playing a role. He knew that at this point, even if the woman had not been with him, he quite likely would have continued the game—on a somewhat more gentle level, he hoped. But even that was not certain. There was something quite exciting in exercising power over helpless victims. He took clips from Elizabeth Gordon's hands willingly, disliking himself for the eagerness with which he did it.

"You start up there," said Elizabeth. "The nipples, of course," she continued as though that were blatantly obvious, "but also the ears, lips, that nice tender flesh of the armpits. Use your imagination."

She held up one of the clips. "There are simply bundles of these little toothed devils. As for me, I'll just start with a few down here between the legs." She looked at Raker with glowing eyes. "We girls do know how to bring about the simply grandest sensations down here, especially on other girls."

They worked at their jobs. The helpless girl's body tugged against its bonds as small whimpers came from her throat. When all the clips were used, Elizabeth stood to survey their work.

"Quite good, Colonel, most inventive. In less time than you think our little lovely here will be speaking to us of her grand experience in unmistakable and delicious tones. And it will get better and better."

Raker, feeling terrible need, moved back to the bed-like platform and slid out of his robe. He knelt and started to lower himself over the body of the spread-eagled girl. Her huge, violet eyes looked up at him, not showing fear, but almost with relief. Perhaps she was to be spared the other girl's misery.

"Oh, no!" It was Elizabeth Gordon's voice. "No, Colonel. Not yet." She was on the upholstered surface, near him, quickly. "That just isn't the way it's done. Not yet." She put a hand on him, at the same time stroking him and pushing him gently away. "They have to earn that. They have to pay for it." Her eyes were huge and bright. "Pain for pleasure. For example . . . ." She placed hands on the girl's breasts, grasping their tips.

"Now I think this superb little creature is too quiet. Don't you?"

She didn't expect a reply. "So let's see if we can't liven up the party a bit."

Her fingers squeezed her nails together. The girl arched up from the bed, a short cry escaping her lips, eyes squeezed tightly shut, and face contorted.

"See?" she asked simply. "But I'm just a gentle woman. Now you . . ." she took one of Raker's hands, "you have such big, strong fingers." She grasped his thumb and forefinger. "Oh yes, such nice, strong fingers." She placed his hand over the girl's breast. "I'll bet you could really get her to sing for us?" She pushed his thumb and finger together.

Almost without thought, Raker tightened his fingers and felt the body stiffen under his grasp. He strengthened his grip, and the body bounced. The girl whimpered, and a gasp of a pain escaped her lips.

"Oh, wonderful," breathed Elizabeth Gordon. "Wonderful. Please, more!" She moved away from the girl and out of Raker's sight. "Don't stop. Let me hear. I'm just at the cabinet getting a little equipment." In a moment she was back at his side. On the surface beside them she placed a short, flexible dog whip, a pair of small tweezers, two stiff bristled brushes and several thick rubber bands.

"For later," she explained. "The brushes are simply marvelous for the circulation, and the cute little elastic bands can be amazingly effective in creating sudden reactions. But for now . . ."

She grasped Raker's other hand and forced it down to the cleft between the bound girl's legs. Knowing what was expected of him, Raker pinched flesh, squeezing and twisting. The girl's soft cries of pain became louder. Elizabeth Gordon dropped to the floor near Raker and pushed at his legs.

Her mouth opened and her lips enclosed him, her tongue working furiously. "More," she mumbled, "more noise."

She quivered with pleasure at the screams of the girl as Raker, lost in the sensations produced by Elizabeth Gordon's practiced skill, tortured their victim's flesh, almost unaware of what his hands were doing or the sounds they brought. All he felt was the glorious thrills which flooded his being. It rose from the moist, warm whirlpool which seemed to engulf him, pulling his entire body down into its tugging, swirling vortex.

...

Later, Raker sat nude in a chair near the bar, drinking a whiskey and water, watching Elizabeth Gordon. She was insatiable, he thought. Absolutely insatiable. It had been hours since he had lost himself in his first encounter with delivering pain for pleasure. And, sexually satisfied to a point beyond his expectations, he had grown tired of the cries of anguish which so delighted Elizabeth Gordon, though those now seemed past. As he watched, he reminded himself that it was not only pain that gave the woman pleasure. She loved the actual act of sex. He had been right in his earlier evaluation. The woman went beyond being bisexual. Sex would be sex, no matter what the person or the object.

She had been from girl to boy to girl and back again, using her hands, her mouth, and the carefully designed instruments of pain which had come with the room, to create cries of both pain and pleasure as she had used their victims in turns and at times together. Raker had shifted, repositioned, regrouped, and retied their merchandise time and again. And, he would admit, it had been interesting!

In fairness to Elizabeth Gordon, Raker admitted that he—and he hoped only to reaffirm his role in her eyes, but he was not sure about that—had introduced some events which had caused her pleasure to be amplified. They had not been, he thought, as painful to their victims as the games invented by the woman. But, he thought, that was probably a cop out. In fact, he had enjoyed the evening. And, at least thus far, there had certainly been no damage to their merchandise. By tomorrow, any reminders would be mostly forgotten.

He felt himself start to respond now as he watched Elizabeth Gordon and the two truly beautiful girls as the nude bodies of the three lay intertwined and writhing gently on the bed to which the blonde girl had been tied. Elizabeth Gordon had been right. The girls had indeed pleaded long and painfully to be allowed to make love to the woman. Their agony and, even more, the indescribable relief from it, had made the girls far more than simply willing partners. They had been almost greedy in paying physical adoration to Elizabeth Gordon's body, and had been rapturously receptive to mouths and hands as they were serviced by her and each other in turn and together.

Raker had joined in their orgiastic abandon. He had performed with extraordinary and greatly appreciated zeal and proficiency. In his present condition it did not matter, though he was aware of the fact that he had hardly been missed when he retired from the game. As he watched, Elizabeth Gordon wrapped an arm around the girl whose head had been moving across her breasts, lips and tongue loving and busy, and then she reached her hand down to gently caress the hair of the other girl whose face was snuggled against Elizabeth's thighs.

"My God," she breathed, "enough. Oh, yes. Enough." She pulled the girls up to hold each of them with an arm. She looked over at Raker, stroking each of the girls gently.

"They learn so fast," she said. "They've become so very eager and expert. Or haven't you tried them?"

Raker knew the woman's words were meant as a dare, or perhaps just to tease.

"I did, indeed, try them, partner. In several ways as you well know." He decided to force a grin. He discovered it was real. "I have tried everything," he said, looking at the woman pointedly.

"Really?" asked Elizabeth Gordon. "I must have not noticed." Her smile and tone said it was lie. She uncoiled gracefully, extricating herself from the arms and legs of the girls which held her.

She reached for the robe she had discarded earlier and thrust her arms into its sleeves. She did not close it, but instead moved across where the young man, after being used—and abused—in several ways, had been retied to the frame. She reached out a hand to touch his bottom.

"Well, well, they're still there," said Elizabeth approvingly, referring to the paddle marks. She stroked the boy softly. "He's really been through quite a lot, and no relief, either." She looked back at Raker. "That's the beauty of it. We let him touch and feel and perform, and make him beg and moan, but with no release." She smiled in satisfaction. "But now, it's time."

She dropped to her knees. Her hand grasped the youth and

she began. Her motion was slow and smooth and sure. The boy responded, muscles twitching, soft moans of pleasure coming from his mouth. And as Elizabeth Gordon felt the first surges, she added a massaging motion to her hand's movements, and at the same time reached with her free hand to grasp the end of the pearl necklace she had inserted in the youth. As she felt the throbbing increase within her grasp, she slowly pulled the long string of pearls from within the boy. His moans increased and his slender, smooth muscled body slumped against his bindings as warmth flooded Elizabeth Gordon's hand. She rubbed the hand against the boy, drying it, and stood.

"You forgot, playmate, a moment ago," she said, facing Raker, "that you haven't completed everything."

"No? I can't imagine what that could be."

She smiled secretively. "One thing. We haven't . . . ." She let the words trail off.

"Now my little boy here will be ready in a short time . . ." she looked up at Raker, as though delivering an aside, "isn't it wonderful how quickly the young recuperate? Yes, he'll be ready in a very short time, but in the meantime," she reached to the floor behind the rack where the youth was tied and picked up something, "come here."

It was a gentle order. She beckoned enticingly.

Raker moved to the woman. She raised hands and grasped him. As he had watched her play with the youth, his diminished and flaccid organ had regained life, and as her hands stroked him gently he felt blood surge. She dipped fingers into the jar of petroleum jelly she had picked up and began to smear it around the swelling muscle.

"I'm flattered," grinned Raker, desire spreading, "and I don't want to offend you, but I don't think that will really be necessary."

Elizabeth Gordon uncoiled easily and rose to her feet. She moved to the boy tied to the frame and smiled wickedly at Raker as her hand smeared the lubricant deep into the crease of the boy's buttocks.

"Oh yes! I think it will. I really do!"

Raker stared at the woman. That, he thought, is not my game.

The woman continued to wait, holding her hand out toward him. The girls she had left were kneeling upright on the bed, watching the others with interest. Their arms were around each other.

What the hell, thought Raker. Why not? He had come this far. He shrugged and stepped forward toward the frame. He was growing accustomed to the use of Vaseline by now.

Elizabeth Gordon moved back toward the bed where the two girls reached for her. She sank to the bed where eager hands slipped off the robe she had donned. The bodies of the three females melded together as one, and they prepared to watch the action from across the room.

• • •

"Well," sighed Elizabeth Gordon. "It was a magnificent night, Colonel. I mean really."

Raker eyed her from across the automobile as they sped back toward the city. He forced a chuckle. "It was indeed quite a night."

She had placed a hand on one of his arms and studied his face.

"You really make a marvelous playmate, Colonel Campbell, or whoever you are. Most satisfying. I'd like to do it again sometime." Her eyes were warm and affectionate, her voice soft.

"And me, Duchess, and me." It had not been difficult at all, he thought, not liking himself for it. "But I'm not sure I can afford your passion."

Elizabeth Gordon smiled luxuriously with renewed memories of the night past. Ah! Those wonderful sounds! "Next time, my good fellow, the treat's on me. You are a most ingenious and inventive man." She was past such hunger, but looked at Raker as though planning a menu for some future banquet.

"And you, my dear Duchess, are persistent. After the pleasure those lovely young people gave you, I'm surprised you insisted on retrussing them before we left."

"Come, Colonel," said Elizabeth. "They were paid for until noon today. There are still a couple of hours to go."

"True," said Raker. "But that's not showing a great deal of appreciation. Especially not with those nasty little clips feeding on their tender flesh."

"Decorations, dear Colonel. Decorations." She snuggled into her seat. "And by now they will be serving as irresistible reminders of the evening for our young people. *If* they are capable of coherent thought by now." She glanced at her watch. "Of course, in time our little toys will probably escape to unconsciousness. Those little clips do cause one to faint eventually, you know."

"I have no doubt," said Raker dryly. "Won't our man Jellico release them?"

"Of course not," replied Elizabeth. The thought was absurd. "We bought them for the entire term. They will be released only when the time is up."

Raker wished he had approached the man with a bribe to release the youngsters once he and Elizabeth were gone. It would probably have done no good. To Jellico, business would be business, and the contract must be fulfilled. Raker discarded the thought.

"Well, then," he said, "your obvious pleasure would seem to indicate that you might be interested in joining my little campaign. Am I correct?"

"Colonel, I am interested in joining you in just about anything."

The words were not said lightly. "Just what is it, exactly, that you want of my brother and me?"

Raker told her.

Elizabeth Gordon's eyes, as he listened, became predatory and feral. Certainly! She would be delighted. She knew her brother would be most happy to cooperate. Just when could they get started?

"As you've said, Duchess, let's not hurry. We have plenty of time."

Now they were his! The Gordons were in. His preparations were complete and it was time for execution. Or perhaps, he thought, I should say *termination*.

CHAPTER 16

As Beverly Martin Raker hung up the telephone in the lobby of his hotel, ending his conversation with Pagan Maguire, he experienced a sense of satisfaction. In the something less than six months since his successful recruitment of Elizabeth Gordon and her brother Alec, his plans had proceeded without a flaw. As he had estimated, the addition of the woman's twin brother to his plot had required only the formality of her so informing the man.

As he thought of his conversation with Pagan, Raker felt a twinge of regret that she had suffered discomfort at the hands of Webb. It was not of great import but he truly liked Pagan and would prefer she experience no hardship because of him. Her involvement had been required only to expedite his use of her dead brother's Irish associates and, as an uninvolved messenger, to help cast the aspect of foreign involvement on his plot. The last was a circumstance to be desired as a way to keep Mitchell off-balance and indecisive.

Now, though it was not at all necessary in view of his phenomenal memory, Raker felt it was time to stop briefly in his alternate lodgings where, as Coleman/Campbell, he would review the circumstances as they now stood. It would be a small luxury which would allow him to savor the current attack on PanGlobal Assurance.

Raker walked from the telephone to the men's room near the front bar of the hotel to find the privacy of one of its cubicles. He locked the door, placed his briefcase on the commode, and began his preparations.

He carefully removed the expertly barbered, distinguished,

gray toupee—so painstakingly handcrafted in Italy—from his meticulously shaved head. From his briefcase he took a small case and from its specialized contents removed the remarkably realistic mustache which he adjusted into position. It was followed by the brushing of dark color into his eyebrows. Examining the results, Raker was satisfied.

Next, he inserted soft, non-absorbent pads into his mouth between lower gums and cheeks. They were held in place with dental adhesive. The effect was a distinctively different shape to his face. Dark tinted contact lenses covered the icy blue of his eyes; carefully measured and shaped pieces of flexible plastic were bent and inserted into each nostril, dramatically broadening his nose.

He was no longer Beverly Martin Raker, but the man Pagan Maguire knew as Owen Coleman. For the sake of convenience he had, after their first meeting, appeared in the same guise to both Elizabeth and Alec Gordon. There were only a few other people in the world who would have recognized him.

Raker removed his expensively tailored, solid gray suit coat and folded it carefully. He took a tweed hound's-tooth patterned jacket from his briefcase and replaced it with the one he had just removed. The jacket went well with his gray slacks. His red and blue rep stripe tie was replaced by a black knit whose knot was just a little too large.

From the pocket in the top of the briefcase Raker took a small flat packet of dark gray silky material. This last was a precisely constructed cover which slipped over the light tan briefcase, covering it entirely, with the exception of the handle. He paused for a moment to review all of his procedures, and checked to see that nothing was being left behind. Only then did he leave the cubicle.

A glance at the long mirror extending over the restroom's wash basins showed him that the modifications in his appearance were quite satisfactory. Even the walk, the posture, and the manner of carrying the head were different. It was Owen Coleman/Ian Campbell who left the hotel and would, after only some minor preparations, check into the Wellington where a reservation awaited. It was there, in a room of that once grand old hotel that he would thoroughly review his plans to avenge the betrayal of T.J. Laughlin those many years ago. The disastrous betrayal which had led to the ruin of Laughlin's mining company.

On that far distant occasion, and only weeks after taking out adequate insurance for his many holdings and operations, Laughlin had experienced a fast and furious series of tragic and ruinous mine disasters. The company had been forced to absorb the immense losses—for there had been no insurance policies in force.

As had been his custom, T.J. Laughlin had paid the premiums for his policies in cash and sealed the deal with a simple handshake. He had received nothing in writing. It was the same action which Raker had taken this very day in sealing his agreement with the ruler of PanGlobal.

The act had been quite deliberate and only fitting.

Those many years ago, the insurance premiums paid by Laughlin had been made to a friendly acquaintance; a fellow hardcase and carouser whom he liked and trusted. After all, the man had done business with Laughlin in the past, but that had been before someone had got to the man.
Laughlin had never seen him again.

The policies had never been issued. There had been no proof that any agreement had ever been made.

The profit must have been quite good, for that man had ceased to exit. It had taken these many years for Raker to discover just who he had become: *Mallory Fleming Mitchell.*

The ones who had persuaded him in his course of action had long ago ceased to live. Raker had seen to that. Now it was Mitchell's turn.

• • •

With the skill born of long practice at subterfuge, and secure in his simple but effective disguise, Raker needed little time to purchase a used suitcase and the clothing he might need to cover any further appearances in his alternate guise. He added several felt-tipped pens and a thick pad of paper which would be sufficient to allow him his practice of setting everything down where he could see it in the planning of each step of his campaigns. A restroom in the bowels of Penn Station gave him privacy to transfer his purchases into the suitcase.

During the taxi ride from the station, Raker, holding his hands below the vision of the driver, wrapped his right hand carefully with an elastic bandage, covering the fingers, but leaving the wrapping loose enough to permit flexibility. As the taxi deposited him at the side of the Wellington, he paid the driver with a bill held between the first and second fingers of his left hand. The tip he left was neither too large nor too small, and Raker would be quickly forgotten by the driver.

At the front desk, Raker apologized for the awkwardness of his signature, necessitated by his injured right hand. The desk clerk was solicitously sympathetic and summoned a bellman to assist the guest with his luggage. Raker's fingerprints would be found on neither the pen nor the registration card if anyone ever cared to check.

With the bellman properly tipped and smilingly departed, Raker waited a moment, then opened the door to place the Do Not Disturb sign on the outside knob. He closed and locked the door. He removed the temporary bandage from his hand, then, with the aid of a small tin of talcum from his briefcase, he donned a pair of surgical rubber gloves. He would carefully wipe the inner and outer door knobs each time he left the room.

He placed a wedge tightly under the door, then crossed the room to raise the window. The action gave him satisfaction. How seldom, anymore, could one have the privilege of raising an old-fashioned window in a hotel? A sliding door onto a balcony or the like, yes. But an old sash window? Seldom. He smiled as he also remembered the tap labeled "Ice Water" in the bathroom. He supposed that at one time it had actually delivered what it proclaimed.

He put his head out the window and studied the sides of the hotel and the buildings across from him. No apparent way to enter his room through the window with any but the greatest difficulty. The buildings opposite, tall gabled and ornately trimmed, offered no vantage point for a shot into the room if he kept carefully away from the window. He expected no such eventuality, but it paid to be certain, just as it paid to know the location of all the fire escapes, just in case. The slight breeze he felt, and the sounds of the city rising from the streets pleased him. He left the window open, but pulled the drapes partly closed. One could never be too secure.

He placed his briefcase on a small table in the corner of the room and his newly purchased suitcase on the luggage bench. After hanging his clothes in the small closet he took out the pad he had purchased, one of the felt tip pens and, after removing the cheap, black, ballpoint pen from the gray suit coat he had been wearing earlier in the day, sat at the table and switched on the table lamp. He glanced at his wristwatch. He would allow himself two hours. The watch, while as efficient and accurate as money can buy, was simple in style and held in place by a tasteful, plain strap. For the same reason, Raker wore no other jewelry, not even a ring. It would be foolish to wear any articles that might later be remembered.

He unscrewed the barrel of the ballpoint pen and removed the ink cartridge. He unrolled the small, thin piece of onionskin wrapped around it, and smoothed it with his gloved hands. He was forced to re-roll it in the opposite direction before it would lie flat on the table at which he sat. The words were neatly printed in tiny letters:

?

TISSOT/S	BECQUEREL/Y	SIOT/B+
SULLIVAN/A	PASCOLI/N	HOTEL/P!
KAVANAUGHT/E	KIDIROT/JC	TRAIN/V!
SUPERIOR/CV	ZANGANO/ABC	TANKER/CJC!

There was a date above each column.

Raker studied the list briefly. It existed for more than just information. His eyes feasted on the top name in the middle column:

Becquerel. The hated name against which his actions were soon to achieve yet another measure of vengeance. The initials following the name of each target represented the first name of his agent, or terminator, as he thought of them. Exceptions were the B+ which designated Brennan and his crew, the ABC which identified the terminator as separate from Alec Gordon, and the JC which Raker considered as the first name of Jean-Claude LeBlanc.

The other multiple initials indicated that more than one person was to take part in the action. The terminations indicated in the first column were already underway. Those in the second column were scheduled for the very near future. The "?" over the third column was the hopeful conjecture of Raker that these actions, though scheduled, might not be necessary.

The first two rounds of terminations were against single targets. The third round would be devastating in its toll of human life. The "SIOT" was, of course, the Shetland Island Oil Terminal. The hotel, to be incinerated by Phillip Cheney, was an incomparably famous one in London. It had been one of the world's greatest hotels. Raker thought of it in the past tense. Over the past months, Phillip Cheney had made careful and undetectable preparations for its near spontaneous demolition. The tunnel would also be the scene of a fire. The tunnel would be one that crossed under the Hudson River. The event would occur at the height of rush hour. Gasoline, and other hotter flammables, loaded into a van which was stalled and blocking traffic, would explode with devastating violence. There would be a chain reaction. The van's driver, a man, would have been picked up by the driver of the car ahead, a woman. The toll of life would be horrendous.

The Gordons would enjoy the spectacle.

As for the train, it would be derailed by an explosion while traveling at high speed across southern Canada. That responsibility would fall upon Victorio Largo. It would not be a happy event.

The tanker would be one anchored far north off the American West Coast. The ship would, in all likelihood, not sink. The oil spill would wreak havoc with the ecology of Pacific beaches and the sea. The task would be undertaken by J.C. Leblanc and Clay Sizemore.

Raker hoped these last strikes would not be necessary. But if so? Then it simply had to be. Anyway, he no longer had any control over Brennan and his crew. Barring a large miracle, the oil terminal was doomed. That was incidental to Raker. What did matter was the top name, second column—Becquerel.

He slowly rewound the thin paper around the ink cartridge and replaced it in the plastic case of the pen. His mind turned to other details and he casually tossed the pen into the open suitcase where it nestled among the other writing instruments he'd bought. He thought of his next scheduled meeting with the Gordons which was set for the following morning. He would meet with Pagan Maguire on the morning following that.

Both meetings would be made in similar fashion. At the prearranged time, Raker would be at the newsstand of the hotel. Whoever he was meeting would enter, buy a newspaper and leave. With his expertise and highly tuned intuition Raker would ascertain that the party was not being tailed and would then follow whoever he was meeting to an open, park-like, concrete square where casual-seeming conversation could be made while both he and the other person appeared to examine the flanking shop windows.

The meeting with one of the Gordons—Alec was scheduled— would be routine. If things worked well, the meeting with Pagan Maguire would be more pleasant. With his own presence and welcome now firmly established at PanGlobal there would no longer be any need for Pagan's involvement. It would please Raker to tell her that her part was successfully ended and that in the near future the Gordons would truly be removed from circulation. He would be relieved to have Pagan safely away from any possible danger resulting from his actions.

Once again he glanced at his watch. The time should be right. He reached out to pick up the telephone and dialed an outside number.

"Home Office," said a pleasant voice, "For whom are you calling, please?"

"Yes, thank you. This is Henninger Stubbings," said Raker, "calling for Researchist Specialties. Do I have any messages?"

There was a slight pause before the reply came. "Did you say Research Specialists, Mr. Stubbing?"

Raker grinned. He had chosen the names to be used with the answering service carefully. There was little chance of duplication.

"Stubbings, with an ending 's'—Henninger Stubbings. And no, ma'am, it's Researchist. Researchist Specialties."

"Just one moment please." The voice was still pleasant. Raker's wait was short.

"Yes, indeed, Mr. Stubbings." The final "s" was emphasized.

"You've had five calls, but no messages. Just the request to have you return the calls in each case. Would you like to take down the names and numbers?"

"Yes," said Raker. "Go ahead."

As the voice read him the names and phone numbers at a carefully rehearsed pace, Raker made no effort to take down any of the information; it was unnecessary as the names and numbers were all fictitious, and Raker, knowing that his detailed instructions had been carefully followed, was certain that none of the callers could be identified—even if their voices had been recorded—without the most painstaking and time consuming effort.

It was doubtful if the National Security Agency—though they certainly had the capacity—would be interested in monitoring non-messages to an answering service. What was important was that there were no messages. It meant that all of his preliminary terminations had succeeded. It was now time for the second meeting with Mitchell and PanGlobal, and approaching the eve of the second round of terminations.

At the thought, Raker leaned back in satisfaction. Yes! This meeting would be the big one. It would be the one that would shatter Mallory Fleming Mitchell's newly regained self-assurance. It would be the start of bringing PanGlobal to Raker's terms. That, or cost the lives of untold hundreds, perhaps even thousands, of totally unwarned, unsuspecting and innocent pawns whose only error had been in choosing PanGlobal as their insurer. Raker had selected the word pawns in preference to victims.

He reached into the still open briefcase and extracted a large envelope. It was addressed to himself, Beverly Martin Raker. Just below the name was a hand-drawn red dollar sign. The envelope had been sealed and then sliced open with the clasp knife Raker carried on his specially designed key chain. He did not remove the contents. There was no need. Raker had written it using the same typing element as that on the other communications he had typed for delivery to PanGlobal.

Raker felt this might well be the final communication he would deliver. On the outside chance that his estimations were wrong, one additional envelope containing yet another message still awaited delivery along with other materials he had instructed his trusted aide, Maria Theresa Chavez, to forward immediately at his notice. It too was addressed to himself. After writing the last messages he had destroyed the typing element. The pieces, crushed to powder, were scattered across the New Mexico desert.

In only a few days, thought Raker, such precautions will not be necessary. Not at all. It wouldn't matter who realized that Raker's was the mind behind the plot. But he wasn't there yet—close, but not there yet. Raker's eyes narrowed.

No matter what, even if Mitchell was ready to meet the terms soon to be delivered, the second terminations must occur. Nothing must stop that. Nothing must save those targets. They must die.

In truth, he was thinking only of the name Becquerel.

He paused in his thoughts, then shrugged. Enough of that. It was time to leave. He checked out the room. Rearrange it, he thought. Make it look as if someone is really living here. Leave enough unmarked clothes hanging in the closet. Leave the suitcase open. The pad could stay on the table. He had written nothing. He had left no fingerprints since entering the room. He busied himself leaving traces of occupancy, surveyed his surroundings, and was satisfied. He removed the thin gloves from his hands and stowed them in a pocket from which he took a handkerchief. It would be used to wipe away the fingerprints he had left on the outside of the door. He picked up his separate briefcase which held his change of identity. He would pick his site for transformation at a later time.

The man who could be identified as Raker must never be seen

around this hotel. He opened the door with handkerchief in hand, wiped away any possible prints, and closed it. Time to return to the Sheraton where he would decide whether to enter his room as a shaved-head visitor, or as his own distinguished self. He smiled at the idea. He must phone Colt, he had decided. Tell him he was making some progress and would meet them, Colt and Mitchell, in the morning. Tell them he might have something worth reporting by then.

He considered the coming evening. A dinner? Yes. A dinner worthy of New York. And with company. He thought of one particular lady. Yes, he would call her. If she did not have a previous engagement then they could—and he smiled to himself as the phrase entered his mind—they could do the town. Some clichés, he decided, are okay. In fact, they would stay at her apartment. As for the lady having a previous engagement? Well, he knew quite well that she would break it. She always did. Yes, it would work out well. The letter would arrive at his hotel in the morning, then he would receive it. It would be, say, left at his door following a mysterious knock. The letter would, of course, be the one he now carried in his inside coat pocket.

•••

To Pagan Maguire, both the street and building chosen as her residence while she was in Manhattan were an anomaly. Situated on what seemed to be either a cobblestone or worn brick lane, the buildings were varied in color, material and architectural design. Their only common bonds were their attachment as row houses, moderately low in height. Dwarfed by the towering skyline of the city, none of the buildings was taller than three stories; a few as low as one. A smattering of trees, bushes, and vines added greenery and color to the street, and if one could ignore the muffled noise of the city, diminished by the seclusion of the small lane, and the blur of traffic rushing past the entry to the south, the area could be imagined a part of a small, old village. That was exactly what it was.

While enjoying the relative quiet of her apartment, its seclusion added to her apprehensions. That feeling was a result of her experience with Harlan Webb and remembered threats he had made prior to her rescue by James Colt. From her experience and knowledge of the terrible actuality of events in strife-torn Northern Ireland she knew that such threats were sometimes—no, often—carried out. And in spite of the talkers, she knew well that Ireland also deserved its reputation as a nation of watchers and listeners and doers.

She was aware of the danger of New York with little traffic on the street, either automobile or pedestrian. The fact increased her suspicions whenever someone loitered, or appeared to study her residence, or strolled by at what seemed to her too slow a pace. At the moment, as she peered surreptitiously past the edge of drapes covering her front window, she speculated on the presence of individuals against a building across the narrow street. She knew that in all probability they were only fellow residents.

Nevertheless, with her native caution heightened by her association with Owen Coleman, and now fully aroused by her encounter with Webb, apprehension approached paranoia, a fact of which she was acutely aware. In spite of the knowledge, she realized that it was better to be overly fearful and alert than to be taken off-guard.

• • •

He had been standing, immobile, for some minutes. Probably, thought Pagan, not nearly as long as it seemed to her. Nevertheless, he was there, had been there for some time, and certainly seemed to be studying her hotel. Her suspicions were increased by the hat the man wore which seemed to be pulled lower than usual, down toward the face. While the distance was too great for her to identify the man with assurance, his general physique and his erect posture reminded her of Harlan Webb. She turned from the window with a murmur of disgust at herself and shook her head sharply enough to send her auburn air into a swinging swirl.

"Come, now, Pegeen, my girl," she said aloud, "mustn't be imagining that spider, Webb, behind every bush." She smiled at the unintended association of nouns. "Or at least against every building."

She couldn't resist one more peek, so again she slid the edge of the drape slightly aside. He was still there. She turned, brow furrowed with concern.

What to do? Call Coleman? No. That was impossible. The only way she could do that would be on the morrow at half six of the evening. Or possibly at the newspaper and tobacco shop at nine the next morning?

But by doing that she would be breaking her schedule with the man. That, she would be most reluctant to do; only in the most dire emergency. He had made that ever so clear. The simple presence of a stranger, and one not really even actually threatening, certainly didn't amount to that. No, it must not be Coleman.

Almost before she had pushed the idea away, the name James Colt sprang to her mind. At the thought, tension eased from her body and was replaced with relaxing warmth.

James Colt, she thought. She moved slowly away from the window, head down, fingers sliding across her lips. Now what about James Colt? She paused in front of a mirror hanging against a wall of her living room—parlor, she would have called it if she'd considered the word.

She stood with her head cocked slightly to one side, studying her reflection. She took her hand away from her mouth and smiled. The smile turned to a short, soft laugh, and she shook her head at her image, then winked broadly.

"Shame on you now, girl, shame on you." She spoke aloud. "Here you are thinking of some way to find a sense of security, and what you do is check to see if you're pleasant looking enough to be attractive to a boyo." She leaned toward the mirror.

"Well, me girl, the truth is you're not exactly ugly, and that you know well." Her expression turned serious.

"But the shame be on you for your vanity. And what am I doing talking to you, anyway? You're a bad conversationalist, so the devil take you." She tossed her head in disdain and turned her back on her reflection. She was smiling with warmth as she walked to the sofa to seat herself. Still, she thought, even if my motives aren't purely for delivering up a sense of security, James Colt would sure now be secure company. And pleasant, to top it.

Pagan Maguire turned and swung her legs up onto the sofa to

stretch out full length, head resting on the arm rest. She considered the situation. Certainly she would be secure for the evening. Coleman had told her of the devices installed at her residence to make certain her doors and windows couldn't be forced without her knowing it. And that fact, coupled with the quite illegal but highly efficient .32 caliber Beretta, model 82/84 DA automatic pistol he had made certain she knew how to use effectively, would keep her secure from no greater a threat than she would probably encounter.

Yes, tonight she would be fine, just fine. But tomorrow? Well, tomorrow, that was another day. And James Colt was most certainly another thing to think about.

• • •

Beverly Martin Raker's evening had been more than simply pleasant. It had been a grand, hedonistic monument to pleasures of the flesh, and with a long-time, respected and loyal friend. It was an event Raker seldom allowed himself when involved in a "project." It was in tribute to the progress of his conspiracy against Pan-Global and Mallory Fleming Mitchell.

Upon arising, very early, he had dressed quietly, and left his night's companion, the lovely, intelligent, still sleeping, and delightful woman, with a gentle kiss on the cheek. It was an act which, unless personally witnessed, would not have been believed by Raker's closest acquaintance.

Returning to his own hotel, Raker prepared for his meeting at Pan-Global, and as his mind organized the upcoming scenario, his memory of the previous evening's pleasures became simply nonexistent.

Finally fully prepared, he sat relaxed and unmoving in a chair, eyes closed with his hands crossed on his lap. And as he sat, all his skills, all his intuitions and all his strengths grew and filled him with fear. He knew when fifteen minutes had passed without looking at his watch. It was time. He lifted the phone, placed his call, and notified Victoria Genn that he was on his way. He added, with the words made more ominous by their gentle delivery, that he had some rather bad news.

He wanted the mood of the meeting set before he arrived.

"Mrs. Genn intimated that you had some rather . . ." Mallory Fleming Mitchell paused briefly, searching for a word. ". . . some rather disturbing information, Mr. Raker." He had greeted Raker at the door, opening it himself, when the man's arrival was announced.

"I think the word I used was 'bad' ," observed Raker, "but yes, I think 'disturbing' will do." As he spoke he walked to the window and looked down toward the city; then he turned to face Mitchell.

"You own this entire building? I mean the whole thing. I mean outright?"

Mitchell bristled slightly. "The whole thing, Mr. Raker. The whole damn thing. All of it. Me, my banks, and whatever influences the other board members think they exert." The expression on his craggy face grew haughty. "The building and the people in it. Own them all."

Raker allowed his eyebrows to rise. "People, Mitchell?"

"People, Raker." It was the first time Mitchell had not used the Mr. when addressing him by name. "And if you don't believe that, then you don't know just how much power this outfit of mine brandishes."

Mitchell's choice of the word interested Raker. "Brandishes," not "wields," that power. The real Mitchell shows through, thought Raker. He said nothing.

Mitchell moved away to seat himself behind his huge desk and look down at Raker. His face was grim as his eyes speared their object.

"You may have misunderstood me, Raker, during our first meeting." He was aware that Raker was meeting his fierce gaze with steely immobility. "I wanted you with us because all of my information assured me that you're the best for the job at hand." He paused, drawing on his inner strength to help give him the will to force Raker to break their eye contact.

"But you certainly aren't the only man who can do the job, and I find your cavalier attitude galling. Most galling. I don't like it, Raker. Don't like it one God damn bit, and it's going to change. Now!"

"Then find them," said Raker. His eyes remained locked on Mitchell's. He didn't move.

Mitchell rolled his eyes upward in a face-saving gesture of exasperation. "Dammit, man," he said. His voice had lost its thunder. "Dammit. Don't you realize just how hard—impossible—it is for someone who's been running the whole show for so long, to be treated so . . ." he paused, realizing he had been about to re-use the word cavalier in some form or another ". . . so brusquely," he finished.

Raker's eyes still had not moved or blinked. "Or do you mean so arrogantly?" he inquired.

Mitchell shrugged. "Perhaps. Perhaps that's it. I'm damned well not used to it, whatever label you put on it. All right, then, man. I need you. I really do need you. And I haven't found anyone else I think can do the job you can. Will that do? Is that what you want? An apology?"

"Apologies serve little purpose, Mr. Mitchell." It was the first time Raker had used the title to the man. "What I didn't like was your innuendo—no, your *insistence*, that you owned people."

Raker turned his eyes away, slowly and deliberately, as though to remind Mitchell that it had not been himself who had broken off the ocular battle. He walked slowly toward the low table, with its chairs, away from Mitchell's desk.

"No one should own anyone, *Mr.* Mitchell. People are not to be owned, or used, or abused. Not unless it is absolutely necessary, and with no other option available for the completion of a specific plan."

He paused, thinking of his actions in London with Elizabeth Gordon. "Or at least toward the implementation of their plans," he finished, perhaps by way of excuse. "Now, sir, will you climb down off that throne of yours and come down here where we can talk and listen and hear each other?" He made his tone much lighter.

Mitchell, showing some relief, rose and walked down toward Raker, and the two men sat across the low table from each other.

"My apologies, Mr. Raker, for my boorishness," said Mitchell, "even if you feel apologies mean little. They come hard to me."

"Accepted, Mr. Mitchell. I now assume you would like to have the information that brought me here."

"Indeed I would. Most certainly. I did not invite either Colt or Webb to be with us at this time. During our short association it seemed that if you had wanted either of them here you would have so instructed Mrs. Genn."

"Perceptive, Mitchell," agreed Raker. "And let's both dispense with the Mr. business. It's time consuming."

"As you wish." There was almost a twinkle in Mitchell's eye.

"The information covers several areas," said Raker, taking the envelope from his pocket. "This envelope," and he held it just out of Mitchell's reach, "was delivered to my hotel this morning. There was a knock on the door. I asked who it was, and when there was no answer I took certain precautions—which I have discovered to be of value in my business—to determine the advisability of opening the door. They required a certain amount of time. When I opened the door there was no one there. This letter had been leaned against the door. As you will see, it was addressed personally to me, and the dollar sign is on the outside of the envelope."

Mitchell, no longer reaching out, eyed the envelope with distaste.

Raker leaned forward for emphasis. "We, or at least you and your organization, have been compromised. And that fact places me directly on the hot spot. Because, obviously, we're dealing with an inside job." He made the words sound like an accusation.

Mitchell, bluster not totally absent, nervousness growing, cleared his throat. "And this, uh, this letter threatens you, then?"

"Not at all, Mitchell. You—it threatens you and your entire group of living people." He used unaccustomed qualifiers for effect. "It was left to inform me that they know of my role, and for me to deliver to you so that you would know what they're after." He tossed the envelope almost causally on the table between them and leaned back.

Mitchell seemed to draw back involuntarily as though afraid the envelope might explode. He cleared his throat once again.

"Then this," he jabbed at the envelope with a forefinger, "this is their payoff demand?" He lifted his eyes toward Raker. "Is that what we call it, payoff?"

"And some kind of payoff, too," said Raker, standing. He waved a hand at Mitchell and the envelope in a manner hinting at disgust. "Read the damn thing, Mitchell. It's there, and it's real, and it won't go away just by you ignoring it." He walked once again to the window.

Mitchell drew in a deep breath and straightened. He reached for the envelope and extracted the pages it contained. He read:

CONGRATULATIONS, RAKER OLD MAN. SO YOU'VE BEEN APPOINTED BY THE GREAT ONE TO DELIVER HIS EMPIRE FROM HARM. HE CHOSE A FORMIDABLE CHAMPION, AN OBSERVATION WHICH I AM CERTAIN WILL NOT IMPRESS YOU, BEING IN YOUR ESTIMATION ALREADY ONE OF THE WORLD'S GREATEST AT ANY AND ALL THINGS.

I AM DELIGHTED TO DISAPPOINT YOU. HAVE AT IT, MY MAN, FOR I AM AWARE OF EVERYTHING YOU ARE DOING. THE FACT IS THAT YOU CAN REALLY DO NOTHING. NOTHING BUT PLAY DELIVERY BOY, THAT IS. HERE ARE THE FACTS:

    1. THE FIRST STRIKES AGAINST CLIENTS OF PANGLOBAL HAVE BEEN SUCCESSFULLY COMPLETED, AND THE POLICIES TERMINATED. ATTACHED ARE THE DATA WHICH WILL IDENTIFY THE TERMINATIONS AND AUTHENTICATE SUCH AS ACTIONS BY MY DIRECTORATE. THE AMOUNT OF LOSS INCURRED DIRECTLY BY PANGLOBAL IS ENCLOSED AS WELL AS THE ADDITONAL LOSS TO RE-INSURERS, AND THEIR IDENTITY. WHILE REPRESENTING ONLY SMALL CHANGE TO SUCH A COMPANY AS PANGLOBAL, IT IS WORTHWHILE NOTING THAT THE PAST CLIENTS REPRESENT A HIGHLY DIVERSIFIED GROUP, SOCIALLY, ECONOMICALLY, AND GEOGRAPHICALLY. THE TIMES AND DISTANCE OF THE TERMINATIONS WILL SERVE AS AN INDICATOR OF THE REACH OF MY ORGANIZATION.

    2. A SECOND ROUND OF TERMINATIONS IS SCHEDULED TO FOLLOW IN THE IMMEDIATE FUTURE. THIS IS NON-CANCELLABLE, AND WILL BE CARRIED OUT. THE PURPOSE OF THIS IS TO DEMONSTRATE MY STRENGTH OF PURPOSE. IT WILL REPRESENT HIGHER LOSSES.

    3. A THIRD ROUND OF TERMINATIONS IS SCHEDULED, THE LOSSES OF WHICH WILL BE RUINOUS. THIS STRIKE MAY BE

CANCELLED UPON AGREEMENT TO TERMS SET FORTH IN THIS COMMUNICATION, AND THE SUBSEQUENT PHYSICAL MEETING OF THESE TERMS IN A LETTER TO BE SET FORTH FOLLOWING THE SECOND ROUND OF TERMINATIONS.

4. ANY EFFORT TO ENLIST OUTSIDE AID SUCH AS POLICE AGENCIES, OR ANY OTHER INVESTIGATIVE, MILITARY, OR PARAMILITARY AGENCIES OR FORCES, WILL RESULT IN THE PRESENTATION TO THE MASS MEDIA OF SENSATIONALIZED EVIDENCE OF THE VERY REAL DANGER IN BEING A CLIENT OF PANGLOBAL. YOU MAY BE ASSURED THAT SUCH EVIDENCE NOW EXISTS, AND WILL CONTINUE TO ACCUMULATE, FOR THE SUBSEQUENT DRAMATIC AND NUMEROUS TERMINATIONS.

5. MY REQUIREMENTS ARE SIMPLE. PAYMENT OF $500,000,000 (FIVE HUNDRED MILLION DOLLARS) TO BE MADE IN A MANNER WHICH WILL BE DIRECTED FOLLOWING THE ABOVE MENTIONED SECOND TERMINATION ROUND. DETAILS OF HOW THIS MEETING OF TERMS MAY BE ACCOMPLISHED WILL BE PRESENTED AT THAT TIME.

6. THE SECOND CONSIDERATION TO BE PAID BY PANGLOBAL WILL BE MET BY FAR GREATER OPPOSTION. IT REQUIRES THAT YOU AND MEMBERS OF YOUR BOARD DIVEST YOURSELVES OF A PORTION OF YOUR CERTIFICATES OF OWNERSHIP IN PANGLOBAL AND ITS SUBSIDIARIES. FOLLOWING THE SECOND ROUND OF TERMINATIONS THE DETAILS OF THIS TRANSACTION WILL BE OUTLINED AS TO WHAT PERCENTAGES MUST BE TENDERED, AND AT WHAT OFFERING PRICE. AS YOU CAN READILY DISCERN, THIS PORTION OF TERMS WILL BE PURELY A SIMPLE BUSINESS DEAL. PLEASE BE CERTAIN, MISTER MITCHELL, THAT YOU WILL RETAIN PRACTICAL CONTROL OF YOUR EMPIRE TO MOST INTENTS AND PURPOSES.

7. IT IS PROPOSED, BUT ADMITTEDLY WITH LITTLE HOPE, THAT YOU AND YOUR BOARD WILL NOT BE THE DIRECT CAUSE OF THE UNTIMELY DEATHS OF THOUSANDS OF TOTALLY INNOCENT PERSONS FROM EVERY AGE GROUP AND WALK OF LIFE, WHOSE ONLY BUT FATAL ERROR HAS BEEN TO PLACE THEIR FAITH AND TRUST IN YOUR ORGANIZATION.

CORDIALLY,

$

P.S. RAKER, OLD CHAP, YOU DON'T HAPPEN TO HAVE ANY INSURANCE
WITH PANGLOBAL, DO YOU? IF SO I WOULD CANCEL IT, POST HASTE.

While reading the lengthy communication, Mitchell had run the emotional gamut from stunned disbelief to near apoplexy. He had now returned to disbelief.

"A joke, Raker. A damned, black-humor, graveyard joke. Someone is having us on." His tremulous hands and voice betrayed his words. He snorted. "Half a billion dollars! They can't be serious."

Raker shrugged. "You don't believe that anymore than I do. He, or they, mean exactly what is said. And it's damn well-planned."

"Then, damn it, do something!" exploded Mitchell. "That's what you've been hired for. That's why you're here. Do something, man, do something." Mitchell talked and his hands flew in circles. No vestige remained of the powerful brutality he had tried to project when Raker arrived.

He stopped in his pacing and turned to Raker.

"Can you? Do something? You said you had other information." His voice approached pleading. "Can you God damn it do something, man?"

As he spoke he had moved to his discreetly concealed bar, opened it, and was pouring a glass from the first bottle of whiskey his hand reached. He tossed it down, poured another and held the bottle up toward Raker.

"You?" He looked at the label. It was Scotch.

"No." Raker shook his head.

Mitchell drained the glass and shuddered. "Damned Scotch. Can't stand the stuff." He reached for the bottle of Crown Royal. "Care for this?"

Raker shook his head. "Nothing. This is hardly the time for a foggy mind." His tone chided Mitchell.

"You're right, of course. Right, quite right," agreed Mitchell. He refilled his glass with the Canadian whiskey, capped the bottle, closed the bar and turned to Raker.

"All right then, all right. Just what in the hell do we do?"

"Sit down," said Raker. "Sit down and shut up. I'll give you the rest of the information I've been able to gather, then I'll tell you what we can do."

Mitchell sat, sipping at his whiskey now instead of gulping it. "I'm listening," he said.

Raker started to talk. "Believe me, Mitchell, I understand the difficulty, the real pain that comes with having your own personal world threaten to disintegrate; with being forced to surrender the almost total power you've wielded." He paused. "Or rather *brandished*," he corrected. He made the word Mitchell had used earlier sound ominous.

Mitchell raised his head, searching for dignity, and pushed the half-full glass of whiskey away from him. "That was an ill-chosen word, Mr. Raker . . . Raker." He corrected himself, recalling their past conversation about the "misters."

"I mean to indicate that all my . . . all the company's . . . employees depend on me, on *us*, for their livelihood."

The explanation sounded weak even to himself. He reached for the glass, hesitated, then pushed it away from him.

"Of little consequence, Mitchell. You are you, but in the present circumstances you must sublimate your innate or developed predilections, and understand that I am going to run this show." He made his voice grate. "That, or I'm out."

As Mitchell squirmed almost imperceptibly, Raker added in a more solicitous tone: "That doesn't mean that you're giving up any of your permanent power. It simply means that you're using your demonstrated ability to delegate authority to achieve the most profitable results." The flattery bordered on the blatant, but Mitchell elected to accept it as a cornerstone on which to rebuild his damaged self-esteem.

"You're quite right Mr.—you're quite right, Raker. Quite right. I've been most successful in appointing the right people for the right jobs." He leaned forward. "Now, just what information do we have, and what are we going to do with it?" He was once again at least an equal.

"We start thinking about whether you will meet their demands," said Raker, mildly.

Mitchell started to rise as a flash of anger dilated the veins at his temples. He quickly composed himself and settled back into his seat.

"Good," said Raker. "That's a first step. Fury isn't going to solve a thing. But there's nothing wrong with good old calculated, controlled anger. So let's stick with that."

Mitchell nodded his agreement.

"All right then. Start making that decision. Do you meet their terms? But consider it carefully. Consider all the ramifications. Start considering whether your eventual decision will meet with the approval of your board." He held up a hand anticipating Mitchell's objection that he "ran the damn board."

"Like it or not, you have a board, and while you assure me that you run your empire, you don't have absolute voting control."

"With proxies, damned near," objected Mitchell.

"Good," remarked Raker. "That'll help. Whatever your decision, your conclusions, nothing can be done about it until after those second 'terminations,' as your intimidators call them, have been completed. Work on it. Go through the formality of telling your board what you're going to do. Use your discretion about how much to tell them.

"Next, take that list of clients' names who we've been told have already been terminated and make certain that they have indeed met the fates so graphically described in the rest of the material you have there and haven't bothered to look at yet." It was true. The reading of the demands in the first section of the communication delivered by Raker had upset Mitchell to a point where he had forgotten the second enclosure.

Mitchell drummed his fingers against the top of the low table, making no move to pick up the material they were discussing.

"Yes. Of course. That must be done." He still made no move to pick up the offending sheets.

Raker separated the pages from the material on the table.

"Then shouldn't you?" He let the question hang.

"Certainly," said Mitchell. "Most surely." He started to rise. "I'll call Mrs. Genn and have her . . ."

"Why go to your desk?" interrupted Raker. "Why not just call her with your pocket pager?"

Mitchell showed surprise mixed with some small hint of guilt. "How—how did you know?" His hand had gone involuntarily toward his belt.

Raker allowed himself a grin, waving a hand to dismiss the importance of the question. "Come on now, Mitchell. You are certainly aware that following the development of advanced bugging apparatus, nullifying countermeasure devices were developed." He took a small, rectangular object from his pocket and held it up toward Mitchell. "This little jewel is one of the more advanced. It can, believe it or not, really sanitize a surprisingly wide area."

"Oh, yes," a-hemmed Mitchell. "Certainly. You of all people would take such precautions, wouldn't you?" He placed his hand against the device attached to his belt.

• • •

In only seconds Victoria Genn opened the door to Mitchell's office. "Yes, Mr. Mitchell?" she asked.

"Mr. Raker has some information for you to check," he said, looking toward the papers.

Raker held the sheets in his hand, not proffering them to Mrs. Genn. He frowned at Mitchell as he addressed the woman. "Yes," he said. "I see you have your pad there." He nodded toward the woman. "Please take down these names. They're all clients of Pan-Global. Check regarding the . . ." he hesitated before continuing ". . . their welfare. Please do it at urgent speed."

Raker read her the names. Dairmud Sullivan, Anthony Quiller-Jones, Aristide Tissot, Robert Emmet Kavanaugh, and Superior Imports Incorporated.

Victoria Genn looked up expectantly. "Is that all?" She did not bother to look at her employer.

"Yes."

The woman smiled at Raker and departed.

"I thought it best to leave these here," said Raker, holding up the papers. "Like it or not, you're going to have to read the information."

Mitchell nodded.

"There is no doubt that the information I gave Mrs. Genn will check out. Those people named are most certainly damned-well now deceased. We'll learn specifically how in a short time. Also we shall quite likely discover just what unfortunate circumstance befell the so-called import company."

"We will learn quite quickly," said Mitchell. "The one thing you can't deny is the efficiency of my organization."

"I'm certain of that," said Raker. "Especially that of your most excellent Mrs. Genn. Remarkably effective woman." As he spoke he once again picked up the papers they were discussing.

"If you won't read this material, I'll give you the guts verbally," and during the next few minutes he went on to detail to Mitchell how, after receiving the requested clearance through Harlan Webb on the previous day, he had utilized PanGlobal's computer storage, interfacing it with his own system, and extracted the information he felt pertinent.

There could be no doubt that the plot against the company, if not entirely an "inside job," certainly required critical connections within the organization. It was why he was delivering his report only to Mitchell, leaving out both Colt and Webb. Even Victoria Genn, he added as an after thought. Everyone was suspect.

"I have run profiles on the entire staff of PanGlobal," continued Raker, "as well as all board members and many other individuals and related firms which might stand to profit at PanGlobal's expense. There are some possibilities that bear further investigation," he told Mitchell. "But for the moment I shall keep that specific information solely to myself. Even from you. If my position has been compromised then anything I tell you, or you tell anyone else, may also reach the ears of the enemy." It amused him that the warning came from the mouth of Mitchell's enemy: himself.

"But you . . . you said that your little device there had cleaned— or was it sanitized?—this office?"

"That's not all of it," scoffed Raker, "and that's only a minor precaution. In that regard there are still long-range listening devices and immensely powerful lenses to aid lip readers. And then there are the people you might let in on things." He watched Mitchell's face and knew that his desire to frighten him was succeeding. He let the man assimilate the information.

"Don't forget," he said, leaning forward for emphasis, "that most rape and murder is committed by acquaintances of the victim. And that, Mitchell, is just what they are trying to do. Rape and murder your company. You should understand that, however, since all of you deal in fear."

Mitchell looked across the table at Raker, hating the man nearly as much as those involved in the plot against his company. He didn't realize he was hating the right man. It was not Raker's words but the air and attitude that infuriated Mitchell.

"Do you, Mr. Raker, truly realize the power I command? The pressures I can bring to bear? Pressures that can bend nearly any organization you've ever heard of to my will?" He turned his back on Raker in contempt of the man's knowledge. "I can raise money in amounts that you can't even imagine."

He turned to let Raker see the satisfied smile on his face. "I can buy any God damned thing in the world—anything."

"Then do it," said Raker, mildly. "Buy off these bastards who've got you scared to death." His smile indicated secret knowledge. "Use whatever parts of the insurance world's trillions that you, your banks, your holding companies and your other world-wide subsidiaries control." He was totally relaxed and obviously enjoying himself.

"Use those companies in those fairytale countries whose laws allow you to pull off any shady deal you have in mind," he continued. He leaned forward, eyes cold and hard. "You'd be damned surprised just how much I know about you and your power, Mr. Mitchell. So you use them. You do just that, and I'll be delighted to withdraw from our agreement and stand by to watch your empire disintegrate."

Mitchell's eyes re-evaluated Raker. "You mention a general figure, Raker. And you guess in generalities which could apply to any large concern. I didn't hear any specifics." It was a dare.

"Other than PanGlobal? How about Universal Trade Company?" inquired Raker. "And then there are Tri-Con Chemical and Supertronics, aren't there, not to mention your four large European, Caribbean and South American banks? That's not mentioning the slightly smaller stuff and your illegally held re-insurance companies." He waved a hand as dismissal of their importance. "Are those enough, or shall I go into some details of your other, and somewhat less wholesome holdings?"

• • •

Mitchell was visibly impressed. He cleared his throat before speaking. "I think I am quite satisfied. You seem to have certain accurate information." Mitchell's arrogance was again obviously diminished. "You will admit, then, that it would be fair to say that I—we, that is—do draw a great deal of water, as they say?"

Raker nodded in easy agreement. "You most certainly do that, Mitchell. And in view of your hostility to my methods, I suggest that you avail yourself of that power and extricate yourself from your current predicament." It mattered little to Raker whether Mitchell maintained their hand-shake contract or not. He had, after all, already achieved total access to the client list contained in PanGlobal's computer system, along with all other information he had desired.

"So I'll just be moving along," he said, rising, "and you go right ahead and take care of your . . ." he paused to emphasize the understatement in his next word, ". . . problem."

While Raker had been talking, Mitchell had moved across the office as far from Raker as he could get.

"Yes, well," Mitchell paused to clear his throat once again. His eyes were busy watching his hands massage the knuckles of each other. "Yes," he repeated, "perhaps I've overstated my position. I'm afraid that I must admit . . ." His voice stopped abruptly as though the words choked him. His eyes flicked toward Raker, anger filled. ". . . must admit," he repeated, "that I need your services." The words came with great difficulty.

Raker laughed. "Don't feel awkward about your hostility," he said, a grin wide on his rugged face. "Your resentment is quite normal. Do you perhaps recall *The Brothers Karamazov*, and the words put in the mouth of old big daddy himself by Dostoevsky? When the old man was asked if he knew a certain party, he replied—if you'll allow me to paraphrase it a bit—'Know him? Certainly I know him. He did me a favor once and I'll never forgive him.' Not forget, Mitchell, forgive. Never forgive him. Quite a psychologist, our Russian writer friend. And that's your position now. Resentment that you need outside help."

Mitchell stared at him without friendship. "Yes," he said, "Quite. How very interesting."

Raker's voice still held a chuckle. "And if I save your company from ruin, then you'll quite probably hate me for the rest of your life, and more than the ones who are threatening you." In time the man would know they were one and the same. Raker's expression grew serious.

"But back to your earlier comment. Are you asking me to reaffirm our agreement?"

"Yes." Mitchell's discomfort was obvious, the word soft and reluctant.

"Very well." Raker opened his briefcase. It no longer contained his alter ego accoutrements. "I've prepared dossiers on several of your key employees who have access to your computers, as well as others of your board members. You will find much of the material quite interesting." He extracted a large manila folder and added it to the papers, still on the table, which Mitchell had not yet touched.

"I will not leave this with you permanently. It is based on the information I extracted from yesterday's procedures." He moved toward the concealed bar where Mitchell had earlier poured his drinks.

"Take your time, study the information. But I don't want to leave it around your place where it might become public. I'll just indulge myself in a little of your fine liquor and do some meditating." His voice was as light as Mitchell had ever heard it.

Mitchell grunted and picked up the folder. He started to read.

The information was not truly important. It had been compiled only to give Mitchell cause for concern. The details were based on highly embellished fact spiced with sinister overtones. By the time Mitchell had digested the information he would suspect everyone.

Everyone except Raker.

• • •

It was midmorning when James Colt began to speculate on the course of events which had left him and Harlan Webb out of the meeting between Mitchell and Raker. The speculation was not alarm, for Colt was self-assured enough to accept that, whatever the reason. It was sufficient. The curiosity, however, remained. He was effectively handling the day-to-day work required to keep the claims functions of PanGlobal at its highly regarded level of efficiency when he received the call from Pagan Maguire.

"I really hate to be the bother of you, Mr. Colt," came her pleasant voice, "but I've some concerns that I really feel I can confide only to you."

James considered the words. If coyness, or acting, it was damned well done. The sincerity was tinged with apprehension.

"Please, Miss Maguire, make it James. You are not bothering me at all, I assure you." He realized he meant it.

"Thank you . . . James. In that case you must make it Pagan." She pronounced the name as it was spelled.

"Or perhaps Pegeen?" inquired James Colt lightly.

"I'd like that," she said. "It's how I think of myself."

"Then just what are those concerns, friend Pegeen?"

She was aware of a sense of pleasure at the unnecessary use of the word friend. "It regards that . . . experience you helped me from back yesterday," she said. "Perhaps I'm just being feminine, but I'm nearly certain that I'm being watched. It is quite disconcerting."

Colt frowned. He had called his men off. It couldn't be Daskalos or his crew. And certainly Webb had enough sense to heed Raker's warning. Or did he?

"What kind of watching?" he asked, careful not to sound doubtful.

"Well now, it's just that the same figure, a man, seems to be spending a lot of time leaning against a building near opposite my place, and by the Virgin, I'll swear his eyes never leave my door."

"Do you recognize him?"

"Well, no. It's his hat, you know. Tugged low over his forehead." She gave a short, nervous laugh. "Now I know that sounds foolish. How can I think he's watching my door if I can't see his eyes? It's just that I feel it." She paused briefly. "And his shape." Her voice trailed off for a moment. "His shape, or at least his stance, posture, well they remind me of . . . of, well, you know."

She meant Webb, of course, thought James Colt. Maybe the stupid bastard is playing some game of his own.

"No," he told the girl, "I don't think it sounds foolish at all. Where is all this taking place? I'll certainly look into it."

"Well now, that's part of the problem," said the girl, her words accompanied with a light, nervous laugh. "I can't be telling you that, can I? Not exactly, I mean. Against my instructions."

Colt did not want her to know he was aware of where she lived. "Then how can I check . . . ?"

"But," she interrupted, "if it's not too much trouble, I could meet you somewhere away from home, and then have you check out the whole area for me. That way I'll not be giving away my exact residence and yet I can lead you past the place the watcher has been doing his watching. Or maybe just his waiting," she said after a short pause.

Colt's mind worked. Barring the invitation being some sort of set-up involved in the scheme against PanGlobal, it gave him a logical reason to learn more about the girl. It would require the concurrence of both Mitchell and Raker, of course, but it would seem that they'd both be glad of the opportunity to further the investigation. Moreover, he was aware of a small glow of warmth filling his chest at the prospect of seeing Pagan Maguire again.

"I think that would be very wise," said James Colt. "Even if your 'watcher' has nothing to do with our friend. There are many others in our fair city who make undesirable advances toward such attractive young ladies. Just where would you suggest I meet you? And at what time?"

In the meantime, he thought, I'll sure as hell have Daskalos check on whether the girl is actually under surveillance.

"I've thought of that," said Pagan. "Would around Washington Square sometime near three this afternoon be convenient?" She laughed with a lilt that brought a smile to Colt's face. "There is always something going on thereabouts, it seems. Musicians, artists, or the man with his lovely crested cockatoo." The square was only a short distance from her residence.

"That will be fine," said Colt. A mischievous tone crept into his voice. "I'll just look for the bird." Raker's influence, he thought idly. A result of the man's lecture about English slang.

"Oh, it might not be there today. You'd better . . ." the girl's voice broke off as she became aware of the play on the word. "I see, Mr. 'Clever' Colt. Bird! Of course. Girl. Well that will be just fine, now. The bird will sure enough be there." Her voice reflected her pleasure.

"One thing," said James. "I will have to make certain that my calendar is clear. Why don't I call you back." He stopped abruptly to correct himself. "Rather, why don't you call me back in, say, thirty minutes so I can make certain I'm free?"

"Oh?" Her tone sounded of lifted eyebrows.

"Believe me, Pegeen, my lass, it will take something approaching the disaster of a third World War to keep me away."

"Very well then, James. I'll ring back in a half-hour. Bye." She hung up without waiting for his reply.

It took only moments for Colt to reach Victoria Genn. All communications with Mallory Fleming Mitchell had to pass through her proctorship.

"Victoria, James here. I need to see the man. It's important. Any chance?"

"Just a moment, James." The line went silent for a moment, then her voice sounded once again. "Come right up. He and our friend Raker will be waiting."

James Colt thanked her. Before he left his office he called Daskalos and gave him instructions regarding Pagan Maguire's residence. Then it was time for PanGlobal again.

CHAPTER 17

"I don't know," said Mitchell, after hearing Colt's account of Pagan's call, and taking in to account his own perception of its implications.

He looked toward Raker whose mind had been racing as he listened to James Colt.

"I think it might be quite fitting," volunteered Raker. "It just might be very helpful." He had weighed the pros and cons of such a meeting between Colt and the girl. In view of her experience with Webb, her fear was probably quite well founded. Why call Colt? He had helped her previously, and she couldn't, or wouldn't, call on "Coleman." That was an indication that she was determined to follow the schedule he had established for their communication with each other. She was demonstrating loyalty and not showing panic. Moreover, Jimmy boy is dependable too, so he'll report to me whatever happens. To top it off, there is no way to connect Coleman with me.

He decided. "Do it," he advised. "Meet her. It may further our cause."

"Shall I question Webb?" asked James Colt.

"Why?" asked Raker. "You'll be finding out who the so-called watcher is anyway, won't you?"

"I'll damn well try," vowed Colt. He nodded at the two men and left to await the call from Pagan Maguire.

Mitchell looked toward Beverly Martin Raker. "Won't that scare off the bastards? Won't that amount to breaking their directive?"

Raker shook his head. "Not likely. She called, remember? Quite possibly at their request." He flipped his hand in dismissal. "No problem."

Mitchell shrugged and resumed reading the reports he had been given by Raker.

As the man busied himself, Raker's thoughts turned back to the meeting between Colt and the girl. There was some chance of trouble coming from the meeting. As a precaution, he should probably put into action, however reluctantly, contingency plans made for just such a development. Yes, he thought with certain sadness. I must consider that.

· · ·

James Colt returned to his office, a pleased smile on his strong, tanned face.

Janet Fremont, his secretary and Person Friday as she liked to call herself, greeted him with deliberately exaggerated surprise.

"My, my," she said. "Aren't we the happy one? Did the great one just give you half the company?"

"Well now, old chum," he replied, smile widening, "just maybe something even better." He leaned forward to pat her on the cheek with easy familiarity, "and none of your nosey business."

"Ah, me," sighed Janet Fremont with feigned exasperation, "infatuation once again raises its lascivious head." She made the mocking "tsk-tsk" sound which so often accompanies such teasing. "Well, good luck to you, dear old ex-bed partner." The fact she could refer so lightly to their past relationship was a strong indication of the depth of both their past and present relationship. At least as far as Colt was concerned.

He drew himself up in theatrical haughtiness and placed a hand across his heart. "Not a bit of it, my suspicious nemesis, I simply have the opportunity to play Galahad, I'll have you know."

Janet Fremont replied with a most unladylike snort. "Hoo-wheee!" she derided. "Wasn't he the chaste one of the round table?" She shook her head in an indication of sympathy for whoever the lady was to be. "Small chance. Knowing you, my sexy James, the only thing she'll get is chased."

The two friends smiled at each other with understanding and affection.

"She'll be calling," said James.

"I'll be putting the call through," replied Janet. It was not yet 11:00 a.m.

PARIS

In Paris, it was late afternoon and Yves Fragonard's feet were hurting. They had earned the hurt. He had been walking, with only brief respite, for more than three hours, and after his lifetime of abusing not only his feet but his entire body, Fragonard had become a sitter and lounger, not a walker.

"Perdition take the two of them," he muttered under his breath. Them both—the beautiful woman and the man. The handsome man. Perhaps, he thought, that is why I am of such anger. Not just the feet. Perhaps it is from my always wanting to be handsome and never having even been lied to in an effort to make me think such was so. He snorted. He wouldn't have believed it for a moment, in any event. Did he not have eyes? Were there not mirrors?

No, Yves Fragonard most certainly was not handsome, he admitted. Interesting of appearance? But certainly! Intriguing? Most surely. Was that not most evident for all to see? Even fascinating. Well, perhaps I carry that too far, he thought, considering the last word. But handsome? No! That is for others. As he plodded wearily along, carefully keeping his distance from his quarry, his mind pursued the subject.

Raker, for example. Was he handsome? Most assuredly not. Perhaps nice looking? Maybe even strongly attractive in a rugged way? Yes. That would be a phrase of moderately accurate description. But not handsome. Just as he, himself, Fragonard. No. One thing was certain, neither Fragonard nor Raker were handsome men. The thought contented him.

He was more than pleased when the young couple paused briefly on the broad sidewalk alongside the Champs Élysées, then turned in through a doorway. At last! An opportunity to lean against a building which would offer some relief to his complaining feet. He approached cautiously, pausing just before he reached the broad window fronting the building. There was enough masonry for him to lean against. He did, sighing. The window next to him was full of posters designed to lure the tired, dissatisfied, bored, or simply romantically inclined, to visit faraway places, or near, by plane, ship, train, or any other method which would result in a commission being earned by the travel agency.

As Fragonard leaned against the narrow column of stone separating the windows on either side of him, he took from his pocket one of the sketchily drawn maps of Paris distributed by various shopping complexes or large department stores and busily engaged himself in appearing to study it. The opportunity to simply not walk was energy-restoring in itself.

He had been following Henri Becquerel and his gloriously beautiful young wife since they had left their luxury apartment alongside and overlooking the Seine. The distance, if walked as the pigeon could fly, was not far. The circuitous route taken by the couple, at the obvious insistence of the lovely lady, had caused him to trudge laboriously through what he considered to be most of central Paris.

If there were a single *arondissment* of tourist-oriented Paris that had not been traversed, Fragonard was certain that the wife would drag her young husband, and thus Fragonard himself, through that small remaining portion. Ah, well!

Their stops along the way, too infrequent and brief, had included a small sidewalk café, a crepe stand on the Miche, and a stop at what he thought of as "the bicycle bar." That was where the man, much to Fragonard's surprise, had ordered a *marc*, something simply not done by wealthy young gentlemen. Moreover, he had seemed to enjoy the rough, raw brandy.

More surprising, the magnificent female creature with him had ordered a *biere de la pression*, of large size. An order placed, loudly and indelicately by their waiter, as *formidable*. The woman had quite enjoyed the huge, foaming vase of beer as much as had her husband his glass of rough spirits. As the couple drank and talked animatedly, they seemed to touch each other often and without conscious thought. Fragonard felt their depth of affection for each other and hated the thought. He liked them; they were what life should be. A small part of his mellowness may have stemmed from the opportunity they had given him to sit and enjoy a drink of his own.

In spite of their preoccupation with each other, they had time for politeness and smiles for others, and their—perhaps hers more than his—obvious delight with everything around them was truly enchanting.

When the couple had paused to purchase some flowers from one of the many street vendors, Fragonard had quickly leaned against a building and assumed an expression of concern or puzzlement as though wondering what his next move should be. The girl had looked up and seen him, then walked to him, smiling brightly.

"Please, my old one, do not appear so sad," she had said. She pulled loose one of the flowers. A five-franc-sized blue blossom, and had carefully inserted it in his lapel through the buttonhole which held his most prized service insignia. She stood on tiptoe to kiss his grizzled cheek and squeeze his arm.

"Becoming," she had beamed. "It enhances your dignity." She put her hands on his shoulders. "A smile please? For me?" she had pleaded.

Touched, embarrassed, and angry at having been caught in such close proximity, Fragonard had forced a smile. The smile had warmed him.

"This old one is not deserving of such attention from so beautiful a lady," he had murmured, inclining his head toward the girl and her watching husband. He did it in a distinguished manner. "I am forever in your debt."

Genvieve Becquerel smiled at him brightly, eyes sparkling with pleasure. She had whirled, taking her husband by his arm.

"Farewell, my father, until we meet again," she had said, blowing him a kiss. Her husband waved as they walked away. "She is so beautiful," Fragonard had mused to himself, "so loving and alive. She is, alas, also the one I must kill."

MUNICH

Wolfgang Grunewald had sat quietly through the entire playing of the glockenspiel. He had watched the colorful performance of the ingenious mechanical figures as they turned and whirled high in the bell tower of the new city hall of Munich. He had sipped slowly at the tall glass of Weiss bier with its floating slice of lemon, enjoying the warmth of the sun which bathed him and his fellow watchers and listeners.

The viewers, or was it the listeners? It depended, decided Grunewald, on your personal preference. Anyway, the crowd was not as huge as he had often seen it, and he was certain that he had selected a chair near the area most often favored by Heinz Keppler, but the man had not appeared.

Assumptions, he had thought, were most definitely a dangerous thing.

His plan to kill Keppler while he sat listening to the music had seemed such a certain thing, simply a cyanide tipped dart, blown from what would appear to be an ordinary pipe.

Keppler was a creature of habit, and he, Grunewald, had simply assumed that the man would always be on hand, a ready and easy target. Not, perhaps, easy for an average assassin, for Keppler was constantly accompanied by two companions whose duties included the responsibility for Keppler's safety. But certainly easy for a man like Grunewald. The only problem was that the man had not followed the script.

The fact disturbed Wolfgang Grunewald's methodical mind. Unless he could determine the reason for Keppler's absence and make suitable adjustments, he would have to redesign the plan of attack. That eventuality offended his inherent inflexibility.

After the performance of the tower's figures and the playing of the music, Grunewald had continued to sit, beer forgotten as his mind carefully sorted out the situation, reviewing what he knew of Keppler and his habits. Keppler, the murdering, vicious killer of innocents. Keppler, the ex-Nazi, or more correctly, still-Nazi.

Suddenly, Grunewald smiled, remembering. The date! The day of the month! That was it. It was the day of the month. One of *those* days of the month. He cursed himself for having forgotten.

Now, some hours later, he lounged easily near the base of the huge memorial at Max Joseph Platz and waited patiently for his watch to indicate 3:00 p.m. When it did, he strolled up Residenzstrasse to the corner of the tiny Viscardigasse, crossed the street, and made his way to the entrance of a sedately decorated, glass fronted tearoom.

He seated himself and placed his order for a cup of hot chocolate.

The tables and chairs were ornate and delicate. The decorations would be considered feminine by masculine standards. Not a hint could be seen that would indicate the location was the former site of the old *Feldherrnhalle*. The edifice had been destroyed by Allied bombs, but the exact site was hallowed to some. It was the landmark near which the *putsch* of Adolph Hitler had come to its dramatic confrontation with government forces.

It had been the beginning of Hitler as the power which he was to become. In commemoration of the event, Keppler and his attendants paid homage to the creature by paying a short visit to the tearoom on the 8th, 9th, or 11th of each month. The reasons for the different dates, at least according to Grunewald's deductions, were that by alternating the dates, the visits would not seem so obviously a ritual; the 11th marked the date originally scheduled for the march, the 8th was when the putsch was actually set in motion at the Burgerbraukeller across the Isar river, and the 9th was the day of actual confrontation.

As Grunewald sipped tentatively at his cup of chocolate, slathered under rich, whipped cream, Keppler and his two companions entered.

They went immediately to a table, ordered, and sat quietly and stiffly, faces set and immobile.

Grunewald seemed not to look at them but his wide peripheral vision allowed him to study the trio.

Foul slime, he thought, to honor a devil. They will now drink their tea, exchange glances which will amount to a salute to their former leader—no! The two with Keppler were too young to have served the beast. They will be the new breed, those led by the old such as Keppler. They will make a salute to their idol. Then they will all rise and leave, without a word having been exchanged.

It happened exactly as Wolfgang Grunewald anticipated. As the men rose he watched their retreating backs, finishing his chocolate, once again comfortable with his plan. This would be one of the few days when Keppler would not be at the *Neus Rathaus*. On the other days he would still attend. Keppler is less flexible than even I, thought Grunewald, aware of his flaw. It will be a great pleasure to destroy the man. Perhaps all of them.

But no, he thought. That I must not do, not when performing for The Colonel. One must never exceed one's authority when working for that one. Never gratuitous harm or death. *Der Oberst* always made that a prime directive. And one must certainly obey *Der Oberst.*

A shame that, really. It would be most gratifying to destroy the entire threesome. Grunewald sighed. Ah, well, better one than none. And maybe at some later date he could rectify the omission.

The thought warmed him.

ROME

To the south, near Rome, Niccolo DelSarto was also making his preparations for the demise of a target selected by Raker. Or, as was the case with Grunewald, *il Colonel* in DelSarto's mind. His target was far less predictable, though no less dangerous, than that of the German.

Ugo Pascoli. Like myself, thought DelSarto, a smuggler. But of far different materials. Where DelSarto confined himself to the illegal transportation and distribution of cigarettes, works of art, and certain invaluable antiquities, Pascoli specialized in the distribution of lethal weapons from whatever source and to whatever consumer. He was brutally efficient, highly paid, and totally immoral. That all of those to whom he made deliveries were engaged in terrorism of one form or another had never entered his mind. If it had it would not have been of even passing interest.

That part of the man, DelSarto understood. It was unfortunate that such men existed, but they did, and weapons would always end up in the hands of those determined to use them. That his business profits allowed him the money to purchase his perverted pleasures through bribery of either children or their criminally avaricious guardians was sufficient cause for DelSarto to feel eagerness in seeing to his—what had The Colonel called it?—oh yes, his termination.

As DelSarto sat uncomfortably in the small Fiat he had parked in a carefully selected lay-by above the city on the hilly road leading up from Rome to Tivoli, he wished he could have driven his far more comfortable Alfa Romeo. That fine automobile, however, would have been far too easy to spot when his quarry finally left his estate and headed, as DelSarto was quite sure he would be doing, for the city. The small, most common Fiat 127 would be far less likely to be noticed. It was the most ordinary car on Italian roads.

It was necessary to DelSarto's plan that he manage a "chance" meeting with Pascoli so that he could arrange to know where the man would be on the day set for his death. Unlike the German, Keppler, there was little pattern to the movements of Ugo Pascoli. What would work, considered DelSarto, was a prearranged meeting around which he could design the method of killing the man.

That such a meeting could be managed, if carefully planned, DelSarto had little doubt. For months Pascoli had been interested in forming a coalition of a sort with Niccoli DelSarto. One which, as Pascoli phrased it, could work to their mutual benefit. After all, were they not both in related businesses? Could not they profit by an exchange of transportation facilities?

Very well. I will discuss the possibilities, thought DelSarto. Yes, I will certainly do that. I will even let him select the site of his . . . termination.

SHETLAND ISLANDS

Although it was midafternoon, the weather at the town of Lerwick in the Shetland Islands was not gentle as was that day's in Paris, or warm as it was in Rome. The sky was gray and the wind was raw and chill as Kevin Brennan strolled one of the town's narrow streets with another man beside him.

The heads of both men were tilted down as they leaned into the near-gale which funneled up the street.

"You're a damn fool to be being here, man, you know that," said Brennan's companion. "It serves no purpose."

Without lifting his face, Brennan smiled, feeling the cold wind against his teeth. "And haven't you heard, now? I have kin hereabouts."

The other man only grunted. The statement was related to the question that so many Irish first ask a visitor to their country when establishing acquaintance. "No time for jokes, man. You're needed. But not here, nor now."

"But it's true," said Brennan.

If the other man had lifted his face, interest could have been seen to light it. "For true now? This is mostly a Norse breed here, they are that."

"And lots of the Viking blood still in our homeland, Cully. Lots of it. As well you know. I'll only say that I feel as safe here as I let myself feel anywhere nowadays."

The man called Cully grunted again. "I'll be accepting that," he said. "And why are you really here?"

"To hear, face to face, that things are well," answered Brennan simply. "Are they?"

"At high cost, they are."

"High cost is it?" asked Brennan. "And how high be that?"

"Two dead. One crippled."

The men walked in silence. They were paid little attention by the few others around them. It was not a day for doing more than getting from where one was to where one was going.

"Evidence left?" asked Brennan, finally.

"We recovered them, God bless. No evidence."

"A flaw in planning?"

"Only the terrible sea," answered Cully. "We were prepared but it was worse than anticipated."

"Any problems in proceeding?"

"None," said Cully simply. "Only waiting for your say. The burnin' and blowin' material in proper place. Controls right enough tampered with and ready to be done in." Cully reached out to grip Brennan's arm and tug him to a stop. He used the man's bulk as shelter from the wind as he lit a cigarette.

"But at terrible high cost," he said as moved back to look Brennan directly in the face. "They were good lads."

"I know," said Brennan, "I know they were, though I don't know yet who they were. But others have gone before them, and many of us will follow. If it's God's will, this blow will be more than they can stomach." By "they" he meant the English government.

"Aye," said Cully. "It may well be that." He looked at Brennan, his face drawn and tight. "And we'll probably lose more."

"That dangerous?"

"'Tis. We'll have to get close enough to use the remote control devices."

"Can I help?"

"You can," said Cully. "You can get back home where you're needed. We'll handle this end, right enough."

The men started to walk once again.

"I'll be setting things in motion myself," said Cully.

"Thought you might," observed Brennan. Then, after a lengthy pause, "Cully, make sure you wait for the token. Don't be going off at half cock. We might have an option."

"Small chance," said the man, "but could be. We'll wait for the sign. Now will you please be gettin' the hell out of here? You're makin' me nervous."

Brennan didn't reply. He was already moving away. As Cully looked after him, he turned a corner and was gone.

No one followed either man. But then why should they? The one was simply visiting relatives he rarely saw, relatives who lived on Mainland, by far the largest of the Shetlands. The other man? Why he was a thoroughly checked-out and highly trusted North Ireland protestant who worked at the Shetland Island oil terminal. He, certainly, would never have anything to do with the filthy, murdering Irish nationalists.

New Orleans

In New Orleans, Louisiana, it was much warmer and far earlier in the day, and Jean Claude LeBlanc was unhappy. Now that damn man, he thought, he don't got no taste at all, no. Not one, I guarantee. With all them good place to eat and drink and play in this New Orleans, he pick them damn hotel which make everything like it is made anywhere else, yes.

He shook his head sadly. LeBlanc and the man he watched were seated in the lounge of the Monte Vista Hotel, he at the bar, his subject at a table. At night the room was a carousel. In the daytime it was simply dull.

From his vantage point J.C. LeBlanc was watching Louis Baptiste Diderot entertain, loudly and crudely, two young women and one large man. The two females squealed their laughter at almost anything Diderot said. The other man with them rarely changed position or expression. It was not his job to be entertained. Only to protect. The women looked as though they would have been far more at home if the lounge had been on Bourbon Street, and much more comfortable if it had been evening.

It was not yet lunch time, but the foursome had already eaten, and in a rather fancy but inferior emporium just down the street. A so-called brunch.

LeBlanc sighed desolately. It could not have been the marvelous Masperos, no? Masperos with its crush of massive crowds, its icy cold draft beer and fantastic, huge sandwiches pillowed high with succulent meat swathed in rich cheese then slid into one of the fiery ovens to allow the cheese to melt down into the tender pastrami or corned beef soon to be covered with the other half of the restaurants incomparable specially-made rolls. The nearly unpunctuated thought made LeBlanc's mouth water. He turned his mind away to other locations.

They could even have gone to Mother's, he thought. On Poydras, up from the unspeakable Hilton. Linoleum on the floors, decor of early poverty and a line for service, but food worthy of a gourmet. Unless, of course, that gourmet preferred visuals to edibles. Or, again, it could have been simply a trip to Molly's Irish Pub for a bowl of their grand Gumbo, or around the corner to the 'Sisters, where Willy could cook and Pearl could serve steaming red beans and rice. No! It wasn't Monday. That would have to wait. Ah, well! It made no matter. Such was don't to be the case, and he—well known as 't Jean LeBlanc—must continue to follow his target.

Still, one never knew. Maybe the evening would bring better taste and better food. It would be too much to hope that it could be a trip across the river to LeRuth's, and New Orleans's finest 'Cajun Creole cooking. It rivaled the finest cuisine in the world. When this affair was done, he, LeBlanc, would certainly go there again, guarantee.

Jean Claude LeBlanc loved his food.

Have patience, 't Jean, thought Leblanc to himself. Have patience, old *ami*. We see what this evening brings. At least it can't be much worse than what I feed on in past, for sure, you bet. And the thought of the food he was being deprived of made it even more important that he stay with his man, Diderot, so that when the time came he would know where to find him and kill him.

Yes. He could wait. And for damn sure, you bet, that man Diderot sure need killing. And that, he, Jean Claude Leblanc, would personal guarantee. 't Jean, as he would happily inform one and all, was a full-blooded practicing cajun.

PARIS

In Paris it was not as warm as in New Orleans, but far warmer than the Shetland Islands. Fragonard, following his face-to-face encounter with Genvieve Becquerel, knew that his continuing to follow them too closely would arouse their suspicions. He withdrew to a distance where he could stay out of their vision, hoping that he could continue to track them without his attentions being discovered.

He watched carefully, eyes studying the stores close by as he walked. He found what he needed. If the couple would only stop!

They did. Stopped to watch a sidewalk artist sketching a child whose mother was having difficulty keeping the youngster still.

Fragonard, moving rapidly, sore feet and all, walked briskly into the store he had found conveniently close. It had not been luck or coincidence. Such market places were numerous. This one had simply been nearest. When he emerged in only moments, the couple was still watching the frustrated artist. He waited some minutes before they continued on their stroll. Their marathon, he reconsidered!

But it now mattered little if they only glimpsed him from a distance. His usual beret had been replaced by a tweed cap and his dark jacket was now wrapped as a parcel carried under his arm, an arm now clothed by the sleeve of a far less somber leather jacket. His posture was erect, his stride was measured and determined, and dark glasses covered his eyes and some of his face. It would have required more than casual observation to have recognized the sad, stooped man that Genvieve Becquerel had kissed and smiled upon.

The flower she had given him had not, however, been thrown away. It was carried, pressed between the covers of the small note-book Fragonard always maintained with him. And Fragonard was not a sentimental man, of that he was nearly certain.

All of that had taken place some time before, and now, as he waited for the couple to emerge from the travel agency, he tried to push personal thoughts of the young wife from his mind. She was an object. A target. That only. He must not forget or even doubt that. Not for a moment. After all, did not he, Fragonard, owe his life to the man to whom he had promised . . . action?

As the young couple came through the door he was watching so carefully, he turned away so they could not see his face. It will be so easy, he thought. So terribly easy. In any sort of crowd one of his huge, powerful, practiced hands could snap the slim, lovely neck of the exquisite girl. She can be dead before she falls, thought Yves Fragonard, and I can be gone before her caring young husband realizes that she has fallen.

The couple, hand in hand, turned away from where Fragonard stood and started up the street toward where crowds were gathered near a row of glass-fronted sidewalk cafés.

He turned to walk his own path. It was in the other direction. It was not yet time.

Tomorrow he would return to the travel agency. As a friend with a gift who wants to have it waiting for the delightful young Becquerels wherever it is they are going, and through charm—or bribe—he would determine their travel plans and destination if they were to be leaving before that day. He would be near them at the scheduled time. And that time was almost now.

• • •

Henri and Genvieve Becquerel were still within a block of Fragonard, still holding hands as they strolled, when Henri stopped suddenly and in the middle of the sidewalk put his hands on his wife's shoulders to turn her toward him. He slid one arm behind her back to draw her close, tipped her face up with his free hand and kissed her, gently and lingeringly, ignoring the passers-by as they, in turn, ignored the young couple. But then, it was Paris.

"You," he said tenderly, "are magnificent, beautiful, exciting, and indefatigable. Would you please allow me to find us a taxi in order that I may rest my weary legs?"

"Poof," smiled the girl, arms still holding him. "You never tire." She rolled her eyes. "How well I've had that proven!" She fluttered her eyelashes in mock coyness. "I know, you just want to get me in the seclusion of a dark automobile so you can ravish me."

"Well, now that you mention it . . . !"

"All right, then, Hank, old horse. I'll call that dare. Whistle us up a cab."

Her husband winced. "That, my lovely little cabbage, is your barbaric ancestry showing. What a terrible, americanized version of the distinguished name, Henri. Do it one more time and I shall resort to that ridiculous name your cultured mama was intelligent enough to substitute for your christened one." He was smiling.

The girl affected a look of horror. "You wouldn't dare . . ."

"So be it." He drew back and beckoned imperiously. "Come girl. Come Jennie. Let us, you and your Hank, find a taxi."

Genvieve Becquerel was, according to her certificate of birth, Jennie Emilia Raker. In resentment, her mother had informally changed the Jennie to the more delicate Genvieve.

It was a fact, of course, which had been carefully withheld from Beverly Martin Raker.

MANHATTAN

In New York City it was past lunch time, but Mitchell and Raker had not taken a break for food. Raker because it didn't matter; he ate only when he wanted to or felt he needed to. Mitchell because his appetite had been ruined.

He had finally finished reading the data given him by Raker. That had been enough. Their only interruption had been when Victoria Genn had brought in the report which authenticated the "terminations" of PanGlobal clients. The combination of information had brought sickening reality to Mitchell and fierce, barely controlled anger to Raker.

Raker knew—hadn't he engineered them?—of the killings. He had not known of the deaths of Sullivan's wife and child. The cold fury he felt at the disregard of his orders that there was to be no "incidental" harm or damage to anyone was mistaken by Mitchell for concern.

Raker forced the anger from his mind. For now. He would deal with Gordon later—at their scheduled meeting in the morning. For the time being let it appear to be what Mitchell wanted to see.

"You were right, Raker. Quite right," said Mitchell, tiredly. "Should have known." His voice was wistful. "Guess I was just hoping against hope . . ." His voice trailed off.

Raker said nothing.

Mitchell made an obvious effort to gather strength with some success. "All right, damn them. They've got us. What do we do now? Pay? Make a deal?"

Raker shrugged. "How can we? They haven't told us how to go about it. Yet."

"True. Yes, quite true. True, indeed." Mitchell forced his body erect. "Then what do we do?"

"We wait. Again." God-damn Gordon! The bastard will have to be taught, thought Raker. Should have known those sadistic perverts!

He caught himself and again forced the thought from him. Enough trouble in other quarters. The girl meeting with Colt, for example. No apparent danger there, at least not for the time. But it was a deviation from the script and he didn't like it.

Colt would report to him, he was sure, and it was doubtful that the girl would, or could, tell anything of any import. Still, best to take no chances. He would put the security "prevent" mode into effect. He could compensate if it was not needed, but best to make certain. He nodded agreement inside himself. It would be his first action when he got away from Mitchell.

"We wait," he repeated, "until we hear just how they want us to meet their demands. Plus, I get the hell out and find which one of your trusted employees," he paused to nod at the material laying on the table in front of Mitchell, "or board members, is behind this thing."

Mitchell paled once again. "You don't really think that one of these—them," he nodded toward the papers, "would, or could, do this?"

"You've read it, Mitchell. They're a far cry from the weaklings you've imagined." He stood and went to the window to look down on the city. "They're damn powerful themselves, Mitchell. Maybe you've managed to run rough-shod over them in your personal and face-to-face dealings, but that's a far thing from what they might do when they're away from you."

Mitchell nodded thoughtfully. "Yes. I suppose they are quite capable of evil." He picked up the papers and started to scan them once again.

Think about it, old man, thought Raker. Dwell on it. By the time you realize the truth it will be way past too late.

"If I were you," said Raker, his voice soft, "I'd be getting ready for anything. The pay-off, for example. I'd also consider the calling of a board meeting."

"Board meeting?" Mitchell sounded more curious than surprised. "Just why should I do that? I'll make the decisions around here."

"Not if what I think is going to hit the fan does," said Raker.

"And just what might that be?"

Raker walked back from the window and seated himself comfortably before answering.

"Try this on for size. First," and he held up a finger, "they're going to want the money paid in a way that will appear a straight business deal. That'll have to be a pay-off on an insurance policy. A little manipulation here and there, careful selection of the insured property—which will not exist—and a policy which won't really have been issued. They're damned well aware that you can do that."

Mitchell started to sputter.

"Hold it. You know you can manage that. You're the insurance expert. I won't try to explain any details; you'll be way ahead of me on that."

He held up a second finger. "Stock from you and your very limited stockholders." He nodded toward the papers Mitchell still held, unconsciously, in his hand. "Through mergers, fed payoffs, blackmail."

"Yes," continued Raker, a sardonic grin curling his lip. ". . . them, your board. You can bet that if you're going to come out of this with a working insurance company, and the hope that none of your other holdings is going to suffer, you'll all be called on to give up part of your interest in this company. Most certainly a seat on the board."

"Impossible," snorted Mitchell. "Wouldn't dare. They simply couldn't ask such a thing." He paused, acute discomfort obvious. "Could they?" he asked. It was almost a plea. "Could they really dare that?"

Raker nodded. "Could, and most probably will. All signs point that way. If they're as clever about it as it appears they are going to be, it will all seem quite legal and above board." He, Raker, would make damn sure of that. He was telling the man exactly what the demands would be. They were, of course, his demands.

"Never!" shouted Mitchell. He banged a fist down on the table.

One more like that, thought Raker, and he'll split the damned thing.

"Never," repeated Mitchell. "I'll not give up control of this . . ." his voice trailed off and a gleam of suspicion showed in his eyes. "Wait a minute, just wait a damn minute." His voice drew out the words. "If you're so certain that one of the board is really behind this thing, then why would they want stock? Why would they want a seat on the board if they already have one?"

Raker let his voice carry a sneer. "Control, Mitchell. Control over your ever-loving company. That's why." He stood and towered over Mitchell so that the man did not have room to rise. "Maybe they're tired of being run over? Ever think of that?"

Mitchell, still angry, lost the look of suspicion. "Yes," he answered softly, "that could be." He nodded his head in agreement with his own words. "One of those sissy bastards, he just could get up enough nerve to buck me."

"Or maybe she?" submitted Raker.

Mitchell looked up sharply. "She? She?" He thought. His eyes narrowed. "By damn man, you may have it!"

Raker still stood close to him, not leaving room for the man to move easily from his chair.

Mitchell, who wanted to stand, instead leaned back in an effort to look comfortable. "Yes, by God," he said. "It just could be.

Only one who's ever had the balls to even try to buck me. Updyke. Good old Edna Mae and all of her jillions." He looked up at Raker with something bordering admiration. "Is that who you have in mind? Edna Mae Updyke? Is she the one?"

Raker moved away to allow the man to resume his dignity. He shrugged. "No answer to that right now, Mitchell. But you can count on one thing: I'll give you all the answers, and damned soon."

Mitchell studied Raker. Had he made a mistake? Had he tried to whip Raker into line when the man almost had the problem solved? Bad mistake, he told himself. Must not underrate this one.

"Very good, Mr. Raker. Very good, indeed." He stood and extended a hand. "Please allow me to apologize for being so boorish earlier. It's just that . . ." He swallowed. "Just that I'm so used to running things that I haven't learned yet when it's to my benefit to let some other back run with the ball."

Analogies, thought Raker. The ploy of the salesman. He waved a hand as though brushing the apology aside. "Understandable, Mr. Mitchell," he said, matching title for title with the man, "quite understandable." He continued, matching repetition with repetition.

Mitchell cleared his throat. "And just when do you think we, that is, *you*, might be able to have something concrete for me—that is, us?"

"*Quien sabe?*" answered Raker. He smiled broadly. "I can assure you that you'll be the very first to know."

That, he thought, is for damned certain.

CHAPTER 18

While James Colt had been waiting for Pagan Maguire's call regarding their meeting—he would not let himself think of it as a date—he had phoned his chief investigator, Augustus Daskalos.

As always, when dealing with each other on the telephone, their conversation was guarded.

"Gus, if you have anything coming down, turn it over to someone else. I'll be needing you personally."

"Right. Any special preparations?"

"Have a car handy, and be ready to spend whatever time I'll need you away from your routine."

"Good as done," promised Daskalos. "Can you give me any idea how long I should have current projects covered?"

"We'll go into that when I see you. Shouldn't be long. Can you be ready?"

"Ready now if you need."

"I'll call. Probably soon."

"Gotcha," said Daskalos. "That all?"

"For now," returned Colt and hung up.

• • •

He had just set the phone down when the intercom chime sounded.

"Yes?"

"Your lady," came Janet Fremont's voice, "on hand at the sign of the flashing light."

He punched the button. "Hi, you," he said.

"Hi yourself," said Pagan Maguire, "and do we have a date, now?"

Colt smiled. She had used the word he had avoided. "That we do, Pegeen, my girl. And at what time shall we make it?"

"As soon as possible," said Pagan. The note of concern in her voice was unmistakable.

"I'm on my way," said Colt. He was surprised at the glow of anticipation he felt.

"And I'm waiting," said the girl. She rang off.

For a moment Colt savored the sense of pleasure before he began to dial Augustus Daskalos.

• • •

The only indication of the controlled fury filling Raker was the too carefully measured pace of his walk as he left the PanGlobal building, nodding curtly and with an air of command at the guard seated behind the desk just inside the exit.

The God-damned Gordons! he thought. The God-damned, irresponsible, sadistic, psychotic Gordons! A woman and a child dead because of them. At least him, Alec. Uselessly, unnecessarily and wastefully dead, and with the full knowledge that Raker would not tolerate such an event.

He kept his walk calm and deliberate, not allowing his anger to show to outsiders in his expression or actions. It was too late to waste time regretting that he had recruited them. That was done and they had served part of their purpose. However, as soon as they completed their second and final assignment, then he would allow himself the pleasure of dispatching them personally. And, he thought, in as unpleasant a manner as he could conveniently arrange—at, of course, the earliest possible moment.

His previous plan had been to turn them over to Brennan's representatives. It now had become a matter of discipline. The thought did little to ease his anger.

Arriving at his room at the Sheraton, he carefully surveyed the several tell-tales he had arranged to determine if any attentions had been paid his belongings, other than normal hotel housekeeping. Satisfied, he turned his attention to the telephone which indicated that he had a message waiting.

Checking with the desk he found that he had received a call

from Maria Theresa Chavez. She had asked that he phone her at his headquarters in New Mexico.

Raker walked to the room's closet and, from the rod used to hang clothes, took what appeared to be an ordinary, round, flat, disc of room deodorant which hung alongside his clothing. Opening his clasp knife Raker carefully sliced through the seam of its colored coating and removed the wax. It could be used again. He removed the contents, and attached it to the telephone.

The device, common enough among the knowledgeable but a secret to the average telephone user, was a line guard which could indicate when more than the normal two phones, or other listening tools, were being used on the line. While unsophisticated compared to other electronic equipment available to him, the "bug" detector was conveniently portable and offered some measure of assurance that his conversations could be conducted without eavesdroppers.

"Prevent Incorporated," came Maria Theresa Chavez's voice. The device indicated the line was safe.

"It's me," said Raker.

"A call, Rake," said the girl. "Long distance. From Paris."

Raker felt a chill of apprehension. "And the message?"

"None. A number for you to call. They left no name, but said it would be fine for you to return the call at any time."

"Thanks, Maria," said Raker. "Anything else?"

"Nope. Things going *muy bien* out here," said the girl. "Any instructions from your end?"

"Not for now. Let you know." Raker's voice sounded detached to the girl.

"Later then," she said. "Take care."

"I'll do that. Be sure and let me know of any other developments."

"You know I will." Her voice was accusing.

"Sorry. Of course you will. Be in touch." He hung up.

It could only be Fragonard, he thought. The message means that the number I'm to call is safe. He wasted no time trying to imagine what the reason for the call could be but rather rang for the overseas operator.

As he waited he let his mind remain in neutral, not projecting. There could be any number of reasons for him to call Paris, he had decided, security conscious. And there could be any number of reasons for Fragonard to be calling him. Not necessarily bad.

He didn't believe that.

SORRENTO

"I have located perhaps where the Becquerel's may be, but not where they are," Fragonard reported. "And regrettably, old friend, I will be totally unable to complete this assignment."

"I see," said Raker. "Is there any indication of just where in Rome one might look?" Fragonard was silent for a moment. Raker could sense his uncomfortable reluctance.

"The Albergo Fontana de Trevi," the man said, finally. Raker was surprised. Becquerel was surely moneyed. The very name meant banking. The hotel mentioned, though with a charming location, was certainly no better than second class. Probably third. The reason must be the location.

"You're certain?"

"I am."

"And for what length of time?"

"Until Friday," replied Fragonard. "A car is to be procured for further travel."

"From what source?" Fragonard's reluctance made Raker feel that he was trying to pluck feathers from a tortoise.

"Again, alas. That has not been given to me."

"I see. Very well."

Raker's mind sped. The couple would be in Rome until the day before the termination was actually scheduled. They could leave for parts unknown in a rental car from an unidentified agency. It was little information. It would have to do, and a replacement for Fragonard would have to be found immediately.

"Please, old friend," said Fragonard, "understand that if I could I would. I cannot." It was a plea.

"I understand, large one," said Raker. His respect for the man was great. It was a feeling reserved for Colt first, followed by Phillip Cheney, the Frenchman, and the marvelous Amazonesque-Aztec princess back in Mexico.

"Your loyalty is commendable. I thank you for it and the information. We will drink together again."

"That will give me pleasure," said Fragonard, relieved at being removed from personal responsibility for killing the girl, but sad that his loyalty had made it necessary to supply the information which would still lead to her death.

"*Au revoir*," said Raker, gently. "Until we meet again."

Fragonard did not answer, and after a moment Raker replaced the telephone on its base, his mind working furiously. Alternative target? Absolutely not. It must be the Becquerel termination. It was the most important. The imperative! Then who?

The answer came. It would have to be the Gordons. Their next scheduled termination was not until the third strike. They could finish Fragonard's assignment, and still be back in sufficient time. It would work! Now, it would become a matter of instilling true fear in the twins. The man must not be killed! He must live to suffer. Hurt? Permissible. Injured? All right. But not killed. The woman? Raker smiled grimly, totally without of humor. He had nothing against her. He even regretted the necessity of her death, but it was the only way he saw to exact revenge against the Becquerel name.

Yes! The Gordons would be the answer. He would give the young wife to the Gordons to do with as they wished. They'll jump at the chance, he thought. A beautiful woman to practice their sadistic pleasures on will make them more than eager. He felt his skin crawl at the thought, but shook it off immediately. It was unfortunate but necessary. Yes, the Gordons it would be. Whatever they did to the girl? That was business. But the man, the husband, the son of his old dead enemy, as well as his wife's old lover! He must live, to regret.

Cold fury, the only sort of anger Raker knew, filled him. Why, he thought, must it always be the innocents who pay? Innocents like the wife? He stood quietly, head down, hand rubbing his eyes. Yes, he thought, it's always the innocents.

His eyes stared blankly at the window, seeing nothing. And even if it is only a token action, I'll have to do something about that. But even as his mind flirted with notions of just what that something might be, he remembered Maguire's meeting with Colt, and its unlikely-but-possible threat to his plan.

After only a moment's hesitation he picked up the telephone and started to dial. The conversation would be most circumspect, but it would be a coded order which would see yet another innocent victim die.

New York City

With James Colt in the passenger seat, Augustus Daskalos guided his automobile down Seventh Avenue through the early afternoon traffic. The car was as nondescript as Daskalos; neither the man nor the vehicle would be noticed in even a small crowd. The similarity did not stop there. Beneath the surface both the man and the car were not what they seemed. The car was powered and geared with a motor and transmission that would have done credit to a full-blown, road-racing machine.

Daskalos was a highly skilled observer and investigator as well as being proficient in the martial arts—a product of careful training, a life of street brawling, and a childhood spent as a young Greek boy in a mixed Greek-Turk neighborhood on Cyprus. While still a teenager, he had emigrated to the relative gentility of New York's Bronx.

"It was a dead end on the house," he told Colt in response to a question. He referred to the house Pagan Maguire was occupying. "It's owned by a real estate company out in Phoenix. They have it leased out on a long-term contract to what appears to be a small company that deals in oil lease speculation and uses it to house visitors to our noble city."

"Appears to be?"

Daskalos nodded. "Yeah. Called the company number as listed and got one of those recorded message things. Left a dummy message that can't be traced to us, and the number of my brother-in-law. They didn't return the call."

Colt made no comment.

"Can pursue it and find out more about the company with some real digging. Didn't think you'd want that from what you said."

"Right, Gus. Good thinking." He glanced at the man. Daskalos never asked questions except those which directly affected his assignments. If he was to know more about the deal, Colt would have to volunteer the information.

"You also pulled your men off surveillance," Colt said. It was not a question.

"Same day you ordered."

"Do this then, Gus. You cover the place, you personally. I think there is a possibility it's being staked out. Stay close but covered, and don't touch unless absolutely necessary. Just watch and protect. Don't let anyone inside the place except the girl." He paused before adding, "and me."

Daskalos's face remained expressionless but there was a smile in his voice. "Right on, boss."

Colt grinned. "Smart ass. Not that way at all."

"Sure," said Daskalos. It didn't matter to him. Colt was as straight as anyone he knew.

"Here will be close enough," said Colt as the car approached to within a short distance of Washington Square. "Hope you can find a place to park this bomb of yours not too far from her place."

"Already got one," said Daskalos. He was grinning.

Colt was not at all surprised. He had become used to Daskalos's efficiency and ability to anticipate. He shook his head in appreciation of his Number One as he closed the car door and walked the short distance to the entrance of the park which was more famous than large.

• • •

From under the stone archway he could see Pagan Maguire seated on the low, circular wall near the center of the square. She saw him at nearly the same instant and lifted a hand to wave. Colt could see her smile clearly as he approached, and the open pleasure on her face.

She stood as he neared and stretched both hands out toward him. For an instant he was tempted to throw his arms around her. Instead he simply took her hands and smiled down at her.

My God, he thought. She's beautiful! Those damned, huge, green eyes. Like emeralds.

Pagan squeezed his hands, then slid gracefully to his side and tucked her arm through his.

"You have no idea how pleased I'm being to see you." Slow down, she thought . . . slow down, Pegeen. "How relieved I am," she contradicted. "Yes, how very relieved."

Colt had only heard the first word. Pleased. "Is that cockatoo of yours about?" he asked.

"No, but there's a right lovely cello player entertaining over there," she declared, motioning with her head as she held on to Colt. "Really lovely music."

Colt could see the man only yards away, cello between his knees, resting at the moment. "He must have been playing just for you," he said. "He certainly doesn't seem to be interested in entertaining me."

"Go on with you, now," smiled Pagan. "Why would anyone want to be playing just for me?"

"Go on with yourself," said James Colt, gently tugging her after him and starting to walk. "With all that beauty, even the pigeons will be serenading you like canaries."

"Oh, James Colt, and aren't you the silver tongued flatterer?" She hugged his arm to her side. "But I love it."

As they walked, the eyes of those they passed followed them. There was no doubt that they made an attractive couple. Maybe they were as handsome and as beautiful as each thought the other to be, and maybe not. It didn't matter. What their eyes saw is what mattered. In any event, many of the women they passed were impressed with the lean, athletic man and his clean-cut, masculine features; his looks weren't the sort to make men dislike him.

All the men looked after the young woman with admiration if not something closer to desire. Their eyes admired her slim ankles and her finely turned calves, as her legs swung freely while she walked, almost colt-like. The sheer, soft wool of her modish skirt clung smoothly to the curve of her hips and outlined the thighs of her forward thrusting legs as she walked. She wore a light weight, white sweater thrown over her shoulders, not concealing the modestly snug fit of her open throated blouse whose silky fabric outlined, without detailing, her fine, high breasts.

"I know I've been acting a bit coy," said Pagan, a faint note of embarrassment in her voice. "In honesty, I'm truly delighted to see you again. And it's not just appreciation for what you did for me when that Webb person was being so persistent." With Colt near, the name of Webb had come easily.

Pagan looked up at Colt as they walked. "You're quite a nice looking man, you know, and I'm proud to be seen with you. I want you to know that before I tell you that I did call mostly because it seemed I had nowhere else to turn. But only mostly."

Colt liked the honesty, but more, he liked the fact that she'd wanted to see him again.

Pagan became more serious. "I swear to you, James, someone has been watching my place. And it has been pretty awful on the nerves. Especially after the affair at your business place."

"Webb? I don't blame you. That was a nasty experience."

"I don't know exactly what I've got myself into," said the girl, "but it seems apparent that it isn't exactly what I've been led to believe."

"I expect that is exactly true," said Colt. "Where is it you'd like for us to go right now?" It wasn't the time to probe or make any further comment.

"I really don't know the area," said Pagan, "only the Square here and a shop or two. You?"

"Then let me be your guide, Pegeen, my girl. I'm practically a native."

"Are you now?"

"Not really," grinned Colt. "Lived here for some time now, off and on. Actually from Philadelphia. But I do know a place or two around here."

"I'll be pleased and ready to follow." Pagan gripped his arm tightly as she looked up at him. "I'm truly glad you're here, James Colt. I mean that. And if you won't think of me as some brazen hussy, I'll confess I'm almost glad that I became nervous enough to call you."

Colt kept a smile from his face. Brazen hussy, indeed. He couldn't imagine any of his female acquaintances using the term except in fun, but it was clear that Pagan used it seriously. He hugged the hand on his arm which was close to his body.

"I think you're an honest delight, Pagan Maguire, and I'm also almost glad you became nervous." He stopped and placed his hands on her shoulders.

"Now, my friend, I just happen to know of a small, slanted floor, quaint and almost cutesy place over on west 4th Street. It's not far from here, and they serve some delicious cappuccino, along with some sinfully rich and creamy midafternoon treats that I think we should indulge in." He cocked his head to one side and pretended a look of disapproval. "After all, we have to put some weight on that skinny frame of yours."

Pagan's smile grew huge. She nodded in mock-sage agreement. "Yes indeed. We really must do that, mustn't we?" She felt the temptation to reach up and touch his cheek. She didn't.

· · ·

It was some time later when James Colt looked across the small table located near the café-curtained front window of the Café Viareggio where they had stopped. He'd listened as Pagan detailed the incidents of recent days which had troubled her. There was little doubt that her fears were real, and evidently with cause. In the past few minutes he'd learned that Pagan Maguire was not the sort of person to exercise her imagination in building fears. Whatever the cause, or more correctly, *whoever*, Daskalos would soon have the answer for it. Only James knew that, however.

In the meantime he felt that he should stay around as added protection. At the idea, he grinned to himself. Just who, he thought to himself, are you bull-shitting? You want to stick around to enjoy the lady's company.

He said, "I wasn't really serious about having to fatten you up, you know." He frowned at the empty plate in front of his companion. "Three? You really ate three of those . . . concoctions?"

Pagan smiled widely. "I did indeed that," she said. She slid a hand down across her flat stomach. "And I'll be having you know that I'll not be gaining an ounce. Really, James, seems as though I have no trouble maintaining my weight. Only have trouble gaining. And what's more I haven't been eating all that well lately." She shrugged. "Must have let the situation affect my appetite." She smiled again, glancing at the empty dish before her. "That's obviously a thing of the past, isn't it?"

"It is, Pegeen, me girl, that it surely is," mocked Colt. His expression grew serious. "I only wish . . ." His voice faded.

"Only wish . . . ?" urged Pagan. "Is it that you only wish you knew just what it is that I'm doing in this affair?"

"Not exactly what I was going to say," commented Colt. He had been about to comment on her obviously high metabolism. "Well, that," he said, "but mostly I was just wondering just how you keep that nice figure?"

"No, you're wondering just what a nice girl like me is doing in this thing. Whatever it is."

"Really?"

"Don't play games, James. Certainly it is. And the answer is, I don't know." Her eyes avoided his. She was obviously discomfited. "I really don't know, James. I can't tell you. It just concerns things—promises that I can't go back on."

Colt studied her lovely face which was obviously pained. "Don't," he said. "Please don't. You don't have to tell me a thing." He patted her hand.

Pagan Maguire jerked her hand away as though it were burned.

"Don't patronize me, damn you," she cried.

Colt pulled his hand away from the center of the table and studied her, saying nothing.

"Oh, James, I am sorry. It's just that the pat seemed so damn . . . well, so damn much like someone calming a pet cat or dog."

"I didn't mean—"

"I know you didn't, I know that. It's just that I'm still a bit high strung. Something like that."

James Colt was sympathetic. "I'd say that you have reason." His voice was calm and sincere. "I think that maybe we can do something about that. How about a nice evening seeing the town?" He reached out to touch Pagan's hands which were now back on the table. Her fingers met and held his.

"Let's pretend nothing like this is happening. We're just a couple of friends who are out for a good time." He was acutely aware of their age difference. It was nothing to the young woman, but a gulf to him.

"Yes," said Pagan, eagerly, without thinking. "Oh, yes. I would like that. But I can't be going out with you in this." She glanced down at her sweater, blouse and skirt. "I'll have to be going home to change. Will that be all right? Will you wait for me.?"

Colt grinned. "You'd better believe it," he said, "as a matter of fact . . ." His voice broke off as he thought better of what he'd been about to say.

"And as a matter of fact, what?"

"As a matter of fact, I wouldn't mind waiting at all," he finished. It wasn't what he'd been about to say. He'd been going to tell her that he could accompany her home for he knew where she lived. She was influencing his judgment. It was not yet time to tell her he knew very well where she lived.

"However," he said, "I don't relish cooling my heels over another espresso or whatever, so . . ." He drew out the last word.

"So-o-o?" inquired Pagan.

Colt became serious. "Will you be worried about that 'watcher' being around?"

She didn't hesitate. "No," she said, shaking her head emphatically. "Not while it's daylight." She paused. That wasn't the truth. She elected to tell it. "Not while I have you about," she amended. She rose. "I'll hurry. You'll be most amazed at just how fast we women can move when we want to." She blew Colt an inconsequential, fingertip kiss, and was gone.

Colt's eyes followed her, admiringly.

She'll be safe, he thought. Daskalos would be on hand now, somewhere around her place. He smiled grimly. If anyone would be in trouble it would be whoever tried to approach the girl.

He glanced at his watch then raised his hand and motioned for the lone waiter to refill the cup which sat empty in front of him. Nothing could happen to the girl while she was so near and so well looked after. And he hoped she would not yet change into something much fancier. He had just remembered something that the clothes she was wearing would be perfect for. It was a true "event," and quite nearby.

The time was not yet three in the afternoon.

ROME

In Rome it was fashionably late for dinner, and although Niccolo DelSarto had not yet dined, he was pleased. His vigil on the road from the cool hills between Tivoli and Rome, waiting for the appearance of Ugo Pascoli, had been time well spent.

When the huge, black limousine had whisked past where he sat parked, it had been quite simple to follow the car into the city where the small size of his own vehicle, his willingness to risk damage to its finish, and the reluctance of Pascoli to have his own machine marred, made it easy for DelSarto to follow the car through the bee-swarm of Rome traffic.

The first stop made by Pascoli was predictable to DelSarto. It was the residence of one of Rome's most notorious procurers. Unfortunately, the man was not just an ordinary pimp. Before the night was over, some child, or children, would be delivered to Pascoli's villa for a night of, to DelSarto's mind, heinous corruption.

The next stops included one along the Via Veneto where Pascoli and his two bodyguards took time for coffee at a favored spot. It was the one popular during the previous season. This year it was being inhabited only by those who weren't aware. It was part of the story of Pascoli. DelSarto sat in the truly "in" spot, only across the famous street. He was welcomed effusively. It was a peculiarity of Rome that such spots gained and lost favor with frightening frequency and irregularity. Pascoli's presence had never been known to help any such place, though his money was welcome. On the other hand, DelSarto could aid in making or breaking such sidewalk spas.

The final stop, at least to DelSarto's satisfaction, came as he followed Pascoli across the Tiber to the Sabatini, in the Trastevere section on the Piazza Santa Maria. Now, certain that Pascoli intended to take his dinner at the fine restaurant, DelSarto waited for what he thought was a proper length of time, then walked to the nearby Galeassi, a favorite *trattoria* where the owner was a special friend. There he could use the telephone with privacy. As long as he had his own *gettone*.

He placed his call to the Sabatini, gave his name, and asked to be connected with the Signore Ugo Pascoli.

"Pascoli?" came a voice filled with doubt.

DelSarto laughed for effect. "Do not be surprised Don Ugo," he said. His voice was almost syrupy with friendship. "It is truly me, Niccolo DelSarto. I was driving by earlier and saw you entering the restaurant. I thought it was time that we get together to discuss that mutually profitable affair you mentioned at our last conversation."

"I'll listen," growled Pascoli.

"Things have not been as good as they could," complained Del-Sarto. "Not bad, you understand—just not as good as they could be. I think it would be well worth our time to at least discuss the subject."

"What do you suggest?"

"Simply that we meet. On neutral ground. With many people about." DelSarto was aware of Pascoli's fear of being ambushed.

Pascoli grunted. "Like where?"

"I thought perhaps at the top of the steps," he laughed. "I can think of few places more public."

There was a short silence. "I'll think on it," said Pascoli.

"Then think fast," said DelSarto, making his voice suddenly hard. "It was your idea. I can make other arrangements if you are not interested."

"When?"

DelSarto named the day and time.

"Alone?"

DelSarto laughed again. "Not if you wish differently. Bring your protection. It will not be necessary. I want the business, not the damage."

Pascoli hesitated. "All right," he said, "but let's make it tomorrow."

"Impossible. I will be out of town. If you can't make it just tell me and I'll make other arrangements."

"No! No. Is good. The time is all right. I will be there."

There was little more conversation. As DelSarto hung up he was elated at the ease with which he had made the arrangements. He had been prepared with alternate plans if his bluff had not worked.

Pascoli would show up, of course, several hours ahead of time with a large complement of men to scour the area, assuring himself that there would be no trap. That really wouldn't matter.

From the roof garden, far across the piazza, on top of the tall, red-brick building on the corner facing the Spanish Steps, Niccolo

DelSarto would, using his favorite rifle and telescopic sight, place a nice, clean hole in the head of Ugo Pascoli. At least it would be nice and clean on the side where the bullet entered.

LONG ISLAND

Admiring glances followed Janet Fremont, James Colt's secretary, as she left the PanGlobal building. Her step was light and lively, carrying her trim, athletic, but undeniably feminine body with graceful ease through the now growing crowds of Penn Station.

There are, she thought, many advantages in being an employee of PanGlobal Assurance. Not the least of which was being able to work for someone like James Colt. She felt a slight twinge at the name.

Not the least of the advantages of working there, her thoughts hurried on, were things like the shuttle limousine which carried upper echelon employees (of which she was considered one) home from work if the distance was not too great, or, as in her case, to their COIT terminal. The hours, in addition, suited her perfectly. Here it was, only just past 3:30 in the afternoon, and she was through for the day. Even though it required over an hour each way, going and coming from work, it was well worth it to live beyond the congestion of Manhattan. Even the ungodly hour at which she had to arise was worth the small nuisance.

The time on the train, with only one transfer required, while normally spent reading was, on this day, devoted to thoughts of James Colt. Though their affair had ended many months before, and the man who had replaced him was now nearly forgotten, Janet Fremont thought of James with concern, and not a little guilt. She brushed that particular thought aside.

She had not met the woman James had been going to see earlier in the day, but she knew the man well enough to recognize the signs of beginning infatuation. If James was attracted, then the girl must be very special.

• • •

"I'm so sorry to disturb you," said the visitor, entering Janet Fremont's apartment.

"I really wasn't doing anything important," replied Janet. Some small irritation was evident in her voice. "Isn't it a little unusual for you to be out this way?"

"Yes. It really is." The visitor was silent as Janet Fremont closed and relocked the door.

"I don't mean to sound rude," said Janet, "but just what is it that can't wait until tomorrow?"

"Just this," said her visitor, holding up an attaché case. "May I?" The words were accompanied by a nod toward a nearby table.

"Of course," she said.

The visitor sat the case on the table, unsnapped the locks, reached into the case and turned. In the hand, now pointed at Janet Fremont, was an automatic pistol. It was, to Janet's practiced eyes, a .25 ACP Bauer automatic. Tiny, barely four inches in overall length, it was quite deadly. Her eyes widened in surprise tinged with fear.

"What in the world . . . ?"

"I must ask you to keep quiet," said the visitor. "I will most certainly shoot you if you don't."

Janet heard the ring of truth in the words. She swallowed and was silent.

The visitor looked around the room, eyes finally picking out a large straight-back chair. "Over here," came the voice. "Now." The tone had become harsh. "Sit."

Janet did as ordered. She felt the cold muzzle of the pistol against her temple. She squeezed her eyes shut. This couldn't be happening to her!

"Don't move a muscle," said the voice. "Don't even twitch. Put your hands on the ends of the chair arms."

Janet hesitated.

"Now!" The pressure of the metal against her head increased. Janet Fremont did as instructed. She watched, the pistol still pointed at her, as the visitor deftly, with only one hand, wound a length of elastic bandage around her wrist and the chair arm. The operation was duplicated on the other wrist.

"Now," said her visitor, "you are going to make a call. I will hold the phone."

"A call?" Janet Fremont was now frightened and bewildered.

"To PanGlobal. Tell the message service to inform James Colt that you will be taking the day off tomorrow. Is that understood?"

"But I . . ."

"Is that understood!" The interruption was harsh. Her fear grew.

"Y-yes," she said. Her voice was muted. The number was dialed, the phone was held against Janet's temple, and she repeated the message as instructed.

The pressure of the pistol's hard metal was withdrawn. "Very good," said the visitor. "Now, however, comes the part I truly dislike." The words were followed by swift movement which found the lower half of Janet Fremont's face swathed tightly with yet another elastic bandage. Her mouth was effectively silenced. As she tried to protest she found that she could hardly make a sound.

"Please understand that I would really prefer not having to do this," said her visitor. The words and tone rang of sincerity.

"Unfortunately, this is really necessary for the plan." The visitor reached out to draw a chair near. "I would much rather give you ether or chloroform or some sort of anesthetic, but you see, we're afraid that traces could be discovered and that could throw some doubt on the case we're building." The voice was genuinely apologetic and the eyes of the visitor showed pity.

Over the next few moments Janet Fremont found herself being bound to the chair more firmly by her upper arms, knees and ankles, in addition to her already tied wrists.

Then, her eyes now bright and wet with fear, she watched as gloved hands reached out and pulled her dressing gown wide open and down, leaving her shoulders and breasts bare.

The visitor returned to the briefcase which had been placed on the nearby table, returned with a spray-topped bottle, and paused to light a cigarette.

"I'm afraid this is the best I can do. It isn't perfect, but it will be better than nothing. It's ethyl chloride. It will certainly help ease, if not stop, the pain."

Hands reached forward and sprayed the liquid across Janet's exposed bosom. She shivered; it felt terribly cold.

"I'm so sorry," said her visitor. Sad, distressed eyes looked into Janet's frightened ones. "I am so very sorry, but it has to be."

• • •

The visitor remembered the anesthetic and sprayed her flesh once again. It didn't really matter; Janet Fremont was unconscious.

The visitor was relieved when sufficient burn marks had been made, carefully put out the second cigarette in the closest ashtray, then surveyed the handiwork. It would do. The pain had not been all that severe. It was the knowledge of the magnitude of the actions that had caused woman to faint, considered the visitor. In a way it was fortunate, as it made the next step less difficult.

Moving behind Janet to avoid looking at her face, the visitor extended gloved hands and wrapped them around her throat. The grip slowly tightened. When the hands were withdrawn, Janet Fremont was dead.

Sympathetic eyes gazed down at the body. It had been a shame, but it had been necessary. And, thought Janet Fremont's visitor, it was well known that the woman had a stubborn streak. It would surprise no one that James Colt had found it necessary to use force in attempting to determine just where she had hidden the evidence that incriminated him in the plot against PanGlobal. The terrible thing was that there was still a good chance that Janet's death would not be turned against Colt. However, the stage had to be set.

The visitor unwound the elastic bandages, then checked for marks they may have left on the body. None were apparent. It was why the elastic bandages had been used. The force which had been used in grasping her wrists just before they were tied would be sufficient to show that it was possible she had been tightly held while being tortured. It wasn't perfect, but then, it didn't have to be. It would serve the immediate purpose.

The visitor removed a folded slip of paper from the attaché case and looked around the room. The book! Fremont had been reading it. It would be perfect. The visitor picked up the paperback and placed the folded piece of paper inside its pages then placed it casually back on the sofa. It would be found if needed. The visitor's eyes once again examined the room. Nothing remained to be done. The cigarettes were left in the ashtray for they were the brand that Colt carried for other people. He did not smoke. As the visitor rewound the elastic bandages and placed them in the attaché case, eyes fell on the body of Janet Fremont.

"I am so sorry," said the voice, softly. "Truly, truly sorry."

It made no difference. Janet Fremont was dead.

CHAPTER 19

Later and far away from the tragic scene of Janet Fremont's murder, James Colt and Pagan Maguire stood alone in Colt's penthouse.

"Oh, James, it's beautiful," declared Pagan Maguire, almost breathlessly, as she gazed wide-eyed out onto the terrace garden of his apartment high above the surrounding streets, and whose vista reached to Central Park. She turned from looking out through the wide, sliding glass doors and faced James Colt. "You didn't tell me you were so terribly rich," she said, almost accusingly.

Colt shrugged. "I didn't earn it," he said. "The family. I just happened to come by it through relationship."

"No matter, that," said Pagan, "you have it and it's truly magnificent." She whirled, arms outstretched, soft, gleaming hair swirling about her head. "All of it. Why I've never seen such . . . glamour." She had halted, searching for a word. "Why, you must feel like a king living here."

"Not exactly," replied Colt, "but I must say that you, my girl, do look a downright princess."

"Do I?" asked the girl. "Do I really?" She assumed a regal pose. "Well let me tell you, my lad, that I certainly feel one right now while I'm here, with you." She closed her eyes in remembrance. "Why that bath of yours is like something out of a cinema about the Roman Empire. I loved it." A small frown crossed her face as she also remembered the ladies dressing gown and assorted cosmetics she had seen in the bathroom.

"Something wrong?" asked Colt.

She smiled. "Nothing," she said, handling what she readily recognized as jealousy. "Nothing at all."

Colt approached her and held her by the shoulders. "You," he said, "are one of the most beautiful creatures I have ever seen." His face told her that he meant what he said. It was, at least, the way his eyes saw her.

"A crayture, is it now," she said, emphasizing the Irish brogue. "What a fine thing to say." She grinned. She felt beautiful. On impulse, as she had wanted to do earlier in the day, she reached up and placed her hands against Colt's face, and their eyes locked.

"Lady," said Colt, voice husky, "we had better be getting out of here, and now. Else I'll be destroying that lovely gown of yours by ripping it from your desirable body." It was said lightly, but there was emotion obvious in the words.

"Well, now. Aren't we the violent one," she said, grinning. "Would you really be doing that? Ripping the gown right off a poor defenseless girl like myself?"

Colt reached for the wrap she'd brought along with her when they came to his apartment. "That, my dear, lovely Pegeen, is a distinct possibility. If it was an old and worn frock I would un-doubtedly do so. And in any event, I'm not going to hang around and find out. I think it will be a far better thing if we simply, if you'll pardon the expression, get the hell out of here." He held out her wrap.

Pagan touched his hands as he placed it around her shoulders. "That, I think, is a very fine compliment," she declared firmly, "and I thank you for it." She glanced over her shoulder at him with a hint of wickedness. "I think," she added.

Colt, who had changed into a dark blue go-anywhere suit, and Pagan Maguire, wearing an expensively simple looking and, thought Colt, downright sexy, black cocktail dress, locked arms and left for their "night on the town."

Anyone watching them might have mistaken them for honey-mooners.

Anyone, that is, except possible watchers who knew them to be who and what they were.

New Orleans

In New Orleans, J.C. LeBlanc had remained, throughout the day, on the trail of his target, Louis Baptiste Diderot. Although the man's habits were not defined enough to set a pattern, it was be-coming increasingly apparent to LeBlanc that Diderot would be an easy hit. Oily confidence oozed from the man as he had made his rounds of the Vieux Carre and ventured into other more remote parts of the city, all the while accompanied by the gaudily attractive women from whose bodies he would not keep his hands, and his tough-looking and surly body guard/gopher.

Since the combined forces of local, state, and federal government had tightened their net around Florida, dope smugglers had been forced to develop other avenues for delivery to the U.S. mainland. They had found Louis Diderot, formerly a small-time pusher and distributor, available and eager. Fortunately, he also had connections with Gulf Coast fishing fleet operators and the other capabilities needed. Diderot was, at present, the largest single importer of illegal drugs into the lower United States.

The vast sums of money Diderot was amassing, as a shielded supplier, would have kept most men more than happy. But Diderot was not only greedy; he was stupid through overconfidence in spite of his cunning slyness. As a result, LeBlanc had witnessed several sales of what he calculated must be either cocaine or heroin.

Too clever to have any of the merchandise actually on his person or in his car, Diderot had all transactions made by his guard who, it became obvious to LeBlanc, would stop at a prearranged location to pick up the material, then walk, followed by Diderot in his automobile, to the delivery point.

The circumstances delighted LeBlanc. "I tell you," said LeBlanc softly, under his breath as he watched the latest transaction, "that man one big damn fool, I guarantee." For in the short periods when the man who was responsible for guarding Diderot was on one of his missions, it would be a simple matter for one as experienced, capable, and fearless as LeBlanc considered himself to be, to open the car door, kill the worthless drug peddler, smile politely at his female companion, and be safely gone before full awareness had reached anyone on the street.

Earlier, on a trip across the river, they had been near the location of the restaurant LeRuth's, of which LeBlanc had dreamed earlier. His mouth had watered as he dared hope that they would stop to eat. The magnificent combination of cajun and Creole cooking was certainly among the world's best. Unmatchable, delicately flavored crawfish pie or simply a bowl of the delicious oyster soup with artichokes! But the car had sped past the restaurant and LeBlanc swallowed his disappointment instead of food.

Now, as he followed Diderot's car back to the Old Quarter, his hopes rose again as they neared Moran's by the river.

Irish by name only, the food was Italian of the highest order, with varied overtones of the finest French cuisine. And the setting, LeBlanc felt, was of the finest. Huge double windows, which on clear evenings like this could be thrown open to admit the moonlit view of the wide Mississippi, and through them the sounds from the busy waterfront LeBlanc loved so much.

The car he was following stopped and backed into a parking spot. He cruised slowly, and watched as the car's occupants left the vehicle and walked toward the elevated restaurant.

A wide smile lit LeBlanc's face. His luck was certainly in. He had felt it necessary to follow Diderot for one complete day, but the thoughts of food had almost made him decide to abandon the chase this evening. Now, such was no longer necessary.

Dinner at Moran's would be a time-consuming affair, so he had plenty of time to place a call to summon a suitable companion, from quite near as a matter of fact, he thought. And they, Jean Claude LeBlanc, and the lovely Simonie Augier, would dine, not simply eat, on this beautiful evening.

The thought pleased LeBlanc. Perhaps, he thought, I will, when the time comes, make it a swift, immediate kill and not one that will take several agonizing minutes to bring the death, as I had planned. He thought of such an action as a gracious gesture.

• • •

Their evening together had been idyllic for both James Colt and Pagan Maguire. Actually, in the unvoiced words of the girl as she remembered the earlier talk of her feeling like a princess, more like a fairytale. She admired not only Colt's appearance, but the air of dignity he wore so well. Would it all end at the witching hour?

To Colt's mind, Pagan Maguire had an aura of regal composure and self-assurance about her that he had never found before, and she still managed to make obvious her subtle sense of humor and total lack of arrogance. Her beauty seemed secondary.

As they faced each other, hands touching across the narrow table beside the window in the lovely nightclub, with its panoramic view of the city below, each thought of the past few hours.

Pagan was glad she had waited to change into a dinner dress until she got to Colt's apartment. "I decided it was too early to change at home," she had said when she met earlier with James, "so I just packed a few things to change into at your place, later. Hope that is all right."

It was perfect. James had taken Pagan on a personal New York tour which included Little Italy, since it was the season of the festival of San Gennaro—and an event not to be missed. She was captivated by the area, the people, the delightful music, the festive mood of gaiety, and the incredibly varied selection of food so temptingly displayed. The last was more than either of them could resist.

Colt had plans for dinner at a very special place. So, with great difficulty, they limited their Italian snacking. Afterwards, they had made their way to James' luxurious apartment to change, and then he'd taken Pagan on a continued tour of a few of the hottest places in Manhattan. Pagan had contented herself with only a glass of wine at each stop, sipping slowly, and often not finishing. She had enjoyed the glamour, nearly as much as the festival they'd sampled, but mostly she had enjoyed the company of James Colt.

• • •

Time had rushed so gently by that it came as a small surprise when Colt realized he was hungry. "My dear little colleen," he said, "I've no doubt that with that voracious appetite of yours, and even with those rich concoctions earlier in the day, to say nothing of our Italian snacks, that we must be ready for a little serious dining."

"I thought you were trying to starve me into submission," replied Pagan. "I'm famished."

"Have you eaten Mexican food?"

"You mean like chile and such?"

"No, no," objected Colt. "Nothing like that. Not tacos, enchiladas. I mean *real* Mexican food."

"I thought those things *were* Mexican."

Colt smiled. It was a chance to show off a little of his knowledge. He knew it was juvenile, but that was the way he felt much of the time when around Pagan.

"They are, in a way, though I doubt if any self-respecting Mexican family down in Mexico ever sat down to dine on what is served up north as a 'bowl of red' and saltines. That is really of old American West, chuck-wagon origin."

"Really?"

"And the versions are endless. The fact is that the dish isn't served all that well, even out in New Mexico where you'll probably find the best Mexican food in the Americanized category."

"Isn't it terribly hot and spicy?"

"Can be. There are many versions. Arizona-style has varieties of chile doctored with tomatoes and other innovative substitutes for the real thing. California is something else again. Then there's the New Mexico version which borders on the purist, and includes dishes formerly unknown even to bordering states. *Quesadillas, chico, carne adovado, posole, quiletes, chimichangas, caldillo* . . ." his voice trailed off as he realized Pagan was smiling broadly.

"You, my lad, are showing off." There was no sting in her tone. "But you do know an awful lot about it."

"Not really," admitted Colt, "but a friend of mine who lives out there does. And he has a tendency to lecture about such trivia from time to time. Fact is, his information is sort of interesting. Anyway, many of those dishes aren't known well outside of New Mexico. Some not even in Mexico proper. It may be the heavy Indian influence."

"Indian? As in curry?"

Colt laughed. "No, as in Pueblo. They were the non-nomadic Amerindians who stayed in one place long enough to develop a more or less ethnic cuisine."

"How about Texas? Isn't that supposed to be the great place for Mexican food?"

Colt rolled his eyes. "Now that," he said, "is tragic. Such a question. What they serve is more properly called Tex-Mex food. Good enough, I suppose, but not even a poor relation of the fine New Mexican recipes.

"They do, however, make some of the best 'bowls of red,' along with those in Ohio, New York . . . Heck, one of the best I ever had was at a little 24-hour place called the Tastee Diner in Maryland.

It can be a real taste pleaser. Still, none of that stuff is what I'm talking about. I'm thinking of some real Mexican food, with no qualifier applied to the front of it. Food such as you find down in Old Mexico. It's a much overlooked cuisine which deserves to be ranked with the worlds finest." He'd heard that from Raker.

Pagan looked doubtful. "I'm not really any kind of gourmet, James. Outside of the world's finest steaks, magnificent ham and seafood, especially those incredible Dublin Bay prawns, native Irish cooking isn't all that fancy. Though it's very good."

"No matter, Pegeen, my girl. The food I'm thinking of will set your mouth to watering. It's truly delicious."

"My stomach has already put my mouth to watering," smiled the young woman. "You just be leading on, me fine lad, and your lady will follow."

• • •

The restaurant Colt had in mind was not far. It had been introduced to him by Raker on one of the man's previous visits to the city. Colt suspected that Raker had helped finance the business which was run by acquaintances from Mexico. The name was *El Paso Del Norte*, the pass of the north. Its location was, of course, in south Manhattan.

"It's lovely," said Pagan. "I've not seen anything quite like it."

James Colt was pleased at her reaction. "And the food is even better," he told her.

The heavy double doors of its entry were dark, tall and weathered, and set into a thick-walled curving arch. With square footage at a premium, the designers had still taken several feet of interior space to create the illusion of a courtyard just inside the doors.

Though on the bottom floor of a tall building, an atrium with artificial light overhead offered a vista of tropical plants native to south central Mexico. A tall and massive back bar sat off to one side. Its dark wood was intricately hand carved. The top of the bar counter gleamed with careful attention and the polish of thousands of drinking hands. It had been shipped from Mexico, and it was claimed that Pancho Villa had taken many drinks at this very bar. There was the slim possibility that it was true. The man drank in nearly as many bars as there were women who claimed to be his wife. And quite possibly were.

The dining areas were small rooms, none with more than three tables, separated by thick walls which extended up only far enough to separate diners. Old-looking, carefully tended wood had been overlaid on the concrete floor, adding to the restaurant's air of authenticity. The color scheme was whitewashed brick, earth-toned tile and dark wood, with splashes of brilliant color for accent.

James and Pagan were welcomed with gracious courtesy. Colt was recognized and remembered as a friend of *Señor* Raker.

As Pagan studied the menu her eyes showed interest. It was printed in Spanish, but beneath each item was a description of the dish, simply stated, without the hyperbole of many lesser eateries.

"Everything sounds marvelous," she said. "Would you mind if I just let you order for me?"

"A pleasure, *Señorita*," said Colt. "There are few items which have a certain amount of heat in them. How do you feel about that?"

"I feel that I should try at least a bit of everything life has to offer," said Pagan. "You just be leading on."

"Very well, *mi amiga*. And shall we start with one of the city's finest margaritas?"

Pagan knew the drink. She hesitated. "I truly prefer just a bit of dry wine," she said. "Do you mind?"

"Of course not. How about Sangria? It's not all that dry, but they start with a decent wine and go from there with their own selections of assorted citrus fruits and a few other secret ingredients."

"You're on," said Pagan. Her eyes were warm on Colt as he placed their order.

• • •

Pagan Maguire placed her hands against her flat stomach and gave an exaggerated sigh. "I am about to burst," she said. "What a marvelous meal. I will never be the same. And I will never forget what Mexican cooking can be. Never again. It was magnificent, James."

Colt smiled. "And it's not quite over," he said.

She groaned. "James! It must be. I can't eat another bite." Colt only continued smiling.

"Well, now," said Pagan, "if you're thinking of that dessert you were speaking of earlier . . . maybe I could force down a nibble or two."

The girl, thought Colt, would never have trouble with her weight. If she had eaten throughout her life as he had seen her eat on this day, and had stayed as slim and trim as she was, it was a continuing miracle.

Their meal had lived up to his expectations. They'd started with a seafood cocktail of abalone and shrimp which boasted a gentle sauce with just a hint of chipotle chile. That was followed with bowls of *Crema de Aguacate*, a soup combination of velvet-smooth pureed avocados and rich, sweet Mexican cream, delicately seasoned, and with tiny, ravioli-like puffs of dough, each filled with a tender piece of asparagus, floating on the surface.

Their entree had been called *Tapado Tlaxcala*. It was a boneless strip of beef loin, slit, then stuffed with a combination of mild, green *poblano* chile strips, leeks, fluffy textured *asadera* cheese, and leaf coriander, then grilled over an open flame fed by dried mesquite wood. A mixed green salad, spiced with wilted spinach, accompanied the steak to help freshen the mouth for each ensuing bite. Bread served with the meal had been authentic Mexican *bolillos*. Crusty outside and moistly layered inside, they were unique.

Now, as the waiter began to prepare the special dessert Colt had ordered, Pagan sipped her rich after-dinner coffee. "This is delicious," she said. "What did you call it? Mexican coffee?"

Colt nodded. "It is good, isn't it? Mexican coffee—a different roast than ours—mixed with Mexican chocolate, and around an ounce of liquor. Half rum and half mescal."

"And with the heavy cream as in our Gaelic coffee," injected Pagan.

"But with a cinnamon stick," defended Colt.

"No matter," she said. "It's wonderful."

As they watched, the waiter lifted the pan he'd been holding over the flaming burner which rested on his cart, drawn next to their table. It contained caramelized milk and sugar, chopped pecans, and banana liquor. As it warmed, the man slid *crepas* into the pan, one at a time, and skillfully spooned the liquid over them, folding and then rolling them in the pan. He gently added fine Herradura Anejo Tequila to the pan, allowed it to warm for a moment, then flamed it. He spooned the blazing liquid over the rolled crepas and served them with a flourish. It was, thought Colt, a fine show. The 92 proof tequila made a wonderful fire.

"Indescribable," said Pagan. Her eyes indicated that she thought the word not adequate. "Truly, James. The best sweet I've ever had. Why didn't someone tell me of such wonderful food before?"

"Because you hadn't met me, my girl," replied Colt. He was delighted. He could not remember ever having enjoying watching anyone eat before.

• • •

Colt emerged from his reverie and became aware of Pagan Maguire's glowing eyes focused on his face. They had not spoken for some minutes.

"A penny," said James Colt, then laughed abruptly. He added, before she could speak, "Now isn't that something? I haven't thought of that old thing in years. Or said it. A penny for your thoughts."

Pagan's smile was as gentle as her eyes. "No penny needed," she said. "I was only thinking what a lovely evening it has been. And hating for it to end."

Colt frowned. "I don't like that thought at all," he said. It was more than just the evening ending. It was the worry of what could be awaiting the girl when she returned home. No, she would have to stay with him. But no! Certainly not. If she were being watched by her employer, that could be disastrous. His concern showed on his face.

"My turn," said Pagan. "A penny."

He forced a smile. "Like you. Not wanting the evening to end. And remembering that I've forgotten some business."

Surprise showed on her face. "Business? At this hour?" It was near midnight.

Colt smiled again. "Not terribly important; a phone call will take care of it. Will you wait?"

"Certainly. I happen to think you are well worth waiting a little while for, James Colt."

He left with a squeeze of her hand and found a phone in the reception area. The call would be to a telephone in Daskalos's car. If he wasn't in the car it would automatically transfer a tone to the ear-piece Daskalos wore, a tone which would not be heard from even inches away. He could then go to his car to return the call or, if Colt held the line open, simply answer. Colt waited.

In less than two minutes Daskalos said, "Me here."

"Were you near?"

"Not far."

"Anything?"

"Negative at the moment. The girl was right, however. Traces abound. Cigarette butts, heel marks on the building across—like that. Nothing."

"Were you made?"

"You know better than that." Daskalos's voice was reproachful.

"No," said Colt. "You wouldn't have been."

"And you? Any escort?"

"No. We were clean."

"Probably pulled off when the lady packed," observed Daskalos.

A possibility, thought Colt. Pagan had left, when she came to rejoin him, carrying a small overnight case. "How about the traces?"

"Checking now. Meantime I'll keep the place covered."

"It's been a long day. Can you get a replacement down there for you?"

"When needed," said Daskalos. "Watch yourself. I'll take care of me."

"Make sure your replacement is a good man."

Daskalos scoffed. "They're all good or they don't work for me."

"I know," apologized Colt. "Check with me in the a.m.?"

"Right." The call was over.

• • •

Colt returned to the table to find Pagan Maguire with her chin resting on her hand, gazing out at the night. "Sorry it took so long," he said. "Turned out fine."

"James," said the girl softly, ignoring his comment. "I've decided. I don't know just what I'm into, and I'm not supposed to let anyone know where I'm staying, but to go from this lovely evening back to that house, and to walk that little street alone, well, I'm just not up to it."

Colt started to speak.

"Wait, please," said the girl. "It would be lovely to stay at your palace, but I'm really not ready for that, and moreover, I must stay near my own place. But I will break instructions enough to let you take me to my street, and the devil take the rules set out for me. Will you?"

Colt grinned in relief. "Will I? You're insane for even wondering. I would do nothing else, princess. Now?"

"Now," she sighed reluctantly, "before it strikes twelve and I find pumpkins and mice all over the place."

Colt stood and held out his hand. He wanted to take her in his arms and kiss her.

Pagan took his hand. Her thoughts matched his.

• • •

Fury at the Gordons still filled Beverly Martin Raker, along with the disappointment which resulted from Fragonard's decision that made it necessary to use them against Becquerel's wife. In Raker's mind, "humane" killing was quite permissible as long as it was performed within the parameter of necessary means toward a specific end. The Gordons' way was intolerable, but he couldn't touch them. Not yet. But tonight? Well, tonight, if only as a token protest against the Gordons and their kind, he would try to find suitable substitutes.

He checked the time. Later would be better. His mind turned to other matters.

In spite of the defection of Fragonard, and the small complication on Pagan Maguire meeting Colt—through fear and understandably so, thought Raker—the plan was proceeding as well as could be hoped.

Following the terminations scheduled to occur within the next few days, and the delivery of his final ultimatum to PanGlobal, he was certain that his demands would be met.

Oh, perhaps it might require the additional strikes as provided for, and the elimination of any one or two recalcitrant members of Mitchell's board, but that now seemed unlikely. Possible, and planned for, but highly unlikely. The thought brought a small smile to Raker's visage. The plan would succeed. With its completion would come the end of the Raker of the past. No more violence. No more wars except corporate ones which, he thought idly, would still allow him the pleasure of plotting, planning, scheming, and adventure. And finally, respectability. Not just acceptance such as he now had as the director of a small but successful and specialized company which was too closely associated with violence, but the respectability of big, truly big, business. With that could come the longed-for association with his daughter.

Finally, he thought, I can face her, make up for all the years I've only seen to her welfare; made sure she was kept apart from me and those who long for my destruction. It would all have been worth it, and perhaps in time, he could even forget the past.

The fact that he had been able to tolerate the fears for his daughter's safety through the years had been, in good part, due to the loyalty and understanding of Arlette Cavour. That incomparable woman had cared for and shielded Jennie from danger and, nearly as important to Raker, the truth about her father. Without the woman, Raker would have certainly lost the girl, either through her disgust, or to those who would use her to get at him.

It had not been easy, but for safety's sake he'd made contact only once a year, and only by telephone, with Arlette Cavour. He was kept informed of his daughter's welfare and progress, and told of what was needed in the way of additional financial aid. To Raker's early gratification, the Cavour woman had done a remarkable job raising the girl, and handling the original monies placed in her care.

It was not through need, but only from a sense of guilt that Raker had continued to contribute to the girl's funds, for Arlette

Cavour had maintained Jennie on the highest level and at the same time managed to increase greatly the funds entrusted to her.

Raker's next scheduled contact with the woman was set for just over three weeks from this day and it was then, Raker felt certain, that he could tell the woman to prepare the girl for the reunion with her father.

With the thought. Raker forced his mind to soft darkness. He rested. His preparations were complete and he would be ready, when the time was right this night, for his strike against those who preyed on the innocent, inept and infirm.

• • •

"I," announced Pagan Maguire, lounging back against the rear seat of the taxi, "am just a wee bit on the tipsy side." She leaned into the curve of Colt's arm around her shoulder. "I have the distinct impression that I have been plied heavily with inebriating spirits." She turned her head enough to smile up at James Colt with deliberately obvious ingenuity.

Colt, his face against her head, enjoyed the fresh, clean scent of her hair. "You," he said, "were plied with nothing. The fact is that I've discovered you are a born guzzler, a toper, a veritable booze hound." His smile was broad. The girl had sipped, in fact, only a few glasses of wine and champagne during their time together.

Pagan sighed. "True," she agreed. "But then I come by it quite naturally, you know. All Irish are drunkards, or haven't you heard?"

Colt's arm tightened slightly around her. "So they say, but I must admit, you make a lovely drunk."

Pagan snuggled against him ever so lightly. "I'm so glad the rain started again," she said. "Maybe that really is from being Irish."

"And I," said Colt, "am glad you brought along that bumbershoot of yours, though God knows where you had it stashed."

"With these days of off-and-on rain you can't believe that one of us drunken Irish wouldn't remember an umbrella, can you?" She made her voice sound incredulous.

"Heaven forbid," said Colt in mock horror, "and it was so badly needed, too." They had walked less than five feet, without cover, to the waiting taxi.

"Well, anyway," said Pagan, "if you'll just let me from out of your clutching grasp there, I have something I want to do." She leaned away from James Colt.

"And what," inquired the man, lifting his arm, "might that be?"

"That is just none of your business for the moment, my fine bucko," smiled the girl, "and be turning your head away."

Colt stared down at her.

"I mean it," she said. "Turn away like a good little boyo." As Colt watched out the side window, able to see little of the passing scene through the falling rain, he felt the girl moving on the seat next to him.

"All right," came Pagan's voice. "You can put that arm back and start paying me some attention once again." She held a small purse on her lap.

"And just what was all that about?" inquired Colt.

The girl smiled slyly. "Panty hose," she said, in almost a whisper.

Colt showed his surprise.

"Nothing like that, silly," said the girl, tossing her head. "Be getting such evil thoughts from your mind." Her smile delightful Colt. "It's the rain. When we get near home, I want to walk barefoot in the rain."

"Home?" asked Colt.

"My place," said Pagan. The pleasure and bantering tone of her voice changed. "I've not changed my mind."

She looked at James with large, serious eyes. "I simply couldn't stay at your place, even if we were so inclined," she continued, "for I must stay near the phone at least part of the night. But James," and she paused to take a breath of determination, "I simply can't go back to my place alone, even if I'm only delivered nearby."

Colt nodded, silent.

"I'll feel safe, once inside, if you'll see me there," she went on. "And, if you'll not misunderstand, perhaps we can even share a final drink. A nice warm punch."

"Punch?"

"Irish punch. You know, Irish whiskey, hot water, cloves, lemon and sugar or honey."

"Oh," said Colt. "A hot toddy."

"No," said Pagan Maguire firmly, "Irish Punch."

"All right," agreed Colt, "Irish Punch." He said it solemnly as he bent forward from the seat.

"Just what," inquired the girl in a moment or two, "are you doing?"

Colt lifted his head to smile at her.

"Please," he said, "don't misunderstand. It's just the socks and shoes. I'm taking them off."

Pagan grinned broadly.

"After all," said James Colt earnestly, "there are some of us men who also like to walk barefoot in the rain."

Pagan Maguire leaned again into the curve of Colt's arm and nestled against him.

Their now-bare feet slid together, touched, and intertwined. Or at least as well as feet can perform the feat.

"I think maybe it's real," said Pagan, softly.

"What?" Colt's voice was as soft.

"This. Us. Here it is, after midnight, and still no pumpkins or mice."

"Or slippers," said Colt, "glass or anything else."

• • •

Martin Raker didn't believe in omens. Quite possibly, if he had, there would have been concern about the recent vagaries of fortune. Neither, however, did Raker believe in fortune or misfortune. At the least a pragmatist, Raker believed only in actuality and fate, inasmuch as the last was simply the ultimate outcome. He was angry. Names had been churning in his mind, forbidden names: Forbes, Kingsford, Leacock, Becquerel. He forced the thoughts to cease. They, of course, were seldom away for long.

It was now well past midnight, and Raker had been pursuing a certain outcome for more than an hour, without success, on a path that had taken him into night-time Central Park, over to the west side of Manhattan, and down toward the south.

The apparently on-the-edge-of-drunk man who fumbled in the pockets of dirty, ill-fitting clothing for money with which to pay for his glass of wine looked little like either Raker or the man others knew as Coleman and Campbell.

The dissolute-appearing figure finally tugged bills and some coins from a pocket, spilled the money onto the pitted and worn bar top, and shoved it toward the mildly annoyed bartender who had decided that this would be the first and last drink for this particular customer. He carefully took out slightly over the correct amount and pushed most of the remaining bills toward the man.

"That'll be your only drink in here tonight," he growled. "Enjoy it."

Raker muttered something unintelligible, lifted the glass and appeared to drink it, spilling a good portion as he did so. He started to turn, paused, then eyed the money on the bar. He picked up each bill individually, holding the money up before his eyes, and counted it with exaggerated care. Apparently satisfied, he folded the bills slowly with seeming difficulty, and placed them in his pocket. Then, weaving ever so slightly, turned and left the grimy, ill-kept bar.

Outside, he paused as though undecided as to which way to go. Finally, he turned and, unsteadily, began to retrace his steps back from the direction in which he had come. Only a few yards from the bar he became aware that others had left, quietly, behind him. He continued up the street, shuffling slowly, ignoring the wet, and maintaining the image of one not quite yet drunk, but certainly well on the way. He was remembering the alleyway not many yards up the street in front of him. His keen ears heard the brush of clothing from across the street, and he knew that followers had crossed behind him. He made his pace even slower, pausing at one point to lean against the side of a building.

As he stood, head down, eyes rolled up slightly in their sockets, he used the extraordinarily developed rods of his eyes to enable him to pierce the darkness ahead enough to see two figures cross back to his side of the street and dart into the alleyway ahead. He was pleased. It seemed that there were still those about who believed in preying on others for little cause.

• • •

The trick with the eyes seeing into the darkness was one available to almost everyone, though too few were aware of the ability to train themselves to take advantage of it. As he neared the small alleyway, Raker forced his body to relax. It was where the attack would probably occur, and no matter how it came, he must be ready. He was. "In here, old man," came the voice. It was a loud, sibilant whisper. It told him they wanted him off the main street, though visibility was limited through the light downpour.

"Now, man, or I knife you bad," came another, gruffer voice. Raker hesitated and appeared frightened. He turned and held up his hands toward the voices.

"No! . . . I have nothing . . ."

"Get in here, turkey," snapped the second voice, "or you be dead."

Raker took a hesitant step toward the voices. "Why you wanna pick on me," he whined, "I ain't got nothing."

"Shuddup, turd," snapped the first voice. "We seen you dump that cash on the bar back there, showing off. We want it. Now!"

Raker was just inside the mouth of the little alleyway. He could make out the forms in front of him. One tall and bulky, the other not as large. The smaller man held a switchblade, its steel casting pale reflections of the faint light from the street.

"Do it! Give!" hissed the smaller of the men. "Or I cut you, 'less Bubba does his karate job on you. And that, my man, is even more hurting and permanent."

"All right," almost sobbed Raker, "here, it's yours."

His hand dropped to his waist as his head rose, and for the first time the two men actually saw his face in the dim light. It was enough, but not in time.

In a stunning, frozen and unearthly moment, both saw Raker's eyes and the terrible grin on their intended victim's face, and they knew. It was as if they were facing all the things they had ever feared: spiders, snakes, sharks, werewolves, vampires, and all such manner of things. But they had no time to react, nor even complete their thoughts.

Raker's fingers had flipped loose the hook that held his special keychain to his belt. The chain flashed out toward the larger of the two men and as its length almost reached his face, Raker's hand snapped back and the bunched keys lashed forward with a whipping action that ended in the man's eye socket. There was a mushy popping sound, mixed with the muffled, metallic click of the keys. Shock and flashing streaks of light filled the man's head. His hands flew to his ruined eye and felt the warm blood pouring out even before the searing pain sent him toppling to the ground.

With a flash of the chain, Raker allowed his momentum to turn his body forward and to the side, and he added whirling speed with one leg as his other came first slightly backward then shot forward and up, knee bent, then snapping forward with incredible force to slam into the side of the smaller man who held the knife. Ribs shattered, and the man was lifted from the ground and thrown some distance backward. The kick had not been aimed simply at the ribs, it had been aimed through the body toward the spine.

Raker, calm and unperturbed, looked down at the two men sprawled moaning on the alley's brick and worn-asphalt surface. He shook his head. Pathetic, he thought. Not them, just that they would think they could achieve a goal so easily.

He bent over the man holding his bloody eye socket. "You," he said, "if you can hear me, tell me, or you'll lose that other eye."

The groaning man curled tightly into a ball. "I hear you, I hear you. For God's sake, man, help me, help me."

Raker smiled gently. "Just wanted to see if you were capable of taking care of yourself and your friend," he told the moaning figure.

He turned to the other man who was lying unconscious some feet away. He saw the knife, still held in an outstretched hand. Raker's face tightened. He approached the limp form and tugged until both arms were stretched forward. He removed the knife from the unconscious man's hand and hefted it, feeling its weight and balance. It would do. Not as good as his own, the one from his childhood, now somewhat thinner and narrower from its years of use and honing, and carefully left at his hotel, but it would do.

It took Raker three strokes. He was an extremely strong and experienced man, but thumbs are tough.

He placed the knife against the pavement, stepped on the blade and broke it off. Then, carefully, he wiped any possible fingerprints from both pieces and tossed them away. He returned to the moaning one-eyed man.

"You, my friend," he said softly, "had better lay off any of that fancy karate stuff in the future. Can't afford to lose your only eye. And your partner there . . . he's going to have a hell of a time using a knife without a thumb on either hand." He studied the two figures.

"Well," he said finally, "I'll be saying goodnight, gentlemen. What you just got is a lesson. Never go out of your way to pick on innocents. Might suggest you try and get yourself and your friend to a hospital. He's bleeding inside. You both might bleed to death, you know. Think there's one not too far away. Or maybe you can find a friendly cop." He chuckled.

Down the street, he stopped briefly at the bar he had left only a few moments earlier. As he stepped inside the bartender looked up.

"No way, old man. You've had your last drink for the night in this place. Out."

Raker smiled. In two minutes time from now his appearance would never be mistaken for what he looked to be at this moment.

"Just thought you'd like to know," he drawled, "there's a couple your customers down the street a half-block or so in a little alley. Looks like they run into a buzz saw or something." He grinned and waved. "You all take care now, you hear?" His step was light as he stepped out through the door and was gone before the bartender and his remaining customers had fully comprehended his parting words.

Beverly Martin Raker's anger had dissipated.

CHAPTER 20

The taxi was moving slowly through the steady drizzle, preparing for a stop sign ahead, when Pagan Maguire grasped James Colt firmly by the wrist.

"Here," she said abruptly. "Please, James, let's get out here."

Colt looked at the glow of anticipation on his companion's face. He could almost read her thoughts. He raised his voice so the driver could hear and informed her that the ride had come to its end.

On the sidewalk, Pagan opened her umbrella, refusing Colt's offer to hold it for them, and they sauntered down the street, through the softly falling drizzle, with the girl slapping at the wet sidewalk with her bare feet, splattering water in front of them.

"It's lovely," she said, then suddenly shoved the umbrella's handle toward Colt. "Here, keep yourself dry," and she spun away from him to step into the ankle deep water flowing against the curb and waded through it with exaggerated effort.

Colt kept pace, grinning at her small antics. "You," he said, "are a genuine nut."

Pagan paused, standing in the flow of water, and turned to him. "Am I?" she asked. "Am I really a nut?"

Colt nodded his head slowly. "Yep. A delightful nut. Here, you hold it." He closed the umbrella and pushed it toward her. He bent over, rolled up the cuffs of his trousers, and stepped off the curb to join her. Arm in arm they splashed happily down the street.

"I feel like Gene Kelly," said Colt.

Pagan nodded, "I know," she said. "*Singing in the Rain*, wasn't it?"

"Seems like." Colt stopped and, turning to Pagan, placed his hands on her waist. His fingers could almost encircle her firm, slim figure. Easily, quite without effort, he lifted her to the sidewalk.

The difference in the elevation brought her eyes almost to the level of his. Their eyes met and held, and slowly her arms came up to encircle his neck, and as they stood quietly in the rain, their heads came together and their lips touched. At first softly and gently, then parted and moist and warm and almost fierce in their pressure.

"Oh, my," said Pagan, breathlessly, drawing her head back, arms still locked behind James Colt's head. "That had to happen, now didn't it?"

Colt nodded soberly. "It did," he verified. "And it's a start," he said.

"And about time," replied Pagan Maguire. She moved backward, pulling Colt up to the sidewalk after her. She opened the umbrella and held it over them. "It's for home we are, boyo, for some warmth, and drying out, and the punch for us."

"Irish punch," agreed Colt, and for a moment wondered just what the hell the two of them were doing, walking at this hour of the morning, on streets that weren't completely safe in the light of day. The rain made chances of confrontation less likely than normal, but the threat was still there.

More important though, Colt knew that from the time they left the taxi and started their stroll on the street, they had been under the watchful and protective eye of Daskalos or of a hand-picked substitute, or both. He had noticed no one, but he knew they were there. Colt's confidence in Daskalos was unshakable.

"I know I really shouldn't," said Pagan, interrupting James's thoughts, "Let you know where I live," she amplified. "It's against orders." She hugged his arm to her. "But I simply can't stand the thought of going back alone." She looked up at her companion. "Do you think he, my employer, would understand?"

Colt considered his answer carefully before he spoke. Perhaps now was the time. "It has to be," he said slowly. "You see, Pegeen, I've known where you live ever since your first visit to the office."

The girl showed surprise. "But I took precautions, I never . . ." Her voice faded for a moment, then she looked at Colt accusingly. "You weren't supposed to do that," she said. "I was told you wouldn't."

"A precaution," shrugged Colt. "Webb had you followed, and my men followed both you and his people."

"For my protection," mocked the young woman.

"Partly," said Colt. "And partly just doing my job. Can you understand that? Just like you were doing your job."

Pagan thought, silently, as they walked. "Yes," she said finally. "Yes, I can understand that. And James . . ."

"Yes?"

"I'm glad you did. It means I'm not giving anything away."

They walked in silence for several moments before she spoke again. "Then, were your men around when I was being watched?"

"No. The man who is handling the problems caused by your mission advised us to pull off. We did. Until today; until your call. Since then, one of my very best men has had your place under surveillance."

"Then I could have gone home alone, safely?"

"Yes," said Colt simply.

Another short silence.

"James," murmured Pagan softly.

"Yes."

"I'm glad you didn't tell me. I'm glad you're taking me home."

Colt's arm slid around her waist, pulling her closer to him. "So am I, Pegeen, my girl, so am I."

They walked slowly through the drizzle, comfortable in their silence, to Pagan 's home.

"Off with that necktie, and out of that wee jacket," said Pagan. "There's kindling and some paper over there," she continued, nodding her head toward the small fireplace against a wall of her living room.

It looked like a purely decorative device to Colt. "Are you sure it works?" he asked, dubious.

"Of course, silly. I've used it. It's a plus."

"And highly frowned upon in our polluted city," said Colt.

"And who's to notice with all the other smoke?" queried Pagan.

"True," agreed Colt.

"You handle the fire, and I'll do the punch," said Pagan lightly.

Colt busied himself at the fireplace, and in short order had a respectable flame flickering. He stood in front of the fire enjoying its small warmth.

"James."

The voice came from behind him, and Colt turned. Pagan Maguire stood near the door of the hallway. She had changed from the chic cocktail dress worn earlier, and had on what Colt, if called upon to give it a name, would have said was a plain, gingham-looking house dress. As he watched, the girl reached a hand to the wall switch and turned off the room lights, leaving only the glow from the fire for illumination.

"Isn't it lovely?" asked the girl. "The fire?"

"It is truly lovely," said Colt, huskily. Reflection of the flames seemed to dance in her tumbled, still damp hair, and in her huge, luminous eyes.

She lifted a hand and motioned with a finger for Colt to come to her. He did.

"This isn't new and fancy," murmured Pagan, eyes lifted toward Colt's own.

"New?"

"The dress." She took his hands and lifted them, placing them at the neckline of her frock. "You said something earlier, remember? *This* dress is old and worn." She took her hands from his and held them at her sides, lifting her head daringly.

Colt's hands slowly tightened their grip on the top edges of the vee neck of the dress and pulled them apart. The dress ripped open to the waist, and Colt pulled his hands down to tear its full length open.

The girl shrugged the ripped dress from her shoulders and the glow of the fire played across her body. She wore nothing under the dress. Her arms came up, reaching out for Colt. James gently pulled her to him and their mouths met. His hands slid gently and softly over her bare flesh, and he could feel the heat build within him at the feel of the velvety body and the flexing of the muscles under the satin smooth skin as the girl responded to his touch.

Pagan's hands clutched at Colt, feeling the strength of this lean body, as she urged him backward toward the fire. She allowed her body to go limp, pulling Colt down to the soft carpet before the fireplace.

Her mouth was buried in the hollow of his throat below his ear, and her voice matched his in huskiness.

"You'd better help me get you out of those damned clothes before I do some ripping of my own," she said, her fingers busy. In moments the two bodies, bathed in firelight, were intertwined and moving, seeking, hunting, and finding. Warmth and fury, pleasure and peace were all intermingled as each tried to engulf, to swallow, to become a part of the other.

It was only the beginning.

• • •

It was daylight. The rain had stopped falling but the threat still remained in the dark gray overcast sky.

To Beverly Martin Raker, the weather made no difference, and as he looked out on the streets below him, watching traffic slowly increase as the city started to come to life for yet another day, he felt a small sense of being at peace.

Perhaps, just perhaps, his foray of the previous evening would help prevent some innocent human being from becoming the victim of senseless, unnecessary violence in the future. Almost certainly from the two cretins who had tried to victimize him. It was not that Raker was opposed to violence or even the sacrifice of the innocents his mind kept referring to. The key to his logic lay in the qualifiers "senseless," and "unnecessary." Certainly he had been forced, and without reluctance, to aggrieve certain uninvolved persons in his past. And certainly at present. But that was different. Each incident had been necessary and for a purpose. He had done all he could, for the moment, to teach others not to engage in incidental, or spontaneous harm. His next lesson would be demonstrated to the Gordons. That would have to be in the future. The near future, he hoped.

Right now, his mind was more involved with the morning's coming meeting with Alec Gordon. He would remind him of his violation of orders in harming Sullivan's family; instill a good portion of fear tempered with the promise of reward for future obedience.

That, he felt, would be assured by the opportunity for the terrible twins to have a victim, a young, defenseless one, the sort they preferred most, to do with as they pleased. The problem would be in making sure that they did not kill Becquerel, the husband of their victim. That, he was confident, he could manage.

He looked at his watch. Only a few hours to wait. He would check in with Mitchell merely to heighten the man's apprehensions, contact Colt to see what had occurred in his meeting with the Maguire woman, then—as Coleman, or Campbell to the Gordons—wait in the newsstand of the appointed hotel for Alec Gordon to make his appearance.

Gordon, following the script as set forth by Raker, would leave the newsstand and following a prearranged route, wait at the meeting point until Raker could be certain that neither of them was followed.

Once again he glanced at his watch. He could call Mitchell now.

He admired the discipline of the man that brought him to his office even before the quite early arrival of the organization's key personnel. Oddly, the discipline was only one of several things Raker admired about the man, though he had no respect for him. However, if Mitchell had not betrayed Laughlin with the false policies on his mines . . . but then, he had of course. It was a subject not to be pursued.

$$\cdots$$

James Colt, through habit and training, woke early and, realizing the ease with which he could be diverted from his duties of the day if the woman beside him wakened, slipped carefully from Pagan Maguire's bed.

He showered, then dressed in silence. He had looked for but not found a razor. It didn't matter. He would stop by his place. As he prepared to leave, his eyes caressed Pagan's sleeping form, finding overwhelming pleasure in the peaceful contentment shown on her face.

Few women, he thought, can possibly be as beautiful so early in the morning without the benefit of any makeup or tending of hair. He felt the temptation growing to move to the bed and take her in his arms.

Damn fool! he thought. Next you'll be imagining that you're in love with her. Now get the hell out of here while you can. He looked at the sleeping woman. He longed to touch her, kiss her cheek at the least, but he shook his head in warning to himself and left to look for the man who would have been watching, guarding them throughout the night.

• • •

The short street appeared deserted. Only parked cars lined the stone-paved lane. Colt walked down toward the corner, slowly, knowing that he would be contacted before he'd gone far. He saw the car before he heard the voice.

"Out early, eh, boss?" It was Daskalos.

Colt saw the man's smiling face peering out from the automobile parked nearby. He had not looked for the car during the rainy darkness of the previous night.

"And tired from a night on the sofa," said Colt, approaching the car.

"Tough," said Daskalos. His tone was noncommittal.

"Thought you pulled off last night," commented Colt.

"Did. Came back at the dawn's earliest light," came the reply. "Thought it best."

"Anything new on the lady's watcher?"

A smile lit Daskalos's plain countenance. "Yeah. There sure enough was one. But not dangerous to the subject."

Colt lifted eyebrows. "Oh?"

"Fellow across the way. Wife nagging about his smoking. Fighting off and on for days. He's been spending time smoking and sulking, leaning against the building."

"You've gotta be kidding."

"Nope. Fact. The only thing he knew about your friend was that she has mighty fine legs."

"You checked?"

Daskalos looked disappointed. "You have to ask? Certainly no possible connection with anything to do with us. Ran him through the computers last night. Accounted for since birth without even a traffic ticket or a late payment. Solid. Hen-pecked a bit. Nothing more."

"Well I'll be damned," said Colt.

"Yeah. Gotta remember that things are often not what they seem," observed Daskalos.

Colt smiled. "And you," he said, slowly and distinctly, "remember that." He glanced back toward Pagan Maguire's doorway.

Daskalos only grunted. "Want to keep somebody around?"

Colt considered the question. "Not during the day," he said, "but come nightfall, yes."

"Done," said Daskalos. "Now, you want a ride?"

"Thought you'd never ask," replied Colt. "First let's grab a bite of breakfast, then to the apartment, Augustus, my man, if you'll be so kind."

Daskalos started the engine. "I'll wait and drive you to the plant, if they'll allow this heap to linger in your fancy neighborhood," he said.

Colt grinned. "I'll get you special dispensation," he said and, relaxing in the seat, his mind gently reached back toward Pagan Maguire.

• • •

It was an unusual beginning of the day for Victoria Genn as she started her day's work. First, there was a message for Colt notifying him that his secretary would not be in at all. Second, Mallory Fleming Mitchell had called and, for the first time in years (except when he was engaged in business which required his presence elsewhere), had informed her that he would not be in until later in the day. Probably *much* later.

It was only minutes after talking to her employer that she accepted the call from Raker which he had placed to Mitchell.

"I'm sorry, Mr. Raker," she said crisply, "but Mr. Mitchell will not be in until later in the day. Is there anything I should know?"

"Yes," came Raker's reply. "Please inform him that I have narrowed my search considerably, and that there is truly a viper in PanGlobal's midst." That, thought Raker, will give the tough old bird something to peck at.

"Is that all?" inquired Victoria Genn.

"Not quite. There is the slimmest possibility that I will have to call upon all of his . . ." he paused as though searching for a word, "connections, later in the day."

"I see," said Victoria Genn, cautiously. "I shall certainly inform him of the fact." It was her turn to pause. "Will he understand?"

"He will," said Raker. "I'm sure, with your most efficient assistance."

"Very well, Mr. Raker. You may be certain that Mr. Mitchell will receive the information."

"I'm sure he will," said Raker, and hung up.

• • •

James Colt was mildly annoyed at the absence of Janet Fremont. Not at the woman, but at the inconvenience. Theirs was an association which greatly simplified his far-reaching duties. Being forced to use a replacement secretary from the company's efficient secretarial pool hampered his effectiveness. He was, somewhat tiredly, arranging the day's schedule when the call arrived from Raker.

"Anything to report?"

"Not really," said Colt. "Nice evening with a nice person. Don't really think she's involved anymore than we've been told."

"You're a good judge, Jimmy lad," said Raker. "If that's your determination, I'll go along with it."

"She's scared to death about everything," continued Colt. "Started with the Webb incident. Turns out the watcher she felt was such a threat was just a neighbor with some problems of his own."

"She able to offer any light on who's behind this thing?"

"None. At least she didn't offer any, as you phrase it. And I didn't pursue it. She did allow me to escort her home which was 'against the rules' according to her."

Colt could not see Raker's frown. So, he thought, she, too, isn't following the script. Minor point, for of course her residence was known. Nonetheless, it was a deviation that might portend further defection.

"No hint as to how or where she was recruited? Or for exactly what purpose?" asked Raker.

"No. Like I said, nothing volunteered, and I didn't press."

"Too bad," observed Raker. "Could use a break of some sort."

"Nothing new on your end?"

"It's narrowing," replied Raker. "I'll know more by tomorrow. Lots of bird-dogging and digging to do right now. I'll be out of touch most if not all of today, but I will check the hotel for messages in case anything worthwhile turns up on your end. Do you plan on seeing Maguire again?"

Colt laughed. "I'd certainly like to. But no plans have been made, and this damned affair has me well behind in regular routine. I'll let you know, of course, if I get with her again."

"Do that," said Raker, "and hang in there, old stud."

"Got it," said Colt, but Raker was no longer on the line.

Damn, he thought, was that an observation about the night before? Couldn't have been. He knew that he and Pagan weren't followed. It was just Raker's way.

The thought demonstrated one of the differences between Colt and Raker. Colt knew it was a possibility that you might be followed. Raker knew that you were certain to be followed.

As he hung up the phone, Raker considered the conversation with Colt. The girl had, evidently, stayed remarkably loyal. The fact that she let Colt know where she was staying was a break in her instructions, though certainly not a serious breach of security. And she had divulged nothing else. Not that she knew enough to endanger the plan, anyway. For the moment her apparent loyalty overbalanced her slight indiscretion and that, probably with cause, could be put down to extreme fear of another encounter with Webb.

Raker considered the point. All right, he decided, I'll take no action for the present, but it is a point not to be forgotten.

He felt a fleeting rush of sadness as he realized that he would really not like to see any harm befall either his friend, James Colt, or the young woman, Pagan Maguire, who must be near his own daughter's age. Still, the foundation for a contingency plan had been set in motion. With any additional cause, it would most definitely be completed.

He studied his watch. It was nearly time for Raker to become Coleman/Campbell, meet Alec Gordon, and send the twins off to complete the job Fragonard had been, evidently, charmed out of performing.

...

Pagan Maguire came awake slowly, warmly and lazily. Without turning, or reaching out, she knew James Colt was gone. There was no sadness in the realization, only a vague sense of incompleteness, for she knew she would see her James again.

Her James. Had it come to that, already? How absurd. She stretched, luxuriously, not minding the thought, remembering the beauty and gentleness of the night. And as she lay quietly, she became aware of growing apprehension.

Oh, damn, she thought. Pregnancy! Wouldn't it be just the thing? Damn again. Since her alignment with Coleman she had stopped taking birth control pills, having no time for such things and seldom even having cause. She was selective in the extreme, but now she'd done it. Wouldn't it just be lovely to find the man, the right man, and drive him away by becoming pregnant. Her mind worked swiftly. Double damn! The timing was terrible. Chances quite high that these were her fertile days.

She sighed. Oh, well, there was an answer, but she didn't like it. It might not be bad, but again, it might mean a day of stomach upset and nausea. Anyway, it had to be done.

In the medicine chest of her bathroom she found the pills where she had, with typical neatness and organization, placed them. Not tolerated in Ireland, she thought, and so readily available here. She took four of the pills in her hand, filled a glass of water, and took them all at once.

Done. That takes care of that. Now to hope for the best; that there will be none of those annoying symptoms of the overdose. A shame, she thought, that so many American women didn't even know of the effectiveness of such an emergency precaution. European women have been doing it for years. She looked in the mirror, liking the glow she saw on her face. "Pegeen, my girl," she said aloud, "if you are going to continue keeping company with your James, then you'd better get with the regimen once again."

She tried a smile, but the gnawing apprehension remained. Of course! Coleman. She had broken her pledge to him. She had let someone from PanGlobal know where she lived. Never mind that he had already known. That had nothing to do with it. She stared at her image in the mirror, no longer liking what she saw. Was there anything else I did? Did I say something, give something away? Damn! She had not kept her faith. She turned away from the mirror and started the water running in the shower. That's not like me, not at all. Forget that I was afraid. I wasn't, for a fact, all that afraid. Most of it was the attraction she had felt for James.

"Damn," she said aloud. She had not only betrayed Coleman—however small the action—but her dear dead brother who Coleman was trying to avenge.

As she showered she came to a decision. She would have to tell Coleman. Today wasn't her scheduled day to meet or call him, but there was the—what did Coleman call it? The 'safe-room?' Yes, there was the safe-room where she was to go in case of an emergency. And while this may not be an emergency exactly, the guilt she felt, mostly because of the memory of her beloved brother, was enough to make it imperative that she tell Coleman just what she had done.

Well, maybe not *exactly* everything she had done.

At the last thought, she almost smiled. She felt better. Now, if those damned pills will just oblige me and lie there quietly.

• • •

By the time Pagan Maguire had finished dressing and taken a breakfast of orange juice, toast, milk and tea, the rain had begun once again. She didn't mind in the least. It reminded her of the silly and childish walk she and her James had taken on the night before, and enjoyed so much.

She selected a waterproof plastic raincoat with a hood, not remembering just where, with her mind on other things, she had put the umbrella the night before. She pulled stylish rain boots over her shoes and prepared to leave. The subway, though she hated riding the filthy thing, was not far, and quickly would deliver her almost to the door of her destination.

ALEC GORDON

The apprehension Pagan Maguire had experienced earlier was far exceeded by what Alec Gordon now felt as he prepared for his scheduled meeting with The Colonel. Though he'd told his sister the name was Ian Campbell, he would always be simply The Colonel, or The Man, to Gordon.

Remembering his instructions to always go past his destination, Alec Gordon had found a garage below 55th Street and was now walking back up 7th Avenue. The chill he felt came not from intuition, but rather from experience. He knew, as well as anyone, how The Colonel felt about anyone being harmed outside the Colonel's directive. And he knew this morning would be an experience he would far rather do without. Nonetheless, he had rather face the man and explain the circumstances which were, after all, perfectly understandable, than try to "gap out" on The Man.

That, as others in the past had learned, amounted to deliberate suicide. There was no option. He would have to face The Colonel and explain that it was, unfortunately, of course, a regrettable accident. He would leave out the fact that he had enjoyed seeing the woman and baby die as well as the man. It had just been too quick.

Head lowered against the rain which was now pelting down with some force, Gordon neared the southeast corner of 55th Street and 7th Avenue. Traffic was heavy, and he waited at the stoplight, head lifted as he looked across the street trying to see if The Colonel was anywhere in evidence.

From the subway stop, Pagan Maguire made her way down 7th Avenue, head lowered against the force of the rain, hood pulled tightly around her head. At the northeast corner of 55th and 7th Avenue, she paused to wait for the traffic light change, lifting her head to watch the light. It was then she saw him.

Her heart seemed to jump inside her body, and the breath left her as though she had been struck violently in the pit of her stomach. She stared in disbelief! She would never mistake that face, now only across the avenue from her, which seemed to be studying something over the side street he was facing. It was him! The murderer of her brother, dear, dead Colin. She stood as though paralyzed.

Oh, my God, she thought, if only I could find Coleman right at this instant. If there were some way I could reach that devil there. If only I had a pistol. Her mind whirled, leaving her seemingly without the power of motion.

The light had changed and traffic blocked her way, even if she had been able to force her legs to move. She watched as the man— no, the very devil himself!—walked across the street and into the newsstand. In only seconds, before she could dare move into the rushing traffic, the man came out once again and started down the side street, away from her. She stared in disbelief, pleading in silent desperation for the light to change so she could follow him. It was at the exact moment the light changed and traffic came to a stop, that the man she knew as Owen Coleman emerged from the newsstand, glanced around him, then started up the street behind the diminishing figure of Alec Gordon.

He's found him, thought Pagan Maguire. Oh praise be to Mary, Coleman's found him and is after him. But the thought was followed with a flood of doubt and fear.

The path! The direction the men were walking, and the way they had left the newsstand! It was the exact way that she was to meet Coleman on the days carefully prescheduled.

Heart pounding, still breathless, Pagan turned and hurried down the street at as rapid a pace as she could manage. Thank the Holy Mother that it was raining, she thought, or I'd have been seen. Coleman misses nothing. But in the raincoat and its snug hood, she was only another pedestrian on the crowded streets.

If she was right, if Coleman was actually going to meet that animal, Gordon, she knew where the meeting would occur. She must hurry to a spot where she could see them, if such a meeting was to be.

Luck was with her at the next corner, and she was able to cross the street without waiting. It should be enough, she thought. Her instruction, and she assumed Gordon's, was not to hurry. Simply to stroll to the designated small concrete park not far off 7th Avenue, and wait until Coleman could determine that they were not being followed.

She knew that her only advantage lay in being, at a distance, virtually unrecognizable in her hooded coat, and through the shrouding downpour. And, moreover, she was not following, but was ahead. She would go on just to a point where, from the small dress shop she recalled to be nearby, she could watch out the window and see if Coleman was actually meeting with Gordon.

The thought of the name caused near physical pain, and she came close to groaning as she found the shop she sought and ducked inside.

"May I help you?" asked a sales clerk.

"Oh! No. Not right now. I'm just looking," gasped Pagan Maguire.

The clerk shrugged. "Let me know."

Pagan watched as Coleman approached Gordon who was already in the small, concrete park-like area which was flanked by tall buildings. They stood, as she had been instructed to do, side by side.

Pagan stared in stunned disbelief. It simply couldn't be! Coleman couldn't be in with them. She watched, eyes wide, as they moved away from the area and started in the direction away from her.

Certainly! The thought flashed into her mind—it must be that Coleman was almost ready to deliver. Was that the word, deliver? To deliver the Gordons to whoever it was that would handle them. That must be it. Certainly. That is most likely the way he would handle it. And now he is going to find the woman. Her spirits lifted, but still some doubt lingering.

She stared after the men until they were out of her vision. She could now leave. But she had to know. It was, now, truly an emergency, at least as far as she was concerned. She had to know.

She would go to the safe-room so designated by Coleman, and there wait for him, and the explanation of just what he was doing with Gordon.

Oh, yes. And to tell him of her allowing Colt to know where she lived.

• • •

"Bloody awful, the prices these sodding colonial thieves charge for parking," said Alec Gordon as Raker stepped into the car and out of the rain from where he had been waiting for the man to retrieve his automobile.

"My money, not yours," growled Raker. "I'm a hell of a lot more interested in hearing about your rampage which violated specific orders."

Gordon felt his stomach squirm as though it were a separate groveling organism. His mind wanted his body to shrink and dodge aside as if the man's words were thrown stilettos. He was aware of the almost physical impact of Raker's eyes.

He started to speak and found his mouth too dry to form words. He moved his tongue back and forth trying to draw moisture.

"Yes. That. Unfortunate." His knuckles were white on the steering wheel. "Unavoidable. Operator error. Hit automatic fire without knowing it." Said aloud, the palliation sounded absurd, even to him.

"Bullshit," said Raker.

Gordon drove, eyes intent on the rain-shrouded streets, the silence unbearable to him.

"All right," said Raker, finally. "I don't believe a word of it, but I'm going to accept it. Once." There was a terrible finality in the way he said the last word.

Gordon became aware that his palms were sweating. It was an improvement over the silence.

"Your sister performed precisely," said Raker. The words were an accusation.

"She enjoyed it," replied Gordon.

"So did you," rejoined Raker. "That's now behind us. Just remember, I said *once*. Any other lapse will be terminative." His tone changed. "Your sister is waiting for us in your little love nest?" The insinuation was wasted on Gordon. The incestuous relationship of the Gordon twins was readily acknowledged by them, almost with pride.

"Indeed," said the man. "I rang from the garage when I retrieved the car."

"You told her to prepare for a little trip?"

"I did."

"Neither of you are foolish enough to try and have a recording device or any such thing about, are you?" inquired Raker.

Gordon was startled by the question. "Neither of us has any known suicidal tendencies," he said.

"Good," said Raker, "now, just a short pause down the road here while I make a parcel pickup and we'll be off." The parcel was a small piece of luggage left at a checkroom in a lower Manhattan hotel. It contained, along with certain other carefully selected contingency items, money.

The rest of the plan would not take long, and the Gordons should be, before nightfall, aboard a jet speeding them to Rome.

CHAPTER 21

Pagan Maguire had been given, upon her arrival in the city, the key to the safe-room and instructions as to its use. No name or number was on the key. All that remained for her to do was discover exactly where the room was. She called the telephone number previously given her and performed the ritual in which she had been rehearsed with the admonition that her call would be reported to Coleman.

Identifying herself to the answering service and telling them that their client was to have a message waiting for her, she was told that she had an appointment. They gave her the name of a person, and a time. The time stated was not, as might be normally expected, on any even quarter or half hour, but rather down to specific minutes. The time was actually the room number. The name was, unsurprisingly to Pagan, the Wellington.

It was where the newsstand was. Arriving there, she paused only to purchase a newspaper to help pass the time and then made for the elevator.

• • •

She found the room to be quite ordinary, and with but little evidence of occupancy. She browsed about idly, time dragging by slowly as she waited impatiently for the return of Coleman. It might, she knew from his previous instructions, be quite a while before he returned. However, as carefully instructed by the man, once she determined that an emergency was important enough for her to use this room, she was to wait, however long, for him to appear.

She sighed, tossed her handbag onto the bed, removed her coat, shook the water from it and hung it in the sparsely filled closet, then seated herself at the small table where Raker had sat as he reviewed the progress of his plans during the past few days.

She glanced at the open briefcase with its spread of papers and jumble of pens. She smiled slightly. Felt tips. She remembered how

Coleman was so careful about leaving impressions on sheets beneath the ones on which he wrote.

How typical of the cautious man, she thought, remembering their first meeting. The memory made her feel more secure. He was so sincere and intent. Certainly, he must be on the verge of bringing in the terrible Gordons. That must be it. He was delivering what he had promised. Yes, that must be the case.

She picked up the newspaper and unfolded it. She would wait.

• • •

"So," said Raker, addressing the Gordons, "that's it. As simple as that. Any questions?"

Alec and Elizabeth Gordon glanced at each other briefly, and then looked back at Raker. They were seated close to each other on a long sofa, the woman holding one of her brother's hands on her lap with both of hers.

"No," she said, eyes gleaming with unnatural brightness. "And you mean we, Alec and I, can do anything with our little target that we want? Did I understand that, Colonel?"

Raker despised them. When their turn came, he might break a rule and make their demise as unpleasant as possible.

"That's correct," he said. The words left a metallic taste in his mouth. "But the husband is to be undamaged."

"Not even a little playing around with him?" pouted the woman as might a child denied its allowance.

"I know you," said Raker, "and your 'playing around.' You have a tendency to let it get out of hand. I would not advise it."

"Oh, my, no," said Elizabeth Gordon. "Not this time. It's too grand an opportunity to muck up." She leaned toward her brother to kiss him on the cheek. "We won't do that, will we, Alec, dear?"

"God, no," said the man, his fear of The Colonel overwhelming his growing sense of anticipated delights. And in the past minutes, even his sister had been made acutely aware of the consequences of any deviation from their commission.

"Heaven's no," agreed Elizabeth Gordon. "Making sure he is aware of the events will be part of the delight." Her voice was a purr. "Maybe just a little discomfort for him, but you can be certain, Colonel, that he'll be left to remember what happens. I'll pledge you my life on that."

"You have," said Raker softly. He opened the case he'd brought with him. "Here's your money for the mission. Fifty thousand dollars. That will more than cover expenses. You have suitable passports and other identification?" It was actually a statement.

They nodded. "Certainly," said the woman. "We are nicely husband and wife on a lovely holiday." She squeezed her brother's hand.

"How nice," said Raker, dryly. "Then that does it. You have their names and the hotel, and you know the company name under which I made your airline reservations." He glanced at his watch. "They will be held for another hour and a half pending passenger identification. Take care of that."

"Yes sir," said Alec. The answer was crisp, military, and not at all sarcastic.

"Let me see the passports," said Raker. The twins exchanged glances.

"Not even for you," said Elizabeth. "And I'm certain you would not want us open to inadvertent exposure." The passports they would use to leave the country would not be the ones they would use in Italy.

Raker eyed her coldly even as he respected her caution. "All right," he said, "that takes care of things quite well." He stood. "I'll expect you back immediately following successful completion of your trip. I'm certain you'll be anxious to get on to your next assignments." He smiled. "More Irish," he said.

The woman actually licked her lips. "We know," she said, and Raker still remembered the glow in her eyes much later, even as Alec Gordon drove him back to near where they had met.

His promise had been made only to be certain they would return for their own terminations.

• • •

Still in the safe-room, Pagan Maguire—with a muttered sound of discontent—folded bulkily in half the newspaper she'd been reading, then tossed it onto the bed where her handbag lay. The world simply can't be all that terrible, she thought. War and killings and rape and all sorts of violence. And continuing pronouncements from the Brits that the IRA Provos were falling apart, even as punishment and death were being meted out by both that group and their adversaries. It was enough to make one give up reading.

She rose and went to the window to gaze out into the grayness. It seemed as if the rain had lessened, and for a moment she watched the rivulets of water run down the steep roof of the old-looking building across the way, and pour in thin streams down to the street below.

Damn the man, she thought. I need to know just what is going on with him and that foul heathen Gordon? She turned from the window and began to pace about. She went to the clothes closet and ran a hand across the plastic raincoat she'd hung carefully away from the few clothes in the small cubicle. Only a few beads of moisture clung to the coat, and there was a sprinkling of wetness below where it hung.

Would there be anything in the room that might perhaps tell her of Coleman's present course of action—anything that may help her learn just what the scheme was that she was playing a role in? With only small feelings of guilt, starting tentatively and growing bolder as she worked, she began to examine the pockets of the coats and trousers hanging in the closet. She found nothing there, nor in the pockets of the two shirts.

She turned to the open briefcase that had attracted her attention when she first arrived. Brave now, she riffled through the papers. Most were blank; what written material she found seemed to be information about methods used by educational and charitable institutions for fundraising. She soon lost interest. It appeared to have no connection with either Coleman, the Irish troubles, or even Pan-Global Assurance. As she dropped the handful of material she'd been examining, her eyes fell once again on the array of felt-tipped pens, and then she noticed among them one that was different.

She stretched out a hand to pick it up. It was a quite ordinary, hard and shiny, retractable ballpoint pen. How odd, she thought—the black sheep of the flock. She immediately thought the comparison was quite foolish. They were all black. Still, it was different. She held it in front of her, thumb clicking the point in and out. Then, on impulse, she unscrewed the top. Her brows knit as she saw the small, flimsy roll of onionskin paper wound around the slim ink cartridge. Her fingers plucked it loose and she unrolled it.

It was only a list of names and initials. It meant nothing to her. But it was a bit cryptic. Perhaps it was important, after all. No, it *must* be important, or it wouldn't have been concealed.

Interest aroused, she took the paper to the table, nearer the light, and smoothed the tiny rectangle flat on the wooden surface and studied the names. Her eyes fell on the name Dairmud Sullivan, and she felt a tiny chill which seemed to prickle her skin. Quickly, she raised herself from the chair enough to pick up the paper she'd been reading. Opening it, she thumbed rapidly through the pages.

There it was! Dairmud Sullivan. She glanced at the small thin piece of paper she'd taken from the pen. The name was the same. A man dead, killed on his boat in the harbor along with his wife and child. Murderously cut down by a hail of bullets, and him a known Irish sympathizer. Was there, *could there be* a connection? Her face grew grim. An American-Irishman dead, and his name on a list hidden by Coleman, whom she had just seen with a murderer of the Irish. She would know. She must know! Her chill of apprehension turned to one of fear.

James! she thought. James Colt. She knew she could turn to him. And it might be a far better thing to do than confront Coleman just yet. She could do that on the phone later. She picked up her handbag and searched it for something to write with, a pen or pencil. Then, even in her fear, she smiled, feeling foolish. She picked up one of the felt-tipped pens from the open briefcase, plucked out one of the blank sheets of paper, and started to copy the list she'd found.

• • •

As Pagan Maguire wrote, Raker opened the door of the car Gordon was driving. He was two blocks from the Wellington Hotel.

"Success," he said, stretching one leg out toward the curb, avoiding the water flowing in the gutter.

"Not to worry, Colonel," replied Gordon. "It will be done, and exactly as you desire." He paused. "Report the same way?"

"Of course," said Raker. "You'll always be notified if there is a change."

"Of course," said Gordon. He waited. If only the man would get the hell out and away from him, and let him get on to more pleasant things. He breathed a sigh of relief only after Raker had stepped out to the sidewalk and closed the car door.

Raker watched the car drive off, unsmiling. He could not afford regret. After all, what must be done, must be done. He could not afford regret and he could not afford sadness. He didn't want the young wife of his enemy's son killed. Certainly didn't want her to have to undergo what she would suffer at the hands of the Gordons, but it had to be. If only there had been some other way. He forced the thought aside, but the sadness remained as he turned to make his way to the Wellington where he could, once again—using the checkroom to keep such things as wigs and pads and money— change from Coleman/Campbell, back to Martin Raker, all around swell fellow, and savior of the PanGlobal empire.

The irony, and the closing circle of success lifted his spirits. The sadness remained.

• • •

Pagan Maguire carefully compared the copy she had made with the note she'd found in the pen. She wanted to be sure that she hadn't overlooked or changed anything, however minutely. It could be something that might make a difference when it was examined by James Colt. Satisfied, she folded the sheet of paper and placed it in her purse, re-rolled the original and replaced it in the pen. James, she thought! Perhaps I'd best call him now. She hesitated, filled with a desire to leave the room, yet wanting to know that James Colt's comforting presence was available.

She dropped the ballpoint back in the briefcase, took her coat from the closet, picked up her purse from the bed, and glanced about the room for any other traces she might have left. The newspaper! She'd dropped it in the wastebasket. Moving quickly, she bent and picked it up, tucking it under her arm. Anything else?

Her eyes again inspected the room. No. That was everything. She started for the door, then suddenly stopped. No. I must let James know. He may leave the office at any moment.

She glanced around, looking for the phone and quickly found it on the bedside table. She didn't need a phone book. She remembered the number very well. Reading the instructions, she dialed for an outside line. Then, as she dialed the number of James Colt, she settled lightly on the edge of the bed.

• • •

As Raker picked up his checked parcel, his mind had dismissed the Gordons and the Becquerel girl for the moment. It was time now to complete preparations for supplying Mallory Fleming Mitchell with the complete demands being made against PanGlobal, and the details of how they were to be fulfilled. For the sake of caution, he must, for the next day or so only, use other checkrooms than the ones he'd been using. No problem, really—there was nothing in the parcels or cases to associate Raker himself with their contents. Not immediately, that is. Still, the gray wig in the package he had just picked could, if discovered, cause some speculation. In a very short time it would not matter, and he would be glad to have them know. But that time was not now. He thanked the checkroom attendant with a tip and started for the elevator.

• • •

The voice that answered the telephone at James Colt's office was not the one that Pagan Maguire had learned to recognize.

"May I speak to Mr. Colt, please," said Pagan.

"May I tell him who's calling?" replied the professionally pleasant voice.

"Maguire. Pagan Maguire."

"Just a moment, please, Ms. Maguire. I'll see if Mr. Colt is in."

The line was silent.

"Please," murmured Pagan, aloud. "Please be there." She waited, seconds stretching into hours.

"Pegeen, my girl," came James' voice filling her with pleasure even in her anxiety. "May I say first, that I think you are one of the nicest things that has ever happened to me?"

"James," she said, "I must see you. It's terribly important."

Colt recognized the consternation in her tone. "What is it, sweetheart?" he asked, not even aware that he had used the last word. It was one that he never used idly. Quickly and succinctly, Pagan told him of her discovery and the association of the Sullivan name.

"Too damn coincidental," said Colt. "Where are you now?"

Pagan hesitated. It might just all be a terrible mistake, after all. And I just can't, she thought, give too much away. What if I'm wrong, and Coleman is really doing right.

"I can't tell you that, James. I just can't, not right now."

"Are you where you found the note?"

"Yes."

"Listen to me, Pagan. Get out of there. Now. Immediately. Don't hesitate. Don't volunteer another word to me. Remember where we had coffee yesterday. The first place?"

"Yes. Of course."

"Go there. Now! Wait for me, and sit away from the window." He thought quickly. Daskalos or one of his men could be there before she arrived. Not inside, but close enough to protect her. Her home would probably be staked out in the very near future. "You'll be safe," Colt continued. "Now go. This instant." He hung up hurriedly to call Daskalos.

Pagan, fears doubled by James Colt's urgent tone, almost slapped the phone down. She whirled, rose from the bed, and was quickly out the door and into the hall. The elevator was only a few steps away. She walked swiftly to its doors. She could hear movement but jabbed at the button anyway.

Raker, inside the rising elevator, continued to review his plans.

CHAPTER 22

It would be convenient, he thought, if the current strike is sufficient. If this is all it will take to convince Mitchell and his board that the only thing facing them past here is simply greater loss. And that most likely will be the case. But one can never assume. Only try to anticipate; never assume. If required, the other terrifyingly destructive terminations would be made. He frowned slightly. Those would destroy many innocent victims. They were the massive strikes. The fault would be Mitchell's.

Raker stepped out into the hallway and turned toward the stairwell. As was his habit, he had exited on a floor other than the one which was his destination. He had, this time, selected the floor one level below where he was going.

• • •

Mildly annoyed, Pagan Maguire waited as the elevator stopped at the floor below her. When it finally arrived and the doors slid open, she slipped inside and relaxed against a wall, knees feeling weak. Colt's urgency had frightened her as, she was sure, he had meant it to. She watched the doors close with a sense of relief. They did not open again until the elevator reached the lobby.

Never an easy task, the chore of finding an available taxi had been made more difficult by the nearly constant drizzle, and after only a few moments of waiting hopefully, Pagan Maguire elected to take the bus—abhorring the terrible subway—to her destination not far from Washington Square Park. She found a seat and drew herself into a mental shell, trying to put her mind in neutral until she felt she could come alive again in the security of James Colt's presence.

• • •

Raker frowned as he paused before inserting his key in the lock of his door. The all-but-invisible gossamer thread was not in evidence in the lock. His eyes swept the edges of the door. The tiny chip of paint which matched the finish of the door was not in place. Maid service? Possible, probable. Still . . .

Raker slid his key into the lock, standing clear of the doorway, turned the key at the same time as he turned the knob and, pushing gently, leaving the key in the lock, backed away quickly as the door swung open slowly and without incident.

Dropping swiftly to the carpeted hall floor, Raker dove headlong and with incredible speed, past the open door, eyes sweeping the room. Silently and with practiced skill he made certain that there was no presence in the room other than his own. His experienced eyes saw the evidence of recent occupation. The bed showed, ever so slightly, the pressure of Pagan's body where she had sat talking on the phone.

In rapid succession Raker found the drip marks of the girl's raincoat, found the tell-tales broken on the pockets of his jackets in the closet, the rearrangement of the papers in his case, and the broken seal on the ballpoint pen—an infinitesimally sheer filament of household cement at the juncture of top and bottom parts of the pen.

Who? It had to be the Gordons or the girl. He had been with the Gordons.

He picked up the phone and dialed his answering service. It required only a few seconds to ascertain that Pagan Maguire, using the name and procedures he had given her, had indeed called in order to use the safe-room. But just how in the hell had she found the pen? The note? Would it mean anything to her?

He brushed the thoughts aside. No conjecture. Facts only.

He dialed the desk. "A call was made from here," he said, identifying himself by his hotel name, "and I seem to have misplaced the number. Would it be possible for you to tell me? I asked such a record to be kept."

It took only a few moments for the record of the call to be found. It was the number of James Colt.

"Thank you," said Raker, his mind working furiously.

Certainly. It would have to be Colt. The only one the girl knew well enough to approach with a problem. Again, and for the last time, Pagan had violated trust. She had interfered past direction, and had not remained as her instruction specifically indicated she must do once she used the room. Too bad. No chances could be taken.

He considered the next step for a moment and decided that even the seemingly innocent call he now must make should not be made from this room, or through his current identity, though he would soon be quite gone, for good, from the place. Any other telephone would do, and the few seconds shouldn't matter.

• • •

At the first available pay phone, Raker placed the call. "We must proceed with the picture hanging," he said, "and immediately." More foolish "code talk," he thought, but this time meaning a frame-up. Foolish or not, it mirrored Raker's caution.

"Of course," came the reply. "There will be no problems. Everything has been carefully prepared."

"Good," said Raker. "See to it. I'll be busy over the next hours. Leave messages." He replaced the phone, waited a moment, and picked it up again. His second call was to the private number of Mallory Fleming Mitchell. If the man was not at home the call would be automatically transferred to his car or office, or most other places the man might be.

Mitchell, when he answered, was already at his office.

• • •

Pagan Maguire was still sipping her first cup of strong, black tea when James Colt walked through the door.

"James," she said, spirits soaring, "I'm so glad to see you. This is awful." Her lovely face was tense with concern and tinged with fear.

"Please," said Colt, seating himself, "don't. You're fine now. No one is going to harm you. Now what can you, *will* you, tell me."

Pagan held out the paper onto which she had copied the list of names found in the pen. "This. The one name, Sullivan, is the same as that of the man killed down in Baltimore, along with his wife and child." She looked at Colt with pleading in her eyes.

"James. Tell me. The truth. Was that man insured by your company?"

Colt hesitated only a moment. "Yes," he said. "He was. And all the others in the first column."

Pagan dropped her eyes and stared at her cup. She seemed to sag. "I was so afraid it would be that." She looked up. "Since I've been sitting here, things have seemed to come together." She looked at Colt earnestly. "I've been a part of a murder plan, haven't I, James? I *have* been, I know it."

"No," said Colt, slowly. "Not part of a murder plan. You've been used." He reached out to take her hands; they were frost-bite cold. "And all you've done is carry communications that could have been, would have been, sent in some other way. What I'm worried about is why? Why were you the one selected to do this? It seems like they've been taking an unnecessary risk."

Pagan was overwhelmed with a feeling of abject misery. "I think I know," she said, quietly. "I'm terribly afraid I know the why of that. And I'm afraid it's not just myself that is being used."

"Can you tell me, Pagan? Can you tell me now everything you know about the affair?"

Pagan was deathly still and quiet for a moment, hardly seeming to even breathe. Finally she sighed. "Yes," she said. "Yes, I think I must tell you, or most of it." She leaned forward intently. "Did I cause any of this James? Did I?"

"No." The answer came quickly. "It would have occurred without you. *Did* occur without you," he corrected. "You were really sort of a smoke screen meant to draw our attention from other things. I really should have seen that from Raker's attitude. He's seldom wrong. He felt you were playing a very small role."

"Raker?"

"A friend, and the man who just might be able to save us, the company and you, from this thing. You'll meet him. I'll tell you more about it later, but right now, tell me what you know."

She did. Over the next few minutes, Pagan Maguire outlined nearly everything that had happened in her associations with Coleman since he'd first approached her in Dublin those months ago. She left out only Coleman's meeting with Brennan. They, Brennan and his crowd, they did not operate over here, she thought, so there was no reason to bring them into it. It was enough that she could confess her desire for vengeance against those causing her brother's death.

"I see," said Colt, finally. "I can understand it, dear," he said, meaning it. He understood well the drive for revenge. After all, he had learned much about that from Raker. And Coleman seemed to be much the same sort of man. Simply on the other side and, hopefully, not as effective. Thank God, thought Colt, that we have someone like Raker to combat the man. If we can only find out who Coleman truly is.

"Will knowing his hotel help?" asked Pagan.

Colt shook his head. "No. Most surely not. He'll have certain knowledge that you were in the room and found the list."

"But he won't," protested Pagan. "I was ever so careful."

"Of no use with people like those," said Colt, "or even someone like me who isn't quite in the league with Coleman's and Raker's. You can bet there were little traps on everything you touched." He shook his head. "No, our bird will damn well have flown from that particular nest. We'll stake it out of course. As soon as I check with Raker." He frowned.

"What?" asked Pagan.

"He'll be after you," said Colt. "Desperately after you, at least until he learns that I have the information. Then he'll be interested in staying away, since you can identify him."

The girl shivered involuntarily.

Colt started to pat her but, remembering her earlier reaction, simply placed his hand alongside her cheek. "No, darling. Don't worry. By the time he knows, you'll be safe. You are now, and you'll have plenty of protection. He'll not get to you. I have good men. One nearby right now. Once we can get with Raker, you'll be safer than ever before."

"I want that," said Pagan, reaching up to hold his hand more firmly against her cheek. "I want to feel that. Oh, I'm so sorry, James, so sorry I ever got into this."

"Don't think of it like that," said Colt. "Realize that by being in on it, even in a small way, you may just have given us the lead we need to stop this thing before any others are harmed. Your involvement may actually save lives."

The words, considered and sorted out carefully by the girl, were enough to bring the ghost of a smile to her tired face. She stretched out a hand, reaching for Colt.

"Oh, I hope so," she breathed softly. "Oh, James, I do hope so."

"First, I'll get you to a safe place," said Colt, "then I'll run that list through the computer to find out if we can determine exactly who those next victims are, and where they are; then I'll get with Raker so we can put an end to this entire thing."

He smiled reassuringly at the young woman.

"Believe me," he said, "Pegeen, my girl, if anyone can clean this thing up, it'll be Raker."

• • •

Colt guided his car through the Queens Mid-Town tunnel and followed the Long Island Expressway, leaving it to reach Northern Boulevard, then cross Queens, out of New York City and into Nassau County. He swung north for a short distance, then began to double back in a westerly direction toward Little Neck Bay.

As the distance from the source of threat lengthened, Pagan Maguire's tensions lessened. She began to feel that Colt's reassurances were based on fact, and that she was not so much guilty as used. Her innate intelligence and toughness of character, limited only by her youth, had allowed her to regain her perspective, and to acknowledge the pleasure she felt from simply being with James Colt, and from far deeper feelings than just the sense of security his presence gave her.

As Colt wheeled the car through stone pillars guarding the entrance to a tree-bordered lane toward a sprawling mansion—what Maguire considered to be the epitome of the word estate—she drew an audible breath of awed wonder.

"Holy Brigid, boyo," said the girl. "Is there no end to the things you possess?"

Colt smiled. "Hardly mine," he said. "I only have what I guess you could call the servant's quarters, that small place away from the main house." He motioned in the direction. "What I pay helps the owners keep up with the taxes."

"Do you come here often? It's so lovely, and so near the water."

"As often as I can." He debated silently a moment before continuing. "This is my safe-house," he told her. "No one knows of it except those I lease it from, and the name James Colt would mean nothing to them. Unless they have some other acquaintance of that name."

Pagan looked puzzled. "I've read, of course, of safe-rooms and safe-houses," she said, "but only in thrillers and spy stories and such. Now here I am involved with two such places right in a row."

"This place goes back a long way with me, Pegeen," Colt told her. "Habit, I guess, has made me keep it. I've never even driven my own car here before." He looked across at her. "At one time, I was what you might call a spy. I was CIA until a few years ago." He was busy closing the garage doors. The car must stay out of sight.

Pagan nodded. "I see. That explains much." She looked at him with interest. "And you'd have been good at it, I suppose. I think that makes me feel even more secure with you than ever." She played with the thought for a moment. "Will we truly be safe here?" she asked.

Colt shrugged. "For a while. Any determined search by really efficient hunters could turn this up. But we'll have this affair settled before your Coleman can manage any such thing." He gave Pagan a reassuring squeeze of the hand. "Come on. I'll show you the place, get you acquainted with its peculiarities, then get back and sort out this list of yours." He looked at her once again.

"Just don't tempt fate. Stay inside, and don't be seen, and above all don't use the telephone. There is an answering recorder hooked up which I'll show you how to use. If a call comes in, monitor it. Answer only if you are certain it's me, and we'll work out a code that will let you know it's truly me and I'm calling of my own free will."

To Pagan Maguire the words were mildly alarming. For all his reassuring, James Colt was obviously concerned about her well being. The thought both pleased and bothered her.

She forced the alarm from the surface of her mind. James would handle it, and well.

Once inside, Colt gave her a quick, efficient tour, repeated his instructions and made her repeat the code he would use when he called. Only then did he call Raker's hotel.

"Sorry," a bland voice told him. "Mr. Raker does not answer his telephone. Would the gentleman like to leave a message?"

"Yes. Please tell Mr. Raker that Mr. Colt called and will call again. If he comes in, would Mr. Raker please leave a number where he might be reached if he did not remain at the hotel?"

"Certainly. Mr. Raker will be so notified."

James Colt and Pagan Maguire kissed. It was a gentle and lingering kiss, and James Colt left. Reluctantly.

It was only a pleasant walk to where he could find a taxi or bus to his next destination. He did not want a record of a taxi picking him up at his "safe-house."

• • •

Knowing that Pagan would have his car for emergency transportation helped make Colt's train ride less annoying than it would have been otherwise. He could return to his "safe-car," the one registered and stored under a name other than his own, and the trip would be more pleasant. By that time he should have information on the names of the list Pagan had copied, have met with Raker, and they would be on the way toward ending the plot against Pan-Global. Foolish or not, the thought helped shorten the trip.

Obtaining a taxi with no little difficulty, Colt made his destination the storage garage where his safe-car was kept to insure that it would be out and ready for him to pick up later in the day. The well-tipped attendant assured him that it would be ready and waiting.

As Colt left the garage, his path took him alongside the Pan-Global building, and James, for one of the few times he could remember, appreciated the convenience of the honor which Mallory Fleming Mitchell felt he had bestowed upon him by allowing him, as the only other person except Victoria Genn and Mitchell himself, the keys that opened the private door and gave access to Mitchell's private elevator.

Exiting the lift on his floor, Colt was moderately surprised to find the hallway and offices deserted. A quick check of his watch told him why. His travel and the time spent with Pagan Maguire had consumed far more of the day than he'd realized. It was well past the normal working hours of the early rising, key personnel of PanGlobal. Only the 24-hour-services personnel would be in the building, along with the large and proficient cleaning crew. It didn't matter; Colt could handle what he needed from his own office.

It took little time. He entered the information from the list, asking the computer only for slightly more than the most basic information regarding the names. Time required for the demanded printout answer was short.

He examined the sheet. Knowing the first column of names had been terminated, Colt had entered, anxious for enlightenment, only the second and third columns. He scanned the list quickly. Four of the names, with their first names and their countries and cities identified, he quickly recognized. They were an unsavory lot, he thought, able to obtain insurance only through PanGlobal and for extremely expensive, high-risk premiums. The policies had then been reinsured, in large part, through Mitchell's covertly owned re-insurers. Colt did not know the firms were owned by Mitchell. Raker did. The subjects of the third strike had been dismissed by the computer as being insufficient information.

The information regarding the top name of the second column struck Colt with almost physical force, stunning him. Following the complete name, Becquerel, H.E., Mrs. (Genvieve), he read: Spouse, Henri Etienne Becquerel: born Jennie Emelia Raker, Geneva, Switzerland, then the accurate birthdate. The information was followed by the quite recent date of her marriage and her present address and telephone listing in Paris.

Colt's eyes stared with frozen immobility at the sheet. There could be no mistake. The name, the age, the place and date of birth all fit. There could be no mistake. Mrs. Henri Etienne Becquerel was the daughter of Beverly Martin Raker.

Colt thought, with stunned shock, that as carefully as Raker had tried to protect the girl, even to the extent of not seeing her or even going near her, and confining any contact with her existence to yearly telephone conversations with the woman to whom he had entrusted her welfare, she had been found and scheduled for death. And evidently, considering the obvious care with which the attack on PanGlobal was being made, well before Raker had become associated with the company. The chance of coincidence was far too great. The girl could only have been selected because of hatred for Raker. The realization shook Colt. They—whoever they were—could not know Raker all that well. If they did, a terrible error in judgment had been made. If anything happened to that girl, the destruction of the world would not be enough to assuage Raker's demand for revenge. The man would be uncontrollable and indiscriminate in his war of vengeance.

The one hope, considered Colt, lay in the fact that knowing in advance, protection could be given the girl. Also, the fact that she had been chosen would help narrow the field of search for the mastermind of the plot against PanGlobal. It must certainly be someone who knows and hates Raker.

Colt picked up the phone and started to dial Raker's hotel.

"Stop right there!" The voice was Harlan Webb's. "Move a muscle, you son-of-a-bitch, and you're dead where you sit." The words came in a snarl.

Colt turned his head slowly to see Webb standing in the doorway. His hand held a .45 Colt automatic, the muzzle trained directly and steadily at James Travis Colt.

"I said don't move, you bastard," snapped Webb.

"What in the . . ."

"Shut your mouth, you treacherous mother-fucker." There was no mistaking the hatred in Webb's voice and the reality of his intent.

Colt stared at him. His only thought was that the man had gone mad.

"I have you, you filthy scum. Caught you dead. And this time even your old buddy-buddy, Raker, can't help you." A wicked smile twisted Webb's lips. "The orders are to shoot you on sight. If I didn't hate your guts so, I'd have shot you in the back. But I want to be looking in your face when I blow it apart."

Colt had gathered his composure. "I have no idea what in the world you're talking about."

Webb snorted in derision, the automatic steady and threatening. "You're something, Colt. Really something. So God-damned straight and fucking pure." He shook his head and it wasn't in pity. He glared at Colt with hatred. "Your own old flame," he said, "your own carefully selected partner and secretary. Maybe the only friend you had."

Colt looked at him, not understanding, the phone in his hand forgotten.

"Come on, you shit," spat Webb, "don't give me that look of innocence. I found her body. You killed Janet Fremont last night sometime. Burnt the hell out of her trying to get back the receipt for the duplicate computer chips of PanGlobal's clients. But she was tougher and more loyal to the company than you ever realized." Webb's eyes burnt with a bright fervor. "She had that receipt, signed by you, and you couldn't force her to tell you where it was. Well, bright boy, she fooled you. If you were as fucking smart as you think you are you'd have found it. She had simply folded it, and was using it to look like a page marker in the book she was reading. She probably put it down when she opened the door to let you in."

Colt was stunned and confused. At the same time he felt a great sense of loss as he realized that Janet Fremont was dead.

"Webb, I know nothing."

"I said shut your stinking mouth." Webb's voice was almost a scream. "You knew well enough," he continued, more calmly. "You sure as hell knew. We found the computer chips in your apartment."

Colt frowned.

"Gotcha," said Webb. "Really gotcha, haven't we, bright boy?"

Colt's mind worked quickly and coolly. The shock had worn off and he realized that he was the victim of a frame, and probably a damn good one. "Who found Janet? And how?" he asked.

Webb grinned evilly. "I told you that, smart boy, me. You're so God-damned wrapped up in self-importance, and so fucking busy sucking up the old man that you don't even know how things work around here outside your own little dream world. It's company policy for me and my security crew to check on the absence, explained or not, of any key personnel and their primary aides." He took a step closer to Colt and raised the gun a fraction of an inch.

"Simple routine," he said, pleased with himself. "I found the body. And the receipt. And then things began to fall into place. It's you behind this whole damned plot."

Colt just looked at him.

"The evidence all added up beautifully. The inside knowledge, your protection of the Maguire girl you were using." He shook his head again, this time with a hint of pity.

"Poor little bitch," he said. "I was wrong there. She had no idea just what the hell you'd conned her into. But you weren't sure how far you could trust her, so you had to go out on a limb to keep me from learning that she already knew you."

"You're wrong, Webb," said Colt, calmly. "What do Mitchell and Raker have to say about all this?"

"Don't count on help there, old buddy-buddy." Webb's face wore a smile of self-satisfaction. "Mitchell has seen the light about using the authorities, and Raker has taken himself out of touch for the day." Webb frowned slightly. "But even if you could lie your way out of it to him, it'll do you no good. You'll be long dead before he comes around. You see, I've been able to convince Mitchell that you're his mullet. Let me assure you that the old man has seen the error of his ways, and when the old bastard goes to work, it's a thing of wonder to see the power he can muster." Webb paused, pleased with his dissertation.

"The old thug has pulled every string at his command, and you are currently wanted by every goddamn law enforcement agency in the country."

He leaned forward to emphasize his next words. "The *authorities*, Colt. The authorities are all out to get you, and the order is to shoot on sight." He grinned. "That's exactly what I would have done, but there's the matter of getting even for your little ambush in my office."

He paused to savor the word. "But mine—my ambush—well, this one is a little different. I'm not going to waste any time bragging to you about what I can do, or how important I am, like you did. I'm just going to kill you where you sit."

He had already talked too much.

Colt's knee pressed the padded plate under his desk and the chiming beeps sounded from the speaker on his desk. It was a seldom-used device which could allow Colt to dismiss unwanted visitors.

Webb's eyes flicked, involuntarily, toward the sound.

The telephone Colt still held lashed out toward the weapon in Webb's hand. The aim was not perfect. The instrument struck the metal only a glancing blow as Webb pulled the trigger.

The blow was enough. The bullet missed Colt's head by almost three inches, and before Webb had time to recover from his surprise, Colt had gathered his legs under him and launched himself at the man. His right hand pistoned out, fingers curled, and palm bent backward from the wrist. The heel of his hand landed on the point of Webb's chin with unerring accuracy and incredible force. Webb was slammed back off balance and his head thudded sharply against the wall. The gun fell from his inert fingers and he slid unconscious to the floor.

CHAPTER 23

Colt's heart was pounding, fear-fed adrenalin pumping through his body. He picked up the Colt automatic from the floor then ran his hands across Webb's supine body. He found what he was looking for. Webb always carried handcuffs.

Colt hauled Webb across the carpeted floor to the small private washroom at the rear of his office. He snapped a cuff on one of Webb's wrists then, opening the doors of the cabinet enclosing the lavatory, locked the other cuff onto the pipe under the bowl. It would do, unless . . . . He bent to go through Webb's clothing with special care, checking for a key that might fit the handcuffs. He found one. He studied the situation. No need to take chances. The bastard was clever enough to have stashed another.

Colt removed his necktie and tied one end securely around Webb's free wrist. He stretched the man's arm out and knotted the other end of the tie securely around the knob of the restroom door. He pulled hard at the fabric, testing its strength. It would do. Maybe, after much effort and no little discomfort, Webb could break the bond. Then, if he did have another key to the handcuffs, he could free himself. By then, however, Colt would be long gone. He dismissed the problem. There were far greater ones to face.

If everything Webb had said was true then he, Colt, was truly in for a world of hurt. And there was no reason to doubt the man. His only error, on this day, had been to talk too much, and be too alert to unexpected sounds. Colt's prime order of the day would now be for him to go under. Or perhaps that would be the second order. First he must get the hell away from the building and get to his stash. His past experience with the CIA, and particularly his associations with Raker, had taught him to always keep money, a second identity, and provisions for at least a minimum change in appearance in an easily accessible and carefully protected location. That he had done.

He thought quickly. Fortunately, because of his concern for Pagan's welfare, he had taken care of his own authentically registered car. When it was found missing, that would be the vehicle others would be looking for. His other safe-car would be waiting. That, too, thanks to Pagan. Then he must get to Raker and after that, to Mitchell. He must get this damn thing straightened out. But not from here. Far too dangerous, for Webb most certainly had his own internal security force alerted. If only he could make it to Mitchell's private elevator, there was hope. That anyone but Mitchell could avail themselves of its use had been kept a carefully guarded secret.

• • •

He made it, undetected. On the street, he carefully matched his stride to that of the other pedestrians. If he could only make it to his safe-car, he would have a certain amount of security. In the trunk of the car was a package, heavily and carefully sealed and addressed as though it were ready to be mailed. Such was the precaution he had taken to keep it from being opened as a result of any incidental stop for a traffic violation or some such eventuality. In the package was an acceptably unkempt wig, far different in style and color from his own well-groomed hair, horn-rimmed glasses, and a driver's license with a different name which matched that of the car's registration, credit cards and other identification. There also was a moderate sum of money which would be sufficient to cover most immediate needs. All together, they should get him to his racquet and handball club where more complete emergency supplies and money were carefully and secretly locked away. Silently and gratefully Colt thanked Raker for the small bit of paranoia which had rubbed off, helping him to take such precautions.

As he made his way thorough the streets his eyes were alert for anything out of the ordinary, and as he surveyed those he passed and those he met, looking at the occupants of cars and hunting for the presence of police, he was, for the first time, without a feeling of pity for the bag ladies and other derelicts his eyes now passed over without really seeing.

Reaching the garage, he found his car pulled to the front and waiting, out of the way. He approached the attendant and expressed his gratitude once again for the special attention, and with spendable thanks.

He removed the package from the trunk of the car, took out the identification papers and money, tucked the glasses into his pocket, held the wig under his coat, placed his own billfold in the container, and carefully re-wrapped and sealed it. The attendant was paying him no attention. Colt was tempted but resisted. It would take only seconds, later, to don the wig and glasses. He was already beginning to relax a bit. He started the engine and swung the car out into the exit lane, waving at the attendant as he pulled from the garage into the flow of traffic.

At the first stoplight he glanced into the rearview mirror and saw the occupants of the car behind him busy talking to each other. He leaned down across the seat, below the line of vision, and slipped the wig on his head. It was followed by the glasses. He straightened. He could adjust the wig as he drove. For the time being, he was relatively safe from recognition as James Colt. He was, instead, Edward Eric Stafford, a newspaper reporter for a small Long Island weekly, visiting the city for the day. The only danger, if the wrong people stopped him, was that the address on his license was that of the house near Little Neck Bay where Pagan Maguire waited, unprotected.

He had to find Raker!

· · ·

It was the waiting time. And even for Raker, with all of his structured discipline, waiting was difficult.

A careful and controlled drinker, though the fact was not realized by more than a few of his acquaintances, Raker, at the moment, understood the pressure behind the often-heard words, "I need a drink." That time, of all times, is not the time to have one. But perhaps a beer? Or possibly just conversation to take his mind off the situation for a brief while?

Raker, as Raker, walked into Rick's Place, hoping that the two bartenders whose company and banter he enjoyed would be on duty. They were.

The light-hearted conversation and pleasant insults the men exchanged, along with two beers, helped pass the best part of two hours.

To Raker, the bar was, in a way, a microcosm of Manhattan. Customers were of nearly every social and economic level. Conversation ranged from superficial trivia through ordinary barroom bullshit to the sagacity of street-wise philosophy. And as he listened—even as he talked—Raker's mind reviewed the circumstances, both present and future.

Colt was taken care of, no doubt of that. The frame, while it certainly wouldn't hold up under close investigation, would be enough to eliminate him. The impressive influence of Mallory Fleming Mitchell would see to that. To harm the plan, Colt would have to show himself. And he would be dead before he could open his mouth. No! Colt would go under and stay. He was good enough to manage that, if he'd stay smart.

Maybe, thought Raker, I should have handled it myself. Simply called him, and taken him out. He had considered doing so, but that Colt had been able to fit pieces together enough to identify Raker as Pagan Maguire's Coleman was a possibility. Raker had no indication of just how much the girl had been able to tell Colt. One thing for certain, Colt was no fool, far from it. At one time almost a prodigy of Raker's, the man was cautious, clever and suspicious. If he had any inkling that Raker was involved, then such a contact could have led to Raker being the victim of any meeting.

No, this way was better. And there was still the girl. Colt, if he had tumbled, would certainly have shared his fears with Pagan Maguire.

She would have to be handled separately. Until Brennan had taken care of the Shetland Oil Terminal, Raker could not afford to have her involved in a manhunt—or was it supposed to be person-hunt, thought Raker, idly—while he, as Coleman, was responsible for her safety. She would have to be taken out in what could be made to look like the work of the Gordons. There was little to fear from Maguire other than the fact that she might be able to identify Raker as Coleman, for she was determined to see her brother's killers taken care of.

Raker smiled at his half-full glass of beer. Hell, he thought, if this will just force Colt to ground for a few days—he and Maguire were most likely together—then it wouldn't matter if Colt and she both knew he was behind the plot. It would be far too late. By then, anyone could know, for he would be in charge. Mitchell would have been whipped into line. There wouldn't be, would never have been, any threat, according to that fine man who would still have some small say in PanGlobal's operation. The girl would be satisfied when he delivered the Gordons and Colt would be happy to be cleared of the frame.

•••

If Colt has not reconciled Coleman with Raker, he will be trying to contact me, mused Raker. If he has it together, he'll try Mitchell first, and finding no welcome, will try to contact someone he can trust in law enforcement. The quietly placed word of the huge bounty to be surreptitiously paid for the man's demise would take care of that.

That would leave only the girl. She would have no credence because of her prior activities, so would be forced, in spite of her fears, to seek out Coleman. If only to find out about the Gordons. She was, he knew, that determined about them, and at that time he could decide what to do about Pagan Maguire.

He took another sip of beer. I do hope, he thought, that they'll just lie doggo until this thing is over. How long will that be? Let's see. Today is Thursday, the strikes are for Saturday. Only three days—two and a half, really. If they lay quiet that long, they may live.

Raker came to a decision. If James hasn't tumbled, he mused—hasn't put it together—he'll call me. In that case, I'll be forced to take him out just to be safe, but I'll give them a chance. I'll stay away until late. Maybe by then something will have developed to make a hit unnecessary. I'll give them that much, he thought. Maybe I owe them a chance.

Otherwise? Well, business is business, now isn't it?

• • •

James Colt drove through the still-wet streets of the city. The rain had stopped for the moment but the skies were still leaden and threatening. There was more traffic, however, than at most times during the past two days, at least pedestrian traffic. Colt circled cautiously through lower Manhattan until he was reasonably certain that he was not being followed. His mind was working furiously.

What step to take first? He must let Pagan know. Or should he? Why frighten the girl? Perhaps a call to re-emphasize that she must stay inside and not let her presence be known? Yes, that would be best for now.

A call to Mitchell? Perhaps he could convince the man that he had been framed. After all, he had been nearly a friend, and certainly Mitchell's most trusted employee, he felt.

Or maybe Raker. Maybe I should go to his hotel, wait there for him. No, too chancy. There was more than a small possibility that in spite of his minor disguise he would be recognized.

Damn! Today of all days for Raker to be out of touch? Let it be Mitchell, then.

• • •

He found a place to park south of Fulton Street and off Pearl. He located a pay phone and started to dial Mitchell's private number. He hesitated. Foolish, he thought. If Mitchell didn't believe the truth, he would damn well have a trace put on the call. By the time I get off the phone and place a call to Pagan, he thought, then I may be surrounded by Webb's authorities.

He dialed his safe-house, allowing the phone to ring two times. It required three to activate the recorder.

He hung up, waited exactly one minute and dialed again. He listened to the recorded message on the answering machine. It was not his own voice. At the sound of the tone he spoke. "This is Shamrock gardening service," he said. "I would like to speak to someone there about the possibility of handling your yard work.

Trees, flowers, shrubs, we do them all." He waited. Pagan should be monitoring the call.

"Yes?" It was what he had told Pagan to say.

"Complications," he told her. "Remember what I said about not spending too much time in the garden?"

There was a pause while Pagan sorted out the meaning.

"Yes," she replied. "I do remember about going . . . there."

"It is even more important, now. And please remember, where some things are concerned, the less light the better." He had warned her to keep the drapes drawn, thus not advertising anyone's presence at the house.

"I remember." Worry and concern were evident in the words.

"Don't worry. I'll take care of things." He longed to say more, to tell her how he felt about her.

"I'll try not." Her tone said she felt the same way.

"Until later then," he said. "I'll be somewhat busy, so it may be later than I planned."

"I'll wait," she said simply.

• • •

Colt depressed the phone's cradle and dialed Mitchell's number. It was the man's private line, answered only by him when Victoria Genn was not at her office to intercept as needed.

"Your money," said Mitchell's voice. He still liked to think he was one of the common folk.

"Colt here. I've been framed. Listen to me . . ."

"You bastard!" Mitchell's voice overrode that of Colt in a near roar. "You lousy bastard. After all I've done for you. It's you—been you all the time. You're the one who's trying to blackmail me. I'll see you dead, you mother-humping, cocksucking, lousy traitor. Dead, do you understand?" The voice was a tremulous screech. "I'll see you flayed alive!"

Colt replaced the phone quietly. Depression flooded him. What Webb had said was true. Mitchell had pulled all the stops. I can be sure, thought Colt, that they're really out for my blood.

Webb's threat about shooting on sight was not an exaggeration. It was simply death waiting.

He thought. Maybe, just maybe . . . . How long had he been on the line with Mitchell? Only seconds. Nowhere near long enough for any tap to have even gotten started. Still, there were systems which could lock onto a phone even after the caller had hung up. Must take no chances.

• • •

Colt returned to his car and drove across town and well away from where he'd made his call. He decided on his next course of action. Lloyd Bilber. A seldom-seen-anymore, but still close friend from his CIA past. Lloyd would be in a position to help him. He found a phone booth and a parking place.

"Lloyd," said Colt, relieved to get the man on his first try. "It's Colt. I'm in deep shit." he said. "I need that favor you keep telling me you owe me." He tried to make his voice light.

"Don't tell me," said the voice. "You don't know just how deep, old partner. You've been sold."

Colt experienced a sudden chill spreading from his stomach. It had reached even this far?

"Can you tell me how deep?"

That's it, thought Colt. If it's reached even to Bilber's agency, then the order is out everywhere. "Can you help?" he asked, without hope.

"Wouldn't if I could," said Lloyd Bilber. "There's no choice. If I was looking at you, I'd have to finish the job without listening. I'm completely covered, and you can bet that anyone who has more than a nodding acquaintance with you is covered the same way. You're a *was*, James, not an *is*. And you can be damned sure that this conversation is being heard."

It was a warning. The line was tapped and a trace was on. Lloyd had done as much as he could. Probably enough to cause himself no little grief.

"Thanks, Lloyd. Try to attend the wake." He hung up and all but sprinted for his car. He had one more try to make. It would have to be from a phone far from where he stood.

• • •

He found suitable parking.

"Lieutenant Davison," he said into the phone. "Is he on duty?"

"He's always on duty," came the reply. "Hold on a sec."

As James Colt waited, he knew this would be his last try. Arne Davison of the New York Police Department would be his final attempt. He was a long-time trusted friend. The trials and triumphs they had experienced together were many.

"Davison," said the voice.

"Arne," said Colt, "listen. Do you recognize my voice?"

There was the slightest pause. "I do."

"Remember the old Rolaids Resort?" asked Colt.

"I do," said Davison.

"Can you get there soon?"

"Can do."

"Do it. Now. I'll explain."

"Done," said Lieutenant Arne Davison. "If you're waiting for me, you're backing up."

Colt managed a tight smile. Maybe, just maybe, it would work. If there was anyone besides Lloyd Bilber who could help, it would be Arne. He must now find another telephone as far away as possible. The line might have been locked onto once again . . . if it had been on the previous calls. Or even if it hadn't.

"Is Lieutenant Arne Davison there?" asked Colt when the phone was answered at the diner near the precinct station. Colt and Davison, who seldom snacked there, had made a joke of its food by naming it the Rolaids Resort.

"Jus' a minit," said the voice that answered.

Colt waited only a moment.

"Davison here"

"Arne, this is Colt. You knew that?"

"Yeh, James. That I sure as hell did. Man, you're blistering. Never seen anyone wanted so much. How the hell y'get so damned popular?"

"Can't spend any time here, Arne," rushed Colt. "Remember that place we spent a St. Patrick's Day. The little narrow one?"

There was silence while Davison thought. "Yeah," he said finally. "I remember. Rocks and stuff?"

Colt recalled how sharp the man was. That was it. Rocks equated with the name of the place. The Treaty Stone. The long narrow bar first introduced to Colt by Raker, with its convenient location on 33rd not far from Madison Square Garden.

"Good. Meet me there. Can you do that? I can explain this whole thing. It's a frame, Arne, a quick and damned good one. But I can prove it if someone'll listen."

"Thought it would have to be that, James. You're not the type." He was silent a moment. "I'm a good listener. What time?"

Colt considered a moment, figuring time and distance. "Eight," he said. "Is that okay?"

"That's fine. Eight. I'll be there."

"I'll be in the back," said Colt. "Behind that lattice work screen."

"Gotcha," said Davison. "Anything else?"

"No," said Colt. "Eight."

"Eight," agreed Davison.

Colt breathed a sigh of relief as he hung up the phone. Finally, someone who would listen. And now, a moment to reorganize his thoughts. There would not have been time to put a tap on the diner's phone. He would have some time for his next call. It would be another attempt to contact Raker.

Mr. Raker had not come back to the hotel yet. Colt slammed down the phone with disgust.

"Damn the man," he muttered. "Where the hell is he when I need him?" Oh well, he thought. At least I've got Arne.

• • •

Lieutenant Arne Davison left the telephone and seated himself at the counter of the diner.

"Sumpin' to eat, Lootenant?"

"Naw," said the man, obviously in a good humor. "Just a cup of that swill you call coffee." He stirred sugar into the cup, then added cream. It should, he thought, disguise the taste even if the cream only turned the brew a dirty, grayish-puce in color. It didn't matter. This was Arne Davison's lucky day. "One hundred thousand," he murmured softly.

"Say sumpin', Lootenant?"

"Nothing," he replied. "Just thinking out loud." He sipped at the cup. One hundred thousand dollars! That was what he would be picking up. And tax free. That was the price to be paid to the man responsible for the death of the "mad-dog-killer," James Colt. Not the capture, mind you, the death. And where the word came from? Well, it wasn't to be doubted.

Yes! He'd sure enough be there at the Treaty Stone to meet his old friend James Colt—along with several of the best shots in the precinct.

Hell! He'd even share some of the loot with them. Probably. Well, anyway, maybe. He looked at his watch. Plenty of time, he thought. Plenty of time. Get there and set up thirty minutes early, and we'll have him dead. His unintended pun amused him. He felt the slight tug of something in his chest. Hell, he didn't really want to see James Colt dead. Shit, he liked the guy. But what the hell, business is business, now isn't it?

• • •

To James Colt, the wait was interminable. Walking would help make the time pass.

He'd left his car in a parking garage well north of his destination. He wanted to minimize chances that through some misadventure there would be any easily checkable record of his safe-house where Pagan Maguire waited. He took his driver's license from his billfold and left it in the trunk of the car. It was the only identification with the address of the house, aside from the car registration which remained in the glove compartment. He retained his credit cards and other identification as a precaution, should he be stopped for some reason or other. If actually apprehended, or killed, a check of the cards would lead to the address of James's apartment, but not to the safe-house and Pagan.

He arrived at the corner of 33rd Street and 7th Avenue shortly after seven o'clock. He debated a moment and then elected to wait, until near time for his meeting, in a lounge of the Statler Hotel which bordered his ultimate destination. It would be far safer, he concluded, to be in a respectable hotel than to loiter on the streets where he might become involved in some minor matter that could lead to greater trouble.

Thanks to his association with Raker, he would not, of course, be in the establishment where he said he would be waiting for Davison, but would watch from inside the doors of the adjacent hotel to make sure Arne wasn't followed.

If only, he thought, Arne will really listen, he is in a position to help clear me of this absurdity. Hell, after all, I can account for all of yesterday. He reconstructed the previous day from the time he met Pagan Maguire until they left the following morning.

Webb said Janet was killed during the night. Even if it had been after he took Pagan home, he could, if necessary, produce the woman as a witness. Of course, that might not be too effective an alibi. She was, in the minds of Mitchell and Webb, highly involved with him. Shit! Then suddenly he brightened. There would also be either Daskalos or one of his men. That would be far better!

He could find out from Arne just when Janet had been killed, and if it was any time before one or two in the morning, then he was cleared.

The thought raised his spirits. It was almost time for him to begin his vigil, watching the doors of the small bar across the street. Suddenly he grinned to himself. I must be getting too much like Raker, he thought. Too suspicious. Why wait? Simply go on across the street and wait among the pleasant people of the Treaty Stone for Arne to show up. He could visit with Tim, the owner, and others he knew slightly. In the happiest of coincidences, Raker might even be there. It was, he knew, too much to hope for, but it was a pleasant thought.

Colt placed more than enough money to pay for his bill on the table and moved to the door. He stopped in surprise. Across the street was Arne Davison nearing the front of the Treaty Stone.

He watched as Davison stopped and turned to the four men who were near him and start talking to them. He was obviously giving instructions. He saw the men nod, and watched Davison motion with his arms as though describing some action or other.

Three of the men took up positions close by the doors of the small bar; one of them started to walk across the street toward where Colt stood. The hair raised on the back of his neck.

I'm set up! There was no feeling of disappointment, only that of mild surprise. Colt was becoming inured to shock. He whirled and moved rapidly away from the glass door.

• • •

The lousy bastard, he thought. Some friend! A knot of fear made its presence known, then grew from the pit of his stomach to fill him. If he was wanted badly enough for a friend like Arne Davison to sell him out, if the price on his head was that great, then there was no hope. None. He rejected the thought.

Forget the fear. Forget the surprise. Just thank your turn of good luck, thought Colt. Be God damned thankful that impulse dragged you out of your seat when it did. Otherwise you'd be morgue meat. Yes, that had been real luck. Maybe there was a chance after all.

I must, he thought, find Raker.

• • •

It had been an easy matter for Colt to leave the hotel unnoticed through another entrance. Davison had assumed Colt, a man as good as his word, would be in the bar. Davison would wait until near eight, then enter. That gave Colt nearly thirty minutes. Enough time to walk back to his car. It took less, including time for yet another call to the hotel in an effort to contact Raker. He was still out and had not been in. Messages were waiting for him.

The best thing, considered Colt, would be to return to Pagan, reassure her, and take the time in the relative security of the safehouse to plan a careful course of action.

As he drove, he realized that he should be grateful to Raker for having made him aware enough of how unforeseen troubles could come from when least expected.

"Be prepared, Jimmy lad," Raker had said, "in one way or another, and often. Never be caught with your old drill punch hanging out. Make damn sure you have another identity to go to."

• • •

Colt's athletic club was located, as planned and carefully selected, on the way to his safe-house. There had been no incident, or even more than a casual wave of recognition, as he entered and easily retrieved the sports bag from his locker. The wig had been replaced with a hat just before Colt entered. He'd kept the glasses on. His presence had been of no special interest to anyone at the club. His sense of security grew.

Now, back in the car, nearing his destination and Pagan, he found reason to hope. At the worst, he thought, I'll get us out of the country and work from there.

Then the thought hit him. Jesus Christ Almighty, came the flash, in my own troubles I've forgotten! I must get to Raker. Not just for my safety and Pagan's; I must get to him and let him know that his daughter is a target for murder.

He felt the urge to drive as fast as the car would go, but his newly refined sense of caution prevailed. He held the speedometer at the legal limit, forcing his nerves to calm.

He must get to Raker. He owned the man that much if not more. He must help save his daughter. Pagan's safety came first, then Raker's daughter second. He grimaced. Or am I only thinking that, he asked himself. Don't I really mean that it's Pagan and myself first? He didn't like the thought.

No, damn it, he told himself. I mean it—the daughter's safety before me. After Pagan, but before me. He liked himself better.

I'll find him, he thought with determination. By God, I'll find Raker this night.

• • •

Since James Colt's telephone call, Pagan Maguire's tension and intuitive apprehension had grown so acute that even her tactile senses caused her discomfort. Her clothing seemed to bind and chafe. However smooth the object she touched, its surface seemed to scrape and grate against the emotionally inflamed nerve ends of her fingers.

Until the call, Pagan had lulled herself into a mood of tranquil escapism. She had admired, in the fading light, the view from the rear windows of the comparative luxury of what James Colt had called his servant's quarters.

Perhaps they were for servants at one time, thought Pagan, but great changes had certainly been wrought. Servants, she conjectured, are seldom offered such opulent furnishings. James had surely been the renovator of the attractive building, separated by some distance from the main house. It certainly bore the mark of the man in what she knew and thought about him. Appointments and furnishings were first comfortable, then decidedly masculine, but without the trimmings of the "super stud" which she had sometimes found in the quarters of a few of the men she'd known, and quickly discarded.

She had passed the time trying to identify the trees and shrubs covering the well-landscaped grounds and had been able to recognize linden and tulip trees, elms, beeches and even a Cedar of Lebanon. There was holly and, in protected corners, rhododendrons and azaleas. In the distance could be seen the sails of boats riding the swells of Long Island Sound. It had been an exercise in observation that allowed her mind to take a short holiday from the pressures and fears and confusion she'd been experiencing over the past two days. Remembering James's advice, she had stayed carefully back from the windows, looking out only from the edge of the drapes.

No, she thought, now forced back to reality, longer than that. If she would only admit it, she had known that something was wrong, that the role she was playing was of far greater import than she'd been led to believe. There was no doubt that Coleman, for all he'd promised, was an unprincipled man and, if all the indications were correct, probably a cold-blooded murderer and blackmailer. A terrorist the equal of those terrible assassins of Ian Paisley and his ilk. And, she admitted, perhaps the more militant arm and offshoot branches of the IRA.

She hadn't told Colt everything. She'd held back the part about Coleman's meeting with Brennan, and the probable involvement of whatever group he represented. She squirmed uncomfortably at the thought, but she realized that it must remain so. She still harbored the hope, if only a small one, that Coleman would perform the service that had enabled him to recruit her in his overall plan—whatever that was. She still hoped he would destroy the Gordons. Until there was no such hope, she would continue to shield Coleman from actual apprehension, and would most certainly not let anyone, even her beloved James . . . !

She started in surprise at her use of the word. That she cared for the man she knew well. But love? Then she realized, for the first time, that such was exactly the case. She was in love with James Colt. The realization only added to her anxiety. She sat on the main room's large sofa, drew her legs up under her, and curled herself tightly, arms hugging her body, chin resting on the back of the upholstered couch, eyes staring blankly out into the night through the broad window where now could be seen only the dark outline of trees and shrubs, and the flicker of distant lights.

The sound of knocking on the door brought her from her reverie. Three raps. A pause. Three raps once again. Another pause, then two quick knocks.

It was James! She heard the key in the lock, leapt to her feet, and was at the door as it opened, and threw her body against James's, winding arms around his neck even before he closed the door.

"James," she said breathlessly, "It's you, God bless. I was so worried." She clung to him as he shut and locked the door.

Colt held her tightly to him. "It's fine," he said, liking the feel of her snuggled against him. "Everything's all right now." He pulled her arms gently from around his neck and, with an arm around her waist, led her to the sofa.

"I was so worried," she proclaimed, voice tremulous. "I was so frightened for you." Sitting, she clung to him, not wanting to give up the reassuring touch of his body. "Did you discover anything? Were those people harmed?"

"I did," said Colt, holding Pagan's head close in the hollow under his chin. "And yes, they were." He had already known that, of course, though he had not told her.

"And the rest of the names and everything?"

"They are all insured by PanGlobal," he mumbled, face buried in her soft hair. "The people at least. The third column didn't offer enough information for identification. They could be anywhere."

"Can they be helped? The people? Saved?" asked Pagan.

"Possibly. Yes, I think so—if I can find Raker." Colt was silent for a moment debating how he should tell her. "They, the people that is, are not really worth a lot of saving, in honesty. Except for one." There was pain evident in his voice.

"Who James? What do you mean."

"Three of the people are men who are involved, or have been involved, in some rather . . . odious activities. Probably only Pan-Global would even have insured them. But the other is a young woman." His pause was more a stumble than a deliberate stop. "She is Raker's daughter."

"Raker?" Pagan's face lifted, a tiny frown of bewilderment on her features. "Oh! Your friend, Raker. The man who is helping to stop all this? Oh, my God, James. How terrible! Can you save her?"

Colt was silent as he considered what he should tell Pagan. He knew a sense of guilt was already gnawing at her, because of her role, however small, in events up to the present.

"Yes," he said, finally. "But I must get to Raker. I can't do it alone." I can't do it at all, the way things are, he thought. He'd have to tell Pagan about the day's events.

He pulled away from her and put his hands on her shoulders, looking into her eyes. "I've been set up, my dear Pegeen. This minute I'm probably the most wanted criminal in this city."

"For what reason? How can they possibly?"

"A frame-up," interrupted Colt. "Do you know the term? I've been framed, and for a terrible crime, as well as made to look like I'm the person behind this whole murderous scheme."

As Pagan stared at him in shocked horror, Colt detailed the day's happenings from the time he'd been accosted by Webb at his office through his attempted contract with Mitchell and his betrayal by Arne Davison.

"But your friends, James, they must know you better than that."

"I would have thought so, Pegeen darling, but it has all been done so cleverly that Mitchell has pulled out all the stops in an attempt to hang me on a meat hook."

"But I can prove you weren't able, couldn't possibly have had the time to do what they claimed. They'll have to see that the scheme is a deliberate attempt to make you appear guilty."

"True, my darling. So I'll have to go out among them and prove it, won't I?"

"But you can't..."

"Can!" interrupted Colt. "Altered appearance is now in order."

"Bosh!" scoffed Pagan. "That silly wig will fool no one, certainly not those who know you well."

"I'm better at changing appearance than that," smiled Colt. "Old time training, you know." He placed his face against hers and kissed her gently, hand stroking her hair.

"You just wait," he said, rising. "When I return from a visit upstairs, you yourself won't recognize me." He lifted the sports bag from the floor where he'd dropped it at Pagan's greeting. He held it up.

"A kit of magic," he told her. "Proof coming up."

Her expression was one of disbelief. "I'll wait," she said, "But I'm not believing it."

"You'll see," he said, mounting the stairs. "You'll change your mind when you see."

Pagan looked after him as he left, fear flooding her body, realizing how much, how very much the man meant to her. She curled herself tightly on the sofa once again, head buried in her arms. She could feel the tears welling in her eyes. "I won't do it," she murmured against the hand she held tightly against her mouth. "I simply won't let him go. I can't. I simply can't." A terrible calmness replaced her fear. She would wait. I can be strong, she thought. I *am* strong. I'll wait and see. Then I'll decide. Her head remained buried in her arms.

It was many minutes later when she heard James's voice. She lifted her head to look at him. The transformation was remarkable. Her eyes widened. Meeting the man she now saw poised at the foot of the stairs, she truly would not have recognized him as her James.

A rumpled, well-used tweed jacket, coupled with a practiced slouch changed his carriage from that of athletic grace to desk-stooped posture. His nose seemed somehow broader, his chin receding the least bit. Hair had been shaved from the top of his head, not slick and clean, but with strands left along the middle of his scalp and brushed back to give the impression of natural and unself-conscious baldness. A fringe of hair remained full and somewhat rumpled at the side and back. Some sort of graying agent had been brushed into the hair above his ears, and the appearance of greater age was enhanced by the horn-rimmed glasses he now wore; the drooping, curved-stem pipe clenched between his teeth added to the overall impression.

As she studied his face farther, she could see that somehow the faint smile lines curving from his nose, out and down toward his mouth, had been ever so lightly enhanced with the discreet and careful use of a shadowing agent. The effect had no hint of makeup, but seemed only to portray a slightly tired, bookish individual who had little regard for his personal appearance.

The results were unnerving to Pagan. It seemed obvious that the change in Colt's appearance would be sufficient to make his identification difficult. But as she studied him while he walked toward her, she realized that it would fool only those who did not know the man well. As effective as the disguise seemed, she became convinced that any extended exposure to those who knew the man at all well would certainly allow him to be recognized. And those persons, it seemed, were the very ones who were so determined to have him killed.

She could not allow him to take the chance. Hurting from the necessity of ridiculing the man she had grown to love, she forced her face into an expression of derision.

"You look a proper Halloween creature," she said. "You might fool a stranger, or someone looking for you, using only a photograph for identification, but you'll fool no close acquaintances. Not for longer than a casual glimpse."

Colt shook his head slowly from side to side. "You're wrong, Pegeen. It will work. Why, I hardly know myself."

"That's flaming nonsense," retorted the girl. "That's only wishful thinking." She approached him and took his hands in hers. "Dear James. Please see that it is still you."

"You're wrong," he repeated. "Look objectively. No one would know this," he pointed his hand to his face and at his clothing. "No one would take this person for James Colt."

Fear for his safety motivated her. "James," she said, speaking carefully and in a measured manner, "you might fool those who have met you face to face for only incidental moments, but you'd certainly not fool those who know you."

Colt frowned. He'd been so certain, but Pagan's obvious sincerity raised some doubt.

"You've only created an image of what James Colt himself may become in time." Her eyes softened and she drew close to him and laid her head against his chest.

"Don't you see that those who know you well, they will see through those years you've added? And that it doesn't matter a whit to us who care that you've grown older and bald, and gray, and wear glasses?"

Colt eyed her, doubt still pervading.

"For certain, my laddie," she reassured him.

Colt, now annoyed, pushed Pagan aside less gently than he had intended and walked to the mirror hanging on the wall near the base of the staircase. He paused in front of the glass to study the reflection.

She was right. He most certainly looked different. But as he studied each point she'd made, he realized the truth of her words. The well-applied, cosmetically created bags under his eyes, and the slight enhancement of the crow's feet and few other lines on his face had converted his image to fit the photograph on the passport he had obtained in years past, and kept renewed. But he was still, to the eyes of a keen observer who knew the real James Colt, himself. The disguise, simple and effective, and at the cost of his carefully styled hair—a process which had not concerned him in the least—had not created another person. Only, as Pagan had said, an older James Colt, at least to those who knew him well—and that would include people like Webb and Arne Davison.

Still, it would probably allow him to pass the perfunctory inspection of searchers working only from photographs such as he might encounter at airports and bus and rail terminals. The odds would be far worse when it came to waiting at the Sheraton for Raker to appear. It was near the heart of where he worked and where more than a few people knew him. He shook off the apprehensions which had accompanied the thought.

"It will do," he said. "It will have to."

"No," said Pagan Maguire. Her voice was soft and determined. "It will certainly not do. You'll go out among those who know you and you'll be shot and killed, and without a thought of what will happen to me, left alone and friendless here in your city." That was the smallest of her concerns, but it seemed that it may be an argument which might persuade James Colt, if he felt for her what she felt for him.

She looked up at him with lovely, huge eyes, for the first time using what she hoped were feminine wiles.

Pagan is right, he thought. If I'm taken, killed, then she would be truly without a protector, and that, he decided, was the role he had assumed. If she were left alone, then God knew what terrible things could await her.

He looked at her, love and concern obvious on his face.

It was the opening Pagan had been waiting for. During the past minutes, she had decided on another course of action, and decided with her full, strong-willed determination.

She stretched out a hand to touch him and as suddenly withdrew it. This was not a time for emotion. She turned her back and walked away, turning to face him only when she and her feelings were insulated by distance.

"Use your head, boyo," she said. Her tone was firm. "You'll walk in to meet your man Raker, and they'll be waiting for you, expecting you, and that will be the end." Her tone almost softened, remembering the friends of her brother who had met the same fate. No, not only the friends of her brother, but of others she had cared for. She shook away the thought.

"Yes, you'll walk in, the great hero, and you'll be suddenly dead, and I'll be left alone to mourn and God knows what all else." She paused, eyes fixed piercingly on his face.

Colt looked at her in silence.

"And we'll all remember how brave you were, and what a grand

and glorious and stupid man." She stepped forward and took Colt by the hands. He was surprised at the strength of her slim, firm fingers. "And that's damned inconsiderate, boyo. And you not all that Irish." Anger was intermingled with sorrow on her lovely face.

Colt started to object.

"Shut your gob, damn you! I'm not done yet!" She glared up at him. "You'll not be running away to become a hero, a dead and grieved martyr. Not while there are other ways to accomplish the ends you seek." Her hands tightened on Colt's own. "Are you hearing me?" she demanded. "Are you hearing what the hell I'm saying, man? Without patronizing or condescending?" She looked up at him then suddenly turned and stalked away.

"Certainly you're not. Another damned know-it-all bastard of a man. Yet another hero, and not even for a cause, but only for the pride of your damned assumed maleness." She whirled about and faced him, hands on her hips and legs spread in an aggressive stance.

"Well, you damned would-be-martyr, you'll listen to me now." Colt's expression sobered, changing from calculation to respect. "It's me that'll be going to find your Raker. And it's me that'll be bringing him back. And if there's to be any martyrdom, then by the Holy Family, it'll sure and be me that'll be mourned. But then, I'll be having none of that, so I'll get the job done." Her face was bright with mixed fury and devotion to purpose. "Are you reading me, man? Do you know I mean it?"

Colt looked at her dumbly. He'd never known such a woman.

Pagan laughed. Loudly and with real humor, reading his thoughts.

"And it's betting I am that I'm the first real woman you've ever met." Her tone softened. "It's care, laddie. I care. And I've less to lose than you. They're not after my life."

Colt considered her words.

"Look at it," said Pagan Maguire, her tone soft and reasonable as though the last exchange had not happened. "Consider. Only the one man is after me, if that. The world's after you. I can go to meet our Raker, and with safety, for if what you've told me is so— and I have no reason to doubt it—then the last place I'll be finding

Coleman is anywhere near Raker. You said yourself that the man must know your precious Raker, you've made that clear. And if Raker is like you say, as effective and dangerous, then Coleman will be staying as far away as possible from the man. And you said yourself he'd be certain to have left the Wellington."

The words were reasonable to Colt. He nodded reluctantly.

"Then there's no question. It'll be me going to find our man," said Pagan with determination.

"But others may be looking for you," objected Colt.

"Whist," scoffed Pagan. "Small chance. I've given no cause to your grand PanGlobal. Only a messenger yet, you said the same. If it's one I have to be looking out for it's only Coleman, and I'm not even sure I have that to fear. And, as I said, he won't be around your man Raker." Her expression and intensity were affecting Colt.

"Don't you see, man?" she asked. "It's the only way. I'll go down, I'll fetch the brute of a savior, and all will be well." Her voice had turned from bluster to plea.

Colt hesitated. "I don't know," he started, "damn it, darling, I can't just sit . . ."

"Sit and be damned," blazed Pagan. "If you don't, you'll stand and die. And I'll not be having that. I love you, damn-you-James-Colt. And I'll not be losing you just yet. Do you ken that, you inconsiderate gillie?"

Colt smiled in spite of himself. He knew he loved the girl. If not until this minute, then certainly now.

"We'll talk about it," he said.

"Talk and be damned," blazed Pagan Maguire. "Now you be sitting down and telling me where it is, and how it is that I can go in and find Raker." She lifted a hand to halt any possible reply. "And as for your change of appearance, just be waiting, darlin' boy, until I show you how a beautiful, sexy thing like herself can put all your disguises to shame." She relented to grin mischievously. "Within the next fifteen minutes you'll not be knowing me, nor will you be wanting to."

"That," said Colt, "I sincerely doubt." He looked at the new Pagan. The strong, equality-demanding Pagan he had known was there but had not acknowledged. He was suddenly aware that she was probably right.

"All right, I'll look," he said at length. "And listen." He looked at her with love and respect. "But you damn well better convince me."

She moved close to him. "That," she purred, "I'm reasonably sure I can do." She reached out a hand. "Perhaps we have the time for a wee hoolie of our own. A hoolie being a lovely, small party of a sort."

•••

They did, indeed, have one. Later, not really convinced but at least certainly satisfied for the moment, Colt listened to Pagan murmur into his ear.

"You rushed me so," she said, "I didn't have much time."

"I beg your pardon," he replied, lazily and with the pretense of offended dignity.

Pagan matched his grin with her own and leaned down to brush her nose against his.

"Foolish man. Not that. Only that when you had me grab clothes and things from the house before you abducted me, I just have this dress and a few things together that I thought I might have to have."

"Oh, that."

"Yes, that." She mulled over her next question. It was on her lips, knowing, yet not wanting to know. "In previous visits to this little hideaway of yours," she inquired, "is it possible that any of your visitors might have left any items I could look at?" She tried to make her tone light.

"I really don't know," said Colt, honestly. There had been a few visitors, of course. None knew him as James Colt. "It's possible," he said. He was familiar with the habit of certain ladies in leaving possessions around as if it were a way of staking a claim.

"I'll check," said Pagan. "And James?"

"Yes?"

"It really doesn't matter. Right now, I hope they did." She paused to kiss him softly. "You'd not be normal if you hadn't had friends come to visit. And whatever happened in your past, at least where the ladies are concerned, well they are most certainly not of concern to me. It's only now that matters."

Colt frowned in concentration. It has been most obvious, for some time, that the Pagan was planning a change of appearance of her own. The fact worried him. But he owed her the chance. "Try the dressing room on the other side of the master bath. The door away from my bedroom. It's on the right side at the end of the hall."

"I know," said Pagan.

"Yes," said Colt. "You do, don't you?" He rose and turned away. "I'll build a fire," he said.

She smiled after him. "I built one earlier," she said. "There are still embers." She was enjoying his obvious discomfort. Understanding the claiming tactics of women, she felt certain that there would be at least a mixed assortment of feminine apparel and other accoutrements available in the dressing room on the other side of the master bath. As James remained silent and fumbled among the logs alongside the fireplace, she went to find out.

She was right.

As Pagan left the room, Colt leaned his head back against the sofa, relaxed and for the moment unworried. His eyes flew open with a start as reality encroached on him.

Raker's daughter! At the least he could try to warn her. He had been too concerned for Pagan's, and his own safety. At least the two of them knew of their danger. The girl, Jennie, did not.

He glanced across the room and located his coat where it lay across a chair back. From a pocket he removed the list of names he'd extracted from the PanGlobal computer. The phone number of the Becquerel's Paris home was there! For a brief moment he hesitated, reluctant to use the telephone. He decided that as long as his call was not to a party directly involved with himself or to someone who might have been alerted about him, using the phone would be safe. Especially in view of the fact that he could dial directly.

It was some minutes before the call was completed. The Becquerel's housekeeper answered. Colt's French was adequate for him to learn that the couple had departed on holiday. If the call was truly as important as the gentleman insisted, he could perhaps find the young people at the Albergo Fontana di Trevi in Rome.

Yes, the housekeeper did have the number of the hotel. In case of emergencies, it was to be understood.

Colt thanked the woman and hung up. Their holiday just may save the girl's life. However, considered Colt, if he could learn where they were so easily then it was only to be expected that her intended assassin could too. Quite probably had already done so and was even now tracking his quarry.

Colt dialed the number in Rome. After many minutes he hung up the telephone. The Albergo Fontana was not answering their phone. Colt glanced at his watch and computed the time difference. It would not be yet six in the morning in Rome. He would try again in an hour or two. Certainly there would be someone at the desk by eight. That should give him plenty of time to warn them.

It was at that moment that Pagan returned.

"I simply hate ostentation." The voice was almost that of Pagan Maguire. "Don't you just, darling?" Her voice was a parody of some sort of affected American accent.

Colt stared in disbelief, both visual and aural. What in the hell . . . ?

"But one must make do with what one has, mustn't one?" continued Pagan. Her face broke into a delighted grin. "Isn't this simply awful, I ask you? Just no style, simply no style at all."

She stood in accepted street-walkers position, weight on one leg, hands on hips which thrust forward suggestively. She had found a wig of blonde curls which now covered her gleaming auburn tresses, and her lovely green eyes now seemed unimportant, lost in the heavy mascara, bright glowing eyeliner, and newly thinned and highly arched eyebrows.

The poor taste demonstrated by the person who had left the wig made Pagan less worried about possible competition.

Colt was nearly speechless. It was several moments before he found his voice, and when he did the first sound was one of awed wonder. Not words. Just sound.

"Great God," he finally managed. "You didn't pluck your own lovely eyebrows, did you?"

Pagan laughed. "Is that your main concern? I think that's flattering. No, I simply shaved a bit here and there. They'll grow, and fast, too. What about the rest?"

"Unbelievable. You look like . . ." he paused to consider his words.

He'd been about to say hooker. But that wasn't exactly the appearance the girl gave. Not with the tasteful pants suit and low heeled shoes. It had been only the overdone makeup and her voice that had led him astray. "Like something nothing near yourself," he finished. "I . . . . Where in the world did you learn that awful accent?"

"From the cine, and the telly," said Pagan. "Passable, now isn't it?"

"Passable," agreed Colt. "Far too passable and a bit unpleasant. It's the sort of affected speech that isn't really admired a great deal."

"I'm sure," agreed Pagan. "But I don't plan on using it more than I have to." She looked down at the two-piece pants suit she'd also found. It fit disconcertingly well. Whoever it belonged to, she would, for all the lack of taste in wigs, seem to have at least an adequate figure. Or better, damn it!

"By the great Finn McCool, I hate polyester," she complained, "but it seems to be in vogue, doesn't it? And more than that, I hate women wearing trousers. Unless, of course, they're in the mountains, on horseback or on a boat where they're quite proper." Her tone of voice echoed the distaste expressed by her words. "But you'll admit that no one hereabouts has ever seen me wearing the ilk of this."

"No," agreed James Colt, "certainly no one can ever say that." Colt, too, liked his women in dresses, though he had not consciously expressed the fact even to himself. It was one of the many things that had first attracted him to the girl.

"Then you'll be admitting there's no one about who will be recognizing me in this get up?"

Colt pondered the question. She was probably right. The few brief meetings with the people at PanGlobal would never, even if Webb had managed to have her photographed, allow the figure standing before him at the moment to be identified as Pagan Maguire.

"No," he agreed, reluctantly. "I can think of no one in the city who would recognize you except possibly your Coleman character. Does he know you well?"

It was Pagan's turn to consider. "He impressed me as being quite observant. But our little time together was not spent studying each other. No," she said tentatively, "I think there is little chance he would penetrate this." She waved a hand at her face and her clothing.

"Anyway," she continued, brightly, "you've said yourself that it's likely your Raker knows him, and that he knows Raker, so if I confine my vigil to Raker's hotel, there's small chance that Coleman will be about."

Colt was forced to agree. They had discussed it earlier. Anyone knowing Raker well enough to hate him would also know that he was far too dangerous to be around.

"All right," he said. "I think perhaps you're right. It may be better for you than for me to wait for Raker."

Pagan's face showed her relief. James would not be exposing himself to the danger of downtown Manhattan. It wasn't just Coleman that was after her boyo.

"Here's what we can do. We aren't too far from LaGuardia. I'll drive you there. Near there at least, to where we can find you a taxi. We don't want one coming here. I'll give you instructions that you can pass on to the driver about the one-way streets that he should take so it will seem as if you know the city well. He'll know the streets, of course, but that can be a help." He looked at the young woman who was listening intently. "Understand?"

"Certainly."

"I'll write a note for you to leave at the desk for Raker. I'll tell him that an Arlette Cavour is waiting for him in the lounge."

"Arlette Cavour?"

"A name important to him. One that will let him know that what's up is urgent."

"I see. Then?"

"Then you can go to the lounge just off the lobby. Try and get a seat at the piano bar where you can see the doorway."

"How will I know him?"

Colt frowned. "That won't matter. He can have the name paged."

"I still want to know."

Colt shrugged. "Distinguished. Tough. Or I should say rugged looking. Taller than he looks because of his compactness. Heavier than he looks because of his height. Moves lightly and with an air of self-assurance that you can't mistake. gray, stylish hair, and eyes that will seem to pin you like a butterfly to a board—icy cold. You'll know him."

Pagan felt a slight chill. "You make him sound threatening."

"Let's just say dangerous when riled," said Colt, "but one of the most dependable men ever when devoted to a cause. And a friend."

"So did you tell me," she said, "of your policeman friend Davidson."

"Davison," corrected Colt. "That's a different case. I'll stake my life on Raker."

"You are," said Pagan Maguire.

"And I've done it before. Anyway, you can wait for him until he shows up." Even as he spoke the words, another thought crowded into his mind. He paused, eyes studying Pagan.

"I'm damned if I like the idea of you sitting there for God knows how long, though."

"Afraid I'll be picked up?"

"No." James Colt took her teasing question literally. "But there's no telling how long you may have to sit there. If it's for any length of time you're bound to draw attention." He shook his head. Suddenly he snapped his fingers. "Now why in the hell didn't I think of that before?"

"What?"

"Rick's Place. It's one of the places Raker favors. It's not much farther than across the street. The bartenders are friends, or at least friendly acquaintances of Raker's. We can leave a note at the hotel that says you, Arlette Cavour, will be waiting at Rick's Place. They know me enough to make it easy to ask. They're the sort who will tuck you into a corner and watch over you until he shows up." He nodded. "I like it. I'll call from somewhere along the way. First, let's get the note done."

He sat down to compose the note. As he wrote he spoke to Pagan. "When you leave downtown, let Raker run things. He'll drive you back. He has access to a PanGlobal car. But don't come back here. In spite of all the precautions he will take, there may be someone around capable of fooling even him. He taught me that. He says that anyone can be had, even himself."

He finished the note and rose, handing it to the waiting Pagan.

She read it, folded it, and placed it in the envelope she'd taken from the desk while Colt was writing. She gave it back to James to address.

"So where do we go, if not here?" she asked.

"I'll show you. First, let's get out and find you a taxi."

• • •

Driving along Northern Boulevard, he explained what he had in mind. "There's a hotel along here where I may be able to find you that cab. It's called the Adria. It's not the nicest of neighborhoods, not by a long shot, but with any luck, and maybe a little bribery, we might find you a ride to town.

"Down the road from there, on the same side, to the east, you'll find a restaurant and bar. I'll drive by and show it to you. They won't be serving food at the time of night you'll probably return, but the bar will be open. Most likely. Have Raker take you there." He told her the name.

"And if it's closed?"

"I'm sure it won't be, not by the time limit I've set for you. Several of New York's finest make it their local."

"New York's finest?"

"Police. Any of them who are members of the Emerald Society."

Pagan showed alarm. "Is that wise, James? Is that really wise? The police around?"

"Purloined letter and all that, my girl. A man running is not likely to seek out the place where hunters congregate. And you'll admit that my present appearance doesn't exactly advertise who I am. Not if only compared to photos or descriptions."

She nodded. He was, at the least, quite different looking than usual.

"If, as you suggested, the place is closed, then have Rake escort you down the street to the Adria. Wait in the lobby or just park nearby. I'll be around somewhere close, watching, to make certain that you're not followed. Then I'll join you. The same applies to the other place. From there we'll all go back to the house where we can plan our next moves. We'll be safe then, for Rake will be there."

"You truly believe in the man, don't you?" asked the girl, "trusting him with the knowledge of your safe-house and all?"

"Completely," said Colt. "And Pagan," he grasped her wrist, "whatever you do, don't tell him about his daughter. You mustn't. Let me do that."

Colt chewed at his lower lip. "She is," he said, "probably the only thing that really means as much as life to the man. If he knows of her danger before I meet him, then in spite of his loyalty to friends, he may be off, leaving us, and we'll still be running. To get to him here where we can all help each other, he mustn't know until then."

"I understand."

"Let's go over it again," said Colt. Concern for the girl was heavy on his mind.

They rehearsed her part until Pagan had it word perfect.

"I think the only thing you have to fear right now is being recognized by Coleman, and that's highly improbable. But you mustn't be seen anywhere except when you leave the cab to enter the hotel, or when John or Joe come to escort you to Rick's Place. As I keep saying, there is no doubt that Coleman knows Raker. His obvious inside connection at PanGlobal means he knows where Raker's staying, so you'll not run into him there."

"Who is the inside contact, James?"

The thought chilled Colt. Yes, he thought. Who is it? Just who in the hell is it? Webb? Possible, but doubtful. Still, that he had held Colt at the point of a gun, ready to kill him, couldn't help Colt now. That could be an indication that he was working against Raker. And there was little doubt about Webb's dislike for Raker. Whatever, there was no mistaking the fear Webb had of the man. So even if the inside contact was Webb, even if he was the man behind the whole scheme, he'd keep his distance from Raker.

"Just who that is," said Colt, finally, answering Pagan's question, "is what Raker is trying to determine right now. Our new information may be of help. First, however, we have to give him the chance to save his daughter, then get ourselves cleared so we can help put an end to this horror."

He held out a hand to her and she took it in hers.

"You're so warm," she said.

"Only because you're so dammed cold," he said. "Scared?"

Pagan dropped her eyes and nodded her head. "Terrified. For you." She lifted her face. "I'm only an incidental," she said. "It's you they're after." There had never been a moment's concern that Colt had really killed the girl he had told about.

"Don't be too certain," warned James Colt. "We could be wrong. The way you look right now, however, you need have no fear as long as you go directly to the hotel, deliver the note, and call Rick's Place. Do you understand that?"

"I do, indeed." There was no fear in her voice.

What a hell of a woman, thought James Colt. What a remarkable, unusual woman. Hell! She's little more than a girl. He'd forgotten just how young she was. Still, one hell of a woman.

Colt stopped along their route to phone Rick's Place. Both bartenders had expressed not only willingness, but even eagerness to watch over Pagan until Raker showed up. They would remain open as long as the law permitted, if necessary, and one of the men suggested that if Raker hadn't shown up by the time they were forced to close, he and his wife would be happy to have the girl stay with them until the morrow.

Colt did not tell them that Pagan, too, was Irish. They would learn that. He did tell them that the matter required a certain amount of secrecy.

The men were pleased with the information. It may be an Irish trait, the love of intrigue.

• • •

Following his phone call, Colt had succeeded in obtaining a taxi for Pagan without driving to the airport. He'd found one when he showed her the location of the hotel. The advance tip he'd given the driver was more than could be considered generous, but that was of little concern to Colt. Pagan's security was all important.

Before they left the safe-house, Colt had given her a small, four-barreled, double-action derringer which did not have or need a safety. It looked to be almost a toy. It most definitely was not.

The weapon was, he told her, untraceable, and she was to handle it only with her gloved hands. It was to remain in her purse, her hand on it, until she was safely delivered to the front door of Raker's hotel. Its use, if she was threatened for any reason, whether from inside or outside the cab, was to be instant, without hesitation. Simply draw and fire. The weapon was a 4 barrel C.O.P., .357 Magnum, just over five inches in length. Colt didn't tell her of the tiny cannon's tremendous kick. It might very well spoil her aim. The first shot, at point blank range, would certainly accomplish the end for which the pistol was designed. Its flaw was that one could not determine which barrel would fire first. With its four chambers full, it didn't matter, not at all.

Yes, Pagan was familiar with derringers. Yes, she would use it if necessary. No, she would not try to simply frighten anyone with it.

Colt was sure she meant what she said.

She did. It was not only her safety, but that of her James, as well.

There was little or even no chance that she would have to use it, Colt assured her, but she must be prepared to do so in any event. She understood.

• • •

As it developed, the cab driver was tired, uncommunicative, and interested only in delivering his fare and pocketing the extra money the long drive and the already generous tip would earn.

The trip was uneventful and allowed Pagan time to sift through her concern that the Gordons must still be made to pay for the death of her brother. It was secondary to her concern for James Colt. She felt some small shame at the thought. But nothing should come before her revenge for Colin.

The plot, the killings of the innocent people must, of course, be stopped. But if Coleman was still planning to keep his word about the Gordons, then he must be given time to do so. Maybe that was what he was doing now! It was a hope against hope. Still, if it were so, then helping Raker save his daughter, plus the time it would take for Raker to clear her James, and protect the others scheduled for killing—that should give the man Coleman the time he would need to destroy the Gordons. That is, if he were going to do it. If, by the time all the other things had been done, Coleman had not done his promised job, then she'd have no regrets about helping Colt and his friend Raker apprehend the man.

She sighed. She was aware that she was dreaming of the things she would like to see. Such dreams seldom if ever came about. She would simply have to do what she could to protect James, and help save the daughter of the man Raker. The rest? That would have to wait. Even the Gordons. After all, she still had her . . . other connections . . . who would like to see them laid to rest. She didn't let herself think that what she wanted was their death.

She relaxed as best she could against the seat, trying to reassure herself that things would, truly, work out, as the cab droned its way toward Manhattan.

Nothing had been heard from the girl, Pagan Maguire, either. Evidently the two of them had not connected Raker and Coleman. He would have known. If they had not done so by now, they probably would not. At least not until Colt talked with him, or the girl saw him. Colt was probably spending his time trying to clear himself of the charges against him, and the bounty on his head. As bright as Raker knew the man to be, he was certain that Colt knew he was wanted dead, not alive. He would have gone completely to ground, taking Maguire with him. On the other hand, he might very well be looking for him, Raker, to help them. That was their terrible danger. If they wanted to live, they must stay away from him. He could not afford to take the chance that they would not make the fatal association.

It had been too bad about the girl, thought Raker. What was her name? Fremont? Yes, Janet Fremont. A shame about that, truly a shame. But that was the price of betrayal.

The main point then, Raker had resolved, was to stay away from Colt and Maguire, or to keep them away from him. It was the reason he'd elected to avoid his hotel, at least until late. He would really prefer that the two nice people live. If they found him, or he them? Well, he just couldn't take a chance. He would have to kill them.

• • •

Upon her arrival at Raker's hotel, Pagan Maguire had received a grunt slightly akin to an expression of gratitude as she added money to the already considerable sum the cabby had received, and as she turned, her stomach seemed to flip and her heart thudded against her ribs. Nausea mixed with fear tore through her body, as acids rose to burn in her chest.

The large figure, only yards away, standing straight and tall, and stiffly erect with military bearing, could only be Harlan Webb.

The man lifted a hand, waved, and took two quick steps forward to grasp the hand of a man approaching. They shook, slapping each other heartily on the back, brushed past the immobile Pagan who had not moved since leaving the cab, and walked into the hotel.

The man had not been Webb. As he turned his face toward her, she'd seen that there was not even a resemblance. It had been only the posture and the build.

Weak with relief, Pagan entered the hotel, left the note with the professionally pleasant clerk, and walked to the telephones. She called Rick's Place, as instructed by Colt, and had her spirits lifted by the reception her call was given. One of the men would be there, immediately, to escort her.

As she waited, she thought that the man Raker must truly be a wonderful person for her James to like and respect him so.

"Please God," she murmured aloud, "let him get the note. Let him come and find me."

After seeing Pagan off in the taxi on her trip to Manhattan, Colt had started back to his safe-house. As he neared the phone booth where he'd made his call to Rick's Place earlier, he was reminded of his previous attempt to phone the Becquerels in Rome.

Perhaps it would be faster to try once again from the booth than from his residence. He could use his telephone credit number although it was in his own name. If through any mischance the call came to the attention of the wrong parties, he would be long gone before they arrived.

• • •

The number still did not answer. The time in Rome was after seven in the morning. Colt's concern grew. He was familiar with the difficulties involved with the Italian telephone system. He may well never complete the call. If he could only find some outside help, someone who'd truly be willing to help, then perhaps he could get word to the couple.

He thought of CIA friends once again. His first attempt had been a bitter disappointment. But what about overseas? Had the word spread there?

He placed a call. It was, once again, to Rome. The number rang!

"Lindgren here." The voice was muffled and thin.

"Harry! James Colt!" His words came out rushed. The man must listen. "I need your help. You must . . ."

"You need a priest," interrupted the voice. "Even talking to you is like breathing cyanide. Dig? Goodbye." The line went dead.

"Damn!" swore Colt. He banged the telephone box with his fist. "Damn!" he repeated, shaking his head in frustration. They won't even listen, he thought. It has reached everywhere. He took a deep breath. Mustn't lose it, he told himself. They're just protecting themselves. The sense of futility remained. He stared blankly at the telephone.

Suddenly his eyes lit with the glimmer of an idea. "I wonder," he mused. "Yes, I just wonder?"

He picked up the phone again and made yet another call. It was to Washington, D. C., to a very private number. It took several rings before the answer came. The voice was sleepy.

"Krylov." The name was mumbled gruffly with one-word bad humor.

"James Colt. Do you remember?"

The voice turned resonant. Deeper, and awake. "Is remember? You have stupid. You t'ink maybe Krylov have forgot old adversary?"

"Knock off the stage accent," said Colt. "I've got a favor to ask." Relief filled Colt. At least it seemed he would be heard.

"A favor, you say? What the hell you think I am, the Godfather?" asked Pytor Krylov. "Is that it? You've crapped in your own decadent, imperialistic bird's nest and want old Petey to sweep out the crap?" There was humor in the voice.

Pytor Krylov was attached to the agricultural mission at the Russian embassy, and had been one of the KGB's respected agents. He and James Colt, while the latter had been with the CIA, had encountered each other in many dealings and developed a wary closeness, mutual respect, and guarded friendship. It was partly based on remarkably full knowledge of each other's activities. "Not exactly, Pete. This is for another cause. Nothing to do with me, and nothing to do with politics or our countries, and not with the old KGB."

"Oh?" The voice was full of doubt. "I know about the heat coming down."

"I'd be surprised if you didn't," said Colt. "This has nothing to do with getting me off the hook."

"Go on."

"Can you get to a safe phone?"

There was a short pause. "I can," said the former KGB agent, "that is if there is such a thing in your totally bugged, police state capital."

"Do it, then," said Colt. "Call me." He knew that giving the man the number of his residence would be the complete end of his safe-house. It might also mean the saving of Raker's daughter. There might be a way to delay the problem.

"Okay," said the Russian, sounding at least as American as Colt. "You're on. Seems as how I might owe you one for that lovely little thing you introduced me to a few years back."

Colt smiled. The reference was not about a woman. It had been information supplied to the Russian, in the interests of both countries, that had prevented what could have been a catastrophic bomb blast directed against the Russian Ambassador. "By the way," he asked, "what do we call the Soviet Union's state security these days?"

"Let's just stick with KGB, everyone remembers that one," Krylov snorted.

"Remember the old home run trick?" Colt asked. There was a short pause.

"Hell yeah!"

"Good going." It meant that he understood what Colt was saying and approved of the code that would follow.

CHAPTER 24

ROME

The man hesitated. The elegant woman's smile was nearly payment enough. Nearly. He took the bills. "So kind," he said. "Would you like to leave a message?"

"Oh, no. We really don't know them, and won't have time to get acquainted. But thank you."

As she left she was relieved. They were, after all, in time. Now, to meet Alec and wait. According to the clerk, the car would be brought from the parking garage and when the nice young Swiss couple collected it and their luggage, they would be followed.

Elizabeth Gordon felt a sense of great anticipation rising within her as she walked from the hotel and past the fountain that nearly filled the small *piazza*. A quick glance at the few people lounging about, reading, or simply watching the water flow over the aging stone was sufficient to assure her that none of them were the quarry she sought.

Even if she had noticed the set of eyes which followed her every move, she would have paid them no heed. After all, she knew she was a striking woman, and was used to such attention.

Alec was parked in front of the church, waiting.

"They are still here," she told him. "Can you leave the car where it is?"

"Not legally, but it can be arranged." He took his wallet from inside his coat. "Stay a moment until I find us a uniformed guardian."

Elizabeth frowned. "Are you certain?"

• • •

Home run stood for four, of course. Krylov would simply subtract four from each number greater than four given him by Colt. The result would be the telephone number Krylov was to call after the numbers were set down, not in order, but alternated from left to right. It was not at all an unbreakable code, but it would do for now.

He gave Krylov the number. "Give me fifteen minutes, then call," he said. He would be at his safe-house by that time.

WASHINGTON, D.C.

The call was nearly on time. "We were tapped," said Krylov's voice. "Don't know just who, but they might have locked on and traced back. You did move locations?"

"I did," said Colt. "Is your phone there hot?" He knew Krylov would have some sort of bug detector.

"Don't seem. You can never be sure with these gadgets. Now what's on your mind?"

Colt explained the situation. Assassins were after a friend's daughter and husband. Nothing to do with the U.S. or Russia. He needed Krylov's help in getting a message to the young couple involved.

"No way, old *bood-ya*. We'll make no direct contacts with out-siders, not even written. It compromises. Any other suggestion I might be able to handle?"

Colt thought. It seemed the Russian was willing to help if the conditions were right.

"You'll deal in the background?"

"The only way."

"How about straight to me. Information only."

Krylov was silent for only a few seconds. "Maybe. If it isn't business."

Colt knew what he meant. "It isn't. How about a stakeout on my subjects, and a check on their movements? They're reported to be about to leave Rome and head for parts unknown."

"Might handle that. Rome, you say?"

"Yes."

"Have good contacts there. Yes, I think I can swing that." Relief flowed through Colt. "Any way you can offer them protection?"

"No way." The comment was sharp. "We're not getting involved in any shooting sprees. Enough bad press from those damn Red Brigades, not even to mention the wounding of papa." He meant the Pope, of course. "Some leg work, maybe, and a report on destination possibly. No more."

"That'll be a big plus," said Colt. "Hopefully enough."

"Ain't it hell," asked the Russian, a smile entering his voice, "when you have to ask the other side for help?"

"Yeah," said Colt. "One hell of a note. But thanks. When will I get the information?"

"Where do you want it?"

"Rome." Even if Raker didn't show up, Colt himself would have to find a way to get there, and soon.

"Old friend, with that flag up on you, you can't even enlist the help of a second Christ, much less get overseas. Think again."

"I'll handle that, Pete. Just get me the information."

"Your funeral. When will you be there?"

"Can't say. As soon as possible. I'm waiting for someone. I'll leave without him if I have to."

"Do I know him?"

Colt realized he shouldn't have said it. Krylov would not work with an unknown variable. He could lie. Krylov would know.

"Raker," he said.

Krylov whistled. "Hoo boy, my friend! The big time. He's heavy duty." Colt could almost hear the man thinking. "All right. He's your friend. He's never come against us directly."

Colt breathed again.

"Listen carefully," Krylov continued. "I'll try for information to be gathered up until your subject's departure. You're on your own after that. Do you know the corner across from the Spanish Steps?"

"Which one? Dell a Croce?"

"Other way—Borgognona. You'll find an olive vendor there. Nine of the morning to afternoon break, then back until probably six or so. Catch him anytime you can make it."

"He's yours?"

"Never mind. He'll have any info I can pull. Do you remember the last drink we had together?"

Colt considered the question. He did. "Yes."

"And the name of the place?" A grunt seemed to be a "yes."

Manhattan

At Rick's Place, Pagan sat at a table by the far end of the bar, her back toward the front entrance, where they would watch her and speak to her whenever possible, but where her face would not be seen by the few patrons seated at the bar.

She had looked at her watch nearly every minute since she had been escorted from the Sheraton. The latest glance had been noticed by the nearest bartender. He moved to stand in back of her and placed a big hand gently on her shoulder.

"It's a hard thing, waiting, it is," he said. "But it'll be over soon."

Pagan looked up at the man over her shoulder. It was the large one. His voice was deep and scarred. The expression on his face was gentle; the face itself was as scarred as the voice. She placed a hand over his large one which still rested on her shoulder.

She smiled slightly. "Thank you," she said. "I know it will. It's just that time won't seem to move."

The large man patted her shoulder and returned to his duties.

• • •

Only a short distance away, across the street, Raker walked into the Sheraton and approached the desk.

He would have preferred to spend the entire night with his evening's companion, but there was simply too much to be done. He was too close to success to indulge himself in pleasure.

It was somewhere around two o'clock. Colt and the girl were quite probably settled in for the night and he wouldn't have to be concerned about them, at least until the following day. Perhaps, by then, they wouldn't represent the threat to his plan that would force him to kill them.

He smiled at the desk clerk. The smile held no warmth. It was simply Raker's "polite" expression.

"Raker," he said. He gave his room number. "Any messages?"

"I'll check, sir." was the polite reply. "Yes sir. Several telephone messages." Slips were handed to Raker. He had expected them.

"And this note delivered not too long ago," added the clerk.

Raker accepted the rectangle of paper, nodded, and stepped away, slitting open the top of the envelope as he did. As he read, a flutter of regret brushed at him and was as quickly gone.

That the note was from Colt, he'd been certain. That it was written in desperation there was no doubt. That would be the only reason he'd use the name Arlette Cavour. Colt was one of the few people he had allowed to know of the woman and her connection with Raker and his daughter.

The woman waiting for him at Rick's Place would be the girl, Pagan Maguire.

So be it, he thought. If he had believed in fate he would have thought that it had just intervened. He would see the girl; she would lead him to Colt. James Colt, the man he probably respected and felt closer to than any other man in the world. Too bad. Now, he would have to kill them. He did not like the thought.

He went to the entrance of his hotel, pushed open the door, and turned to walk the short distance to Rick's Place.

• • •

If Raker had simply passed the girl on the street, her changed appearance would have allowed her to go by without him recognizing her. Under the circumstances, he knew the lone female sitting at the table near the end of the bar to be the girl he sought. Pagan recognized him instantly as he came through the back entrance which she faced. The description James had given her had been quite enough.

Pagan's smile was sweet and affection-filled. The men had been so important to her when she needed them. "Thank you so very much. And sure we'll meet again, God willing."

• • •

She and Raker departed through the door from which he had entered, his arm protectively around her. Outside, on the street, Raker spoke: "How did you get here?"

Damn it! he thought. It wasn't right. The girl was somewhere around his own daughter's age. It just wasn't right that she and his friend James had to die.

The best he could do, when he had them together, was make it quick, merciful, and without talk or explanations or delay. As they walked, Raker wondered just how long it would be before the girl saw through his present appearance—gray haired and clean shaven—and recognized him as the man she knew as Coleman. She was intelligent and aware, and it was probably only her present distress that kept her from being as astute as she would be under other conditions. Recognition quite likely would come. The girl was far too observant.

Conversation stopped while Raker obtained his company car. It was not until they were on the street and driving before Raker spoke.

"Where is it we have to go?"

Pagan told him. "James will be waiting for us. He said to tell you he'd come in after he saw that we weren't followed."

Raker made a noise of appreciation. "He's really learning. Good thinking. Where is the place exactly?"

Pagan gave him the name.

Raker laughed. "A fine idea. Into the lion's den. Very good." It was, in fact, very good indeed, he

thought. For a variety of reasons. Had Pagan been apprehended by someone else and forced to lead them to the location, Colt would have been able to spot the trouble before he walked into it. But it was more than that in the present circumstances. He, Raker, could not now dispose of the girl, then take Colt when he saw him. If Raker arrived without the girl, James would be far too alert to take easily, especially in a bar full of cops. Not that Raker couldn't do it. It was just that the chances against success were far too high.

"James said to tell you he has a special message for you. Something quite personal, and terribly important to you." Pagan's voice was apologetic.

An alarm sounded in Raker's mind. "Personal? Something important? Any idea what?"

"No."

Raker knew she was withholding the truth. He would not pursue it. Colt would tell him—or was it just a ploy to insure Raker's arrival? For the first time, a small doubt about the full extent of Colt's cleverness bothered Raker.

As Pagan glanced at the profile of Raker in the dim light inside the automobile, there was something vaguely familiar about the man. She couldn't place it and brushed the thought aside. Probably just that James had told me so much about him, she thought. She was satisfied.

He was, she felt, certainly a man who seemed capable of helping.

· · ·

It was not yet 3:00 a.m. when Raker pulled into a parking spot at the rear of the restaurant and bar. The lot was nearly full.

Pagan started to open the door and Raker placed a hand gently on her shoulder.

"Wait," he said, "just a moment. I'm nearly certain I have shaken anyone who might have been following us, but let's make sure." It was only an excuse; he was satisfied they had not been followed. He needed the time to think.

The girl, to the present, had given no indication that she was suspicious of his identity. He would have known if she'd tried to hide it. Additionally, she had really done nothing but follow instructions with only minor indiscretions. The inconvenience caused by those had already been mostly covered.

If he could only separate the two, Colt and Pagan, then there might still be a chance that he could allow her to live. He would prefer it. He recognized her fear as sufficient motivation to have followed the course of action she had. That, and her desire for vengeance against the Gordons. The last was an emotion he understood. Raker had, with little difficulty, been able to reconstruct the events that brought the girl to his, or Coleman's, room at the Wellington. Fear of Webb, or her unknown watcher, guilt from taking Colt to her house, and the desire to play it straight had caused her to use the directions he'd given her for contacting him in an emergency. The fact that she must have seen him with Gordon was not as much bad luck as careless planning by himself. It was not a usual thing. It was his own fault in assuming that the girl would never have cause to feel that an emergency existed. Damn assumptions!

No, if the girl could, she must live.

"Pagan," said Raker. "May I call you that?"

"Of course. I've been taking the liberty of calling you Rake as does James."

"Very well. Pagan, I must ask you to do something that may seem strange to you. I have reasons. It is to protect you. Please believe that."

"Of course. James trusts you completely. So must I."

"We'll go inside, as James told you to do, but the moment he shows up, as soon as he comes in, I'll motion, or mention it to you, and I want you to leave us."

Surprise lighted her face . . . "But wh . . ."

"Hear me! It's imperative. Please don't ask why. Just do it. Believe me when I say that your life may depend on it." He turned to face her fully. She was staring at him and there was less chance of being recognized from the front than in profile which was harder to disguise.

Pagan's surprise had given way to fear. There was no doubting the intensity in Raker's words. "I just can't leave James alone, he . . . "

"You can't afford not to leave," interrupted Raker. His words and tone were hypnotic.

Slowly, almost against her will, Pagan nodded her head. "All right," she said slowly. "I will. If it's really so important."

"It is," said Raker. His eyes held the girl's attention. "Listen to me, Pagan. If you don't do exactly as I say, then even I can't help you. Either of you."

"I believe you," whispered the girl, voice tremulous.

"When you leave, go back to your old house downtown. The one where you lived before. Take my car. You'll be safe there."

"You know about that?"

"Of course," said Raker. "All of us do. Remember, I'm the one who is supposed to be running the show."

"Of course," said the girl. "But . . . are you sure it's safe?"

Raker forced a grin. "Safer than anywhere else you can be. Wait there for me. Or James. You'll not be bothered there. I give you my word on it."

Looking into his face, Pagan felt the same security that she had felt with James Colt.

"All right. And can you promise me James will be safe too?"

"If you'll do as I say, the chances will be much better." That was true. "Will you do it?"

It required effort, but when the word came it was definite. "Yes."

"Good. Now, let's get inside and meet our lad."

ROME

Genvieve Becquerel, nee Jennie Emelia Raker, stood at the ill-fitting, double glazed windows in the room on the third floor of the Albergo Fontana, both pair thrown open, as she gazed down on the decaying and littered—but still beautiful—Trevi Fountain. Designed, in theory, to shut out the sounds from the busy *piazza* directly below her, the windows failed completely.

The Piazza di Trevi, so narrow and cramped, and not at all broad and grand as the wide angle photographs one sees on post cards and in motion pictures would have one believe, was already beginning to draw a crowd.

The girl could have thrown coins from the window into the fountain's waters which had only started to flow again since being shut off the night before. It was the case on all but the most special occasions.

As the day went on the crowds would grow, and by dusk the street vendors would have their stocks of useless, flamboyant merchandise piled high on tables, waiting for the artificial lights, the wine, and the magic of the marvelous marble figures and the tumbling waters to make their wares enticing to roving tourists. There also was a cadre of native Romans who loved to linger in the *piazza*.

The girl's eyes scanned the flow of people as they made their way around the army of pigeons, pecking delicately at the grain spilled by drivers feeding horses hitched to carriages. These would soon be busy transporting tourists on circuits of the adjacent area.

Jennie, the golden hair she had inherited from her mother tumbling in shimmering swirls about her robed shoulders, turned her head slightly so that her young husband, still lounging on the bed their night's love making had rumpled, could hear her words.

"They're gone," she said.

"The lack of clatter so tells me," said Henri, his voice good humored with mock severity. "Why in the world did you select this hotel of constant noise?"

The young wife had referred to the very early-morning garbage collectors who seemed to use the *piazza* as their mustering place in the grayness of dawn. The couple had been awakened each morning by their commotion and shouted greetings.

She approached the bed and bent to kiss her husband's forehead.

"Because, my dear Hank, it was here that you first brought me to seduce me and all that good stuff." Her smile matched his.

"Indeed!" replied her husband, delighted in the girl's occasional use of distinctly American phraseology. He considered it a part of her heritage from a father barely remembered and a land she had never visited.

"Not hardly, my little vixen. As I recall, it was you who did the seducing." He put his arms around her and pulled her down next to him. "And anyway, we were married at the time, if you will remember."

"I do," she agreed. "It's just that I prefer to think of it as a seduction. I loved it. And you. And even that terrible racket."

The man's grin widened. They had both enjoyed it, all of it, even the slightly seedy hotel which it was then, and was still, even though having undergone lengthy if not effective remodeling.

"Then," said the young man, "come here and let us renew those old memories."

The girl rose and spun away from him. "Not on your life, buster. Not after last night. I'm famished. Not on this morning will I sit still . . ." she paused to smile, "nor lay still, for another breakfast of bread, lukewarm coffee, and tinned pear nectar. This morning I want a breakfast of fresh orange juice, melon, ham, *pommes frites,* eggs over lightly, and hot, buttered toast."

Henri Etienne Becquerel groaned. "Barbaric!" he said. "Utterly uncivilized." He grimaced, not meaning the words. He, too, occasionally enjoyed the breakfasts introduced to him by his pretty wife.

"But," he continued, sliding from the bed to stand and rest his hands on Jennie's shoulders, "if you insist, then I have no choice."

"Hurry and shower, lazy one," said Jennie, tiptoeing to kiss him on the cheek. She whirled away to return to the window. "I'm already squeaky clean and shining." She gazed out the window once again. "I'm glad the water is flowing now. The fountain looks so tired when it's not."

Her husband looked surprised. "Do you mean it's that time? You should have dragged me up much earlier."

Jennie turned. "We have time. But I do want to linger for a last look around our city."

"I know, little pigeon. I know. I love the sights of the city too, but mainly," and he placed a hand dramatically over his heart, "I have eyes only for you." He gave a deep, exaggerated sigh.

"Liar," grinned the girl, loving both the man and his words. "Now hurry!"

"It is you, my love, who must hurry. I'll be washed and dressed before your seams are straight."

"I have no seams to straighten."

"Then before your panty hose are stretched tightly to your satisfaction," said the man, ducking into the bath.

• • •

He was right. Leaving their room, the couple elected to walk the two flights of stairs to the lobby rather than chance the newly remodeled lift which had even been known to work, on occasion. They stopped at the desk.

"We'll be leaving today," said Henri Becquerel to the man behind the desk. "Would it be possible for me to settle our account at this time?"

"But of course, *Signore*," smiled the man. "Only a moment is required. Will you be leaving now?"

"Not right now," said Jennie. "We want to see a little more of your beautiful city. But we'll leave before long. I've packed our luggage," she paused to glance at her husband to remind him, once again, that the time she had spent packing their belongings was the reason he had been ready to leave the room before her.

"Could you have our grips brought down, and someone available to bring our car from the garage?"

"But of course, *Signora*. Of a certainty." He admired the lovely young woman's fluent Italian. So much better than the French-accented speech of her husband.

"When you return everything will be in readiness."

"Oh," he continued, suddenly. "A telephone message for you." He reached below the desk top and lifted a slip of paper, handing it to the man.

Jennie placed a hand on top of the one her husband had reached with. "Remember?" Her eyes were wide and pleading. "You promised no business."

Henri looked at her and frowned. He glanced up at the desk clerk. "Does the message concern business matters? Has it to do with banking? Money? Anything like that?"

The desk clerk was puzzled, but unfolded the paper and read it. To him, it was most important. It was from a bank in France.

"Yes," he said. "It seems quite important. Banking business."

"Then please destroy it," said Henri. "This trip is to be solely for pleasure."

Jennie squeezed his arm in approval.

The desk clerk shrugged. He had taken down the message shortly after he had resumed answering the telephone in the morning. He would soon be relieved by the day man; it would be he who would answer for the message not having been delivered if such an occasion arose. If the madness was upon these people, it was not his fault. He had tried.

"As you wish, *Signore*. It is done."

"And the bill?"

"Ah, yes," said the desk clerk. The note was forgotten. It required only seconds for him to present the bill. "Will there be anything else?"

"No," said Henri, counting out money, "only the luggage and the car." He added a generous tip and held it out to the man. "Please see that the money is divided correctly?"

"But of course," smiled the man. The sum was large enough that he would actually share a part of it. He watched the couple as they left the narrow lobby, thinking that they were truly a most handsome couple.

Just outside the door, one of the hotel's young porters had overheard the conversation. He knew that the portion of the tip he would receive would not be what he'd earned. His eager and bright young mind went to work. Perhaps, just perhaps, there would be a way he could earn some small additional payment, and to him in person, by the couple who'd proven to be so generous with their money. As had the desk clerk's eyes, his own followed the couple.

He was thinking of *lire*, not their appearance.

• • •

The Gordons had neither traveled together or by that name. Their plane, scheduled to land some time shortly before 9:00 a.m., had been fifteen minutes late. It had caused the Gordons some small concern though they were reasonably certain that their quarry would not be leaving the city at an early hour. After all, the couple was on holiday, and part of such an event should include sleeping late.

Still, it would be better to expedite their trip to the middle of the city. As a result, Elizabeth hired a taxi to take her to the hotel at the Trevi Fountain while Alec took the time to rent a car. The twins had agreed that they would meet on the steps of the church not far from the *piazza*. It was a place where experience told Alec he would be able to find space to park the car at least for a time.

Elizabeth left the taxi near the fountain and walked with deceptively swift strides to the hotel.

"Good morning," she greeted the desk clerk, smiling brightly.

"Good morning, *Signorina*," returned the man, eyes feasting on the attractive woman. "May I be of service?"

"I am so sorry, *Signorina*," said the desk clerk, his eyes sad. "We do not have a French couple residing with us at the moment."

Elizabeth Gordon's eyes reflected her surprise.

"We do have a very nice and most attractive young French-speaking couple, however. Swiss, they are. The Becquerels. A French name, I believe."

Relief flooded Elizabeth. She hid it. "No," she said, hesitantly, "that is not the name. But perhaps they have encountered our friends, what with speaking French and all. Are these Swiss people here now?"

"Unfortunately, no. But they will return." He directed a hand to point behind Elizabeth Gordon. "You see, they still have their luggage to pick up, and an automobile. They plan to journey this very day."

"How nice. What part of your beautiful country are they to visit?"

"They said to Sorrento," said the man.

"How nice, I wish we had the time for the trip."

"Perhaps you could stay to speak with them?" suggested the desk clerk.

"I'm afraid not," smiled the woman, "but thank you so very much." She took money from her handbag and held it out to the man. "You have been so very nice." It was 10,000 *lire*.

• • •

Alec looked interested. "Good information, my darling sister. Most interesting. That will help. Let me take care of our parking space, and then you head for the fountain to watch while I find a place to make a phone call."

"Call?"

"For a *villa*." He smiled down at his sister. "A little private playground for us and our playmates on the morrow."

Admiration showed on the woman's face. "Clever Alec," she breathed. "Oh, yes. A nice, private little playground of our own where we won't be disturbed. Can you do it?"

"Of course. Interhome, or something like it. They handle resort rentals and leases. Leave it to me. Right now you set up watch while I get our parking space properly bribed. I'll ring them from near the fountain."

"Lovely," whispered Elizabeth, plans already filling her head, "absolutely brilliant, dearest Alec." She leaned across to kiss him ardently. No watcher could have possibly thought they were brother and sister.

They walked to the small *piazza* and as Alec went to find a phone, Elizabeth stood, seeming to admire the fountain, but really watching the hotel.

How wonderful, she thought. Just Alec and herself, and the two lovely young people to play with. Any games that she and Alec could devise. A frown marred her features. Well, nearly. The damn Colonel simply would have to put on those foolish restrictions about the man. Oh, well, better than nothing.

Alec returned almost before she was aware that any time had passed. "They show?"

"No. How about your mission?"

"Success. A lovely, though rather expensive property above a small beach, and offering the utmost privacy."

Elizabeth looked at him with interest.

"Their words. Accessible only by parking on the roof and descending a single stairwell. They say it's hardly ever vacant. Seems people love the isolation, no one around to see or hear you."

"Oh, Alec," breathed Elizabeth. "You are a lovely, lucky genius." She squeezed his hand as they looked into each other's eyes. Their time driving, following the Becquerels, could be spent discussing the invention of new methods designed to bring the greatest pain . . . a nice prelude to the ultimate pleasure.

NEW YORK CITY

In New York, Beverly Martin Raker led Pagan Maguire through the doors into the bar and grill where they would wait for James Colt. Even at the late hour, the bar was nearly full. There were no empty stools together which could offer seating for a threesome, or even a couple.

They seated themselves at a table not far from the door and, after asking Pagan's preference, Raker ordered. A beer for him, white wine for her.

The drinks had not yet arrived when James Colt joined them at the table. "Never thought I'd live to see the day when I'd enjoy the sight of your ugly mug," he said, smiling at Raker and extending a hand.

Raker took it. "And me," he said. They shook. Raker glanced

at Pagan, and then turned his attention back to Colt. "Grab a chair and let's hear what's up."

Pagan rose. "James," she started, then fell silent.

"Yes?"

"Rake will tell you," she finished. She looked at Raker, eyes wide and imploring.

He nodded his head. "Now. And this minute."

Colt watched in silent surprise as the girl moved quickly from the table and out through the doors.

"Now what in the hell," he asked, "was that all about?"

"Orders, bucko," said Raker. "I sent her away."

"You what? Who in the hell are you tha . . ."

"Right now," interrupted Raker, "I'm boss! That's who I am. Settle down and listen to me. I'm trying to save your lives, the both of you. I don't think we were followed. Neither do you or you wouldn't be here at the table right now. But we can never be certain, can we?"

Colt nodded reluctant agreement.

"All right, then. I sent the girl away because nobody wants her."

"Bull-fucking-shit," snarled Colt. "I've been trying to call and tell you that the guy who employed her—calls himself Coleman— he's sure as hell after her."

"No he isn't."

"How can you be so sure? I haven't even told you about him yet."

"Now just what in the ever-loving hell do you think I've been doing with my time?" asked Raker. He sneered. "Way ahead of you, old buddy. I've had Coleman pegged from near the start. He isn't the brains. And right now he doesn't even exist."

"Doesn't exist? The hell he . . ." Colt's voice broke off as he studied Raker's composed face. "You mean," he continued, "that you have . . . ?"

"Let's just say that Coleman ain't no more." Raker finished Colt's unasked question. And, he thought, it was true. There was no longer any need for Coleman. Campbell? Perhaps. But Coleman could be gone.

Colt shook his head in admiration. "You clever bastard," he said. "Ahead of us all the way. Any idea who is behind it? And just who in the hell did the frame on me?"

"Everything to its place and time," said Raker. "Yes, and yes. Those are the answers to both of your questions."

"You mean you do have an idea who's behind this thing, and you do know who framed me? Is that what you're saying?"

Raker nodded. "Yup. But I still need the final proof. Not for me, but for Mitchell. I'd take care of it another way, but we can't take a chance on ruining good old PanGlobal, now can we?"

"Okay, I'll buy that. But I'm a hell of a lot more interested in clearing up that frame on me."

"Sure you are," said Raker. He frowned. "But that will take a day or so to pull off. In the meantime the girl will be back at her pad, safe and sound and damn well guarded."

Colt showed concern. "For true?"

"My word on it," said Raker. He meant it. Now, that she was gone, she could do no harm to him. If only Colt would just cool it, go quietly into hibernation for a few days, stay the hell out of the way, then maybe he, too, could live. Raker grinned at his friend and companion.

"God damn it!" said Colt, suddenly. His face contorted into a grimace, pain obvious in his voice. He reached out to grasp Raker's wrist. "I've got terrible news for you. The worst I can think of."

He paused and took a deep breath. His expression was pained, his voice almost cracking. "They've targeted your daughter."

Raker stared at Colt dumbly. His daughter? Targeted?

"She's on the hit list," continued Colt. "Her name is on the next group set for what the bastards call termination."

Colt had never seen such shock on Raker's face. The man sat as though petrified.

"Pagan probably told you about her visit to Coleman's room. No matter. He'd set up a sort of safe-room where Pagan was to go in the case of an emergency. She felt guilty about spending time with me, though she told me nothing. Just browsing, she came across the list. Made a copy. Gave it to me. I checked it out in more detail. Believe me, your daughter is on the list."

"It can't be! There's no way."

"Yes!" Colt's voice was strident, trying to bring reality to Raker. "I checked the names out in enough detail before Webb tried to nail me. It's diamond clear and hard. Genvieve Becquerel."

"That's not Jennie, the . . ." His voice died away as realization came to him.

"The hell it isn't," said Colt. "Genvieve Becquerel." He gave the name its French pronunciation: Zhon-vee-ev. "Jennie, God damn it. Your ex-wife's high-flown French version of Jennie." Agony was mixed with fury on Raker's face.

"Recently married," continued Colt. "Not yet a year. You wouldn't have known, seeing as how you're satisfied with occasional checks with the Cavour woman." The words were an accusation. "It's all there, Rake. Genvieve Becquerel, born Jennie Emelia Raker, Geneva, Switzerland. The right birth date." He handed Raker the printed list.

As he listened, Raker had grown calm. It was the quiet tension of a leopard about to leap. He had recovered from the blow which had sent him reeling. There was no doubt in his mind that Colt's information was correct. He knew the girl, Pagan, had found the list, and that Colt would have checked it.

No, there could be no doubt. And he, Raker, so blinded by fury and the obsession for revenge, had looked no farther than the simple information that his most hated—and dead—enemy's son had a wife who could become a target to bring yet more pain to the Becquerel family. Even if he'd studied the information with greater objectivity, Genvieve would have been glanced over. Probably was! Jennie was his daughter's name.

That Jennie and Henri Etienne Becquerel would get together had never entered his mind. Until he'd seen the hated name on the brief insurance printout, he'd nearly washed it from his mind. Now it all became horrifyingly basic. How natural that the two young people should have grown close: both without parents, both growing up in the same city and same social circles.

With controlled fury, Raker raised his eyes to look at Colt, his mind whirling with options. Time was the problem. There simply wasn't any. His daughter was already off to Rome with her . . . off to Rome, and then to God knows where. The Gordons were there to follow her. Or quite soon would be. He studied his watch carefully, computing the time difference. It was already past 9:00 a.m. in Rome. His daughter may already be well on the road to somewhere else. But where?

"I must get to her," he murmured. He didn't realize he had spoken aloud.

"She isn't in Paris," said Colt, hearing the words. "She's in Rome." Raker looked up in surprise. He knew, of course. But how did Colt know?

"I called Paris to warn her. Their housekeeper told me they are in Rome. At least they were. I called the hotel there, couldn't get an answer until just a short time ago." He'd made his latest call while waiting for Raker and Pagan.

"They were out early for some final sight-seeing, or so the desk clerk said. I left a message telling them that it was imperative they not leave Rome until they received a call from me."

"And?"

"I said the call was from PanGlobal Assurance Group. The husband is into finance and banking. I told the clerk it was very important money business. I'm sure that will intrigue him into returning the call."

Raker thought. Perhaps Colt was right. "When did you call?"

Colt looked at his watch. "It was just a little after eight in Rome."

"Then it's time to be at the phone, or to call again." Raker rose.

"I have a credit number," said Colt.

"So have I," said Raker, already on his way to the phone.

• • •

It required time, but finally a voice came on the line. "*Pronto*," it said. "Albergo Fontana."

"*Buongiorno. Mi vuol mettere in communicazione con Signora Becquerel?*" replied Raker.

Unfortunately, said the desk clerk, the Becquerel's had checked out of the hotel a little while ago. Their luggage, however, did still remain. They would be back.

Yes. A message had been delivered to the young couple. They

had laughed and torn it up. They had said something about it being the second message, and they were going to ignore business matters during their *vacanza*.

The message that Raker then left could not possibly be mistaken for a financial or banking matter. It emphasized that the message concerned a matter of life or death. The *girl's* death.

But of a certainly, said the desk clerk. The message would be delivered with emphasis.

Raker returned to the table. "Well?" asked Colt.

"She's still there, barely. They've checked out, but have left luggage."

"Then there's still a chance."

Raker thought, then said, "Maybe. If they get the message. And if they believe it." He sat and picked up his glass of beer, downing its contents in a gulp. He looked at Colt. "They tore up the message you left."

Colt frowned.

"No business on their vacation, they said. I made my message considerably more urgent. Still . . ."

"Yes?"

"They might not get it, or they might elect to ignore it as a joke of some sort. I'd better get someone else there immediately." But who? He thought. DelSarto would have gone to ground in readiness for his hit.

The police? Absolutely not! The Gordons, who were undoubtedly on the young couple's trail already, would kill the girl at the first sign of interference.

Colt cleared his throat. "I've taken a step in that direction." For some reason he felt awkward in telling Raker that he had called on Krylov for help.

Raker looked up with quick interest.

"I tried an old CIA friend in Rome. No luck. So I got hold of another friend, in Washington." Colt paused briefly. "KGB. He owes me. He agreed to at least have some of his . . . have somebody stake out the hotel. He wouldn't offer any protection. Out of his authority. But he'll spot and leave information at a drop in Rome. I was going to be there as soon as possible, with or without you."

Raker showed a spark of hope. "When can we pick up the info?"

"Me, not we. He trusts me only, among the other side, and that damned little," Colt explained.

"All right, you. When?" Raker asked.

"As soon as we can get there!" replied Colt. "It's your baby. Far as I know I'm still on Mitchell's 'hit-list'. You'll have to handle him. Exonerate me, scare the hell out of him for sure; have him establish your authority, and for God's sake get him to put the Pan Gee jet at our disposal...immediately.

"Then," said Colt, "I'll have arranged to get the information from our KGB angel."

"Will he deliver?" asked Raker

"He'd damned well better," snapped Colt. "He's all we've got."

"Then let's get to it!" Raker rose abruptly and started moving. "I'll grab another phone and get Mitchell. You handle the rest. We'll head to your safe-place soon as we're done here".

• • •

It took less time than anticipated for plans to be sorted out, departure schedules and connections to be made, and then to drive to Colt's house. Now the two men waited only for Mitchell's call. It came.

"Raker," he answered. "Well?"

"Done," said Mitchell's voice. "Things are quite well set up... quite well! Rome knows you're coming and that you're to be in charge." He gave Raker the number of the Italian office of PanGlobal . . . "And Raker . . . be sure to tell Colt that he's now clean."

"And the plane?"

"By two this afternoon."

"So late? I can beat that on a Concorde."

"You cannot, I checked. The time can't be speeded. Minor problem with an engine. You'll still be in Rome sooner than any other way."

Raker forced himself to calmness. "Very well. Good enough, Mitchell. Have you cleared any problems about getting out and in?"

"You'll have no customs problems. It has been arranged. It is really quite simple when you know the right people." Mitchell could not resist the opportunity to remind Raker of PanGlobal's and his own power.

"And we'll leave from . . .?"

"Kennedy. You should be able to lift off before three." Mitchell paused as though waiting for praise.

"It'll have to do," said Raker. That was true. "All right, Mitchell. I'll see what I can do about saving your precious money."

"Yes," said Mallory Fleming Mitchell. "Yes, indeed. Do that."

Raker swung around from the phone, relayed the information to Colt—and then asked him if a drink was available.

"Of course," said Colt. "Name it."

"Just pour," said Raker. "It's one of those times I think I need one." He sank onto a heavily upholstered chair and forced himself to relax.

"Scotch?"

Raker waved a hand. "Anything. With a splash." Colt brought a glass brimming with amber fluid. Raker took it and downed it in a single swallow. "Mitchell's one cold blooded bastard, Colt."

"No more than you, Rake. Just different values."

Raker stared steadily at Colt. A grimace related to a smile twitched his mouth.

"Right on, Jimmy lad. Thanks for the reminder. I've let Jennie's danger cloud my mind." He wiped a hand down from his brow to his chin. It was a gesture Colt had never seen before. Raker's shoulders straightened and he returned to the image of the man Colt knew.

The line was silent. The man was listening. More than that, he heard. For all of his self-confidence, he felt the reality of the threat. This Raker was a mad man, but a frightening mad man. And his orders were from Mallory Fleming Mitchell: "Take the man's word as that of God."

"Yes, sir," he said, biting off the words.

"Make no mistake," said Raker, the syllables as sharp as claws, "I mean every word I say. I will be flying to Rome as soon as possible. I will maintain contacts via radio. Have the company plane met. Keep me informed." He gave the man Colt's telephone number.

"Do not approach the subjects. There will be no attack until after noon tomorrow at the earliest. Understand?"

"I understand. My men are now on the way, even as you talk."

"See to it," said Raker. He did not wait for a reply.

"How," asked Colt, as Raker turned from the telephone, "do you know there'll be no danger until after noon tomorrow?"

Damn!, thought Raker. A slip—small, but nonetheless a slip. Colt had lost none of his sharpness.

"I didn't know," said Colt.

"All right," decided Raker. "Then the other is merely backup. And even if your KGB people don't get to the hotel in time, they should be able to find and track them if they're worth a damn. Even if they miss, we may still need them to nullify the hit team."

"You seem damned sure it's a team," said Colt.

"You can bet on it."

"You said that before," reminded Colt. "How are you so sure?"

"I am sure, James. Damned sure. But right now I'm going to try to phone Jennie again."

• • •

For the first time, it required a wait of several minutes before the call could be completed. As Raker talked, quietly, Colt could see his shoulders sag. He set the phone down slowly and turned. His eyes were hollow with concern.

"They're still out," he said. "There is a new clerk on duty. He didn't know of the message until I told him."

"So? Is their luggage still there?"

"Yes. That offers some hope, I suppose." Colt was not used to the sound of defeat parenthesized by Raker's words.

Colt was uncomfortable and worried. "Quite some time has passed since your call to PanGlobal. Maybe they got their people down there."

"Yes," said Raker. "That's true." He walked to where Colt had left the whiskey decanter sitting out. He poured a large drink and downed it. It was the first time Colt had ever seen Raker take more than two drinks in any one evening.

"Yes," repeated Raker. "There is that. It'll have to do. But I really think we'll have to count on your contacts. The others were short on time." He grimaced. "Damn peculiar to be counting on those who are considered to be 'the other side,' isn't it?"

Colt didn't comment on the observation. "Want to call and check on the PanGlobal people?"

Raker shook his head. "No. I made my point with the man. No sense pulling him off to answer questions that won't help us."

"What we can do is get ready for tomorrow. Sleep, Jimmy, boy. We'll need all the rest we can get." He eyed Colt questioningly. "You have suitable ID to get you out of the country in case Mitchell hasn't pulled off the wolves yet?"

Colt nodded. "Good, and authentic. Just not mine. Clean passport and all."

"Fine. Good. Then let's settle in and wait. I'll take the sofa here."

"Good enough," agreed Colt. "I'll make do with a real bed." He left to go upstairs and join Pagan, but not before he, too, took a large drink.

As Colt left the room, Raker stretched out and forced his mind to calm down. If either man was to be effective, they must be rested. Only by staying that way would it be possible for them to rescue the daughter Raker loved so dearly—if you can truly love someone you don't really know.

He refused to consider that it was his own actions, his own desires, and his own hatreds that had placed her so close to the physical terrors planned for her by the psychotic Gordons.

As he drifted toward sleep he gave fleeting thought to the fact that he might even withdraw his entire plot against PanGlobal if Jennie could be spared.

Might. It was a nice word of limited probability.

His next thought was to decide just which weapons to take from the case in the trunk of his car. He decided to carry the deadly Colt Python Hunter, with the eight inch barrel. Its .357 Magnum power, and its carefully calibrated scope gave it surprising range and great stopping power. The specially designed silencer muted its noise considerably without decreasing its performance too drastically. His additional choice would be the Heckler & Koch, VPOZ,

9mm Parabellum. Its eighteen-shot magazine offered continuing, rapid fire power. He would, of course, carry an extra clip. The two fine pieces complemented each other almost perfectly. Yes, they would do nicely. He felt secure that Mitchell's power would see to it that their luggage and equipment were not carefully examined, if at all, either leaving the country, or entering Italy.

He slept.

He would awaken at the precise moment he had willed his mind to rouse him. He did not dream.

CHAPTER 25

It had been only minutes after Raker gave his instructions to the PanGlobal man in Rome when Jennie and her husband turned the corner from the restaurant where they'd taken several meals on this and their earlier stay in Rome.

They approached the fountain from the *Via del Lavatore*, arm in arm, smiling happily as they spoke of how the waiters always professed such sorrow at their departure, even to the point of tears, whether real or somehow otherwise induced.

"*Signore!*" The voice caused them to halt. It was Renato, the young boy from the hotel, who'd given them pleasant service throughout their stay.

"Good day to you," said Jennie and Henri, almost at the same moment. They exchanged pleased looks. The event occurred often. They thought it was an omen of good luck.

"I have been looking to your comfort," said the boy, his teeth flashing whitely in his smooth, tanned face.

"Yes," agreed Henri Becquerel, "you surely have."

"No, *Signore*," the boy objected. "I mean now. I have taken the liberty of moving your luggage from the hotel into your car, and have it all ready for you to drive from the garage."

Jennie and Henri exchanged quick glances.

"That is quite nice of you, Renato," said Jennie.

The boy looked up at them with large, dark eyes, then lowered them as though embarrassed. "I—that is, they—would not allow me to drive it, the car, to you." He looked up with an assumed air of injured dignity. "Too young, they said. But," he continued with obvious pride, "I made them move the car out to where it will be a simple matter for you to only allow me to close the doors for you, and then you may drive away."

It had required no small amount of skillful talk, accompanied by a small amount of money. Renato felt secure in the knowledge that he would be well recompensed. After all, had he not successfully removed the luggage of the two from almost under the very eyes of the desk clerk? He smiled at the memory of the man momentarily distracted by a telephoned request for service from one of the hotel's other guests.

"How sweet," said Jennie. She looked at her husband. "It is, isn't it, dearest?"

Henri smiled to show it most certainly was. "Truly," he said, "and you shall be most certainly rewarded, Renato, my little Machiavelli."

Renato Grani knew the name. It gave him pleasure that he was being compared with the ultimate layer of schemes.

"This way," he said, and started to lead them, proudly, to where their car was waiting, luggage already stored.

• • •

Elizabeth Gordon placed her hand on the shoulder of Alec who sat next to her at the small table of the café on the corner of the *piazza*. "There!" Her finger was pointing. "Across the way. That must be them."

Alec watched as the couple passed the entrance to the hotel without stopping. "Are you certain? They didn't stop for their luggage."

"That's the boy from the hotel," said Elizabeth. "He just carried luggage out the doors. He took it to their car in the hope of earning a good tip."

Alec frowned. "You're probably right. You said their luggage was sitting along the wall across from the desk?"

"It was."

How perfectly lovely! They were truly a beautiful pair. How nice it would be.

Please, she thought, oh, yes, please. Please let it be those two. Alec appeared at her side, slightly out of breath. "The luggage is gone." His eyes followed Jennie and Henri. "Those are ours, little one." The woman was nearly as tall as he. He slid an arm around his sister's waist. "Yes, indeed. They are ours, and a truly handsome pair if ever I saw such." His hand had slid up to cradle under one of the woman's breasts.

"Yes," agreed the woman, her hand covering her brothers, caressing it gently. "They really are. Oh, Alec. It's going to be lovely."

They separated and turned to walk to their own car which was parked in front of the nearby church. As they opened its doors and got in, watching eyes followed them and continued to watch as first the small red Fiat pulled out of the garage, driven by the male who accompanied the so beautiful young girl. Behind it, the silver Mercedes drove out to follow.

Henri Becquerel was wealthy enough to have afforded nearly any car he wanted to choose. As a man of finance, however, it appeared foolish to waste money on expensive machinery for a short trip to the south when they didn't plan to spend much time in the car anyway.

It was with interest that the observer saw three men approach the small *piazza* of the fountain from three separate directions, each halting at a different corner. They nodded slightly at each other, then one man started to walk toward the Hotel Fontana.

The man entered the hotel and emerged in only moments. He motioned for the other men to come to him. They did.

The observer focused on the mouth of the man who seemed to be in charge. It would have been easier if the words had been in English or Russian, his best languages. Still, he was able to read the lips sufficiently well even though the words were spoken in Italian. "Stupid clerk. Day man off . . . Gone for days . . . doesn't know where they are going."

The observer smiled. Whoever the men were, they were looking for the young couple. And they had not been able to determine where they were going when they left the hotel.

He felt superior to them. It had been a simple matter for him, the trained observer, to read the lips of the young couple as they talked over an early breakfast. They were going to Sorrento.

His attention was diverted when a voice cried, *"Signores!"* He saw the boy who'd guided the two young people approaching the three men. They turned to look at him with distaste.

"Excuse me," Renato said politely, "but I heard you ask inside," he nodded toward the hotel doorway, "about the couple Becquerel." He mispronounced the name. It was close enough.

"Yes," said the man who was obviously the leader, "did ask." He was being terribly careful.

"Well," said Renato, smiling shyly, "although this desk clerk who has only in the hour started work knows not of their destination, I . . ." and he paused proudly, "I was there when the couple told the other desk man where they were going." He had not been there, and had not thought to ask the couple himself. Still, information of some sort should be produced to make these gentlemen feel better. And in order to produce perhaps a reward.

"And that is?" asked the man.

Renato looked puzzled. "I'm sure that I can remember." He stood, frowning intently, in silence.

Light dawned on the face of the man. He reached into his pocket and extracted some bills. He selected one and extended it toward the boy.

"Does this help your memory?"

Renato paused. One more gentle push, perhaps? "It seems," he started, slowly, "it seems . . ." He stopped and shook his head, shrugging.

The man added yet another bill to the one he held out.

Renato slapped a hand to his forehead. The bills disappeared into his other hand. "Ah, yes. The couple are going to the mountains. To the villa of Hadrian and to the Villa D'Este. To enjoy the sights." Who knows, he thought. Perhaps they really were. He shrugged internally. It didn't really matter; he had the money.

"Let's go," said the man, turning to his companions.

"Wait!" called Renato, suddenly reinspired.

"Yes?"

"Would you not like to know of the car they drive?"

The man almost smiled. "No, little thief. That we've already determined." He turned. "Hurry," he said, moving swiftly. The two other men, well behind, hurried to catch up with his rapid walk.

Renato's eyes followed them. I hope, thought the boy, I was wrong. I hope the nice couple does not go to where I said. He did not know of the unclaimed message, or its importance, which his efficiency and mild greed had caused the Becquerels to miss.

•••

The actions and words of all the players were duly entered in the book of the quiet observer. Even he did not know of the message. His job was nearly done. Now he had only to consolidate his notes, make sure they were legible, and turn them in for whatever their use was to be.

At James Colt's former safe-house, it was not yet six o'clock in the morning. He had not been able to sleep. Now, having returned to the living room, he studied the form of Raker which lay stretched out on the sofa, quietly asleep.

How, he thought, can the man rest like that when his daughter is in danger? He realized the thought resulted only from his own inability to disassociate his mind when such was needed. It was yet another gift Raker had. The man was right, he knew. They had done everything that they could do, at least the things Raker felt would not endanger his daughter further. It was only one of the differences that separated the similarities between the two men. It would be Raker who had put aside his turmoil long enough to renew the strength that would be needed for the coming action.

Unless they were already too late.

Why hadn't the phone rung? Why hadn't PanGlobal's people reported back? Why hadn't the daughter acknowledged the message left for her at the hotel? How could Raker simply wait so patiently?

Colt could not. He knew it wasn't likely that his credibility had yet been restored, but he could at least call, using Raker's name. The office in Rome regretted they had received no report from their representatives who were on the mission for the Signore Raker. They would report as soon as word was received.

His call to the Hotel Fontana brought worse news. Yes, the message for the couple Becquerel was still at the desk. Alas, it appeared that they had somehow picked up their luggage without having been given the note. Most unfortunate, but it was not the fault of himself, Celestino Zarfetti. The luggage must have been carried out while he was busy with necessary duties.

Colt slammed the phone down.

At the sound, Raker came instantly awake and alert.

"They didn't get it," said Colt. "They didn't get your message. Their luggage is gone. We've missed them."

Raker's features grew grim. He nodded. "I'm not surprised. They would have called if they had received the note. It was made that urgent. How did they get out without being seen?"

"The clerk says he was busy with other things."

"PanGlobal?"

"No word. Maybe they got there."

Raker shook his head. "If they'd been in time we'd have heard."

"Then what the hell do we do?"

"Nothing. Not until we get there."

"But the police! Surely they could . . ."

"James," interrupted Raker, tiredly, "I've tried to make it clear to you. That would be signing those kids' death warrants." Somehow he seemed to have lost his extreme reluctance in acknowledging the presence of Jennie's husband.

Colt looked at Raker speculatively. "You know more than you're telling me."

"I know a hell of a lot more than I've told you."

"Such as. . . .?"

"Such as some of the people involved in the so-called terminations. Such as the Gordons."

"The Gordons?" Colt's expression was blank.

"Elizabeth and Alexander Gordon. English. Operate in Northern Ireland. They were sure as hell on the CIA's list of baddies."

Colt's expression had changed to one of horror. "Jesus Christ," he blurted. "Those crazies? My God, Rake, are you telling me they're the ones after Jennie?"

"They are," said Raker.

"How can you be sure?"

Raker wanted to shout, Because I sent them! Because I ordered them to kill my own daughter. Instead he said, "Because I've been working at knowing."

"And the others?" Sudden shock showed on his face. "Good

Lord. I'd forgotten. The others. How about the others? How in the hell can we protect them? Have you taken care of that?"

Raker shrugged. "Look at the names, Jimmy boy." He nodded toward the table where he had placed the list. "You should recognize them. Who the hell would want to protect them except their hired hands and associates? And who the hell would insure them except Mitchell with PanGlobal and his hidden reinsurers? You can bet that most of them were forced to get insurance either because of their valuable importance to their associates, or their own vanity. The bastards aren't worth protecting or saving. Pan-Global can stand the loss. The way Mitchell has treated you, you shouldn't mind that."

Colt ignored the admonition. "And Jennie? What has she done that's so terrible. How did she get on the list? Why didn't you try earlier to get protection for her, even if you didn't realize she was your own daughter?"

It had been a slip. Raker's mind told himself that he was becoming careless. "Because, James, I was only finding out about the terminators. I didn't know of the targets until the Maguire girl came up with that list." It would cover it, he thought.

Colt nodded. "I'd forgotten. Still, it isn't right that we become judge and jury, even if those others are rotten."

"Then you do something about them. I'm concerned about Jennie, and only Jennie."

Colt realized that Raker was right. The names on the list, except for the girl, represented people the world could well do without. He had little trouble letting the matter drop. Perhaps, he thought, he was becoming more like Raker than he realized. In fact, he was.

"How about those third strikes? It appears they'll threaten more than just individuals."

"Most likely," agreed Raker. "Probably thousands more. If we can get to Jennie and the Gordons, we may be able to stop those." It was the maybe, once again.

Colt was somewhat mollified. "Still," he said, "I don't see how you can take things so calmly about your daughter."

"What else can I do?" He rose and walked to the window.

"Earlier, Jimmy boy, I almost came unglued." He turned to face Colt. "That was self-defeating. I'll need all the facilities I've got if I'm to stop the Gordons."

"*We've* got," corrected Colt. He looked at his friend. "I'm in this too. Don't forget that you're a friend, my best friend. And the way all these other bastards seem to have been looking at me, probably the only one I can depend on. It's us, Rake. You and me."

Beverly Martin Raker experienced the slightest twinge of conscience. Although he was the cause of Colt's present problems, it was all that his character would allow.

"I know," he said. "And right now, it looks like your contacts are all we've got to hope on." He almost grinned. "Now isn't that a bitch? Here we are counting on the sworn enemies of the good old U.S.A. to pull our heads out of the shit. Whatever happened to the good guys and the bad guys?" He, of course, considered himself one of the good ones.

"Yeah," agreed Colt. "It's sort of like Custer counting on Crazy Horse and the old medicine man Sitting Bull to scout out the Indians."

"You made two contacts?"

Colt grunted an unfunny laugh. "Mistake. No. Only one. Hope he's Crazy Horse, and not just sitting around." He frowned.

"Something wrong?"

"Just thinking—about Custer and the Indians. Hoping my old friendly enemy, Pytor, isn't just setting us up for another Little Big Horn."

"Bad joke, James." He looked pointedly at the top of Colt's recently shaved head. "But you're safe. Looks like you've already been scalped. Now get some sleep, damn it, before you have me as nervous as you."

Colt ran a hand over his head. He had momentarily forgotten he was, at least in theory, in disguise. He was surprised to feel the growing stubble. Had it been that many hours?

"Okay, *cuate*, it's back to the bedroom. And to sleep this time. Call me when you're ready."

There was no answer. Raker was already halfway asleep.

ROME

Just outside Rome it was now past noon. The Gordons were maintaining a discreet distance between themselves and the Becquerels. They were—at least, Alec was—irritated.

"Tourist bastards," said the man. "Why in the hell can't the damned twit take the Autostrada? Why all these sodding back roads?"

"Because, sweetheart, they are being exactly that. Tourists." She reached a hand across to pat her brother's leg. "Don't be upset, darling. We've plenty of time. Somewhere along the way they'll make a stop that will give us the opportunity to become acquainted." She laughed throatily. "Why, such a nice young couple will simply love meeting two pleasant fellow tourists like ourselves. Then tomorrow we can have them to our little villa for a nice, quiet afternoon at the beach."

Alec glanced over at her. "And if they don't buy it?"

"Then we'll simply persuade them by other means." Her voice hardened as she said the words.

POMPEII

The Becquerels finally left the narrow *strada comunale*, and entered the *Autostrada*, much to Alec's relief. The Gordons' opportunity to strike up a conversation came at Pompeii, just as Alec was beginning to doubt his sister's prediction.

They followed the red Fiat through the aging, ill-kept population centers leading toward Pompeii, only close enough to make sure that their distinctive silver Mercedes would not be too readily noticed by their quarry. Alongside the marvelous ruins of the ancient city they saw the Fiat pull up over the curb, into an area in front of a restaurant with its adjoining souvenir shop, flanking the broad thoroughfare.

"They obviously have been here before," said Elizabeth. "That's private property." She watched as a large, magnificently stomached man approached the Becquerels with an effusive greeting.

"Turn in there," she said suddenly. "Next to them!"

"What . . ."

"Do it! Park next to them. It'll be perfect. Leave things to me."

Alec did as instructed. As he turned the car, the man and woman they had been following slid from their automobile, with the man who'd greeted them holding the door for Jennie.

Elizabeth lowered the window of their car as Alec brought it to a stop and called out, her voice bright and friendly. "Is this quite all right?" Her smile was pleasant. "I mean, if it isn't . . ."

The man and the young couple smiled in return. "It is most all right," replied the older man, his English only moderately accented. "I am here to serve. Welcome to my services."

Elizabeth punched Alec with her elbow and motioned with her head. They were to get out as quickly as possible. "Thank you ever so much," she said. "It's so much nicer than looking for a place to park among that huge crowd." She turned her smile on the Becquerels. "I'm so glad we saw you turn in here. We wouldn't have known."

The older man laughed. "Had I but seen you as you passed by, most beautiful lady, I would have blocked the road in order to have your lovely presence here. And please! Do not worry about your automobile. Lock it, don't lock it. Nothing will be disturbed. This is Pompeii, the home of honesty." He frowned, pre-announcing disapproval in his words to come. "This don't Castlemare." He spat. "Thieves there!" He smiled again. "Here, everyone is safe. Please. Come for a glass of wine with me. All of you." He swept his arm out in a gesture of effusive welcome.

It couldn't, thought Elizabeth Gordon, have been more serendipitous. It was perfect! Not only a most unsuspicious reason to approach the Becquerels, but the opportunity to build a small friendship in the company of a host the young couple seemed comfortable and delighted to be with.

Now, it was only a matter of time.

• • •

It was not yet 4:00 p.m. when the Gordons—though not by that name—and the Becquerels exchanged pleasantries, voiced expressions of hope that they would see each other again in Sorrento, and drove away after thanking their host for his great part in making it such a wonderful day.

The Becquerels pulled away first. Elizabeth had Alec waited until their car was well out of sight before they, too, pulled out into the flow of traffic.

Their departure left their host considerably enriched. And not only in spendable wealth. He had really enjoyed the company of the two nice couples. Well . . . at least the company of the two beautiful *signorinas*. It mattered not whether they were married or single. At his age, and with his disposition, any female under the age of 60 was a signorina. He watched the departing cars until they were both out of sight. He sighed, regretting that he had not indulged in at least one small, harmless pinch, and turned his attention to the business of profit.

• • •

"It worked, and beautifully," said Alec, complementing his sister.

"Didn't it just, love? And isn't he the handsome one?"

"And her," said her brother. "Quite the loveliest of girls. Next to you, of course."

Elizabeth patted him to show she was not offended. The two looked at each other, their eyes glowing in anticipation of coming pleasures.

"Shall we look them up this evening?" asked Alec.

"Perhaps. First we need to take a look at the place you've leased. Then stop by a shop or two so that

I may pick up some things for tomorrow."

"Quite," agreed Alec. "Yes. I'd like to help in the selection."

"We'll call," decided Elizabeth. "We know their hotel. Invite them for a private swim on our little beach tomorrow."

"Will they accept?"

"Of course." She thought a moment. "Perhaps we'll just stop by their place and invite them personally."

Alec was still concerned. "And if they don't accept?"

"Silly. Not to be negative. It doesn't really matter, does it? Not really, I mean. We'll be having them out in any event."

They drove in silence, each busy inventing new experiments they might like to try out on their newfound friends.

The girl, thought Alec, was wonderfully shapely and slender. She should look quite pretty stretched ever so tightly so that each feminine muscle would show.

The man, thought Elizabeth, or the girl? Which should I start with? They kept their speed reduced, allowing the Becquerels to reach Sorrento far before they would. Proximity, for now, didn't matter.

$$\cdots$$

"They were really quite nice, weren't they?" Jennie's question came while her eyes absorbed the lovely scenery to her right as their car swept along the curving road carved high into the rocky slopes leading down to the sea.

"Yes," said Henri. "Very."

"Do I hear a bit of hesitancy there?" asked the girl.

"Possibly," said her husband. "Oh, it is not to say that I did not like them. I did." He smiled at Jennie. "It is only that this is really a renewal trip for us. Possibly it should be reserved for that alone."

Jennie considered the words. It was true that the trip was somewhat like a second honeymoon, though the two had not yet been married an entire year. Only nearly.

"Perhaps you're right," she said. "Of course we will not be able to stay away from everyone."

"Oh?" commented Henri, lifting eyebrows and adding a leer to his voice that matched his expression. "Can't we, little one? I know a way that we can make certain . . ."

"You!" said Jennie, sharply, with a light slap at her husband's arm. "You young old lecher." Her smile was delighted. "We came to see and be seen. Not lay and be layed."

"You, perhaps, my dear. As for me . . ."

He let his voice trail off as Jennie leaned against him, careful not to interfere with his driving.

"What do you suggest? We did tell them of our hotel."

"Oh, something nice and illicit. Something like registering under assumed names and pretending that we're not married." It was a game they had played before.

"Why, sir," said the girl, trying to snuggle a bit closer. It was impossible with the separate seats. "How sudden." She looked up and fluttered long eyelashes at her husband. No! Her soon-to-be-lover. She toyed with the thought.

"Yes. I think we should. Can we? I mean passports and all that? And we do have reservations under our own names."

"As a man," said Henri, assuming an air of stiffness, "of banking and commerce, I can assure you that it can be arranged if the price is right. We will simply cancel the reservations, and another couple will be happy fill them." He paused. "Us!"

"Am I worth that? The price?"

Her young husband gazed down at her with loving eyes. "You, my love, are worth any price."

"What name, then?" asked the girl. "What name will we register under. I'd like something absurd and hilarious."

"I must think," said Henri.

"Well?" asked Jennie, after a short silence.

"Quixote. Rosinante and Don Quixote."

Jennie laughed. "How absurd!"

"Is that not what you wanted?"

Jennie nearly giggled. "Yes. But no one will buy it."

"Yes they will," insisted the man. "Of course. We will. *We* will buy it."

"Just a minute there, old friend," objected Jennie suddenly. "That name. Wasn't that a horse?"

Henri made his expression bland and innocent. "A filly, my lovely." He dipped his head to lean across and kiss her hair. "My so lovely, little filly."

What the hell, she thought—she seldom even considered such expressions—she'd not remind her husband that her name, Jennie, was also related to the equine family. The thought brought a smile to her face. She reached over to lay a hand on the arm of her husband. I'm so lucky, she thought. So very, very lucky.

That evening, when the Gordons made their call or paid their visit, there would be no Mr. and Mrs. Henri Becquerel registered at the Ambasciatori.

Neither would they be registered for Raker or Colt to find.

BECQUERELS / GORDONS

Their evening in Sorrento was a delight. Dinner, al fresco, in a garden bordered by an ancient, open-columned marble wall helped set off the exquisite view of Sorrento's harbor by moonlight. Later they walked and looked, and took time to attend and enjoy a musical show which featured a *gruppo folklorica*. The show included audience participation, and it would have been a wonder only if the attractive couple had not been made a part of the show.

They had loved it!

Near the evening's end they found a tiny intimate bar, quite near the town's central piazza. It was a so-called American bar, except it was designed to look like a well-appointed wine cellar. The name was *Au Temp Perdu*.

The quite beautiful young lady who served as bartender fell madly in love, for the fourth time that day. This time it was with the attractive young man with the absurd name.

The handsome, young guitarist who spent most of his evening serenading the golden-haired girl of incomparable loveliness, who was with the quite ordinary man with the absurd name, fell in love with her, quite naturally. It was only the fifth time that week such an event had occurred. He was a most selective person.

The evening had been so nearly perfect, and the young couple so nearly alone although with people—mellow and content—that they were not at all disturbed when they were joined, quite by accident, of course, by the couple they had met earlier in the day.

"Well," said Alec Gordon. "Fancy running into you again."

"Yes," Elizabeth smiled sweetly. "So very nice. How beautiful you both look. And happy."

Jennie returned the smile. They were nice, she thought. "Please," she said, "join us, won't you?"

"Yes, do," said Henri. He meant it, which surprised him.

And in the magic of the evening's mood, the lovely couple Becquerel accepted the invitation to share a private beach the following day, as well as telling their new friends what they had done about changing names. The Gordons agreed that it was quite a clever thing. Their exchanged glances did not agree with their words.

"It does sound good, doesn't it?" asked Jennie of her husband. "Truly. Just us, the four of us, together in the warm sun on this charming coast. Imagine, a private beach."

Henri smiled at her. "It does, little one. And if that is what you desire, that is what it must be."

"Oh, I do," said Jennie. "I really do." She placed her hand on that of Elizabeth Gordon, now seated across from her.

"Yes," she said. "We will be delighted to join you for a swim tomorrow. Say around noon?"

"That will be perfect," said the woman. The money invested in finding out where the young couple was spending the evening had been well worth the cost. It was fortunate that Sorrento is not a large town.

Elizabeth smiled gently at the girl and placed her free hand over the hand which Jennie was touching. "I am glad," she said, gently. "So very glad."

New York / Rome

Raker and Colt's treatment at the airport in New York, both by government and airport officials, had reintroduced the men to the influence of Mallory Fleming Mitchell.

The giant plane which was designed to carry vast numbers of passengers had been modified to accommodate less than fifty, but in considerable luxury. Today it carried only Raker, Colt, and its crew. It had been airborne within ten minutes of the projected time.

Now, for the two men, came the terrible time, the waiting time.

The airplane screeched its way across the Atlantic on the eight-plus hour trip, with Colt's nerves obviously stretched to their limits. Even Raker was showing slight signs of losing some of his composure.

The only evidence, and it would not have been noticed except by those few who knew him at all well, was the continuing series of radioed inquires he sent, asking for information from the Pan-Global force in Rome which was searching for his daughter. And in the several alcoholic drinks he had taken.

To Colt, it was understandable. What agony the man must be suffering. His daughter, his only child, a planned victim of the intolerable Gordons.

It wouldn't be just a matter of killing. Not with those two . . . Colt couldn't find a suitable word. There wasn't one, he thought. Perhaps it would be best to simply institute a manhunt and intercept the Becquerels, even if they were already with the Gordons. Death would be preferable to the horrors their history said the Gordons would inflict.

Colt put the thought from his mind, and looked at Raker. Studying the man's face—tired, drawn, eyes now closed, a fresh glass of whiskey in his hand—he knew that the decision had to be made not by himself, but by Raker.

"I'm fine, Jimmy boy," said the man softly. It was as though he had read Colt's mind; seen him through closed eyes. In a way that had been the case. It was a gift Colt knew the man had.

The eyes opened. "Just thinking." He tossed the whiskey down. "And don't be worrying about the old man. I'm using the booze only as a mild sedative. That was the last one." There was pain etched on his face.

"Will we make it, Rake?" He knew it was a senseless question. "Or should we—you—think about letting someone else try and help?"

"I know what you're thinking," said Raker, softly. "I've had the same thought." He looked up at Colt. "I can't do it. Not yet. Not while there's still time. They . . ." he meant the Gordons, "won't be making their move until noon or after. Today."

"You seem sure of that," said Colt. "Awfully damned sure."

"I am. I told you before. It's their orders in this deal." From me, he thought. His eyes went flat and lifeless with the knowledge.

"Rake, what is it? What in the hell did you think of?"

"Nothing, Jimmy boy," said Raker tiredly. "Nothing new, that is. Just the misery of it all."

Colt nodded his sympathy. "I can only guess. I can't know, of course." He was quiet a moment. "You know, Rake, I'll do anything possible, anything you ask."

"I know," said Raker gently. Colt meant it, he knew, always

did. It would bring more sorrow when the time came to kill his friend. The man's very presence made that most likely. With the last thought came the sorrow, and far sooner than expected.

"Enough," said Raker. Enough talk. "Let's save it, James." He closed his eyes once again. "I've about given up on dear old Pan-Gee. I think it's up to your Indians now."

"Pytor will have arranged something," said Colt. He wished he believed it.

SORRENTO

As their night out in Sorrento drew near its close, Jennie and Henri accepted when their new friends offered to drive them back to their hotel.

"About noon," said Elizabeth Gordon brightly, as their passengers stepped from the car in front of the Becquerel's hotel. "We'll meet you here. We must come to town, anyway. It will be a delightful day."

The woman stepped from the car to embrace Henri and kiss Jennie lightly on the cheek.

Still glowing from the pleasure the day and evening had brought, Jennie's mood was light. "Oh, yes," she said. "We will be looking forward to it."

Henri put his arm around her. "Yes," he agreed, "we will." He meant it. The man and woman had been fine companions during their evening together.

Elizabeth was still smiling when she sat back down in the Mercedes.

• • •

As he pulled from the hotel's drive the following morning, Alec turned to his sister.

"Their car," he said. "Did you find out?"

"Certainly. Stored. We'll have to move it. After."

"Yes," said Alec. "We'll have the keys then. I'll claim it for them so there will be no attention drawn to it. We can also pay their bill at the time, and move the car to another storage area. We

can be long gone from the country before anyone misses them."
He thought. "We'll have to drop off the man somewhere he'll be
easily found and taken care of. You have the stuff to put him out
with?"

"Of course," said Elizabeth.

Alec looked his apology at her. "Sorry. Of course you would.
It's just that I want to be certain that we don't overstep the Colonel's directive."

"Damn the Colonel!" said Elizabeth. She did not mean that
she, too, wouldn't abide by his directive; it was anger at having to
do so.

"You will be careful?" said Alec.

"Certainly," said the woman. "Don't worry, dear. I know exactly what the body can take. Remember? I'm an expert. And with
that young man—with both of them—that will be quite a lot." Her
smooth brow knitted as she considered her words.

"That's the body, of course. Now the mind? Well, that's a different matter." She brightened.

"But the Colonel didn't say anything about that, did he?"

• • •

"We're approaching." The voice was Raker's, heard as if from a
distance by Colt.

"Huh?"

"I said we're approaching the airport. Only a few minutes. You
slept."

Colt straightened, flexing unused muscles. "Yes," he said. "I
did, didn't I? What time is it?"

"5:27, Rome time."

"We're a little off our ETA, but a good job, all in all, I'd say."
Colt rubbed his eyes. They felt red, and they were. "Yes," he said,
"everything old Mitchell uses has to be pretty good to be kept
around. Like you. And me."

"Well," drawled Raker, "we'll see just how far that power of
his reaches, and just how effective it is at a foreign airport at this
time of day." He considered the weapons he had brought with him.
They had not been even looked for at their departure; none of their
luggage had been examined.

"It'll be effective," said Colt. "Don't doubt that. Not at all."

"I think," said Raker, drawing out the words, "that you're right."

Colt heard a reservation in his voice. "But?"

"But if I were Mitchell, I'd sure as hell straighten out his so-called security bunch over here."

"They're new to this sort of thing," commented Colt. "I get the feeling they're really just bodyguards, more or less."

"Less," said Raker, biting off the word. "They missed Jennie. The time we gave them makes that understandable. They also took the word of some kid about her going to Tivoli for the day, which it now seems certain she didn't."

"When did you learn this?"

"While you slept. They finally checked in. Reluctantly. They were foxed. Gave a kid from the hotel a tip for a bum steer." He held out a cup of coffee for Colt.

"They claim to have scoured the hills for the car. No luck. And that's damned well what they needed. They apparently have little ability. Now we're down to only your Indians."

Colt sipped the cup of coffee as he thought. He felt the airplane bank and dip under them, starting its final approach. One of the two flight attendants who had left the men totally alone since Raker's first, curt wave-off, approached and motioned at their seat belts. Colt handed over his coffee and buckled up.

"They'll deliver," said Colt, hoping he was right. He remembered his earlier fears.

"They'd better," said Raker, buckling his own belt. "It's damned near our last hope before we call out the cavalry. Or maybe better, the Marines."

"It'll work," insisted Colt. He looked away from Raker. He didn't like the look on Raker's face. He thought the pain he saw was fear the man felt for his daughter. He couldn't know it was the hatred Raker felt for himself.

"Any shot at contacting your man before the set time?"

"Very little," said Colt, looking up in surprise. "You know that. You know the disciplined way they work."

Raker wiped a hand tiredly across his face. "I know. I'm just reaching out for that last blade of grass to hang on to."

He was silent for some moments. "Well," he said, finally, "It looks like what we do now is wait." He felt the observation was so patently obvious that it bordered on the profound.

"God, I'm sorry, Rake," said Colt, feeling acute helplessness.

Raker looked at him, face grim. "So am I."

· · ·

Their arrival at not-yet-hurried Leonardo da Vinci airport near Fiumicino demonstrated for yet another time Mitchell's influence. Docile officials, accompanied by a stone-faced PanGlobal representative, hurried them past any custom inspection or even declaration, and directly to the sleek black limousine waiting for them on the taxi strip. The time was not yet 6:00 a.m.

A dark-suited man sat behind the steering wheel, the one who had met them opened and held the door of the car for the men. Only minutes after they had landed they were being waved briskly past security guards and speeding toward Rome.

As the car hummed through the slowly lightening morning, Raker questioned the two PanGlobal men sitting in the front seat. They had introduced themselves as Scattoni and Johnson. Scattoni's English was impeccable and American accented; Johnson's was heavily Italian.

Neither Raker nor Colt wondered why.

As the car sped toward the city, Raker's questions were not polite or yet quite insulting, but rather abrupt and searching. His questioning revealed nothing that would help. "All right," he said, finally. "I suppose you did your best. From this moment on you listen only to my orders."

The men in the front seat exchanged glances.

The driver, the man named Johnson, spoke. "*Il capo*, the boss, he's say you wanna come to office. Is correct?"

"Is correct," said Raker. "Who is your *capo*?"

"Fondi," said the other man. "He is the director of security."

"Very good," said Raker. His voice dismissed the men in the front seat.

"Where is your meet to be?" he asked Colt.

"Near the American Express office."

"How far away are the PanGee offices?"

"Not far. Perhaps five minutes by foot. Longer if we try to drive."

"Good. Maybe our luck is turning. Hell, who knows, maybe your PanGee people will come up with something." He didn't think so. He shifted his body to relieve the pressure he felt from both the weapons he carried. The suit had been tailored to conceal the huge Colt revolver.

"We'll freshen up a bit at the office," he said. "Could use a shower and a change of clothes. No time. We'll probably both be a bit rank by the time this is over. No matter." It was almost as if he was talking to keep from thinking.

It seemed that the fate of his daughter now hung on the friendship between Colt and his KGB friend.

A hell of a note, he thought. Here we are depending on a friend whose job it is to preserve and spread communism at the expense of the capitalistic system. And he will be helping, in a way, the largest capitalistic enterprise of its kind in the world. Very funny indeed. That took some sort of friend.

At the thought, a synaptic chill electrified his body and his skin crawled.

Or was the man really a friend at all?

• • •

Epimenio Fondi was a "man aware." In the renovated and restored building which housed the PanGlobal operations in Italy, everything seemed neat, orderly and opulent. With the exception of Fondi's office. It was a study in disorder. Not the disorder of messiness or carelessness, but rather the disorder of swift decision and unhesitating action. As Raker and Colt entered the office the man nodded from behind his paper-littered desk, a phone in each hand as he barked orders. He nodded a greeting and dipped his head toward nearby chairs in an invitation to sit.

As he finished his conversations his predatory eyes flicked from Colt to Raker and back.

"Signore Raker," he said. "I am Fondi." He had determined the correct man.

"We have been mostly unsuccessful in locating your subjects. The men who brought you here were un-thorough in their efforts. They are not experienced in such covert matters."

"And you are?" asked Raker.

Fondi looked at his questioner, measuring him. "I am," he said.

"And what have you determined?"

Fondi shrugged. His collar was open, tie pulled loose. In only a few hours he would be badly in need of a shave, and his eyes were pink rimmed from fatigue and lack of sleep, but still alert.

He formed two fists, extended his arms in front of him and held the wrists together. "Alas, signore, you have tied my hands. I have learned little. No more than has been communicated to you. I continue to search. If you would allow the use of my government's professional hunters the finding could be facilitated."

"Too dangerous," said Raker. "The ones we seek are quite probably in the company of ones who would stop at nothing to complete their mission."

"And that mission is?" As he asked the question, Fondi's eyes studied Colt. "Assassination," said Raker.

"I see," said Fondi. He switched his eyes from Colt to Raker. "Then we must proceed alone. I consider that I have all means at my disposal working at this time. All tourist facilities are being checked with private resources. Also all road stops. We have two reports of a car being seen, the description of which matches the automobile found—by my operatives—to be driven by our subjects. Those reports are being checked for verification at this time."

"And?"

Fondi shrugged once again. "It would appear that the occupants of neither car are who we seek." He turned to a large map of Italy that was pinned to the cork wall behind his desk.

"I consider that we should focus our attention to the east and south. It seems unlikely that our subjects would come to Rome from the north only to return to the north in a rental car. Agreed?"

Raker nodded. "You are likely right. But it isn't certain. You said focus?"

"I did. To the extent of our capabilities, we look all around."

"Then," said Raker, "it seems there is little to do but wait."

"So I have considered," said Fondi. He flicked his eyes toward Scattoni. "The phones," he said. "Tend them while I take a moment to refresh."

He stood and moved from behind his desk. "If you will excuse me, signores, I will attempt to make myself more presentable. Johnson! Some coffee for the gentlemen. Signore Raker, if you are inclined, please review the steps I have taken on your behalf. Do you have Italian?"

"Some," said Raker.

"My movements are outlined in the papers on my desk. Please feel free. I shall not be long." His bow was almost imperceptible as he left the room.

More from curiosity than hope Raker went to Fondi's desk, seated himself and started to scan the papers.

Only steps down the hallway toward the communications center, Fondi, after washing down an amphetamine tablet with strong coffee, slid a battery-powered electric razor over his face while with his free hand he shuffled through papers. He found what he was looking for and let his eyes study it as he finished shaving. He set the razor on a nearby table, seated himself and looked at the wire photo. He placed a hand over the top of the pictured head. The photograph was of James Colt. With the top of the head covered it was easy to see that the bald, or shaven headed, man in Fondi's outer office was Colt. The glasses the man wore were of no importance in changing his appearance.

Yes, thought Fondi. It is the same man. It will avail him nothing, the pathetic disguise. His fingers searched through other papers and found what he was looking for. He knew the coded message by heart. He only wanted to verify his memory.

Yes, it was true. The man who accompanied the most dangerous Signore Raker was indeed worth 100,000 American dollars.

Dead.

* * *

In the following hour and a half, two reports were received at Sorrento's PanGlobal office which tentatively identified Raker's daughter and her husband; each of the reports proved to be unfounded.

Raker and Fondi had agreed that chances were best the young couple would not have planned to drive too great a distance with the late start they'd made. If they were to be found it would most probably be within a three- or four-hour drive.

"Of course," said Fondi, "we must have information as to their location in order to be there. Is that not true?"

"You're tired," said Raker, "so I'll ignore the foolishness of that observation."

Fondi tried a smile. "Only a simple observation of basic fact, Signore. And you are correct, it was foolish. Perhaps made only to fill the time."

Raker nodded. It was probable that Fondi was experiencing a small sample of the infuriating helplessness which infused himself.

"We have one last hope, aside from you," said Raker. "I think you've done your best, but it shows no promise."

Fondi nodded reluctant agreement.

"Within the next half hour or so we will know if our other source has more information." He held up a hand as Fondi started to speak. "Who or what that source, it must be of no concern to you, but if something is there we will need your complete cooperation."

Fondi bowed a promise.

"If we learn nothing . . ." Raker paused before stating his decision, "Then we will be forced to use all your government contacts. That will be our last resort. Probably a fatal one. Better . . ." His voice stopped. Better than what? Better than his daughter being a captive of the Gordons? Yes, of course—far better.

"Yes," he continued, more for himself than the others. "It will be better than doing nothing, no matter what the outcome." The others were silent. Only Raker knew the entire story, but the desperation filling him could be felt by all.

"I want an airplane ready," he continued. "You have one, of course?" It was not really a question.

"Certainly," said Fondi. "More than one. I shall have one ready."

"And a helicopter?"

Epimenio Fondi paused. He was having a hard time keeping his eyes away from Colt. "Yes," he said, "but no. That is we have one, certainly, but it is being repaired, we await replacement of its rotor." He managed to look embarrassed. "A small collision only two days before now."

"All right," said Raker. "A plane will have to do. I'll want it standing by. And cars, if it turns out that our subjects are nearby."

"Most certainly," said Fondi. In fact the helicopter was in excellent working order but he, Epimenio Fondi, may well need it. He must have time to decide how to facilitate the death of the shaven-headed Colt. One hundred thousand American dollars! And he did not want to share it.

The man Raker, however, he was most dangerous. It was something one knew at once. It would be better to pick the time and place when the other, Colt, was alone. Or, perhaps, perform the function from a safe distance? It was only a matter of time and place to Fondi. He had no doubt that the feat would be accomplished.

"Would you like to be supplied with firearms?" inquired the Italian.

If Raker smiled it was sphinx-like, as though he knew something. "No," he said. "That will not be necessary."

Fondi had a terrible moment during which he felt that perhaps the man was reading his mind. He was relieved when Raker spoke.

"Well, then," he said, rising, "I think it's time we were on our way." He looked at James Colt. "Ready?"

Colt stood up. "Yes." It was the first word he'd uttered since they arrived at the PanGlobal office. His contribution would come later when he made contact, hopefully, with the associate of his KGB friend.

"Shall my men accompany you?" asked Fondi.

"No. We'll handle this alone. Walking will be faster than driving, or at least finding a parking place. You will be here as needed, of course?" Again, it was really an order and not a question.

"Of course." Fondi watched as the men left his office. Yes, he thought. Much better to perform the function when he could have the man Raker away. Most certainly. That would be by far the safer course of action.

• • •

It was not yet 8:30 when Colt and Raker arrived at the Piazza de Spagna.

"I think some food and coffee wouldn't hurt us," said Raker. "How about that little café?" He motioned with his head. "We can see the corner from there most likely."

Colt agreed readily.

The small café was close to the Via Borgognono. From the stand-up area near the front window the men could see the corner where Colt was to receive any information through his KGB contact.

The men were finishing their second crusty rolls and cups of milk-thinned coffee when Raker spoke. "I think there is your man," he said. His eyes were focused past the glass window. Colt followed Raker's gaze. A man of seemingly advanced years was trudging slowly up the street, pushing in front of him a wheeled cart atop which lay a large, folded umbrella. The eyes of the two men followed the figure as he paused at the corner and seemed to start readying himself for the day's business of selling olives and cracked coconut from his cart.

In view of the pressure on Raker and himself, Colt was almost embarrassed when he caught himself wondering, idly and irreverently, just where or how the man would hook up to a source of water which would spray across the coconut pieces soon to be on display.

"He's yours," said Raker.

Colt downed the last sip of his coffee and started for the door. He paused for a moment and turned to face Raker. He held up crossed fingers and shook them in hope.

Raker nodded, face grim, and watched as Colt approached the vendor. It was 8:47.

• • •

"*Buon Giorno*," greeted Colt.

"I am not yet open," said the man.

"Did you pick the coconuts yourself?" asked Colt.

The vendor looked up with interest. "What a foolish question. Coconuts do not grow on my farm."

"Neither do olives," said Colt.

"You think they come from Greece?"

"I think they come from Valencia, like the oranges," said Colt. He never got over feeling foolish when playing the identification game.

The vendor smiled. He felt the same way. "You have good friends," he said. "They submit to you information."

"And?"

"First, I am to ask where you last drank with a certain friend."

"Nathan's."

The man nodded.

"I am told to advise you that the subjects you seek have left Rome for a trip to Sorrento." He gave a description of the car and its license number. "I am told to say that there is no information regarding the exact residence, but there was a reference to a hotel from which the sea could be viewed."

"Anything else?"

"Yes. It is only that there were others interested in the same subject. Two separate teams. One a man and woman; the other of three men. The three did not find the subjects. The man and woman followed as the subjects departed from near the Trevi fountain at 11:17 yesterday morning. The car was a silver Mercedes." He gave Colt the license number.

"Is that all?"

"One more thing. A message. Quite short. 'Now we're even.' You are to know who it is from. Is that comprehendible?"

"That," smiled Colt, "is completely comprehendible. Is there any more?"

"Only that I am now open for business," said the vendor. "Some nice olives? Or perhaps freshly cracked coconut?"

Colt hesitated.

"It is not really fresh," said the man. He winked.

Colt smiled. "Thank you," he said. "I think you've done quite enough for me."

The vendor shrugged and began stacking his cart. Colt didn't bother to stay around to watch and discover how the man obtained water for his fountain.

•••

"Well?" inquired Raker. He kept himself in tight control but his voice was stretched high-wire taut.

Colt told him what he'd learned.

Raker slapped his hands together. What was nearly a smile touched his mouth.

"We've got a chance, Jimmy boy. Thanks to your Indians, we Custers just may have a chance. Back to Fondi on the double! Let's get that damn plane!"

•••

"It is not a long trip," said Fondi. "From the office to there is some two hours, even less if there is no mischance."

"Where can we land near there?" inquired Raker.

"I have been considering," said Fondi. "It will be best to fly the amphibian. You may land on the sea at the harbor. You will be directly downtown." Nearly under the town would have been a better description.

"A man of mine is there now. He will start a search for our subjects, and then greet you with his automobile."

He already had a telephone in his hand. "I will give orders to ready the seaplane now, then I will contact my man on site."

"Have him search the entire area," advised Raker. "Our information says Sorrento, but it may be Amalfi, Ravello, Positano. You know. Check them all, but find our people."

"Do not fear, Signore Raker," said Fondi. "It will all be done. The men will now speed you to your airplane. And good luck." He turned his attention to the telephone.

Raker and Colt followed Scattoni and Johnson from the room. As the door closed behind them, Fondi spoke into the phone.

"Have the helicopter ready. I'll be there momentarily," he said. He replaced the phone for a second and then picked it up again. He waited.

"Fondi here. Have the seaplane almost ready. Your passengers are on their way. They will be there within thirty minutes. I want the plane to be gone when they arrive. It is to arrive for their use one hour from now. Understood?"

He smiled at the answer. "Of course. I know you will have to refuel before your journey. You will be flying to Sorrento. And Paoli, be very cautious—these are very important people, they must arrive safely. Be apologetic about the delay. Be sorry that you were on a trip, but glad I was able to communicate with you and facilitate your return for our good friends. I will make it worth your while."

He hung up, smiling. It was all good. It would work. He would be in Sorrento when the amphibian landed. Now, all that remained was for him to select the correct weapon. That would take only a minute.

He did not check the day's communications from New York, not even the one withdrawing the name of James Travis Colt from the profitable "bonus" list.

• • •

As he had done at least every ten minutes for the past two hours, Raker checked the time on his wristwatch. It was now 10:27 a.m. The cliffs atop which Sorrento perched were now visible through the haze.

The six-passenger amphibian had begun its descent, and the pilot was disconcerted. He had delayed his arrival as instructed by his capo, Epimenio Fondi. He would, of course, do no differently. Fondi was not a man one disobeyed.

The pilot, Paoli Orbinati, however, had not been prepared for the American, the one called Raker. The man was impossible. Did he not realize what could result from such abuse of his machinery? Indeed not! The violent, quite obviously deranged and dangerous American had no soul.

The tachometer had been riding the redline since lift off, and the pressure gauge had been held at an impossibly high level. The plane would likely not be able to function after the trip. And worse, they would arrive at a time earlier than that desired by Fondi. The pilot sighed.

He had no alternative. If Fondi knew the American, he would understand. The force of the man was irresistible. One could sense that great harm might well follow too much hesitation with that one. Perhaps, however, he could make two or three false passes before setting the plane down. It was only a thought. The water was quite smooth except for light swells; and anyway, the American would not accept such events. It had become evident to Paoli that the man was an experienced aviator. He sighed again. I will taxi slowly, he thought. I will have difficulty docking. These were only thoughts. He had no intention of doing anything other than his best.

· · ·

"We told them noon," said Elizabeth Gordon as she and her brother slid into the seat of their car. "I hope we're allowing time."

"Not to worry, sister dear," replied Alec. He frowned. "I do hope we don't have to chase them down, however. I hope they're truly looking forward to a nice day with us."

Elizabeth Gordon smiled wickedly. "Yes. Indeed yes. A perfectly lovely day. And I'm sure they will be waiting. They may have intended to avoid us early on, but I feel that after our quite pleasant time with them last evening that they are looking forward to the day."

"I do hope you're right," said Alec. "I'd not like to have the situation complicated."

Elizabeth reached out a hand to pat her brother patronizingly. "Don't concern yourself, dear. They'll be there. Even if they're not, it will be no trouble buying information which will lead us directly to them." Her expression was unworried.

"Can you think of anything we've forgotten? It might be fun to make a stop and pick up any other little gadgets we might need to entertain our visitors while they shop with us."

Alec Gordon shook his head in admiration. "You are truly a talented one, my dear Queen Bess. Forever devoted to your pleasures.

No, I cannot think that we've forgotten anything. Your little shopping excursion yesterday was most complete—and inventive."

Elizabeth affected a pout. "A shame," she said. "It would be nice to browse while I tried to think up some little applications using everyday, ordinary . . ." she paused, seeking a word.

"Gadgets," said her brother. "I liked your choice of that word."

"Yes, it is good, isn't it? Gadgets. It's just that it would be fun to shop with our young friends along, and them not knowing what was going to come about." She lifted a hand to her lips in thought as she guided their car along the narrow road of the Amalfi drive.

CHAPTER 26

"I don't think the pilot liked you," said Colt to Raker.

The two men were striding quickly across the wide base of the long, concrete pier which jutted out into the bay beneath the town.

"No," agreed Raker, not breaking stride. "I had him pushing that plane pretty hard. And I had the feeling he was stalling. How well, or how much do you know about PanGlobal's operation over here?"

"Only what I have to know about it, and only paper data about Fondi. He was around when I joined PanGlobal. I reviewed his background. He seemed efficient and competent from past actions."

"Uh huh," said Raker, noncommittally. "Well, let's climb up and see if his man is there and if they've spotted Jennie."

The men had approached the long narrow steps which Z'd their way up, hugging the sheer cliff that soared up to the town high above the water below.

"Go on," said Raker. "I want to check our tracks." His eyes turned to survey the boat dock behind them.

Colt started up the steps two at a time. He realized that he would have been surprised if Raker had not taken the time to check behind them. He heard Raker's footsteps at his back and then his voice.

"Looks clear. Didn't think there'd be anyone." Suddenly he sensed danger! He lifted his eyes to look above them and in the same instant his voice came in a shout. "Down!"

With the word he dove forward, slamming into the back of Colt's legs. Both men sprawled on the concrete steps.

Colt swept his eyes to the rail high above them. He saw the

man standing there, stiff and still, his arms, holding something, reaching out and down toward him and Raker. In that instant, he recognized the man was Epimenio Fondi.

At the moment he had shouted, Raker had drawn his long-barreled revolver and fired. Colt thought he heard the soft thud of a bullet striking flesh, just before Raker's weapon fired, its sound hardly louder than the slamming of a door. Colt felt pressure against his side and saw the figure of Fondi lift its hands, saw the black, stick-like object fall from those hands and over the cliff railing. The man sank out of sight.

"Bastard!" came Raker's voice. "Should have suspected. I smelled something. He was out for your scalp, Jimmy boy. He kept looking at you. I put it down to your fast growing scalp. He was out for that, James. He was looking for the reward Mitchell posted." Raker had a hand inside his coat.

"Should have known from those looks." He rose slowly, concealing his own weapon beneath his coat. Colt had forgotten Raker had carried it with him all the way from New York after procuring it from the trunk of the car he had driven out to Colt's safe-house.

"Let's get the hell up and away from here. Look curious and don't stop for anything. "Damn!" He winced as he moved.

"Rake! You hit?" Colt kept moving upward, eyes turned back toward his friend.

"Hit. Not bad. Stuffed it with a handkerchief. Keep moving. Let's get somewhere before anyone spots blood."

Everything had happened so suddenly and was over so quickly that the few people nearby were hardly aware that anything important had occurred. The only others on the steps were a man and woman, still a considerable distance above, who were walking down toward Raker and Colt. They'd been busy watching their footing. To them, it seemed only that one of the two men climbing upward had lost his footing and fallen against the other.

As the men passed the couple, with Raker staying behind and close to Colt, using his body to shield any sight of blood, they nodded politely. The couple had the look of tourists.

Raker smiled. "Rather tricky," he said in German.

The man they were passing stood aside, making room for Raker and Colt. He shook his head slightly, hands palm up in a gesture of noncomprehension.

"Sorry," he said, "but we're Americans." Raker had known.

The man's wife—for Raker had noted that their wedding rings matched—smiled slightly as her husband took her arm protectively. They felt that the words the man had addressed to them must have concerned the stairway. The man held the rail carefully as the couple continued their descent.

As they reached the top, Raker and Colt veered to the right, away from a small crowd that had gathered around the motionless figure of Fondi. Their attention was focused on the body. Blood was not yet visible. The Teflon-coated round fired by Raker, with unerring accuracy, had pierced the man cleanly, leaving minimal visible damage.

Externally.

Below, a few loiterers on the pier had found the rifle that had pitched from Fondi's hands as he died. It didn't matter; Colt and Raker were now out of the area of immediate interest.

"Where are you hit?"

"A graze," replied Raker. "Off a rib and into the lat. Annoying but not incapacitating." He was holding his left arm tightly against his side. "I think I have the bleeding stopped enough until I can take better care of it."

"No chance Fondi really has a man waiting for us here?" Colt knew it was a senseless question.

Raker snorted. "None. You know it. The bastard wanted the loot for himself. No, we're on our own. Let's find a place where I can tend this nick in private, then we'll have to start checking hotels ourselves."

The men had reached the Via Correale and turned right toward the Piazza Tasso. Raker considered that around this, the town's main plaza, they could find a pharmacy where Colt could buy some first aid items with which to tend his wound. A private cubicle in the restroom of some *ristorante* or *trattoria* would suffice.

"I have a friend near here," said Colt, "from the old days. He owns a place just off the Corso Italia."

"Is he safe?"

"I've used his help in the past," replied Colt, "and he's a friend. What's more, he knows the area as well as anyone, and has a certain amount of influence."

"Connections?" Raker was interested.

"None better."

Raker's spirits lifted. "You and your friends may just be the saving of—this thing," he said. He meant of his daughter's life.

"I'll stop and pick up some antiseptic and bandages," said Colt. He saw that his companion's face was drawn and the jaw muscles knotted from clenched teeth.

"Any chance your friend will have them?"

"Maybe. Why gamble?"

"No sense advertising our need," said Raker. "Let's chance it. I can wait."

CHAPTER 27

Their walk was not far. Raker stood silently away as he watched Colt greet his friend, a young-looking man with firm, definite features, alert, searching eyes, and a strong, compact physique that just missed being stocky.

As the two men talked, the eyes of Colt's friend kept switching to Raker. He was, Raker estimated, a good many years older than one's first impression would indicate.

"Martin," said Colt, as he and his friend approached, "I would like you to meet my good friend Francesco Vivanti. He, and his brothers and brothers-in-law, own this fine shopping complex of which this delightful *ristorante* is a part. Francesco, this is my close friend Martin." It seemed to Raker that old-world courtesy was to prevail.

He took the extended hand.

Vivanti smiled broadly, teeth gleaming bright against his olive-toned skin. "Hardly a *ristorante*," he said in excellent English. "A snack bar, American Bar, and a salon lounge only, but I am quite proud of it. That, however, is quite enough of the polite stuff. Let's get you taken care of."

He drew Raker by the arm and led him to the rear of his establishment. "There's a comfortable booth here which will offer some privacy for now. I will obtain necessary . . ." he stopped in midsentence as his eyes flicked toward the two young men behind the long, stainless steel-topped bar some six feet away. "I will bring you some merchandise to look at. We'll examine it in my office."

Raker knew what he meant. "And about my search? Did James mention that?"

"Indeed. I commence that immediately," said Vivanti. "If anyone can obtain information in this area, it is myself." It was said without boasting. "A drink may be in order?" His eyebrows went up expectantly. "I have nearly everything."

"I think that is in order," replied Raker. "Any whiskey will do. A large one. James?"

"Yes. The same."

Vivanti moved away and Colt turned to Raker. "I gave him a quick outline. He has the descriptions of the cars and the name of Becquerel. If they are registered, he will find them."

"You trust him, don't you." It was more observation than question.

"Yes. As much as my associations with you have trained me not trust too much." His face showed concern. "How's the—scratch?"

"Tolerable," said Raker. If he was going to say more, his words were interrupted by a commotion at the front door.

Two uniformed figures had moved rapidly and noisily into the lounge. There was one black and one blue uniform. Colt and Raker exchanged glances. Raker's right hand slid beneath his coat to grasp the butt of his revolver.

The black uniformed man was of the *carabinieri*. His voice came in a rush of crisp Italian. He addressed Francesco Vivanti who was now behind the bar.

"We look for two men. Witnesses to an accident by the cliffs."

The eyes of the uniformed men peered toward the rear. They could see the figures of Colt and Raker but not well enough for identification. Hands on their hips, next to holstered weapons, the men started to walk toward the back.

Raker's hand tightened on the butt of his revolver in anticipation of drawing and firing in one motion.

"You look in the wrong place," said Vivanti. His voice was strong and seemed somehow to carry a warning. "My only customers here at the moment came in with me. We drove from my home. Look elsewhere."

The two uniformed men exchanged glances and stopped in their tracks. They relaxed visibly.

"Very well, Signore Vivanti," said the man in blue. He was of the *polizia*. "Our apologies for disturbing you. It is, in any event, a matter of little importance." The urgency of their entry belied their words.

The men touched hands to their caps and withdrew. The exchange fascinated Raker. Francesco Vivanti was obviously more than he seemed.

At the same time Raker remembered about the various uniforms of law enforcement personnel in Italy. One had to have a color-coded program to tell the players, and to determine the range of authority of each group. For the carabinieri and the polizia to work together spoke of important involvements.

"Now, my friends," said Vivanti, setting glasses of whiskey and of water in front of Colt and Raker. "Cin-cin, and let's get on with our work." His eyes studied Raker's face. "Is there need of a doctor?" he asked.

Raker sipped at his whiskey without mixing it with the water. He had started to shake his head. That would have been macho and stupid.

"The search for the young ones first, then perhaps. A trusted one?"

Innocence exuded from Vivanti. "But of course. I will obtain him."

Raker started to speak.

Vivanti lifted his hand. "After," he said. "After I start the search." He smiled. "Drink. And relax. This is the one place you need have no fear to be. They," and he jerked his head toward the door through which the two uniformed men had just left, "will not be back. You're safe here." His smile was disarming.

Raker studied the man's back as Vivanti moved away from the table. He was grateful for Colt's friendship with such a man. He realized he was still gripping the revolver, and released it with a sense of relief. He reached for the glass in front of him.

• • •

It was a late breakfast for Jennie and Henri Becquerel. They were seated on the room balcony of their hotel, relaxed and glowing, fully rested and content, finishing the last of their coffee. It had been *caffee longo* for the man and *ristretto* for Jennie.

"How," asked Henri, elbows on the table, chin resting on his clasped hands as he eyed his wife, "can such a delicate flower as you drink that terrible asphalt?"

Jennie smiled over the rim of her china cup. "When one drinks coffee, my good man, one should drink coffee. Not that diluted mouthwash you've been sipping."

"At least you had the good sense to settle for a civilized breakfast instead of your barbaric ham and eggs," said her husband. They had brunched on *focaccia* and *marmellata*.

Henri reached out a hand to touch his companion. Their teasing about morning eating habits was a continuing game based on affection.

Jennie sighed, eyes gazing toward the sea and the rocky coastline. "Isn't it beautiful?"

"It is," agreed her husband. "Are you certain you wish to spend the day with outsiders? We could find things to do apart from others. After all, are we not the Don and Dona Quixote?"

Jennie felt a temptation to giggle. She did not. "I think not," she said. "You'd probably only end up jousting with some old Roman ruin or other."

"I was thinking of something more like simply going riding." He eyed Jennie with an assumed look of lechery. He had, after all, named her, on the night before, Rosinante.

"Indeed?" replied Jennie, archly, assuming an air of righteous indignation. "Well, I refuse to be considered a brood mare, for your information, and to be so ridden. I desire to wear my sexiest string swim suit and become an object of desire for the males of the Amalfi coast."

"It's a private beach, my little one," said Henri, "and only to be used by us and the other couple."

"True," agreed Jennie. "But he is rather an attractive man, you know."

"True, I suppose. But then so is his companion."

"All right, my love," said Jennie. "Truce! I much prefer to keep my full favors just for you. But I do like the idea of a soft, gentle day at the seaside with congenial companions. It that all right with you?"

"But certainly," said her husband. "And in that event we must prepare. They said about midday, and that is now approaching."

Jennie stood and walked behind her husband to wrap her arms

around his neck while she nestled her face against his head. "I love you, you know," she said softly.

. . .

Raker's face was grim. The medico called by Vivanti was just finishing his work on Raker's wound. It had been more severe than he'd admitted and less than he'd feared. The *Dottore* Chiricozzi had been rapidly efficient, highly verbal, and had explained every step with, what seemed to Raker, great pleasure.

The object—*il Dottore* never once referred to it as a bullet—had indeed scraped past the middle ribs, probably leaving hairline fractures. Entry, however, had been made in the *signore's* pectoralis major, continued down to cut a path through the anterior serratus, followed the curve of the rib cage, and the "object" had come to rest in the heavy muscle of the signore's extraordinarily developed latissimus dorsi. The signore had been extremely fortunate, for the bracial nerve plexus, the brachial and auxiliary arteries had been narrowly missed, as had the subclavianu vein.

Dottore Chiricozzi finished his work with an injection of antibiotics. The only indication that he had even noticed the many other scars on Raker's body came when, preparing to leave, he recommended that the man should perhaps exercise more caution when climbing the barbed wire fences. Was that not the cause of today's wound? The last question was accompanied by a wink as the knowing *Dottore* closed his bag with a click, bowed politely to first Raker, then Vivanti and Colt, and departed.

"There is no couple with the name of Becquerel registered in any hotel along the entire coast," said Vivanti. He had only been waiting for the departure of the medico. He trusted the man, but had no desire to burden him with information he did not need to know.

"You are sure of the facts? The young couple was coming here?" Raker looked at Colt.

"I am reasonably certain our information is correct," he said.

"We will continue to search," said Vivanti. "We will check on anyone remotely answering the limited description you have given us."

It pained Raker that he did not know his daughter well enough to even offer a physical description past that obtained by Colt from the PanGlobal computers, or the few comments made by Arlette Cavour, as that woman told him once a year of how his daughter was growing.

Raker was silent as he continued to button his shirt.

"My associates will continue to scour. We particularly look for the cars. Do not fear. We will find them."

"I appreciate your efforts," said Raker. Time is running out, he thought.

James Colt looked at the man. He had never seen such pain on Raker's face. It was not from physical hurt.

"Please continue," said Raker to Vivanti. "Please find them."

It was the first time, Colt considered, that he had ever heard Raker say "please."

• • •

"Why are you parking here?" asked Alec Cordon.

Elizabeth Gordon looked at her brother slyly. "Foolish boy. We certainly don't want to be seen picking up our prey at their hotel in our own car which can be so easily identified, now do we?"

Dawning awareness showed on the man's face. His sister had parked their distinctive Mercedes at the lot of the *stazonia ferroviaria.*

"So clever of you," said Alec. "You do think of everything, don't you?"

"I hope so," said Elizabeth, almost demurely. "I do hope so. You know this is a really rare opportunity." She tucked her arm in the bend of her brother's elbow as they walked, looking for a taxi. "We actually have carte blanche, with expenses paid and wonderful subjects to work on."

Alec felt her body shiver in anticipation.

"Carte blanche with the girl," he corrected. "Her husband is protected."

"Oh, all right," pouted Elizabeth. "As we wish with the girl, moderation with the man. But that leaves a lot of leeway. He looks sturdy. We'll find out, won't we?"

"With caution, yes," agreed her twin. "With caution." Damn

Raker, he thought. Even from thousands of miles away he still feared the man. He would have to watch Elizabeth carefully. She did get so carried away with her fun.

Each of the twins was silent with their own thoughts as they found a taxi and gave the driver their destination.

"We'll be just in time," said Alec. "It's almost noon." Elizabeth didn't hear him. In her mind she was listening to the moans and screams of the young Becquerels.

· · ·

Francesco Vivanti slapped the telephone down excitedly. "We have them! We have the location." Raker and Colt were on their feet, alert with anticipation.

"Two of my people," said Vivanti, "they report a young couple fitting the age group and driving such a car as we seek, registered at the Ambasciatori under the name of Quixote. That foolish and sentimental Spanish knight. A game they play, perhaps?"

"Who knows?" said Raker. Certainly not himself, he thought. Color returned to his face. "Have you a car?"

"Certainly," replied Vivanti. The keys were already in his hand. "I will lead you. It is only next door. Do you wish assistance?"

"No!" The word burst from his mouth, then his voice softened. "It will be safer for me alone." The men were already moving for the exit of Vivanti's lounge.

"And me," said Colt firmly.

Raker stopped. He looked at Colt from over his shoulder. "Yes," he said after only a second's pause. "And you." He started for the door once again. "Let's get there. Now. How far is it?"

"Quite close," said Vivanti. They reached the street, and Vivanti pointed toward a bright red Ferrari parked in a no-parking zone in front of an official building just across from his shopping complex. "Five, ten minutes at the most." He pointed an arm. "There. On the coast road. You will see it. It is flamingo pink. You cannot miss it."

He stood quietly, watching the car as it sped down the Corso Italia in the direction he had pointed. He didn't know everything, in fact, only a little. He did know it was a matter of life—but not, he hoped, of death.

•••

It was just before noon when the taxi bearing the Gordons turned into the drive of the Becquerel's hotel. Instructing the driver to wait, insuring his cooperation with half of a torn 50,000 lira note, Elizabeth and Alec entered the opulent lobby of the Ambasciatori. They had taken only a few steps inside the heavily wooded and avocado-colored-tile lobby when they saw the Becquerels stepping from the elevator. The girl carried a large nylon beach bag.

Elizabeth, followed closely by her twin brother, hurried forward.

"How radiant you look," she exclaimed, taking the younger woman's hands in hers and leaning forward to kiss her on the cheek. "And you, too," she added, smiling at Henri.

The men shook hands as Elizabeth took Jennie by the arm and gently urged her toward the door they had just entered.

"We've been wandering the town," she continued, "and found ourselves farther from where we parked than we'd anticipated. So we grabbed a cab, and it's now waiting for us."

"Then, by all means," said Jennie, "dismiss him. We'll simply take our car."

"Not at all," protested Elizabeth. "We'll have to pick up our car at any rate. We'll just have the driver take us back to where we parked." Her smile was bright and cheery.

The Gordons, in selecting a taxi, had walked past the small, fuel-efficient cabs and selected one large enough to accommodate the foursome comfortably. They had just arranged themselves in their seats when Jennie spoke.

"Oh, no," she said, her voice tinged with exasperation. "My lotion!" She looked at Elizabeth, expecting understanding. "I burn so easily," she said. "It's a nuisance, but I do have to protect my hide."

She opened the door of the taxi and swiveled in the seat to reach her feet out toward the ground. "It won't take a minute."

Alec turned his head to look at his sister. Elizabeth's eyes were narrow with annoyance.

Oh, well, thought Alec. He sighed. What difference would a few minutes make?

• • •

The red Ferrari raced along the narrow road cut into the cliffs high above the sea. Colt, his eyes intent on the winding pavement, guided the vehicle smoothly through and around the midday traffic.

"It's just ahead," he said, his eyes flicking toward Raker who was seated beside him. "Holding up?"

"No sweat. A little stiff, but I can function." Raker's brows knitted. "The Gordons have to be somewhere around. When we reach the hotel we'll have to play it by ear. You look for Jennie, I'll take care of the Gordons."

"Right. You'll know them?"

"Of course. You just look out for Jennie."

"How will I recognize her?"

Raker was silent.

"How?"

"I don't know," said Raker. "Damn it, James, I simply don't know." His voice turned vicious. "I don't fucking know what my own daughter looks like." Self-accusation was violently obvious.

"Surely you've had pictures. Something."

"No. Nothing. Didn't want them. Too raw a spot." Raker was silent a moment. "Arlette Cavour said she's lovely and blonde. That's it. It doesn't narrow it much, does it?"

"Some," said Colt. He glanced at Raker. "We'll find them, Rake."

"We have to. At least we can find their room. Damned silly stunt, changing names. You get to them. The main thing is that I get to the Gordons."

Colt remained silent as· the car neared the turn into the grounds of the hotel.

• • •

Jennie still had her hand on the taxi door when Elizabeth Gordon reached out to take her wrist gently.

"Don't be foolish," she purred. 'Look at this English-bred complexion of mine. I dare say it's even more vulnerable than your own to old Sol. Why, I suppose I have nearly every sunscreen that's made laying about somewhere. You certainly need have no fear about that."

She exerted a gentle pull on the girls arm. "No need for you to make a trip." Her tug became insistent. "Come on, now," she said. "Let's be getting along. We don't want to lose any time at our lovely strand."

Jennie hesitated for a moment then slid back into the seat.

The driver started the ignition and the taxi pulled out, merging into traffic on its way along the Amalfi drive. Behind it, a sleek, red Ferrari turned into the roadway from which the taxi had just rolled.

As Colt pulled the car to a stop, Raker, eyes sweeping their surroundings, said softly, "Follow my lead. If there aren't any likely prospects in the lobby, or if the Gordons aren't in evidence, we'll make for the room. If I see the Gordons I'll head for them. You keep on the room and don't let those kids out of your sight. Keep them in the room. I can handle the others."

That, he knew, was a certainty. The moment he could speak to them, though his appearance was quite different from what they knew, it would stop them until he could rescind his orders. For the first and only time he was grateful for the terrible twins' perversion. Ordinary assassins would simply have killed the girl as soon as possible and been on their way. The knowledge that the Gordons would go to any lengths to spend hours practicing their savage rites on their victim gave him hope. There was—had to be—hope.

"You look for someone, signore?" It was a bellboy.

Raker forced a smile. "Indeed," he said. "I look for the young couple who registered yesterday." He made his smile friendlier as he told the young man the room number and referred to the foolish name the couple had so playfully chosen. His hand proffered a banknote of large denomination.

The bill disappeared, and the bellboy's smile matched Raker's.

"The couple of which you speak, *signore*, they have only just now departed. Friends met them only moments ago."

Raker cursed their luck. The shock was equivalent to a physical blow.

"Now? Just now? They left together?"

"They did, signore." The young man saw that his news had not been gladly accepted. "Is something wrong?"

"No. No, of course not. I'd hoped to find them here. Can you tell me which way they went when they left? Or the car they took?"

The bellboy widened doleful eyes. "Alas, no, *signore*. I was engaged at the time. I only noticed at all because of the so attractive ladies. I did not see them after they walked out the doors."

Raker whirled, teeth clamped tightly shut. He snapped his fingers loudly. Colt, who had been watching the conversation, advanced quickly.

"Gone! We're only moments late." Raker's voice was cinders-under-shovel rough. "We regroup."

"How?"

"Back to your friend Francesco. Is there any way he can get out an alert on the car?"

"Certainly," said Colt. "But isn't it time now to call out the law?"

"The worst time," growled Raker. "They have the kids. It would be murder. Now we must find the car, and let me take it from there. Believe me, James, it's the only way."

"You know the score. Let's be hooking it, then."

They did.

• • •

The taxi carrying the Becquerels and the Gordons pulled up near the *stazione* and its occupants exited. Alec paid the driver a carefully calculated amount which would please the man without making his passengers particularly memorable. It was an action taken in vain. Gordon did not take into account the Italian appreciation for feminine beauty. The picture of the foursome, or rather the two women, was indelibly etched in the man's memory.

As the two couples walked toward the Gordon's car their talk was animated and breezy, sprinkled with light-hearted laughter. Elizabeth Gordon was especially gay. It was, after all, going to be a simply marvelous day.

• • •

For Raker, miles away, the minutes crawled by like seasons. Both he and Colt felt the despair of helpless futility. It all lay, now, in the hands of Francesco Vivanti and his connections.

As the two men sat, silent and solemn, listening to Vivanti speaking instructions into the telephone, Raker felt drained of hope. It was over. He had failed. His face hardened. He would not fail entirely. Earlier, he had sought vengeance for Mitchell's betrayal of Laughlin. That had been nothing compared to the actions that he would now take. Now, it would be everyone. Everyone and everything. His strike force was still intact, and now there was nothing to stop him.

First it would be the Gordons, and then everyone else he could reach. The world would pay for the loss of his daughter.

The decision gave him no satisfaction even as he thought of the fury he would unleash. There was no price to be paid that could stop him. Only the safe return of his daughter. For that, and only that, would he give up his vendetta.

• • •

"We have news. They took a taxi from the hotel to their car parked on Aranci, and drove to meet the coast road beginning the Amalfi Drive. The cab driver returned, heard of my interest, and called."

"And they are now . . . ?"

Vivanti's smile faded. "At the moment we know not exactly, but somewhere on the coast road. It should be enough. My watchers had been alerted for many minutes even before they drove away. They will be found."

"Will be? No, they *must be*, and soon." He turned to Colt. "Let's hit the road, James." To Vivanti: "Can we check along the road with your people to see if they've been spotted?"

"But of course. I will this moment send notification. My car is known. You will be flagged and given information as you drive. Go now. I will call."

He was on the phone before Raker and Colt were out of the office. It mattered not that new laws had given the Italian police the right to tap phones. He was Vivanti.

GORDONS / BECQUERELS

"Well," said Elizabeth Gordon, face flushed with pleasure, "here we are. Isn't it beautiful?"

"Breathtaking," agreed Jennie Becquerel, nee Raker.

The drive had not covered more than fifteen miles, but the winding, narrow road coupled with the creeping traffic and the roadblock that had been set up to look for two witnesses to an accident back in Sorrento, had required more than forty minutes to navigate.

Elizabeth Gordon had allowed her brother to drive. She wanted the opportunity to sit in the back with Jennie and, as she had said, become better acquainted. At the roadblock a small pistol had been held, ready to fire, if there had been complications. There had not. The foursome had been waved through without trouble.

Alec turned the car off to the right of the coast road and guided it down a moderately steep driveway, onto the roof of the house which was built into the nearly perpendicular mountainside. It had been designed to serve as the villa's parking lot.

The foursome got out of the car and stood facing the sea, allowing their eyes to feast on the beauty of the coast. Far below, through the shrubbery and scattered trees, the small half-moon of volcanic sand beach was being lapped by blue-green water.

"Magnificent," said Henri Becquerel, "truly magnificent. It is so much different knowing this will be our secluded property for a while, and not just an overused, overpopulated tourist beach, overrun by loud people overstuffed into ill-fitting swimsuits.

Alec Gordon laughed. "Indeed. But I think I am safe in observing that neither of our lovely companions need be included in that category."

Henri let his eyes sweep over both Jennie and Elizabeth Gordon. "You are most probably right," he said, hoping there was a leer in his voice. "But shouldn't we really reserve judgment until we see how they fill their costumes?"

"Agreed," said Alec, slapping Henri lightly on the shoulder.

"Men!" sighed Jennie.

"Ignore the beasts," said Elizabeth Gordon. "Now let's not waste one precious moment of this day. Let's get downstairs and get to work."

"Work?" inquired Henri.

- • • •

"Your man Vivanti is thorough and efficient," said Raker. "I'll be damned surprised if he hasn't given those instructions."

Colt nodded eyes on the road. "You're right, he's efficient. But remember, we're at least thirty minutes behind."

"I know," said Raker. "And that's too much. Too goddam much." The Ferrari snarled its way past a crawling truck which was blocking their way.

AT THE CLIFF HOUSE

The entrance to the villa, or cliff house as Jennie thought of it, was reached by a curving iron staircase leading down to the spacious balcony that stretched across the entire back of the house.

Alec Gordon unlocked a heavy, wrought iron gate which guarded access to the balcony and stood aside. Through ingenious engineering, the balcony jutted out to hang over the beach some distance below. The house nestled neatly into the rocky cliff. Anyone so inclined, and with nerve enough, skill enough, and a pair of legs strong enough, would be able to dive from the balcony into the sea below.

"I've never done it," said Alec Gordon who had been watching Henri Becquerel's interested face. "But the shallows drop off quite abruptly, and I expect the water is deep enough to dive into if one is really expert."

Henri laughed. "But no, thank you. I desire to remain unbroken." Jennie, standing at his side, looked at the view with wide eyes.

"It is truly exquisite," she said, turning toward Elizabeth who had lingered behind to relock the iron gate.

"Yes," agreed the woman. "It is, isn't it?"

"How did you ever find something so marvelous?" Jennie turned to her husband. "It is so much nicer than even the hotel."

Elizabeth Gordon, eyes shining bright, put a hand on the girl's shoulder. "Not to worry," she said. "It's now as much yours as ours."

She led the way to the glass-covered rear of the balcony and slid open a door. "Do come in. But watch your step."

Jennie and Henri stepped through the door, looking for the reason for Elizabeth's last words.

"There. In the middle of the room. Seems as though someone has planted bolts of some sort in the lovely wooden floor."

The eyes of the Becquerel's followed the pointing finger of the woman. They saw the eye-bolts screwed into the floor. There were two sets, each spaced two to three feet apart. Each pair was some eight feet from, and facing, each other.

"And the beams overhead, too," smiled Elizabeth Gordon.

The couple raised their eyes and saw hooks set into the beamed ceiling, one hook directly above and between each pair of floor bolts. Ropes were strung through the overhead hooks and stretched toward the far wall where they were secured to still other hooks.

"What in the worl . . . ?" started Jennie, turning toward Elizabeth Gordon.

Her eyes widened in shock as Alec Gordon moved from behind his sister. His hand held a sleekly modern, efficient looking, small automatic pistol. It was a .32 caliber, Bernardelli, Model 80, capable of firing eight rounds without being reloaded.

"You wonder just what in the world they are for." Elizabeth Gordon finished the girl's question. Her voice was a gentle purr. "Well, my lovely dears, we are now going to demonstrate to you just what in the world they are for."

SORRENTO HIGHWAY

Raker's mind was speeding as furiously as the Ferrari. He refused to consider exactly what peril, or even condition, his daughter might be in when they found her. To his mind there was no question that they would find her. Not now. They were too close. It was how best to handle the situation that concerned him.

For certain, he was going to kill the Gordons. That had been decided long before. Only the when, where and how remained to be settled.

He knew that the pair would take as long as they could to kill his daughter. The damage they would most certainly do in the process was a terrifying prospect. He knew that he could stop their actions if he could get to them without frightening them into killing the girl. The last was a horrible possibility, but he could probably overcome it. The problem was James Colt.

If he identified himself to the Gordons in Colt's presence, the man would know at once that Raker was their control. That would be the end of any chance Raker would have to reunite with his daughter. Possibly the end of Raker. That he could not chance, so Colt would have to die.

If the girl was already dead, even seriously or permanently injured, nothing would matter. He would simply destroy everyone and everything he could reach. If she were alive and reasonably well, he would prefer not to harm Colt.

He thought. A possible answer entered his mind. His name to the Gordons was currently Campbell. That would be the name he would use to stop them.

"When we find their location," he told Colt, "I'll approach them alone," he said. "Their control is known as Campbell. The man is the same as the Maguire girl knew as Coleman. If I can hold their attention long enough to get close, I, or both of us, can take them out before they know I've misled them." It sounded weak even to Raker.

"You know a lot, Rake, it seems. How did you miss on your daughter?"

"Wasn't looking," said Raker. "Studying the terrorists, not the victims."

Colt nodded. "I see. That would be your way." The tone expressed neither approval nor disapproval.

Raker studied his face, looking for further reactions.

"What in the hell?" blurted Colt suddenly.

Raker's eyes swung to the front of the car. He saw, in the near distance, the flash of different colored uniforms and the display of men, with automatic weapons, weaving about the line of cars stopped on the road ahead of them.

"A roadblock," he snapped. "A God damned roadblock."

Colt's foot lifted from the accelerator as he pumped the brakes gently, slowing the car. His eyes flicked toward Raker.

"Us? Are they looking for us?"

"Probably," said Raker. His eyes narrowed, mind reviewing options. "What now? We can't outshoot them."

"Hang cool for a moment, Jimmy boy. Maybe it'll work in everyone's favor. Look for that damned Mercedes. Maybe they were caught in the roadblock." Hope was evident in his voice.

Disappointment flowed through him as they came to a stop

behind the last car in line. The Mercedes was not in the row of stopped cars. Two of the uniformed officers were walking toward their own car, automatic weapons across their arms.

Raker eyed the disposition of the other armed men ahead of them, and the traffic on the road ahead. His hand tightened on the weapon stuck in his belt under his coat.

"Get ready, James. When I take these two, fire this machine through there. There's room if you'll use part of the uphill slope. We'll loose a little metal on the way, but should get by. Then drive like hell."

Colt sighed. For Raker he'd try it. "We'll never make it, Rake. Absolutely no way. How about Jennie?"

"She's gone if we don't try," said Raker. "She'll be a long time dying, and in a terrible way."

Colt's left hand gripped the steering wheel, his other on the gear shift knob. One foot held the clutch to the floor, the other poised over the accelerator.

There is, he thought, no other choice. He waited for Raker to draw his weapon—or weapons.

• • •

"Oh, come now, Alec," said Elizabeth Gordon derisively. "You can do better than that. Put a little muscle into it."

Her brother, pulling on the end of a rope, paused a moment in his efforts and drew a deep breath. "Muscle, indeed," he panted. "This sod is heavier than he looks."

He lifted his shoulders in an effort to unlimber them and, drawing a deep breath, pulled fiercely on the rope. "There," he said, securing the end of the rope to the large bolt set into the wall, "how's that?"

Elizabeth Gordon put her hands on the chest of Henri Becquerel who was stretched in front of her, arms secured over his head, legs spread wide apart, and pushed. There was little give.

She smiled at her brother. "That," she said, "is jolly fine." She slid her tongue across her lips. "Now, the fun begins."

Alec joined her, breathing heavily. "Yes," he agreed. "Now begins the fun. Do you want to start with her, or with him?"

Elizabeth surveyed Henri for a moment then turned to face Jennie whose body hung from the beam in the same manner as that of her husband who faced her. She reached out a hand to pat the girl's cheek. "Oh, I wouldn't want to deprive you, brother dear. I'll start with the man. You can have the girl. For now." She lifted a hand and held a slim, pointed knife in front of the girl's frightened face.

"You see, little one," she whispered, "it's going to be a long and delicious session. And a good part of the pleasure is in the peeling." Her smile was evil. "The first peeling will be confined to only those clothes protecting that tender flesh. But later . . . ." She let the threat hang ominously.

She turned and approached Henri. The knife point reached out and slid into the buttoned front of his shirt. "I'll try," she said, sweetly, "not to be too careless while I do this." She fluttered eyelashes at the helpless man. Her hand moved the knife smoothly and expertly, and suddenly the buttons of the shirt were severed, fabric gapping open.

"Do be careful," admonished her brother. "Remember, he is . . ."

"I know," interrupted Elizabeth, voice angry. "Your precious Colonel. I'll tend to this. You just get on with your own peeling." Her eyes were fastened on the skin of Henri Becquerel's exposed chest. She lifted the knife once again.

Alec stood in front of Jennie and reached a hand into his pocket. He withdrew a folded knife which clicked open to expose a length of shining blade at the touch of a button. As he held it forward, Jennie tried to pull her tightly stretched body away from the sharp point. She couldn't move more than a fraction of an inch.

Alec smiled. "This lovely lovely is really touchy," he said over his shoulder. "I think I'll just start here," he continued, sliding the knife forward, "on the seams." The knife touched the girl's side just under her stretched arms. It moved! It sliced easily into the cloth of her blouse.

CHAPTER 28

FINALE

As the uniformed policemen approached the driver's side of the car, Raker prepared to pull the pistol and fire in the same instant. Complete surprise was their only hope. He knew, instinctively, that it would be a futile effort, but he had to try.

"When I move!" he said to Colt. "Get ready." His hand started to move.

"Please, *signores*, allow me to escort you around the automobiles we are checking." The face above the black uniform was smiling. It was one of the two men who had burst in on them earlier only to be admonished by Vivanti.

"I recognize Signore Vivanti's automobile." the man continued. "We have heard of your chase." His eyes looked furtively pleased. "Off the record, of course."

Both Raker and Colt sagged with relief. Vivanti's influence extended farther than even Colt had anticipated.

"The car Signore Vivanti has indicated you seek has passed through our checkpoint. Our instruct . . . ." He paused as he caught himself. "It was suggested that we not interfere with its passage."

"And its passengers?" queried Raker. His voice was strained.

"Quite happy, evidently. Two youngish couples. Quite animated and full of laughter."

"How long ago did they pass?" asked Raker.

The man shrugged. "An hour, less, more." At Raker's obvious displeasure the man frowned. "More nearly forty-five minutes," he said. He had not known it was important.

"Any indication of their destination?" Raker forced the urgency out of his voice. The question was wasted, he knew.

"But of course, Signore." The black uniformed figure shifted his automatic weapon to the curve of one arm and extended the other.

"Only down the road three or possibly five kilometers." His eyes looked knowing.

"My companion was driving to join us and saw them departing from their car parked atop a hillside house just off the road." He rolled his eyes. "Two such lovely ladies are not likely to escape the attention of a man who appreciates beauty, is it not true?"

Adrenalin flowed through Raker. His spirits rose. "It is certainly true," he said, gravely.

Knowing the Gordons, he estimated that they would draw out their operation quite slowly. The very idea of performing their atrocities practically under the noses of the police would heighten their excitement. It could, however, also amplify the early violence of their torture. Still, there was hope. Minutes were important, but it was now possible to spare seconds. He forced himself to calmness.

"You have been most efficient. Your valuable help is most appreciated."

"*Buono*," smiled the man. "It would be beneficial if you would so notify the Signore Vivanti."

"You can count on that. How do we get past that traffic jam ahead?"

The policeman became pointedly officious. "You simply follow me, I shall clear your way."

Colt couldn't resist a sudden urge. "Tell me," he said, "have you found the men that you yourself have been seeking?"

The policeman turned eyes, grown suddenly wary, back toward the car. "No," he said. "I've not located them. I think we shall not." He turned slightly to let both men see his face, and to let them know he knew. "But we shall continue to try." He paused. "Please, do not forget to so inform the Signore that we were helpful. And now, *avanti*!"

Colt steered the car through the path being cleared by the friendly cop. It took longer than he wished it would.

• • •

Elizabeth paused from the physical exertions she so dearly loved. She stood naked and gleaming with perspiration. She held leather straps in her hands that had been split for most of their length into four narrow strips, each strip knotted in several places along its length.

"They are truly a delight, aren't they?" The question was directed at Alec. "Truly quite strong young people. Many would have been gone by now."

"Yes," agreed Alec, face flushed and damp. He held a broad leather strap, not split as his sister's was. "I only wish we could have the drapes and windows open. It seems such a waste, not having that lovely view."

"Foolish boy," chided his sister. "The loveliest view is in here. And anyway, it is delightful enough to know that we are having such fun with the law practically breathing on us." In fact they were some miles away. "It would be stupid to let the sweet sounds we've been eliciting from our guests attract outside attention."

She turned slightly toward her brother and motioned, first at Henri and then Jennie. The two, tied facing each other, sagged as much as their tightly stretched bodies would allow. The flesh of both the man and the girl were crisscrossed with bright, glowing pink welts from their ankles, across their legs and torsos, all the way up their arms. On both front and back.

Elizabeth and Alec had, with professional and practiced expertise, avoided breaking the skin as they had whipped the two nude bodies with deliberately timed and carefully aimed lashes.

Elizabeth reached out a hand to slide it across the chest of Henri, and then down farther. Her fingers found what they searched for and tightened their grip. She squeezed and twisted. Her efforts drew a short, sharp gasp from the man, followed by guttural groans. The sounds delighted her. She released her grip.

"He is so responsive," approved the woman. "But I think you've been a bit too gentle with your little toy there." She moved toward the bound girl. "You are simply wonderful at inflicting agony on men, Alec dear, but I'm afraid it takes a woman to know just how to draw out that sweet song." She reached up to grasp Jennie's hair and pull her head up. The girl looked at her from wide, glazed, hurting eyes.

Elizabeth Gordon smiled sweetly. "Come now, my dear. This has only been a little warm-up. A little tenderizing, one might say."

She dropped the belt to the floor and reached out her strong hands toward the stretched girl's breasts, the sharp pointed nails ready to grip.

As her fingers touched flesh she spoke across her shoulder, her eyes on her subject. "Be a good lad, Alec, and tend to our boy there. I'm sure he feels terribly left out."

A sharp cry was torn from Jennie's throat, and her body jerked desperately as agonizing pain flashed from her nipples to envelop her entire body.

"Perhaps you could give him a nice tattoo with that soldering iron I thought to purchase. Nothing fancy, mind you. Just something simple like his dear little wife's name etched across that lean, flat stomach."

"Nice thought," said Alec. He moved to the table where the twins had carefully laid out their "gadgets."

"Good boy," said Elizabeth, increasing the pressure of her strong fingers and twisting the flesh of the tied girl. She had to raise her voice to be heard over the sounds being made by Jennie.

"Just one thing, my darling sister, would you mind not sending that beautiful little plaything over the edge for a bit? I'd like to have a poke at that while she's still conscious and relatively undamaged, don't you know?" Elizabeth laughed throatily. Her eyes dropped to the aggressive erection which reared between her brother's legs, an angry red, lifting and falling with his heartbeats.

"Of course, darling. I've really only just started. And I do know just how excited you get seeing such a lovely creature teased. I'll be careful."

She turned her eyes back to Jennie's tormented features. The girl's head was shaking from side to side, her mouth open, gasping for breath, eyes squeezed tightly shut against the pain. Elizabeth Gordon's fingers were incredibly experienced instruments for creating exquisite pain.

"I'm turning loose, now," she told the tied girl, speaking softly. "And you'll not believe the results." She started to relax her fierce grip.

"It's truly amazing, the flash that can stab when such stimulus is withdrawn," she told Jennie. She opened her hands and fingers quickly. Jennie's body bounced against her bonds, muscles quivering as a cry rose in her throat.

"Just rest there a moment," she cooed at the girl. She knew Jennie was on the edge of unconsciousness. "I'll just rig up this other little idea of mine and see how you like it. It's a first, but I think you'll find that it will keep you nice and warm while I," and her eyes darted across to fondle her brother's body, "take care of other things."

She moved across the room to the table and her hand lifted a string of decorative lights much like those used to illuminate Christmas trees. She attached an extension cord to the string and approached the hanging girl.

"Now this is novel," she said. "We don't have an electric blanket or the like, but I certainly don't want you to catch your death of cold." She chuckled. "Or even cool off too much." She held up the lights and slapped Jennie lightly on the face, forcing her to open her eyes. "Yes, I think these will do the trick."

Using adhesive tape to secure the cords as she desired, Elizabeth lovingly draped the string of lights around the girl's immobile figure, making certain that each of the bulbs was touching carefully selected points on her body. Finished, she stepped back to admire her handiwork.

"Lovely," she said, "simply lovely. Now, when I plug those in, they will warm you up quite nicely." She reached out a hand and gently patted the girl.

Turning, she went to the wall and started to plug in the extension cord. She paused. It could wait. She noted that her brother was only now satisfied that the soldering iron he was preparing to use on Henri Becquerel was hot enough. That would be fun to watch—and hear.

As Alec stretched out his hand, ready to apply its tip to the skin of the bound man, Elizabeth Gordon moved near him and knelt on the floor at his feet. She reached out her hands and slid them lovingly up her brother's legs, then leaned forward to press her face against him. Her lips moved lightly across his flesh, up and open and seeking.

For the first time, Henri Becquerel screamed.

Alec Gordon was moaning in pleasure. It did not stop the movement of his hand which held the hot iron.

• • •

The long hood of the red Ferrari, now moving more slowly, nosed easily around the curves of the road, the eyes of Colt and Raker sweeping the edge above the gulf of Salerno. They searched for the site described to them at the roadblock. The only traffic on the road was that approaching them.

"You said your man Vivanti had influence," said Raker, not turning his head. "You didn't say that he ran this part of the country."

"He's obviously come a long way," replied Colt dryly.

"Slow!" Raker's voice was sharp. "There! Ahead. The Mercedes. On that white rooftop." He felt electrified, his wound nearly forgotten.

"I see it. It's it, by God. It's it, Rake. Where do we stop?" Colt's voice sounded his excitement.

"Cut the motor. Coast in to the turn off." Raker tried moving his arm on the wounded side. It worked somewhat clumsily but with acceptable discomfort. He would worry about it later. It seemed there might be a later.

"Silence, James. Complete silence until I can scout the situation."

The roof, estimated Raker, would be thick and sturdy, constructed to bear the weight of cars. There would be little chance of their footsteps being heard down below, especially as softly as both he and Colt could move.

"Let's go."

"Careful," came Raker's voice. His voice was soft, almost breathless as he spoke. It was not a sibilant whisper which would carry, but simply low and gentle, meant to be heard for only the two or three feet needed.

"Watch for alarms." He reasoned that a house along the coast, probably left empty for part of the year, would most likely have an alarm system. One probably loud at the site; the other delivered silently to some central protection service.

Colt joined Raker in carefully surveying the rooftop. It appeared that the only entrance would be down the metal stairwell. It was completely covered with a heavy, steel mesh, all the way down to the landing which was suspended in space at the end of the balcony. The roof-high iron gate and adjacent grill-work effectively shut off access to the balcony. It was damn well designed.

Raker suddenly held up a hand in warning. He pointed toward the edge of the roof.

Colt's eyes followed Raker's finger, searching the edge for several moments before he saw what the man had found. A fine, thin, nearly invisible filament was stretched, taut and flush, against the roof molding perhaps a quarter of an inch below the top edge.

"Trip alarm," breathed Raker. "Thin enough the wind won't bother it, but delicate enough that the least pressure will break the safety and trip the alarm." His eyes studied the filament, seeking and memorizing the location of the tiny clips holding it in place. They appeared to be simply nail heads. Raker shook his head.

"Try the gate, James. But soft."

The warning was unnecessary. Colt slipped noiselessly across the roof to lie near the edge. He reached down and exerted gentle pressure on the top of the gate. It was securely locked. He raised himself, turned toward Raker's expectant eyes, and shook his head.

Raker nodded and motioned for Colt to join him.

"Didn't expect more," he said. "Now, lad, gently, and I do mean gently, put your fingertip exactly here." He indicated a spot halfway between two tiny nail heads.

Colt, carefully and expertly, did as instructed.

"Good. Hold it." Raker extended his hand which held his open pocket knife. "It's alive at the end on your side," he said. He cut the line. Colt had been holding his breath. There was no alarm.

"Hang tight until I secure this end," breathed Raker. His hands worked. He lifted them.

"Done. It's secure. You can let go."

Colt breathed.

"And now?"

"Over the edge," said Raker. "There's lots of plate glass on the back. Could see it as I leaned over. Drapes are pulled, however. We'll not be seen."

Colt showed his surprise. "You're out of your mind! The overhang is two feet or more past the edge of the balcony."

"No sweat. I'll go first. When I'm down, you hang over and I'll pull you in." Raker was removing his coat.

"You can't make it, not in your condition. I'll go."

"No way, James. It'll be me. I'm sure of what I can do. I don't know about you. Here." He held his coat out to Colt, his arm on the wounded side still through the sleeve.

"You just hang on to the coat, tightly and silent as a fart in an elevator. I'll slip over the edge holding the roof with my good hand. Just make damn sure you're ready for my weight when I let go. You can drop me low enough that I can swing in and catch the support post. Got it?"

Colt looked dubious, but he knew Raker well enough not to debate it. "Got it."

Raker stretched out, carefully, along the roof, grasped the edge with his right hand, and swiveled his body over the edge.

Colt, stretched prone with his head just over the edge of the roof, held the coat in both strong hands.

Raker lowered his body slowly, his one arm supporting his entire weight until he was at his arm's length. He nodded up at Colt and slowly released his grip. Colt took the full weight, holding him, and Raker hung suspended in space.

Raker reached out a leg and his shoe tip barely touched one of the balcony's roof supports. He had carefully selected the spot from which he lowered himself. His toe pushed. It took several small pushes before his body began to swing. On the fourth swing, his fingers closed on the grillwork of the post. Slowly, carefully, noiselessly, he pulled himself to the rail and slipped over it to the balcony.

The rest was easy. In only a moment Colt stood by his side.

Raker held a finger to his lips, and leaned forward to put his mouth against Colt's ear. "Move when I go in."

Even Colt could hardly hear the words. He nodded and moved to a point away from the sliding glass door at which Raker nodded for him to stay. He reached under his coat and took out his weapon, a flat, compact, Walther P-38K. He held it firmly in his hand and nodded back at Raker.

Raker removed his revolver from his belt where he'd secured both his weapons with his leather key chain. He stood in front of the glass doors and lifted his hand. He paused a second, then thudded it against the glass in sharp knocks.

"Gordons! This is Campbell! Hear me! This is The Colonel. I'm calling it off. I want to see you. Now! This minute!"

• • •

Inside, as Raker's voice boomed through the glass, Elizabeth jumped as though her hands had encountered glowing charcoal. Her face contorted.

"No!" she cried. "No!" It was almost a snarl.

She faced her brother, her eyes bulging, veins showing in her throat and at her temples. "No, Alec! No, no, no! I won't have it! He'll not ruin my pleasures!"

She scrambled across the room on hands and knees to a chair where she and Alec had placed their robes. She snatched at the material and threw it at her brother. "Kill him!" she spat. "Kill the bastard! It's our only chance. Kill him now!"

Alec, mesmerized into action by the ferocity of his sister's tone, lifted himself from the prone body of the girl he had been about to enter. She had been lowered to the floor and tied for his special attentions.

"Now," said Elizabeth, regaining some of her composure. "The robe. A gun. There, on the table." She pointed. As Alec moved she raised her voice, and assumed an attitude of calmness.

"Only a second, Colonel!" she shouted. "Be right there. Was in the tub." She lowered her voice to a whisper. "Kill him!"

Alec nodded. "Through the curtain."

"Fool! You won't get a second chance. Unlock the glass door without drawing the drapes. When he steps inside, shoot him the second you see him—not until. I'll back you." While speaking she had picked up her weapon. It matched the one her brother held.

"Now!" she said.

Gordon flipped the latch on the glass door and stepped back. "Come in Colonel," he called. His voice was unsteady.

Raker slid the door open, revolver lifting from behind his back, and pushed through the curtain. Even at the short range he felt the pain of the first bullet before his mind registered the sound of the shot.

His arm was swinging even as the second bullet struck him. His hand holding the huge revolver slammed into Alec Gordon with fearful power, catching him full on the side of his head. The man's body was thrown its length and more by the force of the blow.

Raker's follow-through spun him to the side, dropping him to his knees as Elizabeth Gordon fired. The bullet hit Raker in the upper chest, higher than she had intended.

Even as she adjusted her aim, James Colt was through the doorway in a swift, powerful lunge that carried him to the woman. His foot lashed out in a vicious kick that knocked the gun from her hand and swept on past to smash into her midsection. She was flung backward, body doubled over, and bounced heavily against the floor.

Colt's eyes swept the room. "My God!" he cried. The words were torn from his throat. He sprang toward the unmoving bodies of the young man suspended from the ceiling and the girl spread-eagled on the floor, pillows pushed under her buttocks.

Raker was on his hands and knees, his face just now turning toward Colt. His eyes were cloudy and a trickle of blood came from his mouth.

"Get her loose, James," he pleaded. His voice was breathy and rasping, almost bubbly. "Get him down." He struggled to rise but slumped back to a sitting position. He watched as Colt did his bidding.

"Is she—are they—?" Raker's eyes were squeezed tight against the sight of his daughter.

"Unconscious," said Colt. "I think they'll make it. They've been badly used, but if there's no more damage inside than seems indicated, they'll be okay." His eyes turned toward Raker. "You?" He didn't like what he saw.

Raker managed to sit up. His fingers felt under his blood-covered shirt front. "Hit pretty good," he said. His eyes seemed to have cleared a bit. "Yes, this time I think they did pretty good." He snorted. "Bastards," he said, almost mildly, "picking on that same side of the chest." He motioned toward the chair still holding Elizabeth Gordon's robe. "Toss me that. I'll rig something to stop this oozing." Blood was flowing freely from his chest.

"I'll do it," objected Colt.

"No! The kids. Take care of them. Blankets. Get them wrapped up. Shock, you know. Then haul them faster'n hell to that doctor friend of Vivanti's."

Colt hesitated.

"Do it," commanded Raker. The authority was still in his voice. As Colt gathered blankets and wrapped the girl and her husband, he studied the marks on their bodies.

"They've been through hell," he said, "but I think your friends were holding back for a long, long session. They didn't want to lose them too quickly. Damned lucky. Your—the girl isn't as badly injured as the man."

Colt's eyes had taken in the marks on the girl and the string of lights on the floor nearby with adhesive tape on the wires. "Looks like they were planning a pretty terrible thing for her." Alec had persuaded his sister to postpone the burning until after his planned rape.

"It would have been one beastly experience," continued Colt. He'd completed his examination of the couple, an examination for which his experience had trained him fairly well. "They'll be all right," he told Raker. "I think you can relax. It's you we'd better worry about."

Raker had finished putting a pressure bandage over his own wounds. He tried to rise and found the chore difficult. Colt started to extend a hand and Raker waved it away. He managed to struggle to his feet and stand somewhat unsteadily.

"You sure, Jimmy boy? She's all right?"

"You know I can't be positive, Rake. It's my best opinion that she's not too bad. See for yourself."

Raker shook his head. "Can't," he said. "I got her into it. I can't." He looked at Colt, his anguish plain on his face.

Colt saw the pain. It was not just from his wounds. "Rake, dammit! You've made up for it. You've done what you set out to do. You've saved these kids. You can let go now."

Raker shook his head sadly. "No," he said. "No, Jimmy boy. I can't." With an effort he straightened and raised his head erect. "You see," he said, "it was all my doing."

Colt was perplexed. "Your doing? Certainly. You saved them. I only helped a bit. You did the saving."

"Don't be slow, James," said Raker quietly. "I'm the one who gave the orders. Me. I'm Coleman. I'm Campbell. I'm the one who set them up, set *you* up." He tilted his head up defiantly. His eyes held Colt firmly. "Now do you understand? It was me."

Colt looked at him blankly in stunned silence. He started to speak and found his mouth too dry. He started again. "You?" The word was brittle. "It was you?" Then he remembered. "By God, it *was* you!"

He had remembered the slight nag of something being wrong just as Raker had called through the door to the Gordons. He had forgotten in the excitement.

Raker had said he was Campbell. That was all right. But he had also said it was The Colonel. The Colonel! Raker's own code name from his mercenary days. It had registered at the moment, but been forgotten.

"Why, Rake? Why for God's sake?" Involuntarily he started forward. Raker raised the revolver his hand still held. He pointed it at Colt.

"Hold it right there, James." The weapon felt heavier than it should. He held it in both hands.

"Get those two kids to the hospital. Come back and I'll give you the whole story." He grimaced. "I'm not going anywhere."

At that moment a groan came from Alec Gordon. His sister had been making feeble, gasping sounds for some time. Raker turned the revolver and fired a shot into Alec Gordon's body. He died instantly.

Before Colt could move, the weapon was trained on him once again. Raker's expression had not changed. "He wasn't going to last long anyway," he said. His eyes glanced at the woman. "Don't worry. I'm not going to waste a shot on her."

He stared at Colt for a moment. "You heard me, James. Get a move on. Get my daughter and her husband to that doctor. When they're taken care of, come back." He coughed, then swallowed with some difficulty.

Blood, thought Colt. He's bleeding inside.

Raker saw the look on his face. He grinned. "Right on, old friend. I'm sure as hell not going anywhere. Now get them out of here. I'll finish up what has to be done."

Colt hesitated only a moment before nodding. Raker was right, he certainly wasn't going anywhere. Or at least not far, not in his condition. He turned and went to the still unconscious form of the girl. He lifted her with deceptive ease and started from the room.

"The key," said Raker. Colt turned.

"The key to the gate. You'll need it. Try that bitch's purse. It's over there on the table with all that crap they had ready to use on those kids." The length of his speech was an obvious effort.

Colt, still holding the girl, managed to find the key. As he left the room, Raker moved slowly across to the inert form of Elizabeth Gordon. She was beginning to show movement as well as making sounds. She would keep for the moment.

Raker turned toward her dead brother and addressed the corpse.

"You are one lucky bastard, Gordon," he said. "Truly one lucky bastard. Lucky to be dead, and I'm sorry about that. I would rather have made other arrangements toward that event." He stood looking down at the body for a moment and then turned to look again at Elizabeth Gordon.

A grim smile twisted his features. "But you," he said, "now you just don't seem to have any luck today at all."

The woman was moving, trying to straighten her body from its doubled position. It appeared to Raker that there were perhaps ribs broken from James Colt's effective kick which had disarmed her.

Grasping the wrists of the whimpering Elizabeth, Raker roughly pulled her arms behind her back. Ignoring her pained protests and using the belt from the discarded robe, he tied her wrists together.

• • •

Colt returned.

"I'm taking the Mercedes," he said. "More room."

"Good," said Raker, his eyes on Elizabeth Gordon. Her eyes were open with an expression of mixed pain and terror.

Colt picked up Henri Becquerel almost as easily as he had lifted the girl. He paused as he reached the balcony.

"I'll be back as soon as possible," he said. "I . . ." he hesitated. "I'll bring a doctor." He wasn't sure there would be any use for one. He hoped so. Not only for Raker's life, but to learn the story. The shock of Raker's admission still confused him. It was true, he knew, but *why?*

Questions could wait until the young couple was safely in medical hands.

"I'll be here," repeated Raker once again. He tried to smile.

Colt carried Henri Becquerel onto the balcony and up the steps. Raker carefully closed the sliding glass door, then turned his full attention to Elizabeth Gordon.

"I think these will do very nicely," he said. "Very nicely indeed." He knelt carefully between the woman's spread legs. "I'll just stuff the nice, trussed bird, and then we'll get on with the roasting." His grin was evil. "It was," he said, "your idea."

It was some minutes before Raker managed to force all the small bulbs on the light string inside the woman, but he managed. He moved slowly away, ignoring her screams of fury and pain. He paused a moment near the light socket before inserting the plug.

He rose with effort, and glanced at the stretched body of Elizabeth Gordon. It would take a minute or so before her sensitive interior membranes began to feel the heat. He stumbled to the table where the twins had stored their array of instruments with which they had planned to draw agony from their helpless victims. He swept the table clean with his arm, glancing around for the coat he'd held when he first entered the room. It was near the door. With effort he retrieved it.

Elizabeth Gordon's cries had lost all tone of anger, had turned to moans, and now were becoming screams of anguish.

He searched in his coat pockets and found what he was looking for. He sat at the table, placed his notebook on the flat surface, uncapped a felt tip pen, and began to write. The note was addressed to James Colt.

As he wrote, Raker detailed everything that had happened up to the present, as well as his reasons for their happening. As his hand sketched the letters, he was aware that his vision seemed to be dimming around the edges.

Elizabeth Gordon's cries had increased to insane screeches. Her body, jerking in convulsions, made thumping sounds as muscles lurched in uncontrollable spasms.

Raker continued writing, paying no attention to the sounds. He didn't even notice when the odor of burning flesh began to fill the room.

• • •

The red Ferrari was still parked above the cliff house as James Colt turned the Mercedes in beside it. He leaped from the car and rushed toward the curved stairway. He was followed by Francesco Vivanti and the fine Dottore who had previously patched up Raker. Colt felt he was bringing good news to the man. His daughter's injuries were not severe, nor were those of her husband. Not nearly as much as Colt had at first suspected. The young couple was now in good hands and resting comfortably.

As he reached the balcony, Colt found the glass door closed. He slid it open and stepped inside. He was met by the odor. He stared with wide eyes at the contorted body of Elizabeth Gordon. What had happened to her was terribly obvious. The end of the cord which led from the body lay unplugged near the wall.

Colt's eyes turned to where Alec Gordon lay. His body was in the same position as when Colt had last seen him. It would have been a miracle otherwise.

Colt heard the men behind him enter the room. He turned to face them and watch their expressions as they surveyed the scene. Neither man showed shock. The doctor, perhaps from force of habit, approached the bodies in turn and gave them a cursory glance.

"Indelicate," he observed, looking down on the body of Elizabeth, "but effective. It would have been painful beyond compare." He shook his head. "Burned to death from the inside out. Remarkable."

Vivanti, after a moment, looked at Colt. "Your friend, he is a thorough and unforgiving man, is he not? He had great anger."

"He did indeed," said Colt. "A very great anger." He looked

around the room, searching for a sign of Raker. His eyes fell on the notebook lying on the table. He picked up the book. Inside, on the first page, he read:

...

James: without your help, my daughter would be horribly dead. I thank you. It's now over for me. The bullets were a little much this time and I'm damned if I'll just lay down and die quietly when that ocean below is so inviting. I've elected to take a nice, last swim if the old legs will shove me out that far. Otherwise, you'll find me down below on the beach or the rocks. Either way, it'll be better.

In this notebook you'll find all the whys and wherefores. I hope you can come to understand. I thought—still think—that I had cause. It's just that I made some terrible errors.

By the time you read this there will be no chance to stop the second round of terminations. The world will be better off because of them. But there are others scheduled. Do what you think best about those, although there is one you cannot affect, so I've left it out. Read this and decide for yourself.

There are three things I'd like to tell you, or ask of you. First, the Maguire girl is truly unaware of anything other than what she has told you. She is one loyal lady. Treat her that way.

Second, please don't tell Jennie about me or any of my involvement in the thing. Third, see to her welfare. You will be well able to afford it. You'll learn how, whether they find my body or declare me dead. You have been appointed general manager of my business, have power of attorney, and are my beneficiary and executor.

Don't object. Just take care of it. Maria Theresa has all the data for you. I'd decided this third thing, long ago, even before I felt I might have to have you done in. Don't know what I'd have done if that had occurred. Glad it didn't. Anyway, Prevent Incorporated now belongs to you, Jimmy boy, whatever the circumstances. Do well by it.

Now, lad, read on. Discover the why, the how, and the who of this mess. Then do as you please. If I'd had a son, I'd have picked you.
Rake.

P.S. You can even call me Beverly.

Colt paused. His feelings were terribly mixed. He placed the notebook in his pocket. He would finish it at another time. It was a moment before he realized that someone was speaking.

It was Vivanti.

"What?" he started, surprised.

"I said that I will take care of disposing of this problem." His eyes flicked toward the bodies of the Gordons.

Colt only stared.

Vivanti tried a small smile. "It will present little problem." He put out a hand and patted Colt's shoulder. "Your friend is not here," he said, quietly. "There is considerable blood on the balcony rail."

Colt looked up at his friend, Francesco. "No," he said, "he isn't here. He . . . he went for a swim, took a little trip."

Vivanti nodded. "His kind do not take well to the waiting for death. They charge." He hesitated. "You loved the man?"

"In a way," said Colt. "And at times hated him. Today, at least."

"His kind are the ones we feel that way about," observed Vivanti. "They are the doers. Perhaps not right doing, but certainly doers."

"There, my friend Francesco, you are absolutely correct." For some reason, Colt felt better.

The men went out on the balcony and looked at the blood-stained rail. "It would have taken a pretty good push to reach out to the deep water," said Colt. "He sure as hell had the legs for it, if he still had enough blood left."

"Those kind, they always have something left," said Vivanti, "always. Never count them out. They have . . ." he shrugged, looking for a word.

"Heart," finished Colt. "Perhaps not tender and gentle, but certainly heart."

• • •

It was over. Nothing could be done about the other deaths that would occur on this day. But perhaps something could be done about *saving* others. Maybe even PanGlobal. The thought did not exactly thrill Colt.

He would finish reading Raker's . . . he stopped. Testament? Will and testament? Was that what it was? Never mind. It didn't matter.

With his death, Raker's terminal policy was over.

• • •

It was more than three weeks before Colt returned to New York. Part of the delay had been occasioned by what he'd learned from Raker's notebook, part lay in Colt making certain that Raker's daughter and her husband were healed and fully recovered from their experience.

Colt had not heeded Raker's wish for anonymity, but instead made the man a hero; the one responsible for the couple's rescue. He successfully hid the fact that PanGlobal Assurance was in any way concerned, or that their peril had been a result of Raker's actions.

The reason for the attack, as advanced by Colt, was that the Gordons were avenging themselves against an imagined wrong done by Becquerel's banking interests.

Jennie felt appreciation and considerable affection toward her recently dead father's memory. It is difficult to feel great sadness for someone hardly known.

• • •

Vivanti had, indeed, taken care of the "problem" at the cliff house. Colt never asked how, but simply spent some time enjoying the man's company.

He had made two phone calls to New York. The first to Pagan Maguire. Following the call she moved from the small house in the village into his apartment. Her stay was only long enough to leave her belongings. She immediately booked passage to Rome.

The second call was to Mitchell at PanGlobal.

Colt told the man that Raker had ended the threat to the company, it seemed, and at the cost of his own life. Mitchell was mildly grateful and said it was convenient that no contract existed which would make it necessary for PanGlobal to pay anything to the man's estate. Colt did not comment.

• • •

Upon Pagan's arrival in Italy, Colt, before doing anything else, made certain that the bounty on his life—denied by Mitchell to have ever been offered—had been lifted. A careful trip to the Rome office of PanGlobal was enough to assure the fact. While there, Colt expressed his regret at the death of their employee, Epeminio Fondi, who had given his life in the course of his duties. He was even able to say the words without the trace of a smile.

What else Colt and Pagan Maguire did during their time together in Italy is no one's business but their own. They did, however, spend a considerable part of two weeks doing it.

• • •

It was the twenty-fourth day since the disappearance of Beverly Martin Raker which found James Colt facing Mallory Fleming Mitchell, who was seated behind his ornate elevated desk. The man was frowning. His fingers drummed on its uncluttered top. The source of his displeasure was Colt.

Mitchell cleared his throat. "Your attitude, James. It is most untypical. Your association with Raker has bred in you a most cavalier attitude. I do not like it. Anymore than I liked that man."

Colt smiled. It was grim and tight. Mitchell had used the same word so often to describe Raker. "Mitchell old man, that is, as they say, your problem. I'm here only to update you before I depart for happier climes."

"Yes," said Mitchell, "yes, indeed. So you say. You did indicate that, didn't you?"

"Why in the hell do you constantly repeat yourself?" asked Colt. Mitchell's thick, twining eyebrows flew up. Colt had never spoken to him in that manner before. He decided to let it pass.

"Habit. Habit, of course. Certainly." He made his tone conciliatory. "I do wish you would reconsider, James. We have had a pleasant relationship in the past. We could again, with some adjustment on your part."

Colt's smile became a laugh. "Bullshit, Mitchell. There's no way. And at any rate, you're just worried that I may open the closet door and let some skeletons rattle loose with tales of how you almost lost your company. Shove it, bucko! I have other things to do, and far better than telling the world about your problems.

"No," he continued. "I'm done with you, and my association with Pan Gee. I've done my part, and I don't owe you a damned thing."

Mitchell tried tact. "Come now, James, come. I know full well that you certainly don't need money. Know well that you are what the poor call loaded, and that you work only because you need a challenge; something to tax your abilities. It's just that I need you, boy. Really need you. There may be others who'll hit on the company like that . . . what was his name?"

"Coleman," said Colt, "Owen Coleman. In cooperation with Ian Campbell."

"Yes. Coleman and Campbell. You're certain they are through? Dead?"

"Quite, Mitchell. They are gone. You need have no fear of those two."

"Yes. Good," said Mitchell.

"They're as dead as Raker." Colt's voice was cold.

Mitchell looked uncomfortable. "Yes, that. Sorry, James. Forgot. He was a friend of yours, wasn't he? Quite sorry. But it was in a good cause."

Colt stood. "You disgust me, Mitchell. Believe it. You don't give a damn about people. Not the clients killed, not even your own employees. You can't even tell me the name of my secretary, the poor girl who was murdered because of your company."

Mitchell averted his eyes. "Don't lecture me, Colt. I have more important things to concern me than one or two people being dead."

"You'd better worry about who killed that girl, Mitchell. Coleman or his alter ego didn't. It was someone else." That fact was true. Just who had done so was the one thing, or at least one of the things, that Raker's last note had not revealed to Colt.

"Don't forget," he continued, "you still have that viper in your nest. We still don't know who sold out to Coleman."

The words pleased him. They, certainly should upset Mitchell. They did.

Mitchell's creased frown showed increased worry. "Damn! You're right. Who? Who was it? Is it?"

Colt rose and started for the door. He shrugged, hand on the knob. "As an old friend of mine would say, *'quien sabe, amigo?'*"

"Wait!"

"Your problem, old timer," said Colt. He lifted a hand and touched it to his forehead in mock salute. "You take care now, you hear?"

As he pulled the door open, he spoke across his shoulder. "A couple of last things, Mitchell. Do you remember the name Laughlin? T.J. Laughlin."

"No," said Mitchell, after a moment's pause.

"Just wondered. You really should. The other thing is something else you should remember. That little game of putting out contracts on people? It works both ways."

Colt was gone, closing the door behind him, while Mitchell digested the words.

EPILOGUE

Elsewhere in the city, Harlan Webb had finished a noontime work-out at his health club. He had showered, dressed, and taken the time to eat a low calorie lunch. He had decided that his clothes were fitting a little more snugly than he liked.

As he walked toward where his car was garaged, he became aware that two men were following him. They made no effort to disguise the fact, and it was typical of Webb that he accost them. He slowed his pace until the men were only a few feet behind him, then suddenly wheeled to face them.

"All right, God damn it! What the hell do you want? Why are you following me?"

The men paused, faces not changing expression. "Mr. Webb?" asked one of the men. His voice seemed to have a singing lilt. "Mr. Harlan Webb?"

"You know damn well I'm Webb. Come off the bullshit. What are you after? And give it to me fast before I . . ."

"Before you what, Mr. Webb?" The flat voice was freezing cold.

Webb suddenly found his throat had closed. It wasn't the words, not even the tone. It was the faces of the two men confronting him: expressionless, tight and drawn, devoid of any emotion.

"We're after bringing you a message, Mr. Webb," said the man who had not yet spoken. His voice was much like the other man's.

"Indeed," said the first speaker, "and it's just that you've done a bad thing, threatenin' and frightenin' and all that sort of thing to the ladies. Lady," he corrected.

Webb's eyes went from face to face. He had placed the soft accent. The voices were Irish. The girl? Maguire? Hell, he hadn't done anything—well, not really, not anything serious. His skin crawled from the terrible quiet on the two faces.

He found his voice. "I've not—that is, I didn't—"

"Hush, now, Mr. Webb. You just hush now. We're not here to be putting a bullet through your knee cap. Not at this time. Anyway, we've really gone to electric drills for that. We'll just be asking you to mind your manners. D'ye ken that?"

Webb tried to speak. He settled for a nod.

"Grand, Mr. Webb. Simply grand. Nice of you to take heed," said one.

"Sure and you can be going now," said the other. Neither man had ever changed expression or tone.

As Webb wordlessly turned and scurried away, the men continued to walk slowly in the direction he had taken.

"I think he has the faith," observed one.

"It would so seem," agreed the other. The men walked in silence for several steps.

"What time is our plane after leavin'?" asked one of the other.

"You have the tickets," said his companion.

"I have that, now haven't I?" He reached into his pocket.

"No worry," said the other man. "Brennan'll not be startin' without us."

"True. But 'tis a fine thing to be lookin' forward to, now isn't it?"

"'Tis."

Much earlier, the men had verified that the Gordons, both man and woman, had indeed been destroyed. The girl's word was good enough for proof. And the Webb creature had been duly cautioned. Their work was now over. At least on this side of the Atlantic.

• • •

James Colt closed the door leading from Mitchell's office and smiled down at Victoria Genn.

"All done, Vicky," he said. "We've parted company, the old buzzard and myself. And nothing lost. But I will miss you."

Victoria Genn looked up at Colt, some little sadness showing in her expression. "I'm sorry, James. You've been my favorite, you know that."

Colt put a hand on her shoulder. "I do. And I thank you." He looked into her eyes and for the first time noted their unique, deep violet color. They were quite lovely, large and wide spaced. Hell, thought Colt, the lady is quite attractive, and I've never taken the time to notice. His thoughts showed on his face.

"Something wrong, James?"

"No. Definitely not. It's just that I've looked at you as Miss Perfect Secretary for so long I've not noticed how lovely you are."

"What a nice compliment," said the woman. She smiled only to lose it to a frown. "I'm so very sorry about Raker . . . your friend. He seemed such a nice person, and so efficient. You must miss him very much."

Colt grinned wryly. "Nice? I'm not sure about that. Efficient? None more so. And yes, I'll miss him very much, Victoria. Very much."

Perhaps from awkwardness in handling her emotions, Victoria Genn had, while talking, unconsciously sliced into one of the letters she had been opening when Colt had emerged from Mitchell's office. She pulled out the paper from inside the envelope.

"Call me now and then?" she asked

"Certainly," said Colt. He watched the woman's face pale.

She had seen the bright red dollar sign at the bottom of the sheet of paper she had just extracted.

Her heart jumped. My God? Was it possible? Was it not ended after all? Her eyes started to scan the typewritten lines.

It was possible, she thought—that sly, crafty bastard! Raker. If anyone could do it, it would be him. Her dear, unique partner-in-schemes, and at-times-in-bed, Beverly Martin Raker.

His plan had very nearly succeeded. Now it seemed it might yet.

She frowned slightly, aware that Colt was watching her. The only thing she truly regretted was having to kill the Fremont girl. But she had tried to make it as painless as possible. And anyway, the girl had betrayed James Colt. It was right that she pay for her deed.

Her hand reached out and picked up the envelope. The postmark could offer a clue as to whether Raker had truly returned, or if the mail had simply been delayed.

"You look terribly distressed, Victoria," said James Colt who had been watching. "Anything wrong?"

She nodded. "It's this," she said, holding up the letter so that Colt could see the red dollar sign.

"I see," said James.

"It's simply terrible," said the woman. Her lowered eyes belied her words. She lifted them to look at Colt. "Whatever can we do?"

"Not we, Vicky. Him. I have separated myself from dear old Pan Gee."

"But this could be terrible," said Victoria Genn. "It could very well be the end of Mr. Mitchell."

"I know," said James Colt.

He smiled, winked, and was gone.